"[An] outstanding, completely engaging tale that will have you on the edge of your seat . . . A must-have for all fans of romantic suspense!"

—THEROMANCEREADERSCONNECTION.COM
REVIEW OF *ANATHEMA*

"Colleen Coble lays an intricate trail in *Without a Trace* and draws the reader on like a hound with a scent."

—*ROMANTIC TIMES*, 4½ STARS

"Coble's historical series just keeps getting better with each entry."

—*LIBRARY JOURNAL* STARRED REVIEW
OF *THE LIGHTKEEPER'S BALL*

"Don't ever mistake [Coble's] for the fluffy romances with a little bit of suspense. She writes solid suspense, and she ties it all together beautifully with a wonderful message."

—LIFEINREVIEWBLOG.COM REVIEW OF *LONESTAR ANGEL*

"This book has everything I enjoy: mystery, romance, and suspense. The characters are likable, understandable, and I can relate to them."

—THEFRIENDLYBOOKNOOK.COM

"Mystery, danger, and intrigue as well as romance, love, and subtle inspiration. *The Lightkeeper's Daughter* is a 'keeper.'"

—ONCEUPONAROMANCE.COM

What Readers Are Saying

"I have always been a hopeless romantic . . . When I began reading your books I couldn't put them down. I love not just the romance but the connection I feel with God when I read your books. It really is incredible!"

—Jennifer

"I just finished *Blue Moon Promise* and it was outstanding! I am so looking forward to *Safe in His Arms*! Thank you for sharing your God-given talent with us."

—Nancy

"I love your books! I am a big fan ☺ You are by far my favorite author."

—Katelyn

"I wanted to let you know that I am reading *Blue Moon Promise* and I can't put it down. I love the way you write! I've read your Lonestar series and I can't wait to read *Tidewater Inn*."

—Jean

"You are such an amazing writer and person. I've been dealing with lots of health issues, and on my 'bad days' I turn to your books to keep me inspired, to keep me thinking positive thoughts, and to help get me through the tough times. Thanks for being an inspiration and for all that you do to include your reader friends in your life."

—Becky

ACCLAIM FOR COLLEEN COBLE

"Second chances, old flames, and startling new revelations combine to form a story filled with faith, trial, forgiveness, and redemption. Crack the cover and step in, but beware—Mermaid Point is harboring secrets that will keep you guessing."

—LISA WINGATE, NATIONAL BESTSELLING AUTHOR OF
THE SEA KEEPER'S DAUGHTERS ON MERMAID MOON

"I burned through The Inn at Ocean's Edge in one sitting. An intricate plot by a master storyteller. Colleen Coble has done it again with this gripping opening to a new series. I can't wait to spend more time at Sunset Cove."

—HEATHER BURCH, BESTSELLING AUTHOR
OF ONE LAVENDER RIBBON

"Coble doesn't disappoint with her custom blend of suspense and romance."

—PUBLISHERS WEEKLY FOR THE INN AT OCEAN'S EDGE

"Veteran author Coble has penned another winner. Filled with mystery and romance that are unpredictable until the last page, this novel will grip readers long past when they should put their books down. Recommended to readers of contemporary mysteries."

—CBA RETAILERS + RESOURCES

"Coble truly shines when she's penning a mystery, and this tale will really keep the reader guessing . . . Mystery lovers will definitely want to put this book on their purchase list."

—ROMANTIC TIMES BOOK REVIEWS

"Master storyteller Colleen Coble has done it again. *The Inn at Ocean's Edge* is an intricately woven, well-crafted story of romance, suspense, family secrets, and a decades old mystery. Needless to say, it had me hooked from page one. I simply couldn't stop turning the pages. This one's going on my keeper shelf."

—LYNETTE EASON, AWARD-WINNING, BESTSELLING
AUTHOR OF THE HIDDEN IDENTITY SERIES

"Evocative and gripping, *The Inn at Ocean's Edge* will keep you flipping pages long into the night."

—DANI PETTREY, BESTSELLING AUTHOR
OF THE ALASKAN COURAGE SERIES

"Coble's atmospheric and suspenseful series launch should appeal to fans of Tracie Peterson and other authors of Christian romantic suspense."

—*LIBRARY JOURNAL* REVIEW OF *TIDEWATER INN*

"Romantically tense, but with just the right touch of danger, this cowboy love story is surprisingly clever—and pleasingly sweet."

—USAToday.com REVIEW OF *BLUE MOON PROMISE*

"Colleen Coble will keep you glued to each page as she shows you the beauty of God's most primitive land and the dangers it hides."

—WWW.ROMANCEJUNKIES.COM

"Colleen is a master storyteller."

—KAREN KINGSBURY, BESTSELLING AUTHOR
OF *UNLOCKED* AND *LEARNING*

"I just read *The Lightkeeper's Daughter*, *The Lightkeeper's Bride* and *The Lightkeeper's Ball*. I could not put them down. I also read the first two books of the Lonestar series and I can't wait to get my hands on the next two. I loved them all!!"

—ADELE

"I finished *Lonestar Angel* and just loved it!! Sure would love for that series to go on and on, keeps getting better and better."

—TERESA

"I just finished the Rock Harbor Series . . . I loved it. You should see my house, laundry, dishes, etc. I haven't done a thing in days. I literally couldn't put the books down. I am off to find *Alaska Twilight*. You are by far my new favorite author. I am from Indiana too, and have visited the UP before. I could almost smell the woods, feel the wind and hear the waves. Thanks for a truly amazing series."

—TANYA

"I just wanted to say thank you for writing the Rock Harbor series. I lost my son in a car accident 12 years ago this month. They waited to bury him when I woke from a coma. I don't remember the accident or barely the funeral. It felt like a nightmare, very unreal and out of body. In your book, she got her little boy back, but she also learned to not be so angry with God. That is something I will always have to work on. I feel very guilty for that, but I am angry. Your book has helped me with that some. I look forward to more in the series, strangely it gave me a peace."

—TIFFANY

"I am so very excited about your new books coming out! I have read almost everything you have put out in the last five years! I am counting down the days till the next Harbor Rock book comes out, and I am pre-ordering *Cry in The Night* this weekend! Thank you so much for all you do! Not only have I enjoyed the story lines, I feel like it's a daily devotional as well!"

—BESS

"I just finished your *Lonestar Sanctuary* novel & LOVED IT! I am a HUGE cowgirl/rodeo fan at heart and worked with troubled children so it really spoke to my heart. I am so glad I have discovered such a wonderful author and will highly recommend your books to my friends and book club!"

—KIM

"The number one gift on my wish list was *The Lightkeeper's Ball*. I read the first two of the Mercy Falls Novels and I LOVED THEM! I'm a huge history nut and I thought that these books were FANTASTIC!!"

—EM

"I just love your books! Rock Harbor is my favorite series. That series has rich plot, deep characterization, gorgeous backdrop, engaging dialogue. And I can't help hoping Bree keeps whispering secrets and suggestions to you about keeping the series going. There's still more to be told!"

—MARY

TIDEWATER INN

A Hope Beach Novel

Colleen Coble

THOMAS NELSON
Since 1798

ALSO BY COLLEEN COBLE

For Erin Healy
Editor extraordinaire and friend

Published in Nashville, Tennessee, by Thomas Nelson. Thomas Nelson is a
registered trademark of HarperCollins Christian Publishing, Inc.

Thomas Nelson, Inc., titles may be purchased in bulk for educational,
business, fund-raising, or sales promotional use. For information, please
e-mail SpecialMarkets@ThomasNelson.com.

Scripture quotations are taken from THE NEW KING JAMES VERSION.
Copyright © 1982 by Thomas Nelson, Inc. Used by permission. All rights
reserved.

Publisher's Note: This novel is a work of fiction. Names, characters, places,
and incidents are either products of the author's imagination or used
fictitiously. All characters are fictional, and any similarity to people living
or dead is purely coincidental.

ISBN: 978-0-7180-7829-4 (Mass Market)

Library of Congress Cataloging-in-Publication Data

Coble, Colleen.
 Tidewater Inn / by Colleen Coble.
  p. cm.—(A Hope Beach novel; 1)
 ISBN 978–1–59554–781–1 (trade paper)
 1. Hotels—Conservation and restoration—Fiction. 2. Kidnapping—Fiction.
 I. Title.
 PS3553.O2285T53 2012
 813'.54—dc23
 2012012625

Printed in the United States of America

16 17 18 19 20 OPM 9 8 7 6 5 4 3 2 1

ONE

Libby Holladay fought her way through the brambles to the overgrown garden. She paused to wave a swarm of gnats away from her face. The house was definitely in the Federal style, as she'd been told. Palladian windows flanked a centered door, or rather the opening for a door. The structure was in serious disrepair. Moss grew on the roof, and fingers of vine pried through the brick mortar. The aroma of honeysuckle vied with that of mildew.

She stepped closer to the house and jotted a few impressions in her notebook before moving inside to the domed living room. The floorboards were missing in places and rotted in others, so she planted her tan flats carefully. She could almost see the original occupants in this place. She imagined her own furniture grouped around the gorgeous fireplace. She'd love to have this place, but something so grand that needed this much repair would never be hers. The best she could do would be to preserve it for someone else who would love it. She itched to get started.

Her cell phone rang, and she groped in her canvas bag for it. Glancing at the display, she saw her partner's name. "Hey, Nicole," she said. "You should see this place. A gorgeous Federal-style mansion. I think it was built in 1830. And the setting by the river is beautiful. Or it will be once the vegetation is tamed." Perching on the window seat, she made another note about the fireplace. "Nicole? Are you there?"

There was a long pause, then Nicole finally spoke. "I'm here."

"You sound funny. What's wrong?" Nicole was usually talkative, and Libby couldn't remember the last time she'd heard strain in her friend's voice. "Are you still in the Outer Banks? Listen, I heard there might be a hurricane heading that way." She dug into her purse for her jalapeño jellybeans and popped one in her mouth.

"I'm here," Nicole said. "The residents are sure the storm will miss Hope Island. The investor is really interested in this little town. And we have the chance to make a boatload of money on it. It's all in your hands."

"My hands? You're the one with the money smarts."

Nicole was the mover and shaker in Holladay Renovations. She convinced owners to dramatically increase the value of their historic properties by entrusting them to Libby's expertise. Libby had little to do with the money side of the business, and that was how she liked it.

"I think I'd better go back to the beginning," Nicole said. "Rooney sent me here to see about renovating some buildings in the small downtown area. He's working on getting a ferry to the island. It will bring in a lot more tourism for the hotel he's planning, but the buildings need to be restored to draw new business."

"I know that much. But what do you mean 'it's in my hands'?" Libby glanced at her notes, then around the room again. This was taking up her time, and she wanted to get back to work. "We're doing the lifesaving station for sure, right?"

"Yes, I've already seen it. We were right to buy that sweet building outright. After you get your hands on it, we'll make a bundle *and* have instant credibility here. I've started making notes of the materials and crew we'll need. But I'm not calling about the renovations. I'm talking a lot of money, Libby. Millions."

That got Libby's attention. "Millions?"

"I stopped by the local attorney's office to see about having him handle the paperwork for our purchase of the lifesaving station. Horace Whittaker. He's got both our names on the paperwork now."

"So?"

"The secretary gasped when she heard your name."

"She knew me?"

"The attorney has been looking for a Libby Holladay. Daughter of Ray Mitchell."

"That's my dad's name."

"I thought it might be. I'd heard you mention the name Ray, but I wasn't sure of the last name."

Libby rubbed her head. "Why is he looking for me? My father has been dead a long time—since I was five."

"He died a month ago, Libby. And he left you some valuable land. In fact, it's the land Rooney thought he had agreed to purchase. So we're in the driver's seat on this deal." Nicole's voice rose.

Libby gasped, then she swallowed hard. "It's a hoax. I bet the attorney asked for a fee, right?"

"No, it's real. According to the secretary, your father was living in the Outer Banks all this time. And Horace has a box of letters Ray wrote to you that were all marked *Return to Sender*. It appears your mother refused them."

Libby's midsection plunged. Throughout her childhood she'd asked her mother about her father. There were never any answers. Surely her mother wouldn't have *lied*. Libby stared out the window at two hummingbirds buzzing near the overgrown flowers.

"Do you have any idea how much money this land is worth?" Nicole's voice quivered. "It's right along the ocean. There's a charming little inn."

It sounded darling. "What's the area like?"

"Beautiful but remote." Nicole paused. "Um, listen, there's something else. I met a woman who looked like you a couple days ago."

Libby eased off the window ledge. "Who is she?"

"Your half sister, Vanessa. You also have a brother, Brent. He's twenty-two."

"My father married again?" Libby couldn't take it all in. This morning she had no family but a younger stepbrother, whom she rarely saw. Why had her mother kept all this from her? "What about my father's wife?"

"She doesn't seem to be around. But there's an aunt too."

Family. For as long as she could remember, Libby

had longed for a large extended family. Her free-spirited mother was always wanting to see some new and exciting place. They had never lived at the same address for more than two years at a time.

"You need to get here right away," Nicole said. "There are a million details to take care of. This is the big deal we've been praying for, Libby. You will never want for anything again, and you'll have plenty of money to help your stepbrother. He can get out of that trailer with his family."

The thought of buying her stepbrother's love held some appeal. They weren't close, but not because she hadn't tried. "I can't get away until tomorrow, Nicole. I have to finish up here first. We have other clients."

How much of her reluctance was rooted in the thought of facing a future that was about to change radically? She never had been good with change. In her experience, change was something that generally made things worse, not better.

Her partner's sigh was heavy in Libby's ear. "Okay. Hey, want to see Vanessa? She'll be here in a few minutes. There's a beach cam out by the lifesaving station, and I'm supposed to meet her there. I'll send you a link to it. You can see her before you meet her."

Libby glanced through the window toward her car. "I have my computer in the car." She tucked her long hair behind her ear and gathered her things. "What does Vanessa think about our father leaving prime real estate to me?" She left the house and started for her vehicle.

Nicole cleared her throat. "Um, she's pretty upset."

"I would imagine. What did you tell her about me?"

"As little as possible."

"I don't know if that's good or bad."

"I wouldn't worry about them. She and her brother are fishing for info though. She mentioned lighthouse ruins and I asked for directions. She offered to show me, but I went out there by myself yesterday. I'm still meeting her today because I knew you'd want to know more about her."

It sounded like a disaster in the making. "I have so many questions."

"Then come down as soon as you can and get them answered. Wait until you see Tidewater Inn, Libby! It's really old. It's on the eastern edge of the island with tons of land along the beach. The inn was a house once, and it is a little run-down but very quaint. It's hard to get out here. Until Rooney gets the ferry approved, you'll have to hire a boat. You're going to love it though. I love this island. It's like stepping back in time. And I've even seen some caves to explore."

"No road to it from the mainland?" Libby couldn't fathom a place that remote.

"Nope. Boat access only."

Her phone still to her ear, Libby opened her car door and slid in. The computer was on the floor, and she opened it. "I'm going to have to get off a minute to tether my phone to the computer. Send me the link to the harbor cam. Don't tell Vanessa I'm watching."

"When can you get here tomorrow?"

"It's about two hours from Virginia Beach?"

"Yes."

Libby doubted she'd sleep tonight. It would be no problem to be in the shower by six. "I'll be there by nine."

She ended the call, then attached the cord that tethered the phone to the computer. She would use the cell signal to watch Nicole's video feed on the larger screen. Then she could watch and still take any calls that came in. Her skin itched from the brambles. She established the connection, then logged on to the Internet. No e-mail yet.

She owned property. The thought was mind boggling. No matter what condition it was in, it was a resource to fall back on, something she hadn't possessed yesterday. The thought lightened her heart. She stared at the grand old home beside her. What if there was enough money from the sale of the inn to allow her to buy a historic house and restore it? It would be a dream come true. She could help her stepbrother. She could buy some Allston paintings too, something she'd never dreamed she could afford.

A woman pecked on Libby's car window, and Libby turned on the key and ran down the window. "Hello. I'm not an intruder. I'm evaluating this gorgeous old place for the historic registry."

The woman smiled. "I thought maybe you were buying it. Someone should restore it."

"Someone plans to," Libby said. What if it could be her instead of her client?

The woman pointed. "I'm taking up a collection for the Warders, who live on the corner. They had a fire in the kitchen and no insurance."

Libby had only two hundred dollars in her checking account, and she had to get to the Outer Banks. "I wish I could help," she said with real regret. "I don't have anything to spare right now."

"Thanks anyway." The woman smiled and moved to the next house.

Libby ran the window back up and clicked on her in-box. An e-mail from Nicole appeared. She stared at the link. All she had to do was click and she'd catch a glimpse of a sister she had no idea even existed. Her hands shook as she maneuvered the pointer over the link and clicked. The page opened, and she was staring at a boardwalk over deep sand dunes that were heaped like snowdrifts. In the distance was a brilliant blue ocean. A pier extended into the pristine water. The scene was like something out of a magazine. She could almost feel the sea breeze.

She clicked to enlarge the video and turned up the speakers so she could hear the roar of the surf. Where was Nicole? The pier was empty, and so was the sea. A dilapidated building stood to the right of the screen, and she could just make out a sign over the door. Hope Beach Lifesaving Station.

Then there was a movement on the boardwalk. Nicole appeared. She smiled and waved. "Hi, Libby," she said. The sound quality was surprisingly good. The sound of the ocean in the background was a pleasant lull.

Libby had to resist the impulse to wave back. Her partner's blond hair was pulled back in a ponytail under a sun hat, and she wore a hot-pink cover-up over her brown bathing suit.

Nicole glanced at her watch and frowned. "Vanessa is late. Like I started to say earlier, I didn't want to wait on her to see the lighthouse ruins, so I went out there alone. I have to show it to you. Wait until you see what I found. You'll seriously freak! Hey, give me a call. This pier is one of the few places where my phone works. Isn't that crazy—an entire island without cell service. Almost, anyway."

Libby picked up her cell phone, still connected to the computer. They could talk a few minutes. Before she could call, a small boat pulled up to the shore. Two men jumped out and pulled the boat aground. Nicole turned toward them. The men walked toward her. There was no one else in sight, and Libby tensed when Nicole took a step back. Libby punched in Nicole's number. She watched her friend dig in her bag when it rang.

When Nicole answered the phone, Libby leaped to her feet and yelled, "Get out of there. Go to your car!"

Nicole was still watching the men walk toward her. "It's just a couple of tourists, Libby," she said. "You worry too much." She smiled and waved at the men.

Libby leaned closer to the laptop. "There's something wrong." She gasped at the intention in their faces. "Please, Nicole, run!"

But it was the men who broke into a run as they drew closer to the boardwalk. As they neared the cam, Libby could see them more clearly. One was in his forties with a cap pulled low over his eyes. He sported a beard. The other was in his late twenties. He had blond hair and hadn't shaved in a couple of days.

Nicole took another step back as the older man in the lead smiled at her. The man said, "Hang up." He grabbed her arm.

"Let go of her!" Libby shouted into the phone.

The man knocked the phone from Nicole's hand and the connection was broken. The other man reached the two, and he plunged a needle into Nicole's arm. Both men began dragging Nicole toward the boat. She was struggling and shouting for help, then went limp. Her hat fell to the ground.

Barely aware that she was screaming, Libby dialed 9-1-1. "Oh God, oh God, help her!"

The dispatcher answered and Libby babbled about her friend being abducted right in front of her. "It's in the Outer Banks." She couldn't take her eyes off the boat motoring away from the pier. "Wait, wait, they're taking her away! Do something!"

"Where?"

"I told you, the Outer Banks." Libby looked at the heading above the video stream. "Hope Beach. It's Hope Beach. Get someone out there."

"Another dispatcher is calling the sheriff. I have an officer on his way to you."

"I'm going to Hope Beach now."

"Stay where you are," the dispatcher said. "We've got the sheriff on the line there. He's on his way to the site. Don't hang up until an officer arrives."

She had to do something. Anything but run screaming into the street. Libby looked at the computer. She could call up the video, save it for evidence. But the stream had no rewind, no way to save it. If she could hack into the site, she could get to the file. The police could save time and get the pictures of those men circulating. With a few keystrokes, she broke through the firewall and was in the code.

Then her computer blinked and went black. And when she called up the site again, the entire code was gone. What had she done?

TWO

Smog hung over the New York skyline and matched Lawrence Rooney's mood. He studied the expansive view from his penthouse office on Fifth Avenue. The senator sitting in the chair on the other side of the gleaming walnut desk had better come through with the promised plum after all Lawrence had done for him.

Lawrence kept his attention away from the senator long enough to make sure the other man knew who was in charge, then turned from his perusal of his domain and settled in his chair. "You have news for me?"

Senator Troy Bassett tugged on his tie, then pulled a handkerchief from his pocket and blotted his damp forehead. "The city is like an oven today," he muttered.

In his fifties now, he had once been handsome, but his blond good looks had been replaced by flab and gray hair. Lawrence had known him since they went to Harvard together. They knew each other's weaknesses all too well. Lawrence had funneled a fortune into getting Bassett elected. But the rewards were coming—now.

"The vote?" Lawrence prodded.

The senator nodded. "Came through. The ferry system will be added next year."

"Excellent." Lawrence sat back in his leather chair. "I will have possession of the land by the end of the summer."

"I thought the old man refused to sell it."

"Luckily for us, he died." How he wished he could have seen Ray Mitchell take his last breath.

Bassett lifted a brow. "Natural causes?"

Lawrence laughed. "Of course. We both know I like to have my own way, but I've never stooped to murder. I've found money talks well enough that it's not necessary." A smile tugged at his lips. "Though there's always a first time for everything."

"You'd met your match in Mitchell though. He was adamant."

"True enough. But his son has no such scruples. He knows when to take a good offer and run with it."

"So he's agreed to your price?"

Lawrence nodded. "He has. I was willing to go up another five million if I had to, but he didn't know that. I got a bargain."

"You always do."

The door opened and Lawrence's secretary stuck her head in. "Mr. Rooney, Mr. Poe is here to see you."

"Excellent. Send him in," Lawrence said. "Stay," he told the senator, who had started to rise. "Poe will bring us both up to date."

Kenneth Poe, in a navy suit and red tie, strolled into the office. Every dark strand of hair perfectly coiffed, he was the epitome of a gentleman. His usefulness to

Lawrence had grown in the past year. If Lawrence had been blessed with a son, he would have wanted the boy to be like Poe. Smart, ruthless, and handsome. He was nearly thirty now and still unmarried. Perhaps it was time to introduce him to Katelyn. Lawrence couldn't imagine a better son-in-law.

"Sir," Poe said, extending his hand. "Senator."

The men shook hands, and Lawrence ticked another box in Poe's favor. He knew how to act around power and had made sure to show respect to Lawrence first. The boy must have taken a class on sucking up. Lawrence liked it.

"I hope you have a signed bill of sale for me," Lawrence said.

Poe settled into the other chair and casually propped one foot on the opposite knee. "Unfortunately, we've hit a snag."

Lawrence frowned at Poe's grave tone. "What kind of snag?"

"It's serious."

When Poe said something was serious, Lawrence paid attention. "How serious?"

"A young woman came to town. Very smart and nosy. She found the cave. I'm not sure if she saw the contents." He glanced at the senator.

Lawrence pursed his lips. "We just need her out of the way long enough for us to get the land signed over. Can you put her in a safe place until we accomplish that?"

"It's already done. But what if that causes even more problems?"

"If it does, we'll deal with it later. I have a great deal

of money riding on this, Kenneth. I won't allow my plans to be derailed by a spelunker. Fix it."

"Yes, sir. I'll do my best."

Poe's best was usually spectacular. Lawrence dismissed his concerns and began to think about what he would do with the money that would come pouring in when he turned Hope Island into the next Myrtle Beach.

* * *

The sailboat was sinking fast, and so was the sun. Two people flailed about in the water below. Chief Petty Officer Alec Bourne sat on the floor of the Dolphin helicopter with his feet dangling over the edge. "Take it lower," he shouted over the roar of the rotors. His Coast Guard team received the call for help twenty minutes ago, and he'd prayed all the way out that they'd be in time.

The hurricane had veered and was going to miss them, but its outer band stirred up fifteen-foot seas, and the small craft below had floundered in the wind and waves. It heeled to the port by about forty-five degrees. This distress call was likely to be the first of several for the day.

Aircraft Commander Josh Holman nodded, and the helicopter hovered closer to the waves pounding at the boat. Alec leaned into the wind. The stinging rain struck his face, and he smelled the salty air as he waited for the signal from Curtis Ireland, his flight mechanic and best friend.

"Stand by to deploy swimmer," Josh barked.

"Roger, checking swimmer." Curtis slapped Alec's chest.

Alec inhaled, then flipped the hinged buckle and released his gunner's belt, the last piece of gear that held him in the helicopter. He shoved off the aircraft. The wind buffeted him on the way down. The waves slapped the air from his lungs and he submerged, then popped to the surface and struck out for the first of the people in the water.

A woman in the sea struggled toward him. When she reached him, she grabbed his neck and nearly took him under the water. "Calm down!" He pushed her away, then grabbed her from behind in the traditional rescue hold. She stiffened, then relaxed in his grip. He gave Curtis a thumbs-up, and the rescue basket began to descend toward them.

"You're going to be okay," he assured the woman.

"We hit a shoal," she gasped, her lips blue. "We've been in the water for two hours."

"It's almost over." He grabbed the basket and got her inside, then signaled to Curtis to lift her to the helicopter while he went after her husband.

Five minutes later he was back aboard the Dolphin too. Mission accomplished. The health service technician, Sara Kavanagh, began to check out the woman's pulse and blood pressure. Both patients were swathed in blankets. They thanked Alec and his crew several times as the chopper veered back to the Coast Guard station, where medical personnel waited to attend the capsized sailors.

On days like this Alec knew he was right where God wanted him. There were other days when nothing went right, or when they lost someone they were trying to save.

He was smiling when he walked to the grassy picnic area of the station with his friends. Alec and Curtis had gone through training together. They were as different as two best friends could be. Curtis was the quiet, thoughtful one of the group. Though he came from money, he never flaunted it. Sara Kavanagh was the only female on their team. Her reserve kept the men at the station from making any inappropriate remarks, and she had earned their trust with her skills. He sometimes wondered if she and Josh Holman would end up a couple. Josh was a jokester and kept the rest of them laughing, but sometimes Alec thought he saw a special spark when Josh looked at Sara.

"You've got three days off, Alec," Josh said. "Gonna leave the island and head for the casino so you can win big and buy me a Jaguar?"

"I think you'll have to settle for a bicycle on what I have," Alec said. "Me and Zach will go crabbing. I hear there have been some good hauls. Maybe I'll make enough to build that back deck."

Sara was pulling food from a sack. "How is Zach?"

Alec's smile faded. He shrugged. "It's only been two weeks. You know how it is with a teenager. One minute he's got a head on his shoulders and the next he's doing something so stupid you think he was raised under a rock. He's sure glad to be back on the island though. He hated Richmond."

"There are bound to be challenges. You've never raised a kid before," Sara said.

"Darrell did most of the raising and I'll figure out the rest. He's all I have left of Darrell."

The small plane crash had been only six months ago, and Alec still missed his older brother with a painful ache. Zach was the spitting image of Darrell at that age too. The kid was a handful for his grandparents, though, and Alec had taken custody two weeks ago. He should have taken him right from the start, but Alec's mother had been adamant that the boy's place was with them. And Darrell had named his parents as guardians.

His cell phone rang and he grabbed it. The station was one of the few places on the island where his cell worked. The call was from his cousin Tom, who also happened to be the sheriff on this rock. "Hey, Tom."

"Sorry to bother you, buddy, but I've got Zach here in jail."

Alec's stomach plummeted. "What's he done?"

"He and some of his friends took it into their heads to spray-paint graffiti on the school. I caught him with the paint. I think you should leave him here overnight. Might teach him a lesson."

The thought of his nephew in jail pained Alec, but he knew his cousin was right. "Whatever you think is best."

"While I've got you on the phone, I need your help. A woman named Nicole Ingram was abducted out at Tidewater Pier."

"Abducted?"

"The Virginia Beach police called me. Her business partner saw it all on the cam."

Alec winced. "That had to have been rough."

"She was hysterical, according to the officer who called me. She's on her way here. Can I get your team to keep your eyes open on this one? The kidnappers took her in a boat."

"Sure thing. You got a description of the woman?"

Tom gave it to him. "Oops, got another call. Don't come until lunch tomorrow to spring your nephew."

Alec ended the call and put his phone away. The others were looking at him with curiosity. "Zach's in jail."

"So we gathered," Curtis said. "What'd he do?"

"Spray-painted graffiti on the school."

"I did that once," Josh said. "It's a rite of passage to adulthood."

"I never did," Alec said.

"Yeah, but you walk on water."

Alec grinned at the familiar joke. Just because he didn't drink or smoke, most of the other men thought he was some kind of saint. The truth was far different.

THREE

The trip to the Outer Banks was a blur, and Libby barely noticed the landscape, though she'd often wanted to go to the Outer Banks. She crossed the Chesapeake Bay Bridge. Route 168 turned into US 158 when she reached the Outer Banks. On her left was the Atlantic Ocean, and on the right she saw Albemarle Sound. The place felt like another world. She ran down her window to drink in the atmosphere of squawking gulls and murmuring surf.

By the time she reached Kitty Hawk, the sun had set. She parked in the Dock of the Bay lot and rushed out. Motorboats and sailboats gleamed in the moonlight where they bobbed in the dark water. There were few people on the dock at this hour, but they were tourists. She stopped everyone she met, but no one had a boat they were willing to use to get her out to Hope Island.

She found herself examining every man she saw, but none looked like either of the men who had taken Nicole. She saw a Coast Guard cutter in the distance and waved her arms, shouting for it, but it cruised on past without noticing her. How was she going to get to Hope Island tonight?

Now that she was here, her driving-induced fatigue fell away. When her stomach rumbled, she realized she hadn't eaten since lunch. She was going to be here all night, so she got a bag of chocolate-covered peanuts from a vending machine and a cup of coffee. Both left her more jittery than before. She eyed the long stretch of water. Maybe a walk along the shore would calm her down. She sat on a rock and took off her shoes, then walked along the soft sand. The salty air cleansed her head, and she prayed for God to be with Nicole wherever she was. Who could have taken Nicole and why?

A boat horn sounded out in the water and the running lights flashed. She wandered out onto the pier and sat down with her bare feet dangling over the water. A fish splashed off to her right, and the sound of the waves rolling onto shore soothed her. God saw Nicole. He was in charge here. Libby had to try to cling to that fact.

With the adrenaline draining out of her, she yawned. Maybe she could sleep for a little while, then she'd find someplace to take a shower. But she sat with her eyes open through the long night. When the sun came up, she got up again and went in search of a charter.

She reached the top of the pier and smiled at a man and woman walking their dog along the beach. The dog sniffed her leg, and Libby stooped to pet it, a cute Yorkie. "You're a sweetheart."

The woman appeared to be in her forties. Her smile lines and straw hat made her look approachable. She wore khaki walking shorts and a red top. She smiled. "It's a surprise to see you here, Vanessa."

Vanessa. Her sister's name. "I'm not Vanessa. My name is Libby Holladay."

The woman's smile faded. "Oh my dear, I'm so sorry. You look so much like a young woman I know on Hope Beach. Pardon me."

"Someone else told me that. Are you from Hope Beach?"

The woman brushed a strand of hair from her eyes. "I used to be. I taught school there for four years. Vanessa was one of my students. It's amazing how much you two look alike."

"I'm trying to find a charter out to Hope Island. Do you know where I might ask?"

"My husband and I are going there in a few minutes. We'd be happy to give you a ride." She put out her hand. "I'm Naomi Franklin, and this is my husband, Earl."

Libby shook hands with them. "That would be wonderful!" She'd been afraid of how much the charter might cost. "What time?"

"Right now," Earl said around a toothpick in his mouth. "Our boat is the *Blue Mermaid*. It's there." He pointed to a big sailboat. I just have to fill the tank and pack the supplies we brought for our summer house."

"She's beautiful," Libby said.

He beamed. "We've only had her a month." He took his wife's hand. "You can take her aboard, honey, and I'll get the supplies."

"What about my car?"

"It's safe here. Just leave it in the lot. You can rent a car on the island. Pricey, but maybe you won't need it for long," he said.

Libby rushed back to her car and grabbed her suitcase, then locked the vehicle and joined them at the dock. Earl helped the women aboard, and moments later the sea spray struck her arms and was dried off by the hot sun.

She stared at the horizon. "How far to the island?"

"About half an hour. You have business in Hope Beach?" Naomi asked.

Libby hesitated. "My partner and I restore historical buildings and sell them. She's been on the island investigating the idea of helping to restore the downtown area."

"There are some beautiful old properties on the island. Many of them have fallen into disrepair, so you'll have your work cut out for you." Naomi tipped her head to the side. "You really do look like Vanessa Mitchell in a most astonishing way."

Libby managed a smile. "They say everyone has a twin somewhere in the world. Have the Mitchells been there a long time?"

"Oh yes. The old Tidewater Inn is the matriarch of the place. Make sure you see it. Since you are into historical buildings, I'm sure you'll be fascinated. It's lovely. Ray Mitchell's dad bought it in the thirties and raised a big family there. Ray bought out his siblings after their father died and turned it into an inn. Not that there are many tourists on the island, but he hoped he could entice families who wanted a quiet getaway."

"Are his siblings still around?" Aunts, uncles, cousins. The idea tightened Libby's chest.

"Just his sister. The rest moved to the mainland." Naomi opened the ice chest. "Water?"

"Sure." Libby accepted the cold, wet bottle and uncapped it. "Is that Hope Island?" she asked when she saw a speck of land in the distance.

"That's it," Earl said.

Libby almost forgot to breathe as the island neared. Why did the island appeal to her so much? She'd never been here, had she? Charming houses lined a small bay with a well-maintained dock. Most of the houses could use a coat of paint and some repair to the gutters, but the village was like something out of a painting from the eighteen hundreds.

"Where can I rent a car?" she asked.

"No need for one, really," Earl said. "Not if you're staying in town. You have a room?"

"Not yet." She ignored the lift of his brow. "Can you recommend a hotel?"

"Tidewater Inn would be your best bet. If you call them, they'll fetch you," Naomi said. "Stop at the general store. They'll give you the number. We don't have a car on the island or we'd run you out there ourselves."

"There's a small lot by the harbor where you can rent a car though," Earl said. "Some people like to explore."

Home. The place felt like home. That was the sensation in her chest.

* * *

The sheriff's office felt deserted when Libby stepped onto the worn wooden floor. "Hello?" she called.

A man in a uniform came down the hallway. He was in his late thirties with dark hair just beginning to get salty. His tanned face was good-natured. "Can I help you?"

"I'd like to see the sheriff."

"That would be me. Sheriff Tom Bourne. Come on back." He led the way to a small office that held a battered desk and a metal filing cabinet, both overflowing with stacks of paper. He lifted a batch of files from the chair opposite the desk. "Have a seat and tell me what I can do for you."

She settled onto the hard chair. "My business partner was kidnapped yesterday."

His gaze sharpened. "You're Libby Holladay, the one who witnessed the kidnapping?"

"Yes. Is there any news?" Surely they had found Nicole by now. Alive, she prayed.

He shook his head. "Nothing. All I found when I got to the lifesaving station was her car. No sign of her. I've called in the Coasties, but they've seen nothing."

"Coasties?"

"Coast Guard. What can you tell me about your conversation? You rushed off before the Virginia Beach police arrived to take your statement."

"I wanted to get here and find her." She described the men she saw, and he took notes. "One man gave her an injection."

"It would help if we could call up the video, but it seems to have been erased from the server."

She bit her lip. Should she admit what she'd done? How much trouble could she get into for that? It was an accident, after all. But didn't the police tend to blame the person closest to the victim?

The phone on his desk rang, and she sat back in the chair while he talked. He rose when he hung up. "I have to go. There's a problem at the jail. Where are you staying? Tidewater?"

She nodded. "I hope to. I haven't called yet."

He reached for some keys and tossed them to her. "I've got an old car I loan out sometimes. Go ahead and take it out to Tidewater. I'll catch up with you there and get it back. Just follow Oyster Road to the end. You can't miss it."

She took the keys and followed him out the door. There would be time to tell him about the video later. Maybe she could find the file and restore it. Then she wouldn't be in trouble.

* * *

The old truck reeked of fish, but it was the smell of money to Alec. The morning's excellent haul would fetch a premium price at the restaurants. But he needed to get to the jail and pick up his nephew. As he maneuvered the truck along Oyster Road just outside of town, he noticed Tom's red Honda along the shoulder. A woman crouched beside a flat tire. Tourist, from the looks of her.

He parked his truck behind the car and got out. "Need some help?"

Her sun-streaked light-brown hair framed a striking face with bold brows and large brown eyes. In her early thirties, he guessed. There was an air of tension around her as if she were about to explode.

She held up the tire iron. "I'm not quite sure how to use this."

"Let me see if I can help." Alec took the tool from her. "Everything okay?" He knelt by the tire and began to remove the lug bolts. "You're driving the sheriff's spare car."

"My business partner is missing." Her voice trembled. "I was watching on a beach cam, and two men kidnapped her right in front of me."

His hands stilled, and he looked up at her. "Nicole Ingram?" He'd gone out last night on the search for the missing woman. All they'd found was her cell phone on the sand, a chilling sight.

She nodded. "She'd told me when she would be at the cam, so I got on the computer. Two guys came ashore in a small boat and took her away. I called 9-1-1, but by the time the sheriff got there, all he found was her car parked along the side of the road. No sign of Nicole."

"No sign of her in any boats that were stopped yesterday either."

She studied him as she fidgeted with her large leather bag. "How do you know that?"

He rose and stuck out his hand. "Alec Bourne. Part-time fisherman and full-time captain in the Coast Guard. The sheriff is my cousin, and he told me about your friend. My crew did a run through the area on one of the boats, but we didn't see anything suspicious."

She grasped his hand in a tight grip. "I'm Libby Holladay. You have to find her."

He checked the spare. "This spare tire is flat too. Tom needs to take better care of this vehicle. Hop in. I'll take you anywhere you need to go. Tom can collect the car later."

She studied his face. "I'm sorry, but I don't know you."

He couldn't blame her for being cautious, especially considering what had happened to her friend. He dug out his Coast Guard ID and held it out. Her fingers grazed his when she took it, and the bolt of adrenaline he experienced nearly made him snatch his hand back. She was beautiful, but he'd seen beautiful women before.

She returned his ID. "Thank you. I'm sorry if I offended you."

"No offense taken," he said while he fetched her belongings from Tom's car. "It's always wise to be cautious." He jerked his head toward the passenger side of the truck. "The door sticks. Give it a jerk." He put her suitcase in the truck bed, then slid behind the wheel of his truck and quickly moved some nets and tackle off the seat.

She yanked on the door, then climbed in. She wrinkled her nose as she shut the door. "I guess you *have* been fishing. The truck reeks of it." She smiled. "Sorry, I don't like fish much."

"You just haven't had the right fish. I went crabbing this morning. Nice haul." He started the engine. "The smell grows on you. Where you headed?"

She hesitated. "I was going to go to the Tidewater Inn, but you can just take me back to town and I'll call them."

"You live in the Outer Banks?"

She shook her head. "Near Virginia Beach."

"Your friend was here on vacation or something?"

She stared out the window. "Or something."

He didn't like the way she didn't look at him. Like she was hiding something. "By herself? She didn't say anything about being worried about someone? No one was following her?"

She shook her head and rested her cheek on the window.

"I get the feeling you're not telling me everything," he said. "I have a nose for deception. Comes with the job."

She finally lifted her head and turned to face him. Her dark eyes were anxious and strained. "It's personal."

He turned the truck into Dead Man's Curve and headed for downtown. "Might have something to do with your friend's disappearance though."

Her face was pale. "Do you know Horace Whittaker?"

Was she in some kind of trouble? "Sure. He was born and raised here on the island. Good man, good attorney."

"His secretary gave Nicole some interesting news. She said my father has left me some property out here."

He tried to think who had died lately. "Who's your father?"

"Ray Mitchell."

Alec raised his brows. "You're Ray's daughter? I never knew he had any other kids except for Brent and Vanessa. You never visited him here. I would have seen you."

"I *thought* he died when I was five." She pressed her lips together and looked down at her hands.

He absorbed the news. So the information that Ray had only died a month ago would have come as a shock. "Who told you that?"

"My mother."

"Your mom lied to you?"

She gave a barely perceptible nod.

He made a quick decision as he parked in front of the jail. "Give me Tom's keys. I'll have a couple of deputies handle the car situation, and we'll go see Horace."

She handed him the keys. "You think he knows what happened to Nicole?"

"He can tell us what he knows of her visit here. Maybe something will point to whatever happened. Though I doubt it's related to your inheritance, I could be wrong. Do your brother and sister know you're here?"

She shook her head. "Seems crazy that I have a brother and sister I didn't know about until yesterday." She stared at him. "Did you see any boats out yesterday at all?"

He shrugged. "Fishing boats. Like I said, we stopped a couple but found nothing suspicious." He got out of the truck. "I'll be right back," he told her through the open window. He'd spring Zach while he was at it and tell the kid to go home and stay there.

FOUR

Libby craned her neck to take in the village of Hope Beach. The main street, Oyster Road, ran straight through to the harbor. Small shops lined the road and displayed wares ranging from beads to beach gear to driftwood furniture. Alec drove the truck past a restaurant with tables on a terrace. There was an ice-cream shop and a coffee shop across the street.

It was a town unlike anything she'd ever seen. She almost felt like she had stepped into a movie about a beach town in the fifties. There were very few cars but a lot of bicycles. So quaint and charming. What a wonderful place to grow up. Live oaks lined the sidewalks, and the street itself was cobblestone. The shop fronts were mostly clapboard. Libby loved it already.

She eyed a Victorian home with decorative siding in the gables. "Why isn't this place on the historic registry? It's like stepping back in time."

"You sound like an expert or something," Alec said.

She stared up at the fretwork on the next house. "I'm an archaeological historian. I work in historic preservation. Some of these places are real treasures."

She glanced back at the man beside her. Alec was a

handsome guy, about six-two with sun-streaked brown hair. His blue eyes were startling in his tanned face, and his muscular frame was from either hauling in nets or working out.

He parked in front of a clapboard house that appeared to be freshly painted. "It's expensive to renovate out here. Material has to be ferried over, and workmen are at a premium. So most make do with what they have or what they can accomplish by themselves."

She continued to stare at the buildings. "That's why they're still intact, then. In college I did my thesis on historic homes in Charleston. I compared contemporary photos that I'd taken to historic pictures I found in the archives. I wanted to show the progress over the years. What I set out to prove was that, historically, homes in Charleston were owned by folks who were too poor to paint but too proud to whitewash. So those places stayed the same."

He nodded. "You might be right about that. Happened here for sure."

She got out of the truck and shut the door behind her. "Why hasn't the charm been destroyed by tourism?"

"Your father gets the credit for that. He owned most of the town, and he refused to sell to outsiders. Some called him a genius and others said he blocked progress."

A rustic sign proclaimed the building to be that of Horace Whittaker, Attorney-at-Law. The place had so much gingerbread in the gables and on the porch that it looked like a fairytale cottage. She followed Alec through the entry and into the foyer, which was surprisingly dim. A young woman in jeans sat behind the counter.

Alec glanced around. "Hi, Mindy. Why are you sitting in here with no lights?"

She rolled her eyes. "Horace forgot to pay the electric bill again. And his bill at the dive shop. That man is so forgetful."

Or so irresponsible. Libby was quite familiar with irresponsibility. Her mother always wanted to play and let the bills take care of themselves. Except they never did.

"They're supposed to turn it on any minute. I don't mind." Mindy held up a romance novel. "I get to read instead of work. At least I have a window." The woman's eyes were sparkling. "You hear about the hurricane? The first one missed us but there's another heading this way."

Alec shrugged. "It's only a category 1. We'll be fine. Listen, is Horace busy?"

The secretary shook her head and picked up the phone. "Horace, Alec is here with a lady to see you." She listened a moment, then replaced the receiver. "You can go on back."

Libby saw the speculation in the woman's eyes. "I'm Libby Holladay."

The woman's eyes widened. "I'm Mindy Jackson. I met your business partner." She put down her book. "I got into so much trouble for telling her Horace was looking for you. He hates to appear incompetent. I was just trying to help though." She tipped her head and stared. "You look a lot like Vanessa."

"So Nicole said."

Mindy winced. "I heard on the radio this morning about her kidnapping. You're the friend who saw the men take her via the cam?"

"Yes."

"I see. Well, welcome to Hope Island, Ms. Holladay. I'm sorry about your friend. Hopefully the sheriff will find her soon."

Libby tensed at the doubt in the secretary's voice. "I'm sure they will," she said. "Did Nicole mention what she'd been doing? Did she seem afraid of anyone?"

Mindy shook her head. "She came in to have Horace help her with some paperwork. But she seemed more interested in the inheritance when she heard about it." She pointed down the hall. "You know the way to his office, Alec." Her tone dismissed them, and she stuck her nose back in her book.

Libby followed Alec down the wide hall. The woodwork was quarter-sawn oak and appeared to be original. The plaster walls were painted an accurate period gray-green. She was sure there were original hardwood floors under the carpet. Alec pushed open a door at the end of the hall, and she glimpsed a man in his fifties behind a massive cherry desk. He looked like Burl Ives with his round face and belly and his pointed beard.

When he spoke, even his voice had that rich Ives timbre. "Alec, can't say I was expecting to see you in need of an attorney." His gaze went to Libby. "Or is it your friend in need of my help?" He rose and extended his hand. "Horace Whittaker."

She put her hand in his. It was warm. "Libby Holladay."

His fingers tightened on hers. His white brows rose. He pointed to the overstuffed leather chairs. "Have a seat. Let me save my work. I'm updating my website and I don't want to lose it."

Libby sat. "You saw my friend two days ago, Mr. Whittaker?"

He nodded. "Call me Horace. It was rather embarrassing that my secretary was so unprofessional." He smiled. "Still, it allowed me to finally track you down."

"You'd had trouble?"

He nodded. "The last address Ray had for you was in Indiana. Your friend said you're in Virginia Beach now?"

"Yes. For the past year." Libby leaned forward. "About my father . . ."

Horace's round head bobbed. "Ray. The town misses him already. He was a great philanthropist, always contributing to those in need. You would have passed the school on the way in. The playground equipment was bought by your father. He's been a driving force in the village for the past twenty-five years."

A lump formed in Libby's throat and she blinked rapidly, determined not to let these men see the emotion that threatened to overwhelm her. If he was so generous to everyone else, why had he ignored her all these years?

Horace wheeled his chair around. "In addition to the old letters, Ray gave me a package for you. It's in my safe." He leaned over a safe behind him, twirled the dial a few times, then popped it open. He reached inside, then shut and locked it again. "Here we are." He held out an irregularly shaped envelope. When she took it, he reached into a drawer and pulled out a shoe box. "Here are the letters."

"What's in this?" She felt the package and couldn't tell what it contained.

"I have no idea. He gave it to me shortly before he died and asked me to put it away."

Libby tucked the envelope into her large bag and put the box of letters on the floor beside it. She wasn't ready to read anything from her father in front of spectators. "Thank you." She leaned forward. "What about my father's second family? They all live here?"

The attorney nodded. "His sister, Pearl, too. She's the town postmistress. She moved into the big house to take care of him before he died."

"What did he die from?" she asked.

"He had a heart attack a year ago and went downhill afterward. He knew his time was short, so he transferred all of his cash to a trust fund for Brent and Vanessa."

"Do my siblings know that I've inherited something?"

"I just informed them last week. Brent was on a trip to England, so I delayed the reading of Ray's will until he got back." Horace nodded. "He's a young hothead, and he demanded that we break the bequest. I told him he didn't have any legal grounds."

She didn't want to admit to herself that her brother's objection hurt. "Is the inheritance so valuable?"

The attorney retrieved a file from his drawer and slid it across the desk to her. "The entire west side of the island as well as an old inn is all yours. Now, it's not as valuable as if it were on the mainland, because progress has passed us by for now. But if tourists ever start flocking here, it could be worth a lot of money. Even in its current state, it's valuable."

She flipped open the folder. The first page was a photograph of a lovely Georgian hotel with porches and balconies. The second was of sand dunes and rolling whitecaps. "My siblings also have an inheritance? A trust fund, you said?"

"Oh yes, they're well taken care of. They each have more than a million dollars in the bank." He steepled his fingers together. "You really should draw up a will. The property is worth well over a million dollars," Horace said. "More if progress ever finds us."

No more money worries for her stepbrother. And that lovely old house she was in yesterday could be hers. She could create a foundation to help preserve the neighborhood. "I think I'd like to set up a foundation after it's sold," she said slowly. "For historic preservation." She sat back in her chair and exhaled. "I suppose I'll need a will too."

"I can draft something simple for you," Horace offered. "So you have something in place for starters."

"That would be nice. Thank you. I can't even think straight right now. I just want to find Nicole. The rest can wait."

* * *

Wind-tossed sand stung Libby's cheeks and arms as she stood on the boardwalk staring out to sea. Gulls swooped low over the water, and a crab scuttled across the wet sand. A few clouds floated on an impossibly blue sky. It should have been paradise.

"It's so beautiful," she said, then shivered. "And so deserted. This is the spot. I recognize the lifesaving station." She pointed to the lone building, a low-slung clapboard structure with a hole in the roof. "You say this belongs to me?"

Alec gestured to the west. "Not the station. That belongs to the town. Just over the hill is Tidewater Inn. You own this stretch clear to the inlet."

"Nicole was here to finalize the purchase of the station. We're going to restore it as a museum for the island." She scanned the area and saw what she was looking for. "There's the cam." It was mounted on one of the posts. She walked directly to it and stopped a few feet away. "Whoever you are, if you have my friend, please don't hurt her," she said. "Her name is Nicole."

Alec's eyes were warm with sympathy when she turned toward him and brushed moisture from her cheeks. "I thought they might be watching. They say an attacker usually goes back to the scene of the crime. And professionals say friends and investigators should try to personalize the victim."

Alec stood with his hands in the pockets of his denim shorts. "It's possible someone's watching. A plea doesn't hurt." He pointed to the final landing before the sand. "Her cell phone was found there. Her rental car was parked along the road with the keys in the ignition."

She winced. "I saw one of the men toss the phone. Would his prints be on it? And what about her hat? I saw it fall off."

"I'm sure Tom is checking that out. I'll do what I can to find her," he promised. "The first thing we have to figure out is where she was staying. My cousin may know." He pulled out his phone and placed a call. "Hey, Tom, I'm with Libby Holladay. Have you found out where Nicole Ingram was staying?"

His voice faded to a drone as she stepped away and stared down the deserted beach. Not a house was in sight of where she stood. No wonder the men had taken Nicole from this location. Gooseflesh pebbled her arms at the thought of what they might be doing to her friend. She swallowed down the wave of nausea that rose in her throat. She had to find Nicole. The most likely reason she was taken was too horrible to contemplate, so she considered whether there might be another reason. Nicole had been poking around about Libby's inheritance. Could there be any connection?

Libby took off her sandals and dug her toes into the warm sand. The sound of the surf washed over her in a rhythm that would have been soothing in other circumstances. Carrying her shoes, she stepped back to find out what Alec had learned. He was just finishing his call.

"Uh-huh. Okay. I'll tell her, thanks." He dropped the phone back into his pocket. "She was staying at the small inn you own. Tom was just about to head out there. We can meet him there and see what is in her room."

Libby glanced around one final time, but there was still nothing pointing her to Nicole's whereabouts. This search was already beginning to feel hopeless.

FIVE

Filtered light struck her eyelids. Nicole groaned and threw her hand over her eyes. The brightness pierced her skull like a knife. She licked dry lips, then pried one lid open, wincing when the brilliance intensified. She rolled to her back, then sat up.

Where was she? The sound of the surf rolled through the small window covered by a grimy curtain. Her head pounded, and she staggered to her feet. Her eyes were beginning to adjust to the light, and she glanced around. She seemed to be in a small building. Overhead were wooden planks, and she could see thatching through the boards. Her sandals and hat were missing, and so was her pink cover-up. She wore only her swimsuit. The dirt floor under her bare feet was cool and damp.

When she put her hand on the door, a rough wooden one, it moved. Surprised it wasn't locked, she stepped out of the shack and onto a mixture of sand and grass. A small beach began twenty feet away. She glanced around and realized she was on a tiny island, barely as big as her yard at home. No other land in the distance as far as she could see. Trying not to panic, she walked along the shore, straining to see something—anything—in the distance. There was nothing but seagulls and waves.

She was incredibly thirsty. Maybe there were provisions in the shack. And what was she doing here? The last thing she could remember was talking to Libby about the inheritance she'd discovered.

She fingered the soreness on her jaw. Ducking into the shack, she circled the perimeter of the space, about sixteen feet square. There was no kitchen, just the small cot and a camp chair. No food or water. Maybe there was a stream on the little island that she'd missed.

She went back into the sunshine and cut behind the shack. No cistern, no stream. Her head spun, and she fought back the rising panic. She'd better get out of the heat and inside. As she skirted the side of the shack, she heard a boat's motor *putt-putt*ing along. Maybe she could get help! She ran to the beach and shaded her eyes with her hand. A small craft rode the waves. Maybe a fisherman?

She shouted and waved. "Help! I need help!"

The bow of the boat headed for the beach where she stood. As it neared, she saw that it held a young man about seventeen or eighteen. The wind whipped his dark hair, and he waved back. When the boat was just offshore, he shut off the motor and threw an anchor overboard. He jumped into the water, and the waves came to midthigh, barely dampening the hem of his black shorts. He reached back into the boat and extracted a box.

She waded out to meet him. When he reached her,

she grabbed his arm. "I'm so glad you came this way. I need help. I don't remember how I got here, but I'll pay you to take me back to Hope Island."

Frowning, he shook off her grip. "I brought you some food and water."

She took a step back. "You knew I was here?" She struggled to make sense of it.

He brushed past her and walked toward the shack. "The water should last a couple days and the food is stuff like bread and peanut butter. Your brother will come get you when the room at the mental facility is ready."

She followed him inside. "I don't understand. I don't have a brother. You're not making any sense."

He set the box on the dirt floor by the cot and opened it. "Like I said, this should last you a few days. I'll be back then with more."

He was going to leave her. She grabbed his forearm and squeezed. "Listen to me! I don't have a brother. You can't leave me here."

He glanced at her, then backed away as if she frightened him. "He said you'd say that. It's only for a little while, until he can get you in. You tried to stick him with a knife, and he can't trust you around people. The mental hospital will have an opening in a couple of weeks. It's for your own good."

His expression was closed. She bolted for the door, slamming it shut behind her to slow him down. If she could get to the boat first, she could get away. She ran to the water and struggled through the waves to the craft, where she threw herself into the bottom of it. Sitting up, she saw him running toward her. She grabbed the rope with the anchor and yanked it up, then scrambled back to try to start the motor.

He reached the water and plunged toward her. She tugged on the rope to start the engine, but she didn't pull it hard enough. Before she could try again, he was at the side of the vessel. She kicked at his hands with her bare feet, but he hauled himself aboard. He grabbed her arm, and she bit his hand. Tasting blood, she bit harder and clawed at him with her nails. He grabbed her hair, tearing the dangling ponytail holder free before he finally seized her.

He shoved her overboard, and she came up spitting salt water. "Please, you have to help me," she panted.

"You are one crazy chick," he said. Using an oar, he pushed the boat away, then turned and started the engine.

She screamed and shouted for him to come back, but he didn't even look at her. Sobbing, she collapsed onto the beach.

* * *

Alec cruised by his house on the way to the hotel. Zach's bike was parked in front of the house, but Alec's gut clenched when he saw Zach tying off to the piling. He'd obviously been out in the old boat in spite of having been grounded. What was he going to do with that kid? Alec couldn't be here 24/7 when he had to work. And Zach was old enough to start taking responsibility for himself.

"I need to stop here at the house for a minute if you don't mind," Alec said.

"Of course. Is that your son?"

Alec parked the truck by the garage just off the street. "My nephew. My brother and his wife are dead, and I've got custody. As of two weeks ago." He shoved open his door.

"I'm so sorry," she said.

"I am too." He led the way to the house.

"Do you mind if I use your restroom?"

"Help yourself." He should have thought to offer. He got out of the truck and led the way to the house.

"Cute," she said, pausing on the stoop. "Built in the fifties?"

He nodded and took a glance at the all-too-familiar two-story. It was white clapboard with gray shutters and a red door. "You're good. I bought it from my parents when they moved to Richmond." He held the door open for her and pointed down the hall to the bathroom. The place was fairly clean. "I'm going to go down to talk to Zach."

His house was right on the harbor, and his fishing boats were docked just offshore. He stepped around to the back by the upper deck, which was anchored into the sand with pilings. Zach climbed down into the rubber boat and rowed to the small dock by the house. The boy had to have seen him standing on the pier, but Zach didn't wave. He probably knew he was in trouble. Alec waited until the raft reached the dock. Tight-lipped, he tied up the rope Zach tossed to him.

Zach stepped over the side of the boat and onto the

pier. He tossed a cheeky grin Alec's way. "I got a job, Uncle Alec!"

Alec's lecture died on his lips. "What kind of job?"

"I'm delivering some supplies." Zach glanced at him from under a lock of dark hair. "I know I was grounded, but Grandpa has been on me to get a job, and this was too good to pass up."

He wanted to ask how the job had come Zach's way while he was supposed to be staying home, but Alec bit back the words. "School is starting again soon. Will the hours be okay?"

Zach shook his head. "It will be over before school starts. It's supposed to last from two to four weeks."

"You should have called me."

"I tried. You didn't answer your phone."

Alec lifted a brow and pulled out his phone. Sure enough, it showed a missed call. Maybe when he and Libby had been in transit to the beach. It hardly paid to have a phone on the island. "Okay, but when you're not working, you still need to be at the house."

Zach brushed past him. "I know, I know. Sheesh, give me a break. I'm doing the best I can."

Maybe he was. The boy was so much like Alec was at that age. Always pushing the boundaries, impatient to be his own man, looking at anyone in authority with derision. At least Zach had a job. That was progress.

"Okay," Alec called after him. "I'm proud of you for getting a job."

Zach just hunched his shoulders and bounded up the stairs to the deck overlooking the water. He plopped down in a chair and pulled an electronic game out of his pocket. The back door opened, and Libby stepped out onto the deck. Alec jogged to intercept her. She'd take one look at Zach and think the kid was a hoodlum. Alec reached the top of the deck as she stepped to where Zach sat.

"You must be Zach," Libby said.

Zach didn't look up from his game. "Yeah."

"Ready?" Alec said. "Your place is about two miles out of town."

Zach looked up then. "The old Mitchell place?"

Libby nodded.

"You're staying there?"

"I own it," Libby said. "I'm Ray Mitchell's oldest daughter."

Zach looked her up and down. "Boy, is Brent ticked. He had plans for that place."

"He's twenty-two," Alec pointed out. "What kind of plans could he have?"

Zach slouched into his chair. "Forget it."

Suppressing a sigh, Alec touched Libby's elbow. "Tom should be there any minute."

She resisted the pull on her arm. "I'd really like to hear what Zach has to say," she said. "You probably already know this, Zach, but I didn't even know I had a brother and sister until yesterday."

His head came up and his eyes widened. "No kidding? Brent didn't say anything about that in the ice-cream shop. Just that some woman he'd never met was going to have the property. Said it was his sister."

"Did he know about me before our father died?"

Zach shrugged. "I don't know."

"I'd like to meet him. And Vanessa. Do they know I'm here?"

"I don't think so. He figures you'll sell the place. There's an investor after it hot and heavy."

"Oh?" There was interest in her voice.

Alec had heard the rumors. Now that the land was out of Ray's hands, everything was liable to change. He didn't know if that was good or bad.

SIX

Sand drifted across the pavement in places. The island was unlike any place Libby had ever seen. Wild, remote, and unbelievably beautiful with white-caps rolling to dunes on one side and tangled maritime forest on the other.

She leaned forward as Alec's truck crested the hill. She caught her breath when she saw the inn standing guard over the empty beach that stretched in both directions. A small but inviting dock jutted over the water. Her chest was so tight she couldn't breathe, couldn't do more than take in the lovely Georgian mansion overlooking the Atlantic. Large trees sheltered it, and it looked as if it had been in that place forever. In a moment, she felt she knew the spot as if it had always been a part of her.

She could almost hear the voices of previous owners in her head. Pioneers, business owners, statesmen. The inn was alive with the history of its past. She couldn't wait to explore, to touch the woodwork and plaster walls.

"Th-This is mine?" she asked, getting out the truck when it rolled to a stop.

"So I hear."

The place clearly needed work, but she didn't care. She stared at the front of the building. "You said it was an inn." She eyed its elegant lines. "It looks like a mansion. It's Georgian. Built in the late seventeen hundreds or early eighteen hundreds."

"It's an inn now. Small, I know. About fifteen suites, I think."

There were two curving staircases up to the porch, one on each side. There had to be two thousand square feet of balconies and porches. Great arched windows looked out on the waves. The place was in serious need of paint, but her mind's eye could see it restored to its earlier glory. How could she bear to sell it? But she had to. For her stepbrother. For Holladay Renovations.

He took her elbow and guided her up the nearest steps. "It used to be a single-family home. There should be some stuff about it in the attic."

No wonder Nicole had said she would love it. Libby took in every angle, every graceful line. "It's so large. Who would build such a magnificent place clear out here?"

"I don't remember all the history, but the builder had some kind of role in early government, and I guess he wanted to impress everyone. Though there weren't many to impress out here but Hatteras Indians. This place is really the beginning of our history as we know it, so it's in the school book about our island."

The porch was expansive, but the floor needed paint. Now that she was closer, Libby saw the signs of decay in the peeling shutters and rotting fretwork. It would take a lot of money to restore this place. Money she didn't have. But oh, how she wanted to keep it.

Alec opened the oversized front entrance. "The lobby is the room to the right."

Sand and salt had scoured the wood floors. Libby ran her fingertips along blistered paint on the plaster walls. She could repair it. She went down through the foyer to what would have been a parlor on the right. Ceilings soared to twelve feet. She glanced up and saw that the plaster drooped in places. It needed to be put back in place with plaster washers and screws. Or replastered altogether.

The reception counter was made of driftwood and marble. The woman behind the counter was in her early thirties. Her dark hair was up in a ponytail that curled down her back. She wore no makeup, and her strikingly beautiful skin didn't need any help. She smiled when Alec introduced Libby.

"I'm Delilah Carter, Ms. Holladay," she said. "I'm so sorry about your trouble. If there's anything I can do to help, just let me know." She rose with a key in her hand. "Let me show you to your friend's room."

"I see Tom outside," Alec said. "I'll join you upstairs in a minute." He walked back the way they'd come.

Libby fell into step beside Delilah. "Did you get a chance to talk to Nicole?"

The woman stepped into the foyer and started up the steps, easily six feet wide. "Oh yes. Lovely girl."

Libby mounted the steps with her. "Did she tell you why she was here?"

"For business, so she said." Delilah inserted the

key into the lock and turned it. She opened the door and stepped aside for Libby to enter. At the first sight of her friend's familiar pink suitcase, Libby's eyes burned. Nicole's pajamas were in a heap on the floor. Her clothes spilled from the top of the suitcase. In the bathroom, her makeup littered the sink counter. Libby picked up her friend's hairbrush and caught a scent of the shampoo Nicole used.

She swiped fiercely at the moisture on her face. Crying wouldn't find Nicole.

* * *

Alec intercepted Tom on the porch. "Any news?"

Tom's lips flattened. "Not about Nicole."

"What's that mean?"

"Ms. Holladay hasn't been truthful with us." Tom took off his hat and wiped his brow with the back of his sleeve. "The reason I can't view the video of the abduction is because it was wiped off the server. The computer's IP address was traced. Libby did it."

Alec's gut clenched. Though he'd known her only a few hours, he would have sworn her innocence and concern were genuine. "So there is no proof her story is even true. The cell phone could have been planted. The car could have been left out there by anyone. We know she only came to town today though, right?"

Tom nodded. "I talked to Earl Franklin and his wife. They met her this morning. But I'm questioning all the charters I know of to make sure she didn't get here a few days ago to lay out her plan."

Alec marshaled all his objectivity. Since when had a pretty face blinded him? "When was Nicole last seen?"

"I was about to question Delilah. No one in town saw her yesterday."

"What about Vanessa? Libby claims she was meeting Nicole."

Tom returned his hat to his head. "I haven't spoken to her yet, but I will. Right now I want to look through Nicole's room and talk to Delilah."

"You haven't gone through her belongings yet?"

Tom shook his head. "My first priority was to find her."

"Delilah just let Libby into the suite."

"Great, just great." Tom jerked open the door and rushed into the house.

Alec followed. He'd sure botched that one.

* * *

"Libby?"

Libby put the hairbrush back onto the sink when Alec called to her from the bedroom. "In here."

When she stepped into the bedroom, she found identical expressions on the faces of the two men in the doorway. Alec was making an obvious attempt to mask his suspicion, but the sheriff's gaze bored through her. She took a step back.

"What have you touched?" the sheriff demanded.

"Nothing but the things in the bathroom." She stepped out of the doorway so he could brush past her. "What are you looking for?"

He glanced around the small bathroom. "You had no business coming in here until I had a chance to clear the scene."

"It's not a crime scene," she said.

"There may still be clues to what happened to her."

He hadn't been nearly so unfriendly at his office. And even Alec was tense. "H-Have you found her?"

The sheriff whirled and glared at her. "You mean her body? Is there something you want to tell us?"

The kidnapping had changed into a murder, and she was a suspect. That was the only possible reason for his change of demeanor. "You found her body, didn't you?"

"What was on that video that you were so eager to make sure no one saw?" the sheriff asked.

His accusing tone made her swallow hard. He knew she'd erased the video. "It was an accident. I was trying to save it so I could show it to the police. The screen went blank and it was gone."

"I might have believed you if you'd admitted it from the first. But you said nothing about it when you were in my office."

"I was going to, but—"

"Right." He turned around and stared at the room. "Delilah, did she touch anything in here?"

"No, sir," Delilah said. "I could see her when she was in the bathroom too. She didn't do anything." The phone rang in the distance. "I'll be right back." She dashed out of the room.

"Alec, take a look in the suitcase. I'll go through the drawers."

Libby curled her fingers into her palms and prayed

that he would find something that would lead them to Nicole and those two men. "Just so you know, I did touch the hairbrush."

Tom looked her over. "Thanks."

Alec pulled shorts and tops out, then dumped out a bag with suntan lotion, sunglasses, and other sundries in it. The sheriff was opening the furniture's drawers and looking through them.

Libby spied Nicole's laptop on the desk and picked it up. "Maybe there's something on this."

The men glanced up. Tom scowled. "I told you not to touch anything. Alec, you know more about computers than I do. Have a look."

Alec lifted a brow and reached out his hand. "May I?"

Surprised he was gentlemanly enough to ask in spite of the suspicion in his expression, she handed it over. "You know anything about Macs?"

"I have one myself." He set the laptop on the desk and opened the lid. Pulling out the chair, he sat down and began to peruse the files. "She has a lot of files on this."

Libby stood behind him and watched over his shoulder. "Sort by date," she said.

He did as she suggested, then leaned forward and read through the sorted files. "What's this one?" He clicked on a file titled "Hope Beach."

The file opened with the picture of a woman. "Who is that?" Libby asked.

"Your sister, Vanessa. Definitely a family resemblance," Alec said, his voice distracted.

Libby drank in the woman's photo before the sheriff blocked her view.

He bent down to read the document. "It's kind of a diary. Ms. Ingram is talking about everything she saw and did since she came. Scroll to the bottom first. Maybe there's an entry for yesterday."

Libby peered over his shoulder and read the entry.

Someone was outside my door last night. He whispered my name. I think it was Brent trying to scare me into doing what he wants. I'll have a talk with him tomorrow.

Libby drew in a breath. "Would Brent have hurt her?"

Tom straightened and stared at her. "Let me handle the investigation."

She clasped her hands together. "Look, Sheriff, I know it looks bad that I didn't tell you about the file, but you're wasting precious time by investigating me. I didn't have anything to do with her disappearance. I can prove where I was when she went missing."

He said nothing at first and continued to stare at her with those accusing eyes. "What kind of proof?"

"For one thing, you can track the time on my cell phone when I called in the abduction."

"You could have disposed of her and gone back to Virginia Beach before you made the call. It's not that far."

Delilah poked her head into the room. "Hurricane warning just came through. That smaller one has veered this way. We need to get the hurricane shutters in place."

"Is the Tidewater in danger?" Libby asked.

"We're on higher ground here so we're safe from the surge," Delilah said, "but we don't know how much wind we're going to get."

"I'd better check in at the station," Alec said. "I'm off duty, but they may need me to begin evacuations. How long do we have?"

"Twenty-four hours or so," Delilah said.

This was her place now. Libby roused herself. "I'll help with the shutters."

* * *

The wind had freshened, but it was far from gale strength yet. The hurricane wouldn't be here for hours, if it even hit. Storms were notoriously capricious. Alec strained to see any sign of movement on the tiny strip of land below as the helicopter powered toward it. He'd already helped evacuate several families to the mainland.

"What's wrong with McEwan?" he asked Curtis.

"Said he thought he might be having a heart attack. The boat is too far away, so they called us."

Alec winced. "We're nearly there. We'll have Sara check him out." She had a manner that generally soothed patients.

The chopper reached an open field just past the pier on the small island below. Though the island had no official name, those in the Banks referred to it as Oyster Island, because some of the best oyster beds were found a few hundred feet offshore. Five families lived on it, all related in some way. McEwan lived in a shanty on the north side. He'd built the place when he was forty and hadn't left the island since. He had to be in his eighties now. He relied on his son to go for supplies. Alec had always liked the old fellow's stories about life in the old days. Alec suspected McEwan had been a rumrunner back in the day.

The rotors were still whirring when he ducked out of the helicopter with Curtis and Sara. They ran through the pelting rain toward the small cabin. The three of them rushed with the stretcher into the building, where they found McEwan moaning on his cot.

"Took you long enough," he gasped. "Ticker's acting up." He hadn't shaved in several days, and the gray stubble added to his pallor. He wore a dirty T-shirt and cotton pajama bottoms that looked like they hadn't been washed in a month.

Sara brushed past the men and knelt by the bed. "Let me take a peek." She pulled out her stethoscope and listened to his heart. "I'm going to give you a shot to relax your arteries," she said. "We'll get you to the mainland where the doctor can look at you, but I don't think it's a heart attack. Might be indigestion or gall bladder."

"I knew I shouldn't have had those raw oysters," the old man said. "They smelled a little nasty."

Alec grimaced. Oysters could contain dangerous bacteria when eaten raw, though oysters found offshore here were generally safe. It was hard to say what the old man had consumed. "We'll get you taken care of."

Once Sara administered the shot, the pain lines around the old man's face eased. Curtis and Sara got him onto the stretcher while Alec gathered a few items from the battered dresser by the bed. "Anything else you need?" Alec asked.

"My gun." McEwan pointed to a shotgun leaning by the door. "And the old suitcase under my bed."

Alec grabbed the gun, then reached under the bed for the battered old metal case. "Here, Sara, you take this stuff and I'll help Curtis carry the stretcher."

"I'm perfectly capable of doing my job." Sara grabbed the bottom of the stretcher.

Touchy. Alec raised his hands. "Suit yourself." Sara leaned in to whisper in his ear. "We'd better take him to the doctor at Hope Island first. I don't think there's time to get him clear to the mainland. I don't like the sound of his chest." Carrying the old man's belongings, Alec led the way back to the helicopter.

"Did that boat get back okay?" McEwan's voice was slurred and his lids droopy.

"What boat?"

McEwan waved his hand to the east. "Saw two men motor by yesterday. They didn't look like no watermen to me. One was yelling at the other one about how to steer. Didn't seem to bother the woman who was sleeping though."

Alec exchanged a glance with Curtis. Two men and a woman? Could it possibly be Nicole Ingram? Or was the old man out of his head? "Where were they headed?"

McEwan's eyes fluttered, then closed. "Out to sea. East."

Alec wanted to ignore the information, but what if the men were heading out to dump Nicole?

* * *

The inn was dark and gloomy with the hurricane shutters closed. Libby had never been in a hurricane before, and the breathless quality of the air added to her unease. "I think I'll sit on the porch and give my stepbrother a call," she told Delilah, who was instructing the housekeeping staff to ready some extra rooms.

Delilah nodded and Libby stepped out into the twilight air with the inn's portable phone in her hand. The sun was almost down and the sound of the cicadas enveloped her as she settled on the swing at the end of the porch. Could the police seriously think she might have hurt Nicole?

Libby put down the phone and clasped her knees to her chest. She had to figure out a way to prove her innocence. As long as the sheriff was investigating her, his attention wasn't on the right person. She should have told him about her mess-up with the computer. Everything was spiraling out of control because of her lapse of judgment. She could kick herself.

She still hadn't opened the items from her father. There hadn't been time, and she wanted no interruptions when she took a peek at the letters and the contents of the envelope.

The sand glimmered in the moonlight. The scene reminded her of when she was a little girl. She and her mom usually spent two weeks along a beach. One year it was California, another year the Texas Gulf, and yet another the cold water of the Pacific Northwest. The various vacations were a kaleidoscope of memories, all slightly hazy with an aura of warmth and love.

That zany woman with the long braid and beads who had been her mother was hard to reconcile with a parent who would lie and deprive her daughter of all contact with her father. Yet that was the situation, if everything she'd learned today was true. But was it?

Libby stood and walked restlessly to the other side of the large porch. No matter what, she knew her mother had loved her. In spite of their constant travels and the many men in her mother's life, Libby's well-being had always been primary. She would cling to that fact for now.

Headlamps pierced the gloom and tires crunched on gravel. Her pulse jumped when she recognized Alec's truck in the glow of the security light. His door slammed, and he went around to the passenger side and helped an old man out.

Libby met them at the foot of the steps. Alec was assisting the man to the inn. "Is he all right?"

"This is Mr. McEwan. He lives on one of the unnamed islands. He had a little bit of angina, but the doctor says he's going to be okay. We generally bring people to the inn during a big blow. I assume that's still okay?"

Libby swallowed her disappointment at his distant tone. "Of course. Let me get the door." She jogged up the steps and held open the front door. "Delilah, we have a guest."

Delilah appeared in the entry. "I'll put him in one of our three downstairs rooms. This way." She led Alec and Mr. McEwan down the hall.

Libby wanted to rush to her room and eat a whole bag of jalapeño jelly beans, but she forced herself to walk back to the swing. Hiding away would make her look guilty.

SEVEN

The windows in Alec's house were boarded, and all they could do was wait. Few of the Hope Beach residents had left for the mainland. Too many times they'd evacuated and then been refused entry to their homes for weeks.

He paced the wood floor in his living room and listened to the wind beginning to pick up outside. The house was on stilts to deal with storm surges, so he and Zach should be okay. It still stood after Hurricane Helene's visit in 1958, a category 3. This was only a 1. Other 3s over the years, Gloria and Emily, had left the house fairly unscathed as well, so he wasn't worried, but he couldn't say the same for Zach.

Zach put down his game, then picked it up again and glanced toward the boarded windows. "You think we'll take a direct hit? And what about the smaller islands offshore? Will they flood?"

The boy's eyes were wide. Alec still remembered the first hurricane he'd gone through. He was just as nervous as Zach.

"We'll be all right," he assured his nephew. "It's

supposed to give a glancing blow to this side of the island. That's all. And God is here with us."

The boy blinked. He got up and paced to the other side of the living room. "That's the thing, Uncle Alec. I've heard that my whole life, but where was God when my parents went down in that plane? If God loves me, then how could he let them die like that?"

At least Zach was talking. "He was with your dad in the cockpit. They are with him now. Being a Christian doesn't mean trouble never comes our way, Zach. It just means God is here, and he gives us the grace to get through the heartache."

Zach hunched his shoulders. Alec could feel the boy's pain. He was an adult, but he'd wrestled with his brother's death too. Why do bad things happen to good people? It was an age-old question, and every Christian dealt with it sooner or later. Poor Zach had been faced with it much too soon.

The phone on the end table rang. Alec glanced at the screen. It was Frank Bowden, Zach's maternal grandfather. Alec's gut tightened the way it always did when he had to speak with the man.

"Hey, Frank," he said. Zach's head came up when he heard his grandfather's first name. Alec shot the boy a reassuring smile.

"Alec." Frank's voice boomed in his ear. "I hear there's a hurricane headed your way. Why haven't you evacuated?"

"I'm needed here to help. We're riding it out."

"We?" Frank demanded. "My grandson is there too?"

"He's fine."

"You have a boat. You could have taken it to the mainland! Or that fancy helicopter you're so fond of hotdogging in."

Alec pulled the phone away from his ear a bit. Frank's voice had nearly deafened him. "Yes, I could have, but it's only a category 1. We'll be fine."

"That's the problem with your family, Alec. None of you ever gives any thought to what's best for everyone. You think things will automatically be all right."

Alec clutched the phone almost tight enough to break it. He couldn't lose his temper. Frank had his own view of the world. It was varnished tightly in place, and no one was going to change it.

When Alec made no comment, Frank huffed. "I want to talk to my grandson."

Without another word, Alec took the phone from his ear and handed it to Zach. His nephew took it hesitantly. He had an uneasy relationship with his mother's dad. No one could live up to Frank's high standards, and Zach had given up trying by the time he was five.

"Hi, Grandpa," Zach said. "No, we're fine. I'm not scared. I want to see what a hurricane is like. It's only a category 1. We'll be fine."

Alec hid a grin and went out to the back deck. The gray waves crashed over the pier and rolled dirty white foam onto the sand. The tide left flotsam behind as it receded for another attack. A dark sheet of rain that was the first outer band of the hurricane was just offshore and would be on him in a few minutes, but he lifted his face to the wind and exulted in God's power.

Such an awesome display. God could choose to spare this little spot or wipe it out. It was all in his control. Alec stared another minute, then the first drops of cold rain struck his face. He returned to the house and got inside just as the deluge hit. The rain thundered on the metal roof. It sounded as though the house was coming in on them, and he began to wonder if he'd made the right decision to ride out the storm. Even a storm this weak could kill.

Zach's eyes were wide and fearful. "Uncle Alec!" His nephew swallowed hard and handed the phone back to Alec. "It's Tom."

Alec took the phone. "Trouble?" he asked his cousin.

"We just got word that high tide is going to hit at the same time in the morning as the storm surge." Tom's voice was tense and clipped. "And Mr. Carter called. Can you evacuate him to the Tidewater Inn?"

It was going to be a long night.

"On my way." Alec hung up the phone. "I need to help some of the shut-ins. You can wait upstairs in case there's a storm surge."

Zach shook his head. "No way! I'm a man now, Uncle Alec. Let me come along and help."

Alec grabbed a yellow slicker and boots. "Get dressed, then." He tossed Zach's gear at him. "Hurry."

He prayed for those caught in this storm. That no lives would be lost. Property could be replaced, but lives were much more precious.

* * *

The storm would be on them soon. Libby sat in a swing on the expansive porch with her father's package in her hands. Bob Marley was crooning to her through her iPod earbuds, and the reggae soothed her ragged nerves as she waited for the rain to hit. The windows were shuttered and ready. The generator was gassed up, and the house hunkered down before the coming storm.

She stared out at the sea. The waves were high, and a few surfers were out braving the massive rollers. Crazy. She watched them for a few minutes, but her task couldn't be delayed forever. Libby pressed the envelope between her hands and felt something hard inside. A small locket with a photo? A bracelet? She couldn't tell. She flipped the envelope over and slipped her finger under the flap. It opened easily. She inhaled, then upended the envelope so the contents slipped out onto her lap. A necklace, a notebook, and a letter fell out.

She picked up the necklace first. There were beads strung on jute. It was quite worn. She rolled one bead over to see an engraved letter on the other side. She could barely make out a *J*. The letters on the other beads had worn off, and she had no idea what it was supposed to spell. The paper might explain, but she found herself a little reluctant to unfold it and read it—almost frightened, though there was no reason for the pounding in her chest. Who was this man Ray? And why had he deserted her?

She laid the necklace on her lap, unfolded the letter,

and glanced at the greeting. *Elizabeth*. No one called her Elizabeth. That made the letter even more special in a strange way. Had he called her by her full name when she was a baby? No matter how hard she tried, she couldn't dredge up a memory of the man who had fathered her. Her gut tightened again, and she pressed her lips together. He was dead and gone, unable to hurt her any longer. These were just words on a page. She moved so the porch light shone on the letter and she forced herself to read.

My dear Elizabeth,

So here you are in my home. Finally, you are where I've longed for you to be these past twenty-five years. My biggest regret in life is that I was not part of your formation, but God assures me he has kept you safe under his wings. I have prayed for you every day of your life, and even now as I face my final days, I desperately pray that you will walk with the Lord. I want to fold you in my arms when you step onto heaven's golden streets.

I know there is so much you don't understand. I trust my sister, Pearl, will fill you in on many of the circumstances that forced me to abdicate my responsibilities. Just know that I have loved you so much even when I've been unable to contact you. I hope the inheritance can make up in some small way for my neglect. I know Brent and Vanessa have never really cared for the inn. Somehow, I believe you will love it as I have loved it. Do with it as you will though. It's yours.

Perhaps you are wondering what this old necklace means. My wife made it for me in 1992, and it never left my neck until I took it off to give to Horace for you. "What Would Jesus Do?" has been the guiding mantra of my life. As you try to acclimatize yourself to the island and to your siblings, I want you to think about those words in all the challenges you face. Every day, I'd like you to jot down when you succeeded in the right responses and when you didn't.

I realize I have no right to ask anything of you. Any rights I might have had were destroyed when I walked away. I make no excuses for my failures. But if you'll wear this necklace and heed its reminder, it would be the greatest of all the possible legacies I might leave you. Much more valuable than the inn and the land.

I pray my God keeps and protects you all the days of your life. That you will walk humbly before him and serve him always. Your siblings will take this very hard, so I ask you to be generous in grace toward them. Extend them as much mercy as you can. The transition into the family will be challenging, and I wish I could be here to help with that. But even though I am absent in the body, I'm rooting for you from heaven. I love you, my dear girl, and always have.

Dad

Libby's face was wet, and she choked back the sobs building in her chest. He'd loved her. All these years when she thought he didn't care, he'd loved her and prayed for her. And had God *really* assured him that he'd kept her safe? She didn't understand any of it. Her father said to talk to her aunt, and tomorrow she would ask Alec to introduce them. Pearl. She liked the name and only hoped she could learn to love this unknown aunt—and even more importantly, that her aunt Pearl would love her.

The jute was rough in her hands. The necklace took on special meaning. Her father had worn it for twenty years. The worn beads had been smoothed by his skin. It was so loved that his fingers had worn off all but one of the letters. But now she knew what they were. *WWJD*.

She lifted it to her neck and fastened it. The beads felt warm, almost alive. She'd become a Christian two years ago, but there was so much about faith that she didn't understand. And she didn't know if she'd ever stopped to consider what a godly response to any tough situation might be. Too often she reacted without thinking. She fingered the beads. What would Jesus do about this place? How was she supposed to know?

EIGHT

Nicole waited in vain for rescue as the wind rose through the afternoon. When the wind had first started to freshen, she was sure someone would be along any minute. But the hurricane was upon her. And she had nowhere to go for safety.

She peered through the single window of the shack. The sea was much too rough for anyone to come now. She was on her own. She opened the door. The sky was downright scary with black clouds blocking the sun. Tossing waves that left her breathless with fear crowded the shack. The flashes of lightning and rolls of thunder were terrifying, but not as frightening as the thought of drowning. If she didn't get higher, she was going to die. The surge was already swirling around her feet. The best she could do with her food and water was put it on the cot, but she feared it would soon be underwater.

She swiped the rivulets of water from her eyes and clung to the door as she stared at the small island. Through the driving storm, she could see a lone palm tree, but the wind had nearly bent it double. No sense in climbing that. More surges of water would be coming through. She had to get on top of the shack. It was her only hope. The sides of the building were rough-sawn boards, but there was a small window ledge that might help her climb. She grabbed hold of the top window frame and hoisted herself up, planting one bare foot on the window ledge. The wind buffeted her back to the ground, and she splashed face-first into the seawater. She came up spitting salt and sand.

Maybe around back she would be protected from the wind enough to climb. Sloshing through the flood, she hurried to the rear. A plastic five-gallon bucket floated in the water. She upended it, then stepped on its bottom and managed to grasp the low roof. As she hauled herself up, the wind hit her again, driving stinging water into her face.

She wasn't going to survive this. Pushing the thought away, she swung one leg onto the roof. She got the other leg up too and lay gasping on the splintered surface with the wind trying to dislodge her. She forced her fingers and toes into every crevice she could find, but it took every bit of strength she possessed to stay atop the shack.

She pressed her face into the shingles and held on. If she fell again, she didn't think she would have the strength to climb, or to survive the night in the water.

* * *

Tidewater Inn seemed to shrug off the effects of the wind, though the storm howled mightily in rage at the way the inn withstood its power. Libby huddled under an afghan on the armchair in the parlor. Mr. McEwan seemed oblivious to the danger as he sat drinking his coffee and eating Delilah's fresh-baked cookies. The roar outside made her shudder. Where was Nicole in all this? Libby could only hope and pray she was all right.

Delilah flipped off the television. "The rain has messed up the satellite signal," she said. "Would you like some cookies, Libby?"

"No thanks."

"I'm always hungry when I'm nervous." Delilah headed toward the kitchen.

Libby rose and paced the Oriental rug that covered the oak floor. *Please, God, don't let Nicole be in any danger from this storm. Let us find her alive and unharmed.*

A thunderous pounding came on the front door. She rushed to answer it. Alec stumbled in with a deluge of rain and wet, salty wind. Libby caught a glimpse over his shoulder of the stormy sky and ocean. Scary. Alec was supporting a wizened old man. Zach was behind him with an older lady almost as round as she was tall.

Alec slammed the door behind them. "I have two more guests for you. I hope that's still all right."

"Of course. We have plenty of empty rooms. Let me fetch some towels." She raced to the laundry room and grabbed a stack of fluffy towels, then hurried back to the parlor where she helped the elderly couple dry off. A thought flickered through her head. What would taking in people cost her? Could these people afford to pay for the room?

"Alec arrived just in time," the lady said. "But I'm worried about my angels."

Alec put his hand on her shoulder. "I had Zach load them in the back of the SUV."

She patted his hand. "Oh, Alec, did you really? You're a darling young man. Could you bring them in?"

"I'll get them." He glanced at Libby and motioned for her to follow him. At the entry, he stopped and folded his arms across his chest. "The lady is Pearl Chilton. Your aunt."

Her pulse kicked. "My father's sister?"

He nodded. "She's a sweetheart. I think you'll love her."

He was still staring at her with a wary expression. "Did you tell her I was here?" she asked.

He shook his head. "I thought I'd leave that up to you."

"Who's the older gentleman? I thought they were married."

"Her neighbor, Thomas Carter. Their houses were both flooded. He was at her house when I got there. Pearl still works as the town postmistress. She's done that for thirty years."

"She's been looking in on my brother and sister since my father died, correct?"

He nodded. "She should have been at your dad's house in town, but she was at her cottage trying to get her angels."

"Angels?"

"Collectible angels. The living room is stuffed with them."

"I can help you bring them in."

"I can handle it. I'll be back in a few minutes." He opened the door and stepped into the driving rain.

Thunder boomed overhead, and Libby shut her eyes against the brilliant flash of lightning. She slammed the door, then took a deep breath and went back to the parlor. Pearl had taken her long hair out of its bun, and the salt-and-pepper tresses lay drying on her shoulders and down onto her huge bosom. Barely five feet tall, she was round as an egg except for the shapely legs revealed by her skirt.

Pearl seemed to realize Libby was staring at her. "Is something wrong, young lady? I have a smudge on my nose?"

Family. She had an aunt, siblings, probably cousins here. Libby couldn't take it all in. If only she knew Nicole was all right, the moment would be perfect.

She shook her head. "I . . . I'm sorry for staring." She walked nearer to the fireplace where Pearl sat combing out her hair. "I'm Libby. Libby Holladay."

Pearl put the comb down. Her gaze searched Libby's face as she heaved herself out of the chair. "Ray's Libby?"

Libby's throat locked, and she nodded.

"Oh, my dear," Pearl said softly. She held out her arms.

Libby leaned forward and was enfolded in soft arms and an immense hug that smelled of lavender and mint. It was all she could do not to break down. Had her father ever held her like this? Once the fervency of Pearl's embrace lessened, Libby pulled away and swiped the back of her hand across her damp eyes.

Pearl's faded green eyes studied Libby's face. "I see your father in you," she said. "You have his dark eyes. I wish he were still alive to see you. Not raising you was his greatest sorrow in life."

Libby couldn't stop the tears that welled then. "I never knew he cared," she choked out. "My mother said he didn't."

Pearl pressed her lips together. "I don't like to speak ill of anyone, but your mother was determined to be free."

Libby sank onto the rug by Pearl's feet and struggled to keep her expression neutral. Just listening didn't mean she was betraying her mother's memory. There were two sides to every story.

Pearl settled back on the chair. Clasping her knees to her chest, Libby watched her aunt's face in the firelight. "What was he like, my father?"

Pearl smiled. "Generous as the day is long. He was always helping other people. I think that's why God blessed him so with material things. He knew Ray would let them run through his hands to other people."

"I—I hear my siblings are not too pleased to learn about me."

Pearl's lips flattened. "Oh, they always knew about you. Ray never made a secret of it. He spoiled them too much though, and they think the world owes them a living. This will be good for them."

Libby's growing impression of her siblings wasn't flattering. How long before she met them? The wind rattled the door. Did her aunt realize that Nicole was her friend? "I'm here to find my business partner, Nicole."

Pearl gasped. "The girl who was taken—she's your friend?"

The compassion in her aunt's voice nearly broke

Libby's composure. She nodded and swallowed hard. "I saw them take her on the beach cam."

"Oh, my dear girl." Her aunt leaned over and hugged her again. "I've been praying for that young woman. Somehow, I think she's all right."

"You do?"

Pearl nodded. "When I pray, I have a sense of peace. You're going to find her."

"I hope so. It's so scary."

Pearl pursed her lips. "What about your mother? Where is she now?"

Libby shook her head. "She's gone. She died a year ago."

Pearl's lips flattened. "She was always a bit of a hippie. I imagine you took care of her—made sure she ate and took care of the house. You have that competent air about you."

Her aunt was perceptive. Libby nodded. "Mom always had a childlike way about her, but she was a good mother. Our house was always fun." *Until it was time to move on to the next town.* "I got a job in a museum when I was sixteen. That's where I learned to love history. I got a scholarship to college and got to follow my dream."

"What are you doing these days?"

"Nicole and I restore historic houses, then sell them. I love preserving part of the past."

Pearl stared at her. "Your father would have been proud of you. I wish he'd gotten to meet you."

Libby was forming a picture of her father that was very different from all she'd been told. But which was right?

NINE

The wind howled and Libby paced through the night. With every rattle of the storm against the windowpane in her bedroom, she prayed for Nicole, then for herself and the siblings she had yet to meet. Where was Nicole riding out the storm? Was she hurt? Would her siblings like her when they got to know her? The questions battered her.

The clock said it should be daybreak, but the black clouds outside blocked the sunrise. She might as well get up. The bedroom door creaked when she opened it, but she doubted the sound would carry above the pounding of the rain against the house. She slipped down the hall to the back stairway that led down to the kitchen. The house shuddered, and she grabbed the doorjamb, then felt along the wall for the switch. The bulb in the stairwell was dim, but its comforting glow lit the rubber-covered stairs.

In the kitchen she fixed some tea, then carried the hot mug to the parlor, where she curled on the sofa with just one light on to push back the dark. The storm still raged outside, but she felt safe and snug surrounded by the possessions of her father.

A shadow loomed in the hall, then Alec spoke her name. "You okay?"

She set her tea on the coffee table. "Did I wake you?"

He shook his head and stepped into the room. "I wasn't sleeping. You had the same idea as me." He held up a Pepsi. "Only mine was easier."

Once he was settled into the armchair, she leaned her head back against the sofa. "I know you're wondering if I did something to Nicole," she said. "I didn't."

"I didn't say you did."

"Your cousin thinks I did. And you're acting differently now. Wary."

He took a gulp of his soda. "You have to admit it looks bad."

"I agree." She held his gaze. At least he wasn't afraid to look at her. "I care about Nicole. That's why I'm here. Will you give me the benefit of the doubt?"

"Okay, I can do that much."

She exhaled when his expression went from cold to lukewarm. "Good." Better to move on to another topic. "I like Pearl."

He wiped the moisture from the soda can. "I knew you would. She's an institution in town. Everyone loves her, even though she knows everyone else's business."

"I noticed that. She already knew my life story."

"She won't repeat it either."

"I didn't think she would." Libby paused, uncertain how much he knew. "She said my mother was adamant about no contact. My father didn't want it that way."

"I'm sure that's true. Ray loved his kids. Sometimes to a fault."

"Did he ever speak of me?" She held her breath, hoping to hear some small snippet of her father's love for her.

He shook his head. "Not to me."

Libby picked up an enameled egg from the table and rolled it in her palms. "According to Pearl, my siblings knew about me. She said my father made no secret of my existence."

"Pearl would know."

She put down the egg and pressed her hand against her forehead. "So much coming at me so fast. I just want to find Nicole, but there's all this other information clamoring to be absorbed. I can't even think."

"You saw the cam late in the afternoon?"

She nodded. "I came right away, but I couldn't find a boat to bring me across the sound until yesterday morning."

"What did you do all night?"

"I sat on the pier. I paced the dock and prayed."

He smiled. "So you're a believer too."

She glanced at him, surprised at the approval in his voice. "Not a very good one. I make it to church about once a month. Maybe that's why this has happened. God is punishing me."

"Forget that idea. Bad things happen even to good people. Life is hard. God never said it wouldn't be. And he's with us in the hard times."

"I feel very alone," she admitted.

"I know Tom will do all he can to find her."

"I might believe that if he will look somewhere other than at me." She finally spoke her greatest fear. "What if they dumped her at sea and she's fighting the waves out there?" He didn't have to answer that. If that was Nicole's fate, she'd be dead by now.

"There's no reason to think that."

She stared at him, caught by a certain tone in his voice. Almost a hesitancy. "Do you know something you're not telling me?"

There was a long silence before he spoke. "Mr. McEwan said he saw two men go past his little island in a boat. He mentioned a sleeping woman."

She sprang to her feet. "Nicole! Did he see Nicole?"

He held up his hand. "We don't know that. I'm going to take a run out there in my boat though. Once the storm subsides."

"Can I come?"

"If you like."

She bit her lip. "Everyone thinks she's dead. I can sense it. I just can't believe that. We have to find her." She willed him to agree with her, but he looked down at his hands.

He rose from the armchair. "I think I'll call into the office and see if I'm needed."

It was clear that he thought Nicole was dead.

* * *

The storm had finally died. Though it was still early, Libby took her mug of tea to the porch. The jute necklace was warm at her neck. She touched it, then opened the notebook her father left. What would Jesus have done yesterday? She grimaced when she realized money had been her first thought when Alec brought in people escaping the storm. Jesus would have been concerned about people, not money. She wrote down yesterday's date and jotted down how she'd failed. Today she would try to do better. She closed the notebook and tucked it into the cloth bag at her feet, then went down the steps to the beach.

Debris littered the lawn, but the old house had withstood the blow like the proud matriarch she was. Libby studied the stately lines of the house. It was so beautiful. Someone would pay handsomely to own this. She walked down the sloping sand. The boardwalk and cam where Nicole had been taken were about a mile down the beach. This stretch of sand seemed to go on forever. Did she dare walk along the shore alone?

Then a figure caught her eye. A man strode along the beach with a clipboard in his hand. Strikingly handsome, he had almost-black hair and broad shoulders. Muscular legs extended from walking shorts. As he neared, she realized his eyes were a vivid blue. He put her in mind of a young Elvis Presley. The breeze lifted his dark hair from his forehead.

She lifted a smile in the man's direction when she saw him looking at the inn and writing in his notebook. "Can I help you?"

He smiled and stopped about four feet from her. "I'm looking over the property for a client who is going to buy it."

Her hackles went up. "Oh? I think you should make sure the owner wants to sell it."

"Oh, it's a done deal," he assured her. "Are you a guest?"

"No, I'm Libby Holladay. The owner."

His smile vanished. "That's not possible. Mr. Brent Mitchell agreed to sell it to me." His eyes narrowed. "What kind of scam is this?"

The proprietary way she felt about the house already was a shock. This was *her* house. "He was unaware until recently that I inherited the house, not him."

He smiled, an obvious attempt to regain his composure. "Then I will direct my client's interest to you." He held out a card. "I'm Kenneth Poe. I have a client who would like to purchase this property."

She couldn't afford to reject his offer. "Why does your client want the property? It's not really a money-making venture at the moment. Tourists have to rent a boat to get here. I had a hard time getting here myself." She decided not to tell him about Nicole's disappearance. It was none of his business.

He shifted his clipboard to the other hand. "I'm sure you see that the place is a monstrosity. It's going to take a lot of money to fix it up. Better just to tear it down."

She gasped. "Tear it down? You have to be joking."

He held up his hand. "Look at the place. Rotting wood, peeling paint, outdated rooms and baths. It would be cheaper to bulldoze it and start over."

"The mansion should be on the historic registry. It will be if I have my way. I've spent my life protecting historic property. I'd die before I saw this place bulldozed."

His smile was entirely too smug. "Come now, Ms.

Holladay. I think we can persuade you. My client is willing to pay you ten million dollars for this property."

The blood drained from her head, and she felt dizzy. *Ten million dollars.* The amount was outside her comprehension. She could buy a house outright, two houses, one for her and one for her stepbrother, here in town if she wanted. She could get a new car before her old clunker died for good. The future stretched out in an enticing way. But to follow that path, she would have to sacrifice an important piece of history. Could she turn her back on her convictions?

She wetted her lips. "I'll think about it."

"You do that. I think you'll see it our way. And my client might be persuaded to give you other incentives, such as a parcel elsewhere to build your own place. I'm sure we can come to an agreement. He's very eager to have this property."

Hope Beach would be just like the rest of the beach towns. There wouldn't be anything unique about this little bit of paradise any longer. Libby couldn't bear the thought, but she couldn't afford to reject it out of hand either. Any other investor would have the same idea, and this one seemed eager to move now.

"Like I said, I'll think about it."

"The offer won't be extended for long. If you don't wish to sell, he'll go after something else. I'd advise you to accept his offer before he loses interest. There are other properties he can purchase."

She bit her lip. "Could I meet with him? See what his plans are?"

Poe shook his head. "I doubt he'd have the time. He would tell me to say take it or leave it."

"I'll let you know next week," she said.

She watched him walk away and chewed her lip. What should she do? That was a lot of money.

What would Jesus do?

TEN

The expansive lawn had been meticulously groomed. The flower beds were in perfect condition for the garden party, and Lawrence smiled with satisfaction. His wife wouldn't be able to complain that he hadn't taken care of his duties as a host.

"How do I look, Daddy?" Katelyn twirled in a gauzy white dress.

His daughter might not be the most beautiful young woman he'd ever seen, but she was elegant and well bred. With her by his side, Poe could go far. Someone needed to be groomed to take over the Rooney businesses. Poe was the first man to come along who Lawrence felt might fill the ticket.

"Like a princess," Lawrence said, kissing her cheek. "There's someone I want you to meet today."

A dimple appeared in her cheek. "Your amazing Kenneth Poe?" she said. "I saw a picture. He's quite handsome."

When she blushed, Katelyn was downright pretty. Lawrence hoped Poe could see her attractions. "There he is now," Lawrence said, waving to Poe, who stood at the edge of the lawn looking around.

"Oh my," Katelyn said. "H-He's like Elvis."

Like Elvis. Lawrence hid his amusement. The girl was already halfway in love. Poe acknowledged the wave with an answering smile and strode across the green carpet of grass with a confident air. Lawrence liked arrogance in a man. Poe had the strength to tame Katelyn. And he'd dressed nicely for the occasion. The suit he wore was an Armani, if Lawrence was any judge—and he was. Poe's tie was silk, and he'd had a fresh haircut.

Lawrence put his arm around his daughter as Poe reached them. "You just flew in, Kenneth?"

He nodded. "My chopper landed an hour ago."

Lawrence put his arm around Katelyn. "Kenneth, my boy, I'd like to introduce you to Katelyn. My one and only heir." He put the emphasis on the last word.

Poe took her hand. "I'm honored to meet you, Ms. Rooney."

"Call her Katelyn," Lawrence ordered.

He noted the way Poe kept control of her hand for a little longer than necessary. The boy wouldn't let any grass grow under his feet. Poe kept his attention on Katelyn too. Smart. They chatted for several minutes, and Lawrence saw how Katelyn flirted. She liked him. And why not? Poe was certainly handsome enough. Their children would be good-looking too. And with any kind of luck, they would possess Lawrence's business acumen.

His wife called to Katelyn over by the food table. "I'll be right back," Katelyn said with a lingering glance at Poe.

Poe watched her leave. "Your daughter is lovely."

Lawrence put his hand on Poe's shoulder. "Feel free to call on her. I'd like nothing more than to have you for a son, my boy."

Poe's eyes widened and he smiled. "I'm honored, sir. Do you think your daughter would be agreeable?"

"I'm sure you could persuade her."

Poe's smile widened and his blue eyes were bright. "I'd like nothing better." He glanced toward where Katelyn stood talking to guests. "Before she comes back, I have some news to report."

"Oh?"

"The property is owned by someone other than Brent Mitchell."

Lawrence shrugged. "Shouldn't be a problem, should it? Offer the same deal to the real owners."

"I did. She was reluctant at first, but I think I can persuade her. It just may take a few weeks until I have her signed contract. The wrinkle is that Nicole Ingram is her business partner and friend."

"Nicole Ingram? That's no problem. She's in my employ."

For the first time, Poe appeared uncertain. "You know her?"

"She's part of the firm I hired to renovate some buildings. You know all about that."

"I know the firm's name. I didn't know the employees."

"What is this about?"

"She's the woman who found the cave."

It wasn't often that Lawrence was unable to speak.

"What did you do with her?" Lawrence held up his hand. "Never mind. I don't want to know. This is getting more and more complicated. Just get the property signed and delivered. I want to break ground by the end of the summer."

Poe nodded. "My thoughts exactly. The thought of ten million dollars was quite an enticement to the owner."

"Just get it done," Lawrence snapped. He nodded toward his daughter, who was approaching with a smile. "You'll be part of my family soon if you get this deal settled."

Emotion flickered in Poe's eyes and his jaw hardened. "I'll do that, sir. You won't be sorry you trusted me with this."

Lawrence's good mood had evaporated. The property would be his no matter what he had to do.

* * *

The winds died by early afternoon. Alec stood surveying the storm damage in the heart of Hope Beach. Libby had insisted on coming with him and Zach when the sheriff called about all the damage. Alec thought she was afraid Nicole's body was going to be discovered floating in the debris, but he prayed she wouldn't be assaulted with such a sight.

At the first glimpse of his house, he thought it had been spared. Then he drove closer, and water sloshed to the top of the truck tires. "I'm flooded," he said, unable to keep the dismay from his voice.

Zach pointed. "Both boats look to be all right though. They're both still attached to their moorings. Listen, can I take out the old boat?"

"The sea is still too rough," Alec said.

Libby grimaced. "It looks like the entire town is a mess." She was staring out the window at the still-turbulent water. "There's no sign o-of Nicole, is there?" Her voice quivered.

He reached over and squeezed her hand. "Tom would have told us if there was." He released her hand and stared at his house. "Guess I'd better see how bad it is inside. You can wait in the truck if you like."

"I'll come." She shoved open her door and stepped into the water.

He took her arm when they reached the front of the truck. He waved at some of his Coastie buddies, who were down the street carrying belongings from a house. The water filled his boots, and he shivered as the cold soaked his jeans. The flood covered Libby's flip-flops and reached nearly to her knees. His spirits sank lower as he pushed open the door and saw the flooded living room. "Gonna be a lot of damage," he said.

"There's plenty of room at the hotel," she said. "Let's gather some things. I'll help."

"It won't take long. You can wait here." Alec went into his bedroom and pulled some jeans and T-shirts off hangers, then scooped up underwear from the bureau. In the bathroom he grabbed toiletries, then met Libby in the hall again. "Let's toss this stuff in the truck and check on the rest of the town."

She nodded and followed him back outside. People were assessing the damage along Oyster Road. He wondered if she knew which house had been her father's. Taking her arm, he pointed down the street. "Your father lived there."

She stared at the two-story house and he tried to look at it through her eyes. Ray had always kept it in top repair, but it was in sorry shape now. The storm surge still lapped a foot up the gray clapboard siding. The sea had deposited debris around the porch and the yard swing. The wind had torn some shingles loose, and they flapped in the last of the wind.

"Aunt Pearl said Vanessa was at a friend's, but is that her?" She pointed down the street.

He followed her finger. "Yeah, that's Vanessa. How did you know?"

"She looks a lot like me."

He glanced at her. Same high cheekbones, same expressive dark eyes. They wore their hair differently, and Vanessa always covered her face with a ton of makeup. Libby was much more natural. "Guess you're right. You want to meet her?"

She shook her head, but about that time Vanessa caught sight of him. "Alec!" She waved to him and sloshed through the water toward them. She was dressed in shorts and a red tank top. The tips of her short hair were purple.

"Sorry," he said. "Should I introduce you?"

"I—I don't quite know what to say. Give me a minute." Libby sounded breathless.

Vanessa reached them. "Is Aunt Pearl all right?

I heard you rescued her last night." She gave Libby a curious glance, then her gaze went back to him.

"She's fine. Where did you ride out the blow?"

"At the church. Brent too. He's there now helping clean up. It's a mess."

"Looks like your house is hit pretty hard too."

She shrugged. "I figured we'd join Aunt Pearl at the hotel. At least it's still ours until the dragon lady comes to claim it." She blew her bangs out of her eyes. "I still can't believe Dad would give our property to some daughter who has ignored him all these years. I want to be out of town when she comes. I want nothing to do with her. Ever."

He tried to interrupt her fierce flow of words, but she barreled over him.

"It's a good thing my *sister* wasn't in residence yesterday, or Aunt Pearl would have been out on the streets."

He could see Libby take a step back. "Uh, Vanessa, there's something you should know."

Libby put her hand on his arm and shot him a pleading glance. He closed his mouth.

Vanessa's face took on a rosy hue, and her voice rose with every word. "I can just see her arriving and trying to lord it over us. I'm going to put her in her place the very first thing. She didn't know Daddy. *She* certainly didn't love him, or she would have come to visit. I hope she just sells the place and stays away. No one here wants to meet her."

"She might not be so bad," he said.

Vanessa's brows arched. "You think the best of

everyone, Alec. I'm sure she's some money-grubbing landlubber who doesn't know the first thing about island living. I hope she realizes that and doesn't bother us any longer than necessary. When we hear she's coming, I think I'll take a vacation."

Libby's face was getting pinker and pinker. Alec didn't think she'd take much more before she blew.

ELEVEN

As Libby listened to her newfound sister rant, her emotions veered between anger and hurt. Why had she thought her new family would be as happy to meet her as she was to meet them? Her aunt Pearl had been welcoming, but Libby was an outsider in this small community.

Vanessa's diatribe finally ended. She turned her attention from Alec and stared at Libby. "I feel like I should know you. Have we met? I'm Vanessa Mitchell."

Libby forced a pleasant smile to her face. "I think I seem familiar because we look alike. And we should. I'm your sister, Libby Holladay."

Vanessa went white. Her mouth opened but only a garbled word came out. Red washed up her face, and she closed her mouth before finally opening it with the strangled statement of "Half sister." Her mouth looked like she'd just bitten into a bad oyster.

"I don't blame you for being upset," Libby said. "Please understand though. I had no idea my father was living. My mother told me he died when I was five."

Vanessa's eyes narrowed, but there was a flicker of uncertainty in them. "I find that difficult to believe."

"It's true. I . . . I wish I'd known him." She held her hand toward Vanessa. "You can't imagine how thrilled I was to find out I have a large family. It's something I've always longed for."

"No cousins or other family?"

Libby shook her head. "My mother never talked much about my father. All she ever said was that he died when I was five, and it was good riddance as far as she was concerned."

Vanessa glared. "Daddy was a wonderful man!"

"So I've heard since I got here to try to find Nicole."

"Nicole?" Vanessa glanced toward the water, then back. "The woman who was kidnapped? You know her?"

"Yes. We're in business together."

Vanessa's glare was still wary. "I met Nicole. I was sorry to hear about what happened to her."

"She told me about you. I was watching on the beach cam to catch a glimpse of you. I saw her taken."

"That must have been hard," Vanessa said, her voice warming for the first time. "I was going to meet her and show her the old lighthouse ruins. I got held up. When I got there, she was gone. I liked her a lot."

"Please don't talk like she's dead," Libby said, tears starting to her eyes. "She's not dead. She's *not*!"

Vanessa bit her lip. "I didn't mean to say she was. I hope you find her."

Alec put his hand on Libby's shoulder. "Don't give up hope," he said.

"I will *never* give up," she said. "She's not going to be another woman who disappears without a trace from an island." The thought of never knowing what had happened to Nicole haunted her.

"Maybe you should contact the media," Vanessa said. "They can get word out. Someone might have seen something."

"That's a good idea," Alec said. "I know a guy who works for the Richmond newspaper. I'm sure I could get him out here."

Libby recoiled at the thought. "Nicole would hate to be the center of a media circus." But would she, really? She'd probably revel in the attention.

Alec nodded. "But if the coverage could help find her . . ."

"We're going to find her soon. I know it." But even as she proclaimed her belief, Libby's pulse skipped. "Maybe you're right," she said, her shoulders sagging. "Make the call."

Alec squeezed her shoulder, then dropped his hand back to his side. "Want us to help you gather some things, Vanessa? We're going back to Tidewater in a little while. Let me call my friend first, then we'll help you."

Libby forced a smile to her face. "I'd like you to come to the inn too. I'm eager to get to know you."

Vanessa's stormy eyes revealed how torn she was. Libby knew the woman wished she could throw the invitation back, but if she did, she'd have nowhere to stay. Pearl's house was damaged as well. It only made sense to join the rest of her family.

"What about Brent?" Vanessa asked. "Is there room for both of us?"

"Of course," Libby said.

"We can stop by and introduce him to Libby too," Alec said. "I need to talk to Zach. I'll be right back."

Libby's stomach plunged at the thought. Zach had already mentioned how upset Brent was about the news that she had inherited.

Vanessa shot a glance Libby's way. "He's not going to be welcoming, just FYI."

Libby kept her smile pinned in place. A soft answer turned away wrath. She had to remember that. "I understand you are both dismayed to find out that you have a sister. I'm not going to push you. I hope you find that I'm not such a bad sister to have."

Vanessa shrugged. "Whatever. Don't say I didn't warn you. He's liable to go off on you. That's all I've heard since Horace gave us the news. Brent had plans for that property."

"I've heard that too. What kind of plans?" Libby asked.

"What difference does it make now? Unless you plan to split it with us?" Hope tinged her words.

"Horace told me our father left you both plenty of money," Libby said, refusing to be goaded.

"But the property you have is what Brent needs." Vanessa turned and squinted. "Here he comes now. He must be done at the church."

Libby turned to look and saw a young man jogging toward them. He wore denim shorts low and loose around his waist in the style she hated. His blond hair fell across his forehead, and his expression was sulky.

She wanted to love this new family, but they were making it difficult.

* * *

Nicole's muscles were cramped from the night on the roof. The hurricane had blown itself out hours ago, but she remained atop the roof. The surge had covered the island, and the water was still a couple of feet deep. The shack was off its foundation, and she feared it was going to float off to sea with her on top of it. The table and chair from inside bobbed in the flood below. Her cot with her food and water also floated in the debris under her feet.

Her eyes burned, and she told herself not to cry. Someone would be along. Surely someone would come. That boy knew she was out here. Nicole would give anything to be in her own tiny room, to look out and see the tired houses across the street, to hear the traffic that she hated. She would never complain again if she got the chance to be home.

The sun was getting hot on the back of Nicole's neck, and her thirst was mounting. She was going to have to get down off this building and see if seawater had leaked into her jug. Staring at the brown swirling water, her courage ebbed. Who knew what was below that roiling surface? Poisonous snakes or spiders came to mind. Hugging her knees to her chest, she tried to talk herself down into the water. There were no snakes out here. Nothing that could hurt her. Though logically she knew that, she didn't want to test it. What if the storm had washed all manner of nasty creatures onto the island?

She licked her cracked lips. Dehydration would kill her if she didn't get down. There was no sense in staying up here out of fear. She rolled onto her stomach and scooted down until her legs hung off the edge of the roof. The plastic bucket was long gone. All she could do was lower herself as far as she could, take a deep breath, then let go.

Her bare feet splashed into cold water. The seawater rushed to enclose her legs up to her thighs. She forced herself not to look down into the swirling water as she slogged through it to her cot. She seized the jug of water. Still full. Hefting it to the light, she examined the cap. Tight. She exhaled with relief, then unscrewed the top and took a swig of water.

The moisture on her tongue revived her. She replaced the cap, then grabbed the cot and dragged it toward the shack. The door was cockeyed now and hung open. Practically swimming, she tugged the cot into the building and glanced around for some way to secure it. There was nothing, so she left it floating there in the water and grabbed her provisions. She would stay on the roof until the water receded

TWELVE

When Alec crossed the street, Zach was sitting in the truck, thumping his hand on his leg in time with the blaring country music. He was oblivious to Alec's approach and jumped when his uncle touched his shoulder.

Zach bolted upright and turned down the radio. "I was about to go looking for you."

"Something wrong?"

Zach chewed on his lip. "I wanted to ask to take the boat out. I know you said no earlier, but the waves aren't all that bad. I have that job."

Alec lifted a brow. "It's still pretty rough out there, Zach. And it's getting late."

"I've been out in worse. In the dark too."

"True. Are the supplies that urgent?"

Zach's gaze cut away. "I need the money. And they're depending on me."

Alec fished in his pocket for the keys to the boat and handed them over. "Okay. Be careful. Wear your life vest."

Zach's smile was big as he jumped from the truck

and jogged through the standing water to the pier. The sea had calmed considerably since they arrived. The flood from the storm surge had gone down a bit too. Now the water barely covered the tops of Alec's boots. But recovery was going to take awhile.

Alec opened the door of his truck and slid inside to make his call.

Earl Franklin answered after two rings. "I was going to call you, Alec," he said, wasting no time with a greeting. "How's it look out there?"

"Rough. Storm surge did more damage than you'd expect from a cat-1. Most of the houses in town have sustained considerable damage."

"Sorry to hear that."

Alec could hear the speculation in Earl's voice. The reporter was probably already planning a feature. "Listen, there's a bigger story here. I think you need to get over to the island as soon as possible."

"What's up?"

"A young woman was kidnapped right off the beach. Her friend was watching via one of the beach cams. So far we've found no sign of her."

"I heard about that. After we left town, I realized we'd given the woman's friend a ride to the island. Tom called to ask me about her."

"I thought you might want to do an article about the abduction, get some publicity rolling. It might help the case."

"You think the Holladay woman killed her and made up the story?"

"Why would you say something like that?"

"She didn't say a word about her friend's kidnapping to us. Seems suspicious."

Alec opened his mouth, then shut it again. He didn't have a good answer to that other than a gut feeling. His fingers curled into the palms of his hands. Surely the crime couldn't be a hoax. But no, Nicole's car was there at the beach. And her cell phone. It would show that a call had been connected to Libby's phone for several minutes.

Unless she had an accomplice.

"Alec? You there?"

"I'm here. All I can tell you is that we're investigating the kidnapping. If you give the case some attention, maybe someone will come forward with information."

"One way or another," Earl said, his voice deep with satisfaction, "it will be all over the national news. Maybe international. I'll head out there as soon as I can. Any chance you can come after me? My sailboat is being repaired. I heard quite a few charter boats were damaged. I might have trouble getting someone to bring me."

"Things are a mess here, and I need to work. If you don't find a charter, call me back and I'll have Zach fetch you after he delivers some supplies."

"Okay, I'll see what I can do first." Earl hesitated and didn't hang up. "Keep an eye on the friend, Alec."

"I will," Alec said. He ended the call. Libby couldn't be guilty of something like that. She was genuinely devastated by her friend's disappearance.

Maybe the hurricane had exposed new leads for

Tom. Alec got out of the truck and headed toward the sheriff's office. His cousin was likely to be out helping the townspeople, but his receptionist would know where he was. He spotted Tom's SUV driving slowly away from the church and waved.

Tom stopped the vehicle beside him. The window came down, and he peered up at Alec. "Something wrong?"

Alec leaned on the side of the vehicle. "I got hold of Earl Franklin. He's coming out to do a piece on Nicole Ingram."

Tom uttered an expletive, and a frown wiped away his smile. "What'd you go and do that for? It will be a media circus. I was careful not to give him any information when I talked to him."

"Every hour that passes puts Nicole in more jeopardy, and you know it." He stared at the sheriff. "Listen, I have a question. Earl said something that got my attention. He seems to think Libby might be involved because she's close to Nicole. You don't suspect her anymore, do you?"

Tom shrugged. "Most homicides are crimes of passion. The murderer is usually someone known to the victim. And we still haven't seen the video of the kidnapping. The tech guy I hired can't find even a piece of that video. All we've got is what Libby told us."

"Well, you found Nicole's phone and car."

Tom nodded. "That's the only reason we're treating it as a real kidnapping." He stared at Alec. "You're in the perfect position to keep your eye on Libby. See if you notice anything suspicious."

"I don't believe she did anything to her friend."

"Well, you can be alert, can't you?"

"I guess so." Alec looked down the road, then back to his cousin. "Did you trace the call between the women?"

"Sure. It lasted four minutes. The only prints on the phone we found at the beach were Nicole's." Tom scowled again. "I wish you'd asked me before you called in the media. I've got enough on my plate with the hurricane damage."

"Sorry."

"I'm sending out a sketch artist to see if she remembers any details about the two men she saw. Let her know they're coming, will you?"

"Sure." Alec stepped back so his cousin could drive on. He watched the SUV's taillights come on, then wink out as Tom rounded the corner toward a group of people picking up the pieces that used to be the town library.

Could she be guilty of something unthinkable? He hoped not. Libby was the first woman who had intrigued him.

* * *

Libby's heart stuttered in her chest. She'd always wanted a brother, but Brent was not quite what she had in mind. He stared at her, then at his sister, as if he sensed the tension between them. Libby smiled at him, but he didn't return it.

"Hey, sis," he said to Vanessa. "You about ready to go out to the hotel?"

Vanessa sent her brother a warning glance. "I'd better introduce you, Brent. This is Libby. Dad's *other* daughter, Libby." She pressed her lips together as if the admission had pained her.

Brent took a step back. His glare pierced Libby, but she kept smiling in spite of the way her chest contracted. "I've been looking forward to meeting you, Brent." She held out her hand, but when he ignored it, she dropped it back to her side.

His gaze swept over her. "You look a lot like Vanessa."

His tone wasn't as hostile as his expression. Not yet anyway. Libby smiled. "I can see that. Vanessa is beautiful, so I take that as a compliment." Her statement didn't change Vanessa's scowl. "We must take after our father. You look more like your mother?"

He shrugged. "Are you staying at the hotel?"

"Yes."

"That woman who was kidnapped two days ago, Nicole? Libby is her business partner," Vanessa said.

His eyes widened. "I talked to her at the ice-cream shop. She didn't say anything about being connected to you. She just said she was looking to restore some of the downtown area for a client. And she asked about Tidewater Inn."

"You told her how disgusted you were about me inheriting, right? That's okay. I know it must have been a shock. I was surprised as well."

He frowned and crossed his arms over his chest. "Dad never mentioned that he was going to do this. So yeah, I was surprised."

"So you wanted to sell the land?" Libby asked.

"Sure. The inn doesn't even turn a profit."

"It doesn't matter now. It's not yours," Vanessa said. "Libby says her mom told her Daddy died when she was five."

"You never saw Dad all these years?" he asked.

"Not that I remember. I'm eager to hear more about him." She tried another smile on him. "I've always wanted a brother."

His eyes flickered. "This is a lot to take in."

He wasn't welcoming her with open arms yet, but she could live with guarded cordiality. "It's a lot for me too. Can I help you grab belongings from the house?"

He shrugged. "If you want." He pointed to the house just down the street. "We live there."

She followed him and Vanessa toward the large two-story, eager to see more than the cursory glance she'd had earlier. The shingle home had been allowed to go gray with the salt. It was newer than the hotel, built in the twenties. The home had been well taken care of and featured an expansive yard that had probably once been meticulously tended, but the floodwaters had left debris everywhere, and some of the shingles were missing. The shrubs and flowers would likely be dead by this time next week, killed by the seawater.

Brent held the door open. "It's a mess. The first floor was flooded. Bedrooms are upstairs."

They trooped through the small entry to the living room. The floor was still damp, and Libby feared the dark floors would warp soon. They were expensive teak, she guessed. One wall had a built-in oak bookcase filled with books. Libby winced to see how waterlogged the books on the bottom shelf were. She longed to examine the books and discover her father's reading tastes. The tables held a few pictures.

She picked up one of a man and a woman standing under a tree. The man had dark-brown eyes and light-brown hair like hers. She liked his open face and contented smile. The woman was lovely with nearly black hair and deep blue eyes. "Our father?" she asked.

Vanessa took the picture from her. "And our mother." Her tone told Libby she didn't want to answer any questions.

Libby wanted to linger and look, but Brent went on through to the stairway, so she had no choice but to follow him up. There were four bedrooms on the second floor, and she started toward the back one.

"That's Daddy's room. You can't go in there," Vanessa said.

Libby stopped with her hand on the doorknob. "I'd love just a peek. I want to know more about him."

Vanessa set her jaw. "Not today. My room is here." It was as if she was willing to expose herself to prevent Libby from invading their father's space.

Not hiding her reluctance, Libby turned and went into her sister's room. The scent of perfume hit her when she entered. Something so strong and flowery that it made her sneeze. Vanessa was feverishly pulling shorts and tops from a bureau and tossing them onto the queen-size bed. The room's polished floors matched the downstairs wood.

"Love the floors," she said. She grabbed a suitcase from the shelf and began packing it.

Vanessa didn't look up. "Thanks." She went to the attached bathroom, then returned moments later with an electric toothbrush and toiletries. She dumped them on top of the clothes in the suitcase. With her hands on her hips, she stared at Libby. "What do you expect from us anyway? That we're all going to be a big happy family now that you've arrived? Forget it! You're not my big sister. You're not anything to me. I don't know you and I don't want to know you."

Libby dropped the top she'd been folding. *Be generous with grace.* "I want to know my family," she said. "Is that so hard to understand?"

"The family has to want to know you too. You can't just force your way in here and expect us to fall on your neck."

Libby rubbed her forehead. "I'm sorry if I've been presumptuous, Vanessa. That wasn't my intention. If I back off, would you agree to trying to be friends?" She held out her hand.

Vanessa stared at Libby's extended fingers and shook her head. "I'm not promising anything. I think the only reason you're here is for the money. There's been ample time to get to know us before now if that's what you really wanted."

Libby dropped her hand to her side and struggled to keep the tears at bay. "I'll see you at the hotel." She turned and plunged through the door and down the stairs to the fresh air outside, free of her sister's vitriol.

She'd tried to honor her father's request, but she'd failed.

THIRTEEN

Every inch of the island was damp and covered with flotsam when Nicole finally descended from the roof. Her face and arms were sunburned from her hours atop the shack, and her tummy rumbled and twisted in its desire for food. She'd eaten half of a peanut butter sandwich, but that was all she'd allowed herself. What if no one came back for days? She would conserve her food and water as much as possible.

Libby had always preached that she should have foresight, but Nicole wasn't sure any kind of wisdom would get her out of this predicament. She kicked a palm frond out of her way and resisted the urge to cry. Tears wouldn't get her rescued. Glancing at the fallen palm fronds, she decided to gather them up. Maybe she could make an outdoor shelter from the sun. She wouldn't be cooped up in the waterlogged shack that smelled of mold and fish.

Once her arms were full of fronds, she deposited them under the palm tree and went back for more. After she'd gathered every frond from the island, she sat down to rest under the tree. The wet ground dampened her shorts almost immediately. Glancing at the water jug, she resisted the urge to drink.

She thought she heard a motor in the distance. Leaping to her feet, she ran to the edge of the water, but at first she saw nothing. Then in the trough of a wave, she saw a boat carrying one person. Shouting and waving, she jumped up and down. The boat was heading for the island like before, and as it neared, she realized it was the same craft as yesterday. The same young man dropped anchor offshore.

She had to convince him to take her off this cursed island. Standing with her hands at her sides, she waited for him to splash ashore. He carried more supplies, so the pain in her stomach would soon be eased. And fruit! She spied apples and oranges in his arms. She salivated at the thought of their sweet taste.

"You're okay," he said. "I was worried the storm surge would carry you off."

"It would have if I hadn't climbed on top of the building." She couldn't take her eyes off the apples. Pink Lady, her favorite variety. "Can I have an apple?"

"Sure." He handed her one.

She bit into it, relishing the sweet yet tart flavor that flooded her mouth. It was all she could do not to moan at the taste. And while she was eating, she didn't have to talk to her jailer. Though she *needed* to talk to him, needed to convince him to let her go.

Wiping her mouth with the back of her hand, she smiled at him. "Were the seas rough?"

"Not bad. I caught some mullets. You want some?"

"I would love some. But how do we light a fire?"

"I brought a lighter."

She watched him slosh back to the boat and return with a box. Inside she spotted fish, a lighter, a knife, and other food items. If she could get the filleting knife, she'd force him to take her to the mainland.

"We'll need firewood. I should have thought of that," he said.

"I have palm fronds. Will that work?"

"No." He glanced back toward the boat. "I can cook it on board, though. There's a grill in the galley." He squatted and grabbed the knife, then began to clean the fish.

Nicole had never wanted anything as much as she wanted that knife. She wanted to leap on him and wrest it away, but he was muscular and she wouldn't have a chance. Even the lighter would do her no good without firewood to burn. She eyed the palm tree. Unless she could manage to set it on fire where it stood.

He finished cleaning the fish, then put the knife in his back pocket and picked up the fillets. "I'll be right back." As he walked toward the boat, the knife slipped to the sand.

She swooped down on the weapon. The handle felt substantial and deadly in her palm. Turning her back to the boat, she tried a few threatening swoops with it in her hand. Could she even bring herself to hurt him? He seemed to believe she was a danger to some imaginary brother. There was no malice in his treatment of her.

She glanced over her shoulder. He was intent on his task, and she caught a whiff of the fish beginning to cook. How could she get this to go down her way? After he returned to the beach, she could back out to the boat with the knife in front of her. He might be afraid to charge her for fear of getting cut. She would have to turn her attention away to get in the boat. Still, she should manage to get aboard before he could wade through the waves. But what if he boarded in spite of her efforts?

All she could do was try. Swallowing hard, she put the knife behind her back and turned when he approached with the cooked fish. "Smells good," she called.

"I'm not the cook my dad was," he said. "I hope it's done. And it's hot and filling."

"Was? Your dad is dead?"

His lips tightened and he nodded. "He died in a plane crash. He and my mom."

"I'm so sorry."

"Thanks." He set the tray of fish on a rock.

"Where do you live? In Hope Beach?"

He nodded. "With my uncle. He's a Coastie." His tone held pride. "I don't want to live anywhere else. I'm a commercial fisherman, like my dad. At least that's what I want to do, if my uncle will let me." He bent down to slide the fish onto a paper plate.

While he was bending over, she shoved him with her foot, and he toppled onto the sand. In a flash, she was running to the boat.

When her feet hit the water, she turned and brandished the knife. "Stay back!"

He'd gained his feet and already stood only five feet away. "You won't cut me."

"Try me!" She wagged the knife blade at him. "I've been kidnapped, half starved, left to rot during a hurricane, nearly drowned. I'm not someone you want to mess with."

She began to back through the waves toward the boat. He stood watching her with a scowl.

"You are just as crazy as they said," he called. "You don't even know which direction is land."

She stopped. "I'll figure it out."

"You don't have enough gas for exploring."

He was just trying to scare her. She continued to back toward the boat. Her bare foot moved and found nothing under it. The underwater hole made her lose her balance, and she fell back into the water. She came up brandishing the knife and sputtering, but he was already at her side.

He snatched the knife from her hand and grabbed her arm. "I was beginning to wonder about what I'd been told, but you just proved how dangerous you are. You tried to cut me like you did your brother." He dragged her back to the beach and left her there.

* * *

Brent and Vanessa were ensconced in rooms across the hall from Libby. After she'd helped to settle them, Alec called her to say a sketch artist was coming. Libby met the artist—a woman—in the parlor and did the best job she could. She could only pray the drawings helped find Nicole.

After the artist left, Libby went to see if she could

help Delilah with dinner. The manager had a suite on the second floor and rarely left the property. Libby had the impression that Delilah had been here a long time and was content with her home. Maybe she could get some information out of the woman.

She found Delilah in the kitchen stirring something that smelled amazing. "Is that she-crab soup?"

Delilah smiled. "It is. This is a special recipe with whipping cream and butter. No flour to thicken it either. Want a taste?" Delilah held out a spoonful.

Libby sipped it and closed her eyes as the rich, buttery flavor hit her taste buds. "It's heavenly."

"I thought you'd like it."

"Can I help with anything? We have a lot of people to feed."

Delilah's eyes widened. "Really? You wouldn't mind? I let our cook take the day off to help with cleanup in town."

"I love to cook, actually. I don't get much opportunity since it's just me and Nicole. She's rarely around anyway. It's hard to cook for one." Libby lifted the CD player in her hand. "I need music though. That okay with you?"

"Of course. I sometimes listen to Beethoven."

"This isn't Beethoven." Libby plugged the player in and started the Counting Crows CD. The lyrics to "Big Yellow Taxi" made her pause. *Paved paradise.*

Delilah stared at her. "Is that what you want, Libby? To see this place become one big parking lot?"

Libby's smile faded. "I don't want that to happen any more than you do."

"So what are you going to do?"

"I don't know yet." She pulled the notebook out from under her arm. "Do you have a menu plan for the next week? I assume our guests will be here that long?"

"A few weeks, most of them," Delilah said. "It sounds like Ray's house is pretty bad, so your brother and sister might be here longer, maybe months."

Months. It would be expensive to feed all of them. Libby mentally counted up the residents. Eight. "Are they chipping in for food?"

"Alec was quick to give me some money for him and Zach. I doubt Vanessa and Brent will contribute. They consider the inn home." Delilah's glance held curiosity. "They know who you are, right?"

"They were less than pleased to meet me."

"Don't take it to heart, honey. It's just a shock. Especially to Vanessa. She's always been a daddy's girl, and she's just jealous."

"Jealous? I didn't even know him."

"But he loved you," Delilah said. "Vanessa realizes that. She never wanted to share Ray with anyone, not even her mother. She's been obsessive about him. So much so that Ray had her in counseling when she was fifteen or so. It got a little better, but this has got to send her reeling."

Was their mother anything like her own? Libby had noticed people often chose the same kind of mates when they remarried. "What about their mother?"

Delilah smiled. "Everyone loved Tina. Ray was nuts about her right up to the day she died." She pointed to the refrigerator. "If you want to fix some salad, go right ahead. We're having grilled lobster, soup, and salad tonight."

Libby winced at how much that must cost. "For so many?"

Delilah stirred the soup. "Zach brought me the lobster and crab. I only had to buy veggies for salad. This is a cheap dinner."

"That was nice of him. Most young men wouldn't have thought of that."

"Alec's brother raised him right. Most folks in Hope Beach look out for one another. Zach's a little troubled right now, but he'll be all right. He's basically a good boy. Trying to find his place in the world."

Libby almost asked about the intriguing Coast Guard captain, but she didn't want to reveal her interest to Delilah. It was much safer to talk about her family.

"How long have you worked here?" She put the salad ingredients on the butcher block in the middle of the kitchen and found a chopping knife.

"Fifteen years. I came here when I was eighteen. I was in foster care and had nowhere to go when I got out of high school. Ray found me crying my eyes out on the pier. When he heard what I was going through, he offered me a job on the spot. At first I was a housekeeper, but I worked my way up. I've been manager ten years in October."

"How many employees are here?"

Delilah stopped and thought. "Three in housekeeping, a groundskeeper, and me."

"I wish I'd known my dad. He sounds like a really great man."

Delilah's eyes glistened. "He was the best."

"You sound a little in love with him."

"Maybe I was." Delilah put down the soup ladle. "I could never take Tina's place, but I would have been willing to try. He never looked at another woman though. Even though I let him know I was available."

"You're much younger."

"I'm thirty-three," Delilah admitted.

"He was in his fifties when he died?"

"Yes, he was fifty-two. But he looked much younger." Delilah shrugged. "The age difference never bothered me. A man like that doesn't come along often."

Libby mixed the greens and vegetables together. "So everyone says." She went back to the refrigerator. "No avocados?"

"There's one in that bag." Delilah pointed to a paper sack on the counter.

"We'll have to get more. I like avocado in everything. I'll make my special avocado dressing for tonight too."

"Sounds great. What about your mother?" Delilah asked. "Do you know much about their marriage?"

"Only that it lasted a short time. They were both young. My mother said he lit out when I was three. I was bitter about it when I was a teenager. Now I find out that my mother lied all those years. She told me he died when I was five. It's pretty devastating."

"I'm sure it is. One thing I know about Ray—he would never shirk his responsibility."

"My mother tried, but she was a kid at heart herself, even at fifty. I was more a parent than she was sometimes. We moved around a lot. I think I went to ten schools in twelve years."

Delilah winced. "Some of Ray's old letters and albums are in the basement. You might want to go through them."

"Oh, I would!" Libby began to chop the avocado.

The thought of learning more about her parents and their lives appealed to her. So much of the time she felt alone, as if a piece of herself was missing. She'd assumed the cause was some dim memory of her father. Even now that she knew he was an honorable man, his abandonment still hurt.

FOURTEEN

The huge living room table felt crowded with so many around it. Alec had never eaten here at the Tidewater Inn when there were so many guests. A white linen tablecloth covered the mammoth table, and fresh flowers made a bright centerpiece. Platters were heaped with steaming lobster, and a white tureen contained the soup he'd just tasted.

"Great meal, Delilah," he said. "No one can make she-crab soup like you."

Delilah smiled and ladled soup into a bowl for herself. "Libby helped. Wait until you taste the avocado-ranch dressing she made from scratch."

Libby was to his right, and she brightened at the praise. "I hope everyone likes avocados."

"Is there any store-bought dressing?" Vanessa started to rise from her seat directly across from the table.

Her aunt Pearl shot her a look that made her sink back into her chair. "I've bought too many avocados for you to think your tastes have suddenly changed, Vanessa."

A dull red crept up Vanessa's neck, and she tipped

her chin up. "I'll try it, I guess." The glance she shot Libby was full of challenge.

Alec wanted to tell her to stop acting like a spoiled brat, but he tucked his chin and took another sip of the soup. "I could live on this, Delilah. But I'm not going to. The lobster looks great."

Libby glanced at Zach. "I hear we have you to thank for this fabulous dinner."

Zach shrugged. "I had a good afternoon on the boat."

She smiled at him. "Modesty. I like that in a man." She turned to her other side to listen to Thomas Carter.

Alec suppressed a grin at the way Zach's shoulders squared when she called him a man. Libby had a way about her that made every man in the room want to impress her. Even old Thomas was busy telling her about the days when he built boats. She listened with the kind of attention that would make any person feel important. Why had she never married? But maybe that was a false assumption. She could be divorced.

Thomas finally ended his story. Libby glanced across the table at her siblings. "Brent, I met Kenneth Poe this morning. He told me about his client's interest in buying the inn."

Brent stiffened and looked up from his plate. "Did he make you an offer?"

"He did." Libby broke off a piece of French bread and dipped it in her soup. "I had no idea this place was worth so much money."

Everyone seemed to freeze. Alec shot her a quick glance. Was she trying to see what kind of reaction she would get? The strain in the room seemed to grow.

How much money had she been offered? A million or two? That would be enough to tempt most people.

"You're not going to sell, are you, honey?" Pearl asked.

"Of course she is," Vanessa said. "She doesn't care about the family. She just wants the money."

"I don't know yet," Libby said. "I haven't had a chance to even think about what should be done. *You* were going to sell," she said, directing a level gaze at Brent before glancing at Vanessa again. "Why is it all right for your brother to sell but not me? Why don't you characterize him as a money grubber?"

"Brent knows this island. He would have done what was best."

"The offer is from the same person," Libby said. "So there is nothing different except who is benefiting."

"Children, let's not argue," Pearl said. "Your father would be very displeased by your attitude to your sister, Vanessa. I'm disappointed myself. We are all family, but you're not acting like it."

"I haven't done anything," Brent said. "Libby, you can do whatever you want. It's your property. Dad seemed to want it that way."

Alec winced at the coldness in Brent's voice, but Libby just nodded.

"Thank you, Brent," she said. "I don't know what I'll do yet. It's a lovely old place. I wish I had the money to keep it. It needs a lot of repairs." She glanced at Alec. "What do you think about a resort going in here?"

He raised his brows. "Resort? We'll need ferry service or a very long bridge to draw in enough people to support it."

"The ferry service is coming," she said. "That's why Nicole was here. We had a client who wanted us to restore some of the more important buildings and make Hope Beach more attractive to tourists."

"It hasn't been announced if it is." He glanced at Brent. "You've heard this?"

Brent nodded. "From Poe. I doubt his investor would be spending that kind of money if he wasn't sure it was happening."

"The island will change," Alec said. "We'll be like Ocracoke. Which is better than Myrtle Beach at least. The tourists aren't overwhelming. It's still a fishing village. We'll survive, whatever you decide."

Delilah's spoon clattered into her bowl. "Easy enough for you to say! This place is my home. It's my *life*." She stared at Libby. "Don't think for a minute that they won't tear this place down. That's what he told you, isn't it?"

Libby nodded. "That's the only thing holding me back. I would have to compromise my passion for historic preservation if I let them do that."

Libby's soft answer defused Delilah's anger. The red faded from her cheeks, and she slumped back in her chair. "Don't do this. I can't bear to leave my home."

Libby bit her lip and looked down at her plate. "I can only promise that I'll consider everything, Delilah. I'm in a hard spot. I don't have the kind of money it would take to restore the inn. Without a major investment, it's going to fall down around your ears." She glanced at Brent. "Why did our father not keep it up? The house in the village is in great condition."

"I can answer that," Pearl said. "The place was due a paint job when Tina died three years ago. Ray had a small stroke, then started letting things slide. The sea is hard on buildings. They need constant maintenance. I told him he needed to spend some time here and make a project list, but he didn't do it. Then his illness turned chronic, and he decided to transfer all his liquid assets to the kids. He wanted to make sure everyone was taken care of."

"I can understand that," Libby said. "But he left me no money for upkeep. It was as if he wanted me to sell it."

"I'm not sure I believe that," Alec said.

"Then why leave me saddled with a house that's in need of so much?"

"Maybe he wanted to see what you were made of."

She absorbed his comment, then nodded. "I suppose we'll never know."

"What you're made of?" Alec raised his eyebrows.

"No. What he wanted me to do."

"If anyone can figure it out, it's you," he said.

Vanessa's head came up and she gave him a sharp glance. He realized he'd let too much of his admiration show. If Vanessa hated Libby before, it was going to be worse now.

* * *

The basement stairs creaked as Libby eased down them. The dank smell was nearly enough to make her turn tail and run, but the promise of the prize contained in the trunk below was stronger than the claustrophobia squeezing her lungs. The bare bulb in the ceiling put out enough light to see the old leather chest right where Delilah had told her it would be, against the wall beneath the shelves lined with jars of canned vegetables.

She was going to grab the albums and letters and run right back to her room with them. The place gave her the creeps. The distant sound of dripping water added to her unease, though the stone floor was dry. The place was free of cobwebs too, so Delilah must keep it swept out.

Libby hurried to the trunk and lifted the lid. The fabric-lined interior smelled of disuse. The trunk was packed with bundles of old letters and photo albums. Her pulse thumped in her throat. Would there be any mention of her or her mother in these old letters? Any photos of her?

A framed picture was in the very bottom of the trunk. Libby held it up to the light. She barely recognized the smiling young woman as her mother. Why had her father kept it all these years? His marriage to Tina seemed to have been ideal. Her mother looked like she was about twenty-five. Young and carefree. Her long, straight hair was on her shoulders, and she wore a buckskin dress covered with beads.

Her mother had been happy but never content with any situation or with any man. She was always striving for the next big thing. Everyday choices had molded her mother. Libby touched the beads at her neck. Her own choices could make her a better person if she chose wisely.

She sorted the contents, then lifted the pile of albums and letters and carried them back up the stairs and to her bedroom. There was no one around. The sun was setting, and she'd arranged to meet the reporter with Alec, so she dropped the mementos on the bed with a regretful glance and went to find him.

FIFTEEN

Libby and Alec sat on the expansive porch at Tidewater Inn after sunset and listened to the ocean. "I thought he'd be here by now," Alec said.

"I don't mind waiting," she said. "It's a beautiful night."

The stars were bright in the night sky, but the moon hadn't risen yet. He kept shooting glances Libby's way. She seemed so at home here.

"What?" she finally said. "Do I have soup on my nose?"

He grinned. "Sorry. I was staring, wasn't I? It's the offer for this place. Would you really sell it, or were you just trying to see what you could find out from Brent?"

"I don't want to sell," she said in a low voice. "But I don't see that I have any choice."

"There's always a choice."

She stiffened. "What would you do?"

"Turn over every rock to find a way to keep it."

"Well, I have another life. The place is gorgeous and historic, I give you that. But sometimes sacrifices have to be made. The money will change my life. And I have a stepbrother who needs help. He was hurt in

Afghanistan and is on disability. I could do a lot of good there." If he would let her. He wasn't eager to have a relationship with her. He'd been a teenager when their parents married, and he had no time for her.

"Life isn't all about money."

"Spoken by someone who has always had enough."

She wasn't going to listen. He peered at the dock as a boat approached. "Looks like Earl is finally here. You ready for this?"

"I'll do anything to help find Nicole."

"You can wait here." He rose and went to the dock. When the boat neared, he caught the rope and tied it to the pilings.

"I'll be back in about an hour," Earl told the captain.

The young man in shorts nodded. He plugged in earphones and settled back in his chair.

Earl was in his fifties with a paunch. His one pride was his thick head of red hair. It had faded with the years, but he still wore it over his ears like an aging Beatle. "She up there?" he asked, jerking his thumb toward the house.

"Yes. Go easy on her though. She's had a rough few days."

Earl chewed on his ever-present toothpick. "Sounds like you believe her story."

Alec shrugged. "I know what it's like to be accused of something you didn't do. I don't want us to assume she's guilty until proven innocent."

"Is Tom going to ask the state for help?"

"Yes. With the hurricane, I think he's overwhelmed."

He fell into place beside Earl, who was walking up the boardwalk to the hotel.

"My story will get some action."

They reached the grand steps. Libby was standing on the porch waiting. Her expression was one of dread. This wouldn't be easy for her, airing her life to the world. Alec sent her a reassuring smile. "This is Earl Franklin," he said when they reached her.

The two exchanged a long look. "It's you." She glanced at Alec. "Earl and his wife gave me a ride to the island," she said. "Naomi thought I was Vanessa."

"You never said a word about your friend having gone missing." Earl's voice held accusation.

She bit her lip. "There was just so much to explain. It seemed easier to say nothing."

Alec already had an uneasy feeling about the exchange. It did seem odd that she wouldn't have told Earl and Naomi anything. Especially Naomi. If any woman had the warm manner that invited confidence, it was Earl's sweet wife. And Libby hadn't made any secret of the incident to him. Alec could see the suspicion on Earl's face.

"There's iced tea," she said, pointing to the table with the refreshments. She resumed her seat in the swing. Tucking one leg under her, she sipped her tea and regarded them over the rim of her glass.

"Don't mind if I do." Earl poured himself a glass from the sweating pitcher. "Ah, nothing like sweet tea." He settled in the rocker and took out a pen. "Hope you don't mind if I record this? It's easier than trying to write it all down." He clicked a switch on the pen recorder without waiting for her to answer. "Can you take me through the events that led up to your friend's disappearance?"

She blinked. "Okay."

She plunged into the story about the client who wanted restoration estimates and ended with what she saw on the beach cam. She broke down again when she got to the part about the men taking her friend. Alec couldn't imagine how he'd feel if he saw someone he cared about being kidnapped and couldn't do anything to stop it.

Earl leaned forward. "Ms. Holladay, did you harm your friend?"

She sat upright, sloshing tea over the side of her glass onto her shorts. "Of course not!"

"You didn't kill Nicole, dump her body in the Atlantic, then call the sheriff with some far-fetched story about an abduction?"

"No, no! You can't possibly believe that." She stared wildly from Earl to Alec, then back again. "Nicole is my friend. I would do anything to find her. Anything!"

"Yet the website with the cam is blank during the time your partner was supposedly kidnapped."

How had he found that out? He must have talked to Tom. Alec wanted to interrupt, but he bit his tongue and let Earl continue his questioning. She'd survive. It *was* strange that the tape had been messed with.

Earl smiled. "I did a little research. You're a computer expert. A person at the historical society said you're their go-to person when they have any computer issues. It's not out of the realm of possibility that you hacked into the cam data and erased that portion of the tape."

"It was an accident." She gulped and held his gaze. "I was trying to save the video. It wouldn't let me, so I . . . I hacked into the system and tried to save it that way. Something happened, and the next thing I knew, the data was gone."

"I see. I must say I thought you'd come up with a more believable story than that," Earl said.

"It's the truth."

Alec watched her face, the way it crumpled, the way tears formed in her eyes.

"I think you've made enough accusations, Earl."

Her fingers inched toward him but stopped before she touched his hand. "I didn't hurt Nicole, Mr. Franklin. If you write a story suggesting that I did, you'll only aid whoever took her."

Earl turned off his tape recorder. "Let me know if you remember anything else." He tucked the recorder into his pocket and strode to the waiting boat.

* * *

The boat carrying Earl back to Kitty Hawk cruised away, and none too soon for Libby. She wanted to throw something, to scream about the injustice of anyone even thinking that she might have hurt Nicole. His blue eyes watching her somberly, Alec continued to sit on the porch with her. He probably still suspected she had done something criminal.

She set her iced tea on the table and paced the

expansive porch. "You said you'd give me the benefit of the doubt."

His sip of tea seemed deliberate, as though he was fishing for extra time before answering. "I am. But it seems strange the data would be missing from the cam."

His doubt was written on his face, and she fought to keep her voice level. "I swear to you I didn't do it on purpose. Yes, I might have caused it. I don't know." She clasped her hands in front of her. "Did you talk to your cousin when we were in town? I want to *do something*! I have to find Nicole."

"With the hurricane, Tom's going to have his hands full. And to be honest, this kind of thing is much more serious than the domestic disputes and traffic tickets he normally deals with. He's my cousin, but I think this is way over his head."

"I'm going to have to find her myself. It's clear no one else is going to do it."

He raised a brow. "You? What do you know about looking for a missing person?"

"Nothing. But I can retrace her steps. Talk to everyone she spoke with. Surely I'll find a clue somewhere. I can't just sit here and wait!" Her voice broke, and she turned her back on him.

She was alone here, and it was time she faced it. The people in the inn shared only her blood. They cared nothing about her. Well, maybe Aunt Pearl cared a little, but her warmth might only be curiosity. Libby refused to entertain the thought that Nicole might be dead.

She sensed rather than heard his approach. His hand

came down on her bare arm, and its warmth made her shiver. She didn't turn to look at him. He had brought that reporter here.

"I'm sorry," he said. "Reporters and law enforcement are trained to look at the person closest to the victim."

She whirled, jerking away from his touch. "Don't call her that! She's not dead, she's not!"

His hand dropped to his side. The wind ruffled his dark hair. "I'm sorry. I didn't mean it that way. She's still a victim of violence. Kidnapping is a violent act."

She shuddered and moved farther away from him. "Earl is going to write a piece suggesting I hurt her, isn't he? He really thinks I killed her and dumped her body in the ocean."

"I'll talk to him. I think he'll be fair."

The breakers rolled over the beach in a hypnotic rhythm. She turned to stare at him again. "Is that what your cousin thinks too? Is he going to taint the state's investigation by implying that I'm guilty?"

"I don't know what Tom is thinking. Look, I'll help you, okay? I'll take some accrued leave. I know everyone in town. It's a good idea to trace Nicole's movements. Someone has to know what happened."

His words were so gentle. Even though she'd screamed at him, he stayed calm. "Why would you do that for me?"

He shrugged. "I was falsely accused once."

"What happened?"

He folded his arms across his chest and moved back a step. "My older brother drowned. We were mulletting with a neighbor. I was about Zach's age. My older brother was named Zach too. He was twenty."

She heard the pain in his voice and wanted to tell him he didn't have to describe what happened, but she found herself holding her breath and wanting to know more.

"Giles, our neighbor, was with us. He was supposed to have checked the fuel in the boat. We were pretty far out and the engine died. No gas. The ship-to-shore radio had broken the week before, and we couldn't call for help. My brother was the strongest swimmer, so he decided to swim for help."

"Oh no," she said softly.

He sighed. "His body was never found. A fishing trawler found us the next morning. As soon as we got to land, Giles started railing at me, saying it was all my fault. If I'd filled the tank, my brother would still be alive. Everyone believed him. The pain and disappointment in my parents' eyes haunted me for years. Still does. They believed Giles instead of me."

"Have you talked with them about it since you've been grown?"

He shrugged. "Pointless now. Even if they believed me, it wouldn't make up for their condemnation back then."

"That's so sad, Alec. It has to have been so hard for you to lose two brothers. And then your parents, in a way."

He went silent for a moment. "Mom keeps the house like a shrine. Everywhere I look I see pictures of my brothers from babyhood to the year they died. In Mom's eyes they are saints now. Something I'll never be."

"And your father?"

"He doesn't say much. Mom rules the household. Her hero worship eventually drove Beth away too. Beth is my younger sister. I don't think she's been home in three years."

"I'm so sorry." She touched his hand. "I've always felt a little unlovable since my father abandoned me. I *thought* that's what he did anyway. Now everything I believed is all jumbled."

He held her hand in an easy grip. "You'll figure it out."

"So will you. I'm already sure that you're a good man, Alec."

A tinge of color stained his face. "Hardly. I was a wild kid. I guess that's why I want to help Zach avoid my mistakes."

"Most of us have to learn the hard way."

Her skin was still warm from touching his hand. He knew what it was like to be misunderstood. She wasn't in this by herself.

SIXTEEN

The rest of the house slept, but Libby paced the rug in the parlor. The grandfather clock in the corner chimed two, but she wasn't a bit sleepy. She should have been. Her last full night's sleep had been before this nightmare started.

What was she going to do if everyone began to look at her as a suspect? How could she clear herself?

"Libby?" Pearl stood in the doorway. A pink night-gown covered her bulk, and her hair was in a long braid. "Are you all right?" She stepped into the room. "You've been tense ever since dinner."

"You'd be tense too if you were accused of harming Nicole."

"What? Who accused you of such a thing?"

"Earl."

"Oh, honey, he's just snooping for something sensational. The truth will come out. You'll see." She beckoned for Libby to come with her. "You're tall. I need some help in my room, if you don't mind."

Libby followed her up the stairs. Helping Pearl would give her something to focus on besides what other people thought of her. When they reached Pearl's room, she looked around. It was very different from the way it had been when Nicole's things were here. Now there were angels everywhere, spilling out of boxes, perched on the dresser top, and heaped on the bed.

She picked up one that held a child in its arms. "How many angels do you have?"

"Oh, I've lost count. Well over two hundred, I'm sure."

"Did you bring them all?"

Pearl picked up an angel still in its box, which was lying beside the bed. "I could hardly leave them in the house, now could I?"

Libby smiled. "Of course not. Why angels?"

"I've always loved stories about angels. I'm sure I saw one once."

Libby found she believed Pearl. "What did he look like? And how did you know?"

"I was ten." She gestured to the window. "It was right out there in the water. I wasn't a very strong swimmer and I got a cramp in my side."

"Oh no."

Pearl nodded. "The surf was high and I couldn't keep my head up. I finally decided I would give up and just go to heaven. My grandpa had died two months earlier and I missed him anyway. So I quit swimming. I said, 'I'm going to heaven now.'"

Libby sat on the edge of the bed with the angel in her hands. "What happened?"

"I felt a hand on my arm, and the next thing I knew I was on my knees in the sand vomiting seawater. I looked around and a teenage boy was walking away.

I called out to him and he turned around and smiled." She paused and her eyes were moist. "I've never seen a smile like that before or since. He said, 'You'll be fine now. It's not your time.' Then he turned and jogged away."

"You'd never seen the boy?"

Pearl shook her head. "He wasn't a real boy. There was something special about him."

Libby wanted to believe her aunt. Even more, she wished she could have an experience like that. She touched the beads at her neck. Somehow God felt more *real* here, on this island. Almost as if he could whisper in her ear at any moment.

Pearl smiled. "How'd we get on that subject? You need to get some rest and I'm blathering about something that happened fifty years ago."

"What can I help you with?"

Pearl pointed to the closet. "The disorder is driving me crazy. It's why I'm still awake at this crazy hour. I want to put some of the boxes of angels on the closet shelf, but I'm too short. There are some boxes in there that could go to the attic. That would leave me enough room. Can you reach?"

"I think so." Libby opened the closet door and eyed the boxes on the shelves. She stood on her tiptoes and pulled down the first box easily. "I think I need a chair for the one in the back."

Pearl brought her the desk chair, and Libby climbed onto it. "Can you flip on the closet light? It's dark in here." When the light came on, she peered to the back of the shelf. "What is this?" She reached in and brought out an envelope. "It's an old letter." She climbed down from the chair and sat on the edge of the bed where the light would allow her to read.

The bed sank as Pearl settled beside her. "It looks like it's addressed to Tina."

Libby opened it. "Did she ever stay in this room?"

Pearl shrugged. "Not that I know of."

Libby pulled out the letter inside the envelope. The writing was in a bold hand that suggested it had been penned by a man. The style was a little hard to read. She held it under the light and read aloud.

"'Tina, I will ruin Ray. You'll see what a huge mistake you've made.'"

Libby stared at her aunt. "Does this make any sense to you?"

Pearl gave a faint gasp. She snatched the note and crumpled it. "It's so old. I don't think we can possibly know what it means."

When Pearl fanned herself, Libby knew her aunt was hiding something. "What do you know?"

Pearl pulled her braid over one shoulder. "Ray had some financial problems a few years back. I never heard what went wrong. He lost about half of his money."

"He still had plenty to leave my siblings."

"He'd already put that money for them in trust funds."

"You suppose someone set out to harm him financially?"

"I can't imagine something so sordid."

"What wrong choice could Tina have made?" Libby wished she'd had the chance to look at the back of the sheet. "The letter is yellowed, like it's old. How long were Dad and Tina married?"

"Twenty-five years the month before Tina died."

"My father didn't wait long to replace my mother."

Pearl started to speak, then closed her mouth and shook her head.

"Was anyone else interested in Tina?"

Pearl rubbed her head. "I think there might have been, but it was so long ago. I just don't remember."

Libby sighed. It didn't matter anyway. This was old news and had nothing to do with finding Nicole.

* * *

Libby lay in the comfortable bed with her eyes open. She'd expected to sleep until at least eight, but something had awakened her. Birds sang outside her window, though the sun was not yet up. The air had the sense that sunrise was just around the corner. She rolled over and glanced at the alarm clock on the bedside table. Five thirty. The sun would be up in half an hour.

She listened again to the sleeping house. What had she heard? Or had it been a dream? She sat up. "Is someone there?"

The sound of running feet came from beyond the door. Her first inclination was to cower under the covers, but she wasn't going to give the person the satisfaction of thinking she was frightened. It was probably Vanessa. Or Brent. She forced herself out of bed and went to the door. There was a folded sheet of paper lying on the carpet. Something inside made it bulge.

Libby nudged it with her foot, and the paper opened to reveal a black blob. She leaped back until she realized it was a dead jellyfish. Why would someone leave this for her? Though she hated to get close, she lifted the paper and carried it into the attached bathroom, where she dumped the jellyfish into the trash. The paper was blank.

She balled up the paper and tossed it into the wastebasket, then pulled on shorts and a top. Whoever had left the creature couldn't make her cower in her room. The beach called, and she could watch the sun come up over the ocean.

The sky was lightening as she stepped onto the porch. A figure loomed to her left and she jumped, then realized it was Alec. "What are you doing up so early?" Mercy, he was handsome in his crisp white shirt and the khaki shorts that showed tanned, muscular legs.

He grinned. "I could ask you the same."

She told him about the jellyfish. "I'm not going to let her scare me."

He lifted a brow. "Her? You think it was Vanessa?"

"Probably. Does a jellyfish have any symbolism?"

He shrugged. "The obvious one is that she's calling you spineless. But that doesn't apply to you. It's clear to all of us that you've got backbone."

She had to smile at that. "I'll admit that it scared me this morning when I found it. But if you tell anyone, I'll deny it."

He grinned and made a zipping motion across his lips.

She pointed toward the whitecaps. "Want to take a walk?"

He pulled his hands from his pockets. "My thoughts exactly."

They jogged down the steps and down the slope to the beach. "I found an old letter last night in the room where Aunt Pearl is staying." She told him what the note contained.

"All that was before my time, but someone would probably know if Tina had another beau. I don't see how that matters now though," Alec said.

"It probably doesn't. I guess I'm just interested in all the history." She paused to peer at a black blob on the beach. "What's that?"

"A mermaid's purse," he said, steering her around it. "Technically known as a skate's egg sack."

She shuddered. "Looks creepy, like some kind of alien." She fell into step beside him again. The murmur of the sea was balm on her soul, and she ran into the gentle waves as far as her knees, letting the water wash away her worries.

"You look happy," Alec said, watching her.

She splashed him with water. "The water's warm!"

He grinned and jogged into the waves with her, then splashed her back. She licked the salt from her lips and smiled. "I'm not going to let Earl's suspicious nature rob me of my peace of mind. I know I'm innocent."

He sobered. "That's good. Because he could do a lot of damage."

"Maybe. But I have to believe the sheriff has enough integrity to look for the real criminals."

"I think he does, but sometimes it's tempting to take the easy way out."

"I'll keep pushing back until he finds the truth." Her high spirits began to sink. Alec's sober demeanor reminded her that she still faced many problems. She didn't even want to see Earl's article.

"What are the plans for today?" she asked. "I want to get started on finding Nicole."

"I thought we'd take the cutter out with my friends. I got permission to search for her, and I talked my boss into allowing you to be on the boat."

"I wish we would find her today." She stared out at the water, which shimmered with gold and orange as the sun lifted its head above the horizon.

He touched her arm. "Don't give up hope."

"I haven't." She rubbed her head. "What made you decide to join the Coast Guard?"

He smiled. "That's an easy answer. I'm happy when I'm on the sea. The Coast Guard rescued us when I was a kid, like I mentioned."

She sobered. "When your brother died."

He nodded. "Riding on that cutter back to land, I knew I wanted to snatch people from the jaws of death the way we'd been rescued. It seemed very noble."

"And is it?"

"Sometimes. When we're successful. Sometimes we're not though. We're not always in time to save lives. Then it's hard, and I feel like a failure."

"I don't think you could ever be a failure." She held his gaze for just a moment, then turned back toward the house. "I think I'll fix coconut pancakes for breakfast."

She couldn't think of a man she admired as much as she did Alec. He was quite a guy. The strain between them was gone this morning, and she prayed it meant he fully believed in her now.

SEVENTEEN

It was ten by the time Alec drove Libby to town to go searching. While Libby ducked into the store to buy some sunscreen, Alec walked across the street to step into the sheriff's office. He found Tom at his desk filling in paperwork.

"Got a minute?" Alec closed the door behind him.

Tom leaned back in his chair. "You bet. What's up?"

"You heard from the state boys on the search for Nicole?"

Tom pursed his lips. "Yeah. There are two detectives coming first of the week."

"Why so late?"

"The state is still reeling from the hurricane, I guess. And their best detective is in Saint Croix on vacation. They're sending him and his partner out when he gets back."

"I guess it will have to do."

"You find out anything by hanging around Libby?"

Alec shook his head. "I think you were right about Earl though. He came in with guns blazing for her last night. He found out about the missing video. Did you tell him?"

Tom frowned. "You know better than that. I wouldn't do anything to compromise the investigation."

"I wonder how he found out, then."

"He might have a contact in the Virginia Beach office. I guess it doesn't matter. It's going to come out sooner or later."

Alec fell silent as he tried to think of how he could convince his cousin to drop his suspicions about Libby. "This morning she said she was sure you had the integrity to dig for the truth. Don't make me think you're less of a man than we both know you are."

Tom flushed. "Come on, Alec, you're letting yourself be fooled by a pretty face. I admit she's a looker, but use your head. Stay neutral and consider that she might be implicated."

"I am. What other evidence have you found about the two men?"

Tom leaned back in his chair. "Two men in a small boat with an outboard motor were seen offshore."

"That reminds me of what Mr. McEwan said." He told Tom about the old man seeing a boat with two men and a sleeping woman.

"Might be our perps," Tom said.

"Did you get a description of the boat? Libby could say if it's the same one she saw. We might be able to track it."

"It was too far for my witness to make out the name or make. Did you ask McEwan?"

Alec nodded. "He said he thought it was a Sea Ray, but he wasn't sure. Said it had some wear and might be a charter boat."

"I'll check out the marinas on the mainland and at Kill Devil."

It sounded like Tom was going to stay objective. The tension eased out of Alec's neck. "Promise me one thing, okay? That you won't prejudice the state boys against her. Let them come in and look at the situation with fresh eyes."

Tom hesitated, then looked down at his desk. "They are already looking at her, Alec. She wiped out the video."

"I believe her story about doing it accidentally."

"I don't know what to believe yet. But we have to consider all possibilities. I need you to promise to keep an open mind and report anything suspicious you see about Libby."

"I know the meaning of duty," Alec said. "I'm not going to hide anything. But we need to find Nicole. Every hour that passes is bad news and you know it."

"I'm doing my best. We're looking too. You have to consider that we may never find her though, Alec."

"I don't want to give up too soon."

"Neither do I."

* * *

The Coast Guard boat rode the waves so well Libby barely felt the swells left from the storm. Nicole had been gone three days. Was she even still alive? Libby stood at the bow of the craft and scanned the sea for any sight of her partner. Alec stood shoulder to shoulder with her and lifted binoculars to his eyes. He'd stopped to change into his uniform.

"We've got the boat for three more hours," he said.

Libby moved restlessly. "I don't think she's out this way. There's nothing here." She'd seen nothing but gulls and whitecaps.

"I don't either."

"If it was the kidnappers the old man saw, could they have had a destination in mind?"

"There isn't much out here but open sea."

"No islands?"

He shrugged. "Just uninhabited bits of sand. Nothing that would withstand a hurricane or support life. Some people picnic on the small islands, but there's no food or water on most of them."

She held out her hand. "Can I borrow your binoculars?"

"Sure." He handed them over.

She adjusted them to suit her and studied the whitecaps. Nothing. Every hour that passed left her feeling more and more hopeless. Where could they turn for information?

She handed back the binoculars. "Could we check the little islands?"

He spoke to Curtis, and the boat veered toward a tiny spot of land to the west. "It will take days or weeks to search them all. It would be insanity to put her on one of them."

"I'm not going to give up. She has to be somewhere. What do you think they did with her?"

He pressed his lips together, then shrugged. "Hard to say. They could have veered toward land at any point and put ashore."

"You don't think they did though, do you? I hear it in your voice. You think they dumped her."

"Libby, we don't know what happened or why they even took her. Anything is possible."

She felt a rising tide of distress and clamped down on it.

"It's too early to give up," he said. "We're going to keep looking."

His tone held determination. She smiled at him. "Thank you."

The craft reached the tiny island. Alec ordered the anchor lowered and the raft readied. "Want to go ashore?"

She eyed the island. It looked deserted. "I'll go."

"It's likely full of bird offing," he warned. "The pelicans like this island."

"I'll manage. Are they nesting?"

"Yes. They breed from March to November. So we may see some fledglings." He helped her into the raft with the others, then rowed ashore. The raft touched bottom and he jumped out, then dragged it to the sand. "Stick with me, just in case." He asked his friends to go the other direction. Josh and Sara went east.

She and Alec went west toward a patch of spindly trees. "Oh look!" She pointed to the ground. "Is that a pelican nest?"

"Yes. There are two eggs. That's common. The parents take turns incubating the eggs." He grinned. "That's the way it should be. The mom shouldn't have to do it all."

"Nice of you to admit it," she said. She glanced at

him out of the corner of her eye as she turned away. Did he feel that way about raising kids? He handled Zach well.

It took less than five minutes to meet up with the other two Coasties. Gulls scolded them as they searched, but the island held nothing.

Sara fell into step beside her. "You doing okay?"

Libby liked the other woman's manner. Calm and confident. "I'm fine. Alec says you're the EMT? Is it hard to work with mostly men?"

"I used to think I had to prove myself, but the guys are fair. They let me pull my own weight." She smiled. "Most of the time."

"Does anyone ever stay on these little islands?" Libby asked.

"Sometimes fishermen will camp out, or teens will party on one. Once in a while a foolhardy mainlander will get it in his head to build a house on one, but it never lasts. The isolation gets to them after a while. Nothing is convenient either. One accident and things can get hairy quickly."

The four of them walked to the center of the island, where Sara pointed out a stash of beer bottles, both empty and full. A cornhole game had been set up, and someone had carved the words *I love Carrie* onto a tree trunk.

"Kids," Josh said. He and Sara headed back to the boat.

"What's that?" Libby pointed to the ground. "Looks like someone built a fire here."

"Probably kids cooking fish," Alec said.

She prodded the ashes with her foot. Nothing but pieces of charred wood.

"Wait." He knelt and sifted with his fingers, then his hand came up holding a pocketknife. He stood, his mouth pinched.

"What's wrong?"

"It's Zach's."

"How do you know?"

He showed her the name carved into the side of it. "He told me he dropped it overboard. This must be a hangout. I'm going to have to have a talk with him."

"You sound discouraged. You're thinking of the beer, aren't you? Boys generally experiment with alcohol."

His mouth was pinched. "He knows better. And he's driving a boat, which makes it worse."

She wanted to ask more, but there was a wall up in his manner. "He seems to love you."

He shook his head. "He's been a handful since his parents died."

"I know they were killed in a small plane crash. Do you know the cause?"

"Dave was an amateur pilot. Their plane went down over a lake in Minnesota. The authorities think clouds rolled in. He wasn't certified for instrument flying."

"I'm sorry."

They boarded the boat and got under way again. She strained to see the next island. Maybe Nicole would be on that one.

"We'll check there too," he said. "But I don't think we're going to find her on an island."

She jutted out her chin. "We have to try."

He glanced at his watch. "Two hours. Then we have to go back. Zach is bringing in fish to feed the town. We'll all need to help."

She wanted to scream that finding her friend was more important than fish, but she swallowed hard and nodded. This man and his friends were helping her. She would be grateful.

EIGHTEEN

The cutter docked at the Coast Guard headquarters in the bay. Alec pointed Libby to the ladies' room, then he walked with his friends across the grassy field toward the parking lot.

"Buddy, you better watch out," Curtis said.

Josh grinned and moved his hand like a diving airplane. "Kaboom! You're about to crash and burn."

Alec stopped and stared at them. "What are you two idiots talking about?"

Josh poked Alec's arm. "We're talking about you, my friend. And that pretty lady. You're already halfway smitten."

"That's ridiculous. I've only known her a few days." He started walking away.

Josh exchanged a long look with Curtis. "We're too late, Curtis. He's gone past denial to defensiveness."

Alec wanted to scowl, but he couldn't hold back the bark of laughter. "I'm just helping her, guys."

"That's what they all say," Curtis said. "I get to be best man though, right?"

"No, I get to be best man," Josh said. He punched Curtis in the arm. "Just because you're a month older, you think you get to do everything."

"No one is best man," Alec said. "There's no wedding."

"You mean we get to come to your house and watch the Dodgers play forever?" Josh whooped. "Now you're talking."

Curtis was grinning as he watched Josh cavort along the lawn. "What do you really think of Libby?" he asked Alec. "Any news on the case at all?"

"Not that I know of." He told his best friend about the disastrous interview with Earl, and Libby's admission about erasing the video.

"That's bad, Alec," Sara said. "You're *sure* it was accidental?"

"I believe her. Why are you asking? Do you know something about hacking?"

Curtis gave an innocent smile. "Well, this is all hearsay, you understand. I've never actually done it myself."

Alec grinned. "Okay, spill it. When did you hack a website?"

"Well, in college, there was this girl I liked. She had a website and I thought it would be cute to hack it and put up a poem I'd written for her."

Sara punched him on the arm. "Get out! You didn't. Poetry? From *you*?"

Curtis grinned. "I did. But the next day I wished I didn't. She wouldn't speak to me. So much for that relationship."

"How'd you learn to do it?" Alec asked.

"I was taking website design. If you know a little, you can do a Google search and get the directions on how to do it. As long as the website doesn't have a good firewall. And many don't."

"What about the cams here? Do they have good firewalls?"

Curtis shrugged. "I'd think so, but with the budget cuts, it's hard to say."

"So maybe a college student could have done it. Or just anyone with a little knowledge."

"Maybe."

"Is IP tracing always accurate?"

Curtis shook his head. "A trace can be misdirected. So you need more evidence than a trace."

Alec gestured to the building. "Here comes Libby."

"When are you going to take her out on a real date?" Josh asked.

"Where would we go? Get a grip, Josh."

"You've got a boat. Take her for a nice, romantic dinner in Kill Devil Hills."

His friend had a point. Maybe Alec would do just that.

* * *

Zach's face was set and strained. Alec eyed his nephew's expression as they stood on the church lawn filleting fish with half a dozen men. Residents from all over the village had brought their gas grills and skillets. Griddles stood ready to cook the seafood, and news of the fish fry brought most of the townspeople to the church with dishes the women had prepared.

Curtis threw a mullet into the bowl. "You think that's enough? We're not going to clean *all* of these, are we? Where'd you get a haul like this, Zach?"

Zach shrugged. "Out past the sandbar. I knew the fishing would be good."

"I think that nephew of yours can read fish minds," Josh said to Alec. He pursed his lips like a fish. "Come catch me. I'll be good eating."

Zach's smile didn't reach his eyes. "Ha ha."

"When are you going to join us in the Coast Guard?" Curtis asked.

"Like, never," Zach said. "I just want to fish."

Josh poked a scale-covered finger at Alec. "Look at your uncle. He serves his country and fishes too. A perfect combination."

Alec wanted to tell them to lay off, but he was curious to see if their ribbing would get Zach to reveal why he was in such a rotten mood. He placed another fillet on the growing mound in the big stainless bowl. But Zach hunched his shoulders and continued to work on the fish. He didn't look at either of Alec's friends.

Pearl hurried across the lawn toward them. "We're going to start cooking the fish. This was wonderful of you to do, Zach. You're a thoughtful boy, just like your dad. He would have done this too."

Zach straightened and smiled. "Thanks, Mrs. Chilton." She patted his cheek. "So polite."

Zach grinned and so did Alec. Pearl could change anyone's frown into a smile.

"I think we're ready to start cooking," Pearl said. "Zach, would you carry the bowl for me? It's about as big as I am."

Zach carried the big stainless bowl overflowing with

fish fillets to the grilling station. A dozen men stood by, ready to start the cooking. The aroma of charcoal made Alec's stomach rumble. Side dishes covered the tables that had been hauled from the church basement.

He loved Hope Beach. It was a gift from God that he'd been able to live here all his life. Good people, good friends—what more did he need in his life? His contentment vanished when he caught a glimpse of Libby. Okay, so maybe he was a little lonely.

Josh nudged him with his elbow. "Look away. Resist the pull."

Alec grinned. "Maybe I don't want to resist."

"Be like me. A confirmed bachelor."

"Right. I've seen you looking at Sara."

Josh folded his arms across his chest. "I don't know what you're talking about."

"No?" Curtis knocked Josh's hat off. "I don't know why you don't ask her out, man."

Josh retrieved his Dodgers hat. "It would mess up the working relationship. What if it didn't work out but we still had to work together? Besides, it's better to be alone. Then I can do whatever I want, when I want."

"In Genesis God says man was not meant to be alone," Alec said, "that a woman completes him. My mom always reminded Dad of that when he complained about something." Alec grinned at the memory.

"All my parents did was fight," Josh said. "Until my mother lit out for somewhere else with another guy. I never saw her again."

"Sara's not like that," Curtis said. "If you don't ask her out, I will."

Josh stiffened. "Oh, come on now, that's not playing fair. She wouldn't go with you anyway."

"Want me to ask and see?"

"No. Just lay off, okay?" Josh's good-natured grin was gone. "I'll ask her if I get good and ready."

Alec had never seen his friend so serious. Who knew Josh's joking hid so much pain? He put his hand on his friend's arm. "Okay, we'll lay off. But think about Sara, okay?"

"Someone mention my name?" Sara was smiling as she joined them. She looked different out of her uniform, happy and carefree with her honey-colored hair blowing in the wind.

Josh shot them a warning glare. "We were just wondering where you were."

She lifted the dish in her hands. "I made my famous sweet-potato casserole. It's about the only thing I know how to cook."

Josh's face was red and he didn't look at her. Alec decided to take pity on him. "Hey, Sara, would you make an effort to be a friend to Libby? I think she feels a little out of place. Her family has been less than welcoming."

"I'd be glad to." A smile hovered on Sara's lips. "We talked a little out on the island today. I'm glad you're interested in her. I like her."

He wanted to protest that he wasn't interested, but they'd all know he was lying.

NINETEEN

Libby stood slightly apart from the happy crowd populating the churchyard. She wanted to be part of the group, but so far no one had taken notice of her. What was it the Bible said about friends? *A man who has friends must himself be friendly.*

She pasted on a smile and approached the closest group of women. "Can I help? I have a really great coating recipe for fish." She targeted her question to the only familiar face, Sara, who'd been on the Coast Guard boat.

Sara smiled. "Hello, Libby. I'm glad you're here. I'm terrible at cooking. What do you need for your breading? I'm a good gofer and I can rustle up the ingredients."

"Cornmeal, flour, paprika, pepper, and onion powder."

Sara held up her hands. "Whoa, whoa, I need to write that down." She pulled a scrap of paper from the purse at her feet and jotted it down. "Be right back."

The other ladies smiled and spoke to Libby as she waited for Sara to return. Their friendliness was a balm to her, and several told her they'd been praying that

Nicole would be found. Her pulse blipped when Alec came across the lawn toward her.

He smiled when he reached her. "You any good at cooking fish?"

"I can fix fish that will have you begging for more," she said. "I have a special breading I use. Sara went after the ingredients for me."

"I can't wait to taste it."

Surely he hadn't come over to make small talk. She searched his expression. "Any news?"

"I've been thinking about that beach cam website. Can we retrace exactly what you did? Did you copy the video to start to save it?"

She shook her head. "I tried to save it to my laptop and it wouldn't work. So I decided to look at the coding and copy it that way. I had just gotten in when it blipped, and everything was gone."

"Maybe someone else was there too. And the trace got misdirected to you. Curtis says it's possible."

"I wish I could believe that. I hate that something I might have done has hindered finding her kidnappers. How can I prove my innocence to the sheriff and everyone else?"

"I don't think you can unless we find the men responsible."

"It feels impossible." She glanced around. "This might be a good time to question people, don't you think?"

"Good idea."

She nodded toward Horace's secretary. "I thought of a few other questions for Mindy."

Mindy was sitting on a lawn chair by herself with a glass of iced tea in one hand and a novel in the other. She seemed oblivious to the hubbub going on around her. Libby had to speak her name for the woman to look up from her book.

Though Mindy smiled, her gaze wandered back to her book, then up again. "I thought you two would be around here somewhere."

"Did your house have any damage?" Alec asked.

She shook her head. "Mine's on a hill. The storm surge didn't reach me."

Alec glanced around. "Is Horace here somewhere too?"

"He and his son both came. His wife is in Virginia Beach." She looked at the book in her hand again.

Libby took the hint. "I am trying to figure out what all Nicole did when she was here. Did she mention any of her activities when you talked to her?"

Mindy thought for a moment. "She went parasailing."

"Who took her out?" Alec asked.

"Brent. I think he was a little smitten."

Libby gasped, and Alec straightened. She stared up at him. "Don't you think Brent would have mentioned that to us? He only mentioned talking to her in the ice-cream shop."

"Yeah, that seems odd."

Libby glanced across the lawn to where Brent stood talking with friends. "I'm going to ask him about it. What day did she go out with him, do you remember?"

"I think it was last Saturday."

Libby started toward Brent, then saw Sara standing

by the grills with a basket of items in her hands. "I'd better do my part with the fish first. Sara went to all the trouble to get me the ingredients."

"I think I want to watch this," Alec said. His lips twitched.

"You think I can't cook?" She tried to put indignation into her tone, but her smile gave her away. "You had plenty of my avocado dressing. Did *you* bring a dish?"

"I can make a mean bowl of microwave popcorn, but that's it," he said. "I don't think there's much demand for popcorn." He took her arm and steered her back to where Sara waited. "I think everyone wants something more substantial."

"I like popcorn," she said. The moment the words left her lips, she wanted to recall them. They sounded flirtatious, as though she was angling for an offer. His fingers seemed to warm as they tightened on her arm, but it had to be her imagination.

He cleared his throat. "Listen, I know your mind is on finding Nicole, but when this is all over, you want—"

"Alec, I need your help," Pearl said. "We need a few more tables hauled up from the church basement."

"Sure thing, Pearl."

Did he sound relieved? Libby watched them go and wished he'd finished his question. Had he been trying to ask her out?

* * *

Brent seemed to be deliberately avoiding him. Alec tried to catch him alone several times during the fish fry. Every time Alec neared him, Brent moved off to talk with another friend.

Libby's fish was a success. She stood talking recipes and food with several of the women from town. It warmed Alec to see how quickly she had made connections. Maybe she wouldn't sell out and leave. She gave a little wave when she saw him, and then spoke to a couple of women before joining him.

"Everyone liked my fish," she said, a trill in her voice.

"It was terrific." He took her arm and moved her out of the way of men carrying chairs back to their cars. "I've tried to talk to Brent, but he's jumping from place to place like a nervous cricket."

"Where is he now?" She glanced around. "There he is. Heading to the street. And he's alone."

"Let's get him." He grabbed her hand and they hurried after Brent. "Brent, wait up!"

Brent appeared not to hear, but he broke into a jog. Alec let go of Libby's hand and ran after him. He reached Brent as the younger man opened the car door. "Hang on there, Brent. We need to have a little chat."

"I'm in a hurry," Brent said. His gaze went past Alec to Libby, who was rushing toward them.

"This will only take a minute."

Her cheeks pink, Libby reached them. "Glad we caught you, Brent. We heard something today and wanted to ask you about it."

"Yes, I took Nicole parasailing, all right?" He shrugged. "It was no big deal."

"Mindy mentioned that she'd told us?" Alec wished

he'd instructed her to keep a lid on it. He would have liked to gauge Brent's reaction to their discovery.

"Yeah. So what?"

The kid was cool. Too cool. Alec couldn't put his finger on why it bothered him. "It's odd you never mentioned it. Were you afraid you'd be implicated in her disappearance?"

"No. I was out of town the day she was kidnapped. Is that all?"

"No, that's not all!" Libby put her hands on her hips. "What is *with* you, Brent? You're oh-so-smooth. Can't you just say what you think for once? Every time I talk to you, I can tell there is so much going on in your head."

"I'm thinking of nothing but my future," Brent said. He pushed his car door open wider.

"I get that my coming derailed some plans. It derailed my life too, but you all seem to forget that. And the other thing you ignore is that none of this is my fault! If I had lobbied for our father to leave me that property, then I could see your attitude. But I didn't."

Brent started to get in the car, but Alec blocked him. "Why didn't you tell us you spent time with Nicole? You never answered that."

"It didn't seem important." For the first time, Brent looked uncertain.

"What are you hiding?" Alec stood in the way of the door shutting. "Come on, Brent. We're not letting you go until you tell us the truth. What did Nicole have to say that day?"

"We didn't spend that much time talking. We were parasailing."

"You traveled together. Did you know who she was?"

Brent's jaw tightened. "I didn't know she was Libby's business partner, if that's what you mean. She asked me about the property, said she had someone interested in buying it. I already had their offer on the table though, so that was no big news."

"Why do you want to sell it instead of keeping it in the family?" Libby asked. "Did you disagree with our father's goal of preserving Hope Beach's peace and quiet?"

"I want to get off this podunk island," Brent said. "With that kind of money, I could go anywhere, do anything."

"You have quite a large amount of money coming even without the inn," Libby said.

"A million dollars will be gone in a heartbeat," Brent said. "That's nothing in today's economy."

What planet was this kid living on? Aware his jaw was hanging open, Alec shut it. "You could go to Harvard, start a business. Buy a house just about anywhere. What do you want to do that would require more than a million?"

Brent's eyes flickered. "You wouldn't understand."

"Try me."

"I'd like to build ships. Cruise ships."

It was a goal Alec could admire. "So get a job doing that. You don't really know anything about building ships. Start at the bottom and work your way up. There's virtue in that. Starting a business when you're ignorant of how to go about it is sure to result in failure."

"It doesn't matter now, does it? I'll have to make do with my paltry million. But don't worry. I'll figure out a way to accomplish my goal." He gave Alec a cold stare. "If you'll move away, I'd like to go."

Alec shrugged and backed off. The guy wasn't going to tell them any more. They watched him leave.

"I think there was something more between him and Nicole," Libby said.

"Me too. Let's talk to Vanessa."

TWENTY

The TV blared in the rec room, where Brent had apparently been in a hurry to watch some kind of shoot-'em-up film starring Bruce Willis. Libby and Alec walked through the inn in search of Vanessa. When they failed to find her, Alec stopped to snag bottles of water from the kitchen. Delilah was whipping cake batter and handed over the spoon when Alec begged for it.

"Have you seen Vanessa?" Libby asked.

Delilah slid the cake pan into the oven. "She said something about going for a swim."

"It's after dark," Libby said. "Isn't that dangerous?"

Delilah shrugged. "She's done it for years."

"Sharks are out now." Libby shuddered at the thought.

"The most dangerous time is just as it's getting dark," Alec said. "That's when they go out to feed."

"Does she know this?" Libby asked.

"Sure. Anyone who lives here knows the danger. But Vanessa isn't one to let anything stand in the way of what she wants to do." The spoon was licked clean and he put it in the stainless dishwasher. "How are you doing for money, Delilah? There are a lot of us to feed."

She hesitated. "Okay."

He pulled out his wallet. "Here's another hundred." He pressed it into her hand.

Libby caught a glimpse of his wallet and realized he'd given her all the cash he had. It shamed her to realize she'd given nothing toward food. Yes, the place was hers, but still. Alec didn't owe them anything. No money had been requested, but he'd handed it over without being asked. More than once.

She had a hundred tucked back for emergencies. This wasn't an emergency, was it? But her fingers dived into her wallet and pulled out the folded bill tucked behind her driver's license. "Here, take this too, Delilah." She had to force herself to release it into the other woman's hand.

When Delilah smiled, Libby felt lighter somehow. Her chest was warm. So this was how it felt to give. When was the last time she'd given so freely? Had she ever done it?

Delilah blinked rapidly and bit her lip. "Thank you, both of you. You're very generous. Some of the folks can't afford to give anything. Old Mr. Carter, for instance. All his pension money is in the groceries that have spoiled in his refrigerator. He feels terrible about it too, poor guy. And Vanessa and Brent can eat me out of house and home. Especially Brent. He expects peanut M&M'S to be in constant supply."

"I'll tell them to kick in some money," Libby said.

"Oh no, don't do that! They'll know I said something."

"I'll just ask if they have," Libby said. "I'll be very diplomatic."

Delilah began to smile. "There's cocoa fudge in the fridge." She pulled open the refrigerator door and pulled out the pan.

"Is this from the box of Hershey's cocoa?" Libby asked. She took a piece and bit into it. The flavor took her back to a time when she'd stand at the stove on a chair and stir the fudge while her mother gave directions. "Oh my goodness, I haven't had this kind of fudge since I was a little girl." She licked her fingers. "I'd better leave before I eat the whole pan."

"You could use a little fattening up," Delilah said.

"I think she looks pretty perfect," Alec said. His face reddened when Delilah laughed. "We could watch the movie with Brent while we wait. Maybe he'll say something more about Nicole."

Libby started to agree, then had another thought. "Which room was my father's when he stayed here? I'd like to look through it."

"Of course." Delilah wiped her hands on her apron. "He had a big suite on the third floor. In fact, his room was the only finished space on that floor." She grabbed a ring of keys hanging on a hook by the back door. "It's locked, so use the red key. It's clean. I make sure of that every week."

Libby's pulse skittered as she took the key ring. "Where are the stairs to the third floor?"

"At the end of the hall, down past my quarters. Take your time. Vanessa won't be in for another hour." Delilah pointed. "Use the back stairway."

Libby led the way up to the second-floor hall, then

back to the third-floor stairs. "Why would he put his suite up there?"

"I think he wanted a retreat where he could play the piano without disturbing anyone," Alec said.

"Piano?"

"He played beautifully. There are some tapes of him playing. They must be around here somewhere."

"I would love to hear one. All of them, actually."

The attic stairs were steeper than the main flights. The stairwell was closed as well. Alec reached past her to flip on the light. The steps creaked as she mounted them to the landing in the attic. It had been beautifully restored to highlight the maple floors, exposed rafters, and large windows that let the starlight shine in.

"How nice," she said, taking in the decor. The chairs went well with the camelback sofa and antique tables. "He had good taste. Chippendale chairs?"

"I think so. You would know better than I would."

There was a flat-screen television mounted on one wall. A bookcase filled with books was on the opposite wall. There was a small kitchenette with a microwave and coffeemaker beside it.

"Looks like his bedroom was through there." Alec pointed to a door on the other side of the cabinets. "Or do you want to look around here first?" He walked over and switched on the table lamps.

The warm glow illuminated the table. Libby frowned and went to inspect the purse. "That looks like Nicole's bag." She picked up the Brighton bag and opened it. Nicole's favorite lipstick, Burt's Bees Fig, was in the top pocket. She pulled out the wallet and glanced at the driver's license. Nicole's face smiled back. "It *is* Nicole's! What was she doing up here?"

* * *

The contents of the purse lay strewn on the coffee table. "Nothing out of order?" Alec asked Libby. The find had shaken her. Her high spirits vanished.

She picked up a piece of paper. "What's this about? It's a note from Mindy asking her to meet Brent for parasailing. Look, Mindy was going to go with them. She didn't mention that. I think we need to ask her how many times she saw Nicole. She hasn't been up front with us."

"I'm going to tell Tom about it too. Something isn't right about all of it. I think Mindy knows more than she's telling. Brent too." He stretched his arm across the back of the sofa. She was sitting close to him. Was it on purpose?

"I'm so tired of trying to figure this out."

Her hair tickled his arm. All he had to do was drop his arm around her and pull her close. What would she do if he tried it? Slap him? He felt as though he'd known her forever. They'd spent more time together in the past four days than he'd spent with the last woman he'd dated for two months. The fragrance in her hair was wonderful. Vanilla maybe? Sweet and enticing. He leaned a fraction of an inch closer and inhaled.

She must have heard him, because she turned her head and lifted a brow. "Is something wrong?"

"I was just smelling your hair," he said, his voice soft.

She didn't slap him. In fact, she leaned a little closer. "Vanilla shampoo," she said.

Her breath whispered across his face. With his right hand, he reached out and twisted a curl around his finger. "Nice," he said. With the back of his hand, he caressed her jaw. His gaze was caught by the glimpse of a necklace under her collar. "Is that Ray's?"

"You recognize it?" She pulled it free of her shirt and held it up. "WWJD. I've been trying to figure out how Jesus would act if his siblings hated him."

"So that's how you've been keeping your cool so well." Ray's legacy continued, even now. The realization stunned Alec.

"I don't know that I've been doing a good job of it. It's hard. My dad's letter asked me to be generous with Vanessa and Brent. I think he meant more than money."

"I'm sure he did. Money never mattered much to him."

"He said to be generous in grace. It would be easier just to share the property with them. Neither of them make it easy. But I'm trying."

No wonder he was so drawn to her. She was remarkable. "Back at the fish fry, I was going to ask you if—"

"What are you doing up here?" Vanessa shouted from behind them. She stood at the top of the stairs.

Libby sprang to her feet. "I'm looking around. How was your swim?"

Nice way to keep her cool. Alec managed not to grin. Her soft answer did nothing to calm Vanessa, who stood with her hands on her hips. Her wet hair hung down her back, and she wore a blue cover-up.

"See any sharks?" he asked.

Her gaze skewered him, and she ignored the question. "This is my father's personal space. You have no business here."

"I own it," Libby said, a steel undercurrent in her voice.

Vanessa strode across the floor to stop two feet from Libby. "So you keep throwing in my face! You may own the property, but you don't own the personal contents."

"Oh, but I do," Libby said. "Ask Horace if you don't believe me."

Tears hung on Vanessa's lashes, and Alec realized she was genuinely hurt. It wasn't anger that drove her. She was covering her pain with outrage.

"You miss your dad, don't you?" he asked her. "Do you come up here often?"

Vanessa burst into tears and covered her face with her hands. "She didn't even know him or love him." She ran to the bedroom and twisted the knob, but it didn't open. She pounded on the door and shrieked, "It's not fair. It's not!"

Libby went to her and put her hand on her shoulder. "Vanessa, I'm sorry. I wish I'd known him. It's not my fault, you know."

Vanessa flinched away. "Don't touch me! It wasn't my fault either, but I'm paying the price."

Libby said nothing. Her hand fell to her side. She bit her lip and turned away.

"You two are sisters, Vanessa. You can build a relationship if you work on it."

Vanessa folded her arms across her chest. "It's too late. I don't want to." She rattled the doorknob. "Give me the key. I want to go in. By myself." Her eyes narrowed, and she stared at Libby's neck. "That necklace. Where did you find it? Up here?" She swiped at Libby's throat.

Libby leaped back. "Our father left it to me."

Vanessa went even whiter. "That's impossible. He knew I wanted it."

"I'm sorry," Libby said. "I can show you the letter. He wanted me to think about the meaning of the necklace every day as I'm working to try to get to know you and Brent."

Vanessa's face worked and her eyes filled again. "That belongs to me. You have no right to it."

Alec winced when he realized what Ray had intended for good was causing more division between the sisters.

TWENTY-ONE

The beads were warm and smooth under Libby's fingers. *What would Jesus do?* The necklace was just a thing. Yes, her father had left it to her, had wanted her to have it. But did it mean even more to Vanessa? Her father had asked Libby to give mercy and grace to Vanessa and Brent. What exactly did that mean?

Libby studied her sister's face. Were those tears of pain or of anger?

Vanessa covered her face with her hands. "Don't look at me like that."

"Like what?" Libby asked. "I'm trying to understand."

"I don't want your understanding. Or anything else from you. I just want my daddy back!" Vanessa whirled and rushed out of the room.

Tears sprang to Libby's eyes too. Alec put his arms around her, and she buried her face in his chest. "What should I do?" she choked.

"What do you mean?"

She pulled away and touched the beads. "About this? Should I give it to her?"

"I don't think I can tell you the right thing to do. What does your heart say?"

"I think Jesus would give it to her." Her voice broke, and she swallowed hard. "It's only a thing. I think I may have already gotten out of the necklace what my father hoped I would. But he wore it for over twenty years. I feel close to him when I'm wearing it. It's all I have of him. So I want to keep it."

"No one is making you do anything. It's your choice."

She studied his kind eyes. "You think I should give it up, don't you?"

He shook his head. "I think Vanessa is acting like a spoiled brat, and I wouldn't give in to her. But she's not my sister. I'm not the one trying to be part of a family the way you are. I don't know what the right answer is."

"I don't either. Vanessa *is* acting like a brat. But I see her pain too. I think I'm going to have to pray about this and see if God will give me some clear direction."

"Let's pray together." His head touched hers.

She closed her eyes and listened to him pray for wisdom and discernment on how to best handle the family dynamics. No other person had ever prayed with her like this, about concerns that mattered so deeply to her. Her spirit bonded with his as they asked God for help.

"Amen," she said when he was finished. "Thank you, Alec. You're a good man."

He shook his head. "I've got lots of faults, believe me."

"I'm not seeing them," she said, holding his gaze. "Thank you for caring enough to pray. I don't know anyone else who would do that."

His fingers touched her chin and tipped her face up. He leaned forward and his lips touched hers. Warmth spread through her belly and up her neck. His lips werc firm and tender. No kiss she'd ever experienced affected her like this one. In his arms she felt safe and treasured. She palmed his face, relishing the feel of the stubble on his cheek. He was all man, yet the tender side of him was so godly, so strong.

She pulled away when Delilah called up the stairs. "Alec, phone call."

"Sorry," he said with obvious regret. "I'll be back." He went down the stairs.

Libby stared at the door to her father's inner sanctum. There was no reason not to go inside. Before she could talk herself out of it, she fitted the key into the door and unlocked it. Her hand shook when she twisted the knob, and her knees were weak. She pushed open the door.

There weren't many windows, so she flipped on the lights to illuminate the dim room. It contained a king-size bed with tan and blue linens. Pillows were heaped at the head of the bed. The walls were painted a creamy tan. The wood floors gleamed. Libby wandered around the room, picking up pictures and examining details. There were many photos of her father with Vanessa and Brent. Also ones of him on a big yacht with his wife.

If only she could have been part of his life. If only there was even one picture of her with her father. Libby turned back toward the door and spied a brown leather Bible on the bed stand. She picked it up and settled on the edge of the bed. The ribbon marked a passage in Hebrews 13. She skimmed it until she saw verse 16 highlighted in yellow.

*But do not forget to do good and to share, for with
such sacrifices God is well pleased.*

She clutched the beads. God didn't mean the necklace. She could share other things with Vanessa. But
even as she argued with herself, a sick roiling in her
belly told her the truth. God had answered Alec's
prayer with a clear message.

The question was whether she could make herself
give up something so precious to her.

* * *

Debris still littered Oyster Road, and folks were out
cleaning their yards. It was going to take a long time
before Hope Beach looked like it did before the storm.
Mud puddles were everywhere, and gulls swarmed the
area, scavenging sea creatures that the waves had left
behind. The air reeked of rotting fish and seaweed.

She sniffed the air. "Smells like the sea on a really
bad day."

"Careful." Alec put out his hand to stop Libby from
stepping in front of a kid on a motorbike.

The wind tugged strands of her shiny hair loose
from the ponytail. She sure was pretty. He'd lain awake
for hours last night reliving that kiss. Their attraction
felt God-ordained to him.

He nodded toward a neat white bungalow that had
been converted into a small café. "Mindy is usually getting an egg sandwich for her and Horace about now.
Let's see what she has to say about the note in Nicole's
purse."

They crossed the street to the courtyard. Live oak trees shaded tables draped with red-and-white cloths. Inside, several residents spoke and nodded greetings to them as they threaded their way to where Mindy sat with lunch in one hand and a novel in the other. Her attention was on the book as she absently took a bite of her egg sandwich.

She looked up when Alec cleared his throat. Her gaze went from him to Libby and back again. She finished chewing and swallowed, then dabbed her napkin to her lips. "You looking for Horace? He's not here."

"Nope. We wanted to talk to you. Mind if we join you?"

She put down her book with obvious reluctance. "I don't have long. Horace will be wanting his egg sandwich in another fifteen minutes."

"This won't take long." He pulled out a chair for Libby, then settled into the one beside her. "We want to ask you a few more questions."

Mindy hunched her shoulders. "I already told you everything I know."

Alec brought out the note they'd found in Nicole's purse. "I don't think so."

Mindy's face went white. Her gaze darted from him to the note.

"Why didn't you tell us you went parasailing with them?"

Mindy bit her lip and looked down at her hands. "It didn't seem important."

"Every detail is important. We have to retrace

Nicole's tracks and find out what happened to her," he said.

Libby leaned forward in her chair. "What did you all talk about?"

Mindy took a sip of her pink lemonade. "Mostly business stuff. She talked to Brent about the sale of the inn."

Libby shook her head. "By then he would have known I owned the inn, not him. So why would Nicole discuss it with him?"

Mindy looked down at her lap. "He wanted to know if she could talk you into giving up your inheritance. He thought she might have enough influence."

"What did Nicole say?" Libby asked.

"That no one would be that stupid."

Knowing Brent the way he did, Alec could only imagine how well that went over. "I'll bet that ticked Brent off."

"Yes." Her admission was barely audible.

So that's why Brent brushed them off when questioned about the parasailing event. If they knew there'd been an argument, he would draw suspicion.

Mindy glanced at her watch. "I need to get back to work." She signaled to the server, who brought her the bill and a white lunch sack. She left money on the table and rose. "You aren't going to tell Horace, are you? He wouldn't like it if he knew I'd gone out with them. She was a client."

"If Brent had anything to do with Nicole's disappearance, it's going to come out sooner or later," Alec said. "You should tell him yourself."

Mindy shook her head violently. "He'd fire me in a heartbeat. I know Brent had nothing to do with it, so I'm safe." She scooped up the bag and headed out through the dining room and into the courtyard.

Alec sat back in his chair. "I think we'd better talk to your brother. He knows more about this than I thought."

TWENTY-TWO

The last of the clouds had rolled away when Libby got out of Alec's truck in the circular drive by the old hotel. She was struck again at the structure's beauty. Someone moved on the expansive columned porch, and she saw Brent leaning on the balustrade. Vanessa was at a table with a coffee cup in her hand.

Libby's stomach tightened at the thought of the coming confrontation. She wanted to love her siblings. That they might be involved in Nicole's disappearance was too horrible to contemplate.

"Steady, let me handle this," Alec said when she drew in a deep breath.

She knew he would be calmer than she was, so she nodded and followed him up the sweeping steps to the grand porch. At the moment, she was glad she hadn't given the necklace to Vanessa.

Brent straightened when they drew near. Libby studied his handsome face. Vanessa was beautiful as well. Their adversarial situation showed no signs of changing. Libby touched her necklace. *What would Jesus do?*

Brent's smile melted away when he glanced at Alec's face. "Something wrong?"

"You tell us." Alec stared at him. "You tried to persuade Nicole to talk Libby into giving up her inheritance. And when Nicole refused, you argued. Two days before she disappeared. That looks bad."

Vanessa joined them at the railing. "Who told you this?"

Alec folded his arms across his chest. "That's not important."

"It had to be Mindy. She was the only other person there," Brent said. "So what? It's no crime to try to convince Libby to do the right thing."

"The right thing." Libby shook her head. "It was the right thing for you. Not for anyone else."

His eyes were cold. "I didn't know you. I still don't. You're a stranger to us and to this town. You don't understand."

"So help me understand! I know it's too much to ask to be part of the family, but the least you could do is treat me with common courtesy."

Vanessa and Brent exchanged a glance. Was it Libby's imagination or did her sister look a little shamefaced?

Alec narrowed his eyes. "So why didn't you go meet her to show her the lighthouse, Vanessa? Because the two of you'd made plans to do away with her?"

"We had nothing to do with her disappearance," Brent said.

The screen door opened and Pearl stepped out. For someone so rotund, she was light on her feet. "What's going on out here?" she asked. "Your voices are carrying to our guests."

"Brent and Vanessa may know more about Nicole's

disappearance than they've been willing to tell us," Alec said.

"Oh dear me, that's not true, is it?" Pearl's gaze went from her nephew to her niece. "What do you know about that girl's kidnapping? Tell the truth now."

Pearl's appearance took all the bravado out of Brent. "We didn't have anything to do with her disappearance, Aunt Pearl."

Pearl's gaze narrowed on him. "Did you ask some friends to put a scare into her?"

He flushed. "I wouldn't do that."

Pearl lifted a brow. "No? I think Jennifer Masters might disagree with that."

"That was different."

Libby didn't like the way he looked down, or the color that came and went in his face. "You've done this before?" If he'd played a prank, then maybe she would have Nicole safe and sound yet today.

He shrugged. "It was just a trick on an old girlfriend."

"Way I heard it, you had two friends grab her and take her to the mainland, where they left her to find her own way back home," Alec said. "I'd forgotten about that. Is that what you did with Nicole? Tell us the truth. We can have her picked up."

"I didn't do anything!"

"Quit harassing Brent," Vanessa snapped. "He had nothing to do with this. Neither did I."

"It still seems odd that you didn't meet her when you said you would," Libby said. "I was watching on the cam. When she was taken, you were already ten minutes late."

"Being late is not a crime." She glanced at her brother.

This was getting them nowhere. The two weren't budging, but Libby didn't get the sense that they were guilty of harming Nicole. "How do you get to the lighthouse ruins you were going to show her?" she asked. "Maybe that's a place to start looking."

"She wasn't taken there," Alec said. "She was on the boardwalk."

"True enough, but we don't know anywhere else to look." Libby wasn't about to let any of them dissuade her. If she had to go by herself, she would. "Can someone direct me to it?"

"I'll take you whenever you want," Alec said. "I think it's a waste of time though. The site is down the shore in an area where no one ever goes. The fastest way to get there is by boat."

"How was Nicole going to get there?" Libby asked. "Were you meeting her in a boat or what?"

They both stared at Vanessa, who put her cup down on the railing and stared out to sea without answering. Libby curled her fingers into her palms. "Vanessa, I've had enough of your attitude. My friend is *missing*. She's been kidnapped. Do you get that? I saw two men forcibly take her away. She was kicking and screaming. One of them poked a needle in her arm." Her voice broke and she took a deep breath. "You'll help me find her or you can get out of my house."

Vanessa's eyes widened. So did Pearl's. Brent just continued to look bored.

"We have no place to go," Vanessa said. "I've spent more time in this house than you can imagine. Dad would roll over in his grave if he heard you threaten us like this."

Her sister's words brought Libby up short. Extend grace, he'd asked. She hardened her jaw. "All that matters to me is finding Nicole. Conflict like this is fruitless."

Vanessa's lips tightened. "I'm not the one who declared war. You think you can breeze in here and take over, but as you pointed out, you didn't even know Daddy. You're no real daughter."

"Maybe not," Libby said evenly. "But I own this place and I say who goes and who stays. So you choose which side you're on and let me know." She slapped her hand to her head. "What's the use? I'm going to go do something useful."

As she walked into the house, she fingered her necklace. Would Jesus have been so harsh? Maybe. He did confront the money changers in the temple. Figuring out how to act in a godly manner was even harder than she thought it would be.

* * *

Libby changed her clothes. Heat gun in hand, she attacked the layers of chipped paint on the trim around the front door. There were easily ten layers of paint on the wood. When it softened and melted, she scraped it off with a putty knife and deposited it in a metal coffee can the gardener had found for her.

"That almost looks fun," Alec said from behind her. "Want some help?"

"I only have one heat gun or I'd take you up on it."

A white SUV pulled into the driveway. A slim woman with auburn curls stepped out of the passenger side. Moments later a stocky man with dark hair was out also and opening the back door on his side. A young boy of about ten joined the woman in the drive.

Libby put down the heat gun. They must be new guests. "Hello," she said, smiling at the family. "Welcome to Tidewater Inn."

The woman was staring at the inn with clear admiration. "I always forget just how beautiful it is until I get here again." She transferred her attention to Libby and held out her hand. "I'm Bree Matthews. You're expecting us."

Delilah had mentioned the family's arrival. It was their third visit in as many years. "We've got your room ready," Libby said. "Can I help you with anything? Call one of the men to help with luggage?"

"I'll help them," Alec said.

Bree pulled the boy beside her. "This is Davy. He's ten now and my big boy. That's my husband, Kade."

Kade was lifting toddlers from car seats in the back. "Be ready," he called. "They've been cooped up and will want to run for the water." He set a little boy and girl on the ground.

"How old are they?" Libby asked.

"Almost two. They're named Hunter and Hannah." Bree smiled and scooped her daughter up as she ran past. "You don't have your swimsuit on yet, honey," she told the child.

"They're beautiful." But Libby's attention was caught

by the gorgeous dog that hopped out of the hatch. "Nice dog." Did they allow dogs in the inn? Delilah had never mentioned their policy.

"This is Samson, my search dog."

Libby watched Alec pet the dog. "Search dog? He finds lost people, like on TV?"

"He's the best." Bree snapped her fingers and the dog rushed over to lick them. "Good boy," she crooned.

Libby stared at the dog. He looked like he had quite a bit of German shepherd in him. "I don't know if you've heard anything about it, but we have a missing woman here. She happens to be my business partner."

Bree's gaze sharpened. "What happened? I haven't watched the news. We've been driving from Michigan and have been playing videos for the children."

Libby told her about Nicole's abduction. "You think he can find her?" Libby petted him and he nosed her leg.

"We can let him try." There was a shadow in Bree's green eyes, but she held Libby's gaze. "A water search is always harder. I want you to understand that. But he has a good nose. We'll do what we can, okay?"

Libby had hoped for utter assurance, but she managed a smile. "I appreciate anything you can do."

Bree glanced around. "Any idea of where to start the search?"

"I can show you where she was taken, but I also know Nicole was down the beach a ways, at some old lighthouse ruins. We haven't searched there yet, and I thought we might look at the ruins too. But let's get you unpacked first. I'll show you to your room."

Delilah had arranged for them to have the only

two-bedroom suite so the children would have plenty of space. Libby hadn't been around kids much, and as the men unloaded the back of the SUV, she found her gaze lingering on the twins. Their dark hair was soft and curly. The little girl had Bree's pointed chin and hairline. The little boy was stocky like his handsome father.

"I want to see the water," Davy announced.

Hannah ran to Alec's leg and tugged on his jeans. "Water," she said, pointing toward the waves.

"We're going, bug," Kade said, touching the boy's hair.

Libby liked Kade already. The way he looked at Bree made Libby glance at Alec from the corner of her eye. Alec was tossing little Hannah in the air while she giggled and screamed, "More!" He seemed to be a natural with the kids. And he'd willingly taken on the raising of his nephew. That couldn't have been easy. Only a rare man would be willing to alter his life that much.

The women corralled the children while the men took the luggage to the room. Bree's mouth curved in a smile. "I like your fellow."

Libby stopped petting Samson, then resumed. "He's not my fellow. I haven't known him very long."

"Sometimes it doesn't take long. He seems like a nice guy."

"He's a good man," Libby agreed.

The men came back out. Kade had a vest in his hand. The dog began to prance around Bree when she took it from him. "Hold still, Samson." She knelt and slipped the vest onto the dog. His tail came up and he looked even more alert. "Someone is ready to go searching."

Samson's ears pricked at the word *searching*. He whined and looked down the beach. "He knows what we're talking about?" Libby asked.

"Oh yes. He loves his job. He acts differently when he's working. Let's go to the location where she was taken. Can you get me something that Nicole has worn? Put it in double paper sacks." Bree handed her two bags. "Our best chance is to go out on a boat and see if Samson can get a scent. But, Libby, it's going to be a long shot, okay?"

Maybe so, but it was a better chance than any other Libby had. She ran inside to grab one of Nicole's shirts. Having another ally had given her new courage.

TWENTY-THREE

Alec stood on the boardwalk with his hands in the pockets of his shorts and watched the freshening wind blow Libby's hair in tangles. As soon as they let the dog out of the SUV, he ran in circles, then back to Bree, who held the bags containing Nicole's shirt. Alec had heard of search dogs, but he'd never seen one in action.

"Where was she when she was taken?" Bree asked. She stood looking around the area.

"Right there." Libby pointed out the camera and the spot where her friend had been standing.

They scanned the same sand dunes, the same rolling ocean that Alec had seen earlier in the week when he'd come here with Tom. The only new items were a crumpled cigarette pack, an empty potato chip bag, and a few Marlboro butts.

Bree knelt and opened the bag. Samson thrust his nose into the bag. "Search, Samson!"

The dog pulled his head from the bag and barked. He ran back and forth across the beach with his nose in the air. Alec's jaw dropped as he watched the dog work. Samson clearly seemed to know what he was doing.

When the dog stiffened, so did Alec, though he didn't know what it meant.

"He's got a scent!" Bree ran after the dog.

Alec and Libby followed. Libby's expression was intent and hopeful, so he rushed ahead of her, just in case whatever Samson was smelling was something Alec didn't want her to find. Samson trailed the scent to the parking lot. He ran to a trash barrel and began to bark.

Alec's gut clenched, and he prayed they wouldn't find Nicole's body in it. "Stand back." He motioned for the women to move back a few feet. Once he got the top off the garbage pail, he put on plastic gloves and began poking through it in spite of the stench. It was only about half full, so he relaxed, sure he wasn't going to find anything at all. The dog had probably gotten sidetracked by the food smells.

"That's hers!" Libby's arm shot past him and grabbed a pink straw hat. She shook off the debris. "I told you I saw it fall off her in the struggle."

"You're sure?" Bree asked.

Libby nodded. "I bought it for her for her birthday. What's it doing in the trash?"

"You shouldn't have touched it." Alec took it in his gloved hands. "Maybe the killers handled it."

The animation on Libby's face ebbed. "It came off her head in the struggle. I don't think they touched it."

"You said they took her right to the boat and off-shore," he pointed out. "You saw them throw her into the boat and move off? They didn't come back for the hat?"

"I saw them leave." Her mouth drooped. "So this means nothing."

"We know the dog can smell her," he said. "Pretty amazing. I guess they could have come back and just thrown it away so nothing looked out of place on the beach. Anyone could have tossed it."

Bree called the dog back to her and had him smell the sack again. "Search, Samson!"

Samson sniffed the air, then ran back to the beach. He barked and raced to a spot near the water, where he began to dig. Alec and the women ran to see what he'd found. Alec knelt to help Samson, but he woofed and nosed at a pair of sunglasses before Alec could dig his fingers into the sand.

Alec held them up. "Nicole's?"

Libby nodded. "I think so."

The dog whined and pressed his nose against Bree's hand. She went through the process of letting him smell the bag again. He ran back and forth on the sand for ten minutes before going back to Bree's side. He whined, then laid at her feet.

"I think this is all he's got," Bree said.

"It was worth a try." Libby glanced at Alec. "Could you take us out tomorrow in the boat?"

"Sure. You think he can find something in the ocean?" Watching the dog work was interesting, but Alec didn't see how Samson could possibly find Nicole in that ocean.

Bree shrugged. "I won't lie and say it's likely. There's a lot of ocean out there and we really don't know where to even look. But Samson has done many other amazing searches successfully, so I want to try."

He appreciated Bree's honesty. Alec nodded. "We'll take my boat out first thing in the morning."

* * *

Libby was too restless to watch the movie playing in the living room. Bree was bathing the children and getting them to bed, so Libby slipped away from the group and went to the third floor again. Her interest in finding out how Nicole's purse had ended up there had resurfaced.

She flipped on the light, then stood in the main living area of the third floor and glanced around. The stairs creaked behind her and she whirled to see Brent stepping into the space.

"What are you doing up here?" he demanded.

"Looking around." She decided against reminding him that she owned the property and could go anywhere she pleased. She'd written in her journal that she hadn't extended much grace after their last encounter.

He scowled at her. "These are Dad's private quarters."

"I know." She gestured to the table. "Nicole's bag is here. Do you have any idea how it got up here?"

"*She* was up here?"

"It appears so. Unless someone put her purse here."

"Have you asked Delilah about it?"

She should have thought of that. "No. But you didn't answer my question. Did *you* know about it?"

His gaze was steady. "You really think I had something to do with her disappearance, don't you?"

She'd had enough of his evasiveness. "Why do you always answer a question with another one? Just answer me, yes or no. Did you see Nicole's purse up here?"

"No. This is the first I've been up here since Dad died. Your turn. You think I'm guilty of something bad, don't you?"

He looked so innocent, so hurt. Was any of it real? Libby wanted to believe him. He was her brother, after all. "I honestly don't know. I'd like to believe you did nothing to hurt her, but you have to admit your lies look bad."

"I didn't do anything to her. It was an innocent outing."

Libby reminded herself how young he was. Maybe she was overreacting. "I know you weren't one of the men who took her. I saw them. But you could have hired the men."

"I could have, but I didn't."

She wanted to know this brother, but she couldn't seem to get through. "You're hard to read, Brent. I want to believe you." She decided that Jesus would lay it all out there, so she gathered her courage. "What do you want, Brent? Do you even care that you have another sister? We're family, you know. We share our father's blood. I want us to learn to love each other."

His eyes flickered when she mentioned love, but then he folded his arms over his chest. "I'm sure you're a very nice person, Libby, but I have one sister and that's enough. You don't belong here. I'm sorry to be so blunt, but you can't show up here and announce you're part of our family and expect it to be so. To us, you're just a stranger."

Though she agreed with the gist of what he'd said, his cold gaze cut her. Her eyes filled, and she turned away so he wouldn't see. "I see. Thank you for being honest." He was still standing there when she regained her composure, so she turned back toward him. "In Nicole's journal, she mentioned that someone whispered to her outside her door. Was that you?"

His jaw tightened. "You're determined to pin something on me, aren't you?"

"Who else would have access here? And it was a male. Be honest with me, Brent. I've learned enough about our father to know he valued honesty and integrity."

His lips flattened. "Fine. I tried to scare her off. Satisfied? But I had nothing to do with her disappearance."

"Why did you want to scare her off? She wasn't hurting you."

His sigh was heavy. "Look, she told me she wanted you to keep the property and develop it yourself. I felt the honorable thing for you to do was to bow out. I still feel that way."

"She wanted us to develop it? That's crazy. Where could we come up with enough money?" Maybe Nicole had been making a play to squeeze more money out of the buyer. Poe seemed determined to have the land.

She held Brent's gaze and found truth there. "I believe you."

His eyes flickered. "Really? Or will those doubts surface again?"

She shook her head. "We've gotten off to a really bad start. Friends?" She reached out her hand.

Brent stared at her extended hand, then quickly touched his fingers to hers and withdrew. "Let's say acquaintances for now."

It was a start.

The steps creaked behind them, then Delilah stepped into the room. She stopped short when she saw them. "I went to the storage shed to look for something and saw the light on up here. I thought someone had forgotten to turn it off. Is everything all right?"

Libby nodded. "I do have a question though." She picked up Nicole's bag. "Do you know how this got here?"

Delilah's lids flickered. "I assume Nicole left it."

"She was up here? Why?" Libby didn't like the thought that Nicole had been poking through her father's things. Maybe this was how Vanessa felt.

"She'd asked to explore the house. I didn't give her any keys and had no idea she would find her way up here, but I must have left the door unlocked when I cleaned the last time. I found her here and chased her out."

"Did she say what she was doing?"

Delilah shook her head. "I think she just wanted to see what was here. She didn't seem to have an agenda, if that's what you mean."

Nicole was as much of a history buff as she was. Libby could see her wanting to poke into every nook and cranny of the attic.

So the purse was a dead end. "I'd like to be alone for a while," she said.

Brent and Delilah exchanged a glance. Brent shrugged. "You're the boss." He went down the steps and Delilah followed.

Libby exhaled and sank onto the sofa. In this place she could sense her father. It would be the perfect spot to have her devotions every day too. His Bible was still on the table where she'd left it. She hadn't had a chance to go through it much. When she picked it up, she realized there was a folded paper, stiff with age, under it.

She unfolded it and discovered it was a map of the island. The old lighthouse site was marked on it. Holding it under the light, she saw someone had written the word *cellar* with an arrow on it near the house structure. Another X marked the wellhead. The place once had several outbuildings too. She was eager to see how much of it still stood. And whether it harbored any clues to Nicole's whereabouts.

TWENTY-FOUR

The sun was barely up, and haze still hung over the waves. Sea spray stung Libby's cheeks and filled her nose with the salty scent of the ocean. She crouched behind the windshield of Alec's boat to avoid a large wave that threatened to wash over the bow. "The sea is strong today."

Bree and Samson rode up front. The dog had his nose in the wind and wore an ecstatic smile. "It's gorgeous out here," Bree called. "Not quite the same as Lake Superior where we live, but close enough. Where are we going?"

Alec pointed to the shore. "The lighthouse ruins. We'll land there. I'll drop anchor, and we'll have to wade to shore. It's got a sandy bottom though, so no danger of getting dunked."

"I'm not afraid of the water," Libby said. In fact, she couldn't think of anything she enjoyed more than being on the sea. Well, other than digging into the history of a gorgeous old house.

The spit of land was narrow, only about twenty feet across. Scrubby bushes and vegetation that had stood up to the salt clung to the sparse soil. The small peninsula widened at the base and joined the main part of the island, where heavier vegetation hid whatever ruins they'd come here to see. Libby scanned the area for a hint of the cover-up Nicole had been wearing. She wasn't sure if she was relieved or sad to see no sign that her friend had ever been here.

The boat touched bottom, and Alec tossed the anchor overboard. Samson dived over the side and swam toward shore. Alec clambered into the shallows, then held out his hand to assist Libby and Bree. Kicking off her sandals, Libby slipped into the water with him. The sea was chillier than she'd expected. The storm must have stirred up the cold from the bottom. She held her shoes out of the water and waded to shore. The sand was firm and smooth under her bare feet. When she reached the beach, she slipped her feet back into her sandals, then looked around.

"Where are the ruins? I don't see anything," she said.

He pointed. "This way."

He led them north, away from the finger of barren peninsula, deeper into the vegetation. Samson barked and ran ahead. Sea oats waved in the breeze, and beach grass fought to hold on in the dunes. Skate cases littered the sand. The sand began to run out and was replaced by thin soil that supported a maritime forest of straggly live oaks pruned by the salt into wedge shapes. Palmettos and loblolly pines marched along the forest.

Libby spied the ruins before he said anything. "There," she said, pointing. The area was still flooded, and she could see only the tops of brick and mortar.

"It was a lighthouse once? There's not much left of it. I expected a standing structure."

"It was knocked over in a big hurricane in the late eighteen hundreds. Legend has it that Blackbeard stormed the lighthouse and captured the keeper's daughter."

"What happened to her?" Bree asked, shuddering.

He shrugged. "No one really knows. Some say Blackbeard loved her and carried her off to his lair in the Bahamas. Others say she jumped overboard and drowned rather than face dishonor. But it's just a legend. There may be no truth to it at all. People have come out here from Hope Beach for generations. Weddings have been held here, ashes have been committed to the sea from here, and babies have been dedicated on this spot. It's almost a shrine to the town."

Libby glanced around. "Why? The place seems so barren."

He propped one foot on the ruins. "Over the years it gained the reputation of bestowing good luck on residents. The first marriage here that I know of was at the turn of the century. That marriage lasted sixty years."

She lifted her chin and sniffed the sweet-smelling air. "It has a welcoming feel in spite of all the ruins."

Advancing to the base of the building, she examined the debris. "Nicole was wearing a pink cover-up over a brown bathing suit. She had on pink flip-flops too. And her hair was in a ponytail."

"I'll take Samson and we'll nose around," Bree said. She pulled a bag of pistachios from her pocket. "Want some?"

Libby grinned and shook her head. She dug into her pocket and held up her jalapeño jellybeans. "I have these."

Bree wrinkled her nose, then she and Samson headed toward the line of vegetation. The dog had his nose down.

Alec walked the perimeter of the ruins and back. "I don't see anything but a few Coke bottles. We'll come back again when the water recedes."

"I'd wondered if she came out here on her own, but I don't see any sign of her."

"How would she get here? It would take an hour to walk from the house," he said.

"She's an avid runner. I imagine she could run along the beach and get here in forty-five minutes. She's not the type to wait for someone else to show her something of interest. I thought she might have come out here the day before to scout it out before coming with Vanessa." She turned and looked out to sea. "Would they have taken her to the mainland? I don't know where we should look."

"The state has put out a bulletin about her. If she's there, someone will see her. This is summer. The coastline is crawling with tourists. It would be hard to take her anywhere without being seen."

"But not impossible if they did it in the middle of the night," Libby said.

"She was taken late in the afternoon."

Libby felt so hopeless. "They could have holed up somewhere."

"True enough."

Libby realized she was grasping at straws. "What about farther out? Are there any uninhabited islands on this side of the island?"

He nodded. "Plenty of them. Some of them barely as big as a postage stamp. I thought we'd check out as many as we can. We can go out in the boat and ask fishermen if they've seen anything too."

"You think she's dead, don't you?" The question tore from Libby's throat.

He stared down at her. "We both know that the longer it goes since she's been spotted, the scarier it is. But I haven't given up hope yet. Someone has to have seen something."

She searched his expression. "You really believe that?"

"I do."

His certainty strengthened her. She glanced back at the ruins. "Are there any photos of the lighthouse before it was destroyed?"

He nodded. "Your dad has quite a library at the old hotel. He was a history buff, and the information about the island and Hope Beach that he has is more extensive than anything the town library has."

It appeared she had something in common with the father who left her.

* * *

Alec led Libby across the street from the harbor to the Oyster Café. It was lunchtime and there would be plenty of townspeople around who might have met Nicole during her stay. Bree had taken Samson to meet Kade and the children for lunch at Captain's Pizza.

"This is such a darling village," Libby said when they stopped outside the café. "I love it. So quaint."

He pushed the door open. The waitress seated them by the window that looked out onto the street where bicyclers zipped past.

"Why do so many people ride bicycles here?" she asked.

He hadn't thought much about it. "Gas is high, and it costs to get a car over here. I guess progress hasn't caught up to us."

"I like it. I'd like to get a bike."

"Your dad has one in the basement of the inn. I'll show you where it is."

She brightened. "I'd like to use his." Her smile faded. "Though it's likely to be one more source of contention with Vanessa and Brent. They don't want me to have anything personal of my father's."

"They'll get over it." He watched her toy with the necklace. "You still have the necklace, I see. I wondered if you would give it to Vanessa last night."

"I think God is telling me to do it, but I'm fighting the idea."

"It's never a good idea to fight God."

"I know." She gave a heavy sigh. "I don't want to do it. I've been praying he makes me willing to obey."

"Good prayer." He looked at the menu. "I think I'll get shrimp grits."

"Crab linguine sounds good," she said, staring at the menu. "Have you had it?"

He nodded. "It's good."

She glanced around the crowded space. "Who might have talked to Nicole?"

He scanned the tables. "I guess anyone in here could have. This is a popular place to eat."

"Maybe the waitress will remember her."

"Maybe." He motioned to the waitress, a pretty woman who was about twenty-five. He should know her name, but he couldn't remember it. All he knew was that she'd moved here from Kill Devil Hills about six months ago.

"What can I get for you?"

He gave their orders. "Did you meet the young woman who was kidnapped earlier this week?"

"Sure did. She sat at that table right there." The waitress pointed to the corner table behind them. "I didn't know her name, but I recognized her face when I saw it in the paper."

"Did she eat alone?" Libby asked.

The waitress shook her head. "Some slick city guy was with her. Real dark hair. Kind of reminded me of Elvis."

"Poe," Libby said. She shot a glance at Alec.

"Could you hear what they talked about?" Alec asked.

"I overheard them arguing a little," the woman said. "She said she thought he wasn't paying enough."

"For what?" Alec asked.

"I don't know. I didn't hear that." The server stuck her pencil behind her ear. "I'd better get this order in."

When the woman walked away, Libby leaned forward. "So maybe she was negotiating for more money for my land."

"Looks like it. When are you supposed to hear from him again?"

"I told him to give me a week. But we didn't set a specific time."

"Did he give you his card?"

Her face lit. "He did. I forgot about it." She dug in her purse and came up with a card and her phone. "My cell doesn't have any bars."

"Neither does mine. We can go over to my house and call after lunch though." Alec's head came up when Tom walked in the door. "Hey, Tom," he called.

Tom had been starting toward a free table, but he changed directions and headed toward them. "Mind if I join you?"

Alec shoved a chair out with his foot. "Have a seat. We just ordered."

Tom motioned to the waitress and gave her his order. He stared at Libby. "I heard you got a search-and-rescue dog team helping. I would have appreciated it if you'd let me know what you were doing before you did it."

She flushed but didn't look away. "I have the right to try to find my friend. You don't seem to be looking."

His jaw tightened. "I'm doing things you don't see."

"No harm in looking on our own," Alec said.

Tom's eyes were dark when he glanced Alec's way. "If you found anything, you contaminated evidence. You know better than that. I would have sent a deputy along with you to retrieve anything you found."

"Fair enough." Though Alec was sure the items they'd found had been dropped by Nicole, what if he was wrong? "We found a couple of things last night, but I'm sure they aren't evidence."

Tom's mouth was pinched. "What?"

Alec told him about the discarded hat and sunglasses. "Someone threw them away. Could have been the kidnappers covering their tracks, or it could have been someone cleaning the beach."

"Where are they?"

"In my truck."

"Alec, that was just plain stupid. I hope you didn't destroy something that might have led us to Nicole."

Alec exchanged a long look with Libby. He had been suitably chastised.

TWENTY-FIVE

Bree and Kade took the kids to explore the town and harbor, and Alec went with Zach back to town to buy some jeans. Worry had drained Libby, and searching for Nicole left her feeling hopeless. What if she never found her friend? Though she tried to kill the thought, it refused to go away.

For days the box of letters from her father had been in her closet. Libby fingered his necklace and decided to gather her courage and read some. But not alone in this room. Maybe with Pearl. She lifted the shoe box from the shelf and stepped into the hall where she practically ran into Vanessa.

Vanessa's eyes narrowed. "What's in the box? That's my father's handwriting on top."

Libby had studied those words for days. *For My Oldest Daughter.* "They're letters he wrote to me."

Vanessa made a grab at the top and flipped it off. "Let me see."

Before Libby could pull away, Vanessa had one of the envelopes in her hand. She stepped out of reach. "I want to understand what this is all about. How could my father prefer you over me and Brent? Surely you can see how I need to figure this out."

Short of snatching the letter back as rudely as Vanessa had taken it, Libby watched as her sister pulled the sheet of paper from the envelope. It took all her self-control to stay calm. "I haven't read it myself. Please give it back."

The other woman lifted a brow but made no move to return the note. She unfolded it.

"Vanessa, that's enough." Pearl stepped from the doorway of her room. "You're being incredibly bad mannered. That was not meant for your eyes. If your sister wants to share it, that's up to her, but the choice is hers, not yours." When Vanessa kept the letter, Pearl stepped closer, plucked it from her hand, and handed it to Libby. "I'm sorry for her rudeness, my dear."

Libby stared at the page. This was an experience she'd wanted to savor, but if she wanted to be part of this family, she was going to have to make an effort. *What would Jesus do?* "Would you both care to look at these with me? We can go back to my room."

The expression on her aunt's face warmed, and the approval Libby saw there convinced her she'd done the right thing. Libby glanced at Vanessa, who shrugged and followed her back into the bedroom. Vanessa glanced around and made a beeline for the four-poster bed that dominated the large room. She kicked off her flip-flops and climbed onto the bed, curling her feet under her.

"This used to be my room whenever we came here

for the night." Her tone made it clear what she thought of Libby staying in the room.

Libby opened her mouth to offer to switch rooms, then closed it again. Vanessa was not going to manipulate her. "It's a nice room." She glanced at the space beside Vanessa, then glanced at Pearl.

Pearl shook her head. "You sit there, honey. It's too high for me." She took the Queen Anne armchair at the foot of the bed.

If not for the tension coming off Vanessa in waves, Libby could almost imagine they were really friends holed up on a rainy night. She looked at the letter in her hand. "This is the oldest one. I would have been fifteen when this came. So he evidently didn't try to contact me before this." She continued to stare at it. Did she even want to know what it said? These communications from her father were a clear sign of how much her mother had lied to her.

"Want me to read it aloud?" Pearl asked.

Libby reached across the bed and handed it to her. "It seems appropriate."

There was something in Pearl's face that caught at her heart. It was as if she knew Libby was about to hear something life-changing. Then Pearl glanced at Vanessa, and that expression intensified. Vanessa's head was down as she traced the pattern in the quilt. Libby tried to summon sympathy for the young woman, but Vanessa's prickly manner made it difficult. It was hard to remember they were sisters.

Pearl unfolded the letter and cleared her throat.

"'My dear Libby. I know I'm breaking the custody agreement by trying to contact you, but I miss you so much. As time has gone on, I've been more consumed by grief over what we have done to you girls. It was wrong. I should never have agreed to the custody split. At the time, it seemed the best for you and Vanessa, but I've regretted it every day of my life.'"

Libby caught her breath. "Vanessa? What does he mean that it's best for me *and* Vanessa?"

Pearl put down the letter. "At last, it's out in the open. I always thought it was the most terrible thing I'd ever heard, but it wasn't my decision."

"What wasn't your decision?"

Pearl glanced from Libby to Vanessa, who was staring at her with the same horror on her face that Libby felt. *Custody split.* Did he mean that she and Vanessa were full sisters? Surely no parent would be so cruel as to split up siblings.

Pearl sighed heavily. "Vanessa is your younger sister."

Libby rose to her knees on the bed. "No, you don't mean we're *sisters*! Full sisters? Not half?"

Pearl nodded. "Vanessa is a year younger than you."

Vanessa scrambled off the bed. "You're lying!" She shot a glance of utter dislike at Libby. "I don't know what you're trying to do here, but this is some kind of scam."

"Vanessa, sit down," Pearl said in a weary voice. "You too, Libby. I can't believe Ray left this for me to untangle. Do you honestly think I'd be part of something unsavory, Vanessa? You know me better than that."

"It's not true, it's not!" Vanessa sobbed. She ignored her aunt's outstretched hand and rushed from the room.

Her knees too weak to support her, Libby sank back onto the bed.

* * *

Several people darted across the street in front of Alec's pickup as he drove slowly through the debris-strewn streets toward the sheriff's office. While he and Zach were at Skipper's Store looking for jeans, a deputy had stopped in to ask Alec to come to the jail. His tone was somber, and he'd said not to tell Libby. Alec feared some new evidence implicated Libby even more than the missing video had.

His cousin was leaning against the doorjamb smoking a cigar when Alec parked and got out of his vehicle. Tom straightened and blew a puff of smoke Alec's way. "Thanks for coming right away."

Alec waved the smoke out of his face. "What's up?"

"I'll show you. Come with me." Tom yanked open the office door.

Alec followed him to the evidence room, down a green hallway. A table in the corner held items that made his heart sink. Bright-pink flip-flops and a cover-up in a matching color. "Those are Nicole's?"

"Seems likely. They washed up on shore a few minutes ago. That woman and her dog found them."

"Doesn't mean she's dead," Alec said quickly.

Tom lifted a brow. "Come on, Alec, you and I both know the odds aren't good. Yeah, she might have lost her shoes in the struggle, but her cover-up is a different matter."

Alec winced. "You call Libby yet?"

"No."

"Why not?"

Tom headed for the door, and Alec followed. His cousin's closed expression sent a prickle of unease up Alec's spine. Tom went directly to his desk and jiggled his mouse. After a few clicks, he motioned to Alec. Alec stepped around the desk and peered at the screen. It displayed the video of the boardwalk where Nicole had disappeared. It displayed only sand and surf at first, then abruptly went black.

Alec frowned. "This the recording of the time she disappeared?"

"Yeah. I checked when Libby arrived in Kitty Hawk. She went to the harbor and tried to rent a boat about nine in the evening. That means she didn't leave Virginia Beach until seven, two hours after she made the call to 9-1-1. Yet she said she rushed off so fast that she didn't talk to the police."

"She may have waited that long for the police, and when they didn't show, she finally took off."

"Maybe." Tom leaned back. "I think we have to consider her as a suspect. And with the items that washed up, we have to treat it as a homicide."

"I can ask Libby why she didn't leave for a couple of hours."

"Don't show your suspicion. Maybe you can trip her up in a lie."

"You really think she harmed her friend?" Alec shook his head. "I don't see it, Tom."

"You and I have both been around long enough

to know the likeliest culprit is usually the most obvious one."

"But not always. I think we need to give Libby the benefit of the doubt." Alec could see by the closed expression on the sheriff's face that he was wasting his breath.

Tom stood. "Look, are you going to help me or not? Or are you too afraid to find out the truth?"

"The truth is never something to fear. But I'm not going to be part of any scheme to railroad Libby."

"I'm not asking you to. Just be on the lookout for anything suspicious."

"I already am."

Tom twirled a pencil in his fingers. "There's more, Alec. I talked to Earl Franklin a little while ago too. Libby's mother died under mysterious circumstances. Libby was held twenty hours for questioning."

Mysterious circumstances. "So? The police were doing their job. She was never charged or you'd have mentioned that first."

Tom banged his fist on the desk and swore. "You're being just as pigheaded as usual, Alec. There's a lot in her past that's questionable."

Alec leaned over the desk toward his cousin. "So investigate, but don't assume she's guilty without getting facts! Otherwise, you're letting a murderer walk."

Tom's face was red. "Let's go tell your lady friend what we've found and see what her reaction is. Maybe that will convince you."

"I'm not the one who needs convincing," Alec said. He hoped that was true.

TWENTY-SIX

Nicole paced the tiny island. Fifty steps to the left of the hut and thirty steps to the right. Then around the back. She was going to go stark raving mad out here. The boy had been here yesterday, so she doubted he would come today. Not when he left enough food and water to last her for several days. She was stuck here under the blazing sun by herself.

She had to get off this island. What would happen if the boy never came back? Or another storm came? She eyed the clouds drifting across the brilliant blue sky. Was there anything she could use for a raft? She darted across the island so fast that her bare feet kicked up sand. Inside the shack, she paused long enough to let her eyes adjust to the dim light filtering through the open doorway and single window. There was no flooring to pry up, only sand. The cot was metal, so it would sink immediately. There was a wooden table. Maybe it would work.

She curled her fingers under the edge and dragged it to the door. It was too wide to pull through the doorway so she turned it on its side and maneuvered it out onto the damp sand. With difficulty, she managed to drag it to where the surf broke on the beach. The waves crashed so hard she wondered if she would manage to get it out to sea. The legs would make it more difficult too. She scoured the beach until she found a rock about eight inches in diameter. Once she got it back to the table, she lifted it over her head and brought it crashing down on the table leg closest to her. It took four whacks to dislodge the first leg. She rolled the table around and continued to batter at the legs until she had all of them free of the top.

Now she had the makings of a raft. And if she could tie the legs together, she might have something that would work as oars. She stared at the trees. There were no vines. She wandered the beach again but found only flotsam and seaweed. Nothing strong enough to take on the crashing waves. Returning to the table, she looked from it to the foaming water. Using single table legs was going to have to do. There was no choice. And she needed to bring water and food with her, but how did she keep it from tumbling overboard while she got the raft out past the breakers?

The sound of the sea rolled over her, powerful and frightening. But she couldn't let fear deter her. If she did nothing, her death was almost certain. If she died in the attempt, at least she was doing *something*. She turned back toward the shack and ducked inside to get peanut butter and water. The peanut butter jar fit in the bra of her bathing suit. She tucked one bottle of water in the front of the bottoms and one in the back, but she didn't have high hopes that they would stay put. If only she had some rope.

Sighing, she grabbed an edge of the tabletop and dragged it into the water, then seized two table legs and tried to hang on to them as she tugged the wood farther into the water. The sea foamed around her ankles, and she waited for the right moment to pull the table through the waves. When the crashing wave receded, she lunged through the water with her fingers gripping the makeshift raft. The waves tried furiously to rip the raft from her fingers, but she managed to hang on. When the water reached her waist, she flung herself atop the table. Tucking the table legs under her, she paddled with her hands for all she was worth. It seemed for every foot she managed to propel herself forward, the surf flung her back toward the island two feet.

The breakers were crashing just ahead of her. She paused her paddling until the right moment, then tried again with all her strength. The waves lifted her, then flung her past the breakwater. The ride smoothed out and the waves didn't threaten to tip her into the sea at every moment. She sat up and examined her circumstances. One bottle of water had been pulled from her bathing suit. The peanut butter had survived the experience, but she had only one table leg. It would be useless by itself. She nearly tossed it overboard, then reconsidered. Her resources were limited out here. She might need it for something.

The island was receding. She flopped to her stomach again and began to paddle with her hands. A fin appeared in the water beside the boat, and she snatched her hands back, then smiled when she realized it was a dolphin. If only the dolphin realized her distress and could help her find land.

The dolphin nosed her makeshift raft. She reached out and touched the mammal's skin. It felt like a warm inner tube. "Can you help me?" she whispered.

The dolphin bumped at her raft again, then flicked its tail and shoved at her raft. The table floated back toward the island. "Hey, that's the wrong way," Nicole said.

The dolphin pushed the raft with its nose again, and Nicole sat up. "Cut that out!" She glanced back at the island. Surely it was much closer. Her chest tightened and she grabbed the table leg and hit the water with it. The splashing didn't deter the dolphin. It continued to shove her back toward the island. Nicole didn't have the heart to actually hit the animal with the table leg. All she could do was splash and scream as the dolphin moved the raft back to the island.

The waves were suddenly higher, and she flung herself to her belly and clutched the sides as the breakers grabbed the tabletop and flung it toward the island. She heard a tearing, grinding sound and was suddenly in the water with salt water burning her nose and throat. She couldn't breathe as the waves rolled her over and over until she came to rest in a foot of water with her knees stinging from scraping the sand.

She sat up and cried out as the waves offered up the pieces of her raft, useless now.

* * *

Pearl carried a silver tray bearing delicate blue-and-white china into the bedroom. "Here you go, honey." She put the tray on the bedside table. "The tea will make you feel better."

"Thank you, Aunt Pearl. You're very thoughtful." Libby stared again at the letter in her hand.

Several hours had passed since Libby realized Vanessa was her sister, but the shock had not lessened. How could her parents have done such a heinous thing? To separate sisters until they were combative strangers was a crime that could not be forgiven. Libby found no charity in her heart toward her parents. God said to forgive seventy-times-seven times, but in this case, even one time was too many.

She fingered the necklace. *What would Jesus do?* Right now, Libby couldn't seem to summon the desire to care.

Pearl touched her head. "There are homemade cookies with M&M'S in them."

Libby flung a letter aside that had contained three pictures of Vanessa winning a swim competition. "Not even chocolate can heal this. We have missed so much of each other's lives. It's monstrous."

Pearl eased her bulk into the chair. "There's nothing you can do to change what is, Libby. All you can do is go forward from here."

"Have you talked to Vanessa?"

Pearl's expression clouded. "She won't open her bedroom door."

"She hates this as much as I do. Maybe more."

"Ray spoiled those children. He would be heartsick if he could see how she is treating you."

Libby rubbed her throbbing forehead. "I can't blame her."

"This is hardly your fault."

Libby stared at her aunt. "Did you try to talk him out of this?"

"Of course." Pearl sat heavily in the armchair. "When he arrived here on Hope Island with Vanessa in tow, I begged him to go back for you."

"Did you know my mother?"

Pearl's eyes filled and she nodded. "She was very naïve and childlike. Once she made up her mind, there was no talking her out of anything. Your mother had been adamant that she wanted no contact with Ray. The only way to do that was for each of them to take a child. She argued that it would only be difficult in the beginning. Once you both forgot, everyone could have a fresh start."

Libby's throat closed. "No wonder I've felt so abandoned. I lost a father and a sister in one blow."

"Your father mourned your loss all his life. Not a week went by but he spoke of you."

Where her aunt's pity had failed to move her, Pearl's words about Ray opened a flood of pain. Libby tried to compose herself. "I don't have any memories of him. What did he like to do?"

"Come with me. I'll show you his pride and joy."

Curious, Libby rose from the bed and followed her aunt into the hall and up a narrow flight of stairs to the third floor. It was a different staircase from the one that led to her father's suite. This space smelled of disuse and dampness.

Libby glanced around the stark space. "No one lives up here, do they?"

Pearl fiddled with a key in the lock of the first door to the right. "Oh no. Once upon a time it was the servants' quarters, but since it became an inn back in the sixties, it's been used only for storage." With a final click of the knob, she flung open the door.

Their feet had left prints on the dust in the halls, but not a speck of dust was in this chamber. Ceilings soared to fifteen feet. The walls were painted a pale lemon, and the wood floors were polished. "What is this place?" Libby asked, peering through the gloom.

"One moment." Pearl felt along the wall, then light filled the room.

Libby's eyes took a moment to adjust, then she gasped as the paintings came into view. "A-Are those real?" She moved close enough to see the brushstrokes. "They look like Washington Allston originals."

"They are. Ray loved the religious ones. He said Allston always chose obscure events in the Old Testament to illustrate how we should live out our faith."

Libby stared at the picture of a young woman sleeping at the feet of an older man. "Ruth and Boaz?" This one was hardly about an obscure event.

Pearl nodded. "He loved it, though it also reminded him that he had failed you. Boaz always did the right thing, in the right order. Ray felt he would never aspire to that high mark."

Libby glanced around the room. "How many did he collect?"

"Five in all."

"They're worth a fortune."

"They are indeed. I'm surprised you recognized them."

"I'm a huge Allston fan. I have a tiny print that's sat on my dresser ever since I can remember." She put her hand to her throat. "Did my father give that to me?"

"The one of *Moonlit Landscape*?" Pearl nodded. "It was his favorite. Though he could never own the original, he has some prints stored in another room."

"So that's why I love Allston," Libby said. "I inherited the love from him."

"He used to take you to art museums, starting when you were six months old. We laughed and told him you were too young, but he carried you from picture to picture, explaining what each painting was and why it was significant."

Libby wished she remembered. How much of her personality and passions had she absorbed from a father she never knew?

"Why did my parents divorce? Why did he leave me behind? Did he love Vanessa more?"

Pearl took her hand and squeezed. "Never think that, honey! Your mother flipped a coin. He got Vanessa, and she kept you."

Libby shuddered at the word picture her aunt's description evoked. "Why would he agree to that?"

"He wanted to take you both, but back then it would have been impossible to get custody of both of you without her agreement. He had no grounds. She told him she only had the energy for one child, that he could take one. It was the luck of the draw."

"So they flipped a coin and ripped a family apart."

Libby didn't want to be bitter. She didn't. But it was hard to come to grips with what had been done to her and Vanessa.

A dog barked. Bree and Samson must have come back. "I think I'll go for a swim and clear my head."

"I'll pray for you, honey. You need to forgive and let go of this."

Easier said than done.

TWENTY-SEVEN

The water beckoned like a lover. Libby dug her toes into the soft sand and watched the waves for a moment. Samson had wanted a walk, so she'd taken him with her. Bree had taken the children to get cleaned up for dinner.

A swim would clear Libby's head, though she knew she should march right back inside and demand Vanessa talk to her. In Libby's wildest dreams she'd never expected to find a sister who hated her. This could have been such a wonderful day. Instead it was a nightmare that she couldn't awaken from.

She pulled off her cover-up and tossed it on the sand. "Want to go for a swim, Samson?" The dog's ears perked at the word *swim*. He danced around her and barked wildly, then ran toward the waves and snapped at the foam.

"Moron," she said, laughing. The dog barked excitedly in answer.

She kicked off her flip-flops and ran into the waves. The shock of the cold water made her gasp, then giggle like she was ten. A breaker rolled toward her, and she waited until the right moment before diving into it.

The force of the current rolled her along the bottom, but she relished its power. When she was in the water, she forgot all her troubles. She surfaced and tossed her hair out of her face. The sea didn't feel so cold now that she was fully immersed. She broke into a breaststroke and crested the next wave. Samson kept up with her as she swam out.

When she turned to look back, she was a hundred yards out. There didn't seem to be a riptide, so she flipped onto her back and let the waves float her along. Sheer heaven. It would be sunset soon, so she wouldn't stay out too long. Sharks would be out.

When the first nudge came on her leg, she thought it was a fish. She straightened to a vertical position and looked around. Then something grabbed her leg and yanked her under the water. She managed to gasp oxygen into her lungs before her head was submerged. Though the salt water burned, she opened her eyes underwater and saw a diver in a black wetsuit. It was too dark to see much detail, but she could make out the person's masculine build and the air tank on his back.

She kicked out with her right foot and hit him in the chest, but the blow didn't make him turn her loose. His fingers squeezed her leg so tightly that it was beginning to go numb. Bubbles rose around her as he dragged her deeper under the waves. He reached the bottom and stood on the sand. She floated just above him with his hand still holding her fast.

He's trying to drown me. The shock of realizing his intention made her release a bit of her precious air into the water. Her lungs began to burn. She flailed to free herself, but he was stronger. Samson would not be able to dive down to help her. If she wanted to live, she had to escape this man. Panic drove all thought from her head for a few moments, then she forced herself to focus.

Think, Libby! Her only chance was to deprive him of oxygen. She lashed out with her foot, aiming for his face. Her heel struck his mouthpiece and it flipped out of his mouth. Bubbles escaped in a flurry. He let go of her legs and grabbed the mask. Lungs burning, Libby shot for the surface. He would be right behind her. She had to get to safety. Her feet pumped, and she rose toward the light.

She didn't think she could hold out much longer. Her vision began to dim, then her head broke the surface. She filled her lungs with air and shook her head to clear it. Shore was more than a hundred and twenty yards away. She struck out for the safety of the sand, vaguely aware that Samson was snarling. A hand grazed her ankle and she kicked hard, then swam to the right and then back toward shore. The diver had the advantage of seeing her from below. It would be a miracle if she escaped him.

Help, Lord! Her muscles were beginning to tire from the exertion, but she kept up the pace. Her starved lungs wanted her to pause and gather in more oxygen, but there was no time. Not if she wanted to live. She dared a glance back and saw a head pop up. The sight galvanized her into swimming even more frantically. The dog growled to her right. He left her side, but she didn't look back until the snarling reached a ferocious level. The dog had his teeth clamped on the man's arm. The diver struck at Samson, but the dog held on.

This was her chance to escape. She swam for all she was worth. The shore grew closer and closer until her knees scraped bottom. She staggered to her feet and practically fell onto the beach. There was no time to recover though. She sprang back up and turned to stare out to sea. Where was the dog?

"Samson!" She screamed his name into the wind. The harsh caw of a seagull was the only answer. She half turned to run to the inn for help, then she saw his head break the waves. He was swimming for shore. There was no sign of her attacker.

She ran a few feet into the water to greet the dog as he struggled to shore. Sinking to her knees, she threw her arms around his neck. He licked her cheek weakly and she half guided, half carried him the rest of the way. They both collapsed onto the sand. Panting, Samson crawled onto her lap.

"Good dog," she crooned. She'd wanted to see an angel, just as Aunt Pearl once had. Samson was that angel today.

. . .

The sun had colored the clouds with red and gold when Alec found Libby sitting on a piece of driftwood. Her face was turned toward the sunset. Her arm was around Bree's dog. They'd been for a swim. He could see that her hair wasn't quite dry and neither was the dog. Alec paused to shake sand from his sandals, and Tom nearly bowled him over in his haste to get to Libby.

"Ready?" Tom whispered.

"I guess we have to be. Libby," Alec called. She turned her pensive face toward them. He knew when she saw Tom because her eyes widened and she inhaled. "Tom has some news," he said.

Her lips tightened and she got up. "You've found her body?" The dog pressed against her leg as though he sensed she needed comfort.

Alec paused to reflect on her answer. He knew Tom would assume she'd asked because she knew for a fact that Nicole was dead. He didn't believe that. "Not her body but some of her clothing. Bree and Samson found it."

"Where? Why didn't she come to tell me?" She'd thought Bree had acted a little strange. She'd been quiet before rushing the children in to get cleaned up, then off to dinner in town without Samson.

Tom grunted. "I ordered Bree to let us tell you." He put his hands on his hips. "What we found were her sandals and cover-up, Miss Holladay. They match the description you gave us."

"Oh no," Libby whispered.

"You were quick to ask if we'd found her body. I suspect it's because you dumped her body out there."

She went white and her fingers stilled in the dog's fur. "That's a terrible accusation. You were both so somber that I assumed the worst."

"Her shoes and cover-up indicate that she's no longer alive," Tom said, his voice harsh.

"I don't believe it." Libby's lips trembled. Her gaze sought Alec's.

Alec saw no guilt in her face. "Tom needs you to identify the belongings he found."

"Pink flip-flops and cover-up?" she asked.

He nodded. "Shoe size matches."

"Where did Bree and Samson find them?"

Tom shot a fierce glance at Alec that warned him to be quiet. "They found one shoe in some rocks and the other twisted with seaweed a few feet away. The cover-up was fifty yards down the beach."

"Maybe the things aren't Nicole's." Libby's voice rose. "Pink is a common color for beach items."

"I want you to take a look," Tom said, gesturing back at his truck in the driveway.

Libby nodded and they trekked back to Tom's SUV. He stuck his head through the open window and withdrew a plastic evidence bag. Without speaking, he handed it to Libby.

The bag crackled when her fingers tightened around it. She loosened the top and pulled out the clothing and flip-flops. "They look like hers. I bought her the cover-up for Easter." Her voice quavered. She turned the shoes over. "See this nick out of the bottom? Her mom's dog chewed them the weekend she got them."

Alec nodded. "Looks like teeth marks."

She closed the top and handed it back. "I think I can say without any doubt that these belong to Nicole."

Tom tossed the bag into the SUV. "I think we have to assume we're investigating a murder, Miss Holladay."

She visibly wilted. "I don't want to believe she's

dead." She turned a beseeching glance toward Alec.

He didn't want to give her false hope. "You have to face facts, Libby," he said, gentling his voice.

"If she's dead, where is her body?" she asked. "Wouldn't her body have washed ashore too?"

Tom shrugged. "I know it's hard to hear, but it's rare to find a body. Fish take care of the remains."

Her eyes filled and she backed away. Alec glanced at his cousin and saw Tom narrow his eyes. Did he think her distress was put on?

"I'd like to ask you some questions, Miss Holladay," Tom said. "What happened to your mother?"

She reeled as though she'd been slapped. "What do you mean?"

"How did she die?"

Libby wetted her lips. "She fell down the basement steps."

"Isn't it true that the police suspected you pushed her?"

"I didn't!" Libby blinked rapidly. "She was drunk."

"You were held for questioning," Tom said.

"They let me go." Her eyes pleaded for them to believe her. "I had nothing to do with it."

"But you were home?"

She sighed and leaned against the SUV. "I was home," she agreed heavily. "But I was upstairs working on some paperwork."

"You lived at home?"

"Someone had to take care of her. If I wasn't there, she wouldn't have bothered with food." She tipped her chin up. "I took care of her. I cared for her for years."

Tom took a step closer to her. "What happened?"

"I heard a clatter. I jumped up and ran downstairs calling for her. When I found the basement door open in the kitchen, I rushed down the steps and found her lying at the bottom of the stairs. Sh-She was lying there with her eyes open. I tried to help her up, but I knew as soon as I touched her that she was gone."

"The policeman I spoke with seemed to think your story was fishy," Tom said. "Why was that?"

Alec could tell Tom already knew the answer but wanted to see if she would tell him the truth. He prayed for Libby to be honest and put to rest any doubts his cousin might have.

She looked at her hands. "We'd had an argument in town earlier that someone overheard."

"And you threatened to kill her."

"It wasn't like that!" She lifted her head and stared at Tom. "I said, 'I could just kill you when you act like that.' That wasn't a threat. It was just a figure of speech. A really awful figure of speech."

"What had she done?" Alec asked gently.

"She insulted the grocery store owner, then threw tomatoes at him. It was an ugly scene. I tried to stop her, but she was like that when she'd been drinking. There was nothing anyone could do. She was the sweetest person when she was sober."

Alec heard the ring of truth in her voice. She'd loved her mother. He glanced at Tom and saw compassion. Tom could tell truth when he heard it.

TWENTY-EIGHT

Libby felt like she'd been tossed around by a tidal wave. Could the sheriff actually suspect that she'd killed her own mother—and that she'd disposed of Nicole? Couldn't he see her heart? She'd started to tell Tom that someone had just tried to drown her, but then she saw the suspicion in the sheriff's eyes. He would think she was making it up to divert suspicion. What a mess.

It was none too soon for her when Sheriff Bourne's vehicle left the driveway and headed back to town. Alec stood at the bottom of the porch steps with his hands in the pockets of his khaki shorts. She'd been hoping to tell him about what she'd discovered from Pearl, but now she didn't have it in her.

Her eyes burned, and she rushed up the steps before she could disgrace herself by showing how much the sheriff's accusations had hurt her. Samson whined and trotted after her.

"Libby, wait! Tom is just doing his job."

"His *job* is to find out who took my friend, not to railroad an innocent person!"

He mounted the steps to the porch and stopped in

front of her. "Look at it from his point of view. Can't you see why he would have some suspicions?"

She was in no mood for his placating tone. "While he wastes his time investigating me, the real criminals are walking free. Don't you worry that the men might take another girl? Someone *you* know and love?"

That stopped him. She could see him processing her question.

"You're saying you don't think it was personal? That Nicole just might have been in the wrong place at the wrong time?" he asked.

"I don't know what to think. You hear of human trafficking though. Who knows but that's what these men intended? How did they know she would be there at that time? Maybe they just came ashore and saw a lone girl and decided to grab her."

He stared at her. "You didn't try to rent a boat until nine."

"What?" She didn't understand the sudden change of subject.

"The night Nicole disappeared. That means you didn't leave Virginia Beach until a good two hours after you called 9–1–1. Why?"

"No. I threw some clothes in a suitcase and left right away. Then I got stuck in a traffic jam from a jack-knifed truck." Her ire rose. "Do you want to check with the state patrol? I came as quickly as I could."

There would be no end to the suspicion and accusation. She was going to have to do this on her own. The realization made her pulse jump. But it wouldn't be impossible. She had years of experience uncovering the history of houses, interviewing previous owners, delving into the secrets of dusty pages. While this would be a different investigation, she had determination and love on her side.

"I can see I'm on my own now." She turned to leave.

"You're thinking about doing this yourself? You'll just make Tom and the state detectives mad," Alec said.

"What other choice do I have? The story Earl wrote is going to hit the papers soon, and we both know it's going to be slanted toward my guilt. The state isn't going to look any harder than the sheriff is. If I want to stay out of jail, I'm going to have to do this myself and find those men. And quickly. Before everyone in town is convinced I'm some kind of killer."

"Let's start with a sketch of what you remember."

"Are you going to help me or accuse me, Alec? I'm having trouble keeping it straight." If he doubted her, she didn't think she could stand it. His opinion mattered way too much.

"I told you I'd help. We've already started. I haven't changed my mind."

She searched his face. "For my father's sake?"

He nodded. "And for the sake of truth. Truth matters."

She relented. Should she tell him about today's attack? "It doesn't seem to matter to anyone but us," she said.

"What do you mean by that? Has something happened today?"

He had an uncanny perception. Where did it come from? She pointed to the rockers on the porch. "Let's sit down. This is going to take a few minutes." What would he think when she told him what their parents had done to her and Vanessa? Would he still idolize her father? And would he believe a diver had really tried to drown her?

* * *

A breeze lifted the strands of Libby's light-brown hair, and the porch light glimmered on her tresses. A few bugs buzzed the lamp. Alec stretched out his legs in the rocker and petted Samson, who rested his head on Alec's knee. The dog huffed with pleasure. If only people were so easily pleased. Libby had her legs tucked under her on the swing. He waited for her to explain what was going through that beautiful head of hers.

He noticed red marks on her ankle. "What happened there?" he asked, pointing.

Her gaze searched his face. She rubbed her ankle. "A diver tried to drown me a little while ago." She studied the marks. "I didn't realize he'd left marks."

He sat forward. "What? Someone tried to *kill* you?"

She nodded. "Samson and I went for a swim. A diver in a black wetsuit dragged me to the bottom and tried to hold me there. I managed to get away, and Samson helped until I got to shore."

He clenched his fists. "Why didn't you say anything to Tom?"

She shrugged. "He has his mind made up."

He pointed to her ankle. "You have proof."

"I didn't realize he'd left marks. And the sheriff would say I scraped it on something anyway."

Alec leaned forward and studied the marks on her skin. "Looks like fingers. We need to show Tom."

She rubbed her ankle, then shook her head. "He'd say I did it myself."

"No, he won't." He grabbed the portable phone on the swing and called his cousin. When he explained what happened, Tom told him to take pictures and bring her into the office tomorrow.

She was watching him talk with shadowed eyes. "What did he say?"

"He believed me. He wants pictures tomorrow and said to take some tonight too. He wants to get to the bottom of this, Libby."

She bit her lip and her head went down. Alec pulled out his phone and snapped several shots of her injury.

The screen banged open and Vanessa stomped out onto the porch. Her hands were curled into fists and her mouth was pinched.

She glared at Libby through narrowed eyes. "Don't think this changes anything! You'll never be part of this family."

"This isn't my fault, Vanessa. Mom and Dad did this, not me."

"Don't call him that! He was Daddy, always."

Alec found their conversation impossible to decipher. "What's going on?"

Libby sighed and leaned back. "It appears Vanessa and I are full sisters."

"You've got to be kidding." He eyed them both. There was a definite resemblance. They'd look alike whenever Vanessa lost the petulant expression she usually wore.

Libby tucked her hair behind her ears. "When our parents divorced, they each took a child. Our mother wanted nothing to do with our father and insisted this was the way it had to be."

"That's nuts," Alec said. This situation gave credence to her story of an atypical mother. "And neither of you knew?"

She shook her head, then glanced up at Vanessa. "Sit down, Vanessa. Standing over me like that isn't going to solve anything."

"Neither will talking." But Vanessa took a hesitant step forward.

Alec left the chair and moved to sit beside Libby on the swing. Vanessa shot him a grateful look. He liked being this close to Libby. The vanilla fragrance on her skin was enticing. "Did you remember another sister at all? Weren't you three when your parents split?"

Vanessa knotted her hands together. "I remember an imaginary friend. Her name was Bee."

"Bee. Lib-BEE," Alec said. "Maybe that was your nickname for her."

Vanessa frowned and shook her head. "I'm sure she was imaginary. She had a monkey named Fred."

"I had a monkey named Fred," Libby said in a low voice. "I still have him. He was a sock monkey."

Vanessa straightened. "He had an eye missing."

Libby nodded. "And his ear had been chewed by the cat."

"I remember that," Vanessa said in a stunned voice. "Do you remember me at all?"

Libby frowned. "I don't have very many memories from childhood. Things were so rocky and constantly in flux. I have only snippets of things, and most of them aren't pleasant."

Vanessa's face clouded and she looked down at her hands. "You'd think you would remember a sister!"

Alec could feel Libby tense beside him. "Stress can damage memories, Vanessa," he said. "Doesn't mean she didn't love you."

"I don't care if she did or didn't," Vanessa snapped.

The screen door opened again and Pearl came out. Her feet were bare under her housedress. "I thought I heard voices out here." She chewed on her lip as she glanced at Vanessa. "Everyone doing okay?"

"Don't tiptoe around it, Aunt Pearl," Vanessa snapped. "How could you keep this from me?"

"If you would have opened your door, I would have talked to you about it."

Alec got up to offer his seat to Pearl, but she waved him off so he sat back down. She leaned her bulk against the porch post. "I'm not staying. This is something the girls have to work out on their own." Her gaze stayed on Vanessa. "I just wanted to assure Vanessa that this is true. I was there. I tried to talk them out of it, but your mother was adamant."

"My mother," Vanessa said, her voice stunned. "I just realized. Tina wasn't my mother!" Her voice broke, and her eyes filled with horror.

"She loved you as much as she loved Brent," Pearl said. "You know she did."

"I can't believe this," Vanessa said. She turned to stare at Libby. "Tell me about our mother. And what was her name? I don't even know her name!"

"Her name was Ursula." Libby held her gaze. "My childhood wasn't like yours, Vanessa. We moved around a lot. Mom was always looking for the rainbow over the next hill. She married again and divorced, then we had a revolving door with men coming and going. She was never happy. She always wanted more and more but never got it. Possessions were important to her, maybe because of her childhood. Still, she loved me more than her things, more than her men. But maybe not more than her beer. In spite of that, my childhood wasn't bad. Just constantly disrupted."

Vanessa winced and turned her attention back to Pearl. "Why did Tina agree to the deception?"

Pearl patted her shoulder. "You started calling her Mama as soon as they were engaged. It just gradually happened. I think your father thought you'd be happier if you didn't remember another mother and sister."

Alec had idolized Ray Mitchell forever. To find he had such feet of clay was indescribably shocking. This kind of tangle was going to be hard to unravel. Alec doubted the women would ever manage to be close. It would take a miracle from God's hand.

Vanessa jumped to her feet and rushed back into the house. Pearl followed, calling Vanessa's name. The seaside cicadas filled the silence as Alec and Libby were left alone on the porch.

Alec stretched his arm across the back of the swing, not quite daring to embrace her, though the thought strangely crossed his mind. "How are you dealing with this?"

She leaned back and her hair brushed his arm. "I don't quite know what to think. It's hard to realize I have a family but that I'm about as welcome as a bedbug. But I don't care about any of this, really. I'm finding it hard to care about anything since Bree found Nicole's belongings. I don't want to believe she's dead."

He hugged her. "I'm sorry, Libby. I wish I could change things."

She swallowed hard and sighed. "Thanks for being here, Alec."

"Does Brent know yet? About you and Vanessa?"

She shook her head. "He's been gone all day. I suppose Vanessa could have called him, but if she did, I don't know about it."

Headlamps pierced the darkness. "I think that's him now."

TWENTY-NINE

Libby could almost imagine they were friends, maybe more than friends, as she sat near Alec with his arm on the back of the swing. Did he feel the connection she felt? He'd offered to help her, and he'd kissed her. With a man like him, that had to mean something.

Brent would be here any minute, but she'd rather sit in the silence than endure more confrontation. Her brother was about to find out he was more alone than he'd thought. Would this change his relationship with Vanessa?

Brent's shadow loomed in the glow from the lamps along the walk, then he walked up the steps to the porch. "You're sitting here in the dark?"

"We have the porch light," Alec said, pulling his arm down.

Libby felt cold without his warmth radiating to her back. Or maybe it was the way Brent's lips pressed together at the sight of her.

"Have a seat, Brent. You've been gone all day and a lot has happened," Alec said.

Brent still stood in the shadows. "I'll stand, thanks. What's up?"

"Libby and Vanessa are sisters," Alec said.

"Sisters? That's not news."

"*Full* sisters. Not half."

Libby listened to Alec explain what they'd discovered today. The deep tones of his voice soothed her. She was still jumping at every sound. Was her attacker out there even now, watching and waiting for the next time? And why had he targeted her? She eyed her half brother. Could Brent want her out of the way so he could inherit? She didn't have a will in place, so by law he and Vanessa would inherit as her closest relatives.

She hated to suspect her own brother, but someone in this town wanted her dead. That someone had already killed her friend, it seemed. Tears welled in her eyes at the likelihood that she would never see Nicole again. She became aware that Alec had asked her something. "I'm sorry?"

"I wondered if you had anything to add?"

She stared at Brent's expressionless face. Though they had only been around each other a few times, she got the impression that he took in everything behind those calculating eyes.

He shifted and she saw what dangled from his hand. Tanks and a regulator. She caught her breath. "Where have you been, Brent?" she asked, noting his broad shoulders. Could he have attacked her himself?

"What's that got to do with anything?" he demanded.

"I see you dive," she said, pointing to his dive equipment.

He glanced down at his equipment. "Yeah, so what? It's the Graveyard of the Atlantic out there, remember? Diving mecca."

"Where were you diving today?"

He gestured. "Out at a wreck offshore. What difference does it make?"

"A diver tried to drown me. Right offshore here. He wore a black wetsuit."

If the thought of her being drowned bothered him, he didn't show it. "Most wetsuits are black."

She stared at him. "Do you hate me, Brent?"

"I don't know you well enough to like or dislike you."

"Did you try to kill me?"

"No." His face was expressionless.

"Can I see your arms?"

He frowned, then shrugged and held both arms out where she could see them under the porch light. The skin was smooth and unmarked. "Samson bit my attacker."

"As you can see, I have not been bitten."

He could have hired someone, but she might as well let it go. Even if he was guilty, she'd never be able to tell.

Tires crunched up the drive. Samson stretched and yawned, then bounded down the steps to meet his owners. Libby followed.

Bree held out her arms. "I'm so sorry, Libby," she murmured. "I wanted to tell you myself, but the sheriff wouldn't let me."

"She can't be dead," Libby moaned, burying her face in her new friend's shoulder.

"Samson and I will do what we can," Bree promised. "We'll help you get to the bottom of this."

Libby lifted her head. "Someone tried to drown me tonight, Bree. A diver grabbed me and took me under. I'm frightened."

Bree went still. "But what could be the motive?"

Libby pulled away. "Money, property? I don't know."

"Don't go anywhere alone until we solve this mystery," Bree said. "I'm afraid for you."

Libby nodded and lifted Hunter from his car seat. "I'm going to stay close to Alec from here on out."

* * *

Libby sat on the porch by herself. It was well past midnight, but she couldn't sleep. She'd seen light coming from under Vanessa's door as well, so she knew her sister was likely just as conflicted. Libby rolled the bead necklace in her fingers. *What would Jesus do?*

God had made it clear what she was supposed to do, but she didn't want to. This necklace meant the world to her. Vanessa only wanted it because she didn't have it. *Be generous with Vanessa and Brent.* Why did her father have to ask that of her? Why hadn't he asked that of them? They were the ones being hurtful. Why should it rest on her shoulders?

Alec's figure loomed in the doorway as he stepped to the porch. "Can't sleep?"

"No. Too much to process today."

He joined her and put his arm on the back of the swing behind her. "Anything I can help you with?"

"It's my dad!" she burst out. "Why did he ask so much of me and nothing of Brent and Vanessa? Why am I the one who is supposed to be generous? Why do I have to extend grace? I'm being pummeled with more than they are."

"I wonder if he knew that you're a Christian? I'm not so sure about Vanessa and Brent. Of course, it's impossible to judge another man's heart, but I've seen no evidence in their lives."

"To whom much is given, much is required." She paraphrased the verse from the book of Luke with a sigh. "Sometimes doing the right thing is so hard."

"What's the right thing you're reluctant to do?"

She pulled the necklace away from her neck and held it to the moonlight. "I have to give this to Vanessa."

"Ah." Alec's arm came down around her shoulders and he hugged her. "One thing I've discovered in my own walk with the Lord is this: when something is really hard but we do it anyway, the rewards are equally great. So if you just suck it up and do what you feel God is telling you to do, you're going to be really glad in the end."

She leaned up and kissed his cheek. He smelled good with some kind of spicy cologne. "Thanks. You're right. I have to do it."

His hand tightened around her shoulders, and before she could pull away, he brushed his lips across hers. The contact sent a warm rush through her. Surely he felt something for her. A man with his integrity didn't go around kissing women willy-nilly.

He pulled back and rested his head on the top of her shoulder. "I'll pray for you."

"That means more than you know." She kissed him

again, relishing the stubble on his cheek. "I'm going to go do it now before I talk myself out of it."

"I'll wait here and pray. Come back down when you're done and let me know how it went."

"You're a great guy, Alec," she said, squeezing his hand. "I'll be back."

Before she could lose her nerve, she hurried inside and up the stairs to her sister's room. The light was still shining under the door. She knocked, hoping her sister wasn't asleep. That would get things off to a terrible start. "Vanessa? Are you still up?"

"I'm up." The door swung open to reveal Vanessa in a red nightgown.

"Can I come in for a minute?" Libby asked.

Her sister shrugged. "Suit yourself." She retreated to the bed, where she flopped on the edge and picked up a bottle of red nail polish.

The room smelled of nail polish too. Libby shut the door behind her. "You're up late."

"So are you. I imagine we're thinking about the same thing."

Was that a hint of warmth in Vanessa's voice? Libby decided to believe it was. "We're real sisters. I can hardly wrap my mind around it."

"Me neither. You might want to see that." Vanessa pointed to an old photo album. "Aunt Pearl gave it to me."

Libby picked it up and flipped to the first page. It showed a young woman smiling into the camera. She had a baby in her arms, and a little girl held on to her leg. "That's Mom. I'm the little girl. You're the baby?"

"I assumed so."

Why hadn't Pearl shown this to her? Libby tried to shove away her jealousy, but it crouched in her chest. She flipped the page to see several other photos. A baby in a crib with an older girl propping a bottle in her mouth, another with the toddler holding the baby on her lap on the floor, and one of a young man holding them both and smiling proudly. She recognized him as their father.

"They look so happy," she said.

"Aunt Pearl says the reality was far different." Vanessa looked up from painting her toes. "I don't remember her at all. Our mother, I mean. You'd think I'd remember my own mother! Do you have any pictures?"

For the first time, Libby looked at the situation from Vanessa's point of view. She'd been abandoned by her mother. She'd even been deceived about *who* her mother was. At least Libby had known the identity of both parents, even though her mother had lied about her father's death.

She nodded. "I have some back in Virginia Beach. I'll have some copies made for you."

Vanessa's expression hardened again. "I guess it doesn't matter. Tina was a real mother to me. She was wonderful. I still miss her."

"I've heard nothing but good things about Tina."

This wasn't going as planned. Vanessa seemed almost unapproachable. Libby inhaled and squared her shoulders. "I came here to give you this, Vanessa." She unfastened the necklace and held it out.

Vanessa's eyes widened and she held out her hand.

Libby dropped it into her palm, and Vanessa's fingers closed around it. "But I thought you loved it."

"I have to admit I didn't want to give it to you, but God told me to." Her voice broke and she cleared her throat.

Vanessa frowned. "And you did it just because you thought you were supposed to?"

"I'm trying to obey what the letters mean. What would Jesus do? Jesus didn't care about possessions. The necklace is just a possession. So it's yours."

Vanessa held the hand with the necklace to her chest. "Thank you." Her gaze searched Libby's face. "Do you think we can have a real relationship?"

"I'd like that more than anything," Libby said. "I'm willing if you are."

"I'm willing." Vanessa fastened the necklace around her neck. "It's going to take time though. We have a lot of catching up to do."

"I have all the time in the world," Libby said.

She couldn't wait to tell Alec that he'd been right.

THIRTY

Alec gave the swing a push with his foot. Libby had been gone half an hour. He'd been praying that she would find favor with Vanessa, that a door to a good relationship might be opened between the two women. He had a sense that God was answering that prayer.

He heard a car and straightened. His stomach tightened when he recognized his truck, driven by his nephew. He rose to confront Zach for breaking curfew. This wasn't going to go well, but it had to be done. He waited under the security light.

The interior light came on when Zach got out of the truck. His whistle died on his lips when he realized Alec was standing on the walk. "Hey, Uncle Alec."

"It's nearly one," Alec said. "Your curfew is midnight."

"I'm seventeen years old. I don't need a curfew."

"Well, you have one anyway. Nothing good happens after midnight. Just things like this." He held out Zach's pocketknife. "I found this on one of the little islands. Along with beer bottles."

Zach snatched the knife from his hand. "I didn't do anything."

"You're saying you didn't have a little beer, have a little fun?"

"There's nothing wrong with that. You telling me you've never had a beer?"

"You're underage."

"And you never drank when you were my age? Come on, Uncle Alec. I've heard the stories about you. You were no saint."

"Which is why I'm trying to keep you from making my mistakes."

The security light illuminated Zach's angry face. He clenched his fists. "I don't have to listen to this."

Alec grabbed his arm as he started past. "You will listen. The next time you're not here at midnight, I'll come looking for you. I imagine it would be embarrassing to be hauled home in front of your friends."

"You wouldn't do that."

"I would and I will. This is a small island. I know every nook and cranny. You won't be able to hide from me."

Zach's eyes narrowed. "I'll run away."

"And you'll end up in a boys' home. Is that what you want? Look, Zach, I'm trying to help you. I know it hurts that your parents are gone. How do you think your dad feels when he looks down from heaven and sees how you're acting?"

Zach took a step back. "I'm trying to make sense of it, okay? I always wanted to be the kind of man my dad was. I idolized him. But what good did it do Dad to try to please God if he was just going to kill him?"

Alec tried to embrace the boy but Zach shook him

off, so he dropped his arms back to his sides. "Integrity has rewards that are more valuable than how many days we spend on the earth."

The boy's face worked to restrain emotion. "If God cared, he wouldn't have taken both my parents. That's just plain cruel. Mom and Dad always told me that God loves me. I wish I could still believe it."

"I can see why you think he doesn't. Psalms says, 'Blessed in the eyes of the Lord is the death of his saints.' I know we miss them, but now they are alive like never before. God doesn't view death in this life the same way we do." Alec thought he saw a sheen of tears in Zach's eyes.

"Is that supposed to make me feel better? It doesn't. I want my dad. I want to come home and hear Mom's voice. No one could make peanut-butter cookies like her. And she *cared*. So did Dad." Zach's shoulders slumped. "I don't have anyone anymore."

Alec put his hand on the boy's shoulder. "You have me. And your grandparents. Plenty of us love you, Zach. Don't shut us out. We're all in this together. We're all hurting."

He opened his arms, fully expecting Zach to turn away. Instead, the boy buried his face in Alec's chest.

"I miss them," Zach said.

Alec hugged him. He struggled to speak past the lump shutting off his throat. "I do too. But we're still family. We will get through this."

Zach pulled away, looking a little embarrassed by his outburst. "I'll try to be home on time tomorrow."

"I'll wait up." He wanted Zach to know the rules still

stood. "Time for bed, bud. We have church in just a few hours."

Zach made a face but said nothing as they walked to the porch. When Zach went inside, Alec settled back on the swing to wait for Libby. The front door creaked, and she burst through the opening with a smile on her face. He rose as she rushed toward him. She launched herself at him, and he caught her and hugged her. The scent of her vanilla shampoo filled his head. "I guess it went well?" He had to grin at her exuberance.

Her arms went around his waist and she hugged him. "It went super, Alec. You were so right."

He didn't want to let her go, but when she pulled away, he released her and led her to the swing. "So tell me about it."

Her face beamed as she told him about the pictures and Vanessa's reaction to the necklace. "It was hard. Really hard. But you were right—my sacrifice opened a door between us. We may never be as close as typical sisters, but we're on the right path. We have a lot to get caught up on. She's going to tell me about Dad, and I'm going to tell her about Mom."

Her voice was full of excitement, and he smiled. "God always comes through."

"I think I've learned more about God this week than I have my entire life," she said. "And it's all thanks to you."

He hugged her. It was a habit he could get used to. "I'm not the Holy Spirit. He was telling you the right thing to do, and you obeyed."

He'd never been able to talk to another woman about God so freely. That had to mean something.

. . .

People of every age and description crowded the pews at church. Fishermen, stay-at-home moms, and shop owners mingled as friends and neighbors. Libby squeezed past Alec to stand in the aisle and shake hands. People eyed her curiously but were a little more standoffish than the last time she'd been in town.

If she were alone for a few minutes, she would slip up to the front and sit in the first pew. Not that God would answer her question of *why*. Libby wasn't ready to accept that Nicole was dead. Not yet. She didn't feel any sense of closure.

Alec touched her shoulder, and she realized most of the people had cleared out. She smiled at him. "Sorry, I was woolgathering."

"You okay?"

She nodded, her throat too full to speak. "I love this church. It was built in about 1890?"

He nodded. "You're good."

"Comes with the job."

His eyes were grave. "I wanted to wait until church was over to tell you. The article in the paper came out today. It's on the front page."

She examined his expression. "It's bad?"

"Yeah." He took her elbow and guided her down the aisle to the front where they settled on the pew. He opened his Bible and pulled out a clipping. "He basically implies you're another Susan Smith."

The woman who drowned her children. Numb, she took the clipping and scanned it. "He talks about my mother's death too, even though I was never charged with that. He's painted me as some kind of monster."

She was stunned. This was even worse than she'd expected. Why would Earl do something so vicious? She'd liked him on the trip from Kitty Hawk. Was this his revenge for her not telling him about Nicole's disappearance sooner?

Alec's expression was pained. "I'm sorry, Libby. This is my fault. I thought he'd help us, not hurt us."

He'd said *us* as though they were one unit. The realization that he sided with her was a comfort she could cling to. "What can we do about this?"

"Not much. Suing him for libel would just draw more attention to it. All we can do is try to find out who grabbed Nicole. And make him look stupid."

"Why are you doing this?" she asked, searching his face for clues.

"Doing what?"

"Helping me. Standing by me. Your own cousin thinks I might be guilty."

He was silent a moment. "You're Ray's daughter. He would expect me to help you."

Not quite what she'd wanted to hear. She'd hoped he'd tell her he liked her. That he believed in her. "You've never said why you idolized my father so much."

He closed his Bible. "Ray was my father's best friend.

He was like a second dad to me. More than that, like a real dad. My father was often busy with his fishing boats. Dawn to dusk, he was out hauling in seafood. Lobster, crab, fish. He never had time to pitch me a ball or take me to the mainland for a game."

"He was working, providing for his family."

He nodded. "Sure. But Ray made time. And when I got into trouble when I was in high school, he turned me around. Forced his way through my rebellion with love and strength. It's because of him that I'm a Christian today."

"Why would he do that? Care about a kid that wasn't his own?"

"I honestly think he was trying to be Jesus in the flesh to me. To do what he could to share his faith through his actions." His gaze searched hers. "And maybe he was trying to atone for what he did to you. I know that's what you're wondering. Why did he help me and not you? Trust me though, Libby. Your dad was a good man."

"So he was a model Christian." She'd been more of a lax one. When was the last time she helped someone out just to bring praise to Jesus? Never. She wanted to do better, though, to shine like Alec did. Her hand went to her neck, but it was bare. No WWJD necklace anymore. Its impact hadn't faded though. She prayed it never would.

His smile was gentle. "Ray was more than a model Christian. He was a conduit for God's love to most everyone he met. I often saw him take bags of food to widows and give money to those in need."

She remembered turning away that woman who was collecting money for the house-fire victims. "He had plenty to give."

"Not in the early days. He always said God would provide for his needs. He just had to be faithful." He smiled. "Tina used to get so aggravated when he'd raid her larder and leave them without food. They couldn't always afford to buy more, so he'd trudge off to the store to buy peanut butter and bread. They always made it though. He would tell her that you can't out-give God."

She couldn't imagine that kind of generosity. If only she'd had a chance to know him.

THIRTY-ONE

"No, no, not that!" Libby stopped the workers from hauling the walnut wainscoting out of the lifesaving station. "I can restore it. It's native walnut."

The man made a face. "Looks ruined to me."

"Trust me, I can fix it."

She directed him to lean it against the far wall, then glanced at her watch. Alec was going to take her and Bree out searching on the boat this afternoon, but she had to get this project started. Once the renovations were complete, she was going to donate it to the town. Just being back to work in some way lifted her spirits. She might not be able to find Nicole, but she could help the town.

Libby wandered through the station. It practically boasted of its previous life. The boats that had carried rescuers to the seas were propped against one wall. One had holes in it, but two were in good shape. The bunks that housed the men were rusty and falling apart, but she could see in her mind's eye an exhibit that would explain the courageous work done here through the decades. The building was good and solid. It deserved to be saved, and her work would bring in visitors.

She climbed the old circular stairs, the iron clanging

under her feet, until she stood in the widow's watch and stared out to sea. The lookout's job would have been monotonous until that moment when a ship broke to pieces on the shoals.

So much history here.

"Libby, someone here to see you," one of the workers called.

She turned her gaze from the sea to the parking lot. The sheriff's SUV was parked by the door. She gulped. The state authorities were supposed to arrive today. Sheriff Bourne had probably escorted them himself so he could watch her squirm. She prayed for strength as she clanged down the steps and found three men in the main room watching the activity.

"You're putting this place on the national registry?" the sheriff asked.

"Yes. It shouldn't be hard. There's so much important history here." She held out her hand to the two agents. "Libby Holladay."

The first man was in his fifties, skinny and wiry with a thin mustache and pale blue eyes. "Detective Monroe," he said, shaking her hand.

The other one also took her hand. His brown eyes were cold and judgmental. He was in his thirties and had an eager-hunter look about him. "Detective Pagett," he said. "We're here to find out what happened to your business partner."

"I'll do whatever I can to help you find her."

"Would you like to step outside so we can discuss this in private?" Monroe asked, glancing at the workers who were watching them.

"Whatever you say." She would not show any fear.

"After you." Pagett held open the door for her.

The hot sunshine on her face gave her strength. She heard the church bells ring out the time, as if God was telling her to take courage. There was a bench outside by the walk, so she headed for it and settled on it. "I've been working all morning, so I hope you don't mind if I sit down."

"Not at all," Monroe said. "Now, about your partner. We particularly want to talk to you about the day she disappeared. Where were you?"

"I was documenting a house for the national historic registry." She told them where it was located. "The new owner wanted us to do the restoration."

"Did anyone see you there?" Pagett asked.

She started to shake her head, then stopped. "There was a lady in the neighborhood collecting money for a family who had suffered a house fire. I don't know her name, but if you talk to the people who had the fire, they will likely know. I think the woman will remember that I was there."

Pagett's mouth grew pinched. "We'd like your permission to examine your bank account."

"That's fine."

His brows rose at her quick agreement. "You haven't withdrawn a large amount of money?"

She laughed. "Do you have any idea what I make? There was never a large amount of money to spend. It's all I can do to pay my expenses."

Monroe took out a notebook. "Let's talk about the call from your partner."

"She called while I was at the old house. She told me I had a sister here, and that if I could log on to my computer, I could have the chance to see her."

"There was an open wireless at your site?" the sheriff asked.

She shook her head, trying not to show her impatience. "No, but I have a card to tether my computer to my cell phone."

"I thought you didn't make much money. That would be an expensive gadget," Pagett said.

"It's part of my work and not that expensive. I get leads on the road all the time and I need to be able to pull up the maps. They're too small to see on my phone." She crossed her legs and clasped her hands over her knee. "Look, detectives, I can tell you think I did away with Nicole, but you couldn't be further from the truth. Find out who took her. It wasn't me. I saw two men."

The older agent had an expression in his eyes that made her hope he was listening, so she targeted her gaze at him. She described the kidnappers and everything she saw. As she talked, she remembered more about the boat and gave them details on color.

Monroe put his notebook away. "We'll get on it, Ms. Holladay. Thank you for your time."

"But don't make any plans to leave Hope Island," Pagett said.

"Trust me, I'm clinging to hope for dear life," she called after them.

* * *

With the sea spray in his face and the sun on his arms, Alec steered his boat toward a small cove down the shore from where Nicole's belongings had been discovered. He cut the engine. "I checked tide and current charts. I think there's a good chance the killers could have been out here when they threw her overboard. The currents would have carried anything placed in the water here to the shore where her shoes and cover-up were found."

Libby's face was pink with the sun, and she had her long hair back in a ponytail. The style made her look about eighteen. "She's not dead, Alec. I know it. We'll find her."

Alec smiled and said nothing. The day stretched out in front of them, and Alec found himself wanting to hang on to every minute. What did that mean? She was becoming way too important to him too quickly. He glanced at Bree and Samson in the front of the boat. The dog was enjoying the ocean breeze but didn't seem to have caught any kind of scent yet.

Libby lifted a pair of binoculars to her eyes and scanned the horizon. "There's nothing out here but ocean. I'm a little disoriented."

The disappointment in her voice struck a chord with him. He'd hoped for more too. He pointed. "The lighthouse ruins are there." He moved his finger to the north. "The lifesaving station where she was taken is there."

"So that's why we're here?"

"I suspect whoever took her brought her out here right away. I suspect they killed her almost as soon as they grabbed her. That's why Bree found her things where she did." When she stiffened, he touched her shoulder. "Whatever happened, her things went overboard out here. The shoes and clothing washed ashore too quickly for them to have let much time elapse."

Her expression grew somber as she stared out at the sea, and he wished he could carry some of her pain. Was she imagining Nicole's last moments here, struggling for survival? No, she was seeing a different scenario. One where Nicole was alive and awaiting rescue.

She let the binoculars hang down from her neck. "Now what?"

He pulled out a currents chart he'd brought. "The only other place where her body might have washed ashore is here." He stabbed a finger to the north of the lighthouse ruins.

"We were there the other day. We walked right past."

"It was flooded then, but the water has gone down now. I'm going to anchor offshore and see if we can find anything." He avoided saying the word *body*.

She swallowed hard. "Okay."

He squeezed her hand. "I won't leave you." He saw Bree turn her back as though to give them more privacy.

Libby stared at him. "Are you for real?"

"What do you mean?"

"I didn't think men like you existed. Strong, steady, spiritual. I think I must have dreamed you."

Her admiring amber eyes brought heat to his cheeks. "I'm just an ordinary guy."

"You're anything but," she said softly. She looked past him to the shore. "Do you think Brent is behind this, Alec?"

He'd hoped she wouldn't ask. Not until he poked around a little more. "It's possible," he admitted. "The money he was promised for the land could corrupt anyone."

"Ten million."

"How'd you know that?"

"Poe offered me the same thing after I arrived."

"What did you tell Poe?" He couldn't keep the dislike from his voice.

"You've met him?"

"Once."

"You don't like him."

He pressed his lips together. "He's out for his own interests."

She sighed. "Isn't everyone?"

"The Bible teaches God first, then others, then self."

"I don't think I've met anyone who followed that."

"Your dad did."

"We're not talking about my dad but about Poe."

He shrugged. "He makes money brokering deals for investors in New York. You could probably get more money if you asked for it."

"Would you sell it?" There was only curiosity in her voice.

"No way. Your dad was adamant about preserving Hope Beach. He owned enough property to keep out most investors. And his influence swayed those who might have sold out. He also snapped up houses for sale, then gave them to deserving families."

Her eyes widened. "You're kidding! He gave away *houses*?"

"Property is cheap here. He wanted to keep the town for the fishermen, the little guy. If he let a market boom start, the only people who could afford to live here would be rich tourists who come for the summer."

She fell silent, her gaze still on the shore. "Poe said I didn't have long to decide. That if I waited too long, his investor would just move on to another property."

"There *is* no other property of its size with beach-front. The state owns much of the shoreline. They'll have your property, or the resort idea is toast."

"That does make it more valuable. How much more do you think I could get?"

She obviously hadn't listened to a thing he'd said. He wasn't sure he had the words or the inclination to dissuade her. If she couldn't see the ramifications of her actions, then she had more of a mercenary heart than he'd thought. "Another five million. Maybe ten."

"You're mad at me," she said. "I'm sorry, but I have to think of my future too. If I keep the inn, how will I even afford the upkeep? There's no money to do the repairs that it needs."

"Some of the men from town would help. I can swing a pretty good hammer." But when he remembered how much needed to be done, he knew his offer wouldn't make much difference.

He motored toward shore. Change was coming to his small island whether he liked it or not.

THIRTY-TWO

A crane swooped low over the water and caught up a wriggling fish. Gulls screeched overhead as Libby waded ashore.

"I love this place," she said. "It's so peaceful here."

Bree and Samson had already disappeared from sight. There was no one around but Libby and Alec, and she found herself walking closer than necessary to Alec. If she had the courage, she'd hold his hand. Her gaze went to the lighthouse ruins. The maritime forest beckoned but not as much as the ruins did.

"You're a historian," Alec said, smiling. "If there's a ruin around, you're content."

"Exactly right." She stepped close to the lighthouse foundation. "What secrets are hidden here? Wouldn't you like to know? The men who manned this lighthouse saved lives, but I'm sure they had hidden heartaches too."

She would rather daydream about lives gone by than face why they were here. What if they found Nicole's body in this place? Glancing at Alec, she saw he understood. Words seemed unnecessary between them. She'd never been with anyone who was so in tune with her.

The wind ruffled his hair. "Can't you just imagine Blackbeard coming ashore where we did?"

"I'd like to live out here," she said. "Maybe I could have the inn moved to this spot."

"Way I hear it, this spot is right where Poe's New York investor wants to build his resort."

She frowned. "Here? I thought it was going to be where Tidewater Inn is standing."

"Who knows. Rumors are floating all around. Ask him." He nodded toward the water.

While they'd been talking, another boat had anchored and sent a dinghy ashore. Poe stepped out of the rubber raft. He shook sand from his shoes, then headed toward them with a set smile.

Libby suppressed a sigh. They didn't have time for this.

"I was told you might be out here," Poe said, stopping when he reached them.

His face was pink with sun, but it only enhanced his good looks. Libby was sure he knew it too. "You came all this way to find us?"

His smile never faltered. "It's a lovely day."

"I haven't had a chance to think about your offer," she said. "I do have some questions though. Where exactly will the resort be built?"

"He has plans for this entire stretch of coastline."

"Even here? This is almost sacred ground," she said.

"Oh yes, most certainly here. With all the legends about Blackbeard, he'll want to capitalize on that. Maybe a wedding chapel." He dismissed the topic with a shrug. "That's not our concern though. We simply need to come to an agreement. I realize you're still looking for your friend, but my client is growing quite insistent. I suspect he'll move on to another idea if you don't make up your mind."

"Nicole is dead," Alec said.

Libby opened her mouth, then closed it again. Protesting wasn't going to change anyone's mind.

He blinked. "Y-You're sure? I haven't heard anything about that. Where was her body found?" Tugging at his tie, he shifted his feet in the sand.

Why would he be so agitated? Was his client that eager to get her land?

"Her belongings were found," Alec put in.

The tenseness seemed to go out of Poe in a rush. "I'm so sorry."

The words seemed sincere, so she decided to accept them at face value. "You understand that selling this property has been the last thing on my mind."

"Of course. But as I said, my client is growing impatient."

"There is no other land for him to buy here, so quit harassing the lady," Alec said. "You and I both know this is his only shot."

Poe's lips flattened and his nostrils flared. "Her father was the one opposed to selling. I'm sure others in town would be willing to let their property go for the right price. Her brother was quick to agree."

"This is the only stretch of beach that can be purchased. The rest is state land."

Poe shrugged. "My client has connections. If he wants state land, I suspect he could get it." He turned to

Libby. "I'm prepared to make an offer of twelve million. But we must sign the deal this week."

"What's the rush?" she asked. "I told you I need to think about it."

"These things take time, and my client wants to start construction this fall."

"I'm sorry, I'm just not prepared to make a decision." If only he would just leave. They had an unpleasant search to make and he was in their way.

"Very well. I'll check back with you in a few days."

She watched him walk stiffly away, then clamber back into the rubber raft. She turned to study the peaceful setting. "So this place will be gone. That makes me sad."

"You have the power to stop it," he said.

"Not really. That's a lot of money to walk away from. I don't think I can do it. I see it upsets you, but I suspect you've never been poor. I think of all the good I could do with that money. And the pantry will always be full."

"My family wasn't wealthy, Libby," he said. "But I don't believe money solves everything. If you don't have money problems, you have health issues or personal problems. God uses whatever means at his disposal to mold and shape us." He took her arm and turned her back toward the ruins.

She'd never thought of it that way before. But she still couldn't see letting go of such an unbelievable sum of money.

They poked through the ruins for an hour without seeing anything of import. On their way back to the boat, she heard a shout. Bree was jumping up and down and waving. Libby broke into a jog.

"Look at this," Bree said, pointing to the ground. "Have you been down there?"

"What is it?" Libby asked, stooping to lift away some bricks. "It looks like a door to the cellar."

"This area used to have a lot of brick heaped up. The storm surge must have moved enough of the debris to reveal the trapdoor," Alec said.

"You didn't know it was here?" Libby asked. She shoved several bricks out of the way. "We might see things that haven't seen the light of day in decades. Can we take a look?"

He began to help her and Bree move bricks. "Probably nothing important, but if you want to explore, we can."

*   *   *

The flashlight in Bree's hand pushed back the shadows and showed water in the bottom of the hole. A rickety ladder descended into the darkness. "Musty," Libby said, wrinkling her nose.

"You can hold the light," Bree said, handing it to her.

Libby peered past her. "Wonder what's down there? When do you suppose the last people were in here?"

Alec flipped on his flashlight. "Late eighteen hundreds maybe. That's when the whole place came down."

Her pulse sped up. No telling what she might find down there.

"There might be rats or spiders," he warned.

She stopped. "I'm not afraid." But her quivering

voice told a different story, so she cleared her throat and forced strength into her tone. "They'll run from us."

He gave her a skeptical glance, then shrugged. "I'll go first and make sure it's safe."

He put the handle of the flashlight in his teeth and began to climb down the ladder. Libby heard the ladder groan several times and held her breath, but the rungs held. His feet splashed into the water, and she trained her light on him to see how deep it was. The water came to his calves.

"It's not too bad," he called up. "I'll hold the ladder if you're sure you want to come down."

"I'm sure," she said. She tucked her flashlight into the waistband of her shorts and began to step down.

Even the ladder felt damp. The musty odor filled her head. She climbed down until she was standing in knee-high water that made her shiver. It was colder than she expected. She plucked her flashlight out and flipped it on. With a little more light, she felt more confident.

"Stay," Bree told Samson. She joined them in the cellar.

Alec swept his light around the room. "Looks like it was a root cellar. There are old jars of canned food down here." He moved to a shelf that held Ball jars. "Looks like pickles."

Libby followed him and peered at the contents. "I think they're still good."

"I wouldn't eat them," he said, his voice laced with disgust.

"Me neither." She followed him, sloshing through

the water to explore the rest of the cellar. Bree was examining the walls.

Old barrels, tools, and items from yesteryear floated in the water or hung on the walls from rusty hooks. She didn't recognize some of the tools and glanced at Alec.

"One of the keepers was a doctor," he said.

Whale-oil casks bobbed in the water. She paused at an overturned case of shelves. There was less water here. Her foot struck something and she looked down to see what it was. Horror froze her in place when she realized a human skeleton lay partially submerged at her feet. Uttering mewling noises, she grabbed Alec's arm. Her muscles finally obeyed her, and she turned and ran for the ladder. She thought Alec called her name, but she didn't stop until she was crouching in the sand and heaving. Samson whined by her ear as if to commiserate with her distress.

A few moments later Alec's hand was on her shoulder. "It's okay," he said, his voice soothing in her ear.

She shuddered. "That was a person." Details she hadn't noticed at the time came back to her. "A woman. I saw a blue sundress." She sat back and swallowed hard, then allowed Alec to help her to her feet.

"I think I know who it is," he said, his voice grim.

Bree clambered up the ladder and stood beside her. "Are you okay?"

"Did you see the skeleton?"

Bree nodded. "It's not Nicole."

"No, no, of course not." She stared into Alec's face,

noting his pallor. This hadn't been easy for him either. "Who was she?"

"I think she was Ray's wife, Tina," Alec said.

Libby stared back at the opening. "Tina? I don't understand. She was murdered? I just heard she died."

Alec turned to look at the cellar hole too. "She went out on a boat ride and never came back. Her skiff was found broken up and half submerged, but her body was never found. So it was assumed she hit a rock and drowned."

"What does this mean?" she asked, trying to take it all in. "How do you know it's Tina?"

"She always wore a dress. And there was a picture of this dress all over town."

She looked at the yawning hole in the ground and shuddered. "D-Do you think someone killed her and threw her down there?"

"That was my first thought. I suppose it's possible she went exploring and got trapped."

"But the boat . . ."

He nodded. "Exactly. Someone would have had to deliberately scuttle the boat."

She hugged herself. "I don't like this."

"Neither do I."

She looked away from the dank hole. "When did she die?"

"Three years ago. The news caused Ray's first stroke, a small one. He loved her very much."

Pity stirred for her father. "I'm glad he's not alive to see this. If she was murdered . . ."

"The press is going to have a heyday with this." He took her arm and turned her toward the boat. "One good thing is that it might deflect attention from your friend's death for a while."

She stopped and clutched his arm. "I want attention to stay on her. That's the only chance we have of finding out who killed her."

"You don't suppose there could be any connection between Tina's death and Nicole's, do you?" Bree asked.

He frowned. "I don't see how."

"Nicole came out here," Bree said. "What if she saw something? Something that put her in danger?"

"Maybe. But she didn't get into the cellar. It was covered over until the storm surge." He stared back at the cellar. "I need to let Tom know about this. I saw a passageway when we were down there. It looked like it went toward those rocks." He pointed to a rocky point of land jutting into the sea. "I've seen a cave there, but I always thought it was shallow and not very big."

He took Libby's arm and led them all to the cave. They waded into the water and out to the rocks, where he pointed out a small opening.

Stooping, she peered into it. "It's bigger than it looks."

Bree glanced into the cave, then glanced at Libby. "Any chance Nicole would have gone exploring?"

Libby nodded. "Oh yes. She explores caves every chance she gets. Last summer she went on a spelunking vacation with some friends. She mentioned finding one here on the island."

Alec's lips tightened. "We might have a connection, then."

THIRTY-THREE

The palm tree provided a little shade. Nicole had been out since morning watching for a boat, any boat, but the sea remained empty. Her stomach growled, and she worked on ignoring it as best she could. The bread was soggy, and the thought of plain peanut butter wasn't appealing. Besides, she had no idea if the boy would even come back. Her eyes grew heavy, so she propped up her head with her arms and closed her eyes for a few minutes.

A gull cawed and she sat back up, rubbing her eyes. When she stared back out to sea, she saw the reason for the gull's displeasure. A boat skimmed the tops of the waves as it headed for her tiny beach.

Scrambling to her feet, she dusted the sand from her legs and hands and went down to meet the boy. He was wary as he dropped anchor and splashed ashore. It was going to take all her persuasion to convince him she wasn't crazy.

"Got your supplies," he said, dropping a sack onto the sand. "See ya."

"Wait!" She ran to catch him.

When he held out his hands to shove her back, she

stopped. "I won't touch you. Just talk to me for a minute, okay? It's lonely out here by myself." Tears sprang to her eyes and she sniffled.

Concern replaced the wariness on his face. "Hey, don't cry. I can stay a minute. Just don't try anything, okay?"

She nodded. "Okay. I'm sorry about before. I was just scared." She searched his gaze. "Is anyone back on Hope Island looking for me?"

"Why would anyone there be looking for you? You're from Raleigh."

She shook her head and decided to go ahead with her plan. The truth. "I live in Virginia Beach. My partner and I have a restoration business. We were hired to restore some buildings in the downtown. My partner's name is Libby Holladay. I'm Nicole Ingram."

He gasped and took a step back. "How'd you hear about that? Did you talk to the Ingram girl sometime?"

"I *am* the Ingram girl. My birthday is July 4. I'm twenty-five. Libby is Ray Mitchell's daughter, but no one on Hope Island knew about her."

His eyes narrowed. "You're lying."

"I'm not." She reached out toward him, but he flinched and stepped back. "Please, check it out. Ask to see a picture of me. You'll see I'm telling the truth. I don't know what all those men told you, but it wasn't true. I was at the boardwalk by Tidewater Inn, and two men kidnapped me. Is Libby in town?"

She was sure of the answer to that. Libby would leave no stone unturned until she stood on this beach and rescued her.

"You don't know anything," he said. "Nicole Ingram is dead. They found her belongings on the beach."

The revelation made her take a step back and gasp. "I fought them. My pink cover-up came off in the struggle. One of them tossed it. And I lost my flip-flops when I jumped overboard. That's all they found, right?"

"I don't know what they found. Just that Nicole's clothes were on the beach."

"Libby didn't believe it, did she? She's still on the island?"

"She's still there. Poking around to try to find out who kidnapped her partner. But I'm not convinced you're the one she's looking for. Your brother told me you were wily and not to believe any story you concocted."

She managed a smile. Even if she didn't get off the island today, he would go back and investigate. He'd find out she was telling the truth. "So don't believe it. Check it out for yourself. Then tell Libby where I am. I'll make sure the police know you were duped, that you weren't an accomplice."

As soon as she said the word *duped,* she knew she'd made a mistake. No guy liked to look foolish.

"I'm not stupid," he said. "You're the stupid one. Trying to snow me with a crazy story like this."

"Look, I know it sounds crazy. But it's even crazier that someone would kidnap me and stick me here in this place. Think! What would be the motive? Locking up a crazy sister? There are places for that. His story makes no sense, and you'd know it if you had any brains at all!" She was past caring if he was mad. Past worrying about hurting his feelings. "You've got to see the truth."

"I'm out of here," he said, turning on his heel. He stomped off toward the boat.

Nicole ran after him and grabbed his arm. "Check it out," she said desperately. "That's all I ask. My picture has to be in the paper. Or online. You'll see I'm telling the truth."

He brushed her hand off. "I'll check it out, and then I'll let you know how crazy you are."

She tried on a winning smile. "What's your name?"

"Zach," he said.

"You have a nice boat."

"Yeah. My uncle likes to fish."

"He's a commercial fisherman?"

He shook his head. "Works for the Coast Guard mostly. Fishes in his spare time."

"And your parents?"

"Dead."

A common bond. "I'm sorry. My dad has cancer, and I'm afraid he won't make it. It's hard."

"What about your brothers?"

She saw where he was going with that. "No brothers. Only two sisters, and they both live in California."

He stepped into the waves. "I gotta go. I'm going to be late."

She wanted to scream and beg him to take her with him, but she forced herself to smile and wave. "Thanks for the supplies, Zach. Don't forget to look up my picture."

* * *

Alec held the door to the sheriff's office open for Libby. He knew by her expression that she dreaded being interrogated by his cousin. "I'll do the talking," he whispered, guiding her toward Tom's office with his hand at the small of her back.

She held her head high as several workers glanced at her curiously. Her courage impressed him. Not many women would have gone into that cellar hole with him. Not many women would hold up under the suspicion she'd been under.

They found Tom at his desk scowling at the computer. He straightened when he saw them. "Hey, what's up?"

"We found something out at the old lighthouse ruins." He pointed to the first chair. "Have a seat, honey." He nearly bit his tongue off when he realized he'd called Libby *honey*. She smiled and didn't seem to take offense, though, so that was good. He sank into the chair beside her. "We could both use something to drink. Got any bottled water?"

"Yep," Tom reached into a small refrigerator behind his desk and extracted two bottles. "You both look pretty puny. I don't think I've ever seen you so white."

"Thanks." Alec uncapped his bottle and took a swig of water. "It was a rough day. The storm surge uncovered a cellar out at the ruins."

"A cellar?" Tom frowned. "I didn't know about a cellar."

"It's been there all along. Remember that pile of bricks toward the back? It was under there. The force of the water moved the bricks and uncovered the trapdoor. Libby, Bree, and I went down to explore."

"And?"

In answer, Alec pulled out his smartphone and pulled up the picture he'd taken. "We found this." He handed the phone to his cousin.

Tom studied it in silence. "No telling how long that's been down there."

"I'd say about three years."

Tom looked up sharply. "Three years? Why would you say that?"

"Take another look. Recognize anything?" When Tom's face stayed blank, Alec leaned forward and poked his finger on the blue dress. "That's Tina's dress."

Realization dawned on Tom's face. "Tina Mitchell?"

"Yeah. A picture of her in that dress was plastered all over the state for a month."

"You're right. Holy cow." Tom sat back in his chair. "How did she get there?"

"We've been wondering the same thing." Alec told him about going back into the cellar and finding the other entrance.

"So anyone who knew about that could have gone in there. How did Tina know? And did she get trapped in there by the tide or something?" His face changed. "No, that's impossible. Her boat was clear down the coast. It had to have been deliberate."

"That's what I thought too. Someone put her body there, probably after they killed her, then scuttled her boat to make it look like an accident. Forensics can maybe tell what happened."

"Or maybe not," Tom said. "Doesn't look like there's much left."

"Nicole was an avid cave explorer," Libby put in. "What if she found the cave leading to the cellar? What if she found the body and the murderer saw her?"

Tom stroked his chin. "Maybe." But he glanced at her with a hard expression.

"It makes sense," Alec said. "Whoever took Nicole didn't keep her long. It was like they grabbed her and disposed of her right away. I'm guessing they didn't want her to tell anyone about the cellar and what it contained."

"Seems a little far-fetched to me," Tom said. "She wouldn't know who anyone was, killer or victim."

"But the minute she reported it, you would have known as soon as you saw Tina. I think there's evidence in that cellar that will lead us to the killers."

"I'll call the state detectives. They have more resources than we do. I don't want to muck up this investigation. Holy cow," Tom said again. "Tina Mitchell was murdered. But why?"

"When we know that, we might know who."

"Ray maybe? No relationship is perfect."

Alec bristled. "Don't even go there. Ray was a good man. The best."

"Even good men snap," Tom said. "You know it's usually the person closest to the victim." His gaze slid again to Libby.

"Not this time," Alec said.

"One of the kids?" Tom suggested. "I remember hearing they were having some battles about Brent's lack of a job. He expected his parents to hand out money, and they wanted him to work."

Alec glanced at Libby. She should tell Tom about the attack and how Brent had a wetsuit, but he knew she wouldn't want to get her brother in trouble.

Libby leaned forward with her hands clasped. "Please, Sheriff Bourne, I didn't kill Nicole. Or my mother. I'm not some kind of monster."

Tom tapped his fingers on the desk. "Can we place Nicole at the cellar?"

"I know she'd been out to a nearby cave. She told me in the call."

But then Tom's face hardened and he stood. "Good work, Alec. Staying close to her has paid off, hasn't it?"

Alec went hot, then cold. He leaped to his feet with his fists clenched. "Let's go, Libby." He held out his hand.

She took it, glancing from him to his cousin and back again. "What do you mean 'staying close to her'?"

Tom was white. "You didn't think he was hanging around because he liked you, did you? I asked him to keep an eye on you."

Alec stared at Tom. Why was he doing this? Libby stared at him with eyes filled with pain. "Libby," he began.

Without a word she turned and rushed for the door. He started to go after her, then turned back to Tom. "Why did you do that?"

"I thought if she was shook up, she might reveal something."

"She's a good woman, Tom," Alec said. "I'd better leave before I bust your face in and you have to throw me in jail for attacking an officer."

He stormed from the office. Libby was nowhere in sight.

THIRTY-FOUR

It was a long hike back to Tidewater Inn, but Libby needed the time to compose herself. She vacillated between anger and hurt. So Alec's support had all been a ploy. She should have known he couldn't be the superstar he seemed. She paused to sniffle and wipe her eyes.

An old Buick slowed and she saw Pearl behind the wheel. The window came down, and her aunt beckoned her to get in the car. Libby went around to the passenger seat.

"What are you doing walking alone?" her aunt scolded. "Especially after what happened to your friend?" She studied Libby's face. "You've been crying. Have a spat with Alec?"

"He tricked me," Libby burst out. "He was just pretending to help me. All the time he was trying to see if I killed Nicole."

"And who told you this?"

"The sheriff." Libby glanced around the car. "You've got a block on the pedals."

"So I can reach them." Her aunt pressed her shoe against the block on the accelerator and the car jerked into motion. "Let me tell you something about our sheriff. Tom idolizes his cousin. But he's also jealous of Alec. Tom knows he'll never be the man Alec is. So he tries to bring Alec down to his own level every chance he gets. I've seen it over and over again."

"But he didn't deny Tom had asked him to find out what he could."

"I'm sure Tom *did* ask him. He likely saw the way Alec looks at you. Tom wouldn't have liked it."

Libby's cheeks heated. "Alec looks at me? What do you mean?"

Pearl laughed. "Oh, honey, a blind woman could see that besotted expression. The guy fell hard right from the start."

"I don't think so." But Libby's heart sped up at the possibility. Could it be true?

"He took vacation to help you. He's been underfoot every moment since you arrived. The man is smitten." Pearl's sideways glance was sly. "I believe he feels as strongly about you as you do about him."

"He's just a friend." Fresh tears blurred her vision. "At least I thought he was a friend."

"Uh-huh. A friend. You can talk to your old aunt. You feel way more for him than friendship."

"We haven't known each other all that long."

"Long enough to recognize the attraction."

"Well, yes. He's unlike anyone I've ever known. I *thought* he was, anyway. Now I don't know."

"You know." Her aunt turned the old car into the drive. "Huh. Looks like we have company."

Libby stared through the windshield. "It's Horace."

The attorney was getting out of his big Cadillac with

a folder in his hand. He mopped his brow as he waited for Libby to step from the car.

"Horace. I wasn't expecting you," Libby said, shutting the car door behind her. She smiled at the older man. "I could use some sweet tea. How about you?"

"Sounds mighty fine, Miss Libby, mighty fine." He held up his folder. "I took the liberty of coming out to bring you the first draft of your will."

"I'd forgotten about it." It was the last thing she wanted to worry about right now, but the man had gone out of his way, so she smiled to hide her disinterest.

"A good attorney never forgets a client's needs," Horace said.

They went up the steps to the porch. "If you want to have a seat on the swing, I'll bring out the tea," Pearl said. "That way you can talk in private. We have a lot of visitors at the moment."

Horace settled on the chair with the cushions. Libby took the swing and tucked her feet under her. They ached from walking. Would Alec come after her? Maybe she should have waited around to talk to him. She was still hurt, but maybe Pearl was right, and Tom was trying to wreck their relationship before it had a chance to start.

"Miss Libby?"

With a start, she realized Horace was speaking to her. "Sorry, what was that?"

He tapped the paper he'd slid toward her on the table. "You want to read over this will?"

She took the paper and began to skim it, though the chore was the last thing she wanted to do. When she got to the part about her beneficiaries, she stopped. "I want to leave half the money to Vanessa."

"And the historic preservation foundation?"

"The other half." She glanced at him. "What happens if I die before this is executed?"

"The laws of the state will prevail. In this case, your next of kin would inherit. That would be Brent and Vanessa."

So Brent would have had motive for drowning her the other night. But was it motive enough to believe that he would hurt her? She hated to think her own brother could be so cold and calculating.

She slid the will back to Horace. "How long before this is ready?"

He pursed his lips. "Just a few days. My secretary is on vacation, and I'm quite hopeless with a computer. As soon as she gets back, I'll have her amend this and draw up the final papers. Is there anything else you'd like to add?"

She toyed with the idea of leaving Alec something. After her near drowning the other day, she'd been thinking about death. No one knew when their time would come. But it was too soon to think that something permanent might develop between her and Alec.

She shook her head. "I think that's it. Thanks for getting to this so quickly. I'd like to wrap it up as soon as possible."

"We'll do that, Miss Libby."

Her aunt bustled through the door with a tray. "Here we go, Horace. I took the liberty of bringing you some cookies as well."

Libby saw Alec's truck kicking up dust behind it on the road. Her pulse jumped, and she rose to excuse herself from Horace.

* * *

Alec waved to Horace as he drove off. Libby vanished inside the house as he started up the porch steps. Clenching his jaw, he followed.

Pearl saw him and pointed. "She went into the greenhouse."

He thanked her and went down the hall to the back of the house. Ray had built the greenhouse for Tina twenty years ago. When she was alive, she grew orchids. They still bloomed in the large, sunny space, though Delilah didn't have the green thumb that Tina had possessed.

"Hey, Libby," he began.

She was standing in front of a particularly beautiful white orchid. She didn't turn when he spoke.

"Look, don't freeze me out, okay? Turn around and talk to me."

"There's nothing much to say," she said, still bending over the flower.

"Tom was out of line."

"Was he? It seems he asked you to keep an eye on me. Or is that not true?" She finally turned and stared at him, her hands behind her back. "Did you suspect that I killed Nicole?"

He didn't want to answer that, but with her somber gaze on him, he couldn't lie. "I had to consider the possibility."

"Is that the real reason you asked Earl to do an article? So he'd dig and find out what you couldn't ask?"

"I wanted to find Nicole. At the time that's all I was thinking about."

"So you agreed to stay close to me and see if I was a murderer?"

"Yes. But I quickly realized you would never hurt anyone."

"I thought we were friends," she said, her voice soft. "I thought you were my only true ally here in town. Now I find out that you were just helping out your cousin. And that hurts."

"We *are* friends." It was much too soon to tell her that he was developing feelings for her that were stronger than friendship. "Please don't let what Tom said derail our friendship."

The hurt in her eyes didn't lessen, but she nodded. "I'll try. I'd like to talk about Tina. Do you have any idea what might have happened to her? Did she have any enemies?"

He'd been trying not to think about her. "It's a puzzle. She was as well liked as your father. He was devastated when she died. Walked the beach for weeks hoping to find her."

"If we figure out who killed her, it may lead us to who kidnapped Nicole. I think it's very possible she found Tina's remains."

"I agree. The first thing we might do is talk to Pearl. She knows more about the town than anyone. And she knew Tina better than anyone else except Brent and Vanessa. I suppose we'd better tell them too."

"It's going to be a hard day for Vanessa. First she finds out how our father lied to her, then she discovers the woman she thought was her mother was murdered."

"You sound sympathetic."

"Of course I am. She's my sister. I'm going to work hard to build a relationship with her."

Pearl stood in the doorway with a tray in her hands. "Anyone want coffee and cookies?"

Her eyes were bright and curious. She was probably dying to know what was going on. "I'll take some," Alec said. "We need to talk to you anyway."

Pearl set the tray on the table. "Libby, I hope you accepted his apology."

"I did," Libby said.

He should have known that Pearl would sniff out any news. "Did Libby tell you we found Tina's remains?"

Pearl's smile vanished. "Tina Mitchell?"

Alec nodded. "There's a cellar at the lighthouse ruins. The storm surge revealed it. She was there." He explained how they'd found the cellar and the other entrance.

Pearl was pale. "So you're thinking Nicole was killed because she found Tina?"

Libby nodded. "Alec says you knew her better than anyone, except maybe the kids. Did she have any enemies? Did she seem worried in the weeks before she died?"

The chair groaned when Pearl settled into it. She frowned as she took a sip of her beverage, which was more cream than coffee. "I told Tom that something was wrong back when she came up missing. He dismissed me. So I was right."

Alec frowned. "What do you mean? What did you see?"

"She was withdrawn, sad. I thought maybe she was suffering from depression and spoke to Ray about it."

"Had he noticed?" Alec asked.

Pearl shook her head. "He'd been gone on a trip. I called him while he was in California. He said she'd been quiet on the phone, but he assumed it was because she was tired from taking care of things while he was gone. He promised to talk to her about it when he got home. He arrived on an afternoon. She went missing that evening."

"So he didn't talk to her about it?"

"I didn't want to bring it up. I was afraid she . . ."

"Drowned herself?" Libby asked. She clasped her arms around herself as if she were cold.

Pearl shivered. "Exactly. I didn't want Ray to blame himself if that's what happened."

Alec tried to remember that time when they were all searching for Tina. "Did you see her with anyone during that time?"

Pearl looked away. "Some rich investor from New York named Lawrence Rooney. He'd come to see Ray but spoke to Tina. He hung around a few days." Her tone was careful.

"What did he want?" Libby asked.

Pearl pressed her lips together. "Tina never said."

"And that upset you because she usually told you everything?" Libby guessed.

"I didn't want to think she would be interested in another man." Her chin jutted. "I still don't think Tina was interested in him."

"Maybe I'll see what I can find out about the guy. There might be a link." This long after Tina disappeared, he feared there would be little evidence left. "Maybe."

Pearl rose. "You realize we need to tell Brent and Vanessa?"

"I know," Libby said.

Pearl sighed. "What a terrible day. I'll send them down to speak with you." She hurried away as if she couldn't wait to leave them behind.

Alec's gut tightened. From Libby's tight expression, he knew she was dreading it too.

THIRTY-FIVE

Vanessa's eyes were red as though she'd been crying. "What's going on?" she asked when she came into the greenhouse, glancing at Alec, then over to Libby.

Vanessa was wearing her father's necklace. Libby hoped it would help her sister through this. "Have a seat."

Brent slouched in with his hands in his pockets. He sank into a white wicker chair by a large geranium. "More drama?" he asked in a bored tone.

Libby pressed her lips together. "There's something you need to know, and we didn't want you to hear this from anyone else. And your perspectives may help Tom's investigation as well."

Vanessa straightened where she sat on the wicker sofa. "What's wrong? You're all so serious."

"There's news about Tina, Vanessa," Libby said.

Vanessa frowned and glanced at her brother. "I don't understand. She's been gone for three years. Why are we talking about her now?"

Libby wished she didn't have to tell them. "Yes, yes, I know. But her remains were found today."

Vanessa's eyes grew wide. Brent inhaled sharply. Libby tried to put herself in her siblings' shoes. No matter how much they distrusted her, they were bound by blood. She needed to help them through this if she could. They were all grieving something.

"Where was she found?" Brent asked.

Libby reached toward him, then dropped her hand. "Out at the lighthouse ruins. In the cellar."

Brent frowned. "There's no cellar."

"It's been hidden all this time. The storm surge knocked debris out of the way. But there's another way in." Libby glanced at Alec. "Would you explain, Alec?"

Vanessa and Brent listened in silence. Their expressions changed to incredulity, then to shock as they realized their mother had been murdered.

"But maybe she just found that cave," Brent said.

Vanessa shook her head. "The boat, Brent. The boat had to have been deliberately scuttled. Otherwise, it would have been found nearby on the shore. Even if she pulled it ashore and then found the cave and the tide dragged it back to sea, it would have been found closer to the ruins. Not where it was."

Tears slid down her cheeks, and she kept her head down. Libby wished she knew the best way to comfort her.

"Exactly," Alec said. "We also have to wonder about Nicole now."

If only Libby had had more time to talk to Nicole that day. So many regrets. "Nicole loved caves. The last time I talked to her, she said she'd found a new cave with something exciting in it. Before she could tell me what that was, the men appeared."

"Did you happen to hear Mr. Rooney talking to your mother?" Alec asked.

"Mr. Rooney? You mean that investor guy?" Vanessa asked. "He took us to dinner in Duck one night. You should have seen his yacht!"

"He was trying to impress Mom," Brent said. "Kept telling her that she and Dad could travel the world, have a house wherever they wanted."

"You didn't like him?" Libby asked.

He shrugged. "Not so much. Mom didn't either. When he tried to pressure her to talk to Dad, she told him to take her home."

"Why did she agree to go to dinner in the first place?" Alec asked.

"You know how Mom was. She didn't like to hurt anyone's feelings. And he'd come all that way to talk to Dad."

"Why didn't he call first and make sure D-Dad was home?" It still felt strange to say *Dad*.

"He did," Vanessa said, her tone implying that she didn't appreciate any criticism of her father. "But Daddy got called out at the last minute. One of his businesses in California burned, and he went to make sure the employees were taken care of."

"So your mother tried to placate the guy by talking to him herself." Alec put his hands in his pockets and paced. "Did you hear what he wanted?"

Brent shrugged. "What they always want. This strip

of land on the ocean. I think this is the guy that Poe represents. He offered ten mil."

Libby bit her lip to keep from telling him the offer had gone up.

"Did your mother seem tempted?" Alec asked.

Vanessa shook her head. "Mom never wanted to leave the island. She didn't care about yachts and travel. It was all Daddy could do to get her to go to Virginia Beach from time to time."

"She was a homebody," Brent agreed.

"And it's not like Daddy was hurting for money," Vanessa added. "He gave her anything she wanted."

"Did they know the state was talking about putting in a ferry system?" Libby asked.

"Oh yes," Vanessa said. "Daddy made several trips to try to talk down the proposal. He was determined not to let them ruin our island."

"How did you feel about that?" Libby asked, glancing at Brent so he would know she wanted to know what he thought as well.

Brent shrugged. "Dad didn't care much for progress, but lots of younger men like me would like to see more jobs. Even tourism would pay a steadier wage than fishing does at times. And what is there here except fishing?"

"Is that why you were going to sell this place?"

"Maybe. If I could have sold it and started a ship-building business here, it would have brought in jobs." His grin was cold. "And it was a lot of money."

Just when she thought she could warm up to the

guy, he turned everything around again. Libby had no idea how to read Brent.

* * *

"Come along, Poe," Lawrence said. He glanced at his daughter. That color dress made Katelyn's skin look like a pumpkin. An unfortunate following after fashion.

Poe rose from the Rooneys' dinner table. "I'll join you in the game room in a few minutes," he said to Katelyn. "All right?"

"I'll be waiting." Her flirtatious glance lingered on him.

Lawrence led the boy to his office. Closing the door behind him, he approached the desk. "I can tell something is on your mind. Has something gone wrong?"

Poe sat in the chair across from the desk. "There's a rumor that Nicole Ingram is dead."

"What? Did you do something to her?"

Poe shook his head. "It wasn't me. Her shoes and cover-up were found, and the authorities are presuming her dead."

"That's not catastrophic, then. They can't blame us for something we didn't do." He eyed Poe. "We didn't have anything to do with this, correct?"

Poe shook his head. "Libby doesn't believe it. She's tenacious. She's got a search-and-rescue dog team there."

Lawrence dismissed the concern with a wave of his hand. "The dog can't tie us to something we didn't do."

"True enough." Poe inhaled and leaned forward. "That's not all though. The cellar has been found. And Tina's remains."

Lawrence bolted out of his chair. "You said no one would ever find her. We should have dumped her body in the ocean." His scowl darkened. "This is your fault."

Poe spread out his hands. "I agree I should have just hauled her body from the cellar when I found it there. But at the time, I was afraid the discovery of her body would heat up the investigation and derail our plan. If they thought she drowned, the hunt would die down. And that's what happened."

"Is there anything you aren't telling me? You didn't kill her, did you?"

"Absolutely not. She must have fallen and hit her head. She was dead when I found her."

"You'd better not be lying."

Poe held his gaze. "I'm telling you the truth. If you have doubts about me, now is the time to say so."

Lawrence looked away and shook his head. He didn't want to alienate Poe when things were going so well with Katelyn. "The problem now is what do we do? Investigators will be poring over that cellar."

"They may not find the cache."

"I'd rather not take the chance," Lawrence said.

"What do you propose?"

"I don't know yet. I'll have to think about it."

Poe relaxed in the chair. "I have an idea."

THIRTY-SIX

When Delilah served the Tidewater Inn guests after-dinner coffee, Alec gestured to Zach and they stepped outside. Over the meal, Alec had caught Zach staring at Libby quite often. Did his nephew see the attraction between them?

"School will be starting soon," Alec said, stooping to pick up an unbroken conch.

Zach folded his arms across his chest. "I'm not going back to school, Uncle Alec."

"Now, Zach," Alec began.

"Don't try to talk me into it. You know I just want to be a fisherman. It's an honest profession. I don't need college to catch fish. I already know the ocean like the back of my hand."

"I know you do. But the world is changing. What happens if the fishing falls off? It's a hard life, Zach. I'd like to see you have something else to rely on. There's plenty of time to try different things. You don't have to set your course right now. At least go to two years of college."

Zach's chin jutted out. "I don't want to. And you can't make me."

The boy—no, Zach was a man now—was in charge of his own destiny. Much as Alec wanted to insist on college, how could he know what was best for Zach? How could any man know what was best for another man? There was no denying that Zach was a natural-born waterman. He was in his element when he rode the seas. His dad, Alec's brother, had been the same way. It was probably why he'd been so hard for their father to handle. Zack, like Darrell, just wanted to be back in Hope Beach.

Alec made one final attempt. "What about online classes? Just a couple to keep learning."

Zach hesitated. "I'll think about it."

"That's all I ask."

"I don't know what classes I'd even take though."

"What about something like marine biology? You'd be good at that, and you'd be helping the ecology." A flicker of interest in Zach's eyes encouraged him. "The Banks have some challenges to face. Maybe you could be part of finding help."

Zach had quit listening. His gaze went past Alec, and Alec turned to see Libby heading toward them with a newspaper in her hand. She looked pale and upset.

"Something wrong?" he asked when she reached them.

She held out the newspaper and he saw it was a New York paper. "The story has been picked up. Front page." She opened the paper to reveal a picture of Nicole.

"I'm sorry," Alec said. It had been a total miscalculation to get Earl involved. The reporter was probably rejoicing at all the interest and might even follow up with more damaging articles.

"I should have expected it," Libby said.

"Can I see it?" Zach asked, holding out his hand. Libby handed it over and he studied the article. Zach handed back the paper. "I'm sorry."

"Thanks, Zach." Her eyes narrowed as she stared at him. His Adam's apple was bobbing, and he didn't meet her gaze. "You are on the water a lot. Would you keep an eye out for anyone suspicious? There were two men. One was in his forties with a cap pulled low over his eyes. He had a beard. The other was in his late twenties. He had blond hair and it looked like he hadn't shaved in a couple of days. He might not always look so scruffy though."

"We did a police sketch. That might help," Alec said. He gave a curious glance at his nephew, who seemed unusually still. "Stop by Tom's office and take a look. Keep your eye out for the men."

"You're sure she's dead?" Zach asked.

Alec shot a glance at Libby. She seemed to be holding together all right. "As sure as we can be without a body," Alec said. "I think I know where the men dumped her." He told Zach about the spot offshore from the old ruins.

"I don't want to accept it," Libby said, her voice quiet. "One minute I'm resigned to it and the next I'm sure she's still out there waiting for me to find her."

"I get out there some. I'll keep an eye out," Zach said. "You think the men were local?"

Alec frowned. "I don't, no. I would vouch for every resident male on the island. This isn't the kind of thing our people would do."

Zach put his hands in the pockets of his denim shorts. "I guess people can hide their true natures sometimes."

An uncommonly perceptive comment from his nephew. Alec sometimes despaired at how little progress he felt he was making in shaping Zach. But hadn't he been the same way when he was Zach's age?

"One of my friends is having a party on the beach," Zach said. "I thought I'd go."

"Be careful." Alec wanted to add *don't drink*, but he knew Zach would hear the implied admonition in his voice. Not that it would matter what he said. Zach would do what he wanted to do. All Alec could do was pray.

Zach nodded and jogged to his old pickup.

"Zach is a good boy," Libby said. "You need to trust him a little."

"I *do* trust him."

"Your tone didn't indicate much trust." She turned to stare out to sea. "I keep thinking that there's something I could have done to stop them from taking her."

"It wasn't your fault," he said gently.

She turned back toward him with a pained expression.

"God is in control of life and death and everything in between, Libby. We can drive ourselves crazy by thinking of all the what-ifs in life."

Her eyes were luminous with tears. "I just feel helpless."

Did he make the first move or did she? He wasn't sure, but the next thing he knew, he was holding her

with her face buried in his chest. It was the most natural thing in the world to press his lips against her
fragrant hair.

* * *

Libby could feel Alec's heart thudding under her ear.
She wanted to preserve this moment and stay in the
safe circle of his arms. Right now it felt as though no
harm could come to her. She'd stood on her own for so
many years that she hardly knew what to make of this
desire to be protected and nurtured.

His hand moved in a caressing motion down her
hair, and he pressed his lips against her forehead.
"You're a special person, Libby," he whispered. "I love
how fiercely you treasure family. You even care about
Vanessa and Brent when they've been nothing but cold
to you."

"Vanessa is warming up."

The scent of man and sea was an intoxicating mix.
She burrowed closer to the solid warmth of his chest.
If she lifted her head, he might kiss her again. Part of
her wanted that, but the fearful side kept her cheek
firmly pressed against his shirt. If he kissed her again,
she might lose her heart completely. Right now, if she
walked away from this place, she might survive. If she
gave too much of herself away, it might destroy her.
And she didn't know what the future held.

His arms gripped her shoulders and he created
a small space between them. His fingers tipped her
chin up. She closed her eyes and held her breath. His

lips were warm and persuasive, and she dropped any pretense of holding on to her dignity. It was too late to hang on to her heart. She kissed him back with all the depth of feeling she didn't know she possessed. The beat of his heart sped up under her right palm, trapped under her. She exulted that she moved him as much as he moved her. Whatever was developing between them was something they both felt.

He pulled away. "Want to go for a walk along the beach?"

She nodded. That was safer than being pelted by feelings she had to resist. They strolled along the dense sand, hand in hand. The companionable silence lulled her. She didn't feel the need to fill it with chatter.

He stopped by a fallen tree, pulling her down with him to sit. The moon glimmered on the water and the salty breeze from the ocean lifted her hair in a sultry caress. "I haven't kissed a woman in a long time. I didn't want you to think I was some kind of Lothario."

She had to smile at the anxiety in his voice. She hadn't even considered that he might worry about that. "Thanks for telling me. I don't even know the last time I went out with a man. I've been too focused on my career."

A smile tugged at his lips. "Glad to hear it."

"What about Zach?" she asked, hoping he wasn't offended by the question. "I got the impression I interrupted an argument."

His smile faded. "You did."

"I'm sure he's still hurting from his parents' death."

"Dave was a fisherman too. He had a charter boat

based in Hatteras. Zach was with him all the time until he died. That's all the kid has wanted to do—be on the water. He wants to be a commercial fisherman. My parents couldn't control him. I think he wants everyone to know how miserable he is."

"So you took him?"

"He landed in jail for vandalizing the school the day before you showed up. So yeah, you could say he's been a handful."

"You were doing your duty," she said.

"It's more than duty. I love the kid. He and I have always been close. Right now, he's pushing me away, but I think that's starting to change."

"He's a good kid."

His glance was warm and tender. "I think so. When he first got here, he was sullen and distant, but he's coming around. He loves the sea. Being a waterman is therapeutic."

"Waterman?" She liked the romantic sound of the word.

"It's what we call men out here who make their living off the water. Fishermen, ferry workers, charter-boat owners."

"So you're a waterman too?"

"We all were. Me, Darrell, even my sister, Beth, works with the sea. She's a marine biologist," he said. "Guess I shouldn't come down too hard on Zach. It's in our blood. He can't help it."

"You don't want him to be a waterman?"

"I want him to have something to fall back on. Fishermen have a hard life fighting weather and tides all the time. They're at the whim of the capricious ocean. When you came out, I was trying to talk him into taking some online classes. He doesn't want to go away to college."

"Maybe he feels safe here. And closer to his parents."

Alec slipped his arm around her waist. "Yeah, I guess so." His lips grazed her forehead. "Why aren't you married? A girl as beautiful as you is usually taken early on."

He thinks I'm beautiful. "I've never been close to marriage. I guess I've been afraid to trust anyone. Dealing with my mom's instability has made me cautious. I've never even had a steady boyfriend. We moved around so much that there was never a chance to develop any kind of relationship."

"You think you can trust me?"

She stared into his face. "Can I?"

"I'm a man of my word, Libby. I'd like for us to see where this relationship might go. Are you game?"

"I think so," she whispered.

His lips found hers again and she turned off the warning in her head.

THIRTY-SEVEN

W e generally don't allow guests in the library,"
Delilah said, unlocking the glass-paned door.
"You're hardly a guest, of course, but I wanted you to
be aware that there are many valuable books in here."

Libby stepped into the room and inhaled the aroma
of old books. Her aunt, Alec, and Bree were right
behind her. Their presence would make the job easier,
though she would have gladly spent hours here alone.
There was nothing she liked better than to delve into
history. She slid her glance to Alec and back again.
Their earlier walk on the beach still lingered in her
heart.

"Do you need me to show you around?" Delilah
asked, her tone indicating she hoped to be released.

"No, I'm sure we'll figure it out."

Libby glanced around the large room. There were
floor-to-ceiling oak shelves on two walls, a desk on the
wall with the window, and a library table against the
other wall. The floors were polished oak. The wood
hadn't been stained, and the naturally light color was
attractive.

"I haven't been in here in years," Pearl said, walking

to the nearest bookshelf. "What do you want to see first?"

"I want to take a look at the history of the lighthouse." Libby's attention was distracted by a picture on the desk of a woman in her fifties with auburn hair and hazel eyes. She was on the bow of a boat with a man and they were both laughing. Her father and Tina looked so happy and carefree.

Libby moved past the picture to study the books. The ones on architecture caught her eye but she forced herself to skim by them. A large book on the Outer Banks looked interesting. She took it to the library table.

"I found it," Pearl said, turning toward her. "This is the oldest one. Ray found it twenty years ago. There aren't many copies in existence, and it's in pretty bad shape."

"What do you hope to find in the book?" Bree asked.

Alec pulled a chair out for Libby. She settled into the chair and gently opened the book. "No one knew about the cellar, but I thought there might be pictures of its history in the book I'd heard about."

"What can I be searching for?" Bree asked, turning back to the shelves. "Any other books we need to study?"

"See if there are any on the history of the island. I know it's unlikely, but what if there are more tunnels that lead to where Nicole might have been taken?" And searching through what had happened in the past might provide a clue to the present.

The paper of the book Libby examined was

brittle and yellow. She checked the front of the book. Published in 1923. "When did the lighthouse cease operation? You mentioned the late eighteen hundreds. Can you be more specific?"

"I believe it was in the hurricane of 1899," Pearl said. "It was known as the Great Hurricane, and we lost many lives. I wasn't born yet, of course, but my grandparents used to talk about it."

The pictures Libby thumbed through were faded but legible. She paused to read some of the text, then continued to skim the book. "Hey, wait a minute," she said. She picked up a piece of paper stuck in the middle of the book. "This is a light bill. In Nicole's name. She was reading this book." She stared at the page marked by the paper. "This shows a cellar door. So it wasn't a secret back in its heyday."

"And it proves she knew about the cellar," Bree said.

Alec stepped behind Libby and leaned over her shoulder to look at it more closely. His breath whispered past her cheek, and she fought the attraction his close presence generated.

He flipped the page and began to read aloud. "'The lighthouse was self-contained. The keeper and his family grew vegetables on a small plot of cleared land and stored the harvest in the cellar.'"

"Just like every other family," Libby said. "That doesn't tell us anything."

She couldn't read, couldn't think, with him so close. His neck was close enough that if she leaned over, she could press her lips against his warm skin. She needed to concentrate on figuring this out, so she shifted away.

"There's more," he said. "Listen to this. 'Blackbeard was said to have escaped through one of the secret passageways from the cellar to the rocky cliffs at the water's edge.'"

"So it mentions the passage you found," Libby said. "And Nicole would have seen this. Knowing her, she was sure to have looked for the cave." She leaned over to read the book. "Passageways, plural. So there is more than one."

"There *were*," he corrected. "No telling if they're still there."

Bree was staring at the book. "The name Blackbeard conjures up all kinds of images of treasure."

"People have searched for his treasures in the Outer Banks for years," Pearl said.

"Could Nicole have heard the legends and decided to look herself? Maybe she decided to hunt by herself."

"It sounds like something she would do," Libby said.

"We can go back there and take a look for other tunnels," Alec said. "Though the tide is wrong right now. We can take a look tomorrow afternoon though."

Libby shut the book. "I want to see if we can find any sign of Nicole."

He looked away and nodded. She knew he was thinking that the kidnappers likely killed Nicole. Libby could only pray he was wrong.

*　*　*

Libby had an hour before she and Bree were supposed to meet Alec at his boat. Libby stepped over the warped floorboards in the living room of her father's house. "I was afraid they were ruined," she told her sister.

"Insurance will replace them," Vanessa said. She still wore the necklace Libby had given her. "Daddy was adamant about keeping up on the insurance." She started for the stairs. "I'm not sure what you're hoping to find in his bedroom."

"I don't know either." Libby followed her up to the second floor. "But someone harmed Tina. Maybe there's a clue in her things to what happened. I appreciate you allowing me to investigate."

Vanessa shrugged and opened the bedroom door. "Here you go. I'll help if you tell me what to look for."

Libby glanced around the room. "Anything out of the ordinary."

The blue comforter on the king bed was smooth. Assorted pillows were heaped at the head. Libby paused at the dresser and studied the pictures. One showed her father and Tina with Vanessa and Brent. They were dressed in red and stood by a Christmas tree.

"That was our last Christmas together," Vanessa said. "Six months later and Mom was gone."

Libby put the picture back. There was a jewelry box beside it. "May I?"

Vanessa nodded. "I used to love to go through Mom's jewelry box when I was a little girl. There's a secret drawer in the bottom." She reached past Libby and lifted out two trays full of necklaces and earrings. The bottom showed no sign of having any compartment.

"Is this the same jewelry box?"

Vanessa nodded. "There's a switch here." She

pressed a spot on the bottom and one edge sprang up. "Mom used to hide notes in it telling me she loved me."

"That's so sweet."

"I still have some." Vanessa lifted the fake bottom from the drawer.

Libby expected to see an empty space, but it contained several folded papers. "Letters or bills?"

Vanessa unfolded one. "This one's a letter."

Libby wanted to read it, but she didn't want to offend her sister. Vanessa had been warming up so dramatically. She could wait until Vanessa offered the information. The letter might be very personal.

Vanessa's frown darkened as she read. She finally handed it to Libby and selected another letter. "This doesn't make any sense. It almost sounds as if . . ."

The paper was stiff in Libby's hand. "As if?"

Vanessa pressed her lips together. "As if Mom had a lover. But that's impossible. She loved Daddy."

Libby held the letter in the light of the window.

> Tina,
>
>   Seeing you again brought back all the love I thought I'd torn up by the roots. Even now I would leave my family if you would agree to do the same. It's not too late for us. Think about it and give me a call if you want to talk.
>
>   Yours,
>   L

"L. Who could that be? First name, last name? Any idea?" Libby asked.

"Not a clue," Vanessa said, still reading another letter.

"Anything in that one?"

"This one sounds angry." Vanessa handed it over.

"Angry? Like in murderous?"

Vanessa's expression was troubled. "Maybe."

Tina,

I can only assume by your actions yesterday that you intend us to be at odds. So be it. You'll find me a cold adversary. I will take what I want and you'll only have yourself to blame for the consequences. Your rejection only strengthens my determination. Your life is about to change.

L

Libby glanced up. "Wow, very ominous."

Vanessa hugged herself. "The tone of the letter gives me the creeps."

"Is that all?" Libby glanced into the jewelry box and saw nothing more.

"Just this." Vanessa held out her hand, palm up. A charm was on her palm.

Libby held it up to the light. "Looks like a stingray or something."

"It's a skate. Mom had a charm bracelet with sea creatures on it. She loved it. The skate was lost a few weeks before she died. She wasn't sure where she lost it."

Libby handed it back. "She obviously found it." Now was the time to ask, but she still hesitated.

Vanessa frowned. "She never mentioned that she'd

found it. Mom loved the skates but shuddered when she saw their egg sacks. She couldn't understand why they had a pretty name like mermaid's purse when they were so ugly. Daddy used to take early walks and pick them all up so she didn't have to see them on her morning run."

"Did you put a dead jellyfish under my door?"

Vanessa's hand closed in a fist. Her lips flattened, then she shrugged. "So what if I did?"

"Were you trying to scare me off or what?"

Vanessa leaned against the dresser. "I'm sorry I did that. I was angry. I thought you'd take the warning and leave. Were you frightened?"

Libby opened a drawer. "More mad than anything."

Vanessa opened her fist and fingered the charm. "It's odd this was in her secret drawer and not back on the bracelet." She turned it over and squinted. "I never realized it was engraved." She walked to the window and held it to the light. "*Love, L.* I know the original wasn't engraved."

"The man who wrote the notes gave it to her."

Vanessa turned back toward her. "And she refused to wear it."

"Which might have added to his anger with her. Let's go see the sheriff."

* * *

Alec took a gulp of stale coffee and shuddered. "Anything from the coroner on Tina's remains?"

The circles around Tom's eyes were pronounced,

and his clothes were rumpled. "He couldn't determine cause of death."

"So no clue to what happened to her."

"Nope. And it being three years ago, I'm having trouble piecing together what happened the day she disappeared. I have the old notes, but we thought her boat hit a rock and she drowned. We didn't treat it as foul play, so there's very little in the file. A statement from a fisherman who saw her speeding toward the old lighthouse ruins is all we have. And he's dead now."

"What about the cellar itself? Anything there?"

"One interesting detail. There was a rope tied around Tina's left ankle. We have no idea if it was put there before or after death though."

The door opened behind Alec, and he turned to see Libby and Vanessa enter the sheriff's office. Neither was smiling.

Libby shot a quick glance his way, then held out two pieces of paper to Tom. "We found these in Tina's belongings."

Tom took the papers and began to read. Alec looked over his shoulder. "Looks like Tina had a secret admirer," Alec said.

"There's this too." Vanessa held out a charm. "Look on the back."

Alec took it and squinted at the tiny lettering, then handed it to Tom. They listened to Vanessa tell them about a lost charm and how this apparent replacement had been in the secret compartment.

"Who is this L person?" Tom asked. "Any ideas?"

"Not a clue," Vanessa said. "Sheriff, you have to find out who did this to Mom."

"I'm working on it, Vanessa."

Alec studied his cousin's expression. He didn't seem to be staring at Libby with suspicion. Maybe he was finally beginning to look elsewhere.

"Ready?" Alec asked. "Bree and Samson should be at the boat by now."

* * *

Bree held the clothing Libby had given her under Samson's nose. The breeze on the water ruffled the dog's thick fur. He sniffed the shirt and whined, then lifted his nose above the bow of the boat. "Search, Samson," she said.

Libby watched in awe. "Can he really find a person by sniffing the air? I thought dogs sniffed the ground."

"Samson is an air tracker. A person gives off skin rafts that float in the air. A trained dog can detect them."

"But it's been almost ten days since Nicole was taken," Alec said.

"He may still get a scent." Bree looked away.

Libby stared at Bree. Hadn't she said something about Samson finding someone after two years? Then the memory clicked into place and she remembered that dogs could smell dead bodies for a very long time. A lump formed in her throat, and she prayed the dog would find a live scent. Something to lead them to Nicole.

The boat accelerated across the tops of the waves. It

was calm and beautiful today, though humidity hung in the air. Bree's curls were a little frizzy from the moisture. Sea spray struck Libby's bare arms and felt good on her heated skin. She prayed for a sign from God today, anything that would allow her to hope that her friend was still alive.

"How can you tell if he smells something?" she asked Bree.

"He'll bark. I'll be able to tell," Bree assured her. "Alec, run the boat in a crisscross fashion across the bay so he gets more exposure."

It seemed they looped back and forth across the water for ages, but glancing at her watch, Libby realized they'd only been at this for two hours. She was beginning to lose hope that they'd find something today.

The dog continued to sniff the air as Alec guided the boat back and forth across the gleaming water. The village of Hope Beach beckoned in the distance. A few people on the pier waved as they scouted the area. Libby waved back, suddenly feeling part of the community.

Samson's ears pricked. He stiffened and barked, straining toward the harbor. "Go that way!" Bree shouted, pointing toward the pier.

Libby's heart pounded. She stood, then nearly fell when the boat accelerated.

"Hang on!" Alec seated his hat more firmly on his head and the boat surged.

Samson was barking frantically. The next instant, he leaped over the side and swam toward a boat. He reached it and tried to paw his way onto it, but it was too high for him.

"That's my old boat," Alec said, frowning. "I don't use it much, but Zach had it out this morning."

His boat? Libby stared at him. Surely he wouldn't have had anything to do with this?

He cut the engine and the craft slowed, then stopped near the dog. He tossed the anchor overboard, then reached down and helped Samson clamber up the ladder. The dog shook himself, spraying water over everyone. He rushed to Bree's side and whined. He strained toward the old boat, a Chris-Craft.

Libby stared at Alec. "What does this mean? The dog is saying he smells Nicole on your boat. Right, Bree?"

"That's right," Bree said, rubbing Samson's ears. "Let's board the boat and let him sniff around."

Alec took an oar and maneuvered the two boats close enough together that they could step from one deck to the other. Samson leaped onto the boat and began to bark. He ran to the side of the boat and his barking grew more frenzied. Bree stepped aboard the old boat, and Libby followed her.

"What's he trying to tell you?" Libby asked.

"It looks like Nicole was here or something of hers is here. He's indicating that area there," Bree said, pointing to the starboard side.

Alec joined them. "That's impossible. She would have had to swim out here and board it. What would be the point?"

"You never use this?" Bree asked.

He shook his head. "Zach uses it sometimes, but he's never met Nicole."

"That we know of," Libby said. She'd rather believe

Zach had a hand in this than the alternative—that Alec was guilty.

"What are you saying?" he asked.

"Is it possible Zach was involved in her kidnapping?" She didn't want to accuse the boy, especially to his own uncle, but the dog's reaction meant something.

"No," Alec said, his voice clipped. "I can't believe you'd even think that."

No one would want to think his nephew would be involved in something so heinous, but Libby couldn't ignore this. "I need to talk to him, Alec. Right away."

"I won't have you accusing him," Alec said. "And based on the reaction of a dog? That's ridiculous."

"Is it? You've admitted that he's been in some trouble."

"Alec, Samson is definitely reacting here," Bree said. "This isn't just some mistake. Nicole was either on this boat, or at the very least, she touched it. He doesn't give false positives."

"Look around," Alec said. "Let's see if there's any other evidence. I can't accuse the boy without tangible evidence."

Her lips tight, Libby opened doors and peered under seats. Under the cushion where Samson stood, her hand touched something soft, and she pulled up a ponytail holder. It still held strands of blond hair. "I have to talk to Zach."

Alec paled. "Don't accuse him of anything," he said. "There has to be some explanation."

"That's all we want," Libby said. "Where is he now?" Zach had left the inn before nine this morning.

"He said he was delivering the supplies for his job and then was going to help do some cleanup around town," Alec said. "There's a group in the square washing the mud off the stores."

He started the engine and guided the boat to the dock. Libby grabbed a post as they neared, then threw the rope around it. She was the first to leap to the boardwalk. Maybe they would find Nicole today.

THIRTY-EIGHT

The townspeople were out in force today. Great strides had been made in the cleanup over the past week. Paint shone clean and free of the mud and mildew. Alec spoke to several neighbors as he searched for his nephew. No one had seen Zach, and Alec began to wonder if the boy had lied about where he was going today.

The business district, such as it was, ended at the juncture of Oyster Road and Bar Harbor Street. A few residents were on Bar Harbor, but Oyster Road just led to the fish house. "Let's check the fish house," he said.

"What's a fish house?" Libby asked, falling into step beside him.

"It's where the fishermen gather and sell their day's catch. Zach likes hanging out there," he said. "I think he feels close to Dave there. I know I do. My brother was always laughing with the other fishermen in there, swapping fishing stories."

The low-slung white building was at the end of a pier where rowboats and water jets docked. He stepped over nets and crab pots on the way to the door of the fish house. The scent of fish was strong.

He nodded to the few men outside the door. "Anyone seen Zach?"

"He's out back helping Rolly unload," one of the men said.

Skirting the building, Alec continued on down the pier, where he found his nephew lifting crab pots off a friend's boat.

When Zach saw him, he frowned. "What's up, Uncle Alec?"

"We need to talk to you. In private." Alec jerked his thumb back toward the street, away from listening ears. Getting a rumor going was all they needed. Zach was getting enough of a reputation as a troublemaker.

Zach wiped his wet hands on his shorts, then slipped on his flip-flops to follow them. He glanced at Libby, who was studying him. "What? Did I suddenly grow horns?" he demanded.

She looked away. "Sorry. We just need to ask you some questions."

They reached the road. There was no one in earshot. Alec put his hands in his pockets. "You know Samson is here to look for Nicole?"

Zach glanced back at the fish house with a longing expression. "Yeah. So?"

"He picked up a scent for her."

That got Zach's attention. "That's good, right?"

Alec nodded. "But the scent is on my old boat. According to the dog, Nicole was on there. So we searched and Libby found something." He glanced at her.

She held out her hand, palm up to expose the pony-tail holder. "This is Nicole's."

Zach went white. He took a step back, then whirled to walk away, but Alec grabbed his arm. He had a sick feeling in the pit of his stomach. "Zach, what did you do?" he whispered.

Zach looked at Alec's hand on his arm. "I didn't do anything. You're always willing to think the worst about me, aren't you?"

"Then how did that hair thing get on my boat?"

Zach bit his lip. "I was going to talk to you about it." His face worked. Then his shoulders slumped. "I just take her supplies," he said. "I didn't know who she was until I saw her picture in the paper last night. Then I didn't know what to do about it."

Libby's face lit. "She's alive? Really, Zach?"

He nodded. "I saw her a couple of days ago. Took her some water and food."

"Where?" Alec asked. He'd figure out what to do about punishing Zach later.

"A little island northwest of here. I have the coordinates."

"Who put her there?"

He shrugged. "I was taking the old boat out to fish. Two guys stopped me and asked if I was looking to make some money. The older man told me that he'd had to stash his crazy sister on an island until he could get her into the hospital he wanted. Said she'd tried to knife him and to be careful because she was dangerous. I was only supposed to drop off supplies every couple of days, then leave."

"That sounds like a fishy story," Alec said.

Zach's lids flickered and he made a face. "He made

it sound plausible. I know now it was stupid for me to believe him, but he gave me all these details and I swallowed his story. And they were paying well."

"Why didn't you tell us when you figured out who she was?"

Zach looked down at the ground. "It was just last night. I wanted to tell you, but I was afraid you'd think I had something to do with it."

"Have they paid you every time you've gone?"

Zach shook his head. "They gave me a thousand dollars to buy food and to pay for my services. They told me what to take her too. I just did what they said."

"I wish you would have trusted me," Alec said. "Come with us. We have to get her."

* * *

Libby could hardly sit still as the boat skimmed the waves. They were so far out to sea that she couldn't see land. Where was that island? She prayed that Nicole was holding on to life, that she would be well and whole when Libby found her.

"Where is it?" Alec asked Zach.

The boy pointed to the horizon, and Libby saw a faint speck that might have been land. They drew closer, and she realized it was a tiny island barely twenty or thirty feet in diameter. How had Nicole survived the hurricane? Libby strained to catch a glimpse of Nicole, but all she saw was a hovel of a building. The place appeared deserted.

"Where is she?" she demanded.

"Maybe in the shack," Zach said. "Though she's usually out as soon as she hears the motor."

Alec took the boat in as close to shore as he could and shut off the engine. Zach tossed the anchor overboard, but by the time it splashed into the water, Libby was already knee-deep in the waves and barreling toward the tiny beach. Bree and Samson were right behind her.

"Nicole!" she shouted.

She rushed to the door of the building and yanked open the door. It took a moment for her eyes to adjust enough to see that the one room held nothing but a few pieces of broken furniture.

"She's not here!" she told Bree, who came in behind her. "Where could she be?" Zach and Alec entered the building.

Zach glanced around. "Her food and water aren't here," he said.

"What does that mean?" Libby asked.

"I brought her a jug of water, peanut butter, canned stuff. None of it is here."

"Has someone else come after her?" Alec asked.

Zach shrugged. "Beats me."

"Who were the men who hired you?" Alec asked. "Didn't you get their names?"

"I didn't know them. One said his name was Oscar Jacobson. The other never told me his name. All I cared about was that they were paying me cash."

"Sounds like a fake name," Alec said.

Bree took Nicole's clothing out of the paper bag and held it under Samson's nose. "Search, boy!"

The dog nosed around the shack, his tail wagging.

He barked at the bed, then ran to the door and around the side of the shack. "He smells her," Bree said.

Libby and Bree followed with the men rushing after them. The dog darted around the island with his nose in the air, then went back to the beach and stood with his tail drooping. He whined when Bree reached him.

"She's not here," Bree said.

"She couldn't have gotten off the island without help," Zach said.

"Look here," Alec said, staring at marks in the sand. "Looks like a raft or something was dragged here."

Bree knelt and touched the indentations. "Could she have built a raft and tried to escape that way?"

"She tried that once before and I found it torn apart on the beach," Zach said. He glanced toward the shack. "Whoa, looks like some of the roof is missing."

"Might she have used the roof for a raft?" Libby asked.

"It would be foolhardy," Alec said. "The ocean is treacherous around here. They don't call it the Graveyard of the Atlantic for no reason. Shoals, rocks—all kinds of things can tear a boat or a raft to pieces in a heartbeat. Would she be foolish enough to try that, Libby?"

She tried not to take offense at his question. "It's not foolhardy to try to escape kidnappers," she said. "Who knows when they might come back?" She turned to Bree. "Could Samson help us find her?"

"Maybe. It's a big ocean out there. He's lost her scent right now, but we could go out and see if he smells anything."

"That's our only option," Libby said. Her voice broke and she swallowed hard. What if Nicole was already capsized and drowning, crying out for help? The thought sent her rushing to the boat. "Come on! We have to find Nicole."

The rest of the crew ran after her, and in moments they were cruising the waves again. Bree gave Samson another refresher sniff, and the dog had his nose in the air. He strained at the bow of the boat. Alec crossed back and forth in front of the area where they'd seen the markings in the sand. Then Samson's tail began to wag. He barked furiously and strained out over the water until Libby thought he might fall in.

"He's got a scent!" Bree called. "Good boy," she crooned. His tail drooped as the boat headed west. "Wrong direction," Bree said. "Try north."

Alec corrected his course, and the dog's countenance perked again. Libby went up to sit by her friend.

Bree saw her and squeezed her hand. "We'll find Nicole."

"I just hope we're not too late."

"I'm praying and I'm sure you are too."

"I am," Libby admitted. "Constantly. But I'm so afraid."

"Put it in God's hands. He loves Nicole. He's out there in the big ocean with her."

The thought comforted Libby. Nicole wasn't alone. No matter what happened, God held her securely.

THIRTY-NINE

The sun beat down on Nicole's head as she sat on her raft. Her skin was tight and hot, and she knew she was going to be hurting from a sunburn later. There was still no land in sight, and she wasn't even sure if she was floating farther out into the Atlantic or nearer to the mainland. All she could do was cling to the boards and hope. How long had she been here? She slanted a glance at the sky. Three hours.

Her food had made the trip past the breakers all right, but though her tummy rumbled, she wanted to save what she had since there was no telling how long she might be adrift. She wiped her forehead and stared at the horizon. Nothing. Her lids grew heavy, and she decided to sleep if she could. On her stomach with her head pillowed in her arms, she listened to the lapping of the waves and felt the gentle rise of the swells under her raft.

Where was Libby now? Her eyes grew heavy and she let them close. Sleep was good.

She wasn't sure what awakened her. Sitting up, she rubbed her eyes. The sun was lower in the sky. It must be nearly four or five. Then she heard it. The sound of an engine. She turned toward the *putt-putt* and saw a boat growing closer in the distance. Leaping to her feet, she screamed and waved her hands. An answering shout came from the boat. Was that Libby? Nicole strained to see. It was!

"Libby, I'm here, I'm here!" Jumping up and down, she could barely breathe for joy.

Nicole recognized only Zach and Libby in the boat. Another man drove, and a woman with a dog stood in the bow. Zach must have realized she was telling the truth and gotten help. She would have to thank him.

The boat reached her raft. The man's strong grip clasped her arm and helped her climb the ladder to the deck, where she collapsed.

Libby sank down beside her and grabbed her in an almost painful grip. "Nicole, I thought they killed you." Her voice was choked.

Tears poured down Nicole's face, and she clung to Libby. "I knew you'd find me. I just knew it."

The two remained locked in an embrace for several seconds, then Libby pulled away and stared at Nicole. "Who did this to you?"

"I don't know. I can't remember anything. I woke up on the island and I've been there ever since. Alone, except when Zach brought supplies."

Libby hugged her again. "I'm so glad to see you. We found your flip-flops and cover-up. Everyone told me you were dead, but I didn't believe it."

"I knew you'd never give up on me," Nicole whispered. "You've always been a rock."

"Let's get you home," Libby said. "We'll get a doctor and make sure you're all right."

Nicole rubbed her belly. "And real food. I'd love a chicken quesadilla."

"I think we can find one of those," the handsome man said.

Nicole glanced at Libby, who was blushing. She was going to have to question her friend about her relationship with the guy.

* * *

After Nicole's checkup at the doctor's office, Tom asked her questions until Libby insisted her friend needed some food and rest. Libby took Nicole to the restaurant while Alec and Bree stayed behind to talk to Tom. Libby was filled with gratitude as she watched Nicole eat. It was a true miracle that they'd found her. Libby filled her in on the events of the nine days.

"Who's the guy?" Nicole asked.

Libby hated the way her cheeks heated at the mention of Alec. "Alec Bourne, Zach's uncle."

"You like him?"

How did she answer that? *Like* wasn't the most accurate word. "Well, he's been a big help. He's been right on the front lines helping to look for you."

"Even though his nephew kept me confined to that island?"

"He didn't know anything about it."

"Are you sure?" Nicole put down her fork. "Wouldn't Zach have been gone? Wouldn't he have taken the boat?

Surely Alec would have asked what he was doing with the boat."

How would she make her friend see? "He's a good man, Nicole. I think you'll like him."

Nicole's eyes flashed. "I don't want to know him, that's for sure. I want to get out of this place and back to Virginia Beach now."

Libby opened her mouth to agree, then shut it again. The thought of leaving this island left a pit in her belly. "We have work to do here. I've started work on the lifesaving station. And have you seen those lighthouse ruins? I love it out there."

Nicole rubbed her forehead. "There's something about those ruins. When I think of them, I get a funny feeling in my stomach."

"Fear?"

Nicole shook her head. "Not fear exactly. Excitement maybe. Oh, why can't I remember?"

Libby reached across the table to squeeze Nicole's hand. "The doctor said you might not ever remember. He doesn't know what drug they used on you, but it might have wiped out that time period permanently. So don't stress about it. If you remember, great. But right now all I care about is that you're here and well."

"I'd like to see the lighthouse ruins. Maybe seeing them will help me remember."

Libby released her hand and signaled for the check. "Do you remember talking to me in front of the beach cam?"

"No." Her eyes widened. "Have you been working

any of our projects besides the station? And have you heard from Rooney?"

"Your investor?" Libby shook her head. "I've been out of the office looking for you."

"You've been checking in, of course?"

"Of course. But no messages from him have come in."

"How strange. He's been pushing so hard for me to get the deal sewed up here."

"He's been trying to buy that property for years, from what I understand."

"I never had a chance to tell him that you own the property he wants and not your brother."

Something about the reference to Rooney nudged at her. Then it hit her. "His first name is Lawrence, isn't it?"

Nicole nodded. "And don't call him Larry. He hates that. It has to be Lawrence. Why?"

Libby told her about the notes she found in Tina's room. "L could stand for Lawrence."

"Or Laban, Lance, Levi, Lloyd, or any number of other names," Nicole said. "Even Libby! That's a stretch to think that Lawrence might be implicated in Tina's death."

"Maybe not. Vanessa and Brent said he was with Tina not long before she disappeared."

"He's going to want to talk to you. You own that property, Libby! You're rich."

"Only if I sell it."

"Of course you're going to sell it. Think of what it would mean. We could expand the business. Or rather I could. You'd never have to work a lick again."

The two of them were worlds apart now, even though they'd only been separated for a couple of weeks. "I've been learning there are more important things than money," Libby said.

"You've changed. It's that guy, right?"

Libby shook her head. "It's my dad." She began to tell her friend about the kind of man Ray had been and all that she'd learned, but Nicole's expression only grew more incredulous.

Explaining a sea change to someone was impossible. Nicole would just have to learn about it by watching her.

* * *

Though she should have been exhausted, Libby couldn't sleep. She finally gave up and went up the steps to her father's third-floor retreat at the Tidewater Inn. The light in the room was already on. Brent was sitting on the sofa with their father's Bible in his hand.

Her first impulse was to demand it back, but she restrained herself and smiled and joined him on the sofa. "Couldn't sleep either?"

He shook his head. "I like to come up here. I feel closer to Dad."

"Me too." Had he been reading Scripture? She hoped so. "I'm sorry I suspected you of hurting Nicole, Brent. I hope you can forgive me."

His brows rose. "It was understandable."

"Will you forgive me?"

"I'm not even sure I know what that means." He rubbed his forehead. "I quit going to church with Dad when I was fifteen. I thought I was too old and wise to swallow all that stuff." He stared at her. "But I've been watching you, Libby. You're different, just like he was. Maybe I'll go back to church."

Her throat closed. If only she could believe she'd had an eternal impact on this brother she longed to love. Her gaze fell on the Bible. *Give it to him.* She resisted the internal nudge. Did she have to give up everything dear to her?

Give it to him.

Her shoulders sagged. How could she resist God? "Would you like to have Dad's Bible?"

His eyes widened. "I know how much you love it. You come up here and read it all the time."

"I know. But there are special passages he's marked that might mean even more to you than they do to me." She leaned toward him and flipped to a high-lighted verse in the worn book. "This is my favorite. Psalm 37:25. 'I have been young, and now am old; Yet I have not seen the righteous forsaken, Nor his descendants begging bread.' I know I'm not old yet, but I believe we are blessed because our father was a righteous man."

Brent's Adam's apple bobbed. "I know that's true." He clutched the Bible to his chest. "Thank you, Libby. I'll never forget this."

* * *

The sun was just coming up, casting a glorious display over the water. Alec sat on the porch railing and inhaled the scent of the sea. The door opened behind him, and he turned to see Libby stepping out dressed in hot-pink sweats with her hair up in a ponytail.

"Couldn't sleep?" he asked. "It's only six."

She shook her head. "It seems incredible that we found Nicole. Thank you for all you did for us."

"I'm glad it turned out so well." He averted his gaze. She was way too pretty this morning. Her eyes shone with excitement. "What's on the agenda for the day?"

"I'm going to go out to the lighthouse ruins with Nicole if she feels up to it. I'm hoping being out there will jog her memory in some way."

"I'll come with you."

She smiled and nodded. "We won't be gone long. I want to show her what I've gotten done on the lifesaving station too. We have a business to run, and it's been neglected for almost two weeks."

She would be leaving soon. He saw it in her expression. "Have you decided what you're going to do about the inn?"

She settled beside him on the rail. "Not yet. I don't want to sell it, but I don't see that I have a choice."

He wanted to protest again, but it wasn't his call. "Uh, could I take you to dinner tonight at Kill Devil Hills? We could take the boat and go to Port O' Call. They've got great crab legs and she-crab soup."

Her smile came immediately. "I'd like that."

The door opened again. Vanessa and Pearl joined them. "I thought we were the only ones up early," Vanessa said.

"You got in late last night. I heard your door after I'd

gone to bed for the second time," Libby said. "I wanted to talk to you, but I was too sleepy to get up again."

"Oh?" Vanessa sat on the top step. Pearl pulled a rocker closer.

Libby leaned against the post. "I wanted to ask you about Tina's meeting with Lawrence Rooney. Did she ever tell our dad what he wanted?"

"You knew about that meeting?" Pearl asked Vanessa. Her voice was high and strained.

Vanessa nodded. "We were there with Mom and Mr. Rooney."

"His first name is Lawrence," Libby said.

Vanessa gasped and straightened. "They talked outside for a minute, and I heard her tell him to leave her alone. I thought it was because he was pestering her about selling the inn. But do you think . . . ?"

Pearl sighed. "He was engaged to Tina when Ray first met her," she said.

Vanessa gasped. "Mom was engaged to another man?"

Pearl nodded. "It was quite the scandal for a while. Tina came to town for a two-week visit with her grandmother and met Ray. It was love at first sight for them both. She broke off her engagement to Lawrence and was married to Ray three months later."

"I imagine Rooney didn't take that very well," Libby said.

"I think Tina was actually a little afraid of him. He threatened to ruin Ray."

Libby leaned forward. "He wrote that note I found in your closet!"

"Who can say for sure, Libby? But yes. It was likely his

doing. He's always been powerful, even back then. His family owns a lot of properties. Ray tried to meet with him about Tina, but Lawrence refused. Over the years he's been a thorn in Ray's side on occasion. He's wanted the Tidewater Inn for all this time. I wouldn't be surprised if he thought he could get Tina back too, at some point along the way. He was an annoyance, of course. But I never thought he would harm your mother."

"I bet he wrote those notes we found in Tina's jewelry box," Libby said to her sister.

Alec shifted on his perch. "Tom needs to know about this. I bet he's going to want to talk to Nicole about Rooney. I'll run into town and talk to him. I'll meet you out at the ruins later, Libby."

* * *

Libby flopped on the sand beside her friend and drew in a deep breath. The long run to the lighthouse had tuckered her out. She turned her head and smiled at Nicole. Her heart overflowed with thankfulness. Nicole was alive! What a wonderful miracle and blessing from God. Nicole had begun to remember what happened to her too, but the men who kidnapped her weren't familiar.

She sat up and inhaled the clear air. "What happened here?"

Nicole stood, dusting the sand from her palms. "I came here the morning before I was kidnapped. Vanessa was going to bring me to see the ruins, but I was too eager to wait on her. I figured I'd let her show me around like I hadn't seen it. There's more here than you know though."

"The cave?"

Nicole nodded. "You know about it?"

Libby pointed toward the cellar opening. "We found it after we saw the cellar."

"Then you know about the treasure?"

"Treasure? All we found was poor Tina."

Nicole smiled. "Want to see? You're going to be excited."

"You're being very mysterious," Libby said, following her friend. "Where is it?"

"In the caves. Just outside the entrance to the cellar. You're going to love this."

"You know about the cellar?" Libby asked.

Nicole nodded. "I found a map in your dad's Bible."

Libby followed Nicole back into the water. They waded through a shallow pool to the base of the rocks.

"You have to dive here to see the opening," Nicole said. She took off her shorts and top to reveal her bikini. "I was snorkeling here and just happened to find it. It's not hard though. Follow me." She held her breath and ducked under the water.

Libby stripped to her one-piece suit and followed. The opening was barely big enough to wiggle through. Nicole disappeared through the hole and Libby went right behind her, determined not to let her friend out of sight. They surfaced in a cave about twenty feet in diameter. The ceiling was ten feet from the surface of the water. Several holes in the rocks illuminated the space, though Libby had to squint to see.

"Bet it gets tight in here during high tide," Libby said.

Nicole nodded. "I wouldn't want to be here then." She swam to the other side and hefted herself onto a flat rock. "This way."

"I can't believe you came in here."

"I had a flashlight with me that day," Nicole said. "Wait until you see this though." She rose and went to the curving wall. "Someone put everything we need right here."

Libby heard a rasp, then light flared from a match. Moments later a light was flickering. "What on earth?" She heaved herself out of the water and went to where Nicole stood. "Someone has put candles and matches in here?"

"Look how old the candlesticks are," Nicole said.

Libby examined it. "It's bronze. Looks late sixteen hundreds maybe."

"It goes with the other things I found. Follow me."

Nicole led her down a long narrow passageway. The sound of dripping became stronger. The floor was damp and slippery under Libby's feet. At one juncture her inclination was to go right, but Nicole led her left.

"Where are we going?"

"The other room is this way. Almost there."

The candle cast flickering shadows onto the wall. Libby wanted to be back in the sunlight instead of this dark, dank place.

Nicole dropped to her knees. "Now we have to crawl."

"How on earth did you find this?"

"I dropped something right here. It rolled under this

ledge and I found the opening." Nicole and the light disappeared under the rocky ledge.

Panicked at being left in the dark, Libby hurried after her and emerged into a larger cave. The candle did little to illuminate what felt like a vast space. A moment later another candle flared to life.

"Look around," Nicole said, smiling. She handed Libby another candle.

This candlestick was also old. Libby held it high and turned toward some objects on the wall to her right. Artifacts leaped out at her: a ship's bell, candlesticks, tin plates and cups, several portholes and helm items. Several cannons were in a jumble. There were many objects she didn't recognize.

She stepped closer. "What is this room?"

"I think it was a headquarters for Edward Teach."

"Blackbeard? Come on, Nicole."

"Look." Nicole stepped to the jumble and held her candle close to the ship's bell. The words *Queen Anne's Revenge* were engraved on the brass.

"Blackbeard's pride and joy," Libby said.

"I found a ship's log too. It says it's Teach's. But I don't see it now. Funny—the stash is smaller than I remember. This stuff is probably worth a fortune to museums. There's no gold or jewels but a wealth of information."

This rich history was more exciting to Libby than gold coins. "I bet the government will want to make this a protected area. Either a state park or a federal one."

"Probably. Archaeologists will have to confirm the artifacts' authenticity, but it all looks real to me."

"But the ship sank offshore somewhere around here. Wouldn't the bell have gone down with it?"

Nicole turned. "You're right. I hadn't thought about that. Did someone find the wreck and bring these things up?"

"Maybe. But this place might be more than a storage room. There are wooden bunks and old blankets. What's left of them anyway." Libby turned to stare at her friend. "It's going to take some professionals to figure this out. Did anyone know you found this? Maybe finding this was why someone wanted to shut you up."

"I don't think so. I only told Horace."

"I think we won't tell the professionals," a man said from behind them. "We won't tell anyone."

Both women whirled. Horace stood with a gun held casually in his hand.

"Horace?" Libby's gaze went to the gun in his hand. "What's this all about?"

"I can't let you ruin all my plans," Horace said. "I'm sorry. I didn't want it to come to this, but you leave me no choice."

Libby saw the determination on his face. "Nicole, the lights!" she screamed as she snuffed hers out between her forefinger and thumb. At the same time she threw herself atop her friend, and Nicole's light went out too. The cave was plunged into darkness. Then a bright light flashed from the gun.

FORTY

Alec told his cousin what he'd discovered about Lawrence Rooney. Tom called the state police in New York, and they agreed to pick up Rooney and question him about Tina's death. Alec thanked Tom and returned to the inn. The visit had taken longer than he'd expected, so he thought the women would be back from their outing to the lighthouse ruins.

He found Bree on the beach with Samson. "Is Libby back yet?"

She shook her head. "I haven't seen them. How long have they been gone?"

"A couple of hours."

"I cried just watching their reunion," Bree said. She rubbed Samson's head. "Reminds me of when I found Davy after thinking for a year that he was dead."

Alec had heard the story. "I have to admit, I thought Nicole was dead. Libby never gave up hope though."

Bree's smile held amusement. "It shows, you know."

"What shows?"

"How you feel about Libby."

His face warmed. "She's a friend."

Bree laughed. "She's more than that and you know it."

"Maybe she *could* be. We'll see where our relationship goes."

Kade and the children came to join them on the beach. Samson rushed to them and licked Hannah's face. The little girl giggled and threw her arms around his neck. The older boy, Davy, ran ahead and splashed into the waves up to his knees. Alec's gaze lingered on the children. He'd always wanted a houseful of kids. What did Libby think about children?

He glanced at his watch. Where were they? Though they could just be lingering at the ruins, he felt a sense of unease. "I think I'll walk toward the lighthouse and intercept them. Lunch will be ready soon, so I'm sure they must be heading this way."

Bree's green eyes crinkled with amusement. "Have fun. I think I'll take the kids to build a sand castle." She put her arm around Kade's waist. "I haven't seen this big guy in days."

He hugged her back. "The twins have been asking for Mommy."

Alec went the other direction. The sand was soft, and he kicked off his sandals. When he still hadn't seen the women after ten minutes, he began to quicken his pace. Some unexplainable anxiety gnawed at his belly.

Someone had put Nicole on that island for a purpose. What if the women had stumbled into more danger? He broke into a run and was breathing heavily by the time he reached the ruins. There was no movement but the rustle of leaves in the maritime forest. The place was deserted, though he saw Libby's and Nicole's clothes on the beach.

He cupped his hands around his mouth. "Libby, Nicole!" His voice rose above the murmur of the waves. He listened, but there was no answering shout.

He walked to the water. The tide was going out, so their footprints were still intact in the sand. The footprints went into the water and didn't come out. What had happened here? Did they swim out to board a boat? If so, why weren't they back at the inn? And why did they leave their clothes? Not for the first time, he wished his cell phone would work on the island.

"Libby!" he shouted again. Where could she be?

He waded a few feet into the water. The waves were gentle today. He glanced at the rocks. The cave. Could the women have gone into it? Libby had said Nicole was an avid spelunker. Maybe she'd coaxed Libby into going in. It would explain the footprints leading back to the water. Could they have gotten trapped in there?

He sloshed through the waves to the mouth of the cave. He peered in but saw nothing. He shouted for Libby. His voice echoed off the stone walls, but he heard nothing. He exited the cave and waded to shore. The cellar door was closed. He opened it and descended as far into the darkness as he could, then shouted again. Still no answer.

Adrenaline gave Alec the energy he needed to make the run back to the inn. He was going to need Samson to help find the women.

* * *

The sound of water dripping penetrated the woozy feeling in Libby's head. She opened her eyes and blinked. A couple of candles flickered in the darkness. "Nicole?" she called out. Where was her friend?

"I'm here," a small voice said to her right.

Libby turned her head and saw Nicole against the wall. Her hands were tied in front of her. "Are you all right?"

"Yes. How do you feel?"

Libby's wrists were bound together. She raised them and touched her throbbing head. Her fingers came away sticky. "I'm bleeding. I think I hit my head."

"He shot you. Horace shot you." Nicole's voice rose.

Libby touched her head again and discovered a furrow. "The bullet just grazed me. I'm okay. The bleeding is stopping."

Clang. The noise across the room drew her attention, and she focused her bleary eyes as Horace used a sledgehammer on the wall.

He paused to wipe his brow. "Sorry about this, girls. I didn't want to hurt Nicole, and I really liked you, Libby. So I'm going to let the sea have you."

"I don't understand," she said, struggling to think through the roaring in her head.

"When I get this hole through, the tide will fill this cave. All evidence will be drowned. And no one will ever discover this cave full of secrets."

"But why? What harm could it do to let the world know about these artifacts?"

When he shrugged and began to pound again, she tried to think of what might happen if the world knew about this place. It would be an attraction to tourists. Knowing what she did about historical preservation, she was sure the government would take it over and run it as well. The state would want to preserve it, likely as a park. How could that be worth murder?

Kenneth Poe. She thought of what he'd said. *This* would be the spot of the new resort. But not if the state had the land. In fact, there would have to be access to the area. There would be no room for a huge resort complex on this side of the island. Poe's investor would not be allowed to purchase it.

Horace was an attorney. Had he been hired to help make sure the deal went through? Was he a partner with Lawrence Rooney? It made sense.

She waited until he stopped pounding again. "You're helping Poe? There's no crime in helping to close a sale."

"You think that's what he wants me to do?" Horace barked a laugh.

Libby weighed this revelation. And then the truth clicked.

"He knows you're a diver. He's paying you to get this stuff out of the cave before the state learns about it and steps in."

He stepped closer. "I don't expect you to sympathize, but I'm nearly bankrupt. Everything was sliding out of my fingers. The money I can get for this loot will save me. I'll be able to keep my boy at Harvard. I won't lose my house in Saint Croix. If this deal goes south, I'm finished. I'll have nothing left. I can't let that happen."

"And an old ship's bell is worth murdering two

people?" Libby couldn't wrap her head around that kind of thinking. "Then why even tell me about the inheritance? You could have destroyed that will and let Brent and Vanessa inherit. They were going to sell to Lawrence."

His eyes narrowed. "That was my intention."

Libby caught her breath. "But Mindy mentioned it to Nicole."

"Stupid woman can't keep her mouth shut. I should have fired her long ago."

Libby struggled to get up and couldn't. "You can always start over somewhere else. Life isn't over just because your money is gone."

He seemed to be listening for a moment, then he shook his head. "It's gone too far now. If you live, you'll turn me in. I'll go to prison. My boy will have to quit college. My wife will have no support. Her family is all gone and I'm all she has. I'm sorry, but it has to be this way."

"We won't say a word, will we, Nicole?" Libby managed a smile. "I like you, Horace. Don't do something you'll never be able to live with."

His eyes filled with confusion, then he stepped back. "We both know you're just trying to save yourself. The minute you got home, you'd be calling Tom. I'm sorry. I really liked your father, you know. I'm glad he's not alive to know about this."

"He's watching from heaven," Libby said. "You think you're doing this in secret? The Bible says we are surrounded by a great cloud of witnesses. And God sees everything."

Horace swallowed. "Don't you understand? I have no choice."

"There is always a choice to do right."

"Not this time. I'm boxed into a corner." He turned back to his task and began to whack at the wall again.

"Wait! You'll destroy all this treasure!"

He paused and turned back toward her again. "I got out what I could, but what's left is nothing compared to my family. And if you hadn't been snooping, I would have had time to transfer all of it to my basement. All but the cannons. So you have no one to blame but yourself." He lifted the sledgehammer again.

Thwack! Thwack! Two strikes from his sledgehammer and the wall began to crumble. He continued to pound until the hole was about three feet in diameter.

"I made it as large as I could so the end is quicker," he said. He dropped the sledgehammer. "Do you want the candles extinguished, or do you want to watch the water pour in? I want this to be as easy for you both as possible."

"Leave them lit, please," Libby said, trying to keep the panic from her voice.

Nicole began to struggle. "Please don't leave us here!"

Regret showed in Horace's eyes. "I'm so sorry," he said. "If I had any other option, I'd take it. God forgive me." He plunged through the door that led to the lighthouse cellar. Moments later the door shuddered and a deadbolt slammed home.

Though her ankles were bound, Libby began to struggle again and finally managed to get to her feet. "We've got to find a way to cut these ropes!" She jumped her way to the wall of artifacts. Surely there was a knife here somewhere. Or an ax. "Help me, Nicole!"

Nicole was crying, but she got on all fours, then managed to get upright. "We can't die here. I don't want to drown!"

"Stay calm," Libby said. "And pray." With her wrists tied together, all she could manage was an awkward sorting through of the artifacts. Bowls, cups, nothing sharp. "There's nothing here," she said.

She glanced toward the door. But no, she'd heard it lock. "Maybe we can hop out through the cave."

"We won't be able to swim."

"Alec will come looking for us. I know he'll look there."

As they moved toward the passage, water began to rush through the opening, faster and faster until the water was swirling around their ankles.

"Libby!" Nicole screamed.

FORTY-ONE

His lungs burning from his run, Alec stopped to catch his breath. He saw Bree and Kade still down the beach a ways. Brent was with them too. "Bree!" He broke into a run again.

She leaped to her feet when she saw him coming. "What's wrong? Where are the girls?"

"Missing." His breath heaving, Alec told her and Kade what he'd found. "Can we take Samson back to search?"

She snapped her fingers for the dog. "Right away." She glanced at Kade with an appeal on her face.

"Go, hon, I've got the kids. I'll be praying."

Relief flooded Bree's face. "You're the best. I'll grab Samson's vest from the SUV." She rushed up the hill to the drive.

"Bring flashlights," Kade called after her.

Brent's eyes were shadowed. "Libby's all right, isn't she?"

"I hope so."

Brent turned and looked out to sea, then back at Alec. "I need to tell you something. I wasn't sure before, but remember that diver who tried to drown Libby?"

"Yes."

"I saw what looked like a bite on Horace's arm the other day. I saw him out at the lighthouse yesterday too. He was in his diving gear. I watched him through the binoculars, but I couldn't tell what he was doing. But he disappeared for a while under the rocks. I think there's a cave there."

Alec couldn't imagine that the jolly, absentminded attorney could be dangerous. "Maybe it just looked like a bite. Horace wouldn't hurt Libby or Nicole. I know about the cave, but I looked in there too."

"I suspect there's more there than you know. He was in there a long time and came out carrying a bag of something."

Bree returned with the flashlights and Samson's vest. "Ready?"

Alec took the flashlights. "Let's go. Thanks for the information, Brent. Tell Tom what you know. Come on, Bree. We'll take the boat." He turned and ran for the dinghy bobbing at the dock. He told himself Libby and Nicole were probably fine, but he didn't really believe his own reassurances. Something was wrong. Libby wouldn't worry them intentionally.

When they finally reached the ruins, he pointed to the cave. "There. The entrance to the cave is there." The boat scraped bottom. He leaped over the side and dragged it onto the sand, then handed Bree one of the flashlights. "Will Samson go in a cave?"

"Sure." She snapped her fingers. "He can sniff their clothes." Kneeling, she pointed to the pile of clothing without touching it. His tail wagging, Samson sniffed the clothing. "Search, boy!"

Samson whined, then his nose went up. He criss-crossed the beach, then barked and splashed into the water toward the rocks. "He's got a scent," Bree said.

Alec ran after him. "I had a feeling they were in there. But I called and they didn't answer." His gut clenched. What if someone had killed and dumped them? He pushed away the unspeakable thought.

The dog had reached the cave opening but seemed unsure about how to enter. Alec ducked down, then clambered onto the ledge. He was dripping wet and realized he'd lost his flip-flops. "Come on, boy. Here, Samson."

Whining, Samson looked back toward Bree. "I'm going too," she told him. She splashed through the opening, then joined Alec on the ledge. "Come on, Samson."

The dog barked, then ducked his head and was inside. Bree helped the dog onto the ledge. Alec switched on the flashlight. The beam pushed back the shadows. "Libby, Nicole!" His shout rebounded off the walls and back at him. The cave floor was cold under his bare feet.

"Search, boy," Bree urged. She flipped on her flash-light as well and joined Alec. After a few minutes of walking, Samson's tail drooped. "Samson seems to have lost the scent," she said.

Alec pointed with his light down the passage. "The cellar is that way, but I checked the cellar."

"Let's check again anyway."

"Okay, this way." He illuminated their path with the

light and led her toward the cellar. A few minutes later, they stood at the door. "Nothing," he said.

"I noticed what looked like a narrow passageway deeper into the rock a ways back. Let's check it out," Bree said.

"I didn't see it." He followed her back until she stopped and shone her light.

"There," she said. "It's narrow, but I think we can get through."

The passage seemed more a crack in the rock. He'd be able to get through, but just barely. "Would they have gone down there? They had no light."

"They might have seen it anyway."

He nodded. "I'll go first." He squeezed through the opening and found that the passageway widened to an even bigger space than the path that led to the cellar. "It's okay!"

Bree came through with Samson on her heels. "Search, Samson."

The dog wagged his tail and trotted forward, but it was clear that he hadn't picked up the scent again. Alec was beginning to feel discouraged. "This is leading through the rock to the ocean on the other side. I doubt we can go much farther." He tipped his head. "Hear that?"

Bree listened too. "Sounds like rushing water. You're probably right. We're going to find an opening into the sea up ahead. We might as well go back." She half turned, then Samson barked. He shot forward. "He's got a scent!"

Alec jerked forward into a run. The dog disappeared around the corner. Alec caught up with him in front of a locked door. There was a padlock on it, and water was pouring from under it. He pounded on it. "Libby!"

Samson's barking was frenzied. "She's close," Bree said. "Libby! Nicole!"

The roar of the water that they had heard was beyond this door. He had to get it open. There was nothing to use to bust off the lock. He heard a woman scream and he tensed. "Libby!" He jerked on the lock, but though it was rusty, it held. He didn't even have a shoe to help.

The flashlight! It was metal. "Hold your light on it," he ordered Bree. She shined the light onto the lock. He battered it with the flashlight that was in his hand, but the lock didn't budge. Moments later, his flashlight was in pieces.

Someone pounded on the other side of the door. Libby cried out, "We're here, Alec! The room is flooding. We're going to drown!"

"There's a lock on the door. I can't get it off. Hang on!" He turned around, looking for a rock, angry with himself that he hadn't thought of that before now.

Bree grabbed his hand. "There's no time! Look!" She pointed and he realized water was seeping out the sides of the door.

He clenched his hands. How was he going to save her?

* * *

Water was pouring through the opening Horace had made. It was now up to Libby's calves. She pounded on the door. "Help us, Alec!" Panic threatened to steal her power to reason. *Breathe.* She took a deep breath, then another. There had to be a way out of here.

Nicole had hopped along the cave floor to join Libby at the door. Her face was grim in the light of the flickering candle. The water was only a few inches from where the candle sat on a chest. When it was gone, Libby wouldn't be able to see Nicole's face.

"Lord, help us," she prayed.

"Are we going to die?" Nicole whispered. "I'm not like you. I never go to church. I haven't given God a thought through most of my life. I'm not ready to die, especially not with all I've done."

Peace seeped into Libby's soul. Whatever happened, God saw them. He held them close in his arms. "All you have to do is ask him to forgive you, Nicole. He's here with us. No matter what happens."

Nicole was sobbing. "I can't. I don't know how." She leaned against Libby.

The weight of her friend's body pressed against her, and Libby lurched to the side. When she did, she heard something splash into the water. Horace's sledgehammer. Had he left it behind? It could knock loose the lock. Would it fit under the door?

She pressed her lips to the crack in the door. "Alec, are you there?"

"I'm here. We're looking for a rock."

"I'm going to try to slide a sledgehammer under the

door. Hang on." She knelt and grabbed the tool with her bound hands. The water was to her neck. She tried to slip it under the door. It stuck. "It won't fit!"

"Try turning it the other way," Nicole said. "Or slide it to a different spot. The bottom of the door isn't even."

Libby did as Nicole suggested. The water was rising fast. It was to her lips and the salt burned the cracks in her skin. She had to submerge to get enough leverage to push the tool. The sledgehammer moved under the door's edge. Almost there. She jiggled it and slid it a few inches the other way. She felt a tug, then Alec pulled it away.

Gasping, she surfaced and sucked in air, but she had to float on her back to get it. The water was above her nose if she stayed on her knees. How could she regain her feet?

"Got it!" Alec yelled. "Step away from the door."

Libby tried to struggle back, but she was only able to move a few inches at a time with the water swirling around her bound hands and feet. "Move away, Nicole," she said as the door shuddered and rebounded with pounding on the other side.

The water was to Nicole's chest. She hopped away, managing to stay on her feet. Hanging on to Nicole's leg, Libby tried to get to her feet but couldn't. The candles sputtered and went out. The darkness wasn't quite complete because a little light came in from the hole where the water poured through. She released Nicole's leg and tried to float. The water seemed to be roaring into the cave now. The sound filled her ears, blocking out all thought. It was like floating in eternity, and she suspected she was about to die. She felt no fear though.

She reached her bound arms over her head, and her fingers touched Nicole's arm. Feeling her way to her friend's hand, she realized the water was nearly to Nicole's neck. The end would be soon. "Please make it painless for Nicole, Lord," she whispered. "Receive us into your arms. Pray, Nicole."

She inhaled what she thought would be her last air, then a strong hand grabbed her around the waist. Alec's lips were against her ear.

"I've got you," he said.

"Nicole!"

"Bree has her. Let's get out of here." He propelled her through the water. "Hold your breath," he said. "We have to dive."

The roof of the cave was just above her. She sucked in as much air as she could manage, then nodded. With his arm around her waist, they dived. She opened her eyes, ignoring the stinging saltiness of the water. The dim light from the opening was just ahead. She saw Bree go through it with Nicole. *Thank you, God.*

Her head bumped the side of the opening, then Alec maneuvered them both through. The current caught them as they exited into open water. Her lungs began to burn with the need for oxygen. She cast her gaze upward. The top of the waves seemed so far away. She wasn't sure she could make it. Her panicked glance at Alec caused him to propel them faster.

Just when she thought she would have to inhale water, her head broke the surface. She dragged in air, then choked when a wave splashed her in the face. Alec still had his arm around her, and they floated in the waves.

He cupped her face with his hands as they floated. "I thought I'd lost you." He kissed her.

She clutched him and kissed him back, relishing the heat that swept through her veins, exulting in the fact that she was very much alive. When he lifted his head, she was even more breathless. "Where are Nicole and Bree?"

"On shore. I can see them." He turned her in the water so she could see her friend waving. Bree and Samson were with her. Libby's limbs went weak.

"Let me see if I can loosen these ropes." He tore at the knots, then shook his head. "They'll have to be cut off. I'll help you." With his arm around her, they began to swim toward the shore.

It was slow going with only one of them able to propel them. She tried to pretend her bound legs were the fin of a mermaid, but it was awkward. Her muscles burned by the time her foot touched sand. Alec lifted her in his arms and staggered to shore with her, where they collapsed in a heap on the beach.

Samson licked her face and barked. "Good boy," she crooned. Nicole dropped to her knees beside her and burst into tears. "It's all right," Libby said. "We're safe."

FORTY-TWO

Tidewater Inn was even more beautiful after Libby's brush with death. It was home already. But what was she going to do about the mansion? She loved it so, but she couldn't afford to keep it up. As Alec guided the boat to the pier, she soaked in the sight of the lovely old Georgian house. She'd never own something so wonderful again.

"Libby!" Vanessa waved from the porch and ran down the curving steps.

Libby nearly fell off the pier when her sister grabbed her and held on as though she'd never let go. "Vanessa?"

"You're okay! I was so afraid when I heard you'd disappeared."

Libby hugged her back. "We're both fine."

Alec hovered at her side as though he feared letting her out of his sight.

"I'll talk to you later," Bree said. "I need to check on the children." Smiling, she went toward the house with Samson at her heels.

Libby followed with Alec close beside her. She wished she dared to reach out and take his hand.

Vanessa was still smiling. "Everyone is inside. The pastor came over to lead us in prayer for your safety."

Libby's gaze went to the necklace around Vanessa's neck. Maybe she'd really begun to think about what it meant. "We needed the prayers more than you know." She told Vanessa what had happened as they walked to the house.

Vanessa stopped at the base of the steps. "I know I've been nasty to you, Libby. I'm ashamed of myself when I remember all the terrible things I said. I'm sorry."

"You were in pain," Libby said. "I understand."

Vanessa shook her head. "I don't deserve for you to let me off the hook so easily. I know we have a long way to go, Libby, but I realized today when I thought you might be dead that I wanted you around. I want to learn what makes you laugh and cry. I want to try to learn to like reggae."

Libby smiled. "I'm not promising anything about oysters, but I'll try."

"It's a deal. You're not leaving, are you? You're staying here?"

Libby's smile faded. "I think I have to sell this place, Vanessa. There's no money for repairs." She gestured to the roof. "Look at the rot going on around the eaves. It's going to take a lot of money to fix it. But I'll split the sale price with you and Brent."

Alec tensed beside her. She wanted to explain her decision, but there was no way to make him understand.

Vanessa shook her head. "I realized today that if this place goes, everything will change. Brent argues that it will be change for the better, but I don't think so. There would be no more long walks on a nearly empty beach. No more pure sound of the waves and wind." Her voice broke. "There has to be another way. How much would it cost to fix it? I have an inheritance. I'll help."

Though the offer touched her, Libby shook her head. "It would be a hundred thousand dollars, I think. I couldn't let you do that. I'll pray about it. Maybe God will show us a way to save it."

Brent opened the door and came toward them. "I brought Tom up to speed. He left to go arrest Horace. It took some talking to convince him I was telling him the truth. Horace has been part of this village forever. He was born and raised here. One of our own."

"I really liked him," Libby said. "I still can't believe it."

"The state police are going to come out and get a statement this evening. Are you up to that?" Brent asked. "You look wiped out."

"Yes. I just want it over with."

"I'll be inside," Vanessa said. "I want to talk to Brent." She joined her brother and they went inside.

Alec slipped his arm around Libby's waist, and they walked up the stairs together. "It's all over. Hard to believe. Now what?" he asked when they reached the porch.

"I'm going to make the biggest mess of chicken faji-tas you ever saw and slather it with guacamole."

He grinned. "I'll even eat the hot sauce with you." His fingers traced the outline of her jaw. "You haven't answered my question."

She couldn't think with his touch igniting feelings

she didn't know existed. "I don't know. I have to sell this place, Alec. You know I do."

"Don't decide too quickly. Are you willing to see what door God might open?"

"When you put it that way, how can I refuse?"

Laugh lines crinkled around his eyes. He bent his head and kissed her, then pulled back. "I think I can sweeten the pot a little. I don't want you to go. I want you to live here where I can take you out to dinner and to the movies."

Her heart was full to bursting. "You mean to see year-old movies?"

His breath stirred her hair. "I want to neck with you in the balcony and I don't care how old the movie is."

Her blood warmed at the expression in his eyes. "I'd like that too."

"I think we have something special, Libby. Something that will last. But you have to stay here to find out. You game?"

"I'm game," she said, suddenly breathless.

* * *

Her family. Libby's gaze lingered on every person around the large dining room table. Mr. McEwan, with his rheumy eyes and sparse hair. Delilah and her no-nonsense love for this place and for Ray. Bree and her family. Old Mr. Carter, who had already grabbed the homemade bread in the middle of the table. Her siblings Brent and Vanessa, already so dear. And Aunt Pearl, whom Libby loved so very much already. Only

Nicole was absent. She'd given her statement to the state investigators, then gone back to Virginia Beach to attend to business. At least she wasn't pressuring Libby to sell the property.

Libby locked gazes with Alec, who was sitting across the table from her. Whatever happened, she wanted to live here on Hope Island, even if it wasn't in the beautiful old inn. This was home now.

Horace was sitting in jail awaiting trial, and everything he'd schemed to avoid would happen to him and his family anyway. Though he deserved his punishment, she grieved for his wife and children. He wasn't leaving a legacy of generosity like her father had. The police had checked out his computer and confirmed he had erased the video of the men he'd hired to get Nicole out of the way. With Horace's information, they'd been arrested too.

The police had discovered that Rooney and his goons hadn't actually killed Tina. She'd fallen and drowned in the cellar's standing water. When Poe found her, he'd panicked and left her there, then scuttled her boat to make it appear she'd been lost at sea. He was also in jail.

"I need your advice," Libby said during a lull in the conversation. "I don't want to sell this lovely old house. But I have no idea how to keep it." Libby listened to the hubbub around her as folks argued against selling the property.

She held out her hands. "Nothing would please me more than to keep Tidewater Inn, but I need some suggestions on *how* to make that possible. I got some quotes on restoration. Material alone is going to be seventy-five thousand dollars."

The group fell silent, and the dismay she saw on various faces made her heart plunge. But she could do a lot with the money from the sale of the property. Help her stepbrother and his family. Fix up the lifesaving station and other historic buildings in town. Help people recover from the hurricane. Buy Alec a new boat. There would be compensations for the blow to her soul if she had to give up Tidewater Inn.

Old Mr. Carter in his straw hat pointed a tobacco-stained finger at her. "I'd like to donate the money you need, young lady." He reached down to the old suitcase beside his chair, the same case he'd asked Alec to rescue during the hurricane evacuation, and it opened to reveal stacks of money. "There's plenty in here for materials if the townsfolk will donate the labor."

There was a group gasp around the table. "I couldn't. It might be years before I can pay you back, Mr. Carter," Libby said. She didn't want charity—she wanted a viable solution.

"Oh good grief, Libby," Vanessa said. "I've been looking at Daddy's art. There's our answer. Sell them."

The Allston paintings. Such an easy answer. Why hadn't she thought of it? "You're right," she said. "They are worth more than I need." She glanced at the dear faces around her. "But what about the town? Is selling better for the town, for progress? We need to be realistic."

"The ferry is still coming," Delilah said. "Tourists will need a place to stay. Why not here? The rest of the town needs to think about what kinds of businesses are lacking and fill the need. We could end up with the best of both worlds. Like Ocracoke."

The ideas began to flow quickly. Libby couldn't stop smiling. She took notes in between bites of chicken fajitas, then later, after the table had been cleared, carried the dessert of flan out to the swing with Alec.

"Hey." He put his flan on his knee and slipped his arm around her. "I told you it would work out. You ready to accept the answer?"

"It's more than I'd hoped for." She touched his cheek with her fingers. "*You're* more than I hoped for."

His gaze held her rooted in place. "I look forward to exploring the future with you. Want to go to a movie tonight? I hear *An Officer and a Gentleman* is playing."

"Now that's *really* old," she said. "But I always sigh when Richard Gere sweeps her into his arms and carries her out of the factory."

"Would you settle for a moonlit ride in my fishing boat?" His smile was teasing.

"Will there be kissing involved?"

"Most certainly," he said.

"Then I accept." She didn't wait for the promised kiss, though, and lifted her face toward his in the moonlight.

ACKNOWLEDGMENTS

This book is a little bittersweet for me. It's my twenty-first project with Thomas Nelson, and Erin Healy has edited all but three of those stories. She's a fabulous writer in her own right, and *Tidewater Inn* is her last book to edit before plunging full-time into her own wonderful novels. Thank you, Erin, for all the things you've taught me in the nine years we've worked together. We have been partners from that first Rock Harbor novel, *Without a Trace*. I treasure your friendship and your wisdom, and I'm so grateful for all the time you've spent on my novels. Love you, girl! I will be screaming from the sidelines for you louder than anyone else as you soar to the heights!

My Thomas Nelson team is my family and I love them and thank God for them every day. They helped me brainstorm this particular book too, and it was so fun to write because of that! Publisher Allen Arnold is loved by everyone in the industry—including me! He's a rock star! Senior Acquisitions Editor Ami McConnell (my dear friend and cheerleader) has an eye for character and theme like no one I know. I crave her analytical eye and love her heart. She's truly like a daughter to me. Marketing Manager Eric Mullett brings fabulous ideas to the table. Publicist Katie Bond is always willing to listen to my harebrained ideas. Extraordinary cover guru Kristen Vasgaard (you so rock!) works hard to create the perfect cover—and does it. And, of course, I can't forget my other friends who are all part of my amazing fiction family: Natalie Hanemann, Amanda Bostic, Becky Monds, Ashley Schneider, Ruthie Dean, Jodi Hughes, Heather McCulloch, Dean Arvidson, and Megan Leedle. I wish I could name all the great folks who work on selling my books through different venues at Thomas Nelson. Hearing "well done" from you all is my motivation every day.

My agent, Karen Solem, has helped shape my career in many ways, and that includes kicking an idea to the curb when necessary. Thanks, Karen, you're the best!

Writing can be a lonely business, but God has blessed me with great writing friends and critique partners. Hannah Alexander (Cheryl Hodde), Kristin Billerbeck, Diann Hunt, and Denise Hunter make up the Girls Write Out squad (www.GirlsWriteOut.blogspot.com). I couldn't make it through a day without my peeps! Thanks to all of you for the work you do on my behalf, and for your friendship. I had great brainstorming help for this book from Robin Caroll. Thank you, friends!

I'm so grateful for my husband, Dave, who carts me around from city to city, washes towels, and chases down dinner without complaint. Thanks, honey! I couldn't do anything without you. My kids—Dave and Kara (and now Donna and Mark)—and my grandsons,

James and Jorden Packer, love and support me in every way possible. Love you guys! Donna and Dave brought me the delight of my life—our little granddaughter, Alexa! I hope she understands soon what her Mimi does for a living as I'm about to embark on a children's book project for her.

Most importantly, I give my thanks to God, who has opened such amazing doors for me and makes the journey a golden one.

DEAR READER,

I'm so thrilled to share *Tidewater Inn* with you! The theme of the story—greed versus generosity—is one that resonates so much with me personally. If you're like me, you struggle to find the balance. No matter what resources God has blessed us with, he expects us to use them to help other people. Money isn't our only resource. Time, talents, and other gifts are to be given generously.

I also wanted to share the personal background of a character in the novel who is very special to me. Pearl is my grandma in the flesh, though the name Pearl is my first teacher in Sunday school. My grandma helped shape me in so many ways. She's been gone over twenty years, but I still hear her voice in my head. I strive every day to be more like her. I learned about Jesus at her knee. She taught me about generosity and loving other people. I owe her so much, and I wanted to share her with you. I hope you love Pearl as much as I loved my grandma! People say I'm just like her, and it's the highest compliment I could have. ☺

I so love to hear from you! Email me at colleen@

colleencoble.com and let me know what you thought of the story.

Love,

Colleen

Discussion Questions

1. Libby had struggled to survive monetarily for years so the thought of having no worries about money was appealing. Money is not evil in itself. What do you think about wealth's influence on our spiritual lives?

2. It often seems our culture doesn't honor the older generation. Why don't we and what are we missing?

3. Vanessa and Brent didn't welcome Libby's intrusion into their lives. How would you feel if you found out you had a sibling you didn't know about?

4. Pearl is based on my grandma, and I smiled just writing her into the story. Her love for me and others was always unconditional. Do you have a person in your life who loves you that way?

5. Ray's biggest legacy wasn't money but a spiritual heritage. What do you hope to leave behind for your family?

6. Libby's struggle between greed and generosity is basically a struggle between selfishness and selflessness. What are some other common things we struggle with?

ABOUT THE AUTHOR

RITA finalist Colleen Coble is the author of several bestselling romantic suspense novels, including *Tidewater Inn*, and the Mercy Falls, Lonestar, and Rock Harbor series.

* * *

Visit her website at www.colleencoble.com
Twitter: @colleencoble
Facebook: colleencoblebooks

THE SUNSET COVE *series*

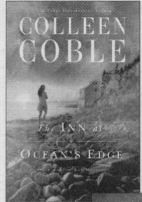

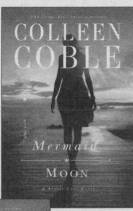

AVAILABLE IN PRINT,
E-BOOK, AND AUDIO

AVAILABLE IN PRINT,
E-BOOK, AND AUDIO

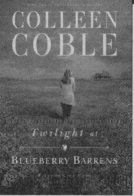

AVAILABLE IN PRINT, E-BOOK,
AND AUDIO SEPTEMBER 2016

THOMAS NELSON
Since 1798

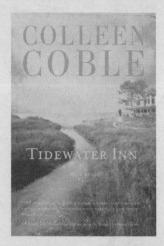
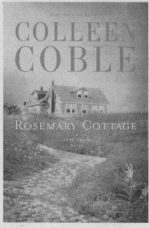

**There is no difference between
love and death
for**

THE NINJA

"Oh, my God!" she heard herself say. It seemed to come from another world.

She stared into a face. The head, like the body, was swathed in a matte black fabric. A tight hood and mask left only his eyes exposed. These were no more than six inches from her own. They were as dead as stones in a pond.

"Oh, my God!" She felt so vulnerable, bent back in a grip she had no hope of breaking and this, more than anything else, terrified her.

When he moved, he was upon her before she could even cry out. She felt his grip shift and it seemed that she was in the grasp of something elemental, like a whirlwind, a force of nature. For surely no man—nothing that was human could have so much power.

No! Please! Take me, don't kill me! Don't! Please! She tried to scream . . . but it was useless. She was powerless against him. . . .

The
NINJA

A NOVEL BY

Eric Van Lustbader

Fawcett Crest • New York

Thanks are due to the following authors, publishers, and agents for permission to use the material included.

Epigraph: Haiku by Matsuo Bashō excerpted from *An Introduction to Haiku* by Harold G. Henderson. Copyright © 1958 by Harold G. Henderson. Reprinted by permission of Doubleday & Company, Inc. *Epigraph:* Lines from *Peter Pan* by J. M. Barrie. Copyright 1928 by J. M. Barrie; renewal copyright © 1956 Lady Cynthia Asquith and Peter Llewelyn Davies. Used by permission of Charles Scribner's Sons. *Page* 30: "All Mixed Up" (Ric Ocasek). © 1978 Lido Music, Inc. International copyright secured. All rights reserved. Used by permission. *Pages* 353, 395, 397: "All My Loving" (John Lennon and Paul McCartney). © 1963 and 1964 Northern Songs Ltd. Reprinted with the permission of Maclen Music, Inc. *Page* 432 (top): "Radar in My Heart" (Bill Nelson) and *Page* 432 (bottom): "Revolt into Style" (Bill Nelson). Used by kind permission of Bill Nelson and Arnakata Music Inc. Worldwide copyright Arnakata Music Ltd. *Page* 433: "I Feel like a Wog" (The Stranglers). Copyright © 1977 Albion Music Ltd. Administered in the United States by Irving Music, Inc. (BMI). All rights reserved. International copyright secured. *Page* 434: "Strange Way" (Rick Roberts). © 1978 Warner-Tamerlane Publishing Corporation, El Sueno Music and Stephen Stills Music. All rights reserved. Used by permission. *Page* 435: "Station to Station" (David Bowie). Copyright © 1976 Bewlay Bros. Music, Moth Music, Fleur Music Ltd.

THE NINJA

This book contains the complete text of the original hardcover edition.

Published by Fawcett Crest Books, a unit of CBS Publications, the Consumer Publishing Division of CBS Inc., by arrangement with M. Evans and Company, Inc.

Copyright © 1980 by Eric Van Lustbader

Calligraphy by Reverend Shunshin T. Kan

ISBN: 0–449–24367–2

Printed in the United States of America

10   9   8   7   6   5   4

FOR SYD
with love

ACKNOWLEDGMENTS

Because, in some instances, I met many of the real people in positions which, of necessity, are in this novel, I wish to state that none of the characters drawn here in any way resemble their real-life counterparts who, without exception, were extremely helpful to me.

I would like to thank:

Dr. Geetha Natarajan, Associate Medical Examiner, City of New York

Lieutenant Jim Doyle, Commander, Village Police, Westhampton Beach

and, especially:

Dr. Michael Baden, former Chief Medical Examiner, City of New York

Thanks to the numerous individuals who assisted me with translations, and to my father, who proofed the manuscript.

Special thanks to Ruth and Arthur for invaluable R&R in Shangri-La.

And to Mom, for her courage.

Natsu-gusa ya
  tsuwamono-domo ga
    yume no ato.
Summer grass:
  of stalwart warriors splendid dreams
    the aftermath.

—Matsuo Bashō

MRS. DARLING. *Dear night-lights*
that protect my sleeping babes,
burn clear and steadfast to-night.

—J. M. Barrie, *Peter Pan*

In darkness there is death.

It was the first thing they had taught him and he never forgot it. He could move unobserved in daylight, too; in other ways. But the night was his special friend.

Now the high piercing sound of the alarm cut through all other nocturnal sounds: the *dree dree dree* of the cicadas, the thunderous crashing of the surf against the gray sand and the black rocks sixty feet below, the wild cry of a disturbed crow far off over the massed treetops.

Abruptly, color gilded the leaves of the ancient spreading sycamore as lights went on inside the house, but he was already away from the car, deep within the concealing shadows of the carefully sculptured hedge. There was little need of this protection now for he was dressed all in matte black: low boots, cotton trousers, long-sleeved shirt, lacquered reed vest, gloves and a hooded mask that covered all his face save a strip across his eyes that had been smeared with lampblack mixed with a fine charcoal powder to eliminate the possibility of reflection; but his arduous training had been too well ingrained for him to take any target for granted. This precluded the possibility of an error in judgment that could lead to a lapse in security.

The porch light came on, insects fluttering around it. The noise of the car's alarm was too loud for him to be able to hear the door opening but he counted off the seconds in his mind and got it dead on....

Barry Braughm stepped into the lemon light of the open doorway. He was in jeans and a white T-shirt. His open fly attested to the haste in which he had dressed. He carried a flashlight in his right hand.

9

From this vantage point on the slight elevation of the doorsill he played the narrow beam around the area of the car. Reflected light from the chrome lanced out into the night and, squinting, he swung the beam away. At this moment he was in no mood to go and fool around with his car—or anything else for that matter.

Not more than a half hour ago he had had a screaming row with Andy, ending up, quite naturally, with him speeding off into the night. Back to the city, Barry supposed. Well, it damn well served him right, cutting off his nose to spite his face. But that was Andy, through and through.

Honest to God, Barry thought angrily, I don't know why I put up with him. And then he shook his head. Yes, you do, he told himself. Well.

He went down the short flight of flagstone steps, careful to give the first one a miss. It was cracked; just one of the things around here Andy had promised to fix this week.

He padded across the wet grass of the lawn to where the car sat, dark and hulking. The wind whistled through the young maple to his left and, farther on, he could just make out the low barrier of the thick hedge. What the hell am I doing with a Mercedes? he asked himself rhetorically. If it had not been for Andy—but Andy loved the creature comforts, wouldn't go anywhere unless it was via first class. That, of course, includes me, Barry thought grumpily. He looked off down the road for a moment as if he might catch a glimpse of Andy's night-black Audi swinging its headlights around the long curve to flood his front lawn. Barry turned abruptly away. Not tonight, he thought. He never recovers this quickly.

He threw the beam of the flash across the top of the hedge as he moved, along the gravel drive to finally send a quick dazzle of liquid light off the car's hood. It grew in intensity as he came up beside the Mercedes.

Goddamned heat, he thought. Always setting off the alarm. And I do not want to sleep alone tonight. Should have thought of that before you called Andy a shit.

He paused for a last look around, then bent and freed the latch, lifting the hood. He gazed into the interior, playing the beam over the engine parts, lingering for just a moment on the battery.

Satisfied, he slammed the hood and went around the car checking the doors, one by one. The seams of glass and chrome

10

vere illuminated as he sought to find any sign of a forced entry. Finding none, he came back to the left side and, bending again, inserted a small metal key into a fixture in the car's side. He turned the key with a quick jerk and silence descended once again. The sound of the cicadas returned and the hiss of the surf gave renewed evidence of its tireless attack upon the slowly eroding shore.

Barry had already turned away on his way back to the house when he thought he heard a brief clatter against the rocks near the verge of the low cliff fronting his property. It sounded to him like the soft noise of running bare feet. He spun around, lifting the flash to scan the area. He saw nothing.

Curious, he went across the lawn and into the high grass which he had never bothered to mow because it was so close to the cliff, emerging seconds later on the slightly elevated portion of land studded with gray slate rocks. He peered along the ridge to both left and right. Directly below him he saw the palely iridescent curl of the tops of the breakers as they rolled noisily in. It's high tide, he thought.

The pain in his chest came totally without warning. He was thrown backward just as if a hand had come out and pushed him and he stumbled along the dew-slick rocks. His arms flew out to the sides to give him balance and the flash spun end over end like a miniature falling star in the night. He heard quite clearly the sharp *pang* as it bounced off the rocks below and arced into the churning sea like some suicidal firefly. His mouth worked spasmodically. He tried to scream but all he could manage was a kind of gasp, insignificant and irrelevant, and he thought he knew what it must be like for a fish on a line.

His arms and legs felt as if they were full of lead and the air seemed to have run out of oxygen just as if he were lost on an alien planet without the protection of a spacesuit. He was incapable of coordinating movement, balanced precariously on the faceted rocks, on the verge of the long drop to the white and black sea. Dimly, he thought he might be having a heart attack and, desperately now, he tried to remember what to do, how to help himself. He died trying to recall....

With the absence of all movement, a shadow detached itself from the wall of the hedge, coming swiftly and silently

11

across to the rocks. Even the cicadas, the night birds wer
left undisturbed by the passage.

The shadow knelt over the corpse and black fingers worke
at something dark and metallic, embedded in the chest jus
under and to the right of the heart. With a last wrench, th
thing was free.

He checked the carotid first, then the eyes, peering in
tently at the whites for what seemed a long time, then th
pads of the fingers.

Softly, to himself, the shadow recited the *Hannya-Shin
Kyō*.

He stood up. The corpse seemed as light as air in his arms
With barely any discernible motion or effort, he launched th
corpse out into the night, over the verge, far enough out s
that it fell squarely into deep water. Immediately the stron
current took it.

Within seconds the shadow had disappeared, having be
come one with the darkness and having left no trace of it
ever having existed.

First Ring

THE GROUND BOOK

West Bay Bridge

SUMMER PRESENT

When Nicholas Linnear saw them fish the bloated blue-white thing out of the water, he turned right around, walking away, and was far down the beach by the time the real crowd had begun to form.

Flies buzzed furrily along the snaking hillock of sand above the high-tide mark. The spindrift, drying, was like a lock of a child's fine white hair. Beyond, the combers rolled in, purple-blue, then white as their tops turned to foam, spending themselves upon the wet sand at his bare feet.

He dug his toes in, very much as he had done when he was younger, but, of course, it did no good. The sea leached away the footing from under him and he grew shorter by inches as the land was eroded by the tide's inexorable progress.

Up until then it had been a quiet afternoon, Dune Road lazy in midweek, even though this was the week after the Fourth of July. He reached unconsciously for the pack of thin black-tobaccoed cigarettes which he no longer carried. He had given up smoking six months ago. He remembered the date well enough because it was the same day he had quit his job.

He had arrived at the agency one chill sullen winter's day and had stayed in his office only long enough to place the ostrich-hide briefcase that Vincent had presented him with for no apparent reason—it was some months past his birthday and longer than that since he had been promoted—on his rosewood and smoked-glass desk that was much too modern to hold anything remotely resembling drawers. Then he went out, turning left, past the curious, upturned face of Lil, his secretary, down the beige-carpeted, rose-neon indirectly lighted hall. When had he actually made the decision? He had no idea, really. On the way in, in the cab, his mind had been empty, his thoughts like ashes swirled in the dregs of last night's coffee. Nothing else seemed to remain.

He went past the pair of female guardians who, like perfectly carved sphinxes before a great pharaoh's tomb, flanked the enormous carved mahogany door. The thing of it was they were damned efficient, too. He gave a brief knock and went in.

Goldman was on the phone—the dark blue one, which meant a conversation with a high-level client, rather than the beige one, which would indicate interoffice brainstorming—so Nicholas stared out the window. They're all high level these days, he thought. There were days when being on the thirty-sixth floor had its advantages, but this was not one of them. The sky was so dense with leaden clouds that it seemed as if a lid had been clamped down on the city. Perhaps, near nightfall, it would snow again. He couldn't think whether that would be good or bad.

"Nick, my boy!" Goldman cried as he cradled the receiver. "It must've been ESP, you walking in now! Guess who that was on the phone? No." He waved one hand. It looked like a duck, eager to take off. "Better yet, don't guess. I'll tell you. It was Kingsley." His eyes got big. They always got big when he was excited. "Know what he said? He was talking my ear off about you and the campaign. The first results are already in. They're 'a dramatic improvement,' he says. Those are his words, the *schmendrick.* 'A dramatic improvement.'"

Nearing sixty, Sam Goldman did not look a day over fifty. He was fit and trim and always tan. This, Nicholas had always supposed, he maintained to set off his shock of brilliant white hair which he wore long and combed straight back. Goldman was enamored of contrasts. His face was somewhat long, lined, pitted slightly on the crown of each cheek. It was a proud face, dominated by large brown eyes, despite the long nose and generous mouth. He wore a blue pinstripe shirt with solid white collar and a navy and maroon Italian silk tie. He knew how to dress, Goldman did. Despite this, his sleeves were rolled partway up his forearms.

16

Looking at him now, Nicholas abruptly knew why this was going to be so hard for him to do.

"I'm glad, Sam," he said.

"Well, sit down, sit down then." Goldman waved him to a beige suede and chrome chair in front of his enormous desk. It was not, perhaps, what he would have chosen himself but all his clients were happy with it.

"No, I'm fine where I am, thanks." Now that he was down to it, he realized that there was just no easy way. "I'm leaving, Sam."

"Leaving? What, you want a vacation already? You've only been creative director for six months—"

"Seven."

"So who's counting? Anyway, you want a vacation? Okay, you got a vacation. Where're you going?"

"I don't think you understand, Sam. I want to leave the company. Resign."

Goldman swiveled around in his chair, stared out the window. "You know, it's going to snow today. On the radio they said no. But I know better. An old campaigner can always tell. My feet tell me. Every time I play tennis. I said to Edna this morning—"

"Sam, did you hear me?" Nicholas said gently.

"That Kingsley. What a schmuck! He may know publishing but he doesn't know shit from advertising. It took him long enough to come here." He swiveled back, abruptly. "You, Nick, you know advertising."

"Sam—"

"Resign, Nicky? Resign? What's this resign? I don't believe it. You have everything here. Everything. You know how much we're gonna net—not gross, mind you, but net—from this one goddamn campaign of yours?"

"I don't care, Sam."

"Two hundred fucking thousand, Nick. Now why would you leave?"

"I'm tired, Sam. Honestly. I feel like I've been in advertising so long that lately—lately, I've been waking up feeling like Count Dracula."

Goldman cocked his head, a nonverbal sign of query.

"You know, like I've been in a coffin."

"You're going back to Japan."

"I hadn't really thought about it." He was far more pleased

than surprised; Goldman was unusually perceptive about these things. "I don't know that it matters."

"Of course it matters!" Goldman exploded. "I think about going back to Israel all the time!"

"You didn't grow up in Israel," Nicholas countered.

"I would have if it'd've been in existence then." He snorted. "But that's irrelevant." He waved a hand again. "History. History is all that matters." A call came through for him and he barked at one of the sphinxes outside to jot it down as a call-back. "Listen, I don't give a good goddamn what we make outa Kingsley, Nicky, you know that. But it's a sign. Can't you see that? You're hot now. I felt it was gonna happen a year ago and now I know I was right. You really want to walk away from that now?"

"I don't think *want* is the right word," Nicholas said. "*Have to* is more like it."

Goldman took out a cigar from a thick wooden humidor, contemplated it. "Nick, I won't bore you by telling you how many bright guys would give their left nut for your job—"

"Thanks," Nicholas said dryly. "I appreciate that."

"Everyone's gotta do for himself." Goldman's eyes regarded the cigar's tip. He took a bite off the end, struck a long wooden match.

"I wish you wouldn't," Nicholas said. "I've given up smoking."

Goldman eyed him, the flame in midair. "Just like you," he said flatly. "Everything at once." He puffed at the flame, flicked the match into a wide glass ashtray. But, unwilling perhaps to admit unconditional defeat, he stuck the cold cigar unhappily in his mouth, chewed on it meditatively. "You know, Nick, I like to think of myself as more than just your boss. It's been a lotta years since I picked you up right off the boat."

"Plane."

Goldman waved his hand. "Whatever." He took the cigar out of his mouth. "As a friend, I think you owe me some kind of an explanation."

"Look, Sam—"

He put his hand up, palm outward. "Hey, I'm not gonna try to stop you from going. You're a big boy now. And I can't say I'm not disappointed, because I am. Why the hell should I lie to you? Only, I'd just like to know."

Nicholas got up, went over to the window. Goldman swung

his chair around to follow his progress like a radar tracking station.

"It's not even very clear to me yet, Sam." He rubbed a hand across his forehead. "I don't know, it's like this place has become a prison. A place to get out of instead of come into." He turned to face Goldman. "Oh, it isn't this *place*, itself. There's nothing wrong—I suspect..." He shrugged. "Perhaps it's advertising. I feel lost within the medium now, as if the electronicization has no meaning for me. As if I've slipped back, somehow, into another age, another time." He leaned forward, a peculiar kind of tension lacing his upper torso. "And now I'm beginning to feel as if I'm adrift, far out at sea where there's no sign of land in any direction."

"Then there's nothing I can do to change your mind."

"Nothing, Sam."

Goldman sighed. "Edna will be very upset."

For several moments their eyes locked in a kind of silent struggle where each, it seemed, was sizing the other up.

Goldman put his thick hands flat on the desk top. "You know," he said quietly, "years ago in the police department of this city it used to be that the only way you got ahead was if you had a rabbi down at headquarters. Someone who looked after you when things got rough or"—he shrugged—"who knows? Used to be the way of the world—all over." He put the unlit cigar into the opposite side of his mouth. "Now, maybe, it's different. Corporations, they don't know from rabbis. You gotta conform. You gotta suck up to all the vice-presidents, get invited to their weekend parties, be nice to their wives who're so horny and unhappy they'd hump a tree if it could tell them how pretty they look; you gotta live in that certain part of Connecticut where they all live in their two-story houses with the semicircular drives. Used to be they had button-down minds; now they got computer minds. That's getting ahead, Nick, business-wise. So they tell me. Me, I wouldn't know. Not firsthand anyway. I'd retire before they'd get me into that kind of trap." His eyes were clear and they sparkled despite the fact that the light was so dull and leaden. "Me, I was brought up with rabbis. They're in my system; no way I can get 'em out now, even if I wanted to." He sat forward in his high-backed chair, his elbows on the desk top, leveled his gaze at Nicholas. "You get what I mean?"

Nicholas looked at him. "Yes, Sam," he had said, after a time. "I know exactly what you mean."

The aching cries of the circling gulls hid the sound of the siren for a time, but, as the ambulance drew nearer, its wailing rise and fall, rise and fall blotted out all other sound. People were running silently along the expanse of the beach, looking birdlike and rather awkward as they tried to compensate for the too soft footing.

He had come out to West Bay Bridge early in the season. In order to survive now, he had to push it all away from him, into a comforting middle distance, not too close, not too far away. The agency, Columbia, everything. Not even a discovery of some drowned corpse was going to interrupt his solipsistic world; it was too much like the city.

Oddly enough, it put him in mind of the call. It had come only a few days after he had left the agency. He had been in the middle of the *Times'* Op-Ed page and his second Irish coffee.

"Mr. Goldman was good enough to give me your home number, Mr. Linnear," Dean Whoolson said. "I trust I've not intruded."

"I still don't understand why you've come to me," he said.

"It's quite simple, really. There has been, of late, a renaissance of interest in the field of Oriental Studies. The students here are no longer satisfied with the superficiality, shall we say, of many of our oriental courses. I'm afraid they view us as sadly out of date in that area."

"But I'm hardly qualified as a teacher."

"Yes, we are well aware of that." The voice was rather dry, like a pinch of senescent snuff floating through the air. But underneath there was an unmistakable note of sincerity. "Naturally we are aware that you do not possess a teaching license, Mr. Linnear, but, you see, this course I have in mind would be perfect for you." He chuckled, an odd, startling sound as if made by a cartoon character. "For us, too, I might add."

"But I have absolutely no familiarity with the curriculum," Nicholas said. "I wouldn't have any idea where to begin."

"Oh, my dear fellow, it's a piece of cake," Dean Whoolson said, his voice now radiating confidence. "The course is a seminar, you see. Taught by four professors. Well, three now that Dr. Kinkaid has fallen ill. It meets twice a week during the spring semester with the four—I'm including yourself, of course—rotating. You see the beauty of it, Mr. Linnear?

20

You can leave the curriculum to the others and stick to what you know better than anyone else in the Western Hemisphere." That strange, oddly likable chuckle came again, reminding Nicholas of mint chocolates and creme sweets. "I don't imagine you would have to concern yourself with overlapping the others' material, would you? I mean to say," he rushed on, as if enraptured by the wholehearted assurance of his own voice, "the kinds of things—uh, insights, as it were—into the Japanese mind are just the added fillip we are looking for. The students would be delighted, no doubt—as would we."

There was a singing discernible on the line in the ensuing silence between them and, faintly, Nicholas could make out the inconstant sibilances of other voices, like ghosts, raised in argument.

"Perhaps you would care to see the campus," Dean Whoolson said. "And, naturally, it is most beautiful in the spring."

Why not try something different? Nicholas had thought. "All right," he had said.

People were still running past him, attracted by the anxiety the wailing siren brought out. A growing knot of curious onlookers hovered, quivering on the borderline between revulsion and fascination, moths circling a flame in an ever-tightening orbit. He concentrated on the sound of the surf, curling and rushing in toward him, calling like a friend, but the human voices, raised in excitement and query, pierced the afternoon like needles. For them it was but a sideshow attraction, a chance to turn on the six o'clock news and say to their friends, "Hey! See that? I was there. I saw it happen," exactly as if it were Elizabeth Taylor and her touring party who had rolled through that particular stretch of surf, and then, as placidly as if they were contented bovines, return to their icy astringent martinis, the sliced pepperoni that someone had thoughtfully brought out from Balducci's in the city.

His house was of weathered gray shingle and coffee-colored brick with neither the pop-eyed Plexiglas bubble windows nor the bizarre cantilevered walls that many of the homes had along this stretch. To the right of the house, the dunes abruptly gave way to flat sand, somewhat lower than that of the surrounding area. There had been, up until early December, a house worth roughly a quarter of a million dollars on that property, but the winter had been fully as foul

21

as the one in 1977—78 and it had been washed away with much of the land itself. The family was still trying to get the insurance money to rebuild. In the meantime, there was more open space to the side than was usual along this densely populated and highly fashionable beach front.

The breakers seemed to be pounding harder as the tide continued to sweep in and he felt the cold salt water licking up his ankles to his calves. The bottoms of his jeans, though turned up several times, pulled heavy with washed sand. He was reaching down to brush them out when a figure barreled into him. He fell backward with a grunt, someone sprawled atop him.

"Why the hell don't you watch where you're going?" he yelled crossly as he untangled himself.

"Sorry, but you don't have to scream, do you? It was a simple mistake."

The first thing he saw was her face, though before that he smelled her perfume, faintly citrus and as dry as Dean Whoolson's voice. Her face was extremely close to his. Her eyes he thought at first were hazel but then he saw that they certainly had more green in them than brown. There were one or two red flecks floating in the left iris. Her skin was creamy and lightly freckled. Her nose was rather too wide, which gave her character, and her lips were plump, which gave her an innate sensuality.

He grasped her firmly under the arms and lifted her with him.

She immediately drew away, crossing her arms over her breasts. "Don't do that." Still she eyed him, made no move to pass him by. Her fingers curled, rubbing the flesh of her arms as if his grip had bruised her.

"Haven't we met before?" he said.

Her lips jerked in a quick quirky smile. "You can do better than that, can't you?"

"No. I mean it. I've seen you somewhere before."

Her eyes darted for a moment over his shoulder. When they again alighted on him she said, "I don't think—"

He snapped his fingers. "In Sam Goldman's office. The fall or the winter." He cocked his head. "I'm not mistaken."

Her eyes seemed to clear as if, with Sam's name, some almost invisible curtain had been raised within them. "I know Sam Goldman," she said slowly. "I've done some free-lance jobs for him." Now she put one long forefinger up to

22

the center of her lips, the clear-lacquered nail burnished by the light. The inconstant sound of the voices down the beach seemed to swell like the roar of a crowd at the advent of a grand-slam home run or a bit of defensive heroics in the outfield.

"You're Nicholas Linnear," she said, and when he nodded she pointed at him. "He talks about you all the time."

He smiled. "But you don't remember our meeting."

She shrugged. "I don't know, really. When I'm involved in my work..." Her shoulders lifted, fell again.

Nicholas laughed. "I might have been somebody important."

"Judging by your reputation, you are. But you just walked away from all of it. I think that's odd."

Squinting up at him, sunglassless, she looked no more than a college girl, as if the sunlight passing through her had somehow illuminated some previously hidden inner innocence. At last her eyes slid away from him. "What's going on up there, anyway?"

"They found a body in the ocean."

"Oh? Whose?"

He shrugged. "I've no idea."

"Haven't you just come from there?" Her gaze slid back from the distance over his left shoulder, touching his face. It was like a cool summer's breeze after sundown. "You must've seen them pull it out." Her eyes were better than arms, keeping him at a carefully measured distance. There was something peculiarly childlike in that, he thought. A hurt child—or scared. It made him want to reach out and touch her reassuringly.

"I left before it happened," he said.

"Aren't you in the least bit curious?" She seemed unmindful of the wind that flicked at the thick mane of her dark hair. "It could be someone from around here. You know how incestuous this place is—we're all from the same business."

"I have no interest in it. No."

She unfolded her arms, put her hands in the front pockets of her cut-off jeans. She wore a plain, sleeveless Danskin top. It was turquoise and set off her eyes. Her firm breasts swelled with her breathing, the nipples visible points. Her waist was narrow, her legs long and elegant. She moved like a dancer.

23

"But you *do* have interests, I see," she said flatly. "How would you feel if I looked at *you* that way?"

"Flattered," he said. "I'd certainly feel flattered."

Justine was an advertising art designer, living four houses down the beach, who found it convenient to work out of the city during the summer.

"I loathe New York in the summer," she told him the next afternoon over drinks. "Do you know that I once spent the entire summer in my apartment with the air conditioning on full and never once moving out of the door? I was deathly afraid I'd get overwhelmed by the stench of dogshit. I'd call D'Agostino and have them send up the food and, once or twice a week, the office would send up this big brawny fag—who was doing the director under the desk during coffee breaks— to take my designs and bring me my checks. But even with that, it wasn't enough and I was forced out. I threw some stuff in a bag and took the first flight out to Paris. I stayed two weeks while the office went batshit looking for me." She turned her head half away from him, sipping at her manhattan. "However, when I got back, the only thing that had really changed was that the fag was gone."

The sun was coming down, the sea devouring its crimson bulk; color lay shimmering on the water. Then, quite abruptly, it was dark: not even the little lights bobbing far out to sea.

It was like that with her, he reflected. Brilliant color, stories of the surface, but what lay beneath, in the night?

"You're not going back to Columbia," she said, "in the fall."

"No, I'm not."

She said nothing, sat back on the Haitian cotton couch, her slender arms spread wide along the back; they went out of the pools of lamplight, seemed dark wings, hovering. Then she cocked her head to one side and it seemed to him as if the ice floe had cracked, coming apart.

"I fell in love with the campus," he said, deciding to answer her by starting at the beginning. "Of course, it was the beginning of February, but I could imagine the red brick walkways lined with flowering magnolia and dogwood, quince in among the ancient oaks.

"The course itself—Sources of Oriental Thought—wasn't

24

really too bad at all. The students at least were inquisitive and, when awake, fairly bright—some of them startlingly so. They seemed surprised that I was interested in them.

"I was curious about this, at first, but as the semester wore on, I came to understand what it was all about. The other professors giving the course had appallingly little time to devote to the students; they were extremely busy researching their latest books. And when they were actually teaching, they treated their students with contempt.

"I remember sitting in on a class just after midterm. Drs. Eng and Royston, who taught the meat of the course, announced at the beginning of the session that the midterm papers had been graded and were ready to be returned. Royston then proceeded to give his lecture. When the bell rang, Eng asked the students to remain seated and, with perfect precision, laid out four piles of papers on the floor at the front of the hall. 'Those students with last names beginning with letters A through F will find their papers here,' he said, pointing to the pile on his right. And so on. Then they had both turned away and left the hall before the first students even had time to kneel, scrabbling through the piles.

"It was degrading," Nicholas said. "That kind of lack of respect for another human being is something I just cannot tolerate."

"So you liked teaching."

He thought that a curious thing to say. "I didn't mind it." He made himself another gin and tonic, squeezed a section of lemon before dropping it into the ice-filled glass. "In the end it was the other professors who made the semester seem long to me. I don't imagine they thought too much of me. After all, the halls of academe are rather closed. Everyone there is bound by the stringency of the situation. 'Publish or perish' has become a cliché as a saying, I suppose. But for them it's a reality which they must face every day." He shrugged. "I imagine they resented me my status. I had all the best parts of their life without any of the responsibilities."

"And Royston and Eng. What were they like?"

"Oh, Royston was okay, I suppose. Rather stuffy in the beginning but he thawed a bit later on. But Eng"—he shook his head—"Eng was a bastard all right. He had made up his mind about me before we had ever been introduced. The three of us happened to be in the lounge one afternoon. 'So you were born in Singapore,' he said. Just like that. Standing over me, peering down at me through his round wire-rimmed spectacles. That's what they must have been; they were far too old-fashioned to be called glasses. He had a curious manner of speech, his words emerging clipped, almost frozen, so that you could imagine them hanging in midair like icicles. 'A disgusting city, if you will pardon my saying so. Built by the British, who had no more regard for the Chinese than they did for the Indians.'"

"What did you say?"

"Frankly, I was too stunned to say much of anything," he said gloomily. "The bastard had hardly said two words to me all semester. He took me quite by surprise."

"You had no snappy rejoinder."

"Only that he was wrong. I was conceived there." He put down his glass. "I asked Dean Whoolson about it subsequently but he merely brushed it off. 'Eng's a genius,' was how he put it. 'And you know how that sort is sometimes. I must tell you, we are damn lucky to have him here. He almost went to Harvard but we snared him at the last moment. Convinced him of the superiority of our research facilities.' He patted me on the back as if I were the department mascot. 'Who ever knows with Eng?' he said. 'Perhaps he thought you were Malay. We all must make allowances, Mr. Linnear.'"

"I don't understand that," Justine said. "You're not Malay, are you?"

"No, but if Eng thought I was, he might have reason to dislike me. The Chinese and the Malays were constantly at each other's throats in the Singapore area. No love lost there."

"What are you?" She seemed abruptly quite close to him, her eyes enormous and very luminous. "There's an Asian hint in your face, I think. In your eyes perhaps, or in the height of your cheekbones."

"My father was English," he said. "A Jew who was forced to change his name so that he could get ahead in business and then, during the war, in the Army. He was a colonel."

"What was his name? Before he changed it, I mean."

"I don't know. He wouldn't tell me. 'Nicholas,' he told me one day, 'what's in a name? The man who tells you that there is some significance in his name is a barefaced liar.'"

"But weren't you ever curious about it?"

"Oh yes. For a time. But after a while I gave up looking."

"And your mother?"

26

"Ah. That would depend on whom you spoke to. She always maintained that she was pureblood Chinese."

"But," Justine prompted.

"But in all likelihood she was only half-Chinese. The other half was probably Japanese." He shrugged. "Not that I was ever certain. It's just that she seemed always to think like a Japanese." He smiled. "Anyway, I am a romantic and it's far more exciting to think of her as a mixture. An unusual mixture given the mutual animosity historically between the two people. More mysterious."

"And you like mysteries."

He watched the sweep of her dark hair, sliding across one cheek, hiding the eye with the crimson motes. "In a sense. Yes."

"Your features are all Caucasian," she said, abruptly switching topics.

"Yes," Nicholas said. "Physically I take after my father, the Colonel." He put his head back on the couch, his hair touching her outstretched fingers for a moment before she moved them back, curling them into a fist. He stared up at the patterned pools of light playing upon the ceiling. "Inside, though, I am my mother's son."

Doc Deerforth never looked forward to the summer. This was a curious thing, he thought, because it was invariably his busiest time. The influx from the city never ceased to astound him, the migratory pattern of almost the entire Upper East Side of Manhattan, as fixed and precise as the geese flying their arrowhead formations south in the winter.

Not that Doc Deerforth knew all that much about Manhattan, not these days, at least; he had not set foot into that madhouse in over five years and then it had been only to pay a brief visit to his friend Nate Graumann, New York City's Chief Medical Examiner.

He was quite content to be out here. He had his daughters who, with their own families, visited him regularly—his wife had died of leukemia over ten years ago, turned to a faded photo—and his work as doctor in West Bay Bridge. Then there was his ancillary M.E. work for Flower at Hauppauge. They liked him there because he was thorough and inventive; Flower kept asking him if he would come to work for the Suffolk County M.E. but he was much too happy where he

27

was. There were friends here, plentiful and warm, but most of all, he had himself. He found that, essentially, he was happy with himself. That did not stop the occasional nightmare, however, from creeping through like a clandestine burglar on the loose. He would still wake up, drenched in sweat, the damp sheets twisted clammily about his legs. Some nights he would dream of white blood but he dreamed of other things as well, dream symbols of his personal fright. At those times he would get up and pad silently into the kitchen, making himself a cup of hot cocoa, and would read, at random, from one of Raymond Chandler's seven novels, finding within that spare inferential prose style a kind of existential calm amid his private storm, and inside of thirty minutes he had returned to sleep.

Doc Deerforth stretched, easing the ache that sat like a stuck pitchfork between his shoulderblades. That's what comes from working all hours at my age, he thought. Still, he went over his findings once again. It was all there, black on white, the words piling together into sentences and paragraphs, but now he was seeing the meaning for the first time, as if he were an Egyptologist who had, at last, stumbled upon the Rosetta Stone.

Another routine drowning, he had thought, when they had called him out to Dune Road. Of course, he did not mean that. The word *routine* had no place in his vocabulary. Life was the most precious thing in the world to him. But he need not have become a doctor to feel that way. Living through the war in the Pacific Theater had been enough. Day after day, from his disarrayed jungle camp during the bitter fighting in the Philippines, he had seen the cascades of small one-man planes guided by their kamikaze pilots as they plunged headlong with 2,650 pounds of high explosives in their blunt noses into the American warships. The cultural chasm between East and West could be summed up by those aircraft, Doc Deerforth had always thought. The Japanese name for them was *Ōka*—the cherry blossom. But the Americans called them *baka*—the idiot bomb. Western philosophical thought had no place for the concept of ritual suicide inherent in the Japanese samurai of old. But that was it, really. The samurai survived, despite all obstacles that had been put in his path. Doc Deerforth would never forget the haiku which, so the story went, had been written by a twenty-two-year-old kamikaze pilot just before his death; this, too, was tradition:

28

"If only we might fall / Like cherry blossoms in the spring—
/ So pure and radiant!" And that, he thought, was how the
Japanese felt about death. The samurai was born to die a
glorious death in battle.

And all I wanted was for the war to end with my skin
intact and my mind unbent.

And it had come to pass, all except for the nightmares that
haunted him like a hungry vampire newly risen from the
grave.

Doc Deerforth got up from behind his desk, went to the
window. Beyond the fluted layers of the oak leaves that
shaded this side of the house from the long afternoon's heat,
he saw the expanse of Main Street. Two or three cars were
lined up for the auto teller at the Colonial-style Fourth Fed-
erated Savings and, farther down, the local DAR meeting
broke like surf from the portals of the library. Just another
weekday in the summer. But that world now seemed a million
miles away, as remote as the surface of another planet.

Doc Deerforth turned back into his office and, scooping up
the manila folder and its contents, went out of the house,
down Main Street toward the one-story ugly red brick building housing the Fire Department and, beyond a courtyard
parking lot, the Village Police.

Halfway there, he ran into Nicholas, who was just coming
out of the automated doors to the supermarket loaded down
with groceries.

"Hello, Nick."

"Hey, Doc. How are you?"

"Fine. Fine. Just on my way to see Ray Florum." They
had met, as most residents of West Bay Bridge did eventually,
along this same Main Street, introduced by mutual acquaintances. It was difficult here, even for the most devoutly re-
clusive, not to make friends even if they were only of the
"Howdy" variety. "Just got back from Hauppauge."

"That body they found yesterday?"

"Yeah." Doc Deerforth turned his head quickly, spat out
a bit of food that had lodged itself between his teeth. He was
glad of this diversion. He felt a genuine fear of confronting
Florum with what he had. Besides, he liked Nicholas. "Hey,
you might've known him. Didn't live too far from you along
Dune Road."

Nicholas smiled thinly. "Not very likely—"

"Braughm's his name. Barry Braughm."

29

Nicholas felt a queer sense of vertigo for just a moment and he thought of Justine's words on the beach the day she had run into him. *You know how incestuous this place is.* She couldn't know how right she was.

"Yes," Nicholas said slowly. "I knew him. When I was in advertising, we worked together at the same agency."

"Say, I'm sorry, Nick. Did you know him well?"

Nicholas thought about that for a time. Braughm had had a brilliantly analytical mind. He knew the public perhaps better than anyone at the agency. What a shock to find him suddenly gone. "Well enough," he said, thoughtfully.

Swinging her around. Slow-dancing into the night, the screen door bang open, the record player sending the music rolling in languorous ribbons, drowning the tide. Moving in stereo.

Her arms had trembled when he had first taken them, guiding her out onto the porch. But it was the right thing to do. The perfect thing. She loved to dance, first off. And it was perfectly acceptable for him to hold her this way, even though, quite clearly, rock was sex and dancing was, subliminally, the same thing. What matter? She would dance.

She shadows me in the mirror
And never leaves on the light . . .

In giving herself up to the rhythms she was sensual, a kind of glossy exoskeleton dissolving at her feet, unearthing an ardor rich with substantive and elemental fury.

Some things that I say to her
They just don't seem to bite . . .

It was as if the music had freed her somehow of her chains, of her wounds—*inhibitions* was a word with far too few ramifications to serve the situation—of her fear, not of him, not of any man, but of herself.

She says leave it to me

30

And everything will be all right.

With her shoulder touching his and the music filling another room, she said, "I grew up reading. At first it was anything I could get my hands on. While my sister, always so good with people, was out on dates, I would be gulping down one book or another. Curiously, that didn't last long. I mean, I kept on reading but I quickly became quite discriminating in what I read." She laughed, a rich happy sound that surprised him in its wholeheartedness. "Oh, I had my phases, yes indeed! The Terhune dog books and then Howard Pyle—I adored his *Robin Hood*. One day, when I was about sixteen, I discovered de Sade. It was rather forbidden reading then and therefore exciting. But beyond that, I was struck by much of his writing. And then I had this fantasy that that was the reason my parents had named me Justine. However, when I was older and asked my mother about it, she said, 'Well, you know, it was just a name that your father and I liked.' It must have appealed to her Continental leanings, I imagine; she was French, you see. But then, oh how I wished that I had never asked her! My fantasy was so much better than the reality of it. Well, what can you expect? They were both banal."

"Was your father American?"

She turned her face toward him and the warm glow from the living room lamps burnished one cheek as if by an artist's brush. "Very American."

"What did he do?"

"Let's go inside," she said, turning from him. "I'm cold."

First there was the large black and white photograph of a rather heavyset man with a firm jaw and undaunted eyes. Printed underneath was the legend: *Stanley J. Teller, Chief of Police 1932—1964.* Next to that was a framed copy of Norman Rockwell's *The Runaway*.

The office was a spare cubicle with double windows overlooking the courtyard parking lot. There was not much to see out there, this time of the evening.

"Why don't you cut the doubletalk, Doc, and run it by me in plain English," Lieutenant Ray Florum said. "Just what's so special about this drowning?"

The subdued crackle of the two-way radio down the hall was a constant background chatter, like being on the telephone with a crossed connection.

"That's just what I've been trying to explain to you," Doc Deerforth said slowly and patiently. "This man did not die of drowning."

Ray Florum sat down in his wooden swivel chair. It creaked beneath his weight. Florum was a big man, both in height and girth, which made him the butt of a series of ongoing jokes batted about good-naturedly among his staff. He was commanding officer of the Village Police of West Bay Bridge. He had a beery-cheeked face on which was positioned dead center, as if it were the bull's-eye of some target, a bulbous red-veined nose. His skin was tanned to the color of cured leather; his salt and pepper hair was cut *en brosse*. He wore a brown Dacron suit not because he liked it but because he had to. He would just as soon come to work in a flannel shirt and a pair of old slacks. "What, then," Florum said equally slowly, "*did* he die from?"

"He was poisoned," Doc Deerforth said.

"Doc," Florum said as he wearily rubbed his hand over his face. "I want this to be real clear, understand? Crystal clear. So perfectly clear that there won't be any possibility of a misunderstanding when I make out my report. Because, besides the State Detectives who, I'm sure you're aware, I'm gonna have to copy on this—and when I do, they're gonna be down here like locusts on a wheat field asking us to do all their goddamned field work and then sucking us dry—besides those sonsabitches, I've gotta contend with the county bastards who're most probably gonna claim that this thing's in their jurisdiction. And, to top it all off, now that you tell me it's a murder, I'm gonna have Flower rumbling in from Hauppauge on his white horse wondering why our investigation is taking so long and when's he gonna be relieved of the stiff, his staff's so overworked." Florum slammed the flat of his hand down on the cover of a copy of *Crime in the United States, 1979.* "Well, this time they're just gonna have to wait long enough so that they're one great step behind me."

A sergeant came in and handed Florum several typewritten sheets and went out without a word.

"Christ, it makes my blood boil sometimes. I'm no goddamned politician. That's what this job calls for. Who the hell cares whether I know police procedure or not. God!" But

32

he got up, still, and came back with a file which he opened on his desk. He ran a hand through his hair, scratched at his scalp. He began to sift through a number of eight-by-ten black and white prints which, even upside down, Doc Deerforth recognized as shots of the drowned man.

"First of all," Doc Deerforth said calmly, "I've taken care of Flower. He won't bother you, at least for the time being."

Florum looked up briefly, inquisitively, then his gaze returned to the photos. "Yeah, how'd you work that little miracle?"

"I haven't told him yet."

"You mean to say," Florum said, as he reached out an oblong magnifying glass from a desk drawer, "that nobody knows about this...murder but us chickens right here in this room?"

"That's precisely what I mean," Doc Deerforth said quietly.

After a time, Florum said, "You know, there's nothing shows up on these photos." He shuffled the photos like a deck of cards until a closeup of the head and chest of the drowned man was on top. "Nothing but a routine drowning."

"You won't find anything there."

"That's what I said."

"Doesn't mean, though, that there isn't anything to see."

Florum sat back in his chair and crossed his hands over his ample belly. "Okay, Doc. I'm all ears. You tell me about it."

"What it boils down to is this. The man was dead before he even hit the water." Doc Deerforth sighed. "It was something that might have been overlooked by even as good an M.E. as Flower." Florum grunted but said nothing. "Look, there is a small traumatic puncture wound in the man's chest, middle-left, and it could easily have been mistaken for a rock scrape which it is not. The puncture led me to take blood samples, one of which was from the aorta, where this type of poison concentrates; it's flushed from the rest of the bloodstream within perhaps twenty minutes of death, by what means I have no idea. It's a highly unusual cardiovascular poison."

Florum snapped his fingers. "Poof! Heart attack."

"Yes."

"You sure about this?"

"About the poison, yes. Otherwise you know I wouldn't

33

have come to you. But I've still got some more tests to run. It appears likely that a sliver of whatever punctured the man's flesh is still lodged in his sternum."

"There's no exit wound?"

"No."

"The fall could have dislodged it. Or the sea—"

"Or it was pulled free after the man fell."

"What you're saying, Doc…" He paused and, pushing aside the photos, consulted a filled-out preprinted form. "This guy, Barry Braughm, an account executive at"—here he named Sam Goldman's advertising agency in New York—"lived at three-oh-one East Sixty-third, was murdered. But in this way? For what reason? He was out here alone. No jealous wife or boyfriend…" He laughed. "He's got a sister in Queens whom we've already contacted and interviewed. We checked on his house on Dune Road. Nada. No sign of it being broken into or even that anything was taken. His car was where he had driven it up and parked it in front of the house as secure as Fort Knox. There's nothing to—"

"There's this," Doc Deerforth said, knowing that, at last, he had come to the moment he had been dreading ever since he had discovered the puncture wound and, subsequently, had pulled the blood from the drowned man's heart. It isn't possible, he kept telling himself, all the while his hands and eyes were running the tests that were confirming it; saying it over and over to himself like a litany against evil. And he felt now rather out of himself, a dreamlike unreality that allowed him to sit in another part of this room and watch himself talking to Ray Florum just as if he were an actor in some film.

Outside there came the sound of a child's laughter, harsh and brittle, transformed by some aural magic into an eerie, other-worldly sound, the mocking shrillness of the macaws' cries in the Philippine jungle.

"It's the poison," he continued. "It's a very specific type." He ran his palms down the sides of his pants. It had been a long time since he had felt his hands wet with sweat. "I came across this particular compound when I was stationed overseas."

"During the war?" Florum said. "But, good God, man, that's thirty-six years ago. Do you mean to tell me—"

"I could not forget this poison, Ray, no matter how many years have passed. A patrol went out one night. Five men.

34

Only one returned and he just made it to the perimeter. We'd heard no shots; nothing but the birds and the buzz of the insects.... It was odd, that kind of stillness, almost creepy; we'd been fired upon by snipers all through the day and every day for about a week." Doc Deerforth took a deep breath before plunging onward. "Anyway, they brought me the man who'd come back. He was a boy, really. No more than nineteen. He was still alive and I began to work on him. I did everything I could, everything in and out of the book, but I was helpless. He literally died before my eyes."

"Dying of this stuff?"

Doc Deerforth nodded bleakly. "The same."

"Do you want me to go?" Nicholas asked her.

"Yes," Justine said. "No. I don't know." She stood behind the couch, her fingers pulled distractedly at the tufted Haitian cotton. "My God, but you confuse me."

"I don't mean to," he offered.

"Words don't mean anything."

He was quite startled to see that her face in profile seemed remarkably different, as if he was seeing her now from the perspective of a different age, some other life. In this respect, she reminded him of Yukio. Of course with Yukio he had always imagined it to be the diverse mixture of her heritage, shrouded in some mysterious world to which he did not belong and to which he had but brought the insight of an alien. That, he knew now, had been a purely Westernized response to what was, quite obviously, inexplicable and it somehow confounded him that here, in the West, it should strike him so differently. Perhaps it was but the passage of time—a certain distancing from the anguish—which enabled him at last to see Yukio for what she really was, to him and to those around him. It was, he thought, the space he had gained from all the ramified, ritualized patterns of his life in Japan, which allowed him to realize the mistakes he had committed, to understand the role of his participation in it all.

Justine stirred on the other side of the couch, as far from him as if she were in another country, and he smelled her fragrance.

"It's late," she said. But it made no sense, was meant, he supposed, to fill a void that was becoming too threatening for her.

35

But this kind of inner tension was one of the things that most intrigued him about her. Oh yes, she was extraordinarily beautiful in his eyes; if he had passed her on a busy Manhattan street, he would surely have turned his head, even, perhaps, followed her into Bendel's or Botticelli before he lost her in a swelling crowd; what else does one do with those kinds of fantasy? When one followed them up, one was invariably disappointed. Then she would have been on his mind for an hour or so. But so what? Physical beauty, he had learned quite early, was the arbiter of nothing, could even be a dangerous and bloody thing. More than anything else, he needed a challenge, with women as well as with all the interests in his life. For he felt quite deeply that nothing in life was worth possessing without a struggle—even love; especially love. This too he had learned in Japan, where women were like flowers one had to unfold like origami, with infinite care and deliberateness, finding that, when fully opened, they were filled with exquisite tenderness and devious violence.

Just the creamy splash of the surf now, the record gathering dust on the immobile turntable. There came the cry of a gull, lonely and querulous as if it had somehow lost its way.

He wondered what he had to do; whether he really wanted to do anything. After all, there was fear inside of him, too.

"Have you been with many women?" she asked abruptly. He saw that her arms, as rigid as pillars, were trembling and that she had brought her head up with an effort. She stared at him, daring him to deride her or, perhaps, revile her, comfirming her suspicions of him and, more generally, of men.

"That's an odd question to ask."

She turned her head slightly and he saw the warm lamplight define the bridge of her nose, slide down into the hollow beneath one eye, at the crest of her cheek. The crimson motes were like points of burnished brass; the right side of her face was entirely in shadow. "Will you answer it?"

He smiled. "Some that I've not cared about. Few that I have."

And all the while she watched his eyes for any hint that he might be mocking her. She found none.

"What is it you wish to know, Justine?" he said softly. "Are you afraid I won't tell you?"

"No." She shook her head. "I'm afraid that you will." Her nails plucked at the nubs of cotton as a musician fingers the

36

strings of a harp. "I want to and I don't want to," she said after a while.

He was about to say, with a smile, that it wasn't so serious but he realized that it was; he knew what she was talking about. He came around the end of the sofa, stood by her. "It's only me, Justine," he said, "who's here. There's only the two of us."

"I know." But it was not enough because she had said it like a little girl who did not quite believe what she was saying, wanting only some outside reassurance for an important inner act.

She broke away from this tight orbit, perhaps feeling the increasing magnetism beginning to influence the balance, and went across the room to stand in front of the large window. The outside lights were still on, and beyond the porch and the fluttering pitiful moths the sea broke endlessly onto the shore, the sand now as dark as coal.

"You know, for some reason this view reminds me of San Francisco."

"When were you there?" he asked, coming around and sitting on one arm of the sofa.

"About two years ago, I guess. I was there for eighteen months, almost."

"Why'd you leave?"

"I—broke up with someone. Came back here. Returned to the East, the prodigal daughter, into the bosom of her family." For some reason that struck her as funny, but the laugh seemed to strangle and die in her throat.

"You loved the city."

"Yes," she said. "Yes, I did that. Very much."

"Then why leave it?"

"I—had to." She lifted her slim hand, then looked at it, surprised that it was in that position. "I was a different person then. Not at all secure." She clasped her hands in front of her, arms extended downward. "I was so vulnerable. I felt— I guess I felt that I couldn't stay there by myself. There was a kind of wind sailing through me." As if it were an afterthought, she said, "It was a stupid situation. *I* was stupid." She shook her head as if she still could not believe how she had acted.

"I've been there twice," Nicholas said. "San Francisco, I mean. I fell in love with it. It's size; its whiteness viewed from Mill Valley." He was watching the thin line of phos-

37

phorescence, almost transparent, that marked the rise of the surf and its subsequent fall to earth, coming in, coming in. "I used to go down to the shore just to watch the Pacific and think: Here are these waves rolling in, rolling all the way across the world from Japan."

"Why did you leave?" she asked. "What made you come here?"

He took a deep breath. "That's difficult to sum up in words. I suppose it was an aggregate of many things, a slow accretion.

"My father, you know, he wanted to come to America. He loved Japan. Fought for it, always. He might have come here himself but—it wasn't his karma, I suppose. It was something he regretted." The spume was like silver lace far away—out there on the bosom of the sea. "If there is a part of him within me, then he's here now and that makes me feel all right."

"Do you really believe that? Life after—"

He smiled. "Oh yes. Oh no. I cannot tell you truthfully. East meets West inside me like swirling currents and there is a kind of tug of war. But about my father, my mother, They are with me, yes."

"It seems so odd—"

"Only because we are here, standing on a porch in West Bay Bridge. If we were in Asia..." He shrugged as if this explanation were sufficient. "And, too, I came here to prove to myself that I could be a Westerner as well as an Easterner. I majored in mass communications at college, launched into the atom age. Advertising seemed a logical choice once I came here and I was lucky enough to find someone who was willing to take a chance on me as a raw trainee." He laughed. "It turned out I was a natural."

She turned her body sideways to the surf, facing him fully. She came and stood next to him. Her long hair swirled, a link; they had not touched. "Do you want me?" she whispered like the tide. "Do you want to make love to me?"

"Yes," he said, watching her eyes, their expanded pupils darkening the green to black. He felt a tightening in his stomach, no longer quite certain of his own ghosts, feeling a filament of fear, a feather brushing the base of his spine. "Do you want to make love to me?"

She said nothing; he felt the nearness of her hand rather than saw it, mesmerized by her eyes, the glowing motes like magnets. He felt its heat, then the tips of her fingers touched the skin of his biceps, curled around the muscles there, firmly but without squeezing, and it seemed to him that the simple gesture communicated so much that it was as if she had never done it before; that it had never been done to him before in just that way. And that first contact was so electrically tender that he felt the muscles of his thighs trembling, a sighing in his heart begin.

He wrapped her slowly in his arms and he was quite certain she cried out, a tiny burst of erotic emotion, "Oh!," the abandoned ardor of the music, just before his lips covered hers. Immediately her mouth opened under his and he felt the length of her body pressing against his, building heat at the fulcrums of breasts, belly and the juncture of her thighs.

How hot she seemed as his lips caressed her long neck, tracing the rounded edge of her collarbone. His hands pulled at her shirt. Her lips were at his ear, her tongue circling, circling like that last hungry gull above the night-dark beach, and she whispered, "Not here. Not here. Please—"

Lifting her arms and the shirt came off; his fingers stroked her spine, the deep long indentation. She shivered and moaned as he licked under her arms, moving slowly to her full breasts, the nipples already hard and puckered.

Her long fingers unfastening the snap of his jeans, her nail clicking together as his open lips covered the upper slopes of her breasts, spiraling inward. "Please," she whispered. "Please." And brought him out of the jeans, already half-erect, stroking him softly to full hardness as he sucked her nipples.

He felt the fear give a last flutter, like a tired sigh, before it evaporated utterly. They sank lower and lower, twisting and trembling with anticipation as the remainder of their clothes came off. Her hands moved to push down the pair of thin silk panties but he stopped her, picking her up from the carpet, one hand under her buttocks, the other at the small of her back, lifted her half onto the sofa, moving between her spread thighs, bending, his opened lips finding their soft inner sides, moving slowly upward, toward the high silk-covered mount. Her fingers were white as they gripped the front edge of the sofa's pillow; his tongue touched the moist silk and she moaned again, her back arching.

He began to lick at her through the thin barrier of the silk and her hands flew to his head, stroking his ears, her wide opened mouth making small involuntary cries as the tension built inside her rapidly. Then he moved aside the sopping silk and buried his face against her. Her nails grazed his back as her long legs jerked convulsively upward. Her ankles locked against his spine. He moved slightly upward to her core, sucked it into his mouth. Her loins rolled upward in powerful thrusts as she cried out, his tongue and lips constantly moving until he felt her shuddering against him, heard her scream, the tenseness dissolving out of her, and wetly, heatedly, she drew him up toward her, her fingers seeking him, her lips wildly on his, wanting him in her now, at this precise moment, more than she wanted anything else, to continue the exquisite heat she felt, to give him pleasure as he had given her.

Her sex felt like a furnace as she guided him into her. She rammed her belly against him as he buried himself to the hilt; they both groaned with the sensation. She surrounded him with her arms, languorously twisting her upper torso so that her lush breasts rubbed back and forth across his chest. She moaned with the intense stimulation to her hard nipples. She licked at his neck as he used his hands on her, all over, increasing her pleasure, riding high within her, and at the end, when she found the tension almost unbearable, when the sweat and the saliva ran down her arms and between her breasts, pooling in her navel, when his frictioning against her was so intense that it took on a kind of third dimension, she used her inner muscles once, twice, heard him gasp, felt herself balancing on the brink, the thudding of their hearts heavy in her inner ear, whispering to him, "Come, darling, come—ohhh!" gasped out as she felt his probing finger, slick with their mingled juices, at the opening of her anus and lost all control, filled with fire all the way up to her throat.

Dr. Vincent Ito stirred the hot chrysanthemum tea steaming in the handleless ceramic cup. Disturbed, several dark bits of crushed leaf swirled upward from the bottom, circling the surface. They reminded him of floaters. They were coming, he knew, had been for a month or so. Those bodies, once people who had leaped or, unconscious, had, perhaps, been pushed into the East River or the Hudson during the long winter months. Consigned to the deep, they had been preserved by the chill at the bottom, undisturbed by the sluggish currents until the beginning of the summer when the water heated up. At thirty to thirty-five degrees Fahrenheit, bacteria would begin to breed, causing putrefaction and gases that would, eventually, bring the body to the surface, and the floater, months after it had gone in, would be brought to him at the Medical Examiner's building.

That certainly did not bother him. Since he was an associate medical examiner, it was merely part of Vincent's life. An important part, he had admitted to himself long ago. The morgue, in the building's basement, with its steel-jacketed doors stacked one atop the other marked by their neat, typewritten cards, the scrubbed gray tile floor, the great scale upon which the corpses were weighed, was where he lived most of his days. There was nothing ghoulish about it, passing the brown and white bodies laid out on the shining gurneys, bloodless, the great T-shaped incisions across the chest from shoulder to shoulder and down across the abdomen, the epidermis thick like leather, the faces as peaceful as if they slept the sleep of the innocent. It had no effect on him. The interest and, yes, the excitement of forensic medicine was, for him, the intricate puzzle of death. Not so much what it was but rather what had caused it. He was a detective whose work among the dead had, many times, aided the living.

Vincent stared out the window as he slowly sipped his tea. Darkness still spread itself before the coming dawn: 4:25. He was always up this early.

He stared out at the city, the lighted empty streets of Manhattan. Far away he heard the grinding of a garbage truck making its lentitudinous way along Tenth Street. Then closer by, a police car siren cut abruptly in, shattering the quietude. But it too, after a time, was gone, evaporating into the darkness. Nothing remained in the night but his thoughts, twisting upon themselves.

He felt trapped. My karma must have been very bad in my last life, he told himself. Japan seemed as inaccesible as if it were in another time. It no longer seemed possible for him ever to find it again, at least the Japan he had left twelve years ago. For him there was no more Japan; it was but a withered flower—calling him still like a siren of the sea.

Nicholas awoke just before dawn. For just a moment, he was quite convinced that he was in his old house on the

41

outskirts of Tokyo, the Zen garden, the oblique shadows on the wall by his head made by the stand of tall rustling bamboo. He heard a cuckoo's brief call, the rush of the morning's traffic into the city, muffled, funneled and yet magnified by the distance and the peculiar acoustics of the topography.

He turned his head, still half asleep, saw a female form asleep beside him. Yukio. She had come back after all, he thought. He had known she would. But now to actually have her here beside him—

He sat up abruptly, his heart racing. A runic chanting, as if from far away across the distance of a sea, abruptly metamorphosed into the drifting crash of the surf, coming clear to him through the open window, the cry of the gulls. Still he knew the meaning of that arcane chanting....

He took several deep breaths. Japan clung to him now like a fine gauzy veil, enmeshing him. What had recalled it to him so intensely?

He looked around, saw the tip of Justine's nose and her soft sensual lips, partly opened as she breathed, the only parts of her not covered by the sheet, blue and white and gray, rippling like the sea. She slept deeply now within its heaving bosom.

What is is about her, he wondered, that pulls me like a current? Oddly, he felt adrift upon the tides. Watching her, the soft rise and fall of her warm body, he knew that he was being drawn back to Japan, into the past where he dared not tread....

An unutterably delicious sensation woke him. He opened his eyes to find her thighs close to his face. He inhaled her musk, realized her lips were around him. Her tongue licked softly, lasciviously, and he groaned. He reached out to touch her but her thighs moved away. He watched, instead, the movement of her mount, tracing with his eyes the highly arched configuration, deeply bisected at its base, the soft curling hair glistening moistly down the center, her flesh as tumescent as his, an arrow of delight.

The pleasure ribboned out before him, a highway endlessly extended. Each time he was on the verge of coming, she used her hands on him, lifted her mouth away, encircling the base until the anticipatory spasms subsided. Then she would resume and the crescendo would begin again, over and over until his legs shook and his heart pounded and he felt as if he were burning with a fever, pleasure pooling and radiating

42

at the same time, leaden with the amount of it running through his pelvis and genitals.

He became aware of her breasts swaying against his belly and he reached down, cupping them, rubbing the nipples until, involuntarily, her thighs opened, rushing toward him. Every touch was now so exquisite that he felt muscles jumping all over his body at each contact. She did something to the head of his penis and he cried out, moving. He clutched at her breasts and she slid up so that his shaft squeezed between them. He buried his face in the crevasse between her thighs, opening his mouth as far as he could as he shot and shot and shot.

Vincent Ito arrived at the Medical Examiner's office on First Avenue at Thirtieth Street at four minutes to eight in the morning. As he pushed through the plate-glass door at the top of the short flight of stairs, he nodded to the uniformed cop on duty and said hello to snowy-haired Tommy, Nate Graumann's chauffeur. As he entered Room 134, he knew he had just enough time to grab a cup of coffee before the morning meeting began.

He turned right through the short hall and into the Chief Medical Examiner's large, crowded office.

Nate Graumann, New York City's Chief Medical Examiner, was a mountain of a man. His eyes were slitted, black and glossy, half hidden within semicircular folds of loose skin, somewhat paler than the color of that around them. His broad nose had been broken once, perhaps in some nighttime street fight in the South Bronx, where he had been born and raised. His hair was salt and pepper but his mustache was jet black. He looked, in short, like a most formidable opponent—which he was, as the mayor and several members of the city's fiscal control board could easily attest.

"Morning, Vincent," he called.

"Morning, Nate." He hurried across the room to the high metal dome of the coffee machine standing like a doge's palace amid the clutter. Hold the sugar, hold the half-and-half, he thought gloomily. I need my caffeine straight this morning.

"Stay a minute, Vincent," Graumann said, as the assignment meeting broke up.

Vincent sat in a green chair across from the littered desk

43

and handed over the cases he had picked out when Graumann asked to see them.

They were friends, away from their labors here, but those times had seemed to shrink over the years. Graumann had been deputy M.E. when Vincent had first arrived here and, it seemed, there had been more time then. Or perhaps it was just that there had been more money. Their workloads increased as the fiscal crunch fell like the side of a mountain upon them. The city had much larger problems than worrying about the people who were daily bludgeoned, knifed, strangled, drowned, asphyxiated, shot, mangled and blown apart on the city's streets or in the bodies of water throughout its environs. Eighty thousand people die each year in New York City and we get thirty thousand of them, he thought.

"What d'you have on at the moment?" Graumann said.

"Uhm. The Morway thing," Vincent said, his brow furrowing in thought, "and the Holloway knifing—I'm due in court on that any moment. The Principal case is about closed—just a few odds and ends left to tie up for the D.A.— the blood analysis should be in this afternoon. And then, oh yeah, Marshall."

"What's that?"

"Came in late yesterday afternoon. McCabe said it couldn't wait so I began working on it right away. Drowning in the reservoir. McCabe thinks he might have had his head held under. They're holding someone on suspicion, that's why she needs the goods right away."

Graumann nodded. "Full load, huh?"

"More than."

"I want you to go out to the Island for a couple of days."

"What? In the middle of all this?"

"If it weren't important I wouldn't be asking," he said patiently, "would I?"

"But what about—?"

"I'll look after your cases in progress personally. And these"—he picked up the two manila folders, tapping their bottoms on the desk top several times as if straightening them out—"I'll give to Michaelson."

"Michaelson is an idiot," Vincent retorted hotly.

Graumann regarded him placidly. "He goes by the book, Vincent. He's steady and dependable."

"But he's so slow," Vincent moaned.

"Speed is not everything," Graumann reminded him.

44

"Tell that to McCabe. She's got the whole office on our case, lately. All those goddamn assistant D.A.s wheedling their way in here mucking things up."

"It's what they're paid to do, I'm afraid."

"So what am I doing out on the Island?"

"Paul Deerforth called late yesterday," Graumann said. "You remember him?"

"Sure. We met last year when I came out to visit you for a couple of days. West Bay Bridge, right?"

"Uhm hmm." Graumann sat forward. "He's apparently got a problem that's over his head. He has ancillary ties to the Suffolk County M.E.'s office." He looked down at his steepled nails, back up to Vincent's face. "He asked for you specifically."

There was a great fish tank along the left-hand brick wall of the living room of Nicholas' house. It was, he estimated, big enough to hold fifty gallons of water. But its denizens were no ordinary guppies or gouramis, for the owners had left to him, the summer's tenant, the care of a multitude of saltwater fish whose brilliant colors electrified the surrounding water just as if they were a flock of boldly plumaged birds flitting through some dense tropical world.

He watched Justine's form through this aqueous lens like a primitive peeping through the foliage at an intruding memsahib.

She wore a red bathing suit cut high along the thighs to resemble a dancer's leotard and thus accentuate her long legs. She had a white towel around her neck as if she had just come from a gym. She licked at a running egg yolk between her fingers as she mopped at the plate with a last bite of toast in her other hand. Popping this into her mouth, she turned to look at him.

"Those aren't yours, are they?" she asked.

He was finished feeding them but unaccountably remained in his crouched position, fascinated perhaps by the distortions of the soft currents created by the fish and the bubbling aerator. The certain air of unreality was comforting although he might be more inclined to think of it as an aspect of fantasy.

"Not mine, no," he said from behind the barrier reef. "They

45

are the house's true owners." He laughed and straightened up. "More so than I, at any rate."

She stood up, brought the plates to the kitchen. "Christ, it's raining." She leaned on the sink with her elbows, stared out the window. "I'd wanted to work outside today."

The rain pattered lightly against the living room windows, the flat roof, coming in from the sea. The light was cold and dark, as patchy as marble.

"Do it here," he said. "You've got your stuff with you."

She came out into the living room, dusted her hands. "No, I don't think so. If I have to be inside, I might as well use the board."

She confounded him, and doing nothing was, in its way, just as bad as taking the wrong turn. He despised hesitation.

"Have you brought any sketches with you?"

"Yes, I—" She glanced away toward the large canvas bag by the side of the sofa. "Of course. Yes."

"I'd like to see them."

She nodded, reached out a large blue-paper-covered tablet, handed it to him.

She wandered around the room while he went from page to page. The bubbling of the tank. The muted hiss of the surf.

"What're these?"

He looked up. She was standing in front of a low walnut breakfront, hands clasped loosely behind her back. She meant the objects he had hung on the wall one above the other, a pair of scabbarded gently curving swords. The top one was perhaps thirty inches long, the one beneath perhaps twenty.

He watched the shadowed line of her spine for a moment, compared it with the one in the sketch he held in front of him. "They are the ancient swords of the Japanese samurai," he said. "The longer one is the *katana,* the killing sword; the other, a *wakizashi.*"

"What're they used for?"

"Combat and *seppuku*: ritual suicide. In ancient times, only the samurai were allowed to wear and use the *daisho,* the two blades."

"Where did you get them?" Still she had not taken her eyes off them.

"They're mine," he said.

She turned her head and smiled. "You mean you're a samurai?"

"In a way," he said seriously and got off the couch. He

46

tood beside her, thinking about the three hours a day he
practiced.

"Can I see," she said, "the long blade?"

Carefully he reached up, took the *katana* off the wall. "I
houldn't do this." One hand on the sheath, fingers of his
ight hand wrapped around the long hilt.

"Why not?"

He pulled slowly, its shining length revealed in a four-
nch span. "The *katana* should be drawn only for combat. It's
acred. Given in the manhood ceremony, christened with its
wn name, it is the heart and soul of the samurai. This is a
dai-katana, longer than the standard sword. Don't touch it,"
he said sharply and she withdrew the extended finger in
alarm. "It would sever your finger."

He saw her reflection in the blade, eyes opened wide, lips
lightly parted. He could hear her breathing beside him.

"Let me see a little more of it." She brushed a stray lock
of hair out of her eyes. "It's beautiful. Has it a name?"

"Yes," he said, thinking of Cheong and Itami. "*Iss-hōgai*.
t means 'for life.'"

"Did you name it?"

"No, my father did."

"I like the name; it fits, somehow."

"There's magic in a Japanese-forged blade," he said, re-
lacing the *dai-katana* in its scabbard. "This particular sword
s almost two hundred years old yet its manufacture is so
superb that it does not show even a year's wear." He replaced
the weapon. "The finest blade the world has ever known or
ever will know."

The phone rang and he went to it.

"Nick. It's Vincent."

"Hey, How are you?"

"Fine. Actually, I'm on my way out to your neck of the
woods—or shore, as it were."

"The Island?"

"Better than that. West Bay Bridge."

"Hey, that's great. I haven't seen you since—"

"March, if you want to know. Listen, I'm going to be staying at Doc Deerforth's in town."

"No you're not. You're staying out here by the beach.
There's plenty of room; you can't swim in town."

"Sorry, but this isn't a vacation, and until I find out what's
going on I'd better plan to stay with the doc."

47

"How's Nate?"

"As usual or thereabouts. There's too much work there fo
all of us."

Nicholas glanced at Justine, who was leafing through he
sketchbook, one hand run through her thick hair. While h
watched, she leaned across the sofa, reached out a pencil from
her bag, began to continue the unfinished sketch she ha
been contemplating.

"Someone there with you?"

"Yes."

"I see. Well, I'll be out late this afternoon." He laughed
his voice sounding for the first time thin and strained. "I
must really be something. Graumann's given me the car *anc*
Tommy. All I have to do is sit in the backseat and take a
nap." He sighed. "Poor me. A few years ago, before the fisca
crunch, I'd be coming out in a Lincoln. Now I have to be
content with a diarrhea-tan Plymouth."

Nicholas laughed. "Give me a ring when you're settled in
and you'll come over for a drink."

"Right. 'Bye."

He cradled the receiver, sat down next to Justine. His eyes
traced the new lines she had made but his mind was far
away.

"I think I see now why you asked for me to come out,"
Vincent said.

"You know what this stuff is?" Doc Deerforth said.

Vincent rubbed at his eyes with thumb and forefinger.
The harsh fluorescent lights hurt his eyes. He reached up,
pulled the gooseneck incandescent lamp closer to the sheets
of paper he had been reading. "I don't quite know what to
think, to be honest."

"The man we just saw downstairs did not die of drowning."

"Of that there is no doubt." Vincent nodded his agreement.
"Whatever he died of, it wasn't asphyxiation."

"As you can see," Doc Deerforth said, indicating the contents of the folder in Vincent's hands, "he had no previous
record of heart failure or any cardiac problem at all; none in
his family. He was a perfectly healthy thirty-six-year-old
male Caucasian, slightly out of shape but—"

"He died of a massive M.I." Vincent completed the sentence. "Heart attack."

48

"Induced, I'm convinced," Doc Deerforth said, bending forward and stabbing at the printed sheet, "by that substance."

"Have you fed it through the computer?"

Doc Deerforth shook his head. "Remember that as far as anyone here is concerned, this is an 'accidental death by drowning,' at least as of now. Anyway, you must be aware that it would do no good at all."

"What about the delay in your report to the C.M.E.?" Vincent snapped shut the folder, handed it over to Doc Deerforth.

"Why, didn't I tell you? I'm having a bit of trouble with the man's family." Doc Deerforth placed the folder under his arm and guided Vincent out of the lab, turning out the lights. The twenty-minute drive back to West Bay Bridge seemed awfully long to him all of a sudden.

Justine sat scrunched down in a far corner of the couch, knees drawn up, arms about her legs. Her open sketch pad lay on the low wooden coffee table in front of them. Across the room, the windowpanes were still teary, though most of the rain had dissipated into a low mist.

"Tell me about Japan," she said abruptly, bringing her face down until it was level with his. Her cool eyes regarded him far from impassively.

"I haven't been back in a very long time," he said.

"What's it like?"

"Different. Very different."

"You mean the language."

"Oh, that's part of it, of course. But it's more basic than that. You can go to France or Spain, have to deal with other languages. But after all, the thought processes are not that much different. Not in Japan. The Japanese confound most Westerners, frighten them, too, oddly enough."

"Not really," she observed. "Everyone's frightened of what they don't understand."

"And then," he said, "there are some who understand right away. My father was one of those. He loved the East."

"As do you."

"Yes," he said. "As do I."

"What made you come here?"

He watched her as the darkness came slowly down, as the world outside turned blue, wondering how she could be so insightful in her questions and at the same time so evasive

49

in her answers. Inside the house, where they sat near the bubbling fish tank, the light was like yellow custard.

"I no longer wanted to be in Japan," he said, recognizing in the simple statement both the truth and the utter insufficiency of the words. But would any words have sufficed? He could not say with any certainty.

"So you came here and went into advertising."

He nodded. "In effect, yes."

"And left your family?"

"I have no family." The words came out cold and hard, as individually devastating as bullets, and she recoiled.

"You make me feel ashamed that I never talk to my sister," she said, turning her face away from him for a moment as if to actively demonstrate her embarrassment.

"You must hate her a great deal."

She spun her head back. "That was a cruel thing to say."

"It was?" He was genuinely surprised. "I don't think so." He looked at her. "Are you indifferent about her? That would be far worse, I think."

"No," she said. "No, I'm not indifferent to her. She's my sister. I—I don't think you could understand," she finished somewhat lamely and he knew she had meant to say something else, only changing her mind at the last instant.

"Why won't you talk about your father? You spoke about him before in the past tense. Is he dead?"

There was a look in her eyes, a kind of reflective opacity as if she were staring into a fire, as she said, "Yes. He's as dead as he could possibly be." She got off the sofa, went over to the fish tank, peering in with a kind of coiled intensity as if she longed to shrink in size and jump into the salt water, becoming one with the crowd idling there. "What difference could it make to you, anyway? I'm not my father's daughter; I don't believe in all that shit." But her tone said otherwise and Nicholas found himself wondering just what it was her father had done to her that she should despise him so.

"What about your sister?" he said. "I'm curious because I was an only child."

She turned away from the tank, the water's reflection in the overhead light dappling one side of her face as if she were submerged, some exotic sea creature attracted by the motion of his descent. He imagined they were at the bottom of the sea, puckered kelp like stately bamboo waving in the deep

50

current's breeze; he imagined they spoke sonically, bone to bone, vibrations batted back and forth like a tennis ball.

"Gelda." Her voice had captured an odd quality that he could not place. "My older sister." She sucked in some air. "You're lucky to be alone; some things shouldn't be shared; some things are better left where they are."

Buried in the sand of the sea floor? he wondered. It seemed irrational to blame her for failing to take him into her confidence yet he found himself annoyed by her obdurate reticence. Abruptly, he felt a tearing need to share her secrets: her humiliations, her childish maunderings, her hate and love and fear; her shame; the core that made this bolt of silk what it was, as different and fascinatingly imperfect as some strange glowing gem. Her mystery pulled him onward and, like a marathon swimmer who has reached his limit and, passing it, finds himself about to go under with the realization that he has attempted to discover and defeat something far too powerful for him, he knew that this same realization was the key to his reaching down to find the unplumbed reserves which would carry him onward to reach the far shore.

But for Nicholas it was somewhat different, for part of him, at least, was well aware of those things which lay hidden there within that interminable beach, and he shuddered to face them again, to gaze upon their hideous countenances. For once before he had come upon them and had almost been destroyed.

They went out of the house in the summer night. The clouds had delivered themselves westward and the sky was at last clear. The stars shone, winking, like ornaments on velvet, making them feel as if the world had wrapped them in a shawl manufactured especially for that occasion.

They strolled along the beach at the waterline, far out, for it was low tide. Their feet picked up the damp sea grapes and their soles felt the brief pain of the fiddler crab shells.

The surf tumbled in low, faintly phosphorescent hillocks that seemed like another world viewed from the wrong end of a telescope. Near to hand, they were alone on the beach; a point of orange, a smokily glowing coal, bespoke a late barbecue in the lee of a dune far down the night.

"Are you afraid of me?" His voice was as light as mist.

"No," she said. "I'm not." She stuffed her hands in the front pockets of her jeans. "I'm just afraid. It's been with me for more than a year and a half, this fear like a diamond shadow-image I can't manage to shake."

"We're all afraid—of something or other."

"Jesus, Nick, don't patronize me. You've never been afraid like this."

"Because I'm a man?"

"Because you're you." She stared fixedly away from him, his muscularity. She rubbed her palms along her bare arms; he thought she shivered. "Oh, Christ."

He bent down, scooped up a sand-encrusted stone. He wiped it off, feeling its ineffable smoothness against his skin. Time had taken away all the edges; time had dictated its shape. Yet the essence of the stone—its mottled color, striations, imperfections of structure, density and hardness—remained. Indomitable.

She took the stone from him and hurled it far out into the water. It struck the surface of the sea without a splash and sank from sight as if it had never existed, but Nicholas could still feel the weight of it where it had rested in the palm of his hand.

"It would be so simple," he said, "if we could approach people we cared for without any past so we could see them without any coloration."

She stood silently regarding him and only a slight tremor along her neck told him that she had heard.

"But we can't," he continued. "Human memory is long; it's after all what brings us together, what causes that peculiar tingling, sometimes, when we first meet, like a faint but unmistakable brush of recognition—of what? A kindred spirit, perhaps. An aura. It has many names. It exists, invisible but unallayed for all that." He paused. "Did you feel it when we met?"

"I felt—something. Yes." Her thumb stroked the back of his hand, tracing the lines of the bones there. "A spark from a flame." She looked down at her feet, at the damp black sand, at the rushing water. "I'm afraid to trust you." Her head came up abruptly as if she had made some decision and was now determined to adhere to it. "My men have been such bastards and—I did the picking, after all...."

"How can I be any different, is that it?"

"But you are different, Nick. I can feel it." Yet she took

52

her hand away from his. "I can't go through it again. I just can't. This isn't a movie. I don't know that everything is going to turn out all right."

"When do you ever know that?"

But she ignored him, continuing, "We're brought up with a kind of romanticism that's so false it leads us astray. Falling in love and marriage is forever. The movies, then TV told us that, even—especially—the commercials. We're all electronic babies now. So then we pass out of 'us' and into 'I'—what do you do when the 'us' doesn't work and the 'I' is far too lonely?"

"You keep searching, I suppose. That's all life is anyway. It's one great search for whatever it is we want: love, money, fame, recognition, security—all of those things. It's the degrees of importance which vary in each individual."

"Except for me." Justine's voice was tinged with bitterness now. "I don't know what I want anymore."

"What was it," he said, "that you wanted in San Francisco?" He saw only her outline, an ebon figure in the darkness, blotting out the starlight where she stood.

Her voice, when she answered, was like a wisp out of time, a cold tendril, slightly unearthly, so that he felt a brief shiver run through him.

"I wanted," she said, "to be dominated."

"I still can't believe I said that to you."

They lay, naked, beneath the sheets in his bed. A beam of moonlight came in through the windows overlooking the sea like an ethereal bridge to another land.

"Why?" Nicholas asked her.

"Because I'm ashamed of it. I'm ashamed I ever felt that way. I don't ever want to be like that again. I reject it."

"Is it so terrible, then, to want to be dominated?"

"The way I wanted it. . . . Yes, it was—unnatural."

"How do you mean that?"

She turned around and he felt the soft press of her breasts against his skin. "I don't want to talk about it anymore. Let's just forget I ever said it."

He took her bare arms in his hands and looked her full in the face. "Let's get one thing straight. I am who I am. I'm not—what was that guy's name in San Francisco?"

"Chris."

"I'm not Chris and I'm not anyone else who's been in your

53

life." He paused, studying her eyes. "Do you understand what I'm saying? If you're fearful of the same things happening then you're bound to see me as Chris or someone else. We all do that at times, unconsciously because we all have archetypes. But you can't do that now. If you fail, if you don't break through now, you never will. And every man you meet will in some way be Chris and you'll never be free of whatever it is you fear."

She broke away from him. "You've got no right to lecture me this way. Who the hell do you think you are? I say one thing to you and right away you think you know me." She got up off the bed. "You don't know shit about me. You never will. Who the fuck cares what you have to say anyway?"

He saw her moving away and, a moment later, heard the bathroom door slam.

He sat up swinging his legs over the side of the bed. The urge to smoke was strong so he turned his mind to other matters. He ran his fingers through his hair, staring sightlessly out at the sea. Even now, Japan lapped at his consciousness. There was a message there, he knew, but because he himself had forced it to be buried so deep, it was slow in working its way upward to the light.

He stood up. "Justine," he called.

The door to the bathroom flew open and she emerged, dressed in a dark tank top and jeans. Her eyes were bright hard points, flashing.

"I'm leaving," she said tightly.

"So soon?" He was amused by her elaborate melodramatics and, too, he did not quite believe her after all.

"You bastard! You're like all the rest!" She turned toward the hall.

He grabbed her right wrist, whirling her back. "Where are you going?"

"Away!" she cried. "Out of here! Away from you, you sonovabitch!"

"Justine, you're acting idiotic."

Her free hand slashed upward, struck him across the face. "Don't you say that to me." Her tone was low, a growl; her face was an animalistic mask.

Without thinking, he slapped her. The blow was hard enough so that she reeled backward against the wall. Immediately, his heart broke and he said her name softly and she came into his arms, her open lips against the tendons of

54

his neck, her hot tears scalding his flesh; she stroked the back of his head.

He picked her up and carried her to the rumpled bed and they made violent love for a very long time.

Afterward, with her lithe arms about him, her legs twined with his, he said quite seriously, "That will never happen again. Never."

"Never," she breathed, echoing him.

He heard the phone ringing in his sleep and drew himself up through the layers from delta to beta to alpha. Just as he awoke, the muscles in his stomach tightened. He turned over and reached for the receiver; beside him, Justine stirred.

"Hello?" His voice sounded furry.

Justine put her arm across his chest; even her nails were warm.

"Hi! It's Vincent." There was a pause. "Say, am I disturbing you?"

"Well, sort of."

"Sorry, buddy."

There was only a singing on the line and he woke up. Vincent was too much a Japanese to intrude yet he would not be calling this early unless it was important. It was up to him now, Nicholas knew. If he said later, Vincent would hang up and that would be the end of it. Justine's head moved into the crook of his shoulder and her face went from light to shadow, the darkness pooling in the dells.

"What is it, Vincent? I suspect this isn't a strictly personal call."

"No. It isn't."

"What's up?"

"You read about the stiff they took out of the water a couple of days ago?"

"Yeah." His stomach rolled over. "What about him?"

"That's why I'm out here." Vincent cleared his throat, obviously uneasy. "I'm at the M.E.'s building in Hauppauge. Do you know where it is?"

"I know how to get to Hauppauge, if that's what you're aiming at," he said shortly.

"I'm afraid I am, Nick."

He felt as if he were abruptly holding onto three pounds

55

of air. "What the hell is going on? Why all the goddamn secrecy?"

"I think you ought to see what we've got for yourself." Vincent's voice seemed strained. "I don't—I don't want to prejudice you in any way. That's why I'm not giving you anything to think about over the phone."

"Buddy, you're wrong about that. You're giving me plenty to think about." He glanced at his watch: 7:15. "Give me about forty minutes, okay?"

"Sure. I'll meet you outside, guide you in." There was silence for a moment. "Sorry, buddy."

"Yeah."

When he put down the phone, he found that the palm of his hand was slippery with sweat.

Nicholas looked again at the sliver of metal under the eye of the microscope, a fractional shaving from the small piece Doc Deerforth had recovered from the breastbone of the corpse.

"Here are the spectrometer readouts," Vincent said, slipping the sheets across the zinc alloy table. Nicholas took his eye from the microscopic fragment. "We ran it through three times to be certain."

Nicholas picked up the sheets, running his gaze over the figures. But he already suspected what he would find there. Still, it seemed incredible to him.

"This steel," he said carefully, "was manufactured from a particular type of magnetic iron and ferruginous sand. There are perhaps twenty separate layers. The size of the fragment makes it difficult to tell. I'm going by past experience."

Vincent, whose eyes had never left Nicholas', took a deep breath, said, "It wasn't made in this country."

"No," Nicholas agreed. "It was manufactured in Japan."

"Do you know what this means?" Vincent said. He sat back, including Doc Deerforth in the discussion.

"What can be inferred from that alone?" Nicholas asked.

Vincent took a folder off the tabletop, handed it to Nicholas. "Take a look at page three."

Nicholas opened the folder, leafed through the pages. His eyes dropped down the typewritten sheet. He sat perfectly still but, abruptly, he could feel the rushing of his blood

56

through his veins. His heart raced. He was nearing that far shore. He looked up. "Who did the chemical analysis?"

"I did," Doc Deerforth said. "There's no error. I was stationed in the Philippines during the war. I've come across this particular substance once before."

"Do you know what this is?" Nicholas asked him.

"I can make a pretty good guess. It's a nonsynthetic poison that affects the cardiovascular system."

"It's *doku*," Nicholas said, "an enormously powerful poison distilled from the pistils of the chrysanthemum. The technique of its manufacture is virtually unknown outside of Japan and even among the Japanese very few know how to make it. Its origins, it is said, lie in China."

"Then we know how the poison was administered," Vincent said.

"What do you mean?" Doc Deerforth broke in.

"He means," Nicholas said heavily, "that the man was killed by a *shaken*—a Japanese throwing star—part of a *shuriken*, a small-blade arsenal—dipped in *doku*."

"Which means we also know *who* killed him," Vincent said.

Nicholas nodded. "That's right. Only one kind of man could. A ninja."

For reasons of security, Doc Deerforth hustled them out of the building. They were careful to take with them all the pertinent readouts and evidence.

Since none of them had bothered with breakfast, they stopped on the way back to West Bay Bridge, pulling into a diner right off Montauk Highway that offered authentic Portuguese food.

Over strong black coffee, broiled sardines and clams in a rich steaming winy broth, they sat and watched the cars silently pass on the highway. No one seemed to want to begin. But someone had to and Vincent said, "Who's the new lady, Nick?"

"Hmm?" Nicholas turned from the window and smiled. "Her name's Justine Tobin. She lives right down the beach from me."

"On Dune Road?" Doc Deerforth said and when Nicholas nodded, he added, "I know her. Beautiful girl. Only her name's Tomkin."

"Sorry, Doc," Nicholas said. "You must be mistaken. This Justine's named Tobin."

"Dark hair, green eyes, one with red motes in it, about five-seven—"

"That's her."

Doc Deerforth nodded. "Name's Justine Tomkin, Nick. At least, that's how she was born. You know, Tomkin, as in Tomkin Oil."

"*That* one?"

"Yep. Her daddy."

Everyone knew about Raphael Tomkin. Oil was but one of his many multinational moneymakers but by all accounts the most lucrative. He was worth—where had he read it? In *Newsweek,* perhaps—somewhere in the neighborhood of a hundred million dollars, the last time anybody had bothered to count; at that rarefied level, there did not seem to be much of a reason to do so.

"She doesn't like him much," Nicholas said.

Doc Deerforth laughed. "Yah. You could say that. She obviously doesn't want any part of him."

Nicholas recalled Justine's words, *He's as dead as he could possibly be.* Now he began to understand the irony of that remark. Still, he was annoyed at finding out this way.

"Now what can you tell me about the ninja?" Doc Deerforth said around a bit of clam flesh.

Outside, a white Ford with black trim pulled up next to the diner. As they watched, a big man with a red face and bulbous nose stepped out and walked toward them.

"Hope neither of you mind," Doc Deerforth said. "I phoned Ray Florum when we got here. He's the commander of the West Bay Bridge Village Police. I think he's got a right to hear what's going on. Okay?" Both Nicholas and Vincent nodded their assent. "Nick?"

"It's okay, Doc," he said as lightly as he could. "It just caught me off guard. I didn't expect her to—" He waved a hand in lieu of finishing.

The door opened and Florum pushed into the diner. Doc Deerforth introduced him around and he sat down. They filled him in.

"Quite literally," Nicholas said, "ninja means 'in stealth.'" Florum poured himself some coffee as Nicholas continued. "Outside of Japan, there is almost nothing known about ninjutsu, the art of the ninja. Even there, it has been poorly

58

documented primarily because it was knowledge that was both utterly secret and jealously guarded. One was born into a ninja family or one gave up all hope of becoming one.

"As you may know, Japanese society has always been rigorously stratified. There is a highly defined social order and no one would even contemplate deserting his station in life; it's part of one's karma, and this has religious as well as social overtones.

"The samurai, for instance, the warriors of feudal Japan, were gentlemen, of the *bushi* class; no one else was allowed to become a samurai or carry two swords. Well, the ninja evolved from the opposite end of the social spectrum, the *hinin*. This level was so low that the transition of that term means 'not human.' Naturally, they were a far cry from the aristocratic *bushi*. Yet, as clan warfare increased in Japan, the samurai recognized a growing need for the specific skills of the ninja, for the samurai themselves were bound by an iron-clad code of *bushido* which strictly forbade them many actions. Thus, the samurai clans hired the free-lance ninja to perform acts of arson, assassination, infiltration and terrorism which they themselves were duty-bound to shun. History tells us, for instance, that the ninja made their first important appearance in the sixth century A.D. Prince Regent Shotoku employed them as spies.

"So successful were they that their numbers increased dramatically during the Heian and Kamakura periods in Japanese history. They concentrated in the south. Kyoto, for example, was dominated by them at night.

"But the last we hear of them as a major factor in Japan is during the Shimabara war in 1637 when they were used to quell a Christian rebellion on the island of Kyūshū. Yet we know they were active all through the long Tokugawa shōgunate."

"Just how wide is the scope of their skill?" Doc Deerforth's nostrils were clogged with the rotting stench of the Philippine jungle.

"Very," Nicholas said. "From the ninja the samurai learned woodsmanship, disguise, camouflage, codes and silent signaling, the preparation of fire bombs and smoke screens. In short, you would not be wrong to consider the ninja military Houdinis. But each *ryu*, that is, school and, in the ninja's case, clan, specialized in different forms of combat, espionage, lore, and so on, so that one was often able to tell

59

by his methods from which *ryu* a particular assassin came. For instance, the Fodo *ryu* was known for its work with many kinds of small concealed blades, the Gyōkku was expert at using thumb and forefinger on the body's nerve centers in hand-to-hand combat, the Kotto was proficient at breaking bones, others used hypnotism and so on. Ninja were also quite often skilled *yogen*—that is, chemists."

There was a heavy silence between them until Vincent cleared his throat and said, "Nick, I think you ought to tell them the rest of it."

Nicholas was silent for a time.

"What does he mean?" Florum said.

Nicholas took a deep breath. "The art of ninjutsu," he said, "is very ancient. So old, in fact, that no one is certain of its origin, though speculation is that it was born in a region of China. The Japanese took many things from Chinese culture over the centuries. There is an element of...superstition involved. One could even say magic."

"Magic?" echoed Doc Deerforth. "Are you seriously suggesting...?"

"In the history of Japan," Nicholas said, "it is oftentimes difficult to separate fact from legend. I am not trying to be melodramatic. This is the way it is in Japan. Feats have been ascribed to the ninja that would have been impossible without the aid of some kind of magic."

"Tall tales," said Florum. "Every country's got 'em."

"Yes. Possibly."

"And the poison you found?"

"Is a ninja poison. Swallowed, it's quite harmless. A favorite method of administering it was to make a quick-drying syrup of it and coat the *shaken* with it."

"What's that?" Florum asked.

"These are part of a ninja's arsenal of silent, easily concealed weapons, his short-bladed *shuriken*. The *shaken* is a star-shaped metal object. Flung through the air by the ninja, it becomes a most lethal weapon. And coated with this poison, the weapon need not even puncture a vital spot for the victim to die."

Florum snorted. "Are you trying to tell me that that stiff was killed by a ninja? Jesus, Linnear, you said they died out three hundred years ago."

"No," Nicholas corrected. "I merely said that that was the last time they were used in any major way. Many things

60

have changed in Japan since the sixteen hundreds and the Tokugawa shōgunate, and the country is, in many respects, no longer what it once was. However, there are traditions that are impossible to obliterate by either man or time."

"There's got to be another explanation," Florum said, shaking his head. "What would a ninja be doing in West Bay Bridge?"

"I'm afraid that's something I can't answer," Nicholas said. "But I know this. There is a ninja abroad here and in all the world there is no more deadly or clever foe. You must take extreme caution. Modern weapons—guns, grenades, tear gas—will give you no security against him, for he knows of all these things and they will not deter him from destroying his intended target and escaping unseen."

"Well, he's already done that," Florum said, getting up. "Thanks for the information." He stuck out his hand. "Nice meeting you both." He nodded. "Doc." And with that he left.

The moment Justine heard the knock on her door she felt her heart sink. She put down her pen and, wiping her hands on a chamois cloth, came away from the drawing board. The light had been just right; she preferred the daylight to the gooseneck lamp clamped to the board, even though its combination of fluorescent and incandescent bulbs gave her a decent approximation of natural illumination.

She let Nicholas in.

"They called you about that body, didn't they?" she said.

He went across the room and sat on the sofa, hands behind his head. "What body?"

"You know. The one they took out of the water the day we met."

"Yes. That's the one." He looked tired and drawn to her.

"Why did they call you?"

He looked up at her. "They thought I might be able to help them find out how he died."

"You mean he didn't drown? But what would you—"

"Justine, why didn't you tell me your father is Raphael Tomkin?"

Her hands, which had been in front of her, fingers interlaced, dropped to her side. "What possible reason would I have to tell you?" she said.

"Do you think I'd be after your money?"

"Don't be absurd." She gave a little laugh but it came out quite strangled. "I don't have any money."

"You know what I mean."

"What difference could it make who my father is?"

"It doesn't, really. I'm more interested in why you chose to change your name."

"I don't think it's any of your business."

He got up, went over to look at what she had been working on. "Nice," he said. "I like it." He went into the kitchen, opened the refrigerator. "That man was murdered," he told her over his shoulder. "By an expert assassin. But nobody knows why." He took out a bottle of Perrier, opened it and emptied it into a glass. He took a drink. "Vincent was called in and he in turn asked for my help, because the murderer is in all likelihood a Japanese; a man who kills for money." He turned around, went back into the living room where she still stood where he had left her. She stared at him, her eyes very bright. "Not a hit man—someone you read about in the papers when there's some gangland killing in New Jersey or Brooklyn. No, this is the kind of man you never hear about. He's far too clever to give himself any notoriety except among an elite core of potential clients. But I really don't know too much about that end of it." He looked up at her as he settled himself on the sofa once more. "Are you getting all this?"

There was silence for a time, just the sound of the surf seeming far away. She moved, at last, over to the stereo, putting on a record. But almost immediately she took the needle off the groove as if the music were some intruder now to be kept away.

"He called me home during my sophomore year at Smith," she said with her back to him. Her voice was flat and dry and contained. "Sent his goddamn private jet for me so I was sure not to miss any of my classes." She turned around but her head was down, her gaze riveted on a paper clip she held, working it back and forth until it snapped apart. "Well, I was, I don't know, I guess 'frightened' is the word. I couldn't imagine what emergency he'd called me back home for. I immediately thought of my mother. Funny, not Gelda; she never got sick. Not like Mother.

"Anyway, I was brought into the study and there he was standing before the fire, toasting his hands. I stood watching him with my loden coat brushed with snow, not even bothering to take it off. He offered me a drink." Her head snapped up and she impaled him with her eyes. "Can you imagine! He offered me a drink as calmly as if we were business partners about to discuss an important deal.

"It's odd, you know. That's precisely the image I had at the time. It was prophetic. 'My dear,' he said, 'I've a surprise for you. I've come across a most extraordinary man. He'll be here any moment. I imagine the snow's delayed him a bit. Come. Take off your coat and sit down.' But I stayed where I was, dumbfounded. 'Is this why you flew me home?' I asked. 'Well, yes. I want you to meet him. He's ideal for you. His family's in the right bracket and quite well connected. He's good-looking and a three-letter man to boot.' 'Father,' I said, 'you scared me half to death over some mad idea that—' 'I scared you?' 'Yes, I thought something had happened, to Mother or—' 'Don't be so idiotic, Justine! I can't think what I'm going to do with you.' I stormed out, furious, and he just couldn't understand what he had done to upset me. It was all done out of love, he told me. 'Do you know how much time I spent making this selection?' he said as I went out the door." She sighed. "For my father, time was always his most precious commodity."

"People don't do that anymore," he said. "Trade off other people as if they were things."

"Oh no?" She laughed sardonically. "It happens all the time, all around." She spread out her arms. "In marriages, when the woman's expected to perform certain duties; in divorces, when the kids are used as bargaining points; in affairs. All the time, Nick. Grow up, will you?"

He got up off the sofa, annoyed at her height advantage. "I'll bet your father used to say that to you. 'Grow up, Justine.'"

"You're a bastard, you know that?"

"C'mon. You're not going to start another fight now, are you? I told you—"

"Bastard!" She leaped across the intervening coffee table, her body crashing against his, her hands flailing against him, but he caught her slender wrists without difficulty, pinioning her.

"Now, listen," he said. "I don't mind horsing around with you, but I told you, I'm not Chris and you're not going to provoke a fight with me every time you want some attention. There're other ways to get it. For instance, you could ask."

"I shouldn't have to ask," she said.

"Oho! So that's it. I don't have ESP. I'm just a human being. And I don't need psychodramas."

"But I do."

"No," he said, "you don't." He let her go.

"Prove it."

"You're the only one who can do that."

"Not alone, I can't." She stared up into his face. Her hand lifted. Her fingertips grazed his cheek. "Help me," she whispered. "Help me."

His mouth covered her open lips.

It seemed highly improbable that Billy Shawtuck would have gotten the nickname "Wild Bill" but nevertheless there it was. He was a ruddy-complexioned man in his early forties, shortish and not even stocky. He always wore long-sleeved shirts, even in the dead of summer when, even out here near the shore, there was more sweat than wind around.

Ask his buddies at Grendel's and they would tell you that was because he didn't like to show off his enormous biceps. Of course, if pressed, they would also tell you he came to his nickname by way of eschewing beers for a double scotch on the rocks every time. Apparently the heat didn't bother him much.

Billy worked for Lilco, riding power lines, and, he always said to those he beat at arm wrestling off-hours at Grendel's, he came by his muscles honestly. "I didn't have to go to no fag gym every day to get these," he'd say, downing the double scotch on the rocks in a swallow and raising his arm to order another. "Shit, my job does all that. Honest work you can sweat at." Then he would shake his head full of sandy hair. "I'm not one of those goddamned desk jockeys."

Grendel's was a local watering hole—almost exclusively blue-collar (the writers had their own favorite)—several miles outside of West Bay Bridge, roadside to Montauk Highway.

Late in the evening, Billy Shawtuck stood in the doorway to Grendel's preparatory to leaving. The sky was turning from indigo to black, the traffic from the highway taking on a spectral quality as headlights and taillights flicked by like the inquisitive eyes of nocturnal animals.

On the top of the steps, Billy took a deep breath and cursed

64

the summer influx. We're all gonna die of carbon monoxide poisoning one of these days, he thought.

Not four paces away, his Lilco truck stood waiting for him, but this evening he was reluctant to leave the cheery warmth of the bar. Music blatted at his back from the juke inside. Tony Bennett singing "I Left My Heart in San Francisco."

You could take San Francisco, Billy thought, take the whole of the West Coast and shove it up your ass. He'd been out there in the Army and had come to hate it. I didn't leave anything there but a good case of the clap. He laughed. But, damn, I'm sure sorry I took this late job. Time and a half is all well and good but some days—well, some days it just wasn't worth it. He had a feeling that this was one of those days.

Sighing deeply, he went down the stairs but not before giving the finger to Tony Bennett and his shit-ass city.

His mood changed, however, as he banged down one of the dark side roads and he began to whistle tunelessly. He didn't think this job was going to take too long.

And, of course, by that time he was thinking of Helene and the stuff he had bought her from the Frederick's of Hollywood catalog. Agh, he thought, maybe it came in the mail today. It was about due.

He was picturing Helene's long-legged frame in the clothes—he laughed: if you could call them that—as he came around the last bend to the beach-front property and saw the black-clad figure step right into the beam of his left-side headlight.

"What the fuck!" He stepped on the brakes and swerved over to the right shoulder. Leaning out the window, he called, "You stupid bastard! I coulda killed you. What's the matter with—"

The door on his side crashed open and it felt as if a tornado hurled him out of the cab. "Hey!" He rolled across the cool tarmac. "Hey, buddy!"

He got to his feet in a boxer's semi-crouch, his fists up in front of his chest.

"Not to fool around, you sonovabitch."

His eyes opened wide as he saw the flash of the long blade in the wash of the headlights. Christ, he thought, a sword. A sword? Jesus, I must be drunk.

A moth battled in the headlight, dazzled, and the cicadas

65

sizzled. Close at hand, the surf hissed and shushed like a nanny calming a crying baby.

He threw a punch. It never connected.

The air in front of him seemed to split apart and vibrate like a beaded curtain.

He felt two sensations almost simultaneously. They were the sharpest, most exquisitely painful feelings he had ever experienced.

Once, just outside the base, he had had a scuffle with an M.P. and the bastard had managed to slash him with a knife, wounding him in the side, before he had had a chance to bury his fist in the M.P.'s face. It was the guardhouse for him for that, but he had never felt so satisfied in his life.

But that pain, that burning was nothing to what Billy Shawtuck felt now. The blur of the blade pierced the night and then pierced Billy. From the top of his right shoulder down across his abdomen to the left side of his pelvis. His guts began to spill out and his nostrils were suffused with a nauseating stench.

"Jesus Chri—"

Then the round wooden pole crashed, whistling like a boy at play, onto his shoulder. He heard the sharp crack as the bones broke but, astoundingly, there was absolutely no pain. Only the feeling that he had been driven straight through the tarmac of the road.

Tears came to Billy's eyes for the first time in years. Momma, he thought, Momma, I'm comin' home.

"I think I know what it is," she said.

Night had come and a strong wind, springing up from the landward side of the house, rattled the trees outside. Far off a boat hooted once and was still. They lay close together on the bed, enjoying the nearness of their flesh, nothing sexual in it; just two beings, together.

"You won't laugh," she said, turning her face toward his. "Promise me you won't laugh."

"I promise."

"If I'm hurt—physically—it prepares me, sort of."

"For what?"

"For the other kind of hurt. The breaking up; the leaving."

"That seems to me an awfully pessimistic view of life."

"Yes, it does."

66

He put his arm around her and she put one foot between his, rubbing his shins.

After a time, he said, "What is it you want?"

"To be happy," she said. "That's all." There is nothing else in the world, she thought, but our linked bodies, our twined souls, and she felt that she had never been as close to anyone as she felt at that moment to Nicholas. Trust had to begin somewhere. Perhaps this was the place for her to start.

She jumped at the sound of an enormous crash that seemed to come from near the front of the house, the kitchen. She cried out as if a cold hand had clutched at her vitals, saw Nicholas sit up, swing his legs over the side of the bed.

He stood up, and as he began to move toward the bedroom door he seemed totally transformed to her. Standing there stark naked, he nevertheless seemed fully clothed, as if his rippling muscles and gleaming sweat-streaked skin were some mysterious raiment cloaking him.

He moved silently toward the lemon light streaming down the hallway. He led with his left foot, his body sideways as if he were a fencer, knees slightly bent, feet not leaving the floor. Down the hallway. He had said not a word to her.

Gathering her wits, she went after him.

His hands were up before him, she saw, their edges reminding her oddly of blades, the fingers as stiff as steel as he moved stealthily into the kitchen.

Past the table, she saw that the window over the sink had been shattered inward and shards of glass gleamed in the light. She dared not move farther on bare feet. The curtains flapped in the wind rushing in through the rent, whipping against the enameled walls.

She watched as Nicholas moved forward, stopped as still as a statue as he peered down at something on the floor on the far side of the table near the window. He stayed in that position for such a long time that she went cautiously across the littered floor to stand behind him. She gasped and turned away. But something drew her eyes inexorably back and she looked again.

On the floor was a black furry mass, large and unmoving. Blood seeped along the floor in several places from under the body, glistening where it shone upon the ruined glass. A strange, astringent smell assaulted her nostrils and she gagged. Her eyes began to tear.

"What—" She gagged again, swallowed hard. "What is that thing?"

"I'm not sure," he said slowly. "Its too big for a bat, at least in this part of the country, and its not a flying squirrel."

The phone began to ring and Justine jumped. Her hands gripped her arms. "I've got gooseflesh," she said. Nicholas remained where he was, staring down at the black thing that had crashed through the window. "Blinded by the light," he said.

Justine went to the far wall and picked up the phone but he seemed oblivious as she spoke for several moments. She had to come back and touch him on the arm. "Vincent wants to speak to you," she said.

He looked at her then, tearing his eyes away. "All right." His voice seemed thick, his thoughts far away. "Don't go near it," he warned as he went to the phone. "What is it?" he said abruptly.

"I tried you at your place," Vincent said. "When there was no answer, I took a chance." Nicholas said nothing. "Look, I know what time it is." His voice rattled against Nicholas' ear, an odd note settled in it. "It's happened again. Florum just brought in another body. They're photographing it now." The wind howling in through the broken window seemed chill to Nicholas. He waited, sweat breaking out on his body. He looked at the mess on the floor: the black-furred corpse, the red blood, seeping still as if seeking something or someone. "Nick, the body has been cut obliquely from shoulder-blade to hip joint as neatly as— It was one cut. Do you understand?"

SPRING / SUMMER 1945 / WINTER 1951

There was a Shinto temple amid the lushest forest Nicholas had ever seen a mere three hundred meters from the extreme eastern edge of his father's land. Then it was another hundred and fifty or so to the house, a large, delicate, precisely orchestrated structure of traditional Japanese design. The front was L-shaped, preceded, as one came upon it, by an exquisite formal garden which, needless to say, required tireless attention and as much love as a small child.

The irony of the location would come later when, on the far side of the long rolling knoll to the west, they would construct an ultramodern eight-lane superhighway to aid the bustling traffic to and from the heart of Tokyo.

The last traces of Japan's military might had been ground to metal powder, its imperial *daimyo* tried and serving time as war criminals. The Emperor remained but everywhere uniformed Americans basked in what they often laughingly referred to as "the atomic sunshine."

Yet Nicholas' history lessons were to begin in another country.

On February 15, 1942, his father told him when he was ten, the British garrison had surrendered Singapore to the attacking Japanese. They held the city for three and a half years until September 1945, when the British reoccupied it. There his father had met his mother, a kind of refugee in the war-torn city. She had been married to a Japanese garrison commander and seeing him blown to bits during the last days of that humid trembling summer perhaps unhinged her for a time.

The first of the British forces were already infiltrating the outskirts of the city and the commander had moved his garrison east to outflank them but, overextending his position, had found himself outflanked. Caught in a murderous cross-fire, he had cut down six English soldiers with his *katana* before the rest had sense enough to step back and loft the volley of grenades. There was nothing left of him, not even bones.

Years later, in an old battered shop selling *ukiyo-e* prints in a tiny Tokyo side street, Nicholas had come across a certain print titled *The End of the Samurai*. It depicted a dismayed warrior's death, his great *katana* flung from his hands by a blast of gunpowder. In that print Nicholas saw, perhaps, the redemption of his mother's first husband, recognizing the historical imperative of that enemy.

His mother had always been a totally apolitical woman. She had married out of love, hardly out of convenience. But with the eventual defeat of the Japanese in Singapore, with the death of her husband, she found that her entire world had exploded into a wilderness that frightened her. This she found utterly consternating. Life, she firmly believed, was for the living. One mourned one's losses and moved onward. Karma. She believed in that above all else. Not a predestiny—she was no fatalist as many Westerners might mistakenly dub her. She knew, rather, merely how to bow before the inevitabilities of life. As the death of her husband.

But this was a time of momentous changes and, like a beautiful flower caught up in an inexplicable maelstrom, she felt adrift in the riot of chattering gunfire and mortar explosions.

She met Nicholas' father, ironically enough, in the very office where her dead husband had carried on the command of his defeated garrison. She had wandered in there as if it were some Buddhist temple, sacrosanct from the flames of war that rose all about her. Perhaps she had come there because it was one of the only places left in Singapore now that was at all familiar to her. Oddly enough, the thought of fleeing the city never entered her mind. Rather, she wandered the lethal city with little regard to her personal safety.

So much of the city had changed that she was confused, no longer certain where the business district was or where her old apartment had once stood. Piles of rubble were everywhere and the streets were flooded with a tide of children, surging and calling, as if in the aftermath of war's bleak nightmare they had been released from some hideous bondage. It recalled to her the happiness she had felt at New

70

Year's festivals when she had been a girl—liberated for a time from the cares and restrictions of the world. And this, too, confounded her.

Thus for many days she had walked the steaming streets, whirling into dark doorways instinctively as she heard the heavy tramping of the approaching soldiers—she was beyond differentiating one side from another. Miraculously, she avoided serious misadventure. Karma, she would say later.

She survived at the sufferance and the pity of those Chinese folk who spied her and fed her almost as if she were a baby, spooning the thin rice soup between her slack lips, wiping her chin every so often, for she could not do even this simple act herself. She relieved herself in the gutters and forgot what it was like to take a bath. Those times when she came across running water, as in the fountains still intact which she stumbled across by chance, she thrust her fingers into the spray, staring at it as if it were something she had never seen before. When it rained, she stood still and stared upward at the billowing clouds, seeking, perhaps, a glimpse of God.

The morning she staggered into the garrison office, Nicholas' father was in the middle of an administrative crisis. Not only were his troops obliged to mop up the last outlying pockets of Japanese opposition but now orders had come down urging him to see to it that his men policed the metropolitan area in an attempt to quell the increasingly violent outbreaks between the Chinese and the Malays who lived constantly in an uneasy half-peace. That left perhaps an hour and a half each day for his men to sleep; it was clearly a situation he could not tolerate and he was in the process of seeking some conciliatory alternative to actively disobeying a direct order. He had, in fact, been sitting in this same wooden slatted chair—the one that had, for the last three years, been the sole property of the dead Japanese garrison commander—since the morning of the previous day.

Except for several hurried trips to the washroom to relieve himself, Colonel Denis Linnear had been right where he was when the dazed woman wandered into his sanctum sanctorum. How she had managed to slip past the three sets of guards he was never able to ascertain to his satisfaction. Yet that particular point only manifested itself to him much later. At the time, he was concerned only with her appearance and, as he jumped up from behind his littered desk, his aides

71

seemed more startled by his movements than by the fact that there was an unannounced woman in the room.

"Danvers!" the Colonel called to his adjutant. "Get a cot in here, on the double!"

The man rushed out and the Colonel was reaching for the woman when she began to fall. Her eyes fluttered closed and she collapsed into his arms.

"Sir?" Lieutenant McGivers said. "About this—"

"Oh, for pity's sake, man, get me a cold cloth," the Colonel barked irritably. "And get Grey in here."

Grey was the garrison surgeon, a tall angular man with a bushy mustache and sun-reddened skin. He arrived just as Danvers was mishandling the cot through the doorway.

"Give him a hand, McGivers, there's a good lad," the Colonel said to the reappearing lieutenant. And together they maneuvered the cot into the room.

The Colonel lifted the woman up, noting her fine Asian features under the layers of dirt and dust, lowered her gently onto the cot.

He let Grey take over then, going back behind his desk, working on the tail end of his problem with one eye cocked across the room until, at length, the surgeon stood up.

"All right, Lieutenant," the Colonel said wearily, "get everyone out of here. We'll reconvene at 0800 hours." He stood up, passing his long fingers through his hair, and crossed to where Grey stood looking down at his patient.

When they were alone in the room, he said, "How is she?"

The surgeon shrugged. "It's hard to say until she comes around and I can run a few more tests. She's obviously suffering from shock and exposure. Several good meals will fix her up, I shouldn't wonder." He wiped his hands on the cloth he had used to clean her. "Look here, Denis, I've a lot of young boys to see. If you suspect a problem when she comes round, have Danvers come and fetch me. Otherwise, I think you know what she needs as well as I do."

The Colonel summoned Danvers and sent him to scrounge up some hot soup and any pieces of boiled chicken he could find. Then he knelt beside her, watching the soft pulse along the long column of her neck.

Thus the first thing Cheong saw when she opened her eyes was the close face of the Colonel. What struck her immediately, she recalled later in recounting the story to Nicholas, were his eyes. "They were the kindest eyes I had ever seen,"

72

she said in her light singsong voice. "They were the very
deepest blue. I had never before seen blue eyes. I had been
outside the city when the British had first come, prior to the
outbreak of the war.

"I often think that it was those blue eyes which so startled
me, brought me around. Suddenly I remembered the long
days after Tsūkō had been killed as if they were part of a
film being run off whole for the first time; the pieces at last
had knit together. I no longer had gauze in front of my eyes
and cotton wool stuffed into my head.

"With that, it all began to pass away from me—as if I
were recalling events from some other person's life—the dark
terrible last days of the war.

"That is when I knew that your father was part of my
karma, in that first moment I saw him, for I have no remembrance of entering the garrison house, of encountering
any British soldiers there before him."

The Colonel took her home at the day's end, in the midst
of the long shimmering emerald and lapis lazuli twilight,
with the city choked with swirling dust, Jeeps clattering
down the streets and soldiers running quick-time along the
sidewalks while the Chinese and the Malays paused in their
homeward journeys, standing quite still, resolute and quiescent and eternal in their cotton drawstring pants and sloping
reed sedge hats.

As usual it was teeming, and the Colonel had the Jeep
brought around, though he was often fond of walking. It took
him twenty minutes on average to make the journey from
the garrison, located near Keppel Harbour, almost due north
through the city to the house he now occupied. As may be
imagined, the command was not overly fond of his making
this trek on foot and thus he was perforce obliged to be accompanied by two armed men from his garrison as escort
from door to door. The Colonel found this a hideous misap-
propriation of precious manpower, but he seemed to have no
choice in the matter.

At first he had been assigned an enormous estate near the
western tip of the city but he soon found that it was hard by
an equally enormous mangrove swamp and being downwind
from it was too much even for him. So he had looked around
and eventually moved to this current smaller but infinitely
more comfortable place.

It was situated on a hill which the Colonel liked quite a

73

bit because when he faced north he could gaze up at Bukit Timah, the island's granitic core and its highest spot. Beyond that dark mass, the hump of some great leviathan, lay the black waters of the Johore Strait and Malaysia, the southernmost tip of the massive block of Asia. On the days when it was particularly hot and humid, when his shirt stuck like hot wax to his skin and the sweat poured from his scalp into his eyes, when the entire city steamed like a tropical rain forest, it seemed to him as if Asia's bulk were sliding slowly downward onto the top of his head, suffocating him in a blanket of endless marshes, mosquitoes and men; the crick in his neck would return, paining him worse than ever.

But this was all before the appearance of Cheong. To the Colonel it was nothing short of miraculous, as if she had come into his room, not from the streets of Singapore, but from the cloud-filled sky. That first evening, when he had turned her over to tiny Pi to be bathed and clothed, and standing by his polished teak desk, taking his first long drink of the day, he felt the tiredness washing away from him like a residue of salt drowned in a hot shower. He thought only that it was good to be home after so long a time at work. Yet perhaps this had been only the most mundane part of it, for when he recalled that time many years later—as he was often wont to do—he was not at all certain of his motivations or his feelings in the matter. He knew only that when she had been brought back to him in his study, when he saw again her face, for the first time since he had left England in the early part of 1940 to come East, he no longer seemed obsessed with Asia. He stood watching her come toward him, feeling like a house bereft of the ghost that had haunted it for so long, now empty, waiting to be filled by new and more substantial tenants. He recognized then his spirit, unchained at last, dancing inside of him and he felt that here before him was his true reason for seeking out the mysteries of Asia.

He studied her face, using the light of the breaking sky, the day's last light, a spurt before darkness fell completely, with the innate fierceness with which he had applied himself to the destruction of the enemy. This was a most formidable talent in the Colonel, one that was highly respected among the Americans as well as the British military and for which he had been amply rewarded by one battlefield promotion after another.

It was not, he felt, a purely Chinese face. This he derived

74

not from any overt configuration of features but by the overall aspect. There was, for instance, nothing classic about that face. This the Colonel found utterly fascinating, not to mention charming. It was oval, longer than it was full. She had high cheekbones, very long almond-shaped eyes and a nose less flat than one might normally expect. Her lips were wide and full and, with those eyes, were her most expressive feature. Later on, he would be able to tell any nuance of changing mood just by a glance at her lips.

Pi had pulled Cheong's long hair back from her face and, having first endeavored to do away with the ragged ends, had tied it tightly back with a red satin ribbon so that it hung down across one shoulder in a long ponytail, so thick and gleaming that the Colonel thought of her more at that moment as some mythical creature come to life. She was, he felt, so densely oriental that it was as if she were the living embodiment of that vast flat crowded land.

"How are you feeling?" He said this in Cantonese and, when he got no response, repeated the question in Mandarin.

"Fine now. Thank you," she said, bowing.

It was the first time the Colonel had heard her speak and he was somewhat startled, never having heard such a beautiful and musical voice before. She was tall, almost five-nine, with a figure as slender as a willow but as shapely as any man could wish for.

"It is most fortunate that I met you," she said, her gaze directed at the floor. She tried in vain to pronounce his last name. "I am most ashamed," she said, giving it up at last. "Pi coached me all through the bath. I am most humbly sorry."

"Don't be," the Colonel said. "Call me Denis."

This she could manage, pronouncing the *D* sound in a way that had no analogue in the English language. She repeated it twice then said, "I shall not forget it, Denis."

By that time, the Colonel knew that he was going to marry her.

When the Colonel received the request by American courier via British liaison to join the American SCAP—the occupation forces—Command in Tokyo as an adviser to General Douglas MacArthur, the first thing he thought of was how he was going to tell Cheong. There was no question of his not taking the assignment. Already he found himself chafing to be in Tokyo.

It was early in 1946 and this part of the world was still reeling from the emotional fallout caused by the explosions at Hiroshima and Nagasaki; the effect was incalculable, the ramifications endless.

He had been married to Cheong for four months and she was three months pregnant. Still he had no second thoughts about abandoning Singapore, which he thought of as much his home as England ever was. Besides the fact that he felt it was his duty to take the assignment at SCAP headquarters he further understood quite keenly the complex problems that had developed within Japan since its unconditional surrender, ending the war, last year and he was eager to immerse himself in what MacArthur had called "steering a bold new course for Japan."

The Colonel deliberated only a moment before he called Danvers in and told him that he was leaving for the day; if anything important came up he could be reached at home.

He arrived at the house to find Cheong taking care of him personally, having shooed Pi away from the doorway at the first hint of the Jeep turning into the driveway.

"You are home early today, Denis," she said, smiling.

He climbed out of the Jeep, dismissed the driver. "I suppose now you'll tell me that I'll be underfoot of the servants cleaning," he said gruffly to her.

"Oh no," she cried, linking her arm in his as they went up the stairs and into the house. "Quite the opposite. I've patted them on the behinds and told them to do the work in the kitchen that they have been putting off for oh-so-long." They went down the hall and into his study where she made him a drink.

"Ah," he said, taking the chill glass from her. "Have they done anything for which they should be punished?"

"Oh no." She put her small hand to her mouth as if shocked by the notion.

He nodded, happy inside himself. "Of course you'd tell me if that were the case, wouldn't you?"

"Not at all." She indicated that he should sit in his favorite chair and when he was comfortably settled within its soft embrace, his long legs stretched out on the carpet before him, one boot set over the other, she knelt at his side. She wore a deep blue brocaded silk robe with a mandarin collar and wide bell sleeves. Where she had obtained this rather remarkable garment the Colonel could not imagine and he had not the bad taste to ask her. "That is none of your concern," she continued. "I am the mistress of this house. Discipline is here my concern as it is yours downtown." She meant at the garrison house. "You must trust me to maintain a perfect aura within our house. Tranquillity is all-important to the health of one's spirit, do you not agree?" And when he nodded, watching her eyes, she continued. "The tranquillity of one's house is not only confined to its location and the servants therein but also to its major occupants." She paused and the Colonel, who had been calmly sipping his drink through all of this discourse, now sat up, placing his glass on the side table by the chair. The Westerner in him longed to take her delicate, capable hands in his, lean toward her and say, "What is the matter, darling? What's troubling you?" This, he knew, he could not do, for in doing so he would shame her. She had obviously spent much time in the preparation of her presentation. He must honor that by allowing her to come to the point as she might. If there was anything the Colonel had learned by being in the Far East for six years, it was patience, for to fail to swiftly learn that lesson was to court peremptory disaster out here where life was so different, seeming only to float upon the bosom of the eternal Pacific.

"You know, Denis, that tranquillity is only one aspect of the harmony of life. And harmony is what all people strive to achieve. Harmony is the basis of a clear mind, of a good and powerful karma." She put her fingers along the back of his hand, which lay along the smooth worn wood of one armrest. "You have such a karma. It is very strong, like the thrown net of a master fisherman." Her eyes looked down at her hands, one atop the other, flashed upward to his face. "I am afraid to do anything to destroy that. But now there is more than one to think of. Our karma have meshed and, intertwined, may be all the more powerful for it, yes?" He nodded again and, satisfied that she had both his attention and his agreement, she said, "Now I must ask something of you."

"You know that you have only to ask me," the Colonel said sincerely. "You, who of all people in this world make me the most happy, can have anything that is mine."

Yet this heartfelt speech appeared to have little effect on Cheong. "This thing I must ask you is very large."

He nodded.

"We must go away from Singapore," she said boldly. Then, seeing that he did not stop her, she went on in a rush. "I know that your work means a great deal to you but this is"— she searched for the proper words that would convey her thoughts—"most imperative for all of us. For you, for me and for the baby." She placed one palm against her lower belly. "We must go to Japan. To Tokyo."

He laughed, struck first by the humor of it and then intrigued by the eeriness.

"This is funny?" she cried, misunderstanding his expression of relief. "It is bad for us to stay here. Most bad. In Japan our karma will flourish, expand. There lies our—what is the English word?—destiny, is that right? Our destiny."

"I laughed only at a rather odd coincidence," the Colonel reassured her. "It was nothing you said." He patted her hand. "Now tell me why we must go to Tokyo."

"Because Itami is there. She is Tsūko's sister."

"I see." She had told him, quite naturally, of her previous marriage but, beyond that, they rarely spoke of this portion of her life. "And what has she to do with our karma?"

"I'm sure that I do not know that," Cheong said. "But I had a dream last night." The Colonel was well aware of how much stock these people put in dream messages. They were not unlike the ancient Romans in this respect. He himself did not, in fact, totally disbelieve in their import. The unconscious, he knew, had more to do with the direction one took in life than most people were willing to admit. And, in any event, dreams were closely linked with the concept of karma and karma was something in which the Colonel had a strong belief. He had spent too many years in the Far East not to.

"The dream was about Itami," Cheong said. "I was in a city. In Tokyo. I was shopping and I turned into a quiet side street. All about me were shops made of wood and paper the way it was in Japan when Tokyo was named Edo and the Tokugawa ruled the shōgunate.

"I passed a shop that had a gaily decorated window and I stopped. In the center of the window was a doll. It was the most beautiful doll I had ever seen. Its aura was very strong.

"She was of porcelain, this doll, white-faced, dressed elegantly in the *bushi* fashion. Her eyes stared at me and I could not look away. 'Buy me,' they said.

"The shopkeeper wrapped her up for me in a silken cloth and I took her home. And, as I was unwrapping her, she began to speak. Her voice was imperious and commanding and very, very firm. She was obviously a lady of a high house.

"It was Itami and she said that we must come to her. She said that we must leave Singapore and come to Tokyo."

"Have you ever met Itami?" the Colonel asked.

"No."

"Did Tsūkō ever show you a picture of her?"

"No."

"Yet you are certain that this doll in your dream was Itami."

"It was Itami, Denis."

He leaned forward at last and took her hands in his as he had longed to do for some time. Her long nails, he saw today, were lacquered deep scarlet. He traced their satiny smoothness for a moment, savoring the feeling. "We will go to Japan, Cheong. To Tokyo. We will meet Itami, just as your dream said."

The smile that spread across her face was like the rising of the sun. "Oh, yes, Denis? This is really true?"

"It is really true."

"Then tell me why, for my spirit is happy and cares not but my mind, my mind cries out to know."

The day before they left, she took him to see So-Peng.

He lived outside the city, to the northwest, in a village of oiled paper and bamboo where no Westerner had ever before set foot. It was not on any map of the region that the Colonel had ever seen. In fact, when Cheong had told him of the location, he had laughed, saying that their destination would be nought but the middle of a mangrove swamp. Nevertheless, she was undeterred and he eventually acquiesced to her wish.

It was Sunday and Cheong insisted that he not wear his uniform. "This is most vital," she had informed him and as he donned his wide-lapeled cream linen suit, white silk shirt and navy regimental tie, he felt somehow spectacularly naked: a daub of crimson in an otherwise emerald jungle, the bull's-eye in an unmissable target. For her part, Cheong wore a white silk dress, embroidered with sky-blue herons, mandarin-collared, floor-length. She looked a dream.

79

There was brilliant sunlight as they left the city; the heat washed over them in slippery waves. A listless breeze brought with it the fetid stench of the mangrove swamps but always from their left. Twice they were obliged to stop, standing perfectly still as long black and silver vipers writhed obliquely across their path. The first time this happened, the Colonel made a move to kill the serpent but Cheong's firm hand upon his wrist deflected him from his purpose.

Far away yet seeming as close to them as the flamboyantly painted backdrop to some stage play, the eastern horizon was fairly choked with dark gray clouds piling themselves into the sky like ungovernable children pyramiding themselves dangerously. Above, the sky was a peculiar yellow; no blue was anywhere to be seen; and now and again silent white lightning flickered and forked through the gray, turning its softness for moments to marble. It was difficult to believe that it was so calm and tranquil here where they walked up the winding road, rising along the spine of a sprawling hillock.

Singapore had long since dropped from sight and, like a ship's anchor sent overboard, it seemed to be absolutely gone, part of another world which they had stepped out of and, passing through some invisible barrier, now found themselves in a land quite apart. At least that was how it seemed to the Colonel on that magical afternoon, how it came to him again and again throughout his life in dreams during the mornings' drowsy early hours.

On the far side of the forested hillock, all indications of the road they had been following disappeared and not even the semblance of a path through the foliage presented itself. Yet Cheong seemed to have no difficulty at all in reorienting herself and, taking his hand, guiding them to the village of So-Peng.

It lay in a leafy shallow hollow with the beginnings of a basalt mountain at its back, a natural barrier behind which, perhaps, only the stormy sea lay.

They came upon one house that seemed in all respects similar to those around it and, having climbed its three or four wide wooden steps up from the mud of the street, now stood upon its foreporch, wide as a veranda in the old South of America, covered against the torrential rains and the baking sun of the seasons. Here Cheong bade him remove his shoes even as she was doing.

The front door opened and they were ushered into the house by an old woman with steel-gray hair, elegantly coiffed, dressed in a long silk robe the color of swirled ash. She put her hands together in front of her breasts and bowed to them. They returned the gesture and, as she stood upright and smiled at them, the Colonel saw that she had no teeth. Her face was lined, to be sure, but the flesh still retained a hint of the vitality and beauty that it had obviously radiated in youth. Her black almond eyes were as luminous as lanterns, shining with the inquisitive innocence of the little girl from out of the past.

Cheong introduced the Colonel. "And this is Chia Sheng," she said without otherwise identifying her.

Chia Sheng laughed, staring at the Colonel's bulk, and shook her head from side to side as if to say, "What can one do with young people today?" She shrugged her thin shoulders and clucked her tongue sharply against the roof of her mouth.

Cheong, the Colonel noted, spoke only Mandarin and, without being told in so many words, he was aware that he should do the same.

They were in a room of some considerable size. No other house he had been in in Singapore, not even the main house of the estate bordering the mangrove swamps that had once been his, could boast of such space. The outside façade, he saw, had little relevance once one was inside.

More odd, however, was the fact that this room was covered in tatami—Japanese reed mats of a specific size by which all rooms in traditional Japanese houses were measured. But more surprises were in store for the Colonel.

Chia Sheng led them wordlessly through this first room, sparsely furnished with low lacquered tables and cushions and little else, down a short dimly lit hallway. Its far wall consisted of an enormous piece of jade so heavily carved that it became a latticework. In its center was a round doorway known, the Colonel had somewhere heard, as a moon gate. These existed in the houses of the very wealthy during the latter half of the nineteenth century on the mainland of China.

Across the moon gate's opening a long bolt of silk hung from a bamboo pole laid crosswise. It was gray. Embroidered upon it was a royal-blue wheel-and-spoke pattern. This seemed oddly familiar to the Colonel, and for long minutes he racked his brain until he recalled that he had seen the selfsame bolt of cloth reproduced in a *ukiyo-e* print by Ando Hiroshige. It was one of the *Fifty-three Stations of the Tokaidō* series; he could not remember the title of the print in question. However, it had shown the design to belong to a traveling *daimyo*. Another mystery. The Colonel shrugged inwardly as Chia Sheng led them through the moon gate, white shot with black and green.

They found themselves in a room only somewhat smaller than the first. On three sides were folding screens of exquisite manufacture, dark colors coming to vibrant life, passing through the years as if they were but veils of smoke.

Scents now invaded his nostrils, the chalkiness of charcoal, the muskiness of incense, and there were others, subtler, delicate cooking oil, tallow and still more impossible to define.

"Please," Chia Sheng said, leading them past a low red lacquered table. Freshly cut flowers in a bowl spread themselves on its center. They disappeared between the ends of two of the screens, which revealed a doorway of blackness, as if it had been cut out of the heart of a piece of onyx.

"The stairs," Chia Sheng murmured and they ascended. It was a narrow spiral staircase with room enough to climb single file only.

The stairwell debouched at length upon a kind of tower which struck the Colonel more as a garret. A green tile roof was supported at the four corners of the structure by wooden beams. Otherwise there was an unimpeded view on all sides save the one where the basalt mountain, like some awesome leviathan out of mythology, loomed close enough to serve as guardian.

As they came into the garret, the Colonel's eyes fell upon a tall figure gazing out at the riding storm, a long glass held to one eye. This was So-Peng.

"Welcome, Colonel Linnear." His voice was rich and deep and seemed to set the garret to vibrating. His Mandarin was oddly accented; in Western terms one might have said clipped. He did not turn around; did not in any verbal way acknowledge Cheong's presence. Chia Sheng, her mission perhaps at an end, left them, silently descending the winding stair.

"Please come over here and stand by me, Colonel," So-Peng said. He wore an old-fashioned formal Chinese robe of the color of mother-of-pearl. It was woven of a material totally unfamiliar to the Colonel, for even the slightest movement of the old man caused its surface to pick up and reflect the fitful light in a most marvelous way.

"Look here," the old man said, thrusting the glass at the Colonel. "Look to the storm, Colonel, and tell me what you see."

The Colonel took the polished brass spyglass, closed one eye and peered through it with the other. Now within the elevation of So-Peng's eyrie, he felt the first tentative touches of the storm they had earlier observed; the wind was rising.

Within the confined circle of his extended vision, he saw the bloom of the clouds, now purple-black like bruises, and, too, the color of the sky behind the storm had changed. The solid-seeming yellow tinge had been struck through with tendrils of a pale green; such a hue the land-bound world could never produce. Deep-throated rumblings could be heard now and again, rolling over the earth like an invisible *tsunami*, a tidal wave. Dutifully, the Colonel related all he saw.

"And that is all you see," said So-Peng. There was no hint of an interrogative in his inflection.

Yes, the Colonel was about to say, that is all I can see. But he checked himself at the last moment, certain that there was something out there that the old man wished him to see.

For long moments he moved the eye of the glass over the terrain an inch at a time but he saw nothing new to report. Still, it nagged at him and he moved the glass upward, scanning. Nothing. Then downward toward the earth. Below the onrushing storm, he saw the women in the rice paddies, the flat wet fields without protection of a single tree or even a makeshift lean-to. Almost in concert, the women bent to their tasks, leaning over, reaching for and pulling at the growing rice. Their skirts were pulled up in the center, tied in huge knots between their bent legs; woven sacks circled their backs so that they had the aspect of beasts of burden; water covered their bare feet to the ankle.

"The women are still working," the Colonel said, "as if the storm wasn't there."

"Ah!" So-Peng said, nodding. "And what does this tell you, Colonel?"

The Colonel took the glass from his eye, lowering it to his side, looking at So-Peng, at his yellow hairless head, the gray wisp of his beard hanging straight down from the ultimate point of his chin, the dark serene eyes regarding him coolly as if from some other age.

"They know something we don't," the Colonel said.

"Hmmm," So-Peng murmured and nothing more. He was fully aware that by "we" the Colonel had meant, however implicitly, Westerners. Yet he now had to make up his mind whether the Colonel was being serious or merely condescending. So-Peng, not unlike every Asian on the continent, had had far more experience with people expressing the latter sentiment. Yet he did not dismiss the Colonel summarily as he very easily might have, so that even at this early stage he must have had an instinctual reaction to this man.

For his part, the Colonel knew only too well that he had come to a crucial nexus in his relationship with Cheong. This man's blessing was imperative for her. Why it had not been necessary at her marriage he could not understand. Yet he knew that for her to depart Singapore, So-Peng had to become an active agent.

That this house, this town were so isolated, so totally unknown to the Western population, made him all the more apprehensive. The Colonel was painfully aware that many Chinese had no great love of Westerners, those barbarian giants from across the sea. That this dislike—indeed this enmity—was, at its core, mostly justifiable, made no difference to him at this moment.

But the Colonel had a great love for these people, for their life, their history, religion and customs, and it was this knowledge, chiefly, which heartened him now, which prompted him to say, "There is no doubt, sir, that we have much to learn here but, too, I feel that the most advantageous of situations involves an exchange, initially, of information but, more important, leads from there to an exchange of—confidences."

So-Peng's hands were inside the wide sleeves of his robe as he crossed his arms over his thin chest. "Confidences," he said meditatively as if the word were some new and exotic flavor he was testing on his palate. "Well, now, Colonel, 'confidences' may have many meanings—inflections and contextual placings determine that. Whereby, my boy, I might be led to believe that you had meant by it, secrets."

"That may not be very far from the mark, sir," the Colonel replied.

"And what," said So-Peng, "makes you think that any such intimacy should be extended to you?"

The Colonel kept his gaze steady, his eyes impaled by those he saw in front of him, and so intense became this look that at length the other's face seemed to disappear, leaving behind that pair of lights swimming alone in the atmosphere, hovering in lambent conversation. "There is, firstly, respect, sir. Then there is knowledge, knowledge sought and assimilated. There is acceptance, of what is and what was—the understanding of one's role within the matrix. Then there is the curiosity to learn the unknowable. And lastly, there is love." This being said, the Colonel relaxed somewhat, knowing that he had spoken his heart, expressed himself in a manner both pleasing to himself and honoring his wife. There was nought else to be done now.

Yet when So-Peng next spoke, it was directed not at the Colonel but at his wife. "Cheong," he said. "I believe that Chia Sheng is calling for you. Her voice drifts up to me in this charged air."

Without a word, Cheong bowed and departed.

The Colonel stayed where he was, silent. Beyond their frail enclosure the storm came on.

"Cheong tells me that you are leaving for Japan shortly."

The Colonel nodded. "Yes. Tomorrow. I have been asked to work with General MacArthur in reconstructing Japan."

"Yes. There is much prestige in such work. A place in history, eh, Colonel?"

"I hadn't thought about that, quite frankly."

"Do you not think," said So-Peng, "that this reconstructing, as you put it, is best left for the Japanese people to decide for themselves?"

"That would be the ideal, of course. But unfortunately certain elements within Japanese society have misdirected them throughout the last two decades." When the other remained silent, the Colonel continued on. "I am certain you are quite aware of their activities in Manchuria."

"Manchuria!" So-Peng scoffed. "What have I or my people to do with Manchuria? It is as a slum on the far side of the world to us. I would just as soon allow the Japanese and the Bolsheviks to fight between themselves for it. Manchuria, from my point of view, would be no great loss to China as a whole."

"But the Japanese sought that land as a foothold into the

rest of China. There they would have built their military bases from which they would expand."

"Yes." So-Peng sighed. "Their imperialist nature saddens me deeply—at least it did when I was a youth. Yes, then it was like a thorn in my side, for the Japanese way is the way of militarism. It always has been; it cannot be otherwise. It is the blood flowing out of the centuries and its imperative cannot be denied, neither by politicians' rhetoric nor by any kind of collective amnesia. Do you understand me, Colonel? The Germans deny their racism now. But how foolish, for how can they? Easier to deny that air is the source of one's life.

"China has nought to fear from Japan nowadays. This I tell you as a—confidence, eh? The pressure now comes from the Bolsheviks and they are to be feared more than ever the Japanese were.

"*Bushido*, Colonel. Do you understand this concept?"

He nodded. "Yes. I think so."

"Good. Then you understand what I mean." He looked out at the sky, entirely gray now and moving, as if some unseen giant were waving a rippling pennant at them. "That is a measure of friendship, did you know that? Good friendship, I am speaking of now—not a friendship as one might find between business associates or neighborly acquaintances. In this kind of friendship, which is rarer these days than one might believe, communication no longer becomes a problem or, as it most often is, a barrier. Do you agree with this notion of mine?"

"Yes, sir, most assuredly."

"Umm. Something told me that you might." He laughed softly, not unkindly. "You know, it was a day just like this one when Cheong first came to me. She was a very small child, not even three yet, I believe. Once there had been quite a large family. I don't know whatever happened to them; apparently no one does, for I made many inquiries over a good many years. All fruitless.

"After a while it did not seem to matter at all. This was her family and I could not have loved her more if she were my own daughter. I have many children and now many grandchildren and great-grandchildren. My goodness, so many is their number now that I sometimes confuse a name with the wrong face. But it is excusable. I am an old man and my mind is otherwise occupied with numerous matters.

"But I may tell you with all candor that among all my progeny Cheong has a special place. She is not the fruit of my loins but she most assuredly is the fruit of my mind, do you follow me? This is where she comes from and you must know this, come to understand it for what it is and what it portends before you leave Singapore."

He was silent for a time now as if he were dreaming of a far-off land or, perhaps, a time long gone. The air seemed to split open and rain slanted down out of the charcoal sky, pattering against the small square roof of the garret, dripping from the diminutive eaves. The green leaves of the trees dipped and shivered under the downpour until, hissing, the world was obliterated as if by a solid wall of water. Leaning slightly over the side, the Colonel could not even make out the lower roof of So-Peng's house. Mist, heavily laden as smoke, drifted up to them. The world was now a gray-green pointillist painting from which only brief shadows emerged as if they were watching the visualization of still-forming thoughts within some godlike brain.

"We seem very alone up here now," the Colonel said.

So-Peng smiled. "One is never truly alone in Asia, is that not so?" He seemed as still as a statue and it seemed odd to the Colonel that this should be so, primarily because the background was in such violent motion. Reflective spray bouncing up off the sill inundated him with a fine mist and he stepped back from the verge a pace, reminded of standing at the bow of a fast cutter on the open seas. "The world is different here," So-Peng continued. *"Our* world is different. We are born with, grow up with, indeed live our entire lives with the concept of eternalness always close to us. This— shall we say intimacy—I have often thought is a two-edged sword. It is indubitably our great strength in life but also— this is another confidence—it is our weakness, I fear, our Achilles' heel when it comes to dealing with the West. I am much afraid that too many of my countrymen underestimate Westerners precisely because they think of them as barbarians, unable to fully grasp the Eastern concepts of man, honor and the nature of time. This can be lethal. Witness the Japanese. Idiotic what they attempted! Glorious but idiotic. But the Japanese know well the nobility of failure. A majority of their national folk heroes would be considered dismal failures by Western standards. It is the nature of their being, the quality of their thoughts that are revered; deeds count for all, in the West. The Protestant ethic, I believe it is called, eh? Well, it is nothing to scoff at, as any Japanese would tell you now. The Protestant ethic is what defeated Japan. It was made to pay dearly for the miscalculation of Pearl Harbor. The United States was truly the sleeping giant; its wrath awesome to behold." He gazed out upon the frantic rain. The air was heavy with moisture. "We as yet lack the necessary understanding of the nature of time. We still look to yesterday when its eternalness was all; we have not yet caught up with the present." He laughed. "But give us time. We are most ingenious people. Once show us the way and there is our salvation. We are an extremely flexible people. Watch out that we do not catch you and overtake you!"

The faraway, dreaming look left So-Peng's eyes as he turned to the Colonel and said, "But my personal views of philosophy are no doubt of little interest to you. Words of wisdom—I do not believe in that phrase. One cannot learn wisdom by sitting at another's feet. One must live one's own life, make one's own mistakes, feel one's own ecstasy to learn the true meaning of existence, for it is different in each individual. Fall down, get up, do it all over again in another context. Experience. And learn. That is the only way.

"So. Enough of prattle. I am like an old woman today. Perhaps it is the weather that has made me so. I am loquacious in storms; perhaps it aids my uneasiness. Monsoon season was always a time of terror for me when I was a child.

"A fair enough introduction. You may wonder, Colonel, as to my cultural origins. Well, my father was Chinese. Not a Manchu, thank heavens, but a cultured, quiet mandarin. He was, originally, a merchant but because of a shrewd mind he soon became an important businessman, emigrating to Singapore when he was thirty-three. Oh, I am from the mainland, certainly; not from here. My mother was a Japanese." His eyes opened wide. "Oh, now, Colonel, you needn't look so surprised. Those things happened from time to time. Not, I admit, with any degree of regularity. No, no. And the true nature of my mother's origin was scrupulously concealed for obvious reasons. Her differing features my father explained away by claiming she came from the north of China, near the Russian border where there is much mixed blood, Mongol and Manchu and heaven knows what else.

"However, of Cheong's origins I have no specific information. Perhaps she knows or then again not. It was never discussed between us. Perhaps, one day, she will tell you. But that, of course, is between the two of you. For myself, I believe it matters little, if at all, for her matrix is here. It is where she grew up; it is what fixed her.

"When one is able to see the matrix from which a precious stone is taken, one is invariably better able to judge the quality of that stone." He shook his head. "But this is a somewhat cold example. Let me give you another. One meets an extraordinarily beautiful woman but, in spending time with her, one gradually finds her behavior somewhat erratic, confusing—in short, incomprehensible. Now, perhaps, one learns, subsequently, that this same woman was the middle daughter of three. It is now possible that one has taken the first step in unraveling the mystery of this beautiful woman's strange behavior. And, of course, the more one learns, the less odd her behavior becomes until, at length, it is perfectly understandable." He sniffed once at the air. "It will be over soon," he said. "Come. Let us descend."

They sat, the three of them—the Colonel, Cheong and So-Peng—around the red lacquered table in the room of screens while Chia Sheng silently served them course after course of food. The Colonel had not in three years seen so much food at once, nor tasted one dish after another so delicious or so exquisitely presented. There was, firstly, every manner of *dim sum*—tiny delicate rice-dough dumplings, filled with a variety of stuffings. Then there was fish soup, hot and spicy without being in the least heavy. Thirdly, there were six kinds of rice, from the simply boiled white to a kind of double-fried version with minced seafood and cooked egg yolk. The fourth course consisted of a cold salad spiced with white horseradish and cucumber. Then came the main courses: hacked fowl, golden brown, crisped, rubbed with coarse salt and herbs; broiled shrimp; hardy langoustes; cracked crabs, their shining carapaces blue and red, fresh from the boiling water. And lastly, great crescent slices of melon, the juice already running down along the sloping sides, onto the clay plates, like the rivulets of an icy stream.

At last they were through and So-Peng, pushing his rind-garlanded plate from him, heaved a deep sigh and patted his stomach. "Tell me about your matrix, Colonel," he said.

And the Colonel told him all about his father, all he had

been told about his mother he never knew, struck down by diphtheria when he was only two. All about his stepmother, whom he despised for no one particular reason but rather for many diffuse ones. He told So-Peng about his feelings at being an only child, a concept that the other found as fascinating and absorbing as he found it strange. About his boyhood in rural Sussex and the road to school which eventually brought him, as it did to most, to London. Of his burgeoning interest in the Far East, his studies and his eventual enlistment.

"And now," said So-Peng, "you are to embark upon a new chapter of your life. You are about to become a politician and more, a maker of history. Very good. Very good. Soon I, too, must leave Singapore for a time. My services are needed elsewhere. Thus this becomes, truly, a farewell party." He paused now, as if waiting for something to occur. Long moments passed in silence with just the lentitudinous dripping from the last of the rain leaving the lush loquat trees that surrounded the house.

Presently Chia Sheng appeared, holding a shadowed object close to her. When she reached the table, she lowered the object into So-Peng's hands. This time she did not leave them but stood silently at his side.

So-Peng held the object before him, chest high, and the Colonel saw that it was a copper box ten inches by perhaps eight across, enameled and elaborately lacquered. On its top was exquisitely painted a fiery, scaled dragon, entwined with an enormous, powerful-pawed tiger.

Still holding the box in midair, So-Peng said, "It is now my duty to apologize to you, dearest Cheong, for being away from Singapore on the day of your marriage to Colonel Linnear. I have thought upon this for many months, deciding what would be most appropriate, for, as you know, everything that is mine is yours also. As it is with all my children." The box was now lowered slowly to the tabletop, where it lay like the most exquisite of jewels, newly mined. "But you mean more to me, Cheong, than all the others, for your love shines all the stronger, all the purer for the hard road you had to endure. No one of all my children, none save you, has ever wanted for anything since the moment of their birth.

"This I have no doubt you already know. But what you are not aware of and what I tell you now is that, of them all, it is your mind alone, which has cleaved most closely to my

90

own. This has touched me deeply, for it has happened naturally, with no urging from myself. It is what you yourself wanted and what you now possess.

"Now, on the point of our last farewell—for I fear that we shall never see each other again—this is for you, for your Colonel, for your child about to be born, for your children yet to be conceived. This I give you gladly, with all my love. It comes from me, from Chia Sheng, from the long line of our families. In all the world there is only one. And its contents, too, are the sole sentinels, their like not to be found in any quarter of the globe. This is my legacy. Use it as you may." His old hands, their long fingers over which the skin was stretched like patinaed parchment, extended, pushing the box slowly across the table until it passed over the center meridian. At that point, as if they no longer wielded any power, they relinquished their hold, withdrawing over the empty red expanse of the table to the old man's lap.

The Colonel, holding Cheong's trembling hand in his, stared into So-Peng's eyes. He meant to say something but, whirling upon itself, his mind paralyzed his tongue and there he sat, on the near side of the table, as if a world apart, watching a man who was obviously as important as he was mysterious, not knowing who he was, what he did or why he might be so important, yet, despite that, understanding it all for the first time.

Both the Colonel and Cheong fell in love with the house and its grounds in the suburbs beyond Tokyo. MacArthur had, perhaps quite properly, requested that the Colonel find suitable lodgings within the city proper, to be more accessible to his work. However, he could find no such place, at least none that could satisfy both him and Cheong.

Thus they traveled outside of the city and, almost immediately, came across the house. It was in an area that had, miraculously, escaped the destruction that had devastated fully half of the city and much of the outlying suburbs.

It lay on the eastern verge of an enormous forest of cryptomeria and pine within which the Shinto temple blossomed like some otherworldly flora whose grace of design, quiescence and natural humility instantly bewitched the Colonel's mind, speaking to him more eloquently than even the country's finest minds of the eternalness and dignity of the Japanese spirit. And always when he came in sight of it he thought of So-Peng.

No one knew who had inhabited the house before the Colonel and Cheong moved in, not even Ataki, the wizened old gardener. It had been there, abandoned, for years, he had told the Colonel, though he had come faithfully every day to tend the grounds, and time had dimmed remembrance. Perhaps, the Colonel thought with a certain degree of resignation, he just did not want to say. In any event, it was now the Colonel's.

The formal garden in front of the house was breathtaking, complete with complexly flowering bonsai trees and a shallow stone pool filled with blue-eyed goldfish with fins like fine, gossamer veils (the Colonel quickly bought a tank, setting it up in the kitchen, one of the house's few Westernized rooms, for their warm winter's sojourn).

In the back of the house was another kind of garden altogether, a Zen pebble rectangle with four jutting rocks placed at significant points by the original artist within the uniform expanse, looking, the Colonel thought, like islands jutting from beneath a perfectly calm sea. However, Nicholas pointed out, when he was old enough to speak, they were most surely mountain peaks rising above a cloudbank: this comment much to the delight of both the Colonel and Cheong. But in any event, the Zen garden was, ironically enough, a place of perfect peace and meditation in a country half-dead, mutilated and charbroiled, struggling now toward a new kind of survival.

Nicholas adored the house and the grounds with an unquenchable passion. He was drawn, over and over, to the Zen garden, where Cheong would often find him sitting thoughtfully, head held in his hand, gazing out over the stark serenity of the rising rocks amid the precisely arranged pebbles. After a time it would be the first place she would look for him.

Nicholas could never decide whether he loved the garden best when he was alone there or when Ataki would come with his water and his rake—to keep the earth beneath from drying out and to make certain that the pebbles were properly aligned—for he adored both the intense solitude of the place ("It's like," he told the Colonel once, "you can hear your soul breathing") and watching the old man's preciseness and deft economy of movement with the pebbles, which were worn so smooth that Nicholas firmly believed that their origin must have been some point on the island's shoreline, for only the constant action of a motion-filled sea could create such stupendous smoothness.

It appeared to Nicholas that the old man's motions were so utterly effortless that he scarcely seemed to expend any physical energy at all. When he was perhaps six he had asked Ataki how it was he moved the way he did, and when the old man answered with one word, "bujutsu," Nicholas went to the Colonel straightaway to ask him what it meant. It was no good badgering Ataki, for he would only tell you what he wanted you to know.

"Bujutsu," the Colonel said, putting down his cup of tea and folding lengthwise the newspaper he had been absorbed in dissecting, "means, collectively, all the martial arts of Japan."

"Then," Nicholas said clearly, "I want to learn bujutsu."

The Colonel regarded his son. He had learned quite quickly that Nicholas never said anything lightly and that now, if he said that he wanted to learn bujutsu, he was quite prepared to take it on; superfluous for the Colonel to tell him how arduous a task it was likely to be.

The Colonel got up from the table and, putting his arm around his son's shoulders, opened the *shōji*—a sliding paper-and-wood wall—so that they could, together, walk outside.

They stood by the edge of the Zen garden but Nicholas noticed, on looking up at his father, that the Colonel seemed to have fixed his gaze far beyond its border, indeed, beyond even the last boundary of their land, to the rising green swords of the cryptomeria forest.

"Do you know, Nicholas," the Colonel said in a rather floating voice, "that within the perimeter of the Shinto temple at the center of the forest lies a park—a small one, mind you—that is said to contain forty different species of moss?"

"I've never been there," Nicholas said. "Will you take me?"

"Perhaps one day," the Colonel replied, his heart aching, for he knew that there was never enough time and he was here to do a job, a monstrous, bloody, awful job that, nevertheless, needed to get done and, furthermore, needed him to get it done right; these years had been more than enough to grind down a man of lesser courage and perseverance than the Colonel. But each time his tired mind seemed on the verge of faltering, he would recall So-Peng and his son, encompassed in the same thought, and he would go on, through another long night and the subsequent longer day until the weekend came and it would begin all over again. "But I have never seen that park either, Nicholas. Few save the Shinto priests of that temple have viewed it." The Colonel took some time now before he continued. "What I mean to say is that you wish to go where few nowadays would wish to go—and there are many specializations."

"I wish only to start at the beginning, Father. That is not so much to ask, is it?" He looked up again.

"No," the Colonel said, tightening his grip upon his son's shoulders. "Not too much." He thought for a moment, his lean face wrinkled along the firm brow. "I tell you what," he said at last. "I'll speak to your aunt about it, all right?"

Nicholas nodded, his gaze lowering from his father's face to the mountains thrusting blindly out of the clouds.

The person to whom the Colonel had referred was, in fact, Itami. Nicholas, knowing her origin, had never really considered her his aunt. Perhaps, after all, this was because he had disliked her for as long as he could remember, and having once formulated this opinion, could not get himself unstuck from it.

It would be no great surprise to learn that his instinctual dislike of her was only an offshoot of how he reacted to the presence of her husband, Satsugai. In a boy who, from birth, had been taught to attain within himself an inner calmness of spirit, like a cool guiding stream, it was most disconcerting for him to come within close contact with Satsugai. He felt, at those times, like an ineffectual moon whirled about by the proximity of a nova. Great turbulent currents, powerful eddies disturbed his tranquillity, and this inability to return to a semblance of inner balance until Satsugai had left frightened him.

On the other hand, his aunt in no way created the same effect in him. She was an exceedingly small and delicately boned woman, beautiful though, in Nicholas' opinion, the perfect symmetricality of her face could not compare to his mother's features.

Itami always wore formal Japanese attire. She was constantly attended to by servants. Her diminutive size made all the more fascinating her rather charismatic nature. She

94

was, the Colonel had told him, a member of one of Japan's greatest and oldest houses, of the *bushi* class. She was a samurai lady. She had been married to Satsugai for eleven years and he, as far as Nicholas knew, was a wealthy and influential businessman.

Then there was Itami's son, Saigō. He was a year older than Nicholas, a large burly boy with deep brooding eyes and a cruel and calculating disposition. He spent much time with his father but, on the many occasions when the two families got together, it was inevitable that Nicholas and Saigō should be thrown together.

It seemed to Nicholas that the other boy hated him almost on sight. Why this should be so he could not imagine. Not until much later. But then he reacted as any boy in any part of the world might to such unadulterated hostility. He returned measure for measure.

It was, of course, Satsugai who had put Saigō up to it. This knowledge, when it came to him, only increased Nicholas' hatred and fear of the man. But then it was also Saigō who introduced Nicholas to Yukio. As it is said, all things in life balance themselves out.

Don't they?

Second Ring

THE WIND BOOK

New York City / West Bay Bridge

SUMMER PRESENT

When the man with the mirrored aviator sunglasses emerged from the depths of Pennsylvania Station on the Seventh Avenue side he did not look around him; nor did he walk immediately to the curb, as did most of his fellow passengers, to wave a raised hand to hail a cruising taxi.

Instead, he waited dutifully for the light to change and, when it did, went quickly across the avenue, ignoring the light rain. By the way he walked and, perhaps because of the rather long black duffel bag slung obliquely across his muscular shoulder, one might have thought he was a professional dancer; he moved as effortlessly and as gracefully as the wind.

He wore a short-sleeved navy silk shirt and cotton slacks of the same deep blue, charcoal-gray suede shoes with almost no heel and soles as thin as paper. His face was rather wide; deep lines were scored downward from each side of his mouth as if he had never learned how to smile. His black hair was bristly and cut short.

On the east side of Seventh Avenue he went by the crowded façade of the Statler Hilton Hotel, crossed Thirty-second Street and, passing up the green and white awning of the Chinatown Express, ducked into the McDonald's next door.

Inside, he went swiftly through the garish yellow and orange interior to a line of telephone booths along one wall. At the side of the extreme left-hand booth was a row of telephone directories encased in steel bindings to discourage theft and vandalism. They hung down in a stand waist-high like quiescent bats in a cave.

The man in the sunglasses pushed up the Yellow Pages book. Its cover was torn and defaced and the bottom edges of a large hunk of the center pages were mutilated as if someone had attempted to eat them. He leafed through the book until he came to the section he wanted. He ran one forefinger down the page. Near the bottom, it stopped and the man nodded to himself. He already knew the address but, out of long habit, liked to double-check his information.

Once more outside, he recrossed the avenue, walking west at a brisk pace along the width of the Madison Square Garden complex, and caught an uptown bus on Eighth Avenue. It was crowded. He stood in the hot and airless interior. The bus smelled from stale sweat and mildew.

At the Seventy-fourth Street stop he swung off and walked up one block. There he turned off Central Park West and headed west toward the Hudson River. The rain had ceased for the moment but the sky remained close and dark, as if hung over from a long night of revelry. The air was completely calm. The city steamed.

He found the address approximately midway between Broadway and West End Avenue on the north side of the street. His nostrils flared for an instant as he mounted the steps of the brownstone. He opened the glass and wood outer doors and stepped into the tiny vestibule. Before him was a modern steel and wire-glass door securely locked. There was a buzzer on the wall of the vestibule which he pushed firmly. Just above it was a discreet brass plate on which was etched TŌHOKU NO DŌJŌ and, above that, a small oval speaker grill.

"Yes?" came a tinny voice from the grill.

The man with the sunglasses leaned slightly to the side. "I wish an appointment," he said.

He waited, one hand already on the knob of the inner door.

"Please come up. Second floor. Around to the left as far as you can go."

The door buzzed and he pushed it open.

He could smell the tang of sweat, tinged with the piquant spices of exertion and fear. For the first time since setting foot in the city, he felt at home. Contemptuously, he tossed this feeling aside. He went swiftly and silently up the carpeted stairs.

100

* * *

Terry Tanaka was on the phone with Vincent when Eileen came up to him. Seeing the look in her eyes, he asked Vincent to hold the line and, putting his palm over the phone, said, "What is it, Ei?"

"There's a man here who wishes to practice today."

"So? We can handle it. Sign him up."

"I think you had better take care of this one yourself," she said.

"Why? What's the matter?"

"Well, for one thing, he's asking to see you. And for another, I've seen the way he walks. He's no student."

Terry smiled. "You see how our fame has spread? That piece in *New York* was great." But when she did not respond, he said, "That's not all, is it?"

She shook her head. "The guy gives me the creeps. His eyes..." She shrugged. "I don't know. But I wish you'd handle it."

"Okay. Listen, give him a cup of tea or something. I'll be right there."

She nodded, giving him a thin smile.

"What was that?" Vincent said in his ear.

Terry uncovered the mouthpiece. "Oh, nothing probably. Just a client who's spooked Ei."

"How is she?"

"Fine."

"And the two of you?"

"Oh, you know. About the same." Terry gave a quick laugh. "I'm still waiting for her to say yes. I've been on one knee so many times, I've worn out four pairs of pants."

Vincent laughed. "We still on for dinner tonight?"

"Sure. As long as it's an early one. I want to see Ei tonight."

"Sure thing. Just some questions I'd like to ask you. Nick was going to come but—"

"Hey! How is he? He called just before he went out to the Island. Has he been loafing all summer?"

Vincent laughed. "Yeah. Until I got hold of him. He's got a new woman, too."

"Good," Terry said. "About time. The ties are still very strong, huh?"

101

"Yeah." Vincent knew only too well what Terry meant. "He sends his love to you and Ei. He'll be in soon, I'm sure, and he'll stop by."

"Good enough. Hey, my new client will no doubt bite Ei's head off if I don't run. See you at seven. 'Bye."

He hung up and went across the room and around the corner to meet Mr. Wonderful.

As Terry came up, Eileen Okura felt some of her apprehension dissipate. She had been startled by two separate elements. First, she had not heard the man's approach. Second, his countenance was unusual. He stood now precisely as she had first seen him, duffel bag on his back, his sunglasses swinging from the thumb and forefinger of his right hand. The skin of his face and his hands was far too white for an Oriental's. But, she saw, as she glanced at his throat where his shirt was open, this snowy color predominated only in those areas, for his chest was a darker, more natural hue. It was as if he had been in some kind of hideous accident. An explosion, perhaps, affecting the exposed areas of his flesh. Yet, for all that, it was his eyes which held her. They looked utterly dead, black stones dropped into a stagnant pool of water, they could not conceivably retain any form of emotion. And it was these same eyes which regarded her now as if she were some specimen, stripped and laid out on a sterile surface, ready for dissection. Eileen felt a brief chill wash over her.

"Watashi ni nanika goyō desu ka," Terry said to the man. How may I help you?

"Anata ga kono dōjō no master desu ka." Are you the master of this *dōjō?*

Terry seemed to ignore the abrupt and therefore extremely impolite mode of the other's speech, said, *"Sō desu."* Yes.

"Koko de renshu sasete itadakitai no desu ga." I wish to practice.

"I see. Which disciplines are you interested in?"

"Aikido, karate, kenjutsu."

"For aikido and karate I can surely accommodate you. But as for kenjutsu, I am afraid that is quite impossible. My instructor is away on vacation."

"What about yourself?"

"Me? I have given up teaching kenjutsu."

102

"I require no instruction. Practice with me for an hour."

"I—"

"It is better than filling out forms."

"That it is. My name is Terry Tanaka. And yours?"

"Hideyoshi."

A name from out of the past. Terry nodded. "All right. Miss Okura will give you the necessary forms. The charge is forty dollars an hour."

The other nodded curtly. Terry half expected him to produce a plastic wallet filled with travelers' checks but instead the man peeled off one hundred and twenty dollars in twenties from a roll he kept in his front right-hand pants pocket.

"Sign there," Terry said, pointing. He nodded toward a small doorway at the far end of the room. "You can change in there. Do you have your own robe?"

"Yes."

"All right. Fine. The *dōjō* proper is one flight up. Which discipline do you prefer to begin with?"

"Surprise me," Hideyoshi said, walking away. He disappeared through the doorway into the darkness of the locker room beyond.

Terry turned his head away, saw Eileen staring at the empty doorway across the room. There were no shadows. The light filtering in through the half-drawn blinds which covered the high narrow windows was diffuse enough to put a patina on her glowing skin. She looked slim and tiny, he thought. A pale ballerina about to perform her half of a difficult pas de deux.

"Who is he?" Her voice seemed like a whisper in the high-ceilinged room. Above their heads came the thump of the floorboards.

Terry shrugged. He was a big man, perhaps six feet, with wide shoulders and narrow waist and hips. His face was flat, the eyes black above very high cheekbones. He told Eileen what had transpired.

"You're not going to do it, Terry?"

He shrugged. "Why not? It's only an hour's practice." But he knew what she meant and his heart was not nearly so light as his words sounded. He was, along with Nicholas, one of the greatest kenjutsu masters now living outside Japan. At thirty-eight, Terry had already spent three quarters of his life studying kenjutsu, the ancient Japanese art of swordsmanship. His reason for abruptly abandoning it within the past year might not be altogether easy for a Westerner to understand.

In the first place, no martial art depended solely on physical discipline. In fact, a great percentage was mental. Long ago, he had read Miyamoto Musashi's *Go Rin No Sho*. It was perhaps the greatest treatise on strategy in all the world. Though written in just a few short weeks before the great warrior's death, its knowledge is timeless, Terry thought. Today, he was well aware, many prominent Japanese businessmen mapped out their major corporate advertising and sales campaigns with Miyamoto's principles in mind.

Just about a year ago, he had picked up the *Go Rin No Sho* once again. But, in reading it, he had now found what he believed to be quite different and darker meanings hidden within the logic and vaults of imagination. To devote oneself so religiously to the domination of others was not, he felt, what life was all about. He had been disturbed by dreams, then, black portents without form or face, all the more real and frightening for that. He had felt compelled to rid himself of the volume, throwing it out in the middle of the night, not even waiting until morning.

In daylight, the feeling had remained. He felt as if he had mistakenly taken a wrong turn in the dead of night and, without warning, had found himself on the lip of a great abyss. There had been a temptation to look over the verge but, with it, had come the knowledge that if he did, he would surely lose his balance and tumble forward into the darkness. Thus Terry had stepped back and, turning away, had put his *katana* away forever.

And then today, this strange man who called himself Hideyoshi appears. Terry shivered inwardly, too much in control to let Eileen see his true emotions. Besides, he did not want to alarm her.

It was surely some kind of omen, for he had no doubt that the man knew well the teachings of Miyamoto. But even beyond this, there was no doubt in his mind that Hideyoshi was a *haragei* adept. The concept, stemming from two words, *hara*, meaning centralization and integration, and *ki*, meaning an extended form of energy, was more than intuition or a sixth sense but, as Terry's *sensei* had said, "a true way of perceiving reality." It was akin to having eyes in the back of your head, amplifiers in your ears. Yet *haragei* could work both ways: being an ultrasensitive receiver also made one an excellent transmitter if one came within a certain distance of another *haragei* adept. Terry had picked this up instantly.

"Just another Japanese off the plane from Haneda," he said nonchalantly to Eileen. He would not, under any circumstances, have told her what he really knew about the man.

"Well, there's something odd about him." She was still staring at the black doorway, which seemed to gape at her like the mouth of a grinning skull. "Those eyes—" she shuddered. "So impersonal, like—like cameras." She took a step toward Terry. "What's he doing in there so long, do you think?"

"Meditating, no doubt," Terry said. He picked up the phone, stabbed the intercom button. He spoke softly and briefly to someone on the third floor, informing him of the new client. He cradled the receiver. "He'll be another twenty minutes at least," he said to her. He stared at her long black gleaming hair. Brushed back and unbound, it rushed like a night-dark stream over her shoulders, down her back in a thick cascade, ending at the tops of her buttocks. She started and he said, "What is it?"

Her head turned. "Nothing. I just felt you staring at me."

He smiled. "But I do that all the time."

"At night, yes." Her eyes stayed serious, her pouty lips firm and straight. "Don't do it here, Terry. Please. You know how I feel about that. We work together and we—" Her eyes met his and for just an instant he felt his heart lurch within him. Was that fear he had glimpsed there lurking like a prowler in the night?

He reached out a hand, pulled her gently toward him. This time she did not resist and, as if seeking warmth, she allowed herself to be cradled, her arms tight around him. She felt safer here, with him so close.

"Are you okay, Ei?"

She nodded wordlessly against his muscles but felt the tears welling up like deep pools within her eyes. Her throat constricted and she could not think why. "I want to come over tonight," she heard herself say and immediately felt better.

"How about every night?" Terry said.

It was not the first time he had said this, though it had been in different ways before. Eileen's response had always been the same, yet now she knew the source of the churning inside her, knew that when he asked her again this evening, as he surely would, her answer would be yes. "Tonight," she said softly. "Ask me tonight." She dabbed at her eyes. "When should I come over?"

"I'm having dinner with Vincent. Why don't you join us?"

She smiled thinly. "Uh uh. There's too much you guys talk about that I have no interest in."

"We'll cut that all out tonight. Promise."

She laughed then. "No, no. I don't begrudge you that. *Bushido* is important to you."

"It's part of our heritage. We wouldn't be Japanese without it. I'm not yet that assimilated into Western culture—I'll never be—that I can forget the history of my people—" He paused, seeing her shudder, her eyes flutter closed.

"My people," her words a ghostly echo. "*Bushido*. I shall die for my Emperor and my beloved homeland." Tears welled from beneath her lowered lids, turning to minute rainbows. Behind them were galaxies of pain. "We survived the great firestorm in March"—her whispered words like the shouted cries of the dying—"when the American armada dropped almost three quarters of a million bombs filled with napalm; when two hundred thousand Japanese civilians were roasted or boiled alive; when half of Tokyo was cindered; when, the following morning, as you walked down the street, the wild wind took the charcoaled corpses and blew them away like dust."

"Ei, don't—"

"We moved out, then, away from the war, to Hiroshima in the south but, quite soon, my parents, terrified by all the rumors, packed me off to my grandparents who lived in the mountains." She looked at his face without really seeing it. "There was never enough food and slowly we began to die of starvation. Oh, it was nothing very dramatic, merely a kind of all-pervading lassitude. I would sit outdoors for hours unable to think of anything. It took me forever to comb my hair because my arms would hurt, keeping them lifted like that. That was for me. But for my mother and my father there was Hiroshima and the light that fell from the sky." Her eyes focused and she looked at him steadily. "What is there for me but shame and hurt? What *we* did and what, in turn, was done to us. My poor country."

"That's all forgotten now," he said.

"No, it's not. And you, of all people, should understand that. It's you and Vincent and Nick who talk constantly of the spirit of our history. How can you celebrate the one without feeling shame at the other? Memory is selective, not history. We are what we are. You can't arbitrarily excise the bad, pretend it never existed. Nick doesn't do that, I know. He remembers; he feels the hurt, still. But I don't think you and Vincent do."

He wanted to tell her of his recent thoughts but he found that he could not. Not now, at least. It was the wrong time, the wrong place, and he had a highly developed sense of these things. Tonight, perhaps. Tonight he would see that it all came down. He watched the diffuse, artist's light on her satin-skinned face, her long slender neck, her slim compact body. It was impossible to think of her as being forty-one; she did not look a day over thirty, even in harsh light.

It was just about two years since they had first met, a year since they had become clandestine lovers—at least as far as those at the *dōjō* were concerned; of course all their friends knew. In that time she had never asked for more, never wanted to know about the future. It was he who, lately, had felt the need for more. And recently he had become aware that, at least partially, the ending of his love affair with kenjutsu had been, simultaneously, the beginning of his love affair with Ei. Now, it seemed to him with pristine logic, that there was nothing more important in life than being with her. The *dōjō*, which he had opened nearly five years ago, was well established and he was more than satisfied that it could run itself for a short while. Time enough for a marriage and a long, leisurely honeymoon somewhere far away. Paris, perhaps. Yes, definitely Paris. It was Ei's favorite city, he knew, and he had never been there. All that remained was for him to ask her. Tonight. Would she say yes this time? He suspected that she would and his heart fairly danced.

"Tonight," he said. "I'll be back by nine, ten if Vincent gets stuck in Island traffic on the way in. But you have a key and some of your clothes are there. Come anytime. But bring champagne. Dom Pérignon. I'll bring the caviar."

It would have been easy for Eileen to ask what this was all for but she felt that it would spoil the moment. There was, after all, plenty of time to find out what she already knew in her heart.

"All right," she said, her eyes very large now.

He turned, abruptly remembering. "I'd better get upstairs and prepare the *bokken*. Soon Hideyoshi will be through with the others and I want to be ready."

Justine's eyes were completely dry. This was something new for her but it brought her no solace. Not when the anxiety had come again, a fierce knot in her stomach, a pressure on her chest, constricting her breathing, refusing to go away. There is nothing wrong, she repeated over and over to herself. Nothing. Absolutely nothing. She shivered, feeling cold. Her fingers were like ice.

She stood in the darkened living room of Nicholas' house, staring out at the mist and rain on this dismal Sunday. Out there, somewhere, was the sea, curling endlessly, but the spiteful rain hid it from her as if it were withholding a bright toy on Christmas morning. She thought about going out there, piercing the mist, finding the ocean for herself, but she lacked, at this moment, the necessary fortitude to brave the weather.

Oh, my God! Oh, my God!

She whirled from the sleeted windowpane, running blindly through the house, groping for the bathroom, and there, at last, she collapsed in front of the toilet, retching.

Her body shook and sweat stood out on her forehead, rolling down into her eyes in tiny stinging rivulets.

After an endless time, when she could no longer stand the stink, she reached out a hand to flush the toilet. It seemed to take all the energy she possessed. But, after that, she somehow found the strength to stand up and bend over the sink. The cold running water fell on her face like bullets from a gun. She shivered, opened her mouth to get the sour taste out. She could not swallow.

Sitting on the edge of the porcelain tub, feeling the cool bar of it striking across her buttocks, she curled over, putting her head in her arms, her arms on her knees.

She rocked back and forth, thinking. *I can't do it. I can't.*

It was her mind now that did the vomiting up. The history of the betrayals unfurling like a hated flag above her head, blotting out all other signs of life. All her men. Timothy, who had been the first, the high school basketball coach. *I'll be gentle, Justine,* and thrusting savagely into her over and over, enjoying the expression of pain on her face, her crying out into the perfect sterile symmetry of the darkened gym; watching his eyes burn with her instant's fear. Then Jodie, the Harvard man with the laughing eyes and the cruel soul. *I want to be a surgeon, Justine*—and already was. Eddie, who was seeing her and his wife on alternate nights; there was nothing he wanted but them both. And then, in San Francisco, there had been Chris. They had come together, igniting like a bonfire, insatiable, insensate to everything and everyone around them. Or was that only the way it had been with her? She could not bear that truth, even now. Dredging it up was like an act of cruel masochism, like opening the edges of a slowly healing wound and probing for the nerve.

She had used her father's name then—and his money. God only knew how much; surely she did not. Wasn't it the money that had made her weak and lazy? So easy to pin down the blame, neatly and resolutely; coming back to her father. How she hated him for giving her—those things: his name (she always wrote the word out on the screen of her mind so that she could make the deliberate typo *fame* which was, as far as she was concerned, no error) and his money. Oh, he wasn't like her. He had an accounting held indelibly somewhere; not that the amount could ever bother him; it was, after all, a tax deduction.

God, this thing makes me nasty and bitter, she thought. As if it's a physical malady that manufactures bile as a by-product. She gagged again but, wrapping her arms around her stomach, she held herself together; there was nothing more to come up; she was empty yet the anxiety made her feel as if she had swallowed a two-by-four whole.

I can't do it, she repeated to herself. *I can't.*

She had taken his money—so much of it—not thoughtlessly but willfully. Because she hated him. But she found that getting it was like having the goblet of wine that was always full no matter how much you drank. What had mattered so much to her was of absolutely no concern to him.

Of course it had mattered very much to Chris, who was the one, after all, who made use of most of the money. At least that was how it had all come down that day when her father had flown in, had come to her house with the battery of local detectives he had hired. It had all been there for her to read in the report. The thing had so shocked her that she had hardly been able to utter a word let alone protest as her father had his men gather up her clothes, all her possessions. He left them to it, hustling her outside and into the waiting limo. She had not said a word all during the flight back east.

Her father, sitting across the aisle in the private Lear jet, was too engrossed in reports to notice. She found that she was not hungry, nor was she tired. She was nothing.

It seemed like a long time ago now. Years could be like lifetimes, never like days. This is what came to her on the plane ride back to New York: she saw their old country house, the one in Connecticut that she had loved so much with the stone walls covered with green creeping ivy, the high leaded-glass windows, the flagstone patio and, across the emerald back lawn, beyond the dirt path, the brick red of the stables, smelling of hay and manure and horse sweat. How she loved that place; it reminded her of England, somehow. Not like the new place on Gin Lane out on the Island. Her father had sold the old house just after Justine's mother had died, paying two and a half million for the estate along one of the most famous streets in all of America.

It was Easter time in Connecticut. She was eight. Gelda had some friends over whom she did not like or just did not want to be with. Her mother was gone, having driven into town to do some shopping. She wandered through the enormous old place, the large bright friendly rooms filled, here and there, by the busy servants preparing for a formal party later that evening. Peering out the window, she discovered that there were a number of cars in the semicircular driveway and, as she went down the long curve of the main stairway to the ground floor, she could just make out voices coming from behind the closed wooden doors to the library. Her hand on the knob, turning, and she pushed.

"Daddy?"

Her father had indeed been inside. He was with a group of men, discussing matters that had no meaning for her.

"Justine," he said with a frown, "you must see that I am busy at the moment." He made no move toward her.

"I just wanted to talk to you." She felt utterly dwarfed by the circle of men. One of them shifted uncomfortably on the couch, the leather creaking under his weight.

"This is not the time. Shall I fetch Clifford." The latter had the form but not the inflection of a question.

She looked around mutely.

Her father reached up and pulled a cord. In just a moment, the manservant appeared.

"Yes, sir?"

"Clifford," her father said. "See that she is kept occupied

until Mrs. Tomkin returns, will you? I can't have any more interruptions. Doesn't Gelda have some friends here?"

"Yes, sir."

"Well, that's the place for her then, eh?"

"Very good, sir." He turned. "Come along, Miss Justine—"

But she had already turned, running down the long high hallway, slamming out through the front door. She could hear Clifford clattering away behind her. She liked Clifford. She spent a lot of her time with him, just talking. But right now she did not feel like being with anyone.

She sped around the side of the house, headed for the stables and was quite out of breath by the time she got there.

They had six horses. Arabians. Her favorite was King Said. He was her horse, to all intents and purposes. But of course the children, though already good riders, were not allowed on horseback or even in the stables without an adult to supervise.

Justine did not really care about that now. She went down the straw-strewn center aisle until she found King Said's stall. She called to him and apparently he heard, for there came to her his slight snorting and stamping; he was eager for a canter. He poked his head out; it bobbed up and down. His powerful neck thrust far above her; his coat shone. She wished that she could reach up and stroke him but she was far too short.

That's when she thought about opening the stall door. She was just lifting the iron latch when Clifford caught up with her.

"Oh, Miss Justine, you must never, never do that—"

But she had already whirled into his arms, clinging to him, crying inconsolably.

The return to New York had presaged a low point in her life. Filled with an anxiety she could not control, she turned in desperation to analysis. At first it appeared to be no help at all. But that was an unfair assessment. It was, after all, a highly subjective one and she was perhaps so low that she could then perceive no change, however minute. It was like lying sleepless in her bed, staring out the window at the east, night still clinging tenaciously, looking at her watch, knowing dawn was not far off but seeing no band of light. Not yet.

It was, in retrospect, really a time of retrenchment. She had no job, could not face that, but she began to sketch, returning to the craft she had once loved. Slowly she built up a current portfolio and, at length, she was ready to go out.

It was not nearly so bad as she had imagined—she had not slept for two nights before the interviews, terrified—and she had gotten a job at the second agency she went to. But doing a job that she liked, she soon found, was not nearly enough (did she know, then, that she was well again?). Of course she knew why. But the thought of becoming involved again was intolerable to her.

Thus it was that she discovered dance. She went to a class one night with a friend from the office and fell instantly in love. Now she channeled her excess energy into her body, adoring the concept of controlled rhythm, the duality of tension and relaxedness that dance afforded her.

Yet it was not only the dance but also its prelude which fascinated her. Her instructor believed in the discipline of t'ai chi as a warmup exercise. With this fundamental core assimilated, Justine found to her delight that she could move into virtually any area of dance she chose, from modern to ballet.

She had been at it for just over a year when her instructor said to her, "You know, Justine, if you had begun the dance when you were a child, you'd be a great dancer today. I say this to you only to give you an accurate idea of where you stand now. You are one of my best pupils because not only is your body responsive but your spirit is within the dance. The greatness is there, Justine, but one unfortunately cannot overcome the advance of time."

She was filled with pride and happiness. But just as important, she knew why. For the first time in her life she felt that she had control of herself as a person; she no longer felt tossed to and fro by the whims of the world. Here, at last, was a control that she could feel directly, that had real meaning for her.

Within the month she had left her full-time job at the agency and had gone into business for herself. The agency still wanted her and she accommodated it. But she was free now to pick and choose the jobs she wanted. She found that within six months of setting up shop she was pulling down triple her old salary in independent billings.

And then she had decided on this house in West Bay Bridge.

And had met Nicholas.

I can't do it. I can't.

She stood up and reeled drunkenly out of the bathroom, down the hallway, using her hands, palms outstretched like a blind person, to guide herself through the house. In the living room she bumped into the bubbling fish tank. All the bright denizens of the deep swam there, tranquil as if anesthetized—blind, deaf and dumb—as beautiful and as unthinking as the vegetation reaching toward the winking surface. She felt another wave of nausea hit her and she turned away, heading for the front door.

I can't make the commitment. I can't trust him. Oh, my God! Oh, my God!

She stumbled out into the rain, tripping down the wooden steps, falling to her knees in the wet sand. It felt like dough, clinging to her jealously.

She crawled a few feet, then, regaining her balance, ran all the way home.

Not long afterward, Nicholas returned from the beach area where they had found the second body. This time they had waited for him.

It was one cut. Do you understand? Vincent had said over the phone. He did indeed understand what that meant. The cut of a *katana.*

The white-skinned corpse was slit from right shoulder, obliquely down to just above the left hipbone. One swing, one cut from the finest blade ever known to man. It could easily slash through armor; flesh and bone were as paper to a *katana* wielded by a master swordsman. Ancient blades had been preserved for a thousand years by succeeding generations of warriors, losing not a bit of their original sharpness or effectiveness; and even today no arsenal in the world could claim such a magnificent weapon as the Japanese *katana.*

This was how the second man had died. He lay, as he had been found, cradled by the soft surf and sand. He had not been in the water very long. There was absolutely no question of his being drowned.

But now they had to revise their conclusions radically. Barry Braughm had obviously not been the ninja's only target. But there seemed, on the surface, nothing to connect the two victims. This man was a worker for Lilco—the Long

Island power company—blue-collar, lower-middle-class background. Nothing in common, nothing at all.

Yet the ninja was abroad, still killing.

Inside, Nicholas threw off the lightweight khaki slicker. His sneakers and his jeans up to the knees were soaked. But this was of only peripheral interest to him. He was thinking of Justine and the thing that had crashed through her kitchen window in the night. He did not dare to think of what it might be. Besides, it made no sense. Still, he had asked her to stay inside in his house and not return home.

She was not there.

He cursed softly and, returning through the living room, scooped up his slicker and headed out the door.

No one answered his knock but, coming down the beach, he had seen the lights burning at the back of the house through the bedroom windows.

He knocked again and, fearful now, tried the doorknob. It gave and he twisted it, went through into the house.

He stopped still as a statue just over the sill, listening and watching the shadows. Someone was home; there was no intruder. These things he ascertained immediately and simultaneously; his training needed no conscious cuing.

He called her name: "Justine."

It was not just the one cut that worried him. Both Doc Deerforth and Vincent had missed the other thing. At least, they had not recognized it for what it was. In leaning over the body, he had chanced to see the top of the left shoulder. The bruise had just begun to darken. He touched it. Below the flesh the clavicle was fractured. Instantly, he was on guard; he had not wanted to alarm the others, even Vincent. If what he believed now was, in fact, the case...

There had been a man. Miyamoto Musashi. Perhaps Japan's greatest warrior. Among other things, he founded the Niten or Two Heavens school—or *ryu*—of kenjutsu. It taught the art of wielding two swords at once. Another aspect of musashi, known as *Kensei,* the Sword Saint, was that he used *bokken*—wooden swords—in actual combat—claiming that he did so because they were invincible.

What all this musing was leading up to was this: the man had been struck *two* blows, not one as Vincent believed. One had been the cut of the steel *katana,* ripping him open, the

114

second had simultaneously crushed his collarbone; this had come from a *bokken*.

"Justine, it's Nick." There was some movement now from the back of the house.

He was beginning to feel as if, having once been surrounded by confetti floating through the air, he was being confronted by a slowly emerging pattern as the shreds fell to the ground.

And what he saw shook him to his core.

Justine became visible, limned in the light from behind her, sweeping through the half-open bedroom door.

"What are you doing here?"

"Justine?" He knew it was her, just did not believe her tone of voice.

"Why did you come?"

"I told you to stay at my house, away from here." He tried not to think of the black furry thing full of blood on her kitchen floor. Tried to calm himself, to ignore the fact, as coincidence, that it was an animal used by ninja as a ritual warning. It did not work.

"I got claustrophobic, all right? I told you I get that way every once in a while."

"It's not safe here."

"What are you talking about? I'm comfortable here. This is my house. *My* house, Nick." With the light bursting through all around her like an aurora, he could not see her gestures. He did not need to.

"I don't think you understand."

"No," she said sadly. "I'm afraid it's you who don't understand." She took a step forward. "Why don't you leave. Please."

"What's happened?"

"There's—just nothing to say."

"There has to be."

"I don't want to talk about it, that's all."

"You're not the only one who's involved here now."

"Nick—nobody's involved."

"You know what I mean."

"Yes, I do. That's why I'm saying this. I'm—just not ready for anything like this."

"Like what?"

"Don't force me to spell it out."

"I just want to know what the hell's gotten into you."

"It's just—you don't know me at all. I'm like this. Change-able. Erratic." She sighed. "Please go, Nick. Don't make a scene."

He raised his hands, palms outward. "No scene." He walked toward her. "I just want some answers."

"You won't find any here. Not today, anyway." She began to turn away from him, back into the light.

"Justine, wait!" He reached out, touched her arm.

"Get away from me!" she cried, hands pushing at him. And then calmly whispered, "Get away from me. I mean it, Nick."

He turned and left her standing there, a silhouette.

Click. Click-click. Pause. Click-clack-click. *Hai!*

As they moved back and forth along the thin line, the diameter of a predetermined circle, Terry felt the fear of an opponent for the first time in his life.

As a master, a *sensei,* fear in kenjutsu was an unknown thing to him. Until now.

It was not so much the fear of defeat—even he had, once or twice, been defeated—though he knew from the opening moments that this man could quite probably take him. No, it was something more subtle than that. It was the manner in which this man—this Hideoshi—fought. Style was imper-ative in kenjutsu; one could tell much about an opponent by the way he fought. Not only where he had studied and with whom but, on a wider scope, just what kind of man he was. For style was also philosophy and, yes, religion. What one respected and what one held in contempt.

Terry was concerned now because he saw in the other's martial philosophy a lack of regard for human life. Ei had been right on target when she had suggested that the man had the eyes of the dead. They were lusterless and as shallow as glass. Nothing, it appeared, resided behind them. Cer-tainly no feeling. And this worried Terry. He had heard of and had read accounts of samurai in feudal Japan—during the 1600s, just after Ieyasu Tokugawa unified the warring *daimyo* by founding the Tokugawa shōgunate, which would last two hundred years—who cared little or nothing for hu-man life. They were killing machines, sent out to do their lord's bidding, loyal to him and to *bushido* only. Yet the code of *bushido* had within it the core of compassion, rigid and unassailable though it was. A core these men chose to ignore. He had often wondered what it was that had so corrupted them.

It seemed oddly fitting that, now, he should be confronted by just such a man. It was as if he had stepped out of another age. Karma, Terry thought.

He moved to his left, attacking, but was at once balked. Now their *bokken* whistled through the air, moving so swiftly that, to the untrained eye, it might appear as if the two combatants were wielding enormous fans, so blurred were the weapons' movements.

Terry moved to one knee, sweeping his *bokken* horizontally, but the other used a vertical block. A less experienced swordsman might then have gone for the kill, using the two-handed vertical sky-to-ground sweep. This would have brought instant disaster, for Terry need only have lunged forward several inches, the point of his weapon piercing the attacker's stomach, to vitiate that lethal blow.

Instead, the other stepped back, forcing Terry to regain his feet to continue the match. There had already been two draws and, as the hour was drawing to a close, this would be the last match. Yet, as he blocked several lightning thrusts, Terry had the uncomfortable feeling that he had not seen this man's complete repertoire of strategy. Truth to tell, he felt as if the other had been toying with him for all of the forty minutes they had been at it.

Annoyed, he struck and struck again. But instead of directly countering, the other's *bokken* cleaved to his as closely as a shadow, moving in concert, always touching. Then they were close together and Terry had his first good look at the other's face. It was just the flicker of an instant, perhaps a tenth of a second when his concentration, his *zanshin*—that is, physical form combined with mental concentration and alertness—wavered. Almost contemptuously, the other flicked at Terry's *bokken* with his own weapon. There was not enough time to react fully and, with the other's *bokken* at his throat, Terry was defeated.

When Justine came out of the bedroom to make herself a drink, it was near sunset. However, looking out the windows at the front of the house, she saw only thick banks of gray clouds, trailing like streamers left over from a wild party, tattered, shredding in the winds aloft. The wan light bleached out all the color from the land. The sand looked solid and lumpy like cooling lead.

She stopped, one hand around the neck of the bottle of rum. There seemed to be a shadow on the porch. Letting go of the bottle, she moved slowly to her right to get a better view. She moved past the center beam between the two picture windows. Curtains fluttered, further obscuring her view. She moved farther to her left and stopped dead still. The shadow had become a silhouette. Someone was out there.

She felt a nameless fear flood her body and, unconsciously, she put a hand up to her throat. Her heart beat like a triphammer and Nicholas' words abruptly came to her. *It's not safe here.* Is this what he meant? She wished now that she had paid more attention to what he had been saying but she had been solely intent on pushing him away, had heard only her own words.

Now she wondered wildly whether she had locked the door after he had left. She thought not but could not be certain. Yet she dared not attract attention by moving to it. She would have to pass directly before the windows. She thought of crawling but was too frightened of making some noise.

Then she thought of the phone. Keeping her eye on the silhouette, she backed up slowly into the hall. She reached down convulsively, almost knocking the receiver to the floor. She went to her knees to retrieve it. She dialed Nicholas' number, closing her eyes, praying he was home. Each solitary ring was like an icicle through her heart. She felt chilled, her flesh raised in goosebumps as she cradled the phone.

She went silently, on dancer's feet, out to the living room, sitting on the armrest of the sofa, staring at the silhouette. She considered creeping out the back door. But then what? Pound on a neighbor's door? And say what? That she was afraid of a shadow?

Abruptly, she felt idiotic, like a madwoman trapped within the nightmares of her own mind. And, after all, there had been no movement of the silhouette since she had first glimpsed it. It could be a chair back or—

She was up and moving without giving herself time to think, to back out. She flung the door open, stepped out on the porch. The air was heavy with the salt of the sea, yet perhaps the humidity was abating somewhat. There was a fresh breeze from the east.

As if she were a mechanical doll, she forced her gaze in the direction of the silhouette.

"Nicholas!" An indrawn breath.

He sat, lotus position, forearms resting easily on the points of his knees, staring seaward.

"What are you doing?" She came around beside him. "Nick?" She stopped, bending down. "What the hell are you doing?"

"Thinking."

"About what?" It was a simple thing to say but, perhaps considering her mood, not a very logical one. She might easily have said, "Can't you do it somewhere else—away from me?" Yet she had not and this surprised her. She wondered that, in finding him there, a guardian of her house—of her, really—rather than an invader, her anxiety had dissipated as easily as a bad dream. In its place was—what? As she pondered this, she heard him say, "I'll have to tell you now."

She reacted better than he might have expected. It was tantamount to saying: You have cancer.

"Are you sure?" she asked.

"I wouldn't tell you if I wasn't. I can't say that I understand it yet but that animal crashing in here was no accident. It was a ninja warning."

"I may be way off base," she said levelly, "but didn't you tell me that one of the ninja's traits was to strike without warning?"

He nodded. "Yes. That was true, most of the time. But there were occasions—a blood feud, for instance, or where it was specifically ordered or where the ninja wished to boast of invincibility—when a ritual warning was given."

"But it's crazy," she protested. "What would a ninja want with me? I've had no connection..." She paused but he said nothing, waiting to see if she would figure it out for herself. He did not think he would have to help her.

She got up off the sofa, walked nervously about the living room, snapping her fingers. She stopped in front of the bar, made herself a long white rum on the rocks without offering him one; she was too engrossed. She came back to the sofa, sipped at it.

119

"There's only one thing I can think of," she said, still somewhat unsure of herself.

"Let's see if we came to the same conclusion."

"My father."

"Your father," Nicholas echoed. "Raphael Tomkin." He got up and poured himself a bitter lemon. "Tell me, what do you know of his business dealings?"

She shrugged. "Not much more than anyone else, I'm afraid. I never took much interest in it. You know, the basic facts. Oil is the mainstay. The corporation is multinational. That's about it."

"In other words, not much."

She winced. "I told you so."

"All right. Let's leave that for a while. Now—"

But she had already put a long forefinger against his lips. "Don't Nick. Don't ask me. Not now. Not yet. Let's leave things the way they are. Please. Please."

He watched her eyes, wondered what he was missing. Perhaps nothing or then again everything. He did not want that. But now he wanted her more and that called for a compromise. It was an uneasy one, at best, he knew. Talking was always better than not talking; that was a fundamental underpinning to all human relationships. Still, perhaps she was right after all and this was the wrong time. He swallowed half of his drink.

"What are we to do now?"

A good question, Nicholas thought, looking at her. The ninja meant to kill her, of that there seemed little doubt. This was something he accepted as a given, although he could not discount the importance of motivation. But there would be no immediate answer to that, thus he put it out of his mind for the moment. What truly concerned him was the nature of the ninja. It was rare enough to encounter a modern-day villain although, as he had indicated to Vincent and Doc Deerforth, a number did operate clandestinely as independent agents on the highest levels. But to find one adept at the Niten school was quite alarming. It was one of the most difficult of kenjutsu styles to master and it might be indicative of other elements. There was, Nicholas knew well, more than one kind of ninja. Was it a coincidence?

"The only thing to do, for the moment, is to stay with you."

Justine nodded. Oddly, this did not fill her with fear. Quite the opposite, in fact. She might even begin to relax with it. God knew, she wanted to. Yes, she thought. I *do* want to.

Suddenly she was feeling much better.

Doc Deerforth was dreaming. He lay on the hammock tied to his porch beams, swaying slightly. The delicate, insistent drone of the unceasing rain had lulled him to sleep.

He dreamed of a forest, gleaming like a great emerald, dripping with moisture. But it was not a place of pleasure or beauty. Not for him. He ran through the tangled underbrush and, from time to time, as he twisted his head to peer fearfully behind him, he caught a glimpse of the hideous beast that pursued him relentlessly. It was a tiger. Fully ten feet long, the beast seemed to move effortlessly through the thick foliage that otherwise sought to pull him down. Its massive muscles worked with astounding fluidity beneath its glossy striped coat. Now and again, Doc Deerforth's eyes would lock on those of his foe. They glowed green in the night like lambent beacons, lighting the way before it. Yet they were not the shape of cats' eyes but the unmistakable oval— epicanthic fold and all—of a human: a Japanese, to be more specific.

. They were the eyes of the ninja Doc Deerforth had encountered just before war's end in the jungles of the Philippines.

Now his way was balked by an enormous stand of bamboo. Every which way he looked, there was no passage forward. He turned to see the man-beast open its mouth. Hot flame poured out like a river, inundating him in a jelly-like substance that clung to him, stinging like a man-of-war. He writhed, slapping at himself to rid himself of the burning substance. Still it clung to him tenaciously as if it was sentient. He had acquired a second skin: a malignancy which now commenced to eat into his flesh. His skin curled and cindered, peeling away to tendon and sinew. This was left him, as the substance saturated him, piercing his bones. These were slowly powdered. And all the while the tiger with the ninja's face grinned at him. Then, as he felt all strength running out of him, as if he were urinating his life away, puddling it on the ground before him, the beast lifted its right forepaw. It was a human arm that had been amputated at the elbow. Above, the skin was black, the muscles gone, the

121

arm—what was left of it—virtually fleshless, as if it had been crisped in some terrible swift blast. The tiger with the ninja's face lifted this limb up to him as if to say, "See this and remember." On the inside of the arm was tattooed a seven-digit number. Camp, he thought over and over. Camp, camp, camp. He was a jellyfish now, shorn of manhood, even his ape heritage. Beyond that, he now swayed in the jungle; when man was still a part of the gravid seas; before the spark; before the first fish crawled to the edge of its world and became an amphibian; before the land was fit for life. In this jungle sea, he drifted with his implacable foe. "See, see, see," said the beast, moving toward him who hung helpless on the tides, the evolutionary avatar. "No!" cried the jellyfish. "Don't you see? You'll destroy everyone!" But, unheeding, the man-tiger was upon him. "This I do for my—"

Doc Deerforth awoke with a start. He was drenched in sweat and his cotton shirt was twisted to one side so that he felt as if he were inside a straitjacket. He gasped, taking several deep breaths. The rain had ceased sometime while he was asleep but water still dripped from the eaves, making him think of the sea and the jellyfish and the ninja and annihilation.

Terry was almost killed on his way to meet Vincent. This, in itself, held no import for him; he was far too busy with his thoughts.

He was thinking about Hideoshi as he stepped off the curb at Sixth Avenue, walking east on Forty-sixth Street. He was meeting Vincent at Michita, a small Japanese restaurant on Forty-sixth between Sixth and Fifth avenues. This place, run in the traditional style—a sushi bar and tatami rooms—was open virtually twenty-four hours a day because it catered, in large part, to the many Japanese businessmen new to the country, still on Tokyo time. It was a favorite haunt of Nicholas', Vincent's and his because they all felt quite at home there.

He was against the light and, in the gutter, he was almost run down by an old rattling Checker cab, hurtling up the avenue. The shrill blast of the horn snapped him out of his reverie and he leaped back onto the sidewalk amid the screech of brakes and the heartfelt curses of the obese, shaggy-haired driver. "Fuckin' asshole gook!" he heard as the taxi swerved past him. He felt the cool breeze of its close passage and then it was accelerating uptown.

This incident, however, did not long deter him from his inner contemplation. Upstairs in the *dōjō*, while he had been preparing his *bokken* for the coming matches, he had observed the man at work on his aikido and, somewhat later, at karate. He had been appalled at the man's strength and agility. Also, it was obvious after but a few short moments that he knew far more about strategy than did Terry's instructors. Since opening, the *dōjō* had rapidly built a reputation as being one of the finest facilities of its kind, not only in America, but in all the world. Much of this, of course, came from Terry's astute selection of *sensei*. To a man, his instructors were top-level masters in each of their specialties. To see them thus handled was disquieting indeed. As he went through Michita's thick blond-wood and iron door, he wondered whether he should tell Vincent of Hideoshi's visit.

Eileen went shopping after leaving the *dōjō*. She went crosstown to Bloomingdale's and bought several new pieces of lingerie. On a whim, she picked up a bottle of cologne she had been meaning to try. On the way back to Terry's she stopped at a liquor store and bought a bottle of 1970 Dom Pérignon.

It was still light when she reached Terry's brownstone. She put the champagne in the refrigerator and threw her Bloomingdale's packages on the wide bed. Returning to the kitchen, she put four eggs up to boil for the caviar, checked to make sure there were enough onions and bread for toast.

Then she went through into the bedroom and, crossing its ample width, into the bathroom, turning on the shower. She undressed and was about to step into the stall when she remembered something. Without bothering to wrap a towel around her, she returned to the living room and put a record on the stereo, turning it up so that she could hear it in the shower.

She sang with the water beating down on her, hearing the distant sounds of the music as if from the far side of a waterfall. She imagined herself on a tropical island, bathing in the turquoise water of a deserted lagoon. She washed her hair and soaped her body, reveling in the slipperiness against her skin.

She cut the water and got out, toweling her hair first. In Terry's full-length mirror, she regarded her naked self critically. She was proud of her body. Her skin was sleek and unblemished, her flesh firm despite her age. Her neck was long and slender, her shoulders as delicate as a china doll's. Her breasts, sloping gently, were still ripe and firm, the nipples dark and long. Her waist was narrow, her hips flaring gently. But it was her legs of which she was most proud. They were long and firm, the muscles taut and supple, the ankles narrow, her feet small. She watched her muscles rippling as she worked the thick blue-green towel over her wet flesh. Her nipples sprang erect at the rough contact and she felt the first beginning warmth as she moved the towel slowly down her belly, between her thighs, back and forth, anticipating Terry's arrival. She loved his hands on her body; they were so soft and gentle and knowing; she abhorred anything rough; he knew she loved that part as much as when he was inside her, both of them moving in concert. She loved to make love to music, the changing melodies, harmonies, tempi somehow enhancing the process. And, of course, the added sounds made vocalizing easier for both of them. She watched the flush of blood throughout her body reflected in the mirror as her thoughts pushed onward, inward. She imagined that Terry was already home, moving around the living room, preparing the caviar and champagne. She dropped the towel as, with one hand, she rubbed her nipples, with the other she probed gently between her thighs.

After a time, she sighed deeply and stepped out into the bedroom. She crossed to the bed and, bending over, slit open the bag. She took out the bottle of cologne, Chanel No. 19, opened it and dabbed it on her richly glowing skin. Then she stepped into the cream silk teddy she had bought, luxuriating in the feel of the sensuous fabric. This was how Terry would see her when he arrived.

She turned down the open doorway and a frown creased her brow. Darkness prevailed there and, while it was night now, the sunset having slipped away while she was in the shower, she was certain she had turned on the lights there when she had come in. Or had she? She shrugged and went through the doorway.

Halfway to the small porcelain lamp on the table next to the sofa, she paused, turning her head. Had there been some movement in the room to her extreme left? Now she saw only clumps of dense shadows. Outside, a cat yowled twice as if it were being skinned alive, then there was the brief clatter of metal garbage can lids in the cement alley on the side of the house, coming clear through the wall. The music was still playing. Henry Mancini. A bittersweet melody that she knew ended the side of the record. Mancini was so romantic.

She crossed to the table and threw the switch; the lights in the bedroom went out. She turned around, oblivious for a moment to the fact that the lamp had not lit. The music was over and she was conscious of the minute sounds of the tone arm lifting, setting down on its cradle and the turntable stopping. There was only one sound now, very close to her, and she realized that it was her harsh breathing.

"Is anyone there?" She felt foolish.

The total absence of sound was infinitely more frightening than if she had heard a voice reply. She looked down at the glowing dial of her watch and all she could think of was: Terry will be home soon.

As if drawn toward the unknown, she went slowly across the living room until she was standing on the sill of the doorway. She peered in, trying to see in the gloom; the curtains were closed and here, at the back of the house, the trees of the backyard intervened behind the closed windows, the working air conditioner, vitiating the lamps from the neighboring houses.

She went into the bedroom, her hand feeling along the wall for the light switch. But before she got to it, she heard the click of the stereo from the other room; heard, after a tiny delay, Mancini's piano and the double bass begin a jazz duet. Soon the drums joined them and then the strings. Last of all was the sax, a crying, almost human voice among the myriad instruments. The music was filled with tension.

She whirled toward the doorway, could not see through it. Something or someone blocked her view. She took a step forward and gasped as something slithered forward in a blur, wrapped itself around her right wrist.

Crying out inarticulately, she stumbled backward. She flung up her arm in an attempt to free herself but the thing—whatever it was—followed her silently, relentlessly; the grip on her wrist tightened until she thought her bones might break.

"What do you want?" she said inanely. "What do you want?" Her mind, numbed by fear, could think of nothing else to say. It was as if the night, through some magical incantation, had become a sentient being.

She felt the edge of the bed against the backs of her knees and, as if this solid barrier brought her back to reality, she launched herself forward. She did not believe in ghosts, not even in the *kami* of her ancestors as tangible objects able to grasp out at the living. Her mouth opened and she bared her teeth, ready to bite into whatever had hold of her.

She felt the solidity of pressure in front of her and bit down. But at that moment her head was jerked backward and upward and her teeth snapped together painfully.

"Oh, my God!" she heard herself say. It seemed to come from another world.

She stared into a face. The head, as, she supposed, was the body, swathed in matte black fabric. A tight hood and a mask that left only his eyes exposed. These were no more than six inches from her own. They were as dead as stones in a pond.

"Oh, my God!" She felt so vulnerable, bent back in a grip she had no hope of breaking, and this, more than anything else, terrified her.

When he moved he was upon her before she could even cry out. She felt his grip shift and it seemed that she was in the grasp of something elemental, like a whirlwind, a force of nature. For surely no man—nothing that was human—could have so much power.

Where his gloved fingers dug into her, they seemed to dissolve her flesh and pulverize the bone beneath. All air was abruptly gone from her lungs; it felt as if she had been thrust to the bottom of the sea. Her insides turned to water. Death rose up on all sides like a specter on an enormous poster. Her gorge rose and she tried to vomit. She retched pathetically against the restraint to her mouth. She tried to swallow and could not. Her eyes were blurry with tears. She blinked wildly, began to strangle on her own vomit.

His face was quite close to hers, but it was as if she had been attacked by an inanimate object suddenly given life. She could smell nothing, see nothing; she had no clue as to what he was feeling, what he might want. She could not even turn her head from side to side, so intense was his grip upon her. Still she struggled merely to swallow and she did, given life once more. But now she saw before her the sloping mountainside in the south of Japan where she had stayed as a child during the last days of the war. She saw as clearly as if she were there again the tall stately pines swaying in the westerly winds, the straggle of *sokaijin* toiling up the long slope, a thin battered line, an exhausted snake that seemed to have no end, no beginning, merely one vast body. She thought of the *zōsui*, the vegetable stew, which had become their staple; the taste of it was strong in her mouth, the smell of the mountain turnips filled her nostrils. She had never thought that she would recall them with such full-bodied accuracy; it was in the nature of human beings to remember pleasure with more clarity than pain.

There was swift movement above her and her silk teddy shredded, parting from her body. She was naked. Her mind was filled up with Terry now because she was quite certain that this terrifying being would rape her; this secret knowledge of why he had come outraged her and calmed her at the same time. Death seemed to stand away, only a visitor to this feast instead of the guest of honor.

She felt his body over hers, not hot, not cool, but somewhere in between. His was not flesh, but neither was it marble. She felt somehow as if she were being lifted into a cradle, the position familiar. She closed her legs, locking her ankles, resisting him still.

So it was with a great sense of shock that she felt him grasp the pool of her thick hair, pulling it up, winding it with one hand into a long twisted cord.

She stared upward, above her head. There was sufficient light for her to see it, standing straight as a sword, blacker than the night.

Then, guided by him, it came down, wrapped around her neck. Until, nooselike, it began to tighten about her throat, however, she failed to understand what was about to happen. But as she fought for every breath, her nostrils flaring because his other hand still covered her mouth, she knew that her body was far from his mind. Was he hard? Would he come? Her mind was like a pond filled with squirming eels, monstrously debating these lewd questions while her lungs filled with less and less air.

No! Please! Take me, don't kill me! Don't! Please! She tried to scream what her mind formed but the words only came out as animal grunts, further terrifying her. It was as if his inhumanity had somehow managed to strip her of her humanity.

The cord of her hair tightened as he heaved on it, arcing

127

his back precisely as if he were making violent love to her. The muscles of her throat spasmed involuntarily; her lungs burned as if with a corrosive. *This can't be happening*, she thought. *I can't die. I won't! No no no no—!*

And then she was fighting, fighting to perform the most basic of functions which had become as difficult as climbing a mountain. Each breath was the most desperate of struggles.

She fought like a tigress, clawing at him with her nails, punching and slashing, using her knees and thighs in an effort to dislodge him, to deflect him from his monomaniacal purpose, but it was as useless as if she were fighting a brick wall. She was powerless against him. He was beyond the living. He was death.

As she choked on her own vomit, rising again like an inexorable *tsunami*, before her eyes bloomed the final firestorm. As her lungs filled with fluid, as she labored still for life, Eileen heard clearly the whistling, abrupt and diabolical, directly over her head and, looking skyward, saw the shadow of the lone bomber, coming like an unexpected eclipse, riding before the sun, saw part of it falling away toward the earth, as if it had contemptuously defecated on the Floating Kingdom, blossoming like a black flower in the bright blue and white sky.

Concussion. The furnace heat of hell. And light like the core of ten thousand exploding suns. Oh, my poor country!

Ashes, floating in the hot wind.

Terry said *sayonara* to Vincent through the taxi's opened window. The day's rain had given the city no relief from the sultry heat and humidity of midsummer. It reminded him of Tokyo.

"I'll call you soon," he told Vincent.

"Right. Let me know if you have any ideas." Vincent leaned his elbows on the sill of the window.

Terry laughed. "I still think you and Nick are making more of this than is there."

"We aren't making up that poison, Terry," the other said seriously. "Or the *katana* wound."

"I don't know, buddy. There are an awful lot of madmen in this city. What would a ninja be doing here, anyway?"

Vincent shrugged, having no good answer.

"See?"

"Hey, Mac," the cabdriver growled, turning around. "Time is money and I ain't got all night. If you're gonna gab why doncha do it on the street, huh?"

"Okay," Terry said, "we're off." He turned his face sideways, smiled and waved to Vincent as the cab pulled away from the curb.

He gave the driver his address and settled back in the seat. Somehow he regretted not telling his friend about the visitor to his *dōjō* in greater detail. He might have, he supposed, if they had not gotten so involved in this case that Vincent had been drawn into. Leave it to him to fabricate something like this. It was the kind of mystery that was just up his alley. Vincent was, Terry suspected, quite bored. Not so much with his job—there were, God knew, enough mysteries there to hold his attention. No, it was more that he was bored with being in America. Perhaps he wanted to go home.

With this, his thoughts turned to Eileen, waiting for him at home. At last all obstacles were washed away. Patience, my *sensei* used to tell me, can often be one's most important weapon. You are too impetuous, my boy. Slow down and enjoy the pace which you yourself set. Abruptly, he remembered the caviar.

He leaned forward, his mouth near the grille bolted to the thick scarred plastic partition separating him from the driver. "Hey!" he called. "I forgot. I've got to make a stop at the Russian Tea Room before you take me to the address I gave you."

The driver cursed and shook his head. "I'm gettin' 'em tonight all right. Couldn't y've told me soona, fella? Now I gotta go back down Ninth an' cut ova—right into the teeth of th' traffic." He spun the wheel and, squealing, the cab swerved in mid-flight. There came the answering blare of horns, mingled with shouts and the screech of jammed-on brakes. Terry's driver leaned out the window and shot his finger into the air. "Fuck off, y'sonsabitches!" he cried. "Why doncha learn how tuh drive, yuh assholes yuh!"

Terry took out a pencil and a piece of paper on the way over to the Russian Tea Room, found himself writing down the name, *Hideyoshi*. Then, after it, *Yodogimi* and, finally, *Mitsunari*. When he had finished, he stared at what he had written as if they were alien scratchings found on the side of a hill.

129

The cab jerked to a halt and the driver turned to him. "Do me a favor, Mac. Don't leave me standin' here holdin' my dick, know what I mean?"

Terry shoved paper and pencil in his pocket and hurriedly left the cab.

It took him only a few minutes to place his order with the maître d' and pay for his two ounces of fresh Beluga. When he returned to the cab, the driver took off as if they were being chased by hijackers. "Gets so yuh can't tell anymore," he said, eyeing Terry in the rear-view mirror, "know what I mean? Guys come into the cab lookin' as straight as can be. They ask yuh to stop and right away they take a powder, couldn't find 'em with a battalion, know what I mean? Used tuh be able to tell, years ago; not now. Want me tuh go through the park?"

"Sure," Terry said. "Yeah. That'll be fine."

It did not take long; the park was as still as a tomb, seeming detached from the surrounding sparkle of the high-rise buildings, pristine in the darkness.

He went up the high stone stairs of the brownstone, whistling softly. He was halfway to the third-floor landing when he began to discern the Mancini music coming through the door to his apartment. He smiled to himself, feeling warm and confident. Ei loved Mancini.

He turned the key in the lock and went in.

Immediately he knew that he must get into the bedroom. He slammed the door and was in absolute darkness, crouched, then rolling and scrambling across the living room.

He had smelled / seen / tasted / felt the differences in the apartment and had acted accordingly. He had heard nothing save the music. Mask, he thought. I might otherwise have stopped before I even opened the door. I'm certain I would have. Goddamn that music!

Eileen! his mind cried out just as he was hit.

He was perhaps three quarters of the way to the half-open doorway to the bedroom. He was struck viciously four times in the first second of the attack. He blocked three successfully but that allowed the fourth to get through. It smashed into him just above his right kidney. All the breath went out of him and he keeled over as his leg went numb. He rolled awkwardly across the floor, simultaneously aware of the low light seeping from out of the bedroom and a heavy sweetish scent.

A blow whistled through the air near his left ear but he was already rolling away from it. The edge of a table exploded against the side of his face, shards chattering through the air like angry insects. He drew his legs up, kicked out with the soles of both feet in concert. He grunted with the effort, heard an answering sound and then he was up and running as best he could, his right leg dragging a bit behind him.

He went through the doorway at full speed, grabbing its edge as he did so, slamming it to behind him. He turned around thinking: Time. I've got to have time.

The broken figure, one leg still upon the bedspread, drove all rational thought from his mind. His legs turned to water and he felt as if the searing edge of a knife blade were prowling through his guts.

Her face was shadowed and dark, shrouded by wayward tendrils of the night-black hair wound tightly around her neck. Her arms were flung upward, over her head; her breasts were covered in vomit. His eyes were drawn to the dark patch between her thighs. There were no marks on her body.

He did not have to touch her to know that she was dead but he bent to it anyway because part of his mind said that he must be absolutely certain. He cradled her head in his lap until he heard the sound from beyond the door.

Almost unseeing, he got up, crossed to the opposite wall. His cold fingers closed upon the cool lacquered leather of the slightly curved scabbard that hung on his wall. He brought it to him with great deliberation; the whisper of the naked blade as he unsheathed it was the loudest sound he had ever heard. Louder even than the splintering of the wooden door as it buckled inward under the enormous force of the karate kick.

The ebon figure stood in the doorway, the *bokken* in his left hand; his right was empty. It was not until this ultimate moment of their confrontation that Terry allowed the thought to surface as a reality. He trembled involuntarily.

"Ninja," he whispered. He barely recognized his own voice, so clogged was it with emotion. "You have chosen death in coming here."

He leaped upon the intervening bed, striking forcefully with his *katana*. It was, he realized instantly, a stupid move, for there was no solid support and therefore not nearly enough power behind the momentum of his strike.

Deftly, with almost no effort, the ninja avoided his strike

without even lifting his *bokken*; no need to cross swords, he was saying. You are not even good enough for that.

The ninja whirled away into the darkness of the living room and Terry had no choice but to follow. Dimly he knew that he was playing into the other's hand; that the background of battle was just as important as the battle itself. He sprinted over Eileen's corpse, his heart constricting, his blood turned to ice. To hell with it! he thought rashly. I can defeat him on any ground. Thus, in his sorrow and his rage, he turned away from all he had been so painstakingly taught.

In the living room where Mancini played on obliviously he saw limned the outline of the *bokken* and immediately went after it.

But the ninja was already in motion, on the attack, and Terry lifted his *katana* into the darkness, bracing for the expected force of the blocked blow against his blade. Thus he was totally unprepared for the violently percussive shock against his exposed chest. He was flung back more than five feet as if by an explosion. He staggered, his ribs and sternum on fire. He ached all the way up to his jaw. "What—?" he coughed, confused.

The ninja was a blur, driving in again. Terry instinctively raised his *katana*, though he was unsure of the point of attack; his vision seemed blurred.

A second blow came against his chest and he flew backward, going down on one knee. The *katana* in his right hand seemed to weigh as much as a human body. His lungs labored and he was disoriented.

The third blow hit him just as he had staggered to his feet. This time he perceived what was occurring even as he was slammed back into the wall. He heard rather than felt a crack as if a roof beam had given out and he felt a curious wetness on his left side. Ribs, he thought dully, his seething mind still filled with what was happening to him. It was like a dream; no possible reality could be so fantastic.

Another blow bounced him off the wall and the *katana* pinwheeled from his grasp, a dead star whirling through space. He glanced down at himself, saw the fractured ribs protruding through his rent flesh. The blood was black as ink, running out of him like tap water down a drain.

It was straight out of the *Go Rin No Sho*. It was the classic Body Strike of which Musashi wrote. Strike with the left shoulder, he wrote, with the spirit resolved, until the enemy

132

is dead. Learn this well. The ninja had, Terry reflected almost disinterestedly. He cared little for his own life now, not with Eileen lying dead in the next room. But to kill this monster, yes, this still had substance for him.

He began to move forward, up the wall, then off it. But his body refused to respond quickly. He reeled, his eyes on the moving ninja, crossing his arms in front of him to ward off the blow.

It had no effect. He crashed backward with a grunt of pain, his sternum splintered from the enormous force of the repeated blows. The bone shot through his body as effectively as shrapnel. He looked up once from where he was huddled against the molding, into the eyes like stones, thinking, Musashi was right after all. The softly swaying Mancini music rang in his ears, recalling Eileen to him. Her warmth suffused him like a lighted fuse, burning its way through him until it reached his brain.

Blood came out of his mouth as he called to her in a voice as fragile as rice paper. "Eileen," he called. "I love you." His head lolled and his eyes slid shut.

The ninja stood dominant in that black void, seeming scarcely to breathe. He stared at the body before him without emotion. For long moments his senses quested for any sound out of the ordinary. At length, satisfied, he turned away, moving silently across the room. From beneath the sofa he drew out his duffel bag and, drawing open the zipper, carefully placed his *bokken* next to its brother on the top of the contents. In one motion he had closed the bag and hefted it, quitting the apartment without a backward glance.

Behind him, Mancini played on, the slow bittersweet melody hinting at lost love, cascading through the room. A deep groan escaped from Terry's cracked lips as he coughed more blood. He lifted his head and, blindly, began to crawl toward the bedroom, not even understanding why, knowing only that he must.

Inch by agonizing inch he moved, crossing the threshold at last, stopping only when he lay panting, drooling blood, beside Eileen's corpse.

Before his face was a cord and, reaching up, he yanked on it. The phone crashed down onto his left shoulder but he was beyond feeling this minute drop within the vast pool of pain that encompassed him. His finger trembling, he dialed seven slow digits. The ringing of the receiver was like the tolling of a far-off temple bell.

But Eileen seemed suddenly so far away from him and he knew she needed him. The receiver slipped through his wet fingers. He crawled across the last miles.

"Hello?" It was Vincent's voice that came dimly through the abandoned instrument. "Hello? Hello!"

But there was no one now to hear him. Terry lay face down on the black fan of Eileen's hair, his eyes open, unseeing and already glazing over, the blood like a second tongue moving from his lips to hers.

In the living room, the music was finished.

Tokyo Suburbs

SPRING 1959—SPRING 1960

Look here, Nicholas," the Colonel said one dark and dismal afternoon. Storm clouds hid the crown of Mount Fuji and, occasionally, forked lightning lit the sky; afterward, the distant roll of thunder.

The Colonel, in his study, had in his hands a lacquered box. On its top was painted a dragon and a tiger, entwined. Nicholas recognized it as the parting gift given to his mother and father by So-Peng.

"It is time, I think, for you to see this," the Colonel said. He picked up his pipe and a zippered pouch of moist tobacco, digging both pipe and forefinger into its depths, filling it. Striking a wooden kitchen match on the edge of his desk, he drew strongly on the pipe, getting it going to his satisfaction before continuing. His long forefinger tapped the top of the box, the tip tracing the lines of the two creatures emblazoned there.

"Nicholas, do you know the symbolic meanings of the dragon and the tiger in Japanese mythology?"

Nicholas shook his head.

The Colonel blew out a cloud of blue aromatic smoke, gripped the pipe stem with his teeth at one corner of his mouth. "The tiger is lord of all the land and the dragon, well, he is emperor of the air. Curious, that, I've always thought. The flying serpent, Kukulkán, of Mayan mythology, though he was depicted as being feathered, was also lord of the air. Interesting that two cultures so far from each other should share a major slice of mythology, don't you think?"

"But why did So-Peng give you a Japanese box?" Nicholas asked. "He was Chinese, wasn't he?"

"Uhm, a good question," the Colonel said, puffing away. "One to which, I am afraid, I do not have a satisfactory an-

135

swer. It is true that So-Peng was from the province of Liao-ning in northern China, but he made it clear to me that his mother was Japanese."

"Still, that doesn't explain the box," Nicholas pointed out. "It's true enough that you were going to Japan, but this box is ancient, not easily acquirable, especially at that time."

"Yes," the Colonel replied, stroking the top, "there is little doubt that this had been in his family—quite probably brought by his mother to China—for some time. Now why should So-Peng give this to us? I mean this specific item. Surely it was no whim; he was not that kind of man. Nor, do I think, was it mere coincidence." The Colonel rose now and stood by the rain-streaked window. Condensation had made the panes into frosted decorations; winter's chill had not totally been left behind.

"I pondered this for a long time," the Colonel said, staring out the windows. He rubbed a small oval, clearing a line of sight as if he were carefully looking out a besieged fortress' apertures. "All the way from Singapore to Tokyo, in fact. So-Peng had asked us not to open the present until we had reached Japan and we respected this request.

"At Haneda Airport, we were met by a contingent of SCAP personnel—we had, of course, flown over in a military transport. However, someone else was waiting for us when we landed. Certainly your mother recognized her immediately and so did I, just by the description I had been given by Cheong of her dream. It was Itami and she looked precisely as your mother had dreamed she did." He shrugged. "Somehow, I was not amazed. One grows used to such... phenomena, here; it's a part of life in the Far East, as I've no doubt you will soon learn.

"I was curious, the rapport your mother had with Itami. It was as if they had known each other all their lives; as if they were sisters, rather than sisters-in-law. There was absolutely no culture shock as there might have been when a young girl brought up in a tiny Chinese village meets for the first time a grand lady of urban Japanese society. Now this was so even though your mother and Itami are totally different kinds of people." The Colonel turned around to face his son. "All the differences you see in them—the warmth in your mother, the steel-like aloofness of Itami; the happiness of your mother, the sadness of your aunt—none of these differences mattered to either of them.

"This, too, I thought about for some time and what I decided was this: although So-Peng told me in so many words that he possessed no knowledge of Cheong's true heritage, yet his present was an oblique way of telling me otherwise."

"You mean Mother is Japanese."

"Perhaps part Japanese." He came and sat down next to his son, putting one hand on his shoulder lovingly. "But, Nicholas, this is something you must promise never to discuss with anyone, even your mother. I tell you now because—well, because it was information passed on to me. So-Peng believed it was important, therefore it must be, though I myself put little stock in that sort of thing. I am English and a Jew, yet my heart is with these people. My blood sings with their history, my soul resonates with theirs. What use is my lineage to me? I want to make this quite clear to you, Nicholas. I did not renounce my Jewish name; I merely dropped it away. Now I suppose it can be argued that this is the same thing. Not so! I did this not by choice but by necessity. England, as a rule, does not like Jews; never has done so. I found, when I changed my name, many doors opened to me that had hitherto been quite shut. There's a moral question to be answered here, I know. Should one attempt to go through? Yes, say I, and devil take the hindmost. But that's my view. And while my soul is with the Japanese, I am neither Buddhist nor Shinto. These religions hold no particular meaning for me, save for scholarly study. In my heart, I have never renounced my Jewishness. Six thousand years of struggle cannot so easily be bought out. The blood of Solomon and David, of Moses, runs in your veins, too. Never forget that. Whether you choose to do anything about it is purely your concern; I would not tamper with so private a matter. Yet it is my duty to tell you, to give you the facts, as it were. I hope you understand this." He gazed solemnly at his son for a long moment before he opened the tiger and dragon box, the last gift of the enigmatic So-Peng.

Nicholas looked down, stared into the brilliant fire of sixteen half-inch cut emeralds.

Nicholas had been studying bujutsu for nearly seven years now and still felt as if he knew almost nothing. He was strong and his reflexes superb; he went through the drills and exercises with a great deal of concentration and assiduousness but without any special love or feeling. This surprised and concerned him. He had been fully prepared for the hard work, the difficulty, for it was exactly this kind of effort which interested and absorbed him the most. What he had not reckoned on was any indifference on his part. It was not, he reflected one day during floor exercises at the *dōjō*, that he had in any way changed his mind about wanting to learn bujutsu. In fact, if anything, this desire had increased. It was—well, very difficult to put. Perhaps there was no spark there.

Perhaps it was his instructor. Tanka was a stolid, solidly built man who believed a great deal in repeated movements and, it seemed, nothing else. Over and over, Nicholas was obliged to perform the same maneuver. Again and again until he felt that the sequence had been engraved upon his brain and nerves and muscles. It was boring work and he hated it. Hated, too, the fact that Tanka treated them as if they were children not yet ready for the adult world.

Ever and again, he would find himself looking over to the far side of the *dōjō* where Kansatsu, the *ryu*'s master, taught individual classes with a select few of the older students. He longed to be there instead of *here* on the dung heap of unspecialized exercises.

He had come to join the same *ryu* as Saigō—as had been said, through Itami's intervention—and it galled him further that his cousin, being older and having joined the *ryu* earlier than Nicholas, was thus far ahead. This point Saigō brought up to him at every opportunity. At the *dōjō* he was openly contemptuous of Nicholas—as were many of the other students, because of his occidental aspect, feeling that bujutsu being one of the most traditional and sacred of Japanese institutions should not be open to a *gaijin,* a foreigner—and never referred to Nicholas as his cousin. However, at home it was quite another matter. He was scrupulously careful to be polite to Nicholas. For his part, Nicholas had given up trying to talk the matter out with Saigō after the third unsuccessful attempt.

Truth to tell, Saigō was a thorn in Nicholas' side at the *dōjō*. When he could have been much help to the other, he invariably went out of his way to make everything more difficult, even going so far as to become the unofficial ringleader of the "opposition."

One evening, the work over with and the showers taken,

138

Nicholas was dressing when five or six of the boys came up in ones and twos until they had surrounded him.

"What are you doing here?" said one of the largest boys. "This is where we sit."

Nicholas said nothing, continuing to dress. Outwardly he took no notice, but inwardly his heart was beating like a trip-hammer.

"Don't you have anything to say?" said another boy. He was small and younger than the others but was seemingly emboldened by their surrounding presence. He laughed derisively. "Maybe he doesn't understand Japanese. Do you think we'll have to speak to him in English like they do the apes in the zoo?" Everyone laughed.

"That's right," the big boy said, picking up the cue. "I want an answer, ape. Tell us why you're here in our spot, stinking it up like a spot of venereal disease."

Nicholas stood up. "Why don't you go off and play somewhere where your jokes will be appreciated."

"Look, look!" cried the small boy. "The ape speaks!"

"Shut up!" said the big boy and then to Nicholas: "I don't care for your tone, ape. I think you've just said something you're going to regret." His right hand chopped downward toward Nicholas' exposed neck without warning. Nicholas blocked it and then they were all crowding into him.

Through the melee he caught a glimpse of Saigō on his way out, oblivious to the raucous disturbance. He called out his name.

Saigō checked and came over. "Hold on!" he called, shouldering his way through the crowd. He shoved them back against the wall, giving Nicholas some breathing space. "What's going on here?"

"It's the *gaijin*," the big boy said, his fists still clenched. "Making trouble again."

"Oho, is that so?" Saigō said. "One against six? Hard to believe." He shrugged, slammed the edge of his hand into Nicholas' stomach.

Nicholas pitched forward onto his knees, his forehead touching the floor as if in prayer. He retched, tried to fill his bursting lungs with air. He gasped like a fish out of water.

"Don't bother these people anymore, Nicholas," Saigō said, standing over him. "Where are your manners? But what can

139

you expect, fellows, his father's a barbarian and his mother's a *Chinese*. C'mon." He led them away, leaving Nicholas alone on the floor with his pain.

She had come with her attenuated procession quite unexpectedly during the middle of the week, throwing the entire household into a state of unmitigated panic, initiated, of course, by Cheong, who felt that the house was never clean enough, the food never fine enough, her family never well dressed enough to suit Itami.

She looked like a tiny doll, Nicholas thought, a perfect porcelain thing to be put on a pedestal inside a glass case, protected from the elements. In fact, Itami needed no such exterior protection; she had a will of iron and the power to promote it, even with her husband, Satsugai.

Nicholas watched clandestinely from another room as Cheong herself performed the elaborate tea ceremony for Itami, kneeling on the tatami before a green lacquered table. She wore a traditional Japanese robe and her long gleaming hair had been put up with ivory sticks. He thought that, at that moment, she had never looked so beautiful or so regal. She was a far cry from the icy aristocracy of Itami, yet perhaps even because of that he had far more admiration for his mother. Of Itami's kind of woman there were plenty in books of photographs he had seen of an older, prewar Japan. But oh, Cheong! There were none to touch her. She carried with her a nobility of the soul that Itami could never hope to attain, not in this life, at least. Though Itami was strong, her magnetism was nothing compared to Cheong's power, for she wielded an inner tranquillity that was as profound as the utter stillness of a hot summer's day, a living jewel, unique. She was, as Nicholas thought of it, of a whole cloth and this he respected and admired above all else.

He had no great desire to talk to Itami but it would have been very bad manners for him to leave the house without acknowledging her presence; his mother would be furious and, quite naturally, blame herself. This he did not want and thus, sometime later in the afternoon, he pulled open the *shōji* and stepped through.

Itami looked up. "Ah, Nicholas, I did not know that you were home."

"Good afternoon, Aunt."

140

"Excuse me a moment," Cheong said, getting effortlessly to her feet. "The tea is cold." For some reason she would not overtly use the servants when Itami was around. She left them alone and Nicholas began to feel uncomfortable under the mute scrutiny of Itami's gaze.

He went over to the window, gazed out at the forest of cryptomeria and pine.

"Do you know," said Itami, "that hidden within the forest is an ancient Shinto shrine?"

"Yes," Nicholas said, turning around. "My father told me."

"Have you seen it?"

"Not yet."

"And did you know, Nicholas, that within that shrine is a park filled with mosses?"

"Forty different varieties, I think, Aunt. Yes, I know of it but I am told that only the priests of the shrine may look upon it."

"Perhaps it is not so difficult as that, Nicholas. I cannot imagine you wanting to become a priest. It does not suit you." She rose, said unexpectedly, "How would you like to take me there? To the shrine and to the park?"

"When? Now?"

"Certainly."

"But I thought—"

"All things may be possible, one way or another, Nicholas." She smiled and called: "Cheong, Nicholas and I are going for a walk. We won't be long." She turned back to him and reached out her hand. "Come," she said gently.

They walked silently until they came to the verge of the forest. There they turned right along the grass for perhaps two hundred meters where she abruptly guided him inward. He found that they were on a narrow but well-worn dirt track through the trees and underbrush.

"Well, Nicholas, you must tell me how you like your training at the *dōjō*," Itami said. She walked carefully in her wooden *geta,* using the point of her lacquered paper parasol as a walking stick to help balance her on the uneven ground.

"It is very hard work, Aunt."

"Yes." She waved a hand as if dismissing this statement. "But this is not something that you had not anticipated."

"No."

"Do you enjoy all the hard work?"

He glanced up at her, wondering what she was getting at.

He had absolutely no intention of telling her of the growing animosity between himself and Saigō. That would not do at all. He had not even told his parents. "At times," he said. "I would wish to move on." He shrugged. "I am impatient, I suppose."

"There are times when only the impatient are rewarded, Nicholas," she said, stepping over a tangled root. "Here, help me the last few feet, won't you?" She gave him her arm. "Ah, there we are!"

They were in a clearing, and as they moved out from the shade of the pines, Itami lifted her parasol over her head and opened it. Her skin was as white as snow, her lips deep red, her eyes as dark as nuggets of coal.

The deep lacquered wall of the temple was awash in shimmering sunlight so that he was obliged to squint until his eyes accustomed themselves to the brightness. It was as if he were gazing at a sea of gold.

They began to walk along the crushed limestone gravel, a blue-white stippled path that completely encircled the temple; one could tread it forever, never getting closer or farther away from one's goal.

"But you have survived," she said softly. "That is gratifying." They had reached the verge of the long wooden steps up to the bronze and lacquered-wood doors which stood open, shadowed, silent, hunkered down comfortably as if waiting for something or someone to arrive. They paused there. She put a hand on his shoulder, so lightly that if he had not seen it, he might not even have felt its weight there. "I had grave doubts when your father came to me, requesting I help gain entrance for you in a suitable *ryu*." She shook her head. "I had no choice but to acquiesce and honor dictated that I make no comment of my own, but I was concerned." She sighed. "In a way I pity you. How strange your life will be. Westerners will never fully accept you because of your oriental blood and the Japanese will despise you because of your occidental features." Her hand lifted into the air like a butterfly and her forefinger gave him a fragile and fleeting touch on the point of one cheek. She stared at him. "Even your eyes are your father's." Her hand dropped to her side; it was as if she had never made the gesture. "But I am not so easily fooled." She turned her implacable gaze away from him, said, "Let us go inside and pray."

142

"Beautiful, isn't it?" Itami said.

And he had to agree. They stood beside a slow meandering brook which tumbled down across moss-covered rocks from a height of perhaps two meters, certainly not more. Everywhere was green, even the water, even the pebbles. To Nicholas it looked as though there were four thousand species of moss here instead of the forty.

"And peaceful," she continued. "It's so peaceful here. The outside world does not exist. Gone." She folded her parasol in the shade of the overhanging cryptomeria. She inhaled deeply, her small head thrown back. "It is as if time itself has dissolved, Nicholas. As if there had been no twentieth century, no expansion, no imperialism—no war." She closed her eyes. "No war." He watched her closely until her eyes flew open, staring. "But there was a war." She turned. "Shall we sit on this stone bench? Good. Perhaps the shōgun—one of the Tokugawas, even—sat just here where we are. There. It gives one a sense of history, does it not? A continuity? A feeling of belonging?" She turned to him. "But not you, I suspect. Not yet, anyway. We are alike in that respect. Oh, yes we are." She laughed. "I see by your expression that you are surprised. You shouldn't be. We are both outsiders, you see, forever cut off from that which we desire the most."

"But how can that be?" Nicholas protested. "You are a Nobunaga, a member of one of Japan's oldest and most noble houses."

Itami smiled at him just the way a predator might and he saw her white even teeth, glistening with saliva. "Oh yes," she breathed, "a Nobunaga, indeed. But that, like a great deal else in Japan, is merely the exterior: the gorgeous lacquered coat which hides the rotting hulk underneath." Her face was no longer beautiful, squeezed as it was by the anguish she felt. "Listen well to me, Nicholas. Honor has fled us here; we have allowed ourselves to be corrupted by the Western barbarians. We are a despicable race now; we have done such hideous deeds. How our ancestors must shudder in their graves, how their *kami* must yearn for the final resting rather than the return to this—modern society."

Her voice had risen somewhat and now Nicholas sat quite still beside her, allowing the air to cool. But she would not or perhaps could not rest now. It had been difficult, he suspected, for her to begin this. But, once she had overcome the initial inertia, nothing could stop her now.

"Do you know what the *zaibatsu* are, Nicholas?"

"By name only," he said, once more uncertain of the ground she had put them on.

"Ask your father to explain the *zaibatsu* to you one day, will you? The Colonel knows a great deal about them and you should know, too." Then, as if it explained it all, she said, "Satsugai works for one of the *zaibatsu*."

"Which one?"

"I hate my husband, Nicholas. And, do you know"—she laughed shortly—"only your father knows why. It is so ironic. But life is ironic. It's a devil withholding from you what you desire the most." Her tiny hands were clenched like baby fists in her lap. "What good being a noble Nobunaga when I must forever carry with me the shame of my great-grandfather? My shame is as inescapable to me as your mixed blood is to you.

"My great-grandfather left the service of the shōgun when he was twenty-eight to become a *ronin*—do you know what that is?"

"A masterless samurai."

"A warrior without honor, yes. A brigand, a thief. He turned mercenary, selling his strong capable arm to the highest bidder. Enraged by this unseemly and dishonorable behavior, the shōgun sent men out into the countryside to track him down, and when they finally did, they adhered to the order given by the shōgun. No *seppuku* for my great-grandfather; the shōgun would not grant him an honorable way to die. He was carrion now; no longer a *bushi*. They crucified him as they did the scum of the land.

"In most of those cases, the offender's entire family is destroyed—the women and all the children so that his family line, his most prized possession, would be stripped from him. Not this time, however."

"Why?" Nicholas asked. "What happened?"

Itami shrugged and smiled wanly. "Karma. My karma which forms the backbone of my life. I rebel against it; it makes me ache, and at night I cry. I am ashamed to say that. I am a *bushi*, a samurai woman, even in this day and age. Some things time cannot alter. My blood seethes with ten thousand battles; my soul resonates to the sweep of the *katana*, its blade, its fearful shades of steel."

She stood up, the parasol blossomed like an enormous flower. "One day you shall understand this. And remember. It is difficult now at the *ryu*. Do not interrupt me. I know. But you must never give it up. Do you hear me? Never." She turned away from him, the soft pastels of the parasol blotting out the smoldering passion in her black eyes. "Come," he heard her say. "It is time we returned to the world."

"This is *Ai Uchi*," said Muromachi. He was holding a *bokken* in his hands. Seven students, Nicholas' group, stood in a precise semicircle around him. "Here at the Itto *ryu*, it is the first teaching; the first of hundreds. *Ai Uchi* means cut the opponent just as he cuts you. It is the timing you will learn here, the one that is basic to kenjutsu. One which you will never forget. *Ai Uchi* is lack of anger. It means to treat an opponent as if he were an honored guest. It means to abandon your life or to throw away fear. *Ai Uchi* is the first technique and it is the last. Remember that. It is the Zen circle."

This was the lesson Nicholas had first been taught upon arriving at the *ryu* seven years ago. He did not fully understand it yet he never forgot it. And in the time that followed, as he practiced with a cold fury the thousand cuts of the *katana* under Muromachi's tutelage; as he learned the moral teaching of kenjutsu; as the knowledge piled itself upon him with dizzying rapidity, he was ever to think of that first lesson and, in pondering it, feel a calmness, stepping into the eye of the storm each time that storm threatened to overwhelm him.

And he repeated the thousand cuts over and over, feeling as if his arms and his legs were wearing grooves into the air until, at last, his reward manifested itself, when his sword became no sword, his intention became no intention and he knew that the first lesson given to him by Muromachi so long ago was, in fact, the highest knowledge.

Still, he was not satisfied. He was thinking of this late one afternoon after practice when he felt a presence in the room. He looked up but saw no one. The room was deserted and yet he could not get it out of his mind that someone was there. He stood up and was about to call out when he thought

145

it might again be several of the boys lying in wait for him and he kept quiet, not wanting to give them any degree of satisfaction.

He began to move around the room in the dusk. The far side of the empty *dōjō* was streaked with dusty sunlight as red as blood, washed in the industrial haze lying low, its tendrils creeping up Fuji's majestic slopes. Rapidly, his assessment changed. While he was quite certain now that someone was there with him, it also came to him that this person meant him no harm. How he had come to this conclusion he could not have said; it was, rather, a purely automatic response.

Light spilled into the corner of the *dōjō*, touching the edge of the clear-lacquered wooden railing, a fat slice of the raised platform behind it, leaving in dense shadow the corner beam. He was watching this pattern of light and shade when a voice said, "Good evening, Nicholas."

The corner shadow had come to life, a figure stepping out of its concealing pocket, into the light. It was Kansatsu.

He was a thin, slight man, his stiff bristly hair already white. He had eyes that never appeared to move yet took in everything at once.

He made absolutely no sound as he came down off the platform to stand in front of Nicholas who, bare to the waist, felt totally tongue-tied. Kansatsu had barely said three words to him since he had come to the *ryu*. Now they were here, together, and Nicholas understood enough to know that the meeting was not accidental.

He saw Kansatsu eyeing him, then the man stepped forward, his outstretched forefinger touching the purple and blue bruise just beneath Nicholas' sternum on the left side.

"These are very bad times for Japan," Kansatsu said. "Very sad times." He looked up. "The war was joined because of economics and our imperialism dictated that we expand beyond our islands." He sighed. "But the war was ill-advised for all that, for it stemmed from greed, not honor. The new Japanese adds the gloss of *bushido* to his actions, I am afraid, rather than allowing his actions to evolve from it." His eyes were sad. "And now we pay the price. We are overrun by Americans, our new Constitution is American and the entire thrust of the new Japan is to serve the American interests. So strange, so strange for Japan to serve such a master." He shrugged. "But, you see, no matter what happens to Japan,

146

bushido will never completely perish. We begin to wear Western business suits, our women wear their hair in the American manner; we adopt the Western ways. These things do not matter. The Japanese is like the willow, bending in the wind so that it should not break. These are merely outward manifestations of our desire now for parity in the world. So, too, do the Americans unwittingly serve our purpose, for, with their money, we shall rise more powerful than ever. Yet we must ever look to our tradition, for only *bushido* makes us strong.

"You wish to become one of us," he said abruptly. "But this"—he pointed to the bruise that had been inflicted by Saigō—"tells me that you have not been entirely successful."

"Success will come in time," Nicholas said. "I am learning not to be impatient."

Kansatsu nodded. "Good. Very good. Yet one must take the necessary steps." He put his fingertips together in front of him, began to walk slowly across the *dōjō* with Nicholas beside him. "I think it is time that you begin to work with other *sensei*. I do not want you to give up your very valuable work with Muromachi; rather I want to add to your current schedule.

"Tomorrow you will begin to work with me," he said, leading Nicholas across the darkened room, "in *haragei*."

Nicholas would always separate his relationship with Satsugai into two distinct sections. The specific point of demarcation was the *zaibatsu* party he attended with his parents. It was, of course, quite possible that this changing perception was strictly a function of his own growing up. On the other hand, he had tended to believe that it was just as much a matter of what transpired there that night.

Satsugai was not a large man, either in terms of height or of bulk. Yet for all that he was nevertheless quite remarkable. He was massive through chest and belly, with squat legs and arms that appeared to be far too short for his body. His head seemed to be cemented onto his shoulders without the benefit of an intervening neck. His head was a perfect oval covered on top by jet black hair cut *en brosse* which, to Nicholas at least, added to his military bearing. His face was flat but not in a typically Japanese manner. His eyes, for instance, were distinctly almond-shaped and as glossily black as hard chips of obsidian but they slanted upward at their outer corners and this oddity, combined with his flat high cheekbones and the deep yellow colors of his skin, bespoke his Mongol heritage. Nicholas could think of him, without much difficulty at all, as some reincarnation of Genghis Khan. This was not so outlandish as it at first might seem for, recalling his history, Nicholas brought to mind the Mongol invasions of Japan in 1274 and 1281. Fukuoka, in the south, was their chief target because of its nearness to the Asian shore. Satsugai, Nicholas knew, had been born in the Fukuoka district and though he was, in all ways, purely Japanese—tradition-minded, wholly reactionary—who could say that his ancestors had not been among those most feared of mounted nomads?

One might think that, in giving all these particulars of his physical appearance, one might thus be able to define the man. Not so, however. Satsugai was, quite clearly, an individual who was born to lead. Being a native of a land dedicated to the idea of duty to the group—family elders, the *daimyo* and, ultimately, the shōgun who represented the concept of Japan more forcefully and in a much more real sense than did the Emperor for a span of some two hundred and fifty years—he was nevertheless forever a man apart. Outwardly, quite naturally, this was not so, for he was totally dedicated to Japan, *his* Japan, and to this end he belonged to many groups, not merely one of the *zaibatsu* conglomerates. Yet it became manifestly clear to Nicholas on the night of the party that, inwardly, Satsugai believed himself superior to others. This, curiously enough, was at least part of the basis for his ability in leadership. The Japanese were born followers; they had been bred to follow with blind obedience the dictates of the shōgun even unto death. Was it so surprising then that Satsugai should find a wide following of fanatic supporters? It was a subtle pillow upon which he slept—had Caesar done otherwise?—but nonetheless it was a prime motivational factor in his life.

Always Itami was by his side. Near him, too, was Saigō as if he were bathing in the energy of a companion sun. However, that night there was a fourth person with them and, from the first moment he saw her, she captivated Nicholas. He leaned over, asked his mother who the girl might be.

"That is Satsugai's niece. From the south," Cheong said.

148

"She has come for a brief visit." By her tone of voice Nicholas could tell that, as far as Cheong was concerned, the visit could not be brief enough. He meant to ask her why it was she disliked the girl but already Satsugai had her in tow and was introducing her to Cheong and the Colonel.

She was slim and tall—willowy, a Westerner might call her. Her dark hair was very long; her eyes seemed enormous, liquid and feral. Her skin was like porcelain, possessing an inner glow quite impossible to duplicate via cosmetics. Nicholas thought she was quite stunning. Her name, so Satsugai informed him when he introduced her separately to Nicholas, was Yukio Jokoin.

She had come with Saigō. He made this plain by keeping within her shadow for most of the evening. Though Nicholas tried, he could not tell whether she wanted this attention or not.

For most of the evening he stewed inside himself, debating whether to ask her to dance. He knew that he wanted to do it; he just did not know what waves his action might cause. Not that he was intimidated by Saigō's close princely protection of her, rather he was burdened by the secrecy of the father, whose relationship with the Colonel was stormy at best.

There was no one's counsel he could seek but his own and, in the end, he decided that he was worrying about something that had significance only for him.

Accordingly, he approached them. It was Yukio herself who provided the opening, for she immediately began to ask him questions about Tokyo, which she had not visited in some time; his immediate impression was that she was fairly well confined to Kyoto and its environs.

Saigō, as might be anticipated, took a rather dim view of his interference and was about to voice his displeasure when his father called for him and, reluctantly, he excused himself.

As he led her onto the dance floor, Nicholas had time to admire her kimono. It was dove-gray with platinum-colored threads running through it. It was embroidered with the design of a midnight-blue wheel-and-spoke pattern typical of the standard of a *daimyo* in feudal times.

She seemed weightless as they danced to the slow music and, holding her close, he felt the heat from her body, the subtle shifting of her flesh beneath the thin kimono.

"We two are both too young to remember the war," she

said, her voice husky. "Yet we are so much affected by it. Doesn't that seem odd to you?"

"Not really." He was breathing in the musk of her skin and it seemed to him as if her very sweat were perfumed. "Isn't history continuous? Incidents don't happen in a vacuum but cause ripples spreading outward, interacting with other ripples, changing their courses and, in turn, being themselves changed."

"My, what philosophy." And he thought that she might be mocking him until she laughed and said, "But I like that theory. Do you know why? No? Because it means that what we do here will affect our histories."

"What, you mean us?"

"Yes. The two of us. A duo. White and black. Yin and yang."

Now while she spoke she had contrived, without Nicholas' being in the least aware, to slide closer to him. Abruptly, as they swayed to the music he found her left leg between his. She pushed discreetly forward and he felt the hot contact with her thigh and then, incredibly, her pubic mound. She continued talking, staring up into his eyes, while she rubbed herself lightly back and forth against him. It was as if they were joined by a hardening fulcrum. Nicholas scarcely dared to breathe lest some precipitous move of his dislodge them from this position. It was an astoundingly intimate gesture, coming as it did in the midst of six hundred or so people, lavishly dressed, still disdainful of new ways or liberal viewpoints. Its highly clandestine nature thrilled him especially when, turning her around, his gaze fell upon Saigō staring at them from the edge of the dance floor, still engaged in a discussion from which his father would not release him. It was the only time Nicholas would think kindly of the man.

They danced for what seemed like endless moments but when, at length, they parted—with not one word exchanged about the intimacy—he was unaware that he would not see her again for nearly four years.

On Sundays the Colonel slept late. This luxury he permitted himself perhaps because, on a day when he did not work, he was delighted to smash routine to smithereens; though he awoke six mornings a week at precisely six o'clock,

150

he rolled out of bed whenever he wished on that first day of the week.

No one disturbed him then save for Cheong, who seemed invulnerable to his infrequent wrath. At times she would stay on the *futon* with him until he was awake but at other times she was up early, working in the kitchen, having shooed the servants away.

Cheong prepared the meals on the weekend. She would have cooked every day, Nicholas knew, because she loved to do it, but the Colonel forbade it. "Let Tai do the cooking," he told her somewhat crossly one day. "That is what she is paid for, after all. Your time should be your own, to do with what you want." "Do what?" she had said. "You know very well what I'm getting at." "Who, me?" She pointed to herself. "Me only ignorant Chinee, Colonel-san." She said this in pidgin English, though she had superb grasp of that language. She bowed to him over and over. The Colonel was exasperated by her parodies—she was a brilliant mimic, picking up individual accents and idiosyncrasies with astounding rapidity—because they struck so close to reality. He did not like to recall those aspects of the hazed Asian shore so close to them across the *genkainada:* the utter disdain with which the English and the Americans alike treated the Chinese and the Malay; as if they were some subhuman species, suitable only for menial and sexual labors. The Colonel had taken Cheong in his strong sun-browned arms and kissed her hard on the lips, holding her tight around, knowing from experience that this was the only way to silence her, that the expression of his anger would only egg her on.

That particular Sunday morning, Cheong was already up and slicing fresh vegetables when Nicholas came into the kitchen.

Oblique bars of sunlight jazzed the windows, turning them sparkly. The drone of a distant plane could be heard, preparing to land at Haneda. Low on the horizon he could see the flying V of the geese, moving away from the ellipse of the rising sun.

He kissed her and her arms went around him.

"Will you go to the *dōjō* today?" she asked quietly.

"Not if Father will be home."

She split green beans. "I think he has a surprise for you today. I was hoping you would decide to stay."

"I felt I should be here," he said. "I wanted to be."

"There may come a time," Cheong said without looking up from her cooking, "when that will not be possible."

"You mean with Father?"

"No, this applies to you."

"I don't think I understand."

"When your father and I left Singapore, So-Peng was already dying. It was to be a relatively slow death and he had much to accomplish before the end. But as he said to me, it would be the last time we would see each other; and he was right." Her hands moved in a blur along the wooden counter, blithely dissociated from her words. "I knew that I must take your father and leave Singapore behind forever; our life lay elsewhere; it lay here. But my heart broke at leaving So-Peng. He was my father; so much more than a father and I so much more than a daughter. Perhaps that was so because we had chosen each other; it was our minds rather than our blood that were the same.

"That day, as we left, I paused on the porch of his house as I had done so many times when, as a child, I was about to go out, when So-Peng put a hand on my arm. It was the first and last time he touched me as an adult. Your father was already somewhat ahead on the street. 'Now you are me, Cheong,' he said to me in the peculiar Mandarin dialect we used only among ourselves in the household."

"What did he mean?"

"I don't know—I only suspect." She wiped her hands, dipped them in a bowl of cold lemon water, began to slice again, swiftly and deftly; this time it was cucumbers. "I cried all the way through the forest until we reached the clearing where the Jeep was parked. Your father, of course, said nothing, though I've no doubt he wanted to; he would not shame me that way."

"Did you have to leave?" Nicholas asked.

"I did, yes," she said, for the first time looking up from her work. "I had my duty to your father. That is my life. I knew it that day and so did So-Peng. It would have been inconceivable to him that I should stay with him, that I should abandon my duty. It could not happen. To abandon duty is to destroy that which makes any individual unique and capable of prodigious feats.

"Duty is the essence of life, Nicholas. It is the only thing over which death has no dominion. It is true immortality."

152

As it turned out, the Colonel had the entire day free and, it being spring, he took Nicholas to the Jindaiji Botanical Park in the city for the traditional cherry blossom viewing.

On the way they dropped Cheong at Itami's; she had promised her she would go with her to see her uncle who was ill.

The morning's haze had lifted and a strong easterly wind had already banished the low-lying mist; wispy cirrus arced like a series of Impressionist paintings newly hung in a museum's vast gallery.

So, too, the park seemed to have been dropped wholesale from out of the heavens. The heavily flowering trees, their long branches bent low under the weight of the palest pink blossoms, took on an ethereal otherworldliness. At other times of the year the park perhaps showed its rather austere beauty. But this was April and the splendor displayed here was breathtaking.

Kimonos and brightly colored oiled paper parasols were much in evidence as they made their leisurely way along the winding paths beneath the two skies, one low and fragrant, the other far out of reach. They stopped at a vendor selling sweet tofu. The Colonel bought them each a portion and they ate the confection slowly as they moved on. Laughing children passed them, indulged by their parents, and young couples, arm in arm. There were many Americans.

"Father, will you tell me something about the *zaibatsu*?" Nicholas asked.

The Colonel spooned a bit of tofu into his mouth, chewed reflectively. "Well, I'm sure you know quite a bit already."

"I know what the *zaibatsu* are," Nicholas said. "Four of the largest industrial complexes in Japan. And I know that for a brief time just after the war many of the *zaibatsu*'s top executives were tried for war crimes. I don't really understand that."

The Colonel was obliged to stoop slightly as they passed beneath low-hanging branches. They might have been flying, passing through rose-colored banks of clouds. Modern Tokyo seemed never to have existed, to be, rather, a manifestation of some science fiction tale. An Easterner walking here at this time would have no difficulty in understanding this. Symbols abounded in Japan, acquiring their own potency. For the Japanese there was perhaps no more powerful symbol

153

than the cherry blossom. It stood variously for renewal, purification, love and ineffable, timeless beauty: basic concepts to the Japanese spirit. All this passed through the Colonel's mind as he decided where to start.

"As in all things Japanese," he said, "the answer is not a simple one. In fact, its origins lie elsewhere: in Japan's long militaristic history. With the beginning of the Meiji Restoration in 1868, Japan made a strong and concerted effort to turn away from both the isolation and the feudalism that marked the two hundred-plus years of the powerful Tokugawa shōgunate. This also meant turning away from the traditionalism which, many felt, was the backbone of Japan's strength."

They turned off to the right, heading down a shallow incline toward a small lake. The shouts of children's voices drifted up to them through the foliage.

"But with this new policy," the Colonel continued, "this Westernization, if you will, came, quite naturally, the eroding of the samurai's great power. After all, they had always been Japan's most stalwart traditionalists. Now they were branded reactionaries, for they vigorously opposed all that the Meiji Restoration sought to create. I know that you are well aware that since 1582, when Hideyoshi Toyotomi became shōgun, only samurai were allowed to wear two swords—the *katana* was the samurai's province alone. Now this was all changed. The Military Conscription Act forbade the wearing of the *katana* and, by creating a national army composed of 'commoners,' effectively did away with the class barrier that had exalted the samurai since its inception in A.D. 792."

For a time they strolled by the side of the lake, its pure chill blue contrasting with the pink-white of the blossoms. Toy sailboats drifted across the water, their white sails billowing, their tiny captains running gleefully at the verge of the land to keep up with their progress.

"However, the samurai were not so easily beaten," the Colonel said. The miniature sails, moving so steadfastly over the water, recalled to him perfect prints out of Japan's internecine past. "A great majority of them fought back directly and, when they were defeated, they formed societies. The main one was called the Genyōsha—the Dark Ocean Society—but there were others such as the Kokuryūkai—the Black Dragon Society. These societies, which are quite active today, are reactionary organizations that believe strongly in

154

imperialism and a manifest destiny for Japan upon the Asian shore.

"Now the Genyōsha was born in Fukuoka and is based there still. But since that part of Kyūshū is this country's closest approach to the continent, it's not very surprising that the Genyōsha should be most virulent there."

Nicholas thought of the Mongol invasions, of the violently nationalistic feelings that must have been nurtured there by such precipitous incursions. And this led him back to thoughts of Satsugai.

They found a bench beside the water, sat down. On the far side of the lake a child held a handful of colorful balloons and, farther away, over the massive treetops, he could see plastered against the sky the quivering fragile presence of a box kite; it was painted in the image of a fire-breathing dragon.

"Having failed in their bid to overtly overthrow the Meiji regime, the members of the Genyōsha next set about subverting the Restoration covertly, from within. They were clever men. They knew that the Meiji oligarchy, which propounded industrialization, would need economic expansion in order to fuel this. To them, this must involve the exploitation and eventual subjugation of China.

"Working within the prescribed political framework of the new Japanese society, the men of the Genyōsha sought to make allies in the highest levels of government. They made their intensive target the members of the General Staff, where a reactionary philosophy was the norm rather than the exception.

"They were aided in this by the upcoming general election of 1882. The Genyōsha made deals with the incumbents. In return for their seeing that these politicians were returned to office, the society was assured that this regime would follow a vigorously imperialistic foreign policy. Accordingly, the Genyōsha hired toughs, importing them into each district of the country. Beatings were not uncommon. It was an election of fear."

Two American Army officers passed by with their families in tow; they wore their uniforms like a badge of honor, treading the ground like the conquering heroes they were. Perhaps they saw where they were, what went on around them, but surely they understood none of it.

"With the implementation of this policy and the success

of Japanese expansion into Manchuria and Shanghai came the vested interests of the Japanese businessman abroad. A growing economy was now crucial to Japan and its rate of growth was prodigious. Out of this caldron rose the four enormous industrial combines comprising the *zaibatsu*."

"Then Kansatsu was right when he said that economics must take as much responsibility as militarism for Japan's road to the war," Nicholas observed thoughtfully.

The Colonel nodded. "In many ways, Japan was a primitive nation by world standards; the Tokugawa had seen to that. But, on the other hand, they understood perhaps better than any others the purity of their country. But I'm very much afraid it's one of the things that MacArthur missed. Oh, he knew enough about the culture to leave the Emperor just where he had always been despite the hue and cry that he be tried and executed as a war criminal. You see, quite apart from the fact that, from the first, the Emperor had done all in his power to aid the Americans after the war, MacArthur was well aware that any attempt to dethrone him would throw Japan into utter chaos; it was a tradition that even the mighty shōguns dared not tamper with.

"Yet also from the first the Americans propounded the myth that the guiding force behind the Japanese war effort came entirely from the military." He licked at his sticky fingers, took out his pipe. "Nothing could have been further from the truth. It was the members of the *zaibatsu* who backed the country into a corner from which war became the only viable economic alternative."

"But what about the Japanese people as a whole?" Nicholas asked. "Surely they did not want war."

The Colonel placed his pipe, unlit, between his teeth. He looked up, watching the gentle bobbing of the laden boughs in the wind. "Unfortunately there is a long history here of the people being led. It comes from being so long in a feudal society, of giving blind obedience to the Emperor, the shōgun, the *daimyo*. It's inbred." He sat upright, half facing his son on the bench, one hand holding the bowl of his pipe. "It's not surprising, then, to learn that there was little concerted antiwar sentiment just before the war. In fact, the Social Democrat Party, who had been openly antimilitaristic in their stand when Japan invaded Manchuria, lost much of their constituency in the 1932 general election. It was the tiny but ineradicable Communist Party that became the lone Japanese voice raised against imperialism during that time. It was little more than a reed in a hurricane; the *zaibatsu* and the Genyōsha had efficiently manipulated key individuals in both the government and the media; war became inevitable."

They both looked up at the sound of running feet. To their left a pair of uniformed policemen rushed down stone steps three at a time, their arms spread wide on either side for balance. People looked up. There was a harsh cry. Children turned; the toy sailboats rocked unattended and unwatched. Several of the American officers hesitated for an instant before taking off after the police. Nicholas and the Colonel stood up and began to drift with the crowd around the left side of the lake.

There was a stand of intervening cherry trees and the foliage was so lush that they could not make out what was happening behind it.

A crowd had formed by the time they arrived, having cut through the grass so as to bypass the crowded stairs. Taking Nicholas by the arm, the Colonel shouldered his way through the throng. Already, at the edges, there was some pushing and shoving. The scuffling was brief, however, as more of the metropolitan police arrived on the scene.

The front line of people parted and they saw an expanse of grass like a glade in a forest. There were cherry blossoms scattered upon the grass as if in a hero's welcome home. Nicholas caught a glimpse of a patterned kimono. At first it appeared gray but then, as he was shoved forward by the thrust of the uneasy crowd, he saw that it was composed of thin waved lines of black and white which, at a distance, blended together. It was trimmed in white.

As more policemen pushed themselves through the onlookers, those already in the glade shifted position. As they did so, Nicholas saw a man kneeling on the grass. His forehead touched the ground littered with blossoms. His right arm was close to his body, the hand invisible within the kimono's folds across his belly. In front of him was a small lacquered rosewood and brass box and a long white strip of silk, partly in shadow.

Behind him, the Colonel gripped Nicholas' shoulders as he said, "That's Hanshichiro!" He was referring to the great Japanese poet.

Nicholas squirmed to get a better look. He now saw the

kneeling man's face between the forest of shifting legs. His hair was iron-gray, his face wide and flat, the features thick. Lines pulled down the corners of his mouth. His eyes were closed. Then Nicholas saw that the silk strip before him was not shadowed but stained. Being porous, it let all the blood through so that it seeped into the earth at Hanshichiro's feet.

"*Seppuku,*" the Colonel said, "is how it ends for the honorable."

Nicholas was still thinking of how incredibly ordered it was. He was used to stories of the war; there, death was messy. But here, how serene, how precise, how much like the tide of time it was, while all around its calmness stirred the agitated waters.

"Are you all right, Nicholas?" The Colonel put his hand lightly on his shoulders, looked down at him concernedly.

Nicholas nodded. "I think so." He looked up. "Yes. I guess I am. I feel—a little strange, as if there's been too much to take in suddenly. I—Why did he do it in the park? He wanted everyone to see."

"To see and take note," the Colonel said. They had quit the lake, climbing into the heights of the park where the trees blotted out even the surrounding paths. Above, Nicholas could still see the wavering dragon, spitting his fire into the air, as if in defiance of the currents that blew him hither and thither.

"He was a bitter man, firmly embedded in the past. He could never reconcile himself to Japan's new path." A dark blue carriage filled with pink twins and pushed by a matronly Japanese woman went past them. "Hanshichiro was a brilliant artist, obsessed. A man of great honor. This was his way of protesting Japan's march toward the future, a future which, he felt, would ultimately destroy it." A young American sailor and his Japanese girl friend approached them from the heights, laughing and clutching each other's hands. The sailor put his arm around the girl, gave her a kiss on the cheek. She giggled and turned her head away. Her hair tossed in the wind, rippling like the dragon's body if he were but articulated.

"There are many others like Hanshichiro," Nicholas said. "Wasn't Satsugai born in Fukuoka?"

The Colonel looked reflectively at his son. He stopped and

dug in his jacket pocket. He withdrew his tobacco pouch, went about filling his pipe, his thumb tamping at the bowl.

Nicholas, watching the dragon float high above him, over the treetops, said, "I've read the Constitution, Father. I know that you had a hand in it. It's not Japanese but it's very democratic. Much more so than the policies of the government today. Politically, Japan's gone far to the right, the *zaibatsu* were never dismantled. Most of the prewar personnel is intact. I don't understand that."

The Colonel drew out a gunmetal-gray Ronson lighter and, turning his back to the wind, thumbed the long flame to life. He sucked three or four times, deeply, almost with a sigh of contentment, before he flipped the top of the lighter closed. "I want to know how you feel before I answer that. Do you care that Hanshichiro is dead? Or that you've seen a man take his own life?"

"I don't know. I really don't." He put his hand along the black iron railing bordering the path, feeling the cool metal against his skin. "I don't know whether it has taken effect yet. It's like a movie, not real life. I didn't know him or his work. I guess I'm sad but I don't know why. He did what he wanted to do."

The Colonel drew on his pipe, thinking of what his son had just said. What had he expected? Tears? Hysterics? He dreaded returning home and having to tell Cheong. She loved the old man's poetry. It was terribly unfair for him to think Hanshichiro's death could touch Nicholas in the same deep way it did him. Their experiences were not the same and neither were the generations; anyway, Nicholas did not yet possess the sense of history that the Colonel and Cheong did. And, of course, he had quite a different perspective on it. For a moment he thought of Satsugai. There wasn't much Nicholas missed. He would have to watch that from now on.

"Although the American party line was to make the military totally culpable for the war," the Colonel said, "it's only fair to say that there was a purge of the *zaibatsu* directly after the war. However, there was so much burning of original documents and deliberate falsification of others that a great many upper-echelon executives slipped through. Others, of course, did not and were tried and convicted of war crimes." They began to walk toward the eastern gate beyond which their car was parked.

"Now the Americans came in here with the best of intentions." The Colonel drew on his pipe, exhaled the blue smoke. "I remember the day we finished drafting the new Constitution and dropped it on the Premier and the Foreign Minister like another A-bomb. They were flabbergasted. It wasn't a Japanese Constitution; its spirit was totally Western, that's certainly true. But it was MacArthur's firm intention to keep the country weaned from its feudal past, which he saw as highly dangerous. Its essence was that all power should be stripped from the Emperor and given into the hands of the Japanese people while maintaining him as the symbol of state."

"Then what happened?" Nicholas asked.

"In 1947, Washington, through MacArthur, did a complete about-face. Rights were withdrawn, certain war-crime convictions were overturned and the leaders of the *zaibatsu* were restored to their prewar eminence."

"It all sounds so contradictory."

"Only if you look at it from a purely Japanese point of view," the Colonel said. "You see, America is deathly afraid of global communism; the Americans will go to any lengths to prevent its spread. Just look at how they've aided Franco in Spain and Chiang Kai-shek out here. Fascism, the Americans feel, is their best weapon against communism."

"Then the Americans deliberately disregarded their own Constitution for Japan, restoring the reactionary *zaibatsu*, guiding us in a right-wing direction."

The Colonel nodded but said nothing. He felt now as if he might never make it to the park gate, as if it were the end of a treacherous overland journey that he no longer had sufficient strength to make. "Let's sit here a minute," he said softly. They went carefully over the low railing, sat on a patch of grass filled with sunlight. Still, it seemed chill to the Colonel and he hunched his shoulders against the wind. Sheets of thinly layered cloud passed, now and again, across the face of the sun, causing brief shadows to dance like ghosts across the wide lawn. The cherry blossoms rustled; a brace of dogs barked like brass being beaten; a brown and white butterfly darted erratically along the top of the grass, a blithe dancer without a partner. The day seemed like a haiku to the Colonel, perfect and sad, bringing tears to the eyes. Why were so many haiku sorrowful? he wondered.

The Colonel had witnessed many deaths in his day: the deaths of men he knew and those he did not. One develops over time a kind of shell against which these personal disasters must bounce away; either that or one goes mad. Until death takes on the unreality of a mime show and one no longer contemplates it.

This death in the park, on this sunny spring day, among the children, the inheritors of Japan, was different. The Colonel felt deflated, like Caesar returning home to Rome from the arms of Cleopatra, from eternal summer to the chill of March. He thought of the eagle circling Caesar's statue in the square; the augury. And it seemed to him that this important death, which he had witnessed, was also an augury of sorts. But what it portended he could not say.

"Are you all right?" Nicholas asked. He put a hand on his father's arm.

"What?" For a moment, the Colonel's eyes were far away. "Oh, yes. Quite all right, Nicholas. Not to worry. I was just thinking of how to break the news of Hanshichiro's death to your mother. She will be most upset."

He was silent for a time, contemplating the pink-white blossoms all around. After a time he felt calmer.

"Father, I want to ask you something."

It might have been a moment that the Colonel had dreaded, but Nicholas' tone of voice was such that his father knew that he had spent much time thinking about the question. "What is it?"

"Does Satsugai belong to the Genyōsha?"

"Why do you ask?"

"It seems a logical question. Satsugai is the head of one of the *zaibatsu*, he is virulently reactionary in his philosophy and he was born in Fukuoka." Nicholas turned to his father. "Frankly, I'd be surprised if he wasn't a member. Wasn't it that which allowed him to be restored to power after the 1947 purge?"

"Ah," the Colonel said judiciously. "Ah. Very logical assumption, Nicholas. You're quite observant." The Colonel thought for a moment. To their left several gray plovers broke from the treetops in a flurry and, circling once, headed west into the sun. Farther away, the dragon box kite was being slowly lowered by invisible hands; the day was almost done. "The Genyōsha," the Colonel said carefully, "was founded by Hiraoka Kotarō. His most trusted lieutenant was Munisai Shokan. Satsugai is his son."

Nicholas waited for a time before saying, "Is that a yes?"

The Colonel nodded, thinking of something else. "Do you know why Satsugai named his only son Saigō?"

"No."

"Remember I told you that, in the beginning, the Genyōsha decided to work within the political framework of the country?"

"Yes."

"Well, they came to that conclusion the hard way. The Military Conscription Act split the Meiji oligarchy into three factions. One of these was led by a man named Saigō. He was the leader of the ultra-conservative samurai. In 1877 Saigō led thirty thousand of his samurai into the field of battle against a modern conscription army put together by the Meiji government. Armed with rifles and guns, they easily defeated the samurai."

"Of course!" Nicholas exclaimed. "The Satsuma Rebellion. I never connected the names before." He broke off a blade of grass. "That was the last samurai uprising, wasn't it?"

"The last, yes." The Colonel got up, feeling at last as if he were ready to face the outside world, Cheong's saddened face. He could not bear it when she was sad.

They crossed the remainder of the park, passed beneath the high gate. Behind them the sky was clear of dragons, the sun lost within the thickening haze that reddened the sky like a drop of blood on a blotter.

That night they both dreamed of the death of Hanshichiro, each in his own separate way.

Third Ring

THE WATER BOOK

New York City / West Bay Bridge

SUMMER PRESENT

The gray concrete blocks of Manhattan shimmered under the late July sun. It was sticky. Nicholas could feel the heat penetrating the thin soles of his summer loafers, making even walking uncomfortable.

He stood near the curb at Seventh Avenue just outside the modernistic marquee of the new Madison Square Garden and Penn Station complex. He glanced up at it, thinking how quickly it had gone out of style. Across from him was the Statler Hilton Hotel and, a block up, the hideous plastic and glass frontage of a McDonald's.

Distractedly, he watched the traffic shooting the lights, weaving lanes; waves of steel. He was thinking of the call that had come in late last night. Vincent's voice had been a terrific blow. Terry and Eileen, murdered. It seemed impossible to imagine. No prowler could possibly have gained entrance to Terry's apartment without his knowing it; he could not have been surprised in that way. How then? Vincent had been peculiarly unforthcoming; his voice had sounded lifeless and, when Nicholas began to press him, he had merely repeated the instructions to be at the Seventh Avenue entrance to Penn Station after taking the first morning train into the city.

The sun burned the streets out of a cloudless sky. Nicholas' shirt stuck to his skin. He ran his fingers through his hair, wishing now that he had had it cut shorter in deference to the heat. The lights were red along the avenue and the heavy air hung like brocaded curtains, stagnant, feeling almost solid with the heat.

It was not Vincent who would be meeting him but, he had been told, a Detective Lieutenant Croaker. Lew Croaker. Nicholas thought he remembered the name. Free time had made *The New York Times* that much more important. A case earlier in the year. Didion. The papers, even the normally staid *Times,* had turned it into a spectacular event, perhaps because it had occurred in the Actium House, the most exclusive new residence building on Fifth Avenue. Croaker had been brought in. He was someone's fair-haired boy; he got a ton of press, especially on the six o'clock news on TV.

The lights on Seventh changed to green and the traffic resumed its herky-jerky flow, dominated by yellow taxis. Out of this mass of dodging confusion a sleek black limo abruptly appeared. Its tinted glass made it difficult to see inside. It slid to a quiet stop in front of him. The back door on the curb side opened and Nicholas saw movement on the far side of the seat. A figure leaned forward, beckoned to him. "Please get in, Mr. Linnear," a vibrant voice said from out of the depths.

As he hesitated, the front door swung silently open and a brawny man in a dark blue business suit with short-cropped brown hair moved forward and guided him into the limo. Both doors swung to with a comfortable *thunk* that bespoke monied engineering and the limo accelerated into the traffic flow.

There was a spaciousness inside not usually attributable to automobiles and a silence that was truly remarkable. Outside, the city glided by as if pulled on velvet runners. They might have been stationary, a backdrop being rolled by them, save for the slight discomfitures of acceleration and deceleration.

The interior was done all in dove-gray velvet and it was, quite obviously, a custom job; nothing was as one might see it on the showroom floor. It was cool and dim, like the interior of an expensive bar. Even the vibration from the massive V-8 engine was kept to a minimum.

There were three men in the car: a driver, the man in the dark blue business suit who sat on the passenger's side in front and the figure in back, on the opposite side of the plush bench seat. This last regarded him now. He was tall and somewhat stocky. He wore a conservative yet impeccable lightweight linen suit. Beneath this, Nicholas could see that there was no fat on him; his bulk was muscle and bone. He had a large head with a somewhat thrusting jaw which, overall, gave him a rather aggressive appearance. This was enhanced by his slanting forehead and short gunmetal-gray hair. His lean cheeks were pockmarked and his deep-set blue eyes, like marble chips, were guarded by black bushy brows. Altogether, Nicholas decided, it was a face that had borne the brunt of many a tough decision and won them all. Nicholas would have cast him as a general and no lower than a five-star.

"Would you care for a drink?" The man beside him had spoken in his commanding voice but it was blue-business-suit who moved, turning his body partway around on the front seat so that his left arm lay along the velvet top like an implied threat. Nicholas found himself wondering what had happened to delay Lieutenant Croaker.

"Bacardi and bitter lemon, if you have it." Immediately the blue business suit opened a small door in the center of the front seat. Nicholas heard the soft clink of ice against glass. He remained calm, though he still had no idea who these people were. He wanted to keep the man talking. The longer he did that, the sooner he would know who he was.

"You don't look much like your photographs," the man said almost disgustedly.

As blue-suit stretched to pour the rum, Nicholas caught a glimpse of the butt of a revolver snug within a chamois holster under the man's right armpit. He turned his gaze away, to the city outside. It seemed a thousand miles away. "That's perfectly understandable," he said. "I've never taken a good picture; not to my knowledge, anyway."

"Your drink," the man in the dark blue suit said.

Nicholas reached forward through the open partition and, as he did so, he saw from certain minute changes in the other precisely what was coming. Curious, he allowed it to happen. As soon as his hand was through the partition, the man lifted the drink away and grabbed at Nicholas' wrist with his other hand. It was a very swift motion yet, from Nicholas' point of view, slow and clumsy. He could have counteracted it in any number of different ways. Instead, he watched passively as the other gripped his wrist, exerting pressure to turn the hand over. The man peered closely at the edge of Nicholas' hand, which was as hard and callused as horn. The man lifted

167

his gaze, nodded to the man beside Nicholas, then handed Nicholas his drink.

Nicholas sipped at the Bacardi and bitter lemon, found it quite good. Swallowing, he said, "Are you satisfied?"

"As to your identity," said the man beside him, "yes."

"You know more about me than I do about you," Nicholas observed.

The man shrugged. "That is as it should be."

"By your standards perhaps." No one wore sunglasses or any kind of glasses, for that matter; no one smoked.

"Those are the only standards that count, Mr. Linnear."

"Mind if I light up?" His right hand moved toward his trousers pocket and, at the same time, blue-suit's left arm stiffened, moving. He shook his head from side to side.

"You don't want to do that, Mr. Linnear," said the man beside him. "You gave up smoking more than six months ago." He grunted. "Just as well. Those black-tobaccoed cigarettes are certain killers."

Nicholas was impressed by the depth of their information on him. Whoever this man was, he was not an amateur.

"Did you know, Mr. Linnear, that an accumulation of high-nicotine smoke can destroy the taste buds?" He nodded as if this statement needed physical confirmation. "It's quite true. A group at the University of North Carolina completed the study." He smiled. "Ironic, isn't it? The campus is virtually surrounded by tobacco fields."

"I've never heard of that study," Nicholas said.

"Well, of course you haven't. The results are quite secret at the moment. They're being timed for release during the annual tobacco growers' convention in Dallas next October."

"You seem to know a great deal about this study."

"I should," the man said, laughing. "It was funded with my money." He turned his head away, letting that sink in for several moments.

"How much do you really know about me?" Nicholas prompted. He was almost certain now; the face remained vaguely familiar, at least parts of it.

The man swung around, impaling him on an icy stare. "Enough to want to talk to you face to face."

It was the piece he needed. "I didn't recognize you at first," Nicholas said. "I'd never seen you without the beard."

The man smiled, rubbed at his clean-shaven chin. "It does make quite a difference, I'll admit." Then his face lost all its warmth and it seemed as if the flesh were carved out of granite; the difference was appalling. "What do you want with my daughter, Mr. Linnear?" His voice was like the crack of a whip. Nicholas wondered what it would be like growing up under that fierce domination; he did not envy Justine.

"What does any man want with a woman?" he said. "Only that, Mr. Tomkin. Nothing more."

Out of the corner of his eye he felt the movement of blue-suit even before it came into his line of vision. He relaxed; now was not the time. The big beefy hands were at his shirt front. Some of the drink slopped over the side of the glass, ran down his trousers leg. Nicholas supposed that this man would have little trouble in picking up his side of a grand piano. While the man held him from in front, Tomkin leaned over. "That's not very smart," he said. His tone had changed again, as quickly and completely as a chameleon switches color. It was now steel covered thinly by velvet. "In any event, Justine is no ordinary woman; she's my daughter."

"Is this how you handled Chris in San Francisco?" Nicholas said.

Tomkin was quite still for a moment; it was a breathless time. Then, without turning his head from Nicholas, he made a small gesture and blue-suit let go his grip. Without a backward glance the man pulled himself into the front of the limo and closed the partition. He turned to look through the windshield.

"So that's how it is," Tomkin said when they were alone. "Interesting." He eyed Nicholas. "My daughter must like you." Then his tone turned acid. "Either that or you're a hell of a good lay. She hasn't been with any man for more than two hours since I brought her back. That's a long time for a girl of her age." Then, as an afterthought, he said, "She's got problems."

"Everyone's got problems, Mr. Tomkin," Nicholas said drily. "Even you." As soon as he had said it, he regretted opening his mouth. His anger had caused that; not a good sign.

Tomkin sat back, sinking into the cushions. He squinted at Nicholas. "You're an odd one. I do a hell of a lot of business with the Japs; even go over there three, four times a year. Never met anyone there like you."

"I imagine that's a compliment."

Tomkin shrugged. "Take it any way you like." He leaned

forward, depressed a hidden stud, and a small desk swiveled out on his side, complete with a miniature gooseneck lamp. Behind the desk was an accordion compartment built into the seat. Tomkin dipped a hand into this, extracted a sheet of paper. It was folded once across its width. He handed it to Nicholas. "Here," he said, "what do you make of this?"

It was a sheet of Japanese rice paper, very fine. Nicholas unfolded it carefully. On it was a symbol, brushed on the center with black ink. There were nine small diamonds surrounding a large circle like satellites about a sun. Inside the center circle was the Japanese ideogram for *komuso*, the beggar-ascetic.

"Well?" Tomkin demanded. "Do you know what it is?"

"Tell me how you got this." Nicholas lifted his gaze from the crest, saw that those cold blue eyes were clouded with a kind of held-in anxiety.

"It came in the pouch." And when he saw Nicholas looking at him uncomprehendingly, he added, somewhat irritably, "The pouch from Japan. Each of our foreign offices has a daily pouch for important messages, when phones are inconvenient or insufficient for relaying data. At first I thought it was some kind of a joke but now..." He shrugged. "Tell me what it is."

"It's a crest," Nicholas said simply. He handed the sheet back to Tomkin, but he would not take it so Nicholas slid it onto the desk. "A crest for a ninja *ryu*—a school." He took a deep breath, weighing his next words carefully, but before he could open his mouth Tomkin was hammering at the smoked-glass partition. Blue-suit turned his head and a part of the glass opened. "Frank, I want to go to the tower."

"But, Mr. Tomkin—"

"Now, Frank."

Frank nodded, closed the partition. Nicholas could see him talking to the driver. The limo turned at the next corner, heading east. When they came to Park Avenue South, they made a left, headed north.

Next to Nicholas, Tomkin eyed the folded rice paper as if something inside it had come to startling life.

Detective Lieutenant Croaker was not happy as he left Captain Finnigan's office early that morning. In point of fact he was on the verge of boiling over. He strode down the fluorescent-lighted corridor, crowded with officers and clerks, in long athletic strides.

"Hey, Lew, wait till I—" But Croaker had already brushed past the sergeant without noticing him and the man shrugged, turned away. Croaker could be like that sometimes and it was best then to stay out of his way.

Reaching his frosted-glass-fronted office, Croaker swung in and pounded his fists against the laminated Formica desk top. Many was the time he had tried to burn holes in the thing with the end of his cigarette. To no avail. That was modern science for you.

He crashed down into the dark green swivel chair. He stared fixedly at the frosted-glass partition but what he was really seeing was Finnigan's fat mick face, those soft dewy blue eyes staring up at him blankly.

"I want to make this very plain to you, Croaker," the captain had said. "The Didion case is a closed book." He raised his pudgy hands in front of his face, warding off Croaker's expected protests. "I know, I know, I put you on it myself. But that was when I thought we could see some quick results. Everyone from the mayor on down was howling for a quick arrest. Then the media jumped all over it; you know what they can do." His hands came down, lying flat on his desk top. Croaker thought they looked like hams ripe for roasting. "You know as well as I do the kind of people who live at the Actium House. People like Cardin and Calvin Klein don't like that kind of thing happening where they live. There was an awful lot of pressure."

Croaker closed his eyes for a moment, counting slowly, one-Mississippi, two-Mississippi, just as he had done when playing football on the streets of Manhattan's Hell's Kitchen when he was a kid. It was either that or belt Finnigan in his fat red nose. His eyes snapped open, they saw the captain leaning back in his high-backed chair, his hands, fingers interlaced, sitting atop his ample stomach. Croaker wondered how many whiskeys the old man had already downed. Inadvertently, he glanced at the spot where the lower right-hand drawer was, where the bottle always lay within easy reach. His gaze swung back to Finnigan's red-veined face. His eyes seemed even more faded in the soft early morning light filtering through the closed shades. Outside, the towers of lower Manhattan rose like blocky giants.

"I know all about that pressure, Captain." His tone revealed none of his hidden emotion. "I've lived with that ever since I joined the force ten years ago. What I don't understand is this sudden switch, this about-face."

"You weren't getting anywhere," Finnigan said equably. "I pulled the plug, that's all."

"Bull! That's a load of—"

"Don't start this with me, Lieutenant." Finnigan's eyes blazed and a thin line of spittle glistened on his protruding lower lip. "I'm in no mood 'for any of your grandstanding." He sat up, leaning forward, and now his small eyes seemed mean and bitter and altogether merciless. "You may enjoy a great reputation with the press. I allow that because it's good for the department as a whole; the public responds well to one name, one face. But don't you ever think that that gives you any special privileges in here or out there." His enormous thumb hooked back over his shoulder, indicating the streets of the city. "I'm onto your little game and it gets no points with me. You love that attention, the media play. You eat it up like a glutton. But that's okay; that I can handle. What I won't tolerate is you treating me as if I'm some kind of idiot, some kind of moral defective." He saw the look on the other's face, jumped on it. "Yeah, that's right: moral defective. You been on the force more than long enough to know the reason why some investigation or other gets snuffed. Someone high up 'requested' it. Okay? So now I've spelled it out for you." His face was red now and the wattles beside his mouth were quivering. "Believe me, I have thought of getting rid of you so very often, transferring you to some other district. But you're too valuable to me. You're good for at least a couple of mayor's citations for me each year. I don't mind telling you I like that; it's good for my record." He stood up now, his thick arms straight columns ending in bunched fists pressed so hard against the desk top that they had gone white. "But I'll be goddamned if I'll ever let you pull a stunt like you did with the Lyman thing. That was officially chocked and you went after it anyway. You made me look like a 'fool to these people here and I'm just lucky that the commissioner didn't hear about it." He lifted a finger as big around as a sausage, shaking it in Croaker's direction. "You'll take this Tanaka-Okura double murder and I don't want to ever hear that you threw a case back at the precinct boys the way you did last night." He coughed thickly, wiped at his lips with a gray handkerchief. "What's the matter?

172

You got something against slants? No. So take it and be happy. Be happy that you've got a case to run with."

Croaker turned to leave but, as his fingers grasped the knob, Finnigan said, "Oh and, Lieutenant, you know how things function around here. Next time don't make me explain S.O.P. to you as if you were some rookie just off the streets, okay?"

It was at that point that Croaker had decided to continue with the Didion thing. Now he knew that he had to do it all on his own. He could confide in no one at the office and, if he used their resources, which he surely would, he would have to camouflage his intent. He looked at his watch, then at the dregs of old coffee in the stained plastic cup on his desk. He was late for the Linnear pickup but right now he did not much care; his mind was still on the Didion thing. Finnigan was right in one respect—he had nothing. But only up to a point. The girl had friends somewhere, it had just proved to be a bitch unearthing them. Now he was close to at least one of them. Matty the Mouth had come up with a lead. But he needed a name, an address, or it was useless to him. This was what he was waiting on now; this was why he was so sensitive to being pulled off the case. It was no good telling Finnigan what he had now; no good at all. It would be like talking to the wall. Which was why Croaker always kept his cases to himself; it was part of the reason why he got Finnigan his mayor's citations each year. So it was the one thing Finnigan did not question. In any case, Finnigan could care less about M.O., it was results he craved. Talk about your gluttons! Croaker grunted as he swiveled around in his chair. Those results gave the whiskey a fine race for the captain's undivided attention.

Croaker cursed and got up. Time to pick up Linnear.

At approximately the same time, Vincent had been at work in the autopsy room. He had not, of course, been on duty when they had brought Terry's and Eileen's corpses in late last night but he had been called right away—Tallas had thought he should know; she had the soundest judgment of all the associates, he thought. Consequently he had arrived in time to hear the tail end of the argument between the two precinct patrolmen who had responded to the call and the

173

detective. He was a big burly son of a bitch and he was giving them a tongue-lashing.

Vincent had not concerned himself with the noise or the rising tempers. He had wanted to make certain. Perhaps it had all been a ghastly mistake—one of the *dōjō's* instructors at Terry's apartment—or . . . but it had been Terry and it had been Eileen. Dead. It was then that he had remembered the frozen-line call. No one there. Could it have been Terry phoning him? He turned sadly away. It did not matter now.

He put them away for the morning, made sure all their clothes and personal effects were properly tagged and bagged for the detectives who would take the case. Then he had gone home to spend an uneasy night.

It had gotten to the point where he was content only down in the morgue. There he could work, logically problem solving, sleuthing his way through the silent mayhem. Sometimes it worked and his report led directly to the arrest of the murderer; at other times he was the only one who could be of solace to the families of the dead who rolled past him each day.

They were like massive hieroglyphs, mute monoliths, waiting to have their arcane messages unearthed. And he the archaeologist of their past.

It was immensely satisfying to him to work here in the dead house, as many physicians called it. But it was such a misnomer, for here, every day, he and his colleagues were hard at work wresting secrets from death's cold grip. They hacked at it, bringing it down to size, demystifying it, bit by bit, until much of its fear was dissipated. What job could claim more importance for the living?

This morning Vincent now stood in the central room, his back to the tiers of stainless-steel doors. A black man, naked and cool, his head at an angle, lay on a gurney to one side. He stood staring at the swinging doors leading into the autopsy room. Behind that barrier, he knew, lay his friend, Terry Tanaka; next would be Eileen. For the first time since coming here, he wondered whether he really wanted to push through those doors. It seemed, all at once, one death too many and he did not feel the same inside anymore. He knew that he wanted to return to Japan. But he felt that to be impossible now, as if he had contracted some dread disease in the West, in the city, in New York, and now transformed inwardly as well as outwardly, he felt as if the culture shock would be the death of him.

Yet, deep inside, he perhaps understood that his only salvation now was to go on. Death had returned to him as it had as a child, a solid wall too high for him to climb over. He knew that he must tear that wall down or go mad and his only path lay within the bright, tidy room inside. There death could be quietly dissected, the wall pulled down one brick at a time until, at last, he would understand what had done this to his friends. For, he found, he wanted desperately to know.

Vincent shook himself and, pushing aside the swinging doors, went in to work on the body. Japan, once a dream, had now departed.

The limo pulled out of the traffic flow in the low Fifties, slid quietly to a stop at curbside. Frank got out first and opened the rear door for them.

They were on a block dominated by the steel exoskeleton of a building that seemed perhaps three-quarters complete. It was set far back from the street and the pavement had been torn up in order to install brick-red tile. A wooden companionway had been erected so that pedestrians would not be inconvenienced by the construction. On the south end of the block an enormous cement mixer was drawn up. Multicolored polka dots had been painted on its revolving barrel. Beside it, an angular crane was in the process of elevating a number of girders.

Part of the building's fashionable black stonework façade was up; chalk marks still crisscrossed some of the blocks, the white and yellow glyphs of the modern world. Still, fully one side was skeletonized like a transparent cocoon beneath which the chrysalis could be seen forming.

They walked along wooden planks laid out while, in the rubble beneath, men with bulging muscles and oil streaked faces drilled with jackhammers like sullen dentists.

They came into the shade of the roofed walkway. The air was filmed with dust which hung chokingly, settling on their hair and their shoulders like dandruff.

A man with a lean dented face approached them. He wore a bright yellow hard hat. "Lubin Bros." was stenciled across the front in blue. He smiled broadly when he recognized

175

Tomkin, extended his hand. He led them off to the right into a mobile home which served as construction headquarters. Tomkin introduced him laconically as Abe Russo, the building foreman. Russo shook Nicholas' hand with a firm cool grip. He handed out hard hats for all of them and they left.

Frank led them into the innards of the structure, through the enormous atrium lobby, then along a corridor where bare light bulbs hung on flex threads and the damp smell of raw concrete filled their nostrils.

Olive-green mats still hung on the walls of the elevator. They took it to the top. In the hall a man as big across as Frank but slightly shorter met them. They went silently down the corridor.

The ceiling was finished, as was the interior wall, in a deep blue fabric, slightly nubby, giving the effect of raw silk. To their right, the outer wall was glass down to the level of their shins, or at least it would be when all the plates were in. Mostly it was a latticework of thin-seeming metal, stained orange by the rustproofing. Beyond was the breathtaking panorama of Manhattan, west and north. First the thick buildings on the opposite side of the avenue, then onward, marching in square-cut rows toward the Hudson River. Looking north, he could make out the depression in the elevated surface of Manhattan that was the south end of Central Park.

The corridor gave out on metal-façaded double doors with ostentatious brass doorknobs in the center of each. To the left, bare wooden doors opened on small offices, floored at this stage only by rough concrete. In several Nicholas could see the huge rolls of carpet, ready to be stapled down.

A warm wind whipped at them, intermittently. It was still hot up here; one could not so easily escape the heat of a summer's day in Manhattan. Soot and grime raced along the bare floor like spindrift, borne on the breeze. The corridor seemed very exposed at this point.

Tomkin paused before the metal doors and looked outward. His arm lifted as if he were about to begin an aria. "Do you see what I see, Nicholas?" He turned for a moment. "I *may* call you Nicholas." But it was a rhetorical question and he continued apace. "That used to be a big world out there. Used to be something for everyone—at least for anyone with guts enough to go out and get it." His arm came down, the fingers curled at his side. "Now it's nothing but a god-damned industrial farmyard. There's no space anymore and

176

no time. Do you know what that means, hmm? I'll tell you. There's not enough out there anymore. We're all strangling each other in an effort to survive. Oho, yes, you heard me right. It's survival now, not just a matter of making a profit. And the world's homogenized." He squinted sideways at Nicholas. "You know what I mean? No? How'd you have liked to've been Marco Polo, eh? Traveling for two and a half years across the endless deadly expanse of Asia; to at last come upon Cathay, a land where no Western man had ever dreamed of, let alone set foot in? Could there be anything in this world to equal such an extraordinary experience? No, I'll tell you a thousand times. No."

He moved forward as if in a trance, put his hands on the spider-web tracery of the steel superstructure. "Do you know," he whispered, "that I don't know how much money I have. Oh, I could hire a staff to figure it out, except by the time they did the figure'd be totally out of date. Anyway, the sum's far too big to think about comfortably." His face glistened now with a thin film of sweat. "There is virtually nothing in this world I can't have if I wish it. Do you believe that?" He turned on Nicholas. His tone of voice had become savage and the veins stood out on one side of his temples, pulsing. "I could have you heaved over the side of this building. Now. Just like that. I could do it with complete immunity. Oh, I might have to suffer through a cursory investigation but that's all." He waved a hand. "But I wouldn't."

"I'm relieved," Nicholas said but Tomkin went on as though he hadn't heard him.

"That would be a rather despotic way to act. A flaunting of my power. It doesn't interest me."

"You sound disappointed."

"What?" He came back from his reverie slowly. "Oh, of course not. But let me tell you, like all great men before me I am concerned by mortality—my mortality." He hesitated. "I want the best for Justine—for both my daughters."

For some reason, Nicholas had the distinct impression that Tomkin had been about to say something else entirely. "Then I'm sure they'll get it," he said.

"Don't patronize me," Tomkin said harshly. "I am well aware of my failings as a father. Justine has problems relating to men and Gelda just divorced her fourth husband and I can't hire enough men to keep her away from the liquor.

I keep jumping into their lives. In and out. That's the way it is. If it's hard for either of them to bear, too bad."

"Justine, at least, doesn't seem to want you jumping in at all," Nicholas pointed out.

"She's got no choice," Tomkin snarled. "I'm still her father whatever she cares to say to others. I still love her. I love them both. We're all fucked up, one way or another; their problems are just more visible than most, that's all."

"Look, Mr. Tomkin—"

"Don't screw up now, Nicholas. Not when we're getting along so well." He spat the words out as if they were burning the lining of his mouth. "Sure she hated it when I jumped in two years ago. But what did she know? Christ, she was up to her armpits in shit." He made a quick violent motion with his head. "She was following that bastard around like he was God himself."

"She told me—" Nicholas began.

"Did she tell you that he ran a male stud service? That he was a speed freak? That he liked men more than women? Did she tell you that he tied her up and beat her before laying her? Did she tell you any of that?" His face was mottled with anger and shame and spittle flew uncontrollably from his lips.

"No," Nicholas said softly. "She didn't."

Tomkin laughed harshly, humorlessly, an animal-like sound. "I'll just bet she didn't." His head was thrust forward and in that position he looked remarkably like a hunting dog on point. Nicholas found himself wondering if he were the prey. If so, Tomkin had bitten off more than he could chew this time.

"You had no business telling me all this," he said. His voice rose dangerously.

"What's the matter? Is your stomach turning at the thought?" He smirked. "Does she disgust you now that you know what kind of woman she really is? Do you hate yourself for ever getting involved with her?"

"It doesn't matter what she did in the past," Nicholas said slowly. "And unless she's living in the past, it has no bearing on either of us." He stared at Tomkin, at the sweating face hovering close in front of him. "I know what kind of person Justine is, Tomkin. I just wonder whether *you* do."

For just a moment, Tomkin's eyes seemed to bulge. Then, abruptly, he seemed in total control of himself once again and all signs of anger slipped away from him. He smiled, clapped Nicholas on the back. "I don't suppose I can be condemned for making certain, can I?"

Nicholas realized just how weak Tomkin was. That was why he made such an overt show of disenfranchising his daughters, because they were so important to him—his immortality. Nicholas wondered whether he was reconciled to not having a son to carry on the line.

Oddly, it was this weakness which prevented Nicholas from disliking the man. He had been taught, at the Itto *ryu*, to seize upon an opponent's weakness and thereby bring him crashing down. But outside the *dōjō*, Nicholas had learned that people often lived their lives, or at least a good part of them, out of weakness. It was what made them human, what made them vulnerable; what made them interesting. Take Musashi, for example. If one believed entirely the *Go Rin No Sho*, one saw not a man but a steel monument, invincible and emotionless. However, there were many stories concerning Musashi. The one Nicholas never forgot was the one where Musashi was defeated by a ninja using a paper fan. Ninja were notorious for their harnessing of odylic forces and this, it was commonly believed, was what made Musashi's defeat so effortless. Nicholas, of course, knew that there was more to it than that. Still, it warmed him to know that the great Musashi, the Sword Saint, had after all tasted defeat.

It would be all to easy, Nicholas knew, to dismiss Tomkin as villainous and have nothing more to do with him. But people's façade were all too often just that. He had touched a nerve and had glimpsed for an instant something else in the man, a spark that humbled him, made him human. Moreover, Tomkin was intelligent enough to realize that he had given away this advantage to Nicholas and now Nicholas was intrigued enough to try to find out why. He did not have long to wait.

"I want you to work for me," Tomkin said easily. "I want you to find out what's going on. I know all about the Yakuza; I've even had a brush with Shōtō. You've heard of him, no doubt?" Nicholas nodded and he went on. "Tough cookie, that one. But I managed. I managed." He put his finger and thumb up, pinched his lower lip thoughtfully. "Don't know anything about ninja, though, and what I don't know about myself I give over to experts." He stabbed a forefinger. "You're an expert on these bastards, isn't that right?"

179

"You could say that."

"Well, I want to hire you, then. Find out what this is all about." He produced the folded sheet of rice paper with the ninja crest painted on it, waved it. "Take the goddamned thing. I don't want it."

Nicholas did not move. "When did you get it?" he said.

"Like I said, came in the Japan pouch, let me see, oh, about a week ago."

A week, Nicholas thought. It could not be a coincidence. Barry's body had been found about that time. Then he had been right. Tomkin was the target. "I think you've been marked for assassination," he said.

Tomkin did not even blink. "All right. It's happened before."

"Not with a ninja."

"No," Tomkin admitted. "But I told you I've had a spot of Yakuza trouble. Nothing I couldn't handle."

"This is different."

"How so? He'll never get to me."

"There are a thousand ways he could do it but don't waste your time trying to figure out how. You'll never do it."

"Is this a sales pitch?" Tomkin's eyes had gone hard. "A little something you just dreamed up to give yourself a raise before you've even started work?"

"I never said I'd take the job."

Tomkin shrugged. "Suit yourself. I've got Frank and Whistle there. I'm not worried."

Nicholas did not even look at them. "Tomkin, if indeed a ninja has been contracted to assassinate you, he'll go right through those two as if they were stalks of wheat."

"Like I said, that's some sweet sales pitch you've got."

"It's no pitch at all. You've made me late for an important appointment. I'm not inter—"

He missed the signal but they were on him, one on each side. Frank's hands hung loosely at his sides, the fingers slightly curled. Whistle's gun was already out. It was a snubnosed .38, not so good at long range but brutal within fifteen yards. They were way inside that now.

Nicholas was in the classic first position of *yoroi kumi-uchi*, originally grappling in armor but today used quite effectively when one was dressed in encumbering Western street clothes.

Whistle's revolver was at the horizontal, his forefinger

beginning to squeeze inward on the trigger. Nicholas stepped forward, jammed his right foot into the man's left instep while at the same time slamming the muzzle of the gun away with the edge of his left hand. There was an explosion and the bullet whined off the inner wall, leaving a gray scar against the blue.

Whistle dropped the useless gun, bringing his right hand upward toward Nicholas' abdomen. He watched it, wide-eyed, as it was halted in mid-flight as if it had come up against a concrete barrier. He winced in pain as it was twisted hard around, felt a hot tearing and then a whiplike snap. At the same instant, Nicholas' left hand smashed into his collarbone and he went down, unconscious.

Frank moved in. He made no move toward the gun under his armpit. His fingers were as straight as boards as he whipped forward.

Nicholas stood motionless, watching the unfolding of the assault. There was plenty of time. He is left-handed, Nicholas thought, and he's expecting karate.

At the point of Frank's attack, Nicholas moved almost languidly, separating the deadly hands. To Tomkin, watching interestedly from the sidelines, it appeared as if he had not moved at all, merely pushed his elbows into Frank's rib cage almost gently. Frank collapsed onto the concrete floor.

"I knew you were good," Tomkin said excitedly. "I knew it! The reports said so, but you often can't trust them. Take other people's work for granted and you find yourself in a hole. Happens all the goddamned time." He stared down at his two incapacitated bodyguards. "Fucking great, that's all." He looked up, extended a hand. "Glad to have you aboard, Nick."

Nicholas stared at Tomkin's face as he moved away down the corridor toward the elevator. "I told you, I'm not interested in working for you." He pressed the button and it glowed. The elevator began its ascent. "You have no respect for people." Tomkin came toward him, stepping over the fallen bodies.

"It's not like that."

"Sure it is. I don't like being manipulated. Any more than I imagine Justine does. I don't owe you a thing, Tomkin. You have no claim over me."

Behind him the elevator doors opened. He stepped inside.

"Wait a minute, Nick." Tomkin reached out a hand.

"Don't call me. I'll call you."

The doors began to close as Nicholas pressed the ground button but Tomkin lunged forward, holding back the doors with his hands. His face was as hard as granite and there was a peculiar feral light in his eyes. "Aren't you forgetting something?" he spat. "It's not only my life that's at stake but my daughters', too. You wouldn't want this sonovabitch to get his hands on Justine, would you? Think about that," he said savagely and let the doors sigh shut.

On the way down, Nicholas recalled the night he and Justine were together, when that thing came through the kitchen window. Red blood and black fur. The Kuji-kiri ninja calling card, meant to create terror, one of the ninja's most useful weapons. The Kuji-kiri, most feared of all the ninja *ryu*. Whose crest was the *komuso* ideogram, circled, surrounded by nine diamonds.

Justine! his mind cried out. He looked up, watching in impatience as the floor numbers flickered by. He wanted to get to a phone immediately.

Outside on the street he saw a dark-haired man with wide shoulders and a pushed-in face. It had character, like a cowboy's. He stood beside a plain white Ford sedan. Even without the removable flashing red light on top, he knew it for a police car. But he had recognized the face. Detective Lieutenant Lew Croaker. He walked out of the shadow of the building's makeshift entrance and, tossing his hard hat to one of the workmen, went down the wooden plank to the curb.

He had used the phone in Abe Russo's portable headquarters. He had thought about calling Ray Florum, the police lieutenant out at West Bay Bridge, but he knew Justine would never stand for it. Accordingly, he got Doc Deerforth's number from Information and spoke to him for several minutes. He had agreed to look in on Justine every so often.

"Linnear," Croaker said as he came up to him in the sunshine, "what the hell were you doing with Raphael Tomkin?" He worked a wooden toothpick between his teeth with two long slender fingers.

"Hello to you, too, Lieutenant." Nicholas nodded.

"Cut the wise dialogue and get in," he said, ducking his

head as he sat behind the wheel. "We've got business to attend to."

Nicholas opened the door on the passenger's side, got in. As soon as his foot was off the asphalt, the car roared off. He pulled at the door, slamming it shut.

"Didn't your buddy Ito give you specific instructions?" Croaker said. He began to weave through the uptown traffic, heading for the left side of Park Avenue and the street divider.

"Tomkin picked me up while I was waiting for you."

Croaker snorted. "Didn't your mother tell you never to get into a car filled with strangers? Jesus! What'd that fucker want with you?"

"I don't have to answer that."

Croaker swung his head around, unmindful of the tenacious traffic. He glared at Nicholas. "Listen, buddy, don't give me a hard time. I'm telling you that if it has to do with Raphael Tomkin it fucking *is* my business, get me? Now give!" He braked savagely, in line to make a left onto the downtown side of the avenue.

"What makes you so interested in Tomkin?" Nicholas was tired of being questioned without having any of the answers.

"Now, look, Linnear," Croaker said, carefully enunciating each word. It was obvious he was holding himself in with an effort. "I'm doing my best to be civil, to treat you with respect. I've got no beef with you. Yet. But today's just not my day; I'm on a short fuse. That means, you being here beside me, it's not your day either. Now be nice and tell me what I want to know. I promise, it won't hurt." He leaned on the horn, turned down Park.

"I'm seeing his daughter," Nicholas said. "He wanted to check me out."

Croaker hit the steering wheel with the heel of his hand, bounced up and down. "Goddamn!" he exclaimed. "Goddamn! Ho!" He shook his head. "What do you know!" Then he swore as he was forced to swerve around a slowly cruising cab. He gunned the Ford and they leaped forward into the semicircle of the overpass at Forty-sixth Street. When they emerged, below Forty-second, he said, "Jesus, I thought I'd pass up the fucking traffic on Second by going down Park but will you look at this." He gestured at the sea of cars gleaming in the sun ahead of them. They were baking in the interior and the air stank of exhaust and overheated oil. "To hell with this!"

He reached out his left hand, started the siren. On top the red light began to flash. "Christ," he said as the cars began reluctantly to part, "summer in New York!"

They turned east on Thirtieth Street and Croaker cut the siren. "Which one is it?"

"Which what?"

"Daughter, Linnear. Which daughter? Gelda, the one who likes Chivas, or is it the crazy younger one—what's her name?"

"Justine."

"Yeah. I can never remember it." He shrugged. "Too pretty for a Tomkin." He turned his head, spat the toothpick out the open window. "Spoke to her once, couple of months ago. She's kinda hard to forget."

"Yes," Nicholas said. "She's beautiful all right." He wished he was with her now instead of being in this melting heat on his way to the morgue. Goddamn Tomkin! he thought savagely. Then he smiled inwardly. You could say this for the bastard, he sure knew his people. Which led him to another point. "You certainly know the family well."

They had pulled up halfway down the block between Third and Second avenues as traffic piled up at the red light. A refrigerated meat provisions truck was in the process of pulling out into the traffic, its nose canted into the flow.

Croaker turned to look at him, one elbow on the sill of the open window. He had gray eyes and thick hair cut rather long, combed straight back. He looked as if he had been through the wars; like a character out of *From Here to Eternity*. "You sure are nosy for a civilian." The line of cars started up, rolling slowly forward after the truck had nosed its way in; it was no faster than a funeral procession. His voice changed gears, softening remarkably. "Guess the old bastard didn't take it too well, you seeing his baby."

"You could put it that way." They had stopped again; the heat was oppressive. "How'd you find me anyway?"

Croaker shrugged. "I got to Penn Station in time to see you gettin' into the limo. Frank's a wiseacre."

"Yeah. I know." Nicholas grinned. "He and Whistle tried their best to evict me from the premises."

Croaker eyed him. "Don't look like it bothered you none."

"I wanted to leave anyway."

184

Croaker threw his head back and laughed. "Linnear," he said, "you just made my day."

They soon came to the source of the slow-up. The gutter gurgled and the street swished with running water. Farther down the block four or five shirtless kids, their pants rolled up to their knees, danced about an open fire hydrant. Croaker rolled up his window and they splashed through as if they were in a car wash.

"Do you miss it?" Nicholas asked.

"What? Miss what?" Croaker took them through the intersection on the amber, accelerated.

"Smoking." He had noticed the ends of the other's fingers on his right hand were yellowed.

"Goddamn right I miss it," Croaker growled. "Why'n hell d'you think I chew these goddamned MintyPicks? Huh! You think I've got time to eat with all the shit coming down in this city? I ain't been in a proper bed in three days." He hung a left onto First Avenue and, with a squeal of brakes that must have left several inches of rubber on the city's asphalt, he pulled up in front of the turquoise-glazed brick façade of the Chief Medical Examiner's office. He double-parked and they went up the steps.

Croaker led them over to a desk, flipped open a brown plastic case to display his badge and I.D. to the receptionist. The man nodded when Croaker said, "Dr. Ito," and dialed a three-digit number on the telephone on the small desk.

He looked up as he cradled the phone. "Dr. Ito will be right up, Lieutenant. He's in the morgue."

Croaker looked around, watched the policeman on duty for several minutes. He did not know the man.

Vincent came out. He was wearing a green lab smock that tied in back. "Hello, Nick," he said gravely. He shook Croaker's hand. He led them back the way he had come, past the identifying room with its hydraulic lift to the morgue and down a set of stairs to the basement.

There was no smell at all down here; Nicholas had always imagined it would stink from disinfectant and formaldehyde. It was silent save for the monotone drone coming from behind a set of swinging doors; an autopsy was in progress. Vincent went to the bank of stainless-steel doors, drew two out. Then he described in detail what he had found.

"It was no ordinary intruder who found them," he concluded. "You see how the sternum and rib cage are fractured?"

"Christ," Croaker said. "I've never seen anything like that. He looks like he's been battered with a baseball bat."

Vincent shook his head. "Nothing so crude, Lieutenant. It was a human body."

Croaker snorted. "Idiotic! A human body by itself couldn't cause such extensive damage in such a short amount of time. The man must've had fists like hammers."

"No fists," Vincent said.

Croaker stared at him. "I'm sure this is leading somewhere, Doctor."

"Lieutenant," Nicholas said. "Terry was a *sensei,* a master of kenjutsu, karate, aikido. No man alive could get close enough to him to kill him, unless..."

"Unless what? I want to hear this." Croaker crossed his legs, leaning nonchalantly against the bank of doors.

"There is a kenjutsu technique, perfected and written about by Miyamoto Musashi, Japan's greatest swordsman. It's called the Body Strike, for obvious reasons. Using one's shoulder—"

"This guy must have been built like a tank," Croaker said.

"On the contrary," Nicholas said, "his stature could have been quite a bit smaller than Vincent's. We are not so much speaking of pure physical strength now, Lieutenant, but of an inner strength."

"Look, Linnear, the only inner strength I've ever seen is from David Carradine in 'Kung Fu' and I didn't believe a bit of it."

Nicholas smiled. "Then we must begin to educate you, Lieutenant."

Croaker stood up, said, "Then you agree with Ito here. You think these two were killed by a Japanese."

"Well, I can think of a small number of Occidentals who are kenjutsu *sensei.* But none of them could kill this way. This is a spiritual killing that would be far beyond them."

Croaker stared down at Terry's smashed chest. "Ain't nothing spiritual about this, my man. This is the work of a pile driver."

"Was there any kind of a murder weapon found in Terry's house?" Nicholas asked.

"Just a sword—"

186

"Terry's *katana*," Vincent interrupted, his gaze shooting the message, "lying by his side."

"Yeah," Croaker said. "But no blood on it; nothing like that. No other possible weapon that could've done *that*. But that don't mean shit. The guy could've taken off with it."

"He didn't," Nicholas said. "Lieutenant, killing has been a high art in Japan for almost two thousand years. In another time, it was a way of life for the Japanese. And today, though there is the modern Japan which stands in its place, still the old ways remain. Still there is *bushido*, the Way of the Warrior."

"Yeah? What the hell is it, then?"

Nicholas laughed. "I don't think I could explain it in a few minutes."

"That's okay, I've got bags of time." He extracted a MintyPick from his breast pocket, rolled it between his teeth. "I ain't eaten in much too long. What say you and I talk this out over a meal?"

Nicholas nodded and Croaker turned to Vincent. "Say, Doc, I'll sign for the bags while I'm here."

"Right." Vincent went around the corner to the small alcove where a number of polythene bundles waited for collection by the police: homicide victims' effects and clothes. Vincent brought two bundles back to Croaker, gave him a form to sign.

Croaker looked up, giving Vincent back his pen. "I'll be in touch," he said.

Nicholas' call had made Doc Deerforth uneasy, and while Nicholas had been brief, he'd given more than enough for Doc Deerforth to chew on.

He had appointments until twelve-thirty but, directly his last patient said good-bye, he left the office and drove out to Dune Road. He had been in constant touch with Ray Florum, of course, but there had been no progress on the two murder cases and, reluctantly, he had had to let the county detectives in. Not that it would do any good, Doc Deerforth thought sourly as he drove across the steel drawbridge onto Dune Road, the county people were like the Keystone Kops, all gung-ho and no expertise.

He turned right and settled back. Gulls rose, wheeling over the water on his left, circling above the two stories of

The Crosstree, Dune Road's newest condominium. It was tan and dark brown with a maze of outside staircases on this, the landward side. Soon the condominiums gave grudging way to private houses.

The thought of the ninja haunted him all the way out to Justine's house. Ever since he had become aware of the evidence, he hadn't had a decent night's sleep. In dreams he would return to the steaming jungles, to the mortar fire by day, the sniper's fire by night. But it was one specific night he dreaded most of all and even in his dreams he fought against remembering. Soon, he knew, he would have to resort to chloral hydrate to knock himself into a dreamless abyss.

He parked the car on the side of the house, took the elevated slatted-wood pathway over the dunes and scrub grass to the beach. He went up the stairs, knocked on the screen door. Behind him the water surged and, down the beach, he could hear the cries of children as they ran into the surf. A shaggy dog barked, leaping along the sand in pursuit of a wobbling Frisbee. The beach was a patchwork of oiled bodies, brightly colored blankets and striped sun umbrellas. A cool breeze blew in off the water and, for a moment at least, there came the drone of an airplane.

Justine came to the door, opened it. She smiled. "Hi. What brings you out here?"

"Nothing special," Doc Deerforth lied. "I was out this way and thought I'd say hello. Haven't seen you since the beginning of the summer."

Justine laughed as she stepped back to let him in, "Thank God that allergy doesn't last for long. I couldn't endure it all summer." She went into the kitchen. "Would you like a drink?" And when he nodded, she added, "Gin and tonic?"

"Fine."

She went about fixing it.

"Seems quiet around here," he said. "Had any visitors?"

"What?" she said over the sound of cracking ice. "I can't hear you?"

He went into the kitchen. "Any visitors lately?"

She handed him his drink, began to make hers. "Only Nicholas." She tasted it. "Umm. But that's the way I like it. I've never been comfortable with a lot of people, not at home at least." They went into the living room, sat on the sofa. "In business, it's different. I don't like to mix the two."

Doc Deerforth nodded. "I know what you mean. I don't like to either."

She regarded him over the rim of her tall glass. She pressed the condensation against her lip, rolling the glass. "Tell me, Doc," she said. "You didn't come all the way out here to exchange pleasantries, did you?"

"I came to see how you are."

"I'm not ill," she pointed out.

Doc Deerforth smiled. "I didn't say anything about that. This isn't a business call."

"I see." Her eyes wouldn't let him get away. "Did Nicholas call you?"

He laughed, relieved. "You know, you remind me of Kathy, my youngest. Nothing gets past her, either." He shook his head. "Nicholas called this morning."

"I wish he'd called me instead," Justine said. "I wish he hadn't gone into the city."

"He had to, from what I gathered." Doc Deerforth put his drink down. "Anyway, you could've gone in with him."

She shook her head. "Too much work and, besides, they were his friends. I'd just be out of place. I've got no desire to tag along after him." She took a sip. "We each have our own lives. Where they touch, well—that's where we love. The involvement—we're like two fiercely spinning wheels, each with its own orbit. We lean toward each other, we touch hesitantly, we calculate how far each of us can go without disturbing the orbits."

"What happens if you go too far," Doc Deerforth said, "and your—orbits, as you put it—are disturbed?"

Justine unfolded herself, went across the room to stare out at the hot beach and the cool curling surf. "In that event," she said, her voice as thin as a ghost's, "I'm afraid it would be disastrous."

"The girls will take care of you, m'sieur." The maître d' moved a little to his right, lifting an arm toward the steep dark staircase. He touched his thin mustache with a forefinger, stroked it.

"You know, I thought you'd take me to that place on Park," Nicholas said. "You know, downtown." They were in the low Fifties on the East Side.

"You mean the Belmore Cafeteria?" Croaker said. "Jesus,

189

I leave that to the undercover bastards. Christ, I wouldn't go there for a proper meal."

It was quiet on the second floor; only a table near the door was occupied. The far end of the room was on an elevated platform beside a row of windows.

The two waitresses were pretty. They wore dark Danskin tops and short skirts. They spoke in accents.

Croaker requested a window table and one waitress led them up the steps. She left them with menus after taking their drink order.

"How long did you know Tanaka?" Croaker asked. His eyes scanned the opened menu.

"About six years," Nicholas said. "We met in kenjutsu class."

"Here?"

"Yeah. I still go there. I'll take you after lunch."

"Part of my education, huh? Humm, I think I'll take the bacon and eggs." The girl came up, placed their drinks on the table; a Kir for Nicholas, a dark Myer's rum on the rocks for Croaker. Croaker gave her his order, Nicholas ordered the same. When she had left, he continued. "This *dōjō*. Where'd Tanaka get the bread for it?"

"Worked mostly, I expect." Nicholas took a long swallow of the Kir. "And I think he had a bit of money when he came over here. His mother had left him some before she died."

"How much?"

Nicholas shrugged. "I have no idea. His family was wealthy but there are nine children."

"Where are they?"

"As far as I know, they're all in Japan. Terry was the only one who left."

"And the father?"

"Killed during the war."

"Um hum." He shook his head. "Still, it takes an awful lot of cash or collateral to open up a business here."

"What are you getting at?"

Croaker shrugged, took a pull of his drink. "You know about bread. You need, you get. Sometimes it ain't so easy to pay it back. People get antsy; they don't want to wait."

Nicholas shook his head. "The only business partner Terry had in the *dōjō* was Chase Manhattan and he paid them off nine months ago. The *dōjō* was thriving."

"Someone wanted in."

190

"Uh uh. Lieutenant—"

Croaker lifted a hand, palm outward. "Just going over all the possibilities. You so sure he was straight? I mean, you weren't with him twenty-four hours a day."

"I didn't have to be. I knew him. Believe me, there's no illegal involvement. At least, not in the way you think."

"Which leads us back to *bushido*, right?" He was interrupted by the food. He waited until the waitress had gone before he said, "You know, Linnear, for those two stiffs being your friends you certainly aren't broken up about it."

Nicholas sat perfectly still. A pulse beat strongly in the side of his neck; a cool wind seemed to blow through his brain. There were haunting echoes, as if he were hearing the words of his ancestors carried to him through the corridors of time. Beneath the table, his fingers were as stiff as knives, his thigh muscles like steel. He required no blade, no concealed weapon. There was only himself, as deadly a killing machine as ever was created in any country at any time.

Croaker was staring into his eyes. "It's all right," he said softly. He gestured with the tines of his fork, laced with running yolk. "Your food's getting cold." He went to work on his own and never knew just how close he had come to being killed.

There was anger and then there was anger. Just as there were insults and there were insults. Lew Croaker was just another dumb Westerner, Nicholas told himself as he ate. He had no idea what he was doing or what effect his words would have. He had said what he had in order to find out, to read their effect in Nicholas' face. There should have been no reaction at all. Bujutsu had taught him that. But it had been a long time and he had been off his guard because he had been with a Westerner.

Which just goes to show you, Nicholas thought. Danger comes cloaked in many forms. Not that he thought of Lew Croaker as any kind of danger, far from it. But, he realized, ignorance brings its own kind of danger and Croaker had unwittingly put his head on the block. *Why* would have had no meaning if Nicholas had killed him then or merely disabled him.

Croaker glanced up at him from time to time as they ate, as Nicholas tried to define the complex concept of *bushido* to him. Obedience might be the basis but, to Western minds at least, that word had such a pejorative nature that it seemed like the wrong beginning. Because *bushido* was defined not only by sociology and religion but by history, too. To Americans, who thought in terms of two hundred years when it came to their own country, the concept of centuries seemed like deep water indeed.

Still, Croaker seemed to absorb it all quite seriously, his interest deepening as Nicholas progressed. At the end, over coffee, Croaker sat back, took out a MintyPick. His eyes wandered for a time, then he said, oddly, "I got an old lady, who drives me bats. She's never around when I get home."

"According to you," Nicholas said. "you rarely get home."

Croaker took a swig of the coffee, winced, poured in cream. He broke open a packet of granulated sugar, stirred it in. "I don't know what it is but I just can't seem to get used to it straight." He took a swallow, nodded approvingly, looked up. "All right, I *did* say that, yeah. What I mean is, the odd times I *do* come home, it makes it all the worse, y'know?"

"You need a new job," Nicholas said pointedly.

"Nah. I think I need a new lady, is all. See, Alison's an endocrinologist. She's been working on a project for three and a half years. It must be a bitch 'cause I don't think they're any closer now than they were when they started." He rolled the toothpick around his mouth, from one side to the other. "Recombinant DNA."

"Clones, huh?"

Croaker liked that; his face brightened. "Yeah." He laughed. "She's building an army of super-fuckin-humans. Gonna make you an' me obsolete, Jack." He laughed again. "Nah, nothing so dramatic. They're trying to find a way to alter the DNA in a mother's womb so people with hereditary diseases can have children." He brooded over his coffee for a while. "Things haven't been too good for a while. I think it's time to get out."

"So get out," Nicholas said.

Croaker looked up. "Yeah." There was an awkward silence. "Listen, about what I said before—"

"Let's go," Nicholas said, standing up. "We've got an appointment and it won't do to be late."

* * *

192

It was cool and dry inside without the benefit of artificial air conditioning. It was as if they were far below the surface of the earth where it was naturally cool. The summer sun could not penetrate this far.

The walls were of enormous stone blocks, quite thick, so as to be able to retain the coolness even on the hottest of days; there was a second story to take the brunt of the sun.

Over the sounds of their movement, Croaker could hear faint echoes, like calm voices heard at the bottom of a pond through the intervening water; he could not understand the words but he knew they were there. As they moved closer, he could begin to discern other sounds as well: wordless noises as precise as close-order army drill, recalling to him the long days of basic training in that remote dusty town in Georgia.

"Film and television discovered the martial arts some years ago," Nicholas said as they proceeded, "and turned them into a circus entertainment. As a result, they're taken about as seriously as professional wrestling over here. At best, they are quite misunderstood by Americans." Nicholas stopped and turned to Croaker. "The Way is not mere killing. That is a purely Western notion. You pull out a gun and boom! you destroy life. That is not the Way. The basis of all bujutsu is internal."

They began to walk again and the sounds came nearer now. Croaker thought he heard the rhythmic slap of bare feet against wood, the crack of wood against wood as if a giant were playing an outsized percussion instrument.

"Bujutsu is not something to be taken lightly, Lieutenant, I assure you," Nicholas continued. "It is neither a conjurer's trick nor a parlor game amusement but deadly serious." He turned his head. "I trust I'm not being redundant. I'm merely being careful. You see, the average Westerner will never see nor even hear about the true bujutsu adept. Why should he, since the adept neither wishes for nor gets any kind of publicity.

"Despite its violent nature, bujutsu is more in sync with religion—Zen and Shinto specifically—than it is with, say, sports. It is a way of life, governed by *bushido*. An adept would commit *seppuku*—ritual suicide—rather than break the code. Everything in life, Lieutenant—*every thing*—is subject to *bushido*. I hope you can understand that."

"I'm not certain that I do," Croaker said truthfully. Yet something swam at the edge of his consciousness, tantalizing

193

him. He wondered what it was, then shrugged mentally, le[t] it alone. Straining after it, he knew, would only push it fur ther away.

"It's not surprising." Nicholas gave him a bleak smile tha[t] contained no warmth. "For some Westerners it takes year[s] to understand." He was a bit ahead of Croaker now. "Fo[r] others"—he shrugged—"it never comes at all."

There was nothing in the world that could make Geld[a] Tomkin Odile cry, yet she felt close to tears now. She stoo[d] in the coolness of her Sutton Place apartment, looking ou[t] at the bright sunshine turning the East River solid. It migh[t] have been a river of salt for all the reality it had for her. Th[e] familiar view looked as flat as a painting and as unappetiz ing. Perhaps it was a painting, after all, she thought, but sh[e] knew that she was not thinking clearly. That was the on[e] thing she was happy about; what she had been searching for The Chivas was no longer sufficient; and, she thought wryly it's bad for business. Grass was no damn good. She had foun[d] that out a long time ago. Because she could control it an[d] she needed something that controlled her. Hallucinogen[s] were useless to her and opium merely knocked her out. The[n] she had found that codeine pills in conjunction with the whis key were just what the doctor ordered. She laughed sardon ically at that.

The phone rang in the room behind her, a soft burrin[g] that was as much a part of the atmosphere of the place a[s] was the long leather couch whose surface could only b[e] warmed by contact with naked flesh.

Gelda stared out the window in no hurry to answer the phone; it would continue to ring until she picked it up; if she were not at home or did not want to be disturbed, the machine would have intercepted the call after the first ring. It was Pear who needed her. She could afford to wait.

She wished now that she could cry, but even through the mist of the spirits and the drug she found herself dry, her in terior as sere and forbidding as a desert bleached by the sun.

She turned and walked silently across the deep sapphire wall-to-wall carpet of the bedroom. Through the open door she saw the vast expanse of the umber leather couch and the terra-cotta carpet which dominated the living room—or her work room as she preferred to call it: they rarely wanted to use the bed anymore.

Her thick hair was like honey and, as she passed through a bar of sunlight, it took on the luster of rich silk. She wore a forest-green natural satin robe, loosely belted, which clung to her like a second skin, showed off her ample cleavage, her long legs, but which concealed those parts of her body which, in her most private thoughts, she despised. There was not a single mirror up in the entire apartment, not even over the sink in the bathroom, yet she had a closet full, stashed away; it was a popular item.

She picked up the phone. "Yes."

"Darling, what took you so long?" Pear said in her ear. "Something horribly naughty?"

"Not naughty enough." Gelda closed her eyes.

Pear chuckled. "That's my girl." Her voice changed gears abruptly. "G, are you all right?"

"Sure, why?"

"You haven't been out much lately. Some of the girls were asking, that's all. They miss you."

"I miss them, too," Gelda said, wondering whether she meant it or not. "I've been thinking a lot, Pear."

"My dearest darling," Pear said patiently, "you know that thinking is no good for the soul. You've got to get out more; go to a couple of parties."

"You know I don't do that sort of thing," Gelda snapped.

"Please. I wasn't soliciting." Pear's voice seemed pained now. "My darling, I care about you. Genuinely care."

"I'm worth a lot to you."

"Now you forget that kind of talk, G." It was Pear's turn to snap. "You are just being contrary. I know that and I forgive you that statement. There aren't many people I care about in this world—Lord knows, none of the girls—but you're one of them."

"I'm one of your girls," Gelda said stubbornly.

She heard Pear's exasperated sigh on the other end of the line. "Darling, need I remind you *again* that it was you who sought me out? Yes, I provide your clientele, but they're a very special breed, you don't need me to tell you that. One thousand dollars a night is nothing to look down your nose at. You could perhaps make more by the hour but what's the point, darling? That won't make you happy and this does. But I can hardly say that you are one of my *girls*. My God, what a difference! People *ask* for you, my darling. That's the difference."

195

"Do you have something for me?" Gelda asked woodenly

Pear sighed again, giving up for the moment. "Yes. Dare The actress. You remember—"

"I remember."

"She only wanted you."

"All right."

"Do you have everything you need?" Pear inquired.

Gelda thought for a minute. "The chaps were just cleaned but the silk—"

"I'll have Lawless come by with it this afternoon. Anything else?"

Gelda was thinking about the enormous Remington Navy six-shooter with the long octagonal barrel and the polished hardwood stock under her expert guidance. It wasn't called a six-shooter for nothing. "Yes," she said dreamily, "a half a pound of lox and four bagels." She paused for a moment. "Pear, be sure you tell him no onions; not when I'm working."

Pear laughed in her ear. "That's more like it. You know tonight's going to be more pleasure than business."

There was that to look forward to at least. She turned to look out the window at the bright brittle sunshine. The phone slid from her grip. The river of salt winked at her, dazzling

The room itself was constructed entirely of wood. Only wooden pegs and glue had been used in the laying of the boards, shiny with clear lacquer.

It was a rectangle, wider than it was deep, with a high ceiling. The light was soft and well defined in every corner of the room.

It had the look of a gymnasium save for the raised dais with its low wooden railing that ran across the width at the rear of the room. Otherwise it was devoid of furniture or other accouterments.

There were a dozen men in white cotton leggings and shirts, lined up six against six opposite each other. Each held a polished wooden stick, round with a shallow hilt guard. Croaker would have thought of them as swords had it not been for a total lack of cutting edge or sharp point. The men were maskless. All were Japanese. Most were in their early or middle twenties though he saw one teenager and two who were obviously nearer forty.

A man dressed in gray stood between these two groups,

near the stairs leading up to the low dais. He was small in stature. He was hairless, making a judgment of his age somewhat more difficult. Croaker put it somewhere between forty and fifty. The man gave a piercing cry and the two lines advanced two quick steps, engaging each other in what looked to him like ritualized combat using the wooden sticks.

"This is a kenjutsu class, Lieutenant," Nicholas said. "The finest in the Western Hemisphere and parts of the East as well."

Croaker watched, fascinated, as the men advanced and retreated, attacked and parried, crying out in unison. But it all seemed so slow and methodical that he could not see how any of it could be at all useful in a fight.

In moments there came a soft bell tone and, at a sharp command form the *sensei*, the men stepped back and, lifting their swords in unison, bowed deeply to each other. Then they wheeled and broke up into quiet groups. Some walked to the sides of the *dōjō* and sat on their heels, others bent and stretched where they were. All seemed totally involved in these minute actions.

Nicholas took Croaker across the polished floor to where the kenjutsu master stood. He bowed and, in Japanese, said some things to the small man, who bowed again and extended his hand toward Croaker.

Uncertain, Croaker took it. It was as hard as a block of concrete. The man smiled.

"This is Fukashigi," Nicholas told Croaker. "Consider yourself introduced."

Croaker let go the man's hand, said, "What happens now?"

"Watch," Nicholas said.

Fukashigi looked off to his left, spoke in rapid Japanese. A student uncoiled himself and, first pausing to pick up another wooden sword, came quietly over. He bowed to Nicholas, handed him one of the weapons. Fukashigi spoke to him for a short time and at the end his head bobbed once. *"Hai!"* he said in assent.

The student was tall and lanky, with a hard face and quick intelligent eyes. Both he and Nicholas adopted an opening attitude, feet as far apart as the width of their shoulders, knees slightly bent, both hands on the hilts of their wooden swords.

"Now," Nicholas said to Croaker, not taking his eyes from the student, "there are five attitudes in kendo and only five:

upper, middle, lower, right side, left side. The first three are decisive; the last two, fluid, used when you encounter an obstruction overhead or on one side. However, this is not the Way. To master the technique, you must have what is commonly known as the 'attitude—no attitude.' That is, adapt from one to the other as the situation dictates *without thinking* so that your motion from the beginning of the contest to the end is one uninterrupted fluid motion: like the sea. The five elements, Lieutenant, are crucial to kenjutsu."

And he attacked the student with such blinding speed and ferocity that Croaker literally jumped.

"Approach from the middle attitude," Nicholas said and he performed it again, slowed down immensely, the motions now magnified. He lifted his sword so that its "point" was in the student's face. The man immediately attacked and, as he did, Nicholas, with minimal motion, slashed the other's sword to the right, riding it away from him.

Nicholas stood with his sword high above his head, the upper attitude. The student struck forward and, at the same time, Nicholas cut downward.

Nicholas lowered his sword. The student attacked once more, moving his sword upward. This time the student blocked him but in that same instant Nicholas' sword freed itself from the block, cut across the other's upper arms in a soft tap.

The student immediately moved to attack, coming in from the right side. Nicholas moved his sword until it was on his left side, below his waist. As the student attacked him, his sword flashed upward, scoring along the length and, crossing over, he cut across the man's shoulders.

Now the student attacked from the right and, adopting the left-side attitude, Nicholas again cut upward. Blocked, he slid gracefully into the upper attitude, delivering what would, in actual combat, have been a killing blow to the top of the student's head.

They both stepped back, bowed to each other.

"You see," Nicholas said, turning to Croaker, "the basics of kenjutsu."

"But you're just using wooden practice swords," Croaker said. "You can't hurt anybody—"

"On the contrary, these *bokken* are every bit as deadly as the *katana* is. They—"

But in that instant he had whirled, somehow sensing the

198

ual attack from both the student at his side and the *sensei* directly behind him. The student had already been disarmed with one cut and Nicholas was deep within battle with Fukashigi by the time Croaker had time to react to the situation. That would be about a tenth of a second, he calculated lazedly. My God, I saw the attack coming before he did!

The clash of the *bokken* filled the room but the contestants' movements were so swift that they were a mere blur. Croaker stared carefully but, try as he might, he could not distinguish one movement from the next, so fluid were they. He recalled Nicholas' analogy of this movement to the sea and he understood.

Then there came a momentous crashing as Fukashigi landed a ferocious overhead blow against Nicholas' upraised sword. Nicholas was not moved backward, however, and as he stood immobile, the *sensei* sprang backward as lightly as a current of air, preparing himself for a second attack. But as the sword moved backward to gain momentum for the forward thrust, Nicholas was there, extending himself outward like a river, his own sword following precisely the path of the other's and, beating down the "point," stabbing inward at the *sensei's* head. It touched the tip of the nose but, at the same instant, Fukashigi's left fist was at Nicholas' face in a blow that might have broken his nose and stunned him.

Both stepped back, bowed to each other. Neither of them seemed to be breathing hard.

Doc Deerforth had left. Justine sat over her drawing board working on a design that had eluded her for four days. Once or twice she seemed to have it conquered only to see it slip away from her as she sketched it out. It was like trying to catch a minnow with your fingers, she decided. At length she threw down her pen in disgust, ripped the sheet of tracing paper off its pushpin anchors and crumpled it up.

She went into the kitchen, fixed herself a tuna fish sandwich. She chewed at it without really tasting it, thinking of where she had gone wrong; surely the concept was sound enough. She washed the last of the sandwich down with a half glass of orange juice.

She was dressed in a Danskin bathing suit. For a moment she stood staring at the drawing board as if it were her enemy. Dangerous, she thought. She knew the signs.

She grabbed a towel and went out the door onto the beach. She ran now, dropping the towel onto the sand, high-stepping into the breakers, pushing herself through the heavy drag of the cold water until, seeing a wave looming high over her, ready to crash, she dived into its green side.

In solitude, she dimly heard its thunder over her, felt the slight quake of its violent passage. Then she was borne upward on the swell. She launched out with cupped hands and kicking legs, stroking powerfully outward, feeling the stretch in her lower back, her shoulders, her thighs. Bubbles streamed like molten metal from the corner of her mouth and she glided effortlessly upward, breaking the shivering surface, blinking, gulping air before she went under again.

Nicholas filled her thoughts and, despite what she had told Doc Deerforth, she considered going into the city. She hadn't heard from him. Surely that meant he was busy. God, she didn't want that anymore. But she wanted him, couldn't help it. She continued to stroke outward, coming up just long enough to catch sweet air. When she was far enough out, she turned to her right to parallel the shore.

She found herself thinking of the long black and gold lacquered sheath hung on his wall. In her thoughts, she went across the room and, on tiptoes, reached up slowly, freeing it from its hook. It was heavy, satiny, perfectly balanced. She put her left hand around the end of the sheath, her right around the long hilt of the *katana*. Nicholas' *katana*. Inch by inch, as she exerted slow pressure, she saw the gleaming steel appear before her wide-open eyes, extending in a crescent horizon. It was a silver dazzle, blinding her, an enormous erection that continued to grow under her ministrations. Breath caught in her throat. Her heart pounded. The pumping blood sang in her ears. And the cool wash of the sea was like a caress over her swimming body. Her nipples erected and she felt an excitement stir between her legs. Still kicking, she put one hand down, cupped her mound. She moaned. Bubbles flew like birds thrown across the sky.

She felt a wash of cold water spiraling up her legs against her working thighs. It was so much like the stroking hand of a lover that, startled, her eyes flew open. The current encompassed her aching loins, now snaked up her torso. She rolled over. It was then that she felt the pull. At first it was only the tiniest of tugs but abruptly, as the tide and her swimming took her along, it wrenched at her.

Her impulse was to gasp but she clamped her teeth shut in time. The undertow was pulling her inexorably out to sea. She tumbled in its grasp, not end over end but around, as if she were a cylinder. Dizzied, she struck out blindly for the shore. She was an excellent swimmer and her breath capacity was good. Still, her first priority was to gain the surface.

Whirling, she struck out upward but made little headway. The grip upon her was as real as if a sea serpent had appeared from some unseen abyss and had wrapped its slippery coils about her.

She broke the surface, gasping and coughing. But in doing so she had lost ground to the sea. She tried to lift her head, shake her eyes clear of the stinging salt water so that she could get an accurate fix on the shoreline. She was jerked under.

She began to panic. Her stomach heaved and she shivered, not even swimming now but merely struggling futilely. Why hadn't she screamed when she was in the air? She tried to rise again but the fierce grip would not let her. She sank. And in sinking, found her way home. Near the murky bottom the stillness was absolute. She wondered at this for a moment, her mind still trembling in fear until she realized that the tug of the current was gone. She reached out blindly, encountered rock. She pulled, keeping herself at this level, and began to make her way into shore.

Her lungs turned to fire and once her left thigh seemed seized in a cramp. She let it fall loose for a moment, relaxing her muscles, and it subsided. She went on scuttling over the bottom like an enormous crab. She desperately wanted to shoot upward to the surface but her terror of the undertow was absolute. She pushed on. Her eyes felt as if they were popping out of their sockets and an unquiet wind blew in her ears, roaring.

At last she felt the warmth of the shallower water and, simultaneously, the gentle push of the tide onto the rising sand.

She sprang upward, uncoiling her body fully, breaching the surface, sounding like a whale. She gasped and snorted, her insides turning to jelly. She felt the sand against her soles and, as she came out of the water, she found her legs would not support her. She fell to her knees and a wave inundated her. She fell over.

She heard the sound of raised voices as she vomited seawater into the surf. Then strong hands had her under her armpits. Her head hung down on her chest and she coughed.

"Are you all right?"

She tried to nod, only vomited again, heaving wretchedly. She felt the dry sand against her back. She was aware of her whole body gasping. She felt as if she would never get enough air inside her. Her lungs worked like bellows and the sound was so harsh and rasping to her ears that she might have been an asthmatic. There was a folded towel behind her head, elevating her face. A pins-and-needles tingling broke out along her cheeks and lips. She tried to raise her arms but they felt as if they belonged to another person. There was no strength left within her.

"Take it easy," someone said above her. "Take it easy."

She closed her eyes, feeling as she did so a kind of kinetic vertigo as one does after stepping off a violent ride at an amusement park. In her mind, she still spun in the grip of the undertow. Gradually this faded and, as it did so, her breathing began to return to normal.

"Okay now?"

She nodded, not daring yet to speak.

"Live around here?" It was a feminine voice.

She nodded.

"We've called for a doctor."

"I'm all right," she said. Her voice sounded strange to her.

"He'll be here in a minute."

She nodded, closing her eyes again. She thought of Gelda and the time at the seashore when they were both in the water. Perhaps Gelda was nine; she was six. They were playing and, as a joke, she had poked Gelda in the ribs. Her sister had turned to her, a look of fury on her face, and, reaching up her arms, had clamped her hands onto the top of Justine's head. Down Justine had gone, under the water. At first it was all right. But then she wanted to get up, to breathe. Gelda held her down. She struggled, but still Gelda would not relent. In her mind, she pleaded with her sister, then she reviled her. When at last Gelda had let her up, she was hysterical. She ran from the water, crying, right into her mother's arms. She had never told anyone what Gelda had done to her but for a week she would not look at, let alone talk to, her sister. Gelda's only response had been to silently gloat.

202

Justine opened her eyes to find Doc Deerforth bending over her, talking to her. She reached up and, shuddering, cried against his chest.

When Lieutenant Croaker left Nicholas outside the *dōjō*, he called in through the car radio to see about messages. McCabe wanted him to call back—that was no doubt about the Tanaka-Okura thing; Vegas had dropped by to talk; and Finnigan wanted a progress report.

He was rolling crosstown and the traffic was fierce. "If you can still catch Vegas, tell him I'll be back around four-thirty, okay?" He did not want to speak to the D.A. yet and as for Finnigan—fuck him!

No other calls. Croaker tried to clear his mind of the anticipation. But oh, how he wanted that call to come in. "That's it," he said. "Patch me through to Vincent Ito at the M.E.'s, will you?" The heat sat on wavy lines along the street. He wiped at his sweating forehead. When Vincent came on the line, Croaker set up a dinner. Vincent suggested Michita and gave Croaker the address.

Croaker went through Central Park at the Seventy-second Street Transverse and, moments later, he had pulled up outside the three-story brownstone that housed Terry Tanaka's *dōjō*. There he interviewed all of the instructors. He called for a police artist to draw a composite of the strange Japanese who had visited the *dōjō* on the afternoon of the double murder. None of the people he interviewed had seen the man before or since. None knew where he had come from. The aikido *sensei* recalled his name as Hideyoshi, but that meant absolutely nothing to Croaker. Still, it was conceivable that the man was the killer or was, at least, tied in with him in some way.

It was well after four by the time he was finished. There had been no prints at Terry's save for the two victims', but he called for a print team to dust the *dōjō* anyway. It was not good practice to overlook any possibility, however remote. Who knows, he thought, we may be lucky and pull something. Then he asked for a detective sergeant to canvass the block to see if any neighbor had seen the man.

In the office he checked in with Irene, threw the two polythene bags of clothes and personal effects of Terry and Eileen into a corner.

He checked for calls. Nothing.

He was about to open the bundles for tagging when his doorway was darkened by Vegas. He was an enormous man with a full beard and eyes like points of lightning. His skin was so black it took on blue highlights in the fluorescent lighting of the station house.

"Hey," Croaker said, turning his head.

"What it is." Vegas' voice was like the rumble of distant thunder.

"Heard you wanted to see me."

"Yowsah."

"Take a seat."

Vegas sat down with a grunt. He wore faded jeans, Texas cowboy boots and a gray and black cowboy shirt with pearl snaps. "I gots to get outa there," he said. He meant Narco. "I am being driven up the fuckin' wall."

"Sallyson?" He was the captain.

"You mean Captain Ahab." Vegas snorted. "The fuckin' bastard's ready for the funny farm." He leaned forward, his elbows on his long thighs. "Look, Lew, I want in here. Homicide."

Croaker looked at his friend. He had known Vegas for a long time. They had been hooked up in plenty of wild busts; did each other favors all the time and never did one lightly. "Finnigan's not an easy sonovabitch to take, my man," Croaker said seriously. "He is one mean motherfucker."

"Don't make no nevermind to me, Jack," Vegas said. "Long as I get away from Narco—those boys ain't funny no more."

Croaker squinted up at him. "Let's see. Homicide's not the only answer. Why, you could slip right into Vice, no trouble at all."

Vegas' face looked pained. "Sheeit! Sure, I could make a bundle, takin' my part of the grease each month. Only trouble is, you sawed-off sonovabitch, those fuckers don't allow no black man in on the big-time scam, you dig? They don' want me over there."

"Well, Vegas, I sure as hell don't know whether Finnigan would want you either."

"You know he's an okay motherfucker when it comes to skin, Jack. Wassamatter, don't you want to work with me?"

Croaker laughed. "I sure as hell would love it but right now the old man ain't too pleased with me."

"Shit! That ain't no big thing. You know how he is. Next

time you land a big one an' the mayor hands him another bronze pin, he'll be back kissin' yo' white ass."

Croaker grinned. "Maybe so. Maybe so."

"Ain't no two ways about it, Jack."

Croaker longed to tell Vegas about the Didion case: his suspicions and what he was working on. It was only procedure, after all—you needed a backup in any operation—but he knew that he could not do it. Not that he did not trust the man—they had saved each other's lives too many times for trust ever to be a factor. It was unfair to the other man. It was one thing for Croaker to put himself in departmental jeopardy, quite another to rope someone else in unwittingly.

Croaker reached out, slapped the other's leg. "Okay, you got it. I'll ask Finnigan soon's I think the times's right and we got a chance of him not biting my head off."

Vegas gave him a wide grin. "I dig. I dig." He got up, towering over Croaker. "You lay it on him an' we'll see what pops up. Meanwhile, this is one nigger that's got to hit the streets again. Sallyson's given us all quotas to fill, dig? Sheeit!" He turned and waved. "Later."

"Lay one on for me," Croaker said.

Vegas smiled. "Only on the prettiest one, Jack."

"I don't know, Nick, it seems as if I've been here for a hundred years." Vincent looked down at the peanut he was shelling. "It's funny but Tokyo seems like a dream to me, nothing more."

"You ought to go back, then. If only for a vacation."

"Yeah, I suppose I should." He popped the peanut into his mouth.

They walked down the tired stone steps into the Central Park Zoo. They strolled over hexagonal tiles, smelling the mingled musk of the animals in the heat. They walked north, toward the Monkey House.

"But I won't. I know that now."

"There's nothing stopping you. Nothing at all."

Vincent shook his head. They went down the stone steps to the plaza. On their left, beyond the great empty cage meant to house the avians, they could see the Seal Pond, where now several new sea lions dove and dashed alongside the elderly female, the lone survivor of happier years here. "It's my family, Nick. My sisters. If I went back, I would have to see them. Duty. I can't face them. Not now. Not after what I've become."

Near the Monkey House a swarthy man with a thick mustache and a sailor's hat stood next to a pair of green metal cylinders. He made helium balloons in front of the wide eyes of a group of children. Each time he did it, it seemed like a giant sucking in his breath.

"What have you become?"

The other turned his head. "That's just it. I don't know anymore. But I'm not what I once was. I've been assimilated; I feel as if I've been corrupted by this place. My values have changed. The traditions are crumbling around me." There was a crowd in front of the gorilla cage watching delightedly as the family inside was hosed down by a female attendant. The mother reached out and, putting her palm against the water, sprayed the onlookers. There were squeals and the crowd broke apart momentarily. Laughing, they surged back toward the cage. Next door, the haughty orangutan looked on unperturbed, studying the odd creatures through the bars of his cage as if for research for a book.

"Come on," Nicholas said lightly. "I remember when we first met. You, Terry and me. It was at Michita, remember? We were all kind of lost then—all in the same way. Which is why, I suppose, we all coalesced at that spot." He smiled, or tried to at least. "A bit of home." He shook his head. "But what was it that brought us together? Was it merely that we were all slightly homesick? I don't think so."

"Eileen used to say that it was the martial spirit which linked us. Like a magical umbilical. I think she must have thought we were like children in that way."

Nicholas shook his head. "No. You're wrong there. She respected that in us. She didn't—I suspect *couldn't*—understand it. But she recognized its power and would not interfere. That was why she always declined to come when the three of us got together. She knew she would be out of her element even though we would make every effort to make her feel comfortable. Terry told me once that she said she thought she'd only inhibit us and she was right."

"I don't know," Vincent said. "It all seems so far away to me now as if we were talking about the customs of Finland. I'm not sure whether *I* understand it anymore."

"That's just talk—so many meaningless words. The way a Westerner would think. Open your mind and you'll still feel it. Being here can't make it go away." He seemed to be telling himself as well as Vincent. "We were born in the land of the martial spirit. It binds us more powerfully—timelessly—to one another than a blood bond. What has been taught us will never leave us, you know that. You're still the same person, at the core, who got off that JAL plane twelve years ago."

"Oh no, I'm not. Not by a long stretch. I don't talk the same, I don't think the same way. America has changed me and the process seems irreversible. I can never go back. I no longer belong to Japan and I don't feel like I belong here. The West has taken something very valuable from me, snatched it away while I wasn't looking."

"You can get it back. It's not too late."

Vincent looked at him, put his hands in his pockets and walked on. They were near the arch on top of which perched the famous clock that chimed in each hour with a parade of animals dancing in a semicircle. Beyond was the Children's Zoo, its bright laughter and clip-clop of hastily running feet.

"I haven't told anyone this, not even the police. I got a dead-line call the night Terry and Ei were murdered." He looked up. "But the more I think about it, the more certain I am that I did hear something, after all. Some music."

"Do you remember what it was?"

"Yeah. I'm pretty sure it was Mancini." He did not have to add that Mancini was Eileen's favorite composer.

Vincent shivered. "It was like Terry was calling to me from beyond the grave." He lifted a hand hastily. "I know. I know. I don't believe in that kind of thing. But, damn it! It was as if he was trying to tell me who did it."

"You mean he *knew* the murderer?"

Vincent shrugged. "Maybe I'm making too much out of it. I don't know anymore. I just wish—I wish you had been in the city that night, that's all. Christ, they were your friends, too!"

Nicholas said nothing, stared at the smiling children eating ices, sticking out their patinaed tongues at the solemn apes. He wished he felt something. Grief was a useful emotion; better that than carrying it around with you like a hunchback. He felt an abrupt stillness as if he were at the eye of a raging hurricane. Safe and protected, he nevertheless was witness to the devastation going on all around him. Was there a way to stop it? He knew a way, most definitely, but

207

he was reluctant to take it. Vincent was still looking at him, as if by his gaze alone he would wrench some confession from Nicholas' bowels. It had to be done, then. As he knew it from the moment the deal had been proposed. There was obligation; there was duty. Vincent was right. They were his friends.

Vincent touched his arm. "Sorry, old friend," he said. "It's me. I'm on edge. You can see it. Jesus, it's not fair to take it out on you." He smiled thinly. "You see how Westernized I've become."

Nicholas returned the smile with more warmth than he felt. "No. You were right. Neither of us has forgotten the importance of obligation and duty."

"Listen, Croaker's invited me to dinner. Why don't you join us? At the place."

"All right." Nicholas nodded. "I'd like that."

Vincent glanced at his watch. "Back to the salt mines. See you later."

Nicholas searched through the park for a phone, finally went out on Fifth Avenue. He called Justine. Doc Deerforth answered.

"What's the matter?" Nicholas said. His heart was racing.

"A slight accident. Nothing to worry about. But I think you ought to come out if your work permits."

"What happened?"

"Justine was caught in the undertow. She's all right."

"Are you certain that's what it was?"

"Reasonably. What do you mean?"

"Were there other people around? Did anyone see anything suspicious?"

"There were plenty of people. A neighbor helped drag her out of the surf. No one mentioned anything else."

"Can you stay with her until I get there? I'll take the first train out." He looked at his watch.

"Sure. There's nothing pressing. My service knows where I am. But if there's an emergency—"

"I understand. Doc—tell her I'll be there."

"When she wakes up. Don't worry."

He hung up and hailed a cab, took it to Penn Station. Downstairs at the Long Island Rail Road counter he bought a ticket, found that he had twenty-five minutes to spare. He called Tomkin. There was a considerable delay. He stared out at the passing parade of people, scanning unconsciously. A pair of teenagers struggled with enormous backpacks and, just behind them, a young woman stood against a pillar waiting impatiently to be met. He wondered whether it was her boss who was late.

"Nicholas?" The voice came crisply into his ear.

"Tomkin."

"I'm glad you called. Have you thought about my offer?"

Bastard, he thought. Bastard to bring Justine into it. But now he knew that Justine *was* a part of it. He hated to be in this position. Methodically, he calmed himself. "I've thought about it. I'll start work for you today."

"Good. Why don't you come up to the tower and—"

"No. I'm at Penn Station. I'm taking the next train out to the Island."

"I don't understand—"

"There's work to do out there. Justine's out there."

"I see."

"I'm sure you do," Nicholas said savagely. "I'll be in touch tomorrow."

"Nich—"

The voice was cut off as he cradled the receiver.

The man was on the job. He had come to work for Lubin Bros. over a week ago. He had been assigned to a construction site on Ralph Avenue in Brooklyn until Manucci had turned up sick and he had been transferred to the Park Avenue job. Tomkin was paying extra to make certain construction did not fall behind schedule and the management of Lubin Bros. was doing everything in its power to keep things moving along. That included making sure there was always a full complement of workers.

The man worked tirelessly at every assignment he was given. He was a good worker and spoke very little; no one noticed him. When he reported that day, his mind had been filled with his work of the night before: early morning, that is. It was a way of thinking about today's assignment. Some new wrinkles were needed, and while his forebrain was recounting last night's work, the subconscious dissected the present problem.

It had been no trouble at all to gain access to the Actium

House subbasement parking lot; he had come in in the empty backseat of a Lincoln Continental which had disgorged its passengers at the street-level entrance. Then it had simply been a matter of waiting.

Tomkin's limo had come down the ramp at ten minutes after three in the morning. He was a notorious insomniac and spent the better part of each weekday night in his office at the new building.

The powerful headlights had scored the roof of the lot, then dipped as the limo came down the last part of the ramp. The motor thrummed quietly in the dark as the chauffeur rolled it to the parking space and slid in. The motor died.

The man knew by heart the next movements of the chauffeur, but even so he waited a full hour after the other had left. Time was one element that he had plenty of now. It could be the best of friends or the most implacable of enemies, thus he treated it with respect. It never paid to be hasty.

At last he uncoiled himself and moved toward the limo. He was like a shadow on the prowl. In seconds he had the back door of the car open and closed again. Inside, he used a pencil flash and a surgeon's scalpel. Where the plush carpet met the edge of the rear seat, he scored a line with the scalpel. He made a second cut so that the two were in a T shape. Then he peeled back the small flaps and inserted a round object no more than half an inch in diameter and, using an odorless resin epoxy, he closed the flaps carefully. Next he turned his attention to the phone. He opened the box and, ignoring the receiver, placed a second disk on the inside wall of the box. He sat in the backseat precisely where he knew Tomkin sat and opened the box, looking down at the receiver. He could not see the disk. Satisfied, he closed the box. He turned off the pencil flash and let himself out of the limo. Within twenty seconds he was walking down Fifty-first Street, hunched over in his black nylon windbreaker. In all, he had been in the limo precisely nine minutes.

Now as he worked on the riveting in the atrium lobby of Tomkin Industries, the man worked on the problem of getting upstairs.

At lunchtime he took the outside cage elevator up as far as it would go, one floor below Tomkin's office. Here the hallways were still raw plaster. Pencil marks were strewn about like engineering graffiti. The corridors were deserted but he was careful enough and there were numerous doorways to plunge into. Every so often he paused and, completely still, listened to the sounds of the building. He would know instantly if there was the slightest change.

He was not worried about his face. There was flesh-colored putty on his cheeks and the bridge of his nose had been built up. Treated cotton rolls were placed in his mouth between gums and cheek. Too, his posture had changed from the man who had entered Terry Tanaka's *dōjō*. He had become slightly stoop-shouldered and he walked with a noticeable limp, as if one leg were shorter than the other. This was due to an inch lift in his right shoe. Disguising one's face was all well and good but there were myriad ways one could be identified by an expert. One had to be as meticulous about all parts of the body as one was about the face—the overall image. A disguise had to be total. One needed only the slightest alterations, however, because the idea was camouflage and it did not do to overdo specific characteristics.

He found the fire stairs, went carefully up to the top floor. Here there was much activity. Both workers and Tomkin's staff were present. All the better, he thought.

Tomkin's office, a full corner of the floor, was nine-tenths complete but it had priority because he was already working out of it. Therefore lunch breaks were not observed up here. The morning shift went down to eat while a swing shift arrived to continue the work. The man was just in time to join them. He walked past the steady gaze of Frank, who stood just inside the thick metal doors to the office. This was hardly the most difficult part. It was doing what he had to do in plain sight of everyone.

The answer, of course, was easy. He merely had to look as if he knew what he was doing and no one paid him the slightest attention. It might even have been amusing, the way in which he performed the most clandestine of movements out in the open like the living embodiment of "The Purloined Letter," if he had allowed himself the luxury of feeling. That, however, was quite impossible for him in this context, thus it was merely an object of intellectual curiosity like a peculiarly striated rock brought home from a summer field trip.

He had, of course, to work in fits and starts: that is, to work on what was his own in between what he was given. This presented no problems other than extending his time in the office.

211

He turned it, however, to his own advantage, as was his wont, by using the time to memorize the contours, the tiny nooks and crannies, the open spaces and the closed. He found where the wall was baffled and where it was bare beneath the paint and plaster; where the wiring went and the placement of all of the electrical outlets; where the circuit breakers were and where the auxiliary lighting. At the moment none of these things fitted in with his plans but one never knew when the knowledge might be crucial. Meticulous planning was essential; however, one always had to build into one's plans a bit of leeway because events had a peculiar way of determining themselves and often, *too* often, a random element—an extra guard, a rainstorm, even an unexpected sound; a minute thing that could not be foreseen—slipped in. One never knew.

By one-thirty he was finished and, still under the jaundiced eye of Frank, he went out with the rest of the swing crew. Out the metal doors, they turned to their right, heading toward the outside cage elevator one floor below. As he was turning the corner, the elevator at the end of the hallway sighed open and Tomkin, accompanied by Whistle, appeared.

The man paused for a moment, his dead eyes glittery. How easy it would be, he thought languidly, to take him out now. Whistle dead on his knees and the big man tumbling through the hot air to the unfinished pavement below. He liked it; it had a certain irony to it. But he did not admire it and that made all the difference in the world. It was not elegant, for one thing, and, for another, there would be little terror in it for Tomkin: just the brief moments he would be airborne, the hot wind in his face while the rubble of the sidewalk reached up for him. What would Tomkin think of in those instants, the man wondered. God? Oblivion? Hell? The man shrugged inwardly. It made little difference. He could understand none of these Western concepts. There was only karma for him. Karma and the *kami* he would inhabit when he died, waiting the prescribed time until he returned in another body, in another life, carrying his karma with him.

This concept of life that was so basic, so fundamental, was, he knew, beyond the conception of men like Tomkin. This did not make him any easier to kill; the doing was just that much less absorbing. It was the mechanics of the penetration, the sowing of the terror which occupied part of his mind; the act of killing itself would mean as much to him as stepping on

212

a cockroach. After all, that was what Tomkin was. He could never be called a civilized man.

As to the eventual escape, the man knew that on this assignment there was a possibility that it would not happen. It did not faze him in the least, for it was something toward which he had prepared all of his life. To die as a warrior was life's highest aspiration, after all, for history recorded the manner of one's death and it was in this that one was remembered forever, not how one lived one's life.

Not that he might ever be caught eliminating Tomkin. It was the other half of his plan: the part that made it all worthwhile. He was being paid a small fortune to take out Tomkin, but money meant very little to him. In fact, when he had arrived to take a look around—as he had put it to his then potential employers—he had not been certain he would take the assignment. But he had come upon something so startling, so irresistible that he could not refuse. He had learned early to take what life gave. He was being given something now that was so fantastic that he found himself salivating at the prospect. To turn away from such an opportunity would be a crime. The chance would never come again. The setup would never be so sweet.

And this had been the second reason for not taking Tomkin out at this moment. Besides, it would, by necessity, have to be sloppy; this kind of total improvisation went against his grain. He could do it and do it well but he resisted it. He hated to mop up all the loose ends after the fact. He liked things clean and neat; in another life he might have made a superb diamond cutter.

So it was that he just took a long hard look at Tomkin as he strode down the hallway unaware that death was at his left hand.

Then the man had moved on, down the unfinished corridor, ducking a loose loop of wire flex hanging from an open panel in the ceiling. In a moment he was through the door to the fire stairs, off the floor.

Once down in the atrium lobby, half in shadows, he poked a finger in his ear as if scratching an itch. In the canal was now placed a flesh-colored plastic sphere, flattened on the outside. It was totally undetectable. He touched the top of it with the tip of his index finger and began to listen.

* * *

213

Nicholas felt it as he turned away from the line of shining chromium phones along one wall of the station: that premonitory tickle at the base of his neck. He began to walk calmly toward a bookstore though he had had no intention of going in there. It was merely the way he was headed and he did not want to make any sudden alterations in his movements. He stood by the window, however, instead of going into the open door. People passed him going in and out. There was a short line at the cash register; there was a sale on, 20 percent off the top ten paperback best sellers.

He stood at a slight angle, not looking inside but using the plate glass as one would a mirror. He watched covertly a good section of the station behind him. Observation was made difficult by the poor refraction, the glare of the lights, the distortion of image caused by the glass itself. He accepted all of these and made allowances.

It was not good to stay here too long. He glanced at his watch. He still had fifteen minutes and he had no reason to sit for that time on the waiting train. Especially not now.

He walked away from the bookstore window, moving diagonally across the station. An old woman, her suitcase on wheels, crossed his path and two sailors in crisp whites passed him, one spinning the tail end of a lewd joke to the other. The young woman at the pillar was no longer there; either she had met her date or had given it up; three dark-haired children squired by a dour-looking woman scampered along, laughing and teasing each other. A man in a dark windbreaker stood by the bank of lockers, a lit cigarette dangling from one corner of his mouth. Opposite, a man in a camel-colored suit flipped through the pages of the current *Hustler*, putting it down as a man with a tan briefcase came up to him. They shook hands and walked off.

Nicholas entered a Nedick's, wedged himself in next to a fat man devouring a slice of coconut cream pie. A dollar bill and some change were on the counter before him; his lips were dotted with pie crust and flecks of ersatz cream. The man ignored Nicholas as he sat down on the stool. He ordered a frank and an orange drink. The columns of the place were mirrored and Nicholas used these to continue his covert surveillance while he ate. He got his food, paid for it.

The feeling was still there, unmistakable. There was only one explanation. He was being observed by a *haragei* adept. The receiver was also a transmitter; there was no way to

214

damp the two-way effect. This one had just come too close, that was all. Careless. And foolish.

Nicholas wiped his lips with the stiff napkin, took one last look in the mirror and went out. He had just over five minutes before the train left and in that time he would have to flush the adept. He had no thoughts now about missing the train; his overriding concern was for Justine. She was most assuredly in danger and he felt totally impotent being so far from her. It was one thing asking Doc Deerforth to look in on her once a day, quite another for him to be there when an emergency arose. Nicholas, rightfully, trusted no one but himself in such a situation.

He had one more thing to do. He went to the phones again, called Lieutenant Croaker.

"Yeah." The voice was harsh and rushed.

"Nicholas Linnear, Lieutenant."

"What's up?"

"I'm on my way back out to the Island. Justine's had some kind of accident."

There was some silence. Nicholas was still checking the vicinity.

"Croaker, there's someone following me."

"Seeing shadows or just too much TV?"

"I haven't seen anyone—yet."

The singing along the line seemed like a live thing, the only thing to make a sound.

"How do you know there's anyone there?" Croaker asked finally.

"You might not believe me if I told you."

"Try me."

"Its *haragei*. Bujutsu training. It's a kind of ESP. A way of looking at the world, sensing things—you might even call it an enlarged sixth sense."

Nicholas half expected a joke but none seemed forthcoming from the other end of the line.

"Who do you think it is?"

"The ninja."

There was an indrawn breath. "Stay there, Linnear. I'll be right over."

"No good. He'd never stay put that long. Besides, he'd smell you a block away."

"We can't just sit tight."

"Believe me, it's the only way. Leave him to me."

215

"To you? Where the hell do you come into it?"

"I think he's after Tomkin; Justine, too. That's why I'm going back out."

"Since when did you get interested in Tomkin's life?" The voice held a hard edge to it now.

"Since I'm working for him. Today."

He heard the indrawn breath in his ear. "Shit! Listen, you mother-fucker—"

"No, you listen, Croaker. You have no idea of what you are up against. No idea at all. I tried to give you a taste of it today at the *dōjō* but I guess it's true what they say about Westerners, they're too thickheaded ever to be educated."

He slammed the phone down and went to join the crowd moving down the stairs to Track 17. His scalp tingled all the while. Just as he left the lower level, he thought he caught a glimpse of a face. It was only a glimpse. A ghostly flash, the pale crescent of a face in semiprofile. Something about it stuck with him. He thought fleetingly of reversing his course but the crush of people was enormous.

Then he was on the train, at a window seat. The feeling was gone. Had it ever been there? He knew better than to ask that question of himself. But why would the ninja be following him? There had to be an answer but he was unable to come up with a satisfactory one.

There was some jostling in the aisles as last-minute passengers squeezed on board. The air conditioning cut out for a moment and someone moaned. The lights blinked and then full power came on. Everything appeared as it should be.

The bell rang and the doors slid shut with a sigh, sealing them in. A moment later, the train had started up and the platform began to slide away. He looked out the window. A black man was sweeping up at the end of the platform. Nothing but patterns of light and shadow dictated by the controlled speed of the train.

Then the city was behind him and he was thinking about Justine. He began to doze, his head against the windowpane.

"Tickets, please."

He started awake, his mind filled with that pale crescent of face, the features oddly indistinct as if he were staring up at the moon through a summer night's mist.

* * *

Gelda was laughing. When she laughed her breasts shook, and when her breasts shook, Dare said, she was at her most sensual.

Dare could always make Gelda laugh, which was one of the reasons Gelda enjoyed her. Her body was the other reason.

Dare's skin was a golden brown all over, deeply tanned with no bikini lines. Perhaps it was the natural color; Gelda never inquired. She was tall, taller at least than Gelda, who was not a small woman. She was long and lean without being thin or overly muscular. She had kinky blond hair which she wore long. It was quite natural.

Dare's legs were even longer than Gelda's. More slender, to be sure, but exquisite just the same. She had small, perfectly round breasts high on her chest, a narrow waist, slender hips. She was boyish and feminine at the same time; there was no touch of the bull in her or in how she dressed. She loved the Old West: the sun-browned masculinity, the fluid musculature of the galloping horse, but most of all she loved the lawlessness.

As Pear had said, this was more pleasure than business.

"I almost found one this time, G," she was saying now. She lay back languidly in the tub; the strong scent of violets was in the air. Gelda knelt by the side of the tub, working the crystal faucets. Water crashed onto the white porcelain, between Dare's spread legs, against the thick tangled bush of hair now darkened to the color of caramel by the moisture. Behind them, on the wall, the stained chaps hung like an effigy waiting for the fire to consume it.

"But, you know," she continued, "even when it was about to happen, I didn't really believe it."

"What happened?" Gelda increased the hot water just a bit.

"What happened?" Dare wailed. "My wonderful Texan, my great Longhorn, my rider of the range turned out to be a fag." She put her elbows outside of the tub, wiggled her ass against the water as it crept up her body. "He cried in bed with me; told me women intimidate him." She put her head back, closed her eyes, luxuriating in the wet warmth. "Oh, I'll never find one." Her eyes flew open, as gray as Gelda's were topaz. "But, you know something, I don't think I care anymore." Her voice had lowered to a husky whisper. "I've got you and there are things in this world that shouldn't be any realer than that." Her arms lifted and she held them out. "Come in here, darling. It's cold outside."

Gelda stood up, slipped off the peach satin robe which hung from her shoulders. It slid to the tile floor with a sensual whisper and Dare shuddered to see her thus naked before her.

Their hands touched as Gelda stepped into the steaming tub and Dare moved to accommodate her.

"There's no one like you," Dare whispered. "Not anywhere." She stroked Gelda's shoulder, the upper slope of her breast. "It wouldn't make any difference how much you charged."

Gelda's fingers stroked the other's thigh through the water, using just the tips of her long nails. "And what," she said softly, "if I didn't charge anything at all?"

Dare's brow wrinkled in a frown and Gelda's forefinger smoothed the skin. "Don't do that," she said.

"It might have mattered," Dare said, "in the beginning. Now I don't suppose it does." She shrugged. "The studio gets the bill anyway but even if they didn't..." Her wide lips curled up in a smile. "I come to see you, darling. It just happens that you cost money. Who cares? It comes in, it goes out. You're better than a gram of coke or Russian sable by a long shot."

Gelda smiled. "I suppose that's a compliment."

Dare laughed. "You know it is." She looked around. "Where is it?"

Gelda's fingers continued their stroking, softly but insistently. A muscle high up in Dare's thigh jumped and she gasped. Gelda knew her pulse rate was rising. "There's plenty of time, darling. Relax. It's in a safe place." Her fingers stroked the supple flesh. "It'll come out when you're ready."

Dare's head turned, her hands cupped Gelda's bountiful breasts, her thumbs moving back and forth against the large nipples, feeling them erect. "Uhm," she whispered. "That's what I love about you: the duality. The fire and ice, the soft and the strong, the bitch and the little girl."

"I'm only a mirror," Gelda murmured.

"No, that's not true, not with me you're not. I know you love it as much as I do. You can fool all the men but with women it's different. I can tell. You want me as much as I want you."

Gelda's nails delicately parted Dare's nether lips, probing

218

slowly inward, carefully keeping away from the clit. "You're the only woman I've wanted this way," she said.

Dare's hips were pumping, setting off the waves which lapped at the sides of the tub. They were their own universe. The moon's transit, setting off a series of tidal waves.

Gelda worked her other hand around underneath Dare's buttocks, stroking the cleft.

"Oh, oh, oh!" Dare twisted her upper torso, began to suck on Gelda's nipples. "Ahhh!" The breasts popped out, coated with saliva. "When I'm filming, I lie in bed at night and think of you. I masturbate while I think of your big breasts, your long legs, your wide cunt. Oh, my God!" She clutched at Gelda's shoulder as she felt the first friction against her clit. "Oh, now, now, now!"

Gelda reached her hand over the side of the tub, brought the Remington into full view. Dare's eyes were round and luminous, clouded with lust. "Let me," she whispered throatily and Gelda let her lick the opening of the barrel. "Oh, more!" But Gelda had pulled it away and, holding Dare down as she began to struggle slowly, so slowly, she inserted the end between the lips of her vagina. "Ahhh!" Dare arched her hips upward and the barrel slid into her, all the way, until the hard protrusion of the hammer mashed against her clit. Gelda needed only to waggle the Remington back and forth twice before she felt the oncoming spasms of delight in Dare. She waited, holding on, licking at her hard nipples as she soared up the orgasmic curve. Dare's body was superbly responsive and she could accurately gauge when she would hit the peak.

Dare convulsed upward, breaking at last Gelda's hold on her, and as she did so Gelda pulled the trigger. Once. Twice. Six times. And with each shot, Dare cried out as the air-propelled jets of hot water inundated her.

The bathroom was awash in water. Dare shuddered as if with the ague. She wrapped her arms around Gelda, her lips between her breasts, whispered, "Leave it in, leave it in." Her eyelids fluttered. "Oh, my God." Her breasts heaved as if she had just run a marathon.

"Do it again," she said. "Do it again."

Vincent met Lieutenant Croaker promptly at six-fifteen under Michita's wooden awning. Because of its location, the restaurant was already crowded with people eating a hasty pre-theater dinner.

The place was L-shaped, dark with wooden walls separating the tables. There was a sushi bar to their left as they walked in which curved around to the shorter leg of the L. It was perhaps three-quarters full. Vincent saw a lone American.

They were led into the rear of the restaurant. Here there were no Western tables but rather a series of private tatami rooms. These traditional areas were covered by the reed mats and contained no chairs, only one low table around which diners sat cross-legged. The tatami rooms were screened by a series of *shōji*.

Vincent ordered sake for both of them as they slid off their shoes and climbed into the room. A waiter left buff-colored menus on the gleaming wooden table, went to get their drinks.

Croaker put a manila folder on the table, took out two eight-by-ten sheets and placed them side by side in front of Vincent. "Ever see this man before?"

They were police artist sketches of a man in his thirties, oriental, wide nose, flat cheeks, anonymous eyes. His hair was long.

Vincent studied the drawings carefully before he shook his head. "No, but to tell you the truth, I'd be surprised if I had."

"Why?"

"This is the man who came to Terry's *dōjō* the day he and Eileen were murdered, right?"

"How'd you know that?"

The sake came and they were silent while the waiter filled the tiny cups. When he had gone, Croaker looked inquiringly at Vincent.

"I had dinner with Terry that night," Vincent said slowly. "I did most of the talking." His voice had turned rueful. "Now I'm sorry I did because Terry obviously had something on his mind. He spoke briefly about a Japanese who had come in to practice that day. Karate, aikido and—kendo." He sipped at his sake and one hand waved. "I'm only putting this together now as I talk to you. You see, Bennoku, the *dōjō's* regular kenjutsu *sensei*, has been on vacation for about ten days. If that man came to Terry for kenjutsu there was only one way he could possibly be accommodated. By Terry himself."

Croaker shrugged. "What's so odd about that? Linnear told me that Tanaka was an expert at kenjutsu, a—*sensei*, did you call it?"

Vincent nodded. "Yeah, but what Nick obviously *didn't* tell you is that Terry had put his *katana* away. He had what I can only describe as a spiritual change of heart. He no longer found pleasure in kenjutsu; he no longer practiced it."

"When did this happen?"

"I'm not really certain. Perhaps as long as six months ago."

"Then why didn't Linnear tell me?"

Vincent poured more sake for them both. "To tell you the truth, I'm not sure Nick knows. He's—well, he's also had a kind of spiritual change of heart, only he's still going through his and I don't know what it entails. We're still very close, he and I, and he was close with Terry, too, but he'd withdrawn somewhat. I'm sure Terry had the opportunity to tell him but I rather think he chose not to." He shrugged. "Anyway, if this is the man"—he tapped the drawing—"he'd be disguised. I might know him or Nicholas might but we'd never be able to tell you from one of those."

Croaker nodded. "Okay." He began to put them away.

Vincent put a hand out. "Why don't you wait until Nick comes? It couldn't hurt for him to see it."

"Linnear called me late this afternoon. He went back to West Bay Bridge. His girl had an accident." He finished putting the drawings away. "Nobody saw this bastard going in or out. Not at the *dōjō* or Terry's apartment."

"I'm not surprised. This man's a professional. A highly dangerous professional. I'm afraid you don't know what you're up against here."

"That's just what Linnear told me," Croaker growled. "I don't like hearing it."

"It's the truth, Lieutenant. You'd better face facts. This guy can put away just about anyone he chooses."

"Even Raphael Tomkin?"

Vincent nodded. "Even him."

"It's been tried a dozen times," Croaker pointed out. "By professionals."

Vincent sighed. "This professional is different. We are not

talking about a hit man from Detroit or wherever they manufacture them."

"Jersey City," Croaker said with a thin smile.

"Yeah, well, this is a ninja, Lieutenant. Next to a professional hit man he's Houdini, Superman and Spider-Man all wrapped up into one." Vincent tapped the table with the tip of his forefinger. "The man's a sorcerer."

Croaker stared into the other's eyes, trying to find some hint of irony. He found none. "You're serious, aren't you?"

"At the risk of sounding melodramatic, deadly serious."

The waiter returned and they ordered dinner along with more sake. "Take your time," Vincent told the waiter, who nodded and went out.

"Linnear took me to a kenjutsu *dōjō* today," Croaker said.

"Which one?"

"I don't know the name of it. I met the *sensei*. Man named Fukashigi."

There was an odd look in Vincent's eyes. "You're quite a privileged person. Very few Westerners are allowed entrance. And for Nicholas to take you..." He whistled silently.

"Yeah," Croaker joked. "And that was after I'd insulted him. He certainly doesn't hold any grudges."

Now Vincent's eyes were sad and he said, "It was not for him to be angry but for you to know that you have now lost face."

"Lost face? What do you mean?"

"Simply this. Relationships are based on respect—mutual respect. With that comes trust. And obligation. I will not ask you what you did—no, don't tell me, I have no wish to know—but I will say that if you have offended him then his respect for you has lessened."

"What the hell do I care what he thinks of me?"

"Ah, well, perhaps you don't." Vincent smiled. "If that's the case, no more may be said of the matter." He deliberately took a sip of his sake, refilled the cup.

Croaker cleared his throat and, after a time, said, "Finish your last thought."

"I was merely going to say that it is not up to Nick to forgive you—that he has already done, otherwise he would not have taken you to see Fukashigi. It is up to you to seek to restore the former balance."

"How would I do that?" Croaker said suspiciously.

"Ah, if I knew the answer to that one, I'd be quite the wise man." Vincent shook his head. "And tonight, Lieutenant, I'm not feeling wise at all."

There was a man at the sushi bar with invisible putty on his face. It built up his flat cheekbones, flattened his wide nose, deepened the sockets of his eyes. Even his mother would not recognize him and she had been a most intelligent woman.

He was halfway through a plate of sashimi when Vincent and Lieutenant Croaker entered the restaurant and were shown to a tatami room. He did not turn his head but caught them in the periphery of his vision.

Several moments later, he pushed his plate delicately away from him and walked the length of the room to the rest room. The place was dark and crowded, buzzing with conversation. He had to pass the tatami rooms to get there. The rest room was empty. He washed his hands, peering at himself in the mirror. The door opened and two men walked in. The man went out, past the thin *shōji* walls. He paid for his meal and left.

Outside in the heat of the summer night, he hailed a cruising taxi. He had to make four switches before he found one suitable for his purposes.

At precisely 8:18 P.M. officer Pete Travine pulled the patrol car over so that the right side wheels scraped the curb. It was his second pass down Twenty-eighth Street and he was certain now that what he saw in the alleyway between a brownstone and a tailor shop had not been there when he had made his first pass twenty minutes ago. He had been thinking of the old days, when all cops rode in tandem. Now, because of the city's serious ongoing fiscal crisis, they were still experimenting in certain areas with solo patrols, despite concerted PBA opposition.

The radio squawked intermittently, but there was nothing in his vicinity. He put the blue-and-white in park and got out a flashlight, played it over the darkened alley. The beam of light hovered over a line of garbage cans painted silver. It was quiet here: no pedestrians, only the soft susurrus of the light traffic along Lexington.

He opened the curbside door, slid out. With one hand he unsnapped the top of his stiff leather holster, the guard he wore while driving.

He went cautiously across the sidewalk, his flash flicking the darkness. There was an open grille gate leading to four or five steep concrete steps to the alley proper. The right wall—the brownstone's—was blank for all of its three stories. The left wall had windows beginning on the second story of the building. There were apartments over the tailor shop. Odd lighting, subtly kaleidoscopic, leaked from these. Television sets were on.

Travine went down the steps. He thought briefly of calling in but rejected it. He wanted to have something concrete for them.

Past the line of garbage cans was deep shadow but something protruded partway out into the semi-light casting strange shadows upward along the brick wall. It was these that Travine had seen and questioned.

He stood over the shape now. He took his hand from his gun butt, crouched and reached out to touch it. An old burlap sack covered the shape partway but this close Travine could see the face, one cheek to the wall. Two fingers at the side of the neck confirmed that the man was dead.

Travine got up and, without disturbing anything, went up the stairs to the street. He looked both ways. A couple passed, arm in arm, walking downtown along Lex. There was no other movement. He called in, then phoned the M.E.'s office. "I don't want this to wait until tomorrow," he told the associate on call. "I want something tonight."

Then he went back to the body to I.D. it but there was nothing. No wallet, no money, no cards, nothing. Yet the man was obviously no derelict. He touched the body again. Not yet cold. He stood up. In the distance the night was split by the sound of sirens, growing louder.

Through fingerprints, they were able to establish the identity of the man. That took a little over three hours and at that time they began to wonder what had happened to his taxi.

Vincent came out of Michita looked for a cab.

He was not a little drunk and not in the least bit ashamed of himself. He felt as light as a balloon despite the sultry

224

steaming night. All the cares and worries which had clung to him, weighing him down for months had sloughed away, dead skin shed.

He walked a little unsteadily, realizing it, curious about it, even happy with it. He'd needed this loosening up.

He breathed in the heavy night air, leaden with exhaust fumes, the odors of fried cooking from the corner coffee shop. He felt as if he were on the Ginza in Tokyo, with its bustle, its crowds, its bright neon jungle advertising nightclubs and Western products.

He watched people streaming by him, feeling a bit giddy. He fought down the impulse to giggle and then thought, why not? He giggled out loud. No one appeared to notice.

He began to walk west. Traffic from Sixth Avenue sounded like surf breaking against a far-off shore. He thought of Uraga where the ships of Admiral Perry had docked in 1853, ending two hundred and fifty years of Japanese isolationism. The mysterious surf rolling in toward the Floating Kingdom. Better if we had not given in to that Pacific overture. Far better. The ageless barrier holding Japan in magical thrall had been breached. It was a mythic tale, as all of Japanese history tended to be, throwing larger-than-life shadows on the screen of memory.

Down the block, almost at the corner of Sixth, a cab started up, pulling slowly out from the curb, coming toward him. Just before it pulled abreast, its hack light went on. It caught his eye, a spinning jewel in the night. He was still in Japan.

He waved at it drunkenly and it pulled over to the curb. A Checker, big and roomy. And air-conditioned.

It was a custom job, not fleet-owned. Inside, there was no plastic partition and the front seats were beige leather buckets.

Vincent gave the driver his address and settled back. The cab started up.

Even in the crowded modern streets of Tokyo, Vincent was thinking, amid the urban clutter, the European business suits, one would abruptly come upon an ancient Shinto shrine tucked away somewhere between two buildings. One could hear the ghostly tinkling of the bronze bells, sewn in a vertical strip, green with the patina of time; one could smell the incense gently swirling the air. For those moments the exhaust fumes, the pollution were eliminated and the soul of

225

ageless Japan reigned unsullied by Western encroachment, summoning the ancient gods.

It was dark in the cab. He gazed out at the glowing lights of the city, realized that they were moving quite slowly. He leaned forward. "Hey," he said, "I'd like to get home within the hour."

He saw the back of the driver's head move and, raising his gaze, saw his eyes in the strip of the rearview mirror. He saw that the man was Japanese, looked for his name on the I.D. card on the extreme right of the dashboard. The light was out and he could not make it out. He spoke to the driver in Japanese, apologizing for his rudeness.

"That's all right," the man said. "It's been a hard night for everyone."

They had come around onto Forty-fifth, heading west. The taxi swung right at the corner onto Eighth Avenue. Here the street was lined on both sides by a combination of junk food restaurants and sleazy porn theaters. The sidewalks were filled with hookers looking to feed their habits, black con men, low-grade pushers and Puerto Rican strong-arm boys: the vast white underbelly of the city in all its gritty, sorrowful splendor.

The driver went through one intersection on the change, hit a red light on the next.

"It's a night like home," Vincent said in Japanese.

"No one wanted it," the man said. "It should never have come."

Vincent thought again of Perry's four warships, riding in the harbor at Uraga. Perhaps he's right, he thought. We never should have—

The driver had turned around. His face was blue and green in the dancing garish lights from a movie theater. His mouth opened in a smile. A black oblong that might have belonged to a Nō mask. The eyes were like stones, radiated no possibility of warmth or friendship. This contrast between smile and animosity made him appear to leer frighteningly. Vincent was reminded of the first Nō play he had seen with its terrifying demon's mask; at least that was how it seemed to him at the age of six.

There was something odd about this face but in the low light he couldn't tell—he leaned forward. It seemed as if the skin on the man's face was blotchy as if—

He drew back, his mind stunned at what it had perceived.

226

But his reflexes had been dulled by the alcohol and, even as he retreated, he saw the man's face ballooning out toward him like the wedge of a viper. The cheeks billowed and the lips curled into an O. A fine mist shot from the aperture, caught him in mid-gasp. He had already inhaled some of the spray before he stopped breathing.

Croaker sat in the tatami room, cross-legged, his head propped on one fist, after Vincent had left. He called for more sake and thought savagely about going home. He gulped at the liquor. It was cold and he waited patiently for the fresh bottle. He liked the stuff. It had hardly any taste but generated a hell of a high.

He didn't want to go home. No, no, he thought. That's not it. I don't want to go home to Alison. This both surprised and annoyed him. Surprised because even though he had known this might be coming for a while, it had now surfaced so strongly, so blatantly. Annoyed with himself because he had allowed things to slip this far. It wasn't even that he was angry with Alison, he thought. He just didn't want to have anything to do with her anymore. He wondered for a time that two people could feel so much together for a time and then, later, not feel anything at all. Part of the human condition, he concluded philosophically, but a hell of a part.

The sake came and he allowed the waiter to pour the first cup. He downed it, immediately poured himself another. He itched to call Matty the Mouth but he suspected that if he did he might break this Didion thing to smithereens. It seemed to him now that the entire case was balanced on one shining point: getting the name and address of this broad.

He didn't have to close his eyes to be able to picture again Angela Didion's apartment, but he did so anyway. He went over it all again.

The first thing he noticed when he walked in was the smell. Sickly-sweet, it was ether combined with what? The darkened living room had given up nothing but in the bedroom he saw the American Indian bone pipe and, sniffing it, had smelled the opium. Tasted it on the tip of his tongue. Very high grade indeed. Hardly street stuff. But then this was Angela Didion's bedroom and a woman who was purportedly the world's highest-paid model could hardly be expected to have anything but the best—of everything. He didn't touch the pipe; he didn't touch anything.

Slipping on his surgeon's gloves, he crossed to the closet opposite the enormous bed. The bedroom was done all in midnight blue. from the silk wallpaper to the satin lampshades. There was only one lamp on when he had come in, next to the bed. He left the room that way.

Carefully he opened up the sliding door. Inside he found silk dresses by Calvin Klein and Ferragamo. There were six fur coats, ranging from a full-length dyed Russian sable to a spectacular three-quarter silver lynx. Below, shoes from Botticelli and Charles Jourdan.

On the deep-pile rug between the bed and the closet was a black silk teddy. He skirted that on the way to the bed. It was a custom-made affair, moon-shaped. The sheets were midnight-blue percale but the rumpled comforter was covered in silk. It lay around Angela Didion's ankles like dark surf, ready to claim her.

She lay half on the bed, half off. Her head was in midair, the long honey-blond hair streamed over her head, pooling on the floor. She was made up. Her eyes were mascaraed, her cheeks blushed, her lips painted. She was naked save for a thin gold chain which she wore around her waist. There was no other jewelry. She lay on the left side of the bed. The right side was empty but the pillow on that side was indented as if someone had lain there. There were stains on the sheets, still damp. There was no blood. A pillow was wedged beneath the small of Angela Didion's back.

Someone had done quite a job on her. Bruises, just beginning to darken, lay like boils along the sides of her neck, her chest and rib cage, her stomach. Her back was arched as if in ecstasy. There was no expression on her face whatsoever. No sign of pain or fear—or of passion.

It should have been grotesque, would have been with any other victim—Croaker had seen too many like it. But this wasn't anyone, it was Angela Didion. She must have been an extraordinary woman, Croaker thought as he stood staring down at her corpse, because her beauty transcended even this degradation; even death. Croaker knew that he was looking at a magnificent piece of humanity and it saddened him that it should have been destroyed so recklessly. He felt that about most of the bodies he found, if they weren't the punks

228

who got blown away by their own cupidity; the city breathed easier without them.

He tore his gaze away from the bed and, going around it, knelt beside the black silk garment on the carpet. In this twilight of the room, it was almost invisible: black against the deep blue that was almost black itself.

Dipping one forefinger down, he lifted it up slightly. Bending, he touched his nose to it, breathed in, caught the faint whiff of a perfume. He got up, crossed to Angela Didion's dressing table. He passed over the ivory comb and brush set, the tortoiseshell oval vanity mirror, the odds and ends of mascara, eyeliner, blush, powder, creams, taking them all in as he did so. There were two perfume bottles on a silver tray against the wall. Joy and Bal à Versailles. He sniffed at both of them, one at a time, slowly. Then, to make certain, he returned to the silk teddy, confirming for himself that it emanated another perfume; that it bore the imprint of another woman.

It had taken time and a lot of hard work but, in the end, Matty the Mouth had come through. Now it was this woman's name and address Croaker was anxiously waiting for. Angela Didion's lover. Or, more accurately, one of them. She could not, of course, have been the murderer. Judging from the size of the teddy, she was far too small to have inflicted such terrible wounds on another human adult. *There were no instruments used*, the M.E. had said, *other than the fists*. That meant someone strong and with a massive build; some of the bruises were quite large.

No, this woman was no murderer but, Croaker was convinced, she had been a witness to the murder. She knows, he thought now. She knows. And she's scared shitless of what she's seen. No one had gotten to her. No one would but Croaker. He must see to that.

Come on, Matty, deliver the goods. He found his hand trembling against the table, stared down at it as if it belonged to someone else. He knew he wanted this conviction badly. More than he had wanted any other in his career. And the hell of it was, he knew who had killed Angela Didion. Knew it as surely as he knew his own name. But without this witness, there was nothing: nothing but conjecture and theory and circumstantial evidence that McCabe wouldn't even touch, let alone ask for an arrest. Jesus, he hated counting this heavily on someone else but he had spent seven years

229

cultivating Matty the Mouth and now it looked as if it would finally pay off. If he came through. *When* he comes through, Croaker corrected himself. Think positively.

Which all led him back to this ninja. The case was going nowhere, spinning on its own momentum. That, Croaker knew from long hard experience, was extremely dangerous. It meant he had no handle and *that* meant he had no control. People tended to get severely hurt when that happened.

And then there was the problem of Nicholas Linnear. Vincent had been right, he felt instinctively. Linnear had been highly offended by what he'd said. It had been a stupid thing to say. He had known it as soon as he had said it. Now he realized that Linnear might be the key to the case. *He knows more about the ninja than anyone in or out of Japan*, Vincent had said toward the end of the evening. *Trust him. He knows what he's talking about.* Now he's working for that bastard Tomkin, Croaker thought. He had a strong urge to back off then, to let events happen without him. Perhaps Tomkin would fall. But that, he knew, he could never do. It was not the way he wanted it to happen. And then there was the consideration of the four other deaths. If the ninja was after Tomkin, why had he killed four people who did not know the man, let alone have any kind of association with him? No one seemed to know the answer and there was certainly no one on the force he could talk this over with. It came back to Linnear again. If anyone might have a clue, he would.

Croaker looked at his watch, thought about calling Linnear, then quickly changed his mind. The telephone wasn't the right medium and, anyway, he was too high to be able to think things through with enough clarity to satisfy himself. He sighed, finished off the bottle of sake. He'd had enough.

Still he could not face the thought of going home. Yet he wanted a woman. Into his mind swam an image and abruptly he was as hard as a bar of iron. Her face seemed familiar but where had he seen her before? Perhaps nowhere. Perhaps on some billboard. The image had surfaced from deep inside of him. Perhaps she was long gone. Or, again, had never even existed.

* * *

Vincent exhaled in a rush, attempting to free his lungs of the mist. It was a useless gesture, his mind knew, yet his body would not be denied its chance.

His eyes began to burn and tear. He reached blindly for the door handle. The cab started up as the light changed. He leaned on the handle, got it open on the second try. The city rushed in on him as he half tumbled out. His foot caught for a moment and then he was free, rolling along the street for a moment while horns blared. He could hear the harsh squeal of brakes and muted shouts. Then he was up and running clumsily, slipping on dogshit as if it were a banana peel. He balanced himself with his arms outspread and hit the curb, sprinted up onto the sidewalk.

Behind him he could feel the looming presence of the Checker cab as the driver pulled hard over and jumped out.

"Hey!" he called. "Come back! I want my fare!"

Vincent stumbled along the crowded street, bumping into people. Black faces turned, wide-eyed, to stare.

He's a cool bastard, he thought as he was spun around by an enormous black man with an open shirt and tight maroon pants. "Hey, man! Be cool. Watch yo'self."

He wove in and out of the crowd, wondering how long he had. He had no illusions about what he had inhaled. Even without the characteristic odor, he would have known it was a neural toxin.

He turned his head but could not see his pursuer. He took a chance, darted off the curb, trying to hail a passing cab—it was no good expecting a cop to pop up here. But immediately he saw the man stalking him along the periphery of the crowd and, spying him, he leaped forward.

Vincent whirled, darting back into the thick of the throng on the sidewalk. He began to run again but this, he knew, would only spread the toxin more quickly. Already his heart was pounding furiously and the tips of his fingers felt numb: a bad sign. Yet the man was pursuing him so perhaps there was a chance he had not inhaled a sufficient amount of the poison.

Death was very close now, Vincent knew. It rode his shoulder like an expectant predator. He realized now just how much he wanted to live; how strong the drive was still inside him. This knowledge came like a revelation and it buoyed him for a time. He would need all his wits to overcome this

231

demon, he knew. He was overmatched but he put this thought out of his mind as he ran on and on into the spangled night.

He cut to his right, stumbling off the curb, but again he was balked by the man. No good. A cab was definitely out.

He coughed as he ran now, trying to retch. He felt as if he could not get enough oxygen into his system. His arms felt weak and he had to force his legs to work. He heard a harsh shout from behind him and the sound of running feet. He pushed his way frantically through the crowd, his mind whirling, trying to alight on some— The mist. What a fool he'd been! It was being absorbed through the pores of his skin—the burning should have told him. Inhaling was only peripheral.

Have to find...He was aware of how terribly exposed he was here on these mean streets where no help would be forthcoming. A restaurant was no good: too well lighted. He needed someplace dark.

It was right in front of him. He put on a last burst of speed, feeling his heart pounding painfully as if it were being overworked.

He skidded to a stop in front of a movie theater. In front was a billboard dominated by a cutout of a blonde with large breasts. Beneath it, a blown-up newspaper review of the film. "An erection!" proclaimed a banner. "Highest rated!" Vincent shoved a man away from the ticket booth, threw a bill at the man inside the booth. He pushed through the turnstile, ignoring the shouts. "Hey mister! Wait! Your change!"

Into the darkness, smelling from mildew, stale sweat and dried sperm. Hazy images moved on the screen and there was the sound of heavy breathing, magnified by the speakers, amplified throughout the theater. There was a liquid sound and a moaning.

Vincent blinked several times, adjusting to the low light. He looked for the men's room, found that it was two flights up, past the balcony. He didn't think he could make it.

He moved cautiously along the rear aisle, past two people standing, watching the screen. He came upon a bank of machines. Popcorn. Candy. Soda.

He dug in his pants pocket, fumbled out two quarters. He rolled them into the slot, stabbed a button at random. He waited impatiently while the waxed-paper cup clattered down, followed by the soda and the syrup. He stuck his hand in, caught the shaved ice as it came down the vertical chute. He rubbed the ice over his face. He blinked and blinked, feeling the cold water running into his eyes, over his face. Perhaps he had got to it in time. The ice was like a soothing balm, diminishing the pain. There *was* a chance. The cab had been air-conditioned, the windows closed, but he had gotten out very quickly. He tried to judge the overall time, gave it up as hopeless.

He turned his head to look at the doorway. Someone came in, someone went out. They were shadows to him. Was his pursuer here already? There was no way of knowing and here, in the rear, he was a perfect target.

He turned into the theater proper, went quickly down the aisle. His vision had seemed to clear and he could see men sitting as still as statues, staring at the screen filled with writhing bodies.

He slipped into a row midway down, moving to his right all the way over until he was wedged against one wall. In the darkest part of the theater he sat down. The floor was sticky; the place smelled of accelerated age. His head swiveled around. People were coming and going. Flickering light played over their faces. He turned back.

His hands had begun to shake but this might be because of the increased adrenalin. His mouth was dry and his breathing raspy. Otherwise, he felt better than he had before. Obviously the dose had been less than lethal. He tried to relax, breathing deeply, but his side hurt intermittently, perhaps from the frantic running. Meanwhile, his mind was going over the alternatives. There didn't seem to be many. Having come in here, he was now quite effectively trapped. The ninja, too, was here somewhere. If he made a move to leave, he would be dead before he got halfway to the door.

He would have to fight. It was the only alternative. He was not a *sensei* or a *haragei* adept as Nicholas was—or Terry had been. He turned his mind away from Terry: that way led to despair; if Terry had been defeated...

But Terry had been surprised and then there had been Ei to think of. Vincent was forewarned. He needed time and he was getting it; he was feeling better every moment. Think! he screamed at himself. You've got to get out of this somehow.

There were people in back of him, to his left. Shadows moving in the aisle, up and down, bobbing; rustling as people sat down or got up. Someone slid into his row, one seat away from him, and he stiffened, his eyes sliding that way so that he could see...a youngish businessman, clean-cut, Brooks

233

Brothers suit, thin leather attaché case on his knees. A model businessman.

Vincent removed his attention, went back to thinking. Something touched his arm and he jumped, turned his head. It was the businessman, clean-shaven, reddened cheeks, lived just over the river along the Jersey Palisades perhaps with the wife and two kids, the dog and the two cars. The man was tapping him gently on the arm. He leaned forward, his eyes searching Vincent's. He whispered something but Vincent could not hear him over the amplified moaning. He leaned over, across the vacant seat between them. "Want to move over here next to me?" the man said hopefully.

Vincent stared at him dumbfounded for a full minute until he shook his head violently from side to side, withdrew.

He wiped at his forehead and his fingers came away wet. But he knew what he had to do now and all he could do was wait.

There was a movement along the aisle; a shadow had stopped at the end of his row. Vincent turned his head slightly but all he saw was a black blotch. The businessman who had propositioned him was moving slightly in his seat, his hands invisible under the shield of his attaché case; it was too warm to carry a raincoat.

Someone was coming into Vincent's row now and he held his breath, his heart pumping furiously. Was it the ninja? The figure moved slowly, approaching Vincent. He looked up. The man was just on the other side of the engrossed businessman. He saw a glint of reflected light from the screen dance off the man's eyes. It was the ninja. He bent, said something to the businessman, who moved his legs, not taking his eyes off the screen.

He was coming. Vincent prepared himself for what he had to do. It would take speed and strength and— Now the man was at the seat next to Vincent's. He did not sit down.

Now was the time. Now!

Vincent moved. Nothing happened. His eyes bulged in disbelief. He was paralyzed!

He struggled to lift his hands but his arms were immobile, as if they had been encased in lead while his attention had been elsewhere. He tried to stand up but there was no feeling in his legs. No feet, no ankles, nothing. Then he knew with a swift unalterable certainty that the spray had never been meant to kill him but merely render him motionless.

The shadow loomed over him, blotting out all light. He heard animal cries, lustful sobs; he felt the movement over him with exaggerated slowness, watching calmly and detachedly as the ninja leaned over him and gently put one forearm against his left clavicle. He felt the pressure and his eyes blinked. Perhaps the tip of one finger twitched where it lay on the wooden arm of the seat. There was no fear in him, no sorrow, only an image of Japan, of a rocky seashore outside of Uraga with its ramshackle houses, the pure white sails of the fishing boats as they set sail against the red and yellow sunrise. He saw the lone pine standing on the bluff, limned by the light, a dark sentinel standing watch over its homeland.

The other forearm broke against the left side of his face, pressing at his ear. The force was enormous. The first arm held the rest of his body immobile. Homeland expanding outward, outward into—*snap!*

Tokyo Suburbs

AUTUMN 1963

"This is the perfect place to watch the sun set," Cheong said. She turned to Tai, handed her the lacquer tray. Tai, bowing, took it and silently left them alone in the kitchen.

"You see, I had your father take the *shōji* out and put the glass in." She gave a little laugh. "It scandalized Itami, of course. She would never do a thing like that in *her* house." She sighed, perfectly serious now. "Sometimes your aunt can be extremely trying, I am most ashamed to admit."

"Itami is not blood, Mother."

She put a slender hand over his and smiled. "Sometimes, Nicholas, the spirit is more binding than the blood. You may find such a thing out for yourself as you grow older." She took her hand away. "Are you hungry?"

"Yes."

"Good. Tai has made your favorite." She showed him.

"My favorite is *dim sum*," he said. "Tai does not make them as well as you do, though you tell her what to do."

Cheong laughed and, leaning over, kissed his cheek. "All right," she said lightly. "This weekend I'll make you *dim sum*."

"How many kinds?"

"Enough," she said. "Enough."

She stared out the window. The sky near the horizon was as lemony as custard but, high aloft, the blue was as deep as midnight. "You do not get to see this sight often enough, do you?"

"Bujutsu takes a great deal of time, Mother."

"I know." She hesitated fractionally. "Your school work isn't suffering." It did not seem to be a question.

"There's no problem."

"You know, my father"—she called So-Peng her father

just as if he had sired her—"used to say, it makes a great deal of difference where you have been. Your ancestors live on in your blood."

"I don't know," Nicholas said. "I have a number of American friends who do all they can to break away from such things. You know, their parents and—"

"Then you tell me, my son, if their ancestors have not set the course of their lives?"

He looked at her, thinking that she must, after all, be quite correct.

"Everything your grandfather was, am I," Cheong said. "This he bequeathed me long before I left Singapore with your father. In Asia, this is quite special, quite"—she sought for the proper word—"unique. Now I am able to do the same thing for you."

"But I know so little about him."

"In time you will learn. You are young yet."

"But you were far younger than I am when you began to—"

"Those were different times. Dangerous times. I am very grateful that you could be spared such misery. No one should have to suffer so." Her beautiful face broke into a smile. "But let us speak of more pleasant matters."

I want to know, he told her in his mind. I very much want to know what happened. But, of course, this was something he could not say to her. Never. If she chose to tell him one day...But she would not. He doubted whether even his father knew. Only Cheong and So-Peng. And he was long dead now.

"Your aunt asked about you today," she said, breaking into his train of thought. "She always does when you are not around."

"It was kind of her to think of me."

"Yes." Cheong smiled and touched him. "You should tell her that. It will make her most happy."

"I cannot think—that is to say—"

"Nicholas, Itami thinks of us—all of us—as part of her family. She is very fond of you."

"Sometimes—it's very difficult to know with her."

"Yes, well, people are complex. They need getting to know. Seeping in. Patience. This is, perhaps, difficult for you. Your father makes it so. He is patient and impatient." She shook her head, as if bewildered. "Very inconstant, yes. This is still strange to me." She stroked the nape of his neck. "You are

238

so much like him in that way. He does not make friends easily as most foreigners seem to do. But then, he is no foreigner. Asia is his home, as it is mine. We are both children of the East, forging our own pasts."

"It sounds so difficult, so complex."

She smiled. "We could live no other way."

Increasingly now, Satsugai and Itami came to dinner. His aunt had always been somewhat of a fixture around the house—Cheong saw to that. However, now her husband began to accompany her more frequently.

Listening to Satsugai talk, Nicholas began to understand how Japan had been led blindly into the disastrous war by this man and others like him in the powerful *zaibatsu*. Not that Satsugai ever spoke of events before the war or even of the war itself. As far as he was concerned, the war might as well never have occurred. Ostrichlike, he seemed utterly blind to the still quite visible scars strewn throughout the cities and the countryside.

"The communists have always been a problem in Japan, Colonel," Nicholas recalled his saying one chill autumn evening. The sky was darkening from russet to plum and there was a bitter edge to the wind as it moaned through the pines and the neighboring cryptomeria, a harbinger of the coming winter. A fine rain fell obliquely, streaming against the large study windows, rolling like silent tears. One wretched wren puttered nervously in a tightening circle beneath the inadequate awning of a carefully pruned hedge just outside the window where the rain had caught like pearls on the oval overlapping leaves, a liquid spider web spun in glistening precision across the expanse of the foliage. The wren kept its head cocked, eyeing the sky, impatient to be off.

"The Party is not so large, even now," the Colonel had replied. He tamped down the tobacco in his pipe and carefully lit up. Sweet blue smoke filled the room.

"My dear Colonel," Satsugai said, "one cannot use mere *numbers* to define danger, especially here in Japan." He spoke as if Nicholas' father were some tourist to the country. "One must take into account the *virulence* of the enemy. These are more than dedicated people we are discussing. They are fanatics to the cause of world communism. One mustn't make the mistake of underestimating them. That is the way they achieve their first foothold."

The Colonel said nothing, being busy achieving the proper

draw on his pipe. It was an umber, rough-hewn brier with a curved stem and a high bowl. It had been with him all through the war and, as such, had become quite dear to him. It was a private symbol to him and, though he had well over twenty-five pipes in his collection, this was the one he invariably smoked now.

One gets some peculiar notions in war, the Colonel thought. Perfectly understandable really because, in the end, when the days are dark with death and the overcast nights filled with a jungle terror, when commanders are mowed down by machine-gun fire and mates are blown to bits by mines a pace away from you or slit from throat to navel by a silent invader, those peculiar notions are all that stand between you and utter madness.

The Colonel had gotten it into his head that as long as he had that pipe, as long as he could pull his hand away from the hot grip of his smoking Sten gun, reach inside his uniform pocket and feel the irregularity of the outside of its bowl, everything would turn out all right.

He recalled with vivid clarity the morning in the early summer of 1945 when his unit had begun its assault on the perimeter of Singapore. They had just broken camp and were making their way slowly southward, the units in constant walkie-talkie contact.

In the jungle, the Colonel had reached for the comforting bowl of the pipe, found it gone. He paused, peering at the ground behind him, but could find nothing in the muddy tangle of gnarled roots but centipedes and leeches. A creeping sense of panic had overcome him and, without thinking further, he called for his men to backtrack with him until they had returned to the camp area. He found the pipe half-buried in the silty soil and, brushing it off, was about to order his men out when he heard the first of the rolling reports. The ground shook as if in an earthquake. Southward, they saw the violent geysering of earth and foliage, stained red.

Silently, the Colonel waved them out and they crept forward, zigzagging through the dense jungle only to find the entire company ripped apart; those who had not been caught in the cleverly planted mine field had been taken by sniper fire. The Colonel felt in his pocket for the pipe. The brier was warm under his callused fingers. He hefted his Sten gun and took his men west, through the stinking mangrove swamp, skirting the bloody deathscape, before turning south again.

240

In the dead of night they came upon the Japanese encampment from the rear. They took the perimeter guards out without a sound, stringing them up in the trees as mute witnesses. The Colonel sent half his men into the southeast. At 0400 hours precisely, the Colonel and his men opened fire from their position just south of the encampment. Lead sizzled the air and the Sten guns smoked merrily. Fully half the encampment went down under that withering fire. The other half were not so fortunate. They retreated directly into the line of fire of the second contingent of the Colonel's unit. Caught in a cross-fire, they danced like pyschotic marionettes until their bodies literally disintegrated.

At another time the Colonel might have thought it a terrible waste of precious ammunition, but not that searing blast-furnace night; a *Walpurgisnacht*.

"Satsugai," the Colonel said calmly, the war still vibrating behind his eyes as he languidly blew out a cloud of aromatic smoke, "you know the history of your country as well as anyone, I daresay. Communism is not a reality for Japan, you know that. There is far too much tradition against that kind of idealized egalitarianism. The idea of commune-izing Japan is ludicrous; the people would never stand for it."

Satsugai's face held a hint of a steely smile. "Whatever I believe is of little importance, *hai?* It is what the Americans believe that matters. They understand the communist menace; they know that we of the *zaibatsu* are this country's greatest bulwark against communism. You can't fight it with liberal reform. Your MacArthur found that out in 1947."

The Colonel's eyes blazed. "We all had high hopes for the future of Japan, then—"

"Hopes, Colonel, are for the naïve," the other said blandly. "Realities must be faced. The mainland is only just across the *genkainada* from Fukuoka. Their threat is quite real, I assure you; they will never stop trying to infiltrate, to subvert the government of Japan. That's why we require firm measures and the strictest enforcement of regulations. Liberalism cannot be tolerated here. Surely you can recognize that."

"I see only a country being twisted for the ends of certain interests, just as it was during the war."

For a moment the eyes of the two men locked and it was as if sparks flew from the dynamic friction of the contact.

"If things had been the way they are now in 1873," Satsugai said softly, "the *seikanron* would never have gone down to defeat." He was speaking of the Genyōsha's advocacy of a military campaign against Korea in that year. Its failure to be passed instigated the first overt act of violence by the Genyōsha against the Meiji government, an attempted assassination of Tomomi Iwakura. "Do not forget, Colonel, that if the *seikanron* had met with success there would have been no fighting in Korea; the communists, when they came, would have been bottled up in Manchuria. As it is"—he shrugged—"the Americans hurl themselves from war to war without any wholeheartedness."

"How do you mean?"

"It's obvious, isn't it? You yourself fought in the jungles of the Asian continent. There American tanks and artillery and even large-scale bombing are not the answer. The communists are far too well organized and, in any event, they have a virtually inexhaustible supply of men."

"Vietnam is no concern of ours." The Colonel's pipe had gone out but he appeared not to notice.

"Excuse me, my dear sir"—Satsugai crossed his legs, smoothing down the center crease of his worsted trousers—"but in that I must say that you are most certainly wrong. If Vietnam falls, Cambodia must certainly be next and then what happens to Thailand? No, the so-called Domino Theory is all too real a possibility; a chilling one, at that."

The Colonel appeared to be half asleep. His cold blue eyes were hooded, the irises dark beneath. His cold pipe was still stuck firmly in the corner of his mouth. He listened to the hypnotic rattle of the rain against the windowpanes, on the eaves, his thoughts filled with history.

So much idealism. It had started out that way, in any case. But MacArthur was such a paranoid bastard. By 1947, the time of the American "reverse course" in Japan, the United States was no longer so desirous of strict war reparations as such. After all, Japan was demilitarized; that was enough. What began to concern them more and more was that Japan should become their watchdog against communism in the Far East and to this end they began two separate but contiguous courses of action. First, they restored many of the formerly suspect powerful right-wing politicians and businessmen to power and, second, they poured millions of dollars into the Japanese economy until now over 80 percent of the old prewar structure and industry were back in operation. In doing so, they allowed a totally *Japanese*-inspired campaign to scour out suspected communists and leftist radicals, doing what they had done in Spain and Iran and South America. Over and over. Only this time, it had hit home.

Outside, the wind had picked up, throwing the rain in hard brittle bursts against the windowpanes. There was no color left in the low sky.

That small but intrepid group of men so full of enthusiasm in 1945, certain that their far-reaching vision for a truly democratized Japan, free from feudal encumbrances, was the correct choice for the country. How naïve we all were! the Colonel thought sadly, echoing Satsugai's words. All of them, all my friends are gone now. He watched the rain streaking the glass like tears, cold and forlorn. A violent eddy of wind caught the wet leaves that had fallen since Ataki had last been at the house, sent them skimming through the air, whirling and spinning like miniature airships of alien design. In his twenty-three years in the Far East, the Colonel never felt more like an alien than he did now. His isolation seemed to him both complete and irreversible. One by one, the members of that inner circle of minds linked in friendship, that core of policy advisers to MacArthur, were either transferred or dismissed. In truth, they were unaware of the political machinations that went on around them or of the increasing instability of MacArthur himself. Still, they had hung on tenaciously, even after the reversal in 1947, hoping against hope that their combined influence could help stem the tide and return the new Japan to the beginnings of democratization. Now, in retrospect, it was so obvious; easy to see just how impotent they had been all along. Policy had been determined on the other side of the world and they were expected to implement, not comment. No one had told them that in the beginning. Terlaine had spoken out and had been summarily dismissed; McKenzie had been crushed, transferred back to the States; and Robinson had left two years ago, retired, having been ground down into the dirt as long as he could take it. Only the Colonel remained, the iron man, outwardly the same. But inside he was sick at heart and terribly disillusioned. He could not bear to believe that his life's work had been utterly meaningless; that what he had fought for so long and with such unwavering intensity would never become a reality.

But the Colonel could not give up, even now; it was simply not in his nature to contemplate such a thing. He had thought

243

that he had been cleverer than all the rest; he had an ace to play, after all, that the others knew nothing about.

It seems, he thought, that I've played the game and lost. The fox somehow outsmarted me. But it's not over yet. It can't be. I won't let it.

The germ of the idea had come to him the day after Satsugai had been arrested by the SCAP Military Police late in 1946. Ostensibly, there was nothing the Colonel could do about it. Satsugai was well known in Japan, a powerful reactionary who was head of one of the monstrous *zaibatsu* combines. It was inevitable that he should come under suspicion and, subsequently, be arrested as a war criminal.

Itami withstood the shame stoically, as she withstood everything else in life. But Cheong was hysterical. That night, as they lay in bed, she pleaded with the Colonel to intervene. He was high up in the SCAP hierarchy, an adviser to General MacArthur himself. Surely there was some way he could help Satsugai.

"My darling," he had said, "matters are not as simple as that. This is a highly charged time. Besides," he added reasonably, "Satsugai may indeed be guilty of all they say he is."

But this only served to further infuriate Cheong. "It does not matter," she said simply. "He is family."

"You mean therefore he is no criminal?"

"Yes."

"Darling, you're talking foolishness."

"Maybe so." Her voice was quite serious, containing the undercurrent of strength the Colonel recognized. "But I tell you that your duty is to your family and if there is a way to help Satsugai you must do it. *Kakujin wa hombun wo tsukusa neba narimasen.*" Everyone must do his duty.

Cheong is a most intelligent person, the Colonel thought, but she can be inordinately stubborn at times. He had known there was no way to deflect her from her purpose; knew, too, that there would be no peace for him at home until he had proved to her that he had done his best to enforce his influence.

He had fallen asleep with that thought in his mind and had awakened just before dawn with the idea blooming already.

There *was* a way to free Satsugai, he was quite certain of that now, but to implement the plan would involve tremendous risk. He had no doubt that he could talk the SCAP tribunal into going along with him. It was purely a matter of whether he wanted to go ahead with it.

In the end, he knew he had little choice. He already understood the precariousness of the advisory board of which he was a member and now he thought of his plan as a kind of insurance policy against the day his job should go sour.

He knew a good deal about Satsugai's background; in fact a good deal more than Satsugai himself was aware. The Fukuoka connection was too obvious to ignore. The Genyōsha had never been an outlaw organization in Japan; records were not too difficult to unearth. The Colonel had taken a clandestine trip south to Kyūshū and had found out the truth. Satsugai was a Genyōsha leader.

At this particular point in time, that sort of information was incendiary. If it came to the attention of the SCAP tribunal, it would not matter how many incriminating documents Satsugai had destroyed in time, he would be executed.

However, the Colonel had absolutely no intention of divulging that piece of information to anyone. In any event, Satsugai's death would serve no purpose. The society would simply elevate another member and go on with its work. That work was totally counterproductive to what the Colonel perceived as the correct course toward Japan's future. He wanted the Genyōsha destroyed. If Satsugai were exonerated, he would be a dog on a leash—the end of which the Colonel had firm hold of. Sooner or later, Satsugai would lead the Colonel home to the center of the Genyōsha.

The Colonel turned his gaze from the weeping glass into the warmth of his study. He watched the slanted Mongol eyes of his adversary, so well trained that he could see nothing below the surface, nothing that the man did not want him to see.

It seemed a long time ago, the Colonel thought now, that I let him go and he has led me nowhere. He has known from the beginning. He knew what I wanted. I have managed to neutralize him as a force but he has otherwise stymied me. The Colonel felt a deep sadness inside himself. It was always his game to win, he thought. I was a fool to think otherwise.

That Satsugai hated him came as no surprise to the Colonel. After all, they were from opposite sides of the political spectrum. And while the Colonel understood better than any Westerner in Japan the importance of the maintenance of its

245

traditions, its heritage, knowing that without those things the country would disintegrate, yet he also understood that the kind of traditionalism that Satsugai represented was as evil and self-serving as anything could be in Japan. This was a country of heroes, he knew, not of villains. Those were few and far between. At that moment as he stared into those baleful eyes across the warm expanse of his study, the Colonel knew that he had missed something elemental in the puzzle. There was a piece missing that was, he was convinced, the key to it all. He had believed that he had pierced Satsugai's secret life many years ago and all his actions since then had stemmed from that assumption. He now suspected that assumption, was angry at himself for having been so easily fooled. He played with me as if I were a child, the Colonel thought furiously.

It gave him little comfort at the moment that, by his intervening, he had put Satsugai in an agonizing situation. He was in debt to the Colonel, a man he despised. It was an intolerable situation for a Japanese, yet Satsugai bore it well. I have to give him that, the Colonel thought.

My God, he thought, what is it that he has hidden from me all these years? The old warrior is shrewd yet. And then the Colonel understood what he must do. There had already been too much time wasted in an obviously fruitless plot. He had, as Satsugai himself had just said, to face reality. And the reality of this situation was that he must break the stalemate in whatever way was possible. There was only one way now.

The Colonel knew only too well that, as far as Satsugai was concerned, he was invulnerable. He could, for instance, insult Satsugai and the other would not—could not—take action against him. There was an obligation to be met. Satsugai must grin and bear it. The reverse, however, did not hold true.

For a brief moment, the Colonel was filled with a deep regret. Nicholas was still so young. There had been so little time and there were promises he had made that could not now be kept.

The Colonel stared out at the wide expanse of his property, the trees dripping with moisture, bending in the wind. He looked for the wren but it had long gone, perhaps preferring the storm to idleness. So much beauty out there, but this day he could feel no joy.

"What have you learned from the *Go Rin No Sho?*" Kansatsu said one day at the *dōjō.*

"Some of it is obviously quite useful," Nicholas said, "though it's mostly common sense."

"Many consider it a revelatory work." Kansatsu's tone was entirely neutral, giving Nicholas no clue as to whether or not *he* thought it was so important. His eyes glittered like glass, quite opaque. Behind him the long afternoon slid into the muffled mauve of twilight. The sun was lost in a steep bank of haze; the resulting light, reflective and diffuse, suffused the sky, laminated the trees until the world seemed monochromatic.

"I almost wish you hadn't given it to me."

"Could you be more specific?"

"Well, there is something—I don't know—disturbing about it."

Kansatsu said nothing, merely stood waiting. Behind him, the soft clash of *bokken,* the exhaled breaths in unison, filled the place.

"Some might say its purity is its ultimate virtue," Nicholas said carefully. "But, to me, it's more of a monomania. There is something intrinsically dangerous in that."

"Can you tell me what, precisely?"

"Exclusion."

As if he had been thinking of this all the time, Kansatsu said, "Do you know anything of the life of Musashi?"

"Not really, no."

"Miyamoto Musashi was born in 1584," Kansatsu said seriously. "As you no doubt know, this was not the best of times for Japan. There was and had been terrible internal strife brought about by the constant internecine warfare waged by the numerous *daimyo.*

"Musashi was a *ronin,* little more than a brigand, really. His family came from the south, in Kyūshū, but by the age of twenty-one he had traveled north to Kyoto and there fought his first battle, decimating a family which had, years before, been responsible for his father's demise.

"There are many, many tales told concerning Musashi and one must be most careful in reading these accounts. As is the case with most historical figures from this country's feudal past, Musashi's history is awash with myth. This blurring of fact and fancy is all well and good for the reader wishing simple entertainment. But for the serious student of history—and this should include all who study bujutsu—it can be a dangerous trap."

"But myth sometimes sustains the samurai," Nicholas said.

"Not so." Kansatsu's tone was emphatic. "It is history which must sustain the warrior. History and duty, Nicholas. Nothing more. Myth cannot enter into it, for myth distorts judgment. Even the senses become infected then.

"In bujutsu we deal with most serious matters. The defense of life, yes, but that is not all. Methods of dealing death occupy us daily and there is, literally, no known number to that catalog. One cannot be taught these things without the concomitant use of responsibility. And myth is the chief eroder of this responsibility. Without *bushido*, you see, we would be nothing more than ninja, common criminals stalking the streets. And it is so easy to slip into myth. So very easy."

He put his hand out, indicating that Nicholas should sit. "You have come a long way," he continued. "Your technique is flawless and your capacity for learning seems inexhaustible. However, I believe you have gone as far as you can here. There remains for you but one more hurdle and it is the most difficult. In fact, I must tell you that most students who have come this far never go any further.

"Nicholas, you must now find that hurdle within yourself and make the leap. I can no longer aid or even guide you. Either it will be there or it will not."

"Does this mean you want me to leave the *ryu*?" Nicholas found that he was having difficulty swallowing.

Kansatsu shook his head. "I mean nothing of the sort. You are perfectly free to stay here for as long as you wish."

Nicholas knew that he was missing something and, furiously, he backtracked over the conversation, trying to think what it was. Kansatsu did not seem disappointed with him. On the contrary, there was a subtle undercurrent of excitement running through him. Think! What had he missed?

Kansatsu stood up. "In lieu of a lesson today," he said. "I'd like you to give a demonstration for the class." He stared down at Nicholas. "Come along now."

He went out into the center of the floor, clapped his hands

together once. All sound, all motion immediately ceased and all heads turned expectantly toward him, student and *sensei* alike.

Kansatsu picked four students at what appeared to be at random. They were all last-year students and among the biggest physically in the *ryu*. All were older than Nicholas.

Kansatsu turned and beckoned to Nicholas, who walked out to stand beside him. In his right hand he carried a *bokken*. "Please form up around Nicholas," Kansatsu said to the students; they moved around him in a rough circle. Kansatsu beckoned to a *sensei*, who gave over his *bokken* to the master. Kansatsu delivered this up to Nicholas. "Now," he whispered so that only Nicholas could hear, "we shall see how well you have digested the words of the Niten *ryu*, Musashi's school."

He backed away, leaving Nicholas, a *bokken* in each hand, surrounded by the four students. They were all armed with single *bokken*. All of them had been at the *ryu* longer than he.

Darkness falling like a final curtain and he encircled; the stealthy pad of bare feet against polished wood; a sun orbited by four bright moons.

The dragonfly.

It was but one of the *tai-sabaki*, the circular movements consisting of glides and spins developed by Musashi's Two Heavens *ryu*.

He had seen this and others performed to perfection by Kansatsu countless times. He had read about these in numerous texts which the *sensei* had given him. He had, even, practiced some on his own. But never in combat.

He must let the strategy of the others dictate his first movements, for only by the convergence of their attacks could he successfully use the *tai-sabaki* and only the *tai-sabaki* would give him a victory against four opponents.

Two came at him, one on each side, both raising their *bokken* in the traditional two-handed kenjutsu grip. Crying aloud, they slashed at him simultaneously.

It was the reverse butterfly. He whirled in an arc and, as he did so, his right-handed weapon swept down, slamming against one student's thighs. At the same time, the second weapon was rising and he continued the swirling motion of his torso, sweeping the rising *bokken* against the second student's windpipe. Both crashed to the ground, were replaced by the second set of adversaries. He had half a mind to use the waterwheel here but changed his mind as the vectors changed, feinting it only.

He split them, whirling still, and, his back arched, his right *bokken* stabbed end first into the midsection of the student on his left while his left-hand weapon blurred upward, slamming into the last student's. His *bokken* clattered to the floor. It was the interlacing cross, one of the most difficult of the *tai-sabaki*.

He returned to stillness, his *bokken* poised, quivering the air as if they had a life of their own and wished now to see more action.

"Saigō," he heard Kansatsu call. The four students quitted the field. Saigō stepped into it. He came to the *ryu* now less and less frequently. Nicholas did not know to which *ryu* he belonged; no one seemed to. But he knew that it was none of the ones in the Tokyo area.

Without warning, Saigō ran at Nicholas. His *katana* was still sheathed but in a blur it was out, extending outward and down toward Nicholas. Saigō had become adept at, among other things, iaijutsu, the art of the "fast draw." The object was to incorporate the unsheathing of one's *katana* into the actual thrust against an opponent. The *iai sensei* could kill his enemy before that person was ever aware that he had drawn his weapon.

One moment Saigō was unarmed, the next—perhaps a tenth of a second later—he had struck with lethal force. But even as he had used the *iai* draw Nicholas had been swiveling backward on his right foot so that he now faced Saigō with his left side only. The blow, which had been meant for Nicholas' heart, now swept down into empty air and with his left-hand *bokken* Nicholas made contact, sweeping the *katana*'s blade up and away from him, swiveled again so that for an instant his back was to his opponent, driving the blade away still, using the other's momentum. Then he had completed the circular sweep and his right-hand *bokken* slashed into Saigō's exposed left side. The waterwheel.

He stood now with the entire class watching him, his feet spread, his *bokken* on either side of him, staring down at Saigō's sprawled form. There would be, he knew, a wicked purple welt raising the flesh where he had hit the other which would stay with him for more than a week.

There was absolute silence in the room; the kind of still-ness that weighs on the ears until it becomes in itself painful.

Nicholas saw nothing but the face of his cousin staring up at him. Never in his life had he seen a look which contained so much hate. Nicholas had caused him to lose face in front of the *ryu;* he, a graduate, felled by one of the pupils. The intensity of their silent private war was such that for a moment it appeared as if lightning might light the room.

Then Kansatsu had clapped his hands twice and the on-lookers broke up; class was out for the day.

Nicholas found that he was trembling, the muscles jump-ing as if out of control under the sheath of his skin. Tension and adrenalin both still coursed through him, having been released in enormous quantities by the stress situation. His mind knew that that was over but his body needed more time to accommodate itself to a return to normalcy.

He breathed deeply, in and out. It was like a shudder.

When he returned home that evening, it was not any of the servants who opened the door at his approach. Nor was it Cheong. It was, rather, Yukio.

He had not seen her in three years and then it was only one brief afternoon at a family funeral. It had been three and a half years since their incendiary meeting and he had never forgotten her.

She bowed. "Good evening, Nicholas." She wore a dove-gray kimono with platinum-colored threads running through it vertically. It had a midnight-blue wheel-and-spoke pattern that recalled the signs of the feudal *daimyo.*

He bowed in return. "Good evening, Yukio."

She stood aside for him to enter, her eyes on the floor in front of her. "You are surprised to see me."

He put his bag down, never taking his eyes off her face. "I haven't seen you in years."

"Aunt Itami brought me this afternoon while you were at the *dōjō.* I came up to stay with them but the house is being partially remodeled, including the spare bedroom."

He took her through the house, out the back *shōji.* They stepped out into the night in the Zen garden.

It was clear, just a few stray clouds rising like wisps of smoke low on the horizon. The full moon was enormous, its reflected light turning the air aqueous; everything was

251

bathed in blue shadows. He watched the soft light limn her profile, throwing her eyes into deep shadow. She might have been a statue at the Shinto shrine hidden within the cryptomeria. They might have been underwater.

A nightingale called softly from the treetops high over their heads, and farther away came the long lonely hoot of a snow owl.

"I've never been to Kyoto," he said. It was where she lived.

"You must come sometime." Her head turned slightly. She was staring at the mountains of the rocks, raising themselves like living entities above the lawn of round stones. Her voice was like velvet in the night. They stood quite still, not touching. "It's very beautiful."

Not as beautiful as you, Nicholas thought. He felt his heart beating hard. "I still remember what happened."

She turned to face him and the moonlight glinted off her pupils. "What do you mean?"

Now he felt a fool. "At the party." He paused. "When we danced...."

She laughed a bit self-consciously. "Oh, that. I had forgotten."

He felt a bit deflated. He had felt before that part of her coming here was because of him. He saw how idiotic that notion was now. That one incident had happened three and a half years ago. Why should she remember it?

"Was Saigō at the *dōjō* today?"

"Yes. I hadn't seen him for some time. He's joined another *ryu*, I expect."

"Perhaps that's why he goes to Kyūshū a lot."

He stared at her. "Kyūshū?"

She nodded. "It's my uncle Satsugai's doing, I'm certain. They're always plotting this or that when they're together. I can't imagine that Saigō would get it into his head on his own to go so far away. Anyway, it's a secret, I know that much."

"How do you know that?"

"I asked Aunt Itami once and she made out as if she hadn't heard a word I'd said."

"I'm sure it's nothing, then."

Yukio merely shrugged, putting her arms across her breasts. "Can we go in? I'm hungry."

They went into the house and Nicholas excused himself. He went off to his room and, throwing off his dirty robe,

252

padded into the bathroom. He turned on the shower, stepped inside the stall. Someone as traditional as Itami would, perhaps, prefer the bath but Nicholas had no such predispositions.

It was good to feel the hot water on his body and he began to soap up, his thoughts on the day at the *dōjō*. He had wanted to talk to Kansatsu after the match with Saigō but that had proved impossible. Why hadn't he mentioned the match to Yukio? There had been ample opportunity when she had brought up Saigō. He shrugged, dismissing the thought.

He turned his head, curious. A shadow had been thrown against the frosted glass of the shower stall. It condensed in size. The person was coming into the bathroom.

He turned off the water, opened the door.

He stood perfectly still. Water beaded his skin, glistening in the fluorescent light of the bathroom, which had turned her skin opalescent.

"You are quite beautiful," Yukio said. She was naked. She held a baize bath towel over one arm. She did not offer it to him.

He watched her face for any sign of what she might be thinking. He thought of her words. He saw hunger in her eyes.

He was seventeen and she two years his senior. In terms of chronology it wasn't much but now it seemed like light-years. Despite all his training, his careful schooling, his cool intellect, he felt lost beside her, as if she were some doorway to a world for which he had been totally unprepared.

She took one step toward him. Her lips opened and she said something. It might have been as mundane as "Do you want this?" He couldn't tell. One leg was extended in front of the other, as his had been earlier at the *dōjō* as the beginning of the interlacing cross. Her tiny ankle, the flesh of the calf, the extended knee, the long sweep of her thigh.

Something inside him, high up at the top of his brain, seemed to rise up, beginning to float away, as if someone unknown had chopped at the last cables holding him to the earth. It went twisting away, diminishing in size with such rapidity that he forgot that it had ever been a part of him.

"Come here," he said thickly and his hand reached out, brushing the towel from her arm. It pooled on the glistening tile floor as her arms lifted to him.

"Yukio." But a breath.

253

Her breasts were high and round, the dark nipples long and already very hard. Her narrow waist, her creamy belly. The dark mound of her mons was highly arched.

Her arms came around him and he enclosed her open mouth.

She slid her body against his, not using her hand at all, only her lips against his own, down his neck, back upward again, almost desperate in their urgency. Her breasts rubbed along the wet flesh of his chest, picking up the moisture; her mound was against him, gently massaging.

Her lips were at his ear and he heard her whisper, "Turn on the water."

He half turned, reaching behind them both to spin the taps. Hot water gushed down, inundating them, and as he turned back to her, he found that he was already deep inside her. He gasped. By what magic had she accomplished that? Sensations rolled like liquid thunder upward from his groin, engulfing him.

As he began to move against her, he saw her head float back, upturned, the wet hair cascading down like a stream at midnight. Her face was in the rush of water, her eyes rolling backward, and her mouth wide open in a soundless scream. He could hear panting. Her arms came up, reaching over their bobbing heads to grasp the slippery chrome spout. Her knuckles turned white. Her thighs rose until they were locked around his waist and he was supporting her with his body. Her belly ground in hard circular movements as if she could not get enough of him and he was obliged to put his hands on her waist so that she wouldn't throw herself from their wet connection. The fierce heavings of her body mounted. It was like trying to hang on to a wild animal in the shuddering throes of death.

She began to scream now and abruptly he understood why she had wanted the water on. The pleasure was becoming unbearable and his legs began to tremble with the effort and the straining for release. Dimly he became aware that she was saying something to him.

"Hit me," she moaned. "Hit me."

He thought that in this state he must have misheard her but she repeated it over and over, a litany. Her breasts shook, rivulets of moisture ran down her supple flesh. Her body was arched backward, her hands still gripping the spout, their bodies pistoning frantically.

She was gasping and moaning and he didn't think that he could hold out much longer. Her body seemed bottom-heavy. "Please!" she cried to him. "Please, please, please!" But he would not raise a hand to her. "I know," she gasped out, her lips against his ear. The hot rain crashing against them, her hard nipples scraping his chest. "I know what happened today—at the *dōjō*." Her voice was ragged and there were uneven gaps between the words. Still, he heard her. "I know—oh! Hit me, darling. Hit me!" And then, savagely, "I fucked Saigō, just as I'm fucking you now!"

He struck her then, as she wanted him to, indeed, as she needed him to do.

"Oh!" she cried out, her body arching. "Oh, oh, oh, darling! I'm going!"

And, in that moment, he felt a ring of muscles deep inside her gripping him, clamping his flesh in exquisite torment, and he too cried out, his legs giving way at last. Her fists slipped from the spout and they collapsed to the bottom of the stall, the water on them, all around them, the steam rising. Her arms came around him, pulling him hard against her, both of them still in orgasm.

The clouds were on fire.

The sun, sliding downward in its arc, broke across the oblique shoulder of Fuji, turning the sky the color of crimson. As quickly as it had come, the flare faded as the sun dipped behind the mountain and all that was left was traces of pink, slowly healing wounds on the undersides of the passing clouds. Soon they had turned gray. The lights were lit.

Kansatsu sat cross-legged in the center of the *dōjō*. Nicholas faced him. Nothing was said. The students, the other *sensei* had departed for the night. These two stayed on, breathing.

"Tell me," Kansatsu said at last, "what you have learned from the *Go Rin No Sho*." His eyes remained closed.

"There is good in it," said Nicholas. "And evil."

"That is rare, Nicholas."

"On the contrary, *sensei*."

"So?"

"I don't think anything in life is all good or all bad."

Kansatsu opened his eyes and nodded. "You have learned well, Nicholas. You are an astute student. It is a bad idea to rely too heavily on one discipline or one strategy set. This quickly becomes ingrained and one's thinking stagnates. Rely only on the situation that presents itself. If you let notions of strategy dictate to you, you will surely be defeated." He closed his eyes again. "You would be surprised, Nicholas, at the number of quite good students who make that mistake. *Sensei*, too."

For a time there was silence between them. From outside Nicholas heard the muffled cough of a car starting. It drove off, the beams from its headlights swinging briefly across his field of vision. Darkness returned. A plover twittered, took off in a soft clatter.

Nicholas cleared his throat. "I have read it all."

"And what do you think?"

"To be truthful, I don't know what to think."

"Do the ninja interest you, Nicholas?"

"Yes."

"Then why do you hesitate?"

"I didn't know I had."

"Then you had better look inside yourself."

He thought for a moment. "I guess I feel I should have said no."

"Ah."

"Ninjutsu seems a forbidden topic."

"Arcane, yes. Forbidden, no." Kansatsu stared at Nicholas across the small space between them. "Even here in Japan, there is surprisingly little known about the ninja. They are from a segment of society about which no Japanese can be proud. But ninjutsu is an ancient art. It came from China, or so it is commonly said. I do not think that anyone could tell you with absolute certainty.

"The ninja were not bound by the Way of the Warrior. *Bushido* was only a word to them. Their rise was swift. Because they were so successful, the *bushi* used them more and more. As their wealth increased, so did the sophistication and diversity of their techniques. There came a time, then, when the samurai came to the ninja to learn. Thus the Way became perverted.

"There are many *ryu* in Japan. More than in any official governmental count. Among these, the variety of disciplines taught is virtually limitless. Good and evil are sometimes propounded indiscriminately." He did not have to ask if Nicholas was following his line of thought. Darkness, now; the clouds obscuring the moon. Only man-made lights shone.

"To be a true champion, Nicholas, one must explore the darkness, too."

That evening, Cheong took Nicholas aside. They went into the Colonel's study. It smelled of tobacco smoke and leather. Along with the kitchen, it was a Western room in an otherwise very traditional Japanese house.

Cheong sat sideways on the high-backed wooden chair in front of the Colonel's roll-top desk. Nicholas sat on the leather couch, near her.

"You are happy that Yukio has come to stay with us." It was not a question.

"Yes," he said truthfully. "Is there anything wrong with that?"

Cheong smiled. "You are growing up but you are still my child. I think I have a right to ask. You don't have to answer me, you know."

His eyes dropped to his hands for a moment. "I know that," he said softly.

She leaned forward, enclosed his hands in hers. "My darling, you have nothing to fear from me. Whatever you and Yukio do is between the two of you. Your father may not approve but he sees different things than we do. He is still a soldier and, therefore, mistrusts everyone and everything."

Nicholas looked at her. "He mistrusts Yukio. But what—"

Cheong shook her head. "It doesn't matter, don't you see that? It's a blind spot he has. Never mind. I'm quite certain he mistrusted So-Peng in the beginning."

She turned and, opening a drawer in the desk with a key, she produced the dragon-and-tiger box that was So-Peng's parting gift to her and the Colonel. With deft, economical movements of her fingers she opened the box.

"You see," she said in a hushed voice, "there are fifteen." She meant the emeralds. "There were sixteen, originally. One bought this house." She looked up at him. "I'm sure your father told you the story of this present." Nicholas nodded and she continued. "What he didn't tell you was its meaning. I'm not certain whether even he knows it fully." She shrugged. "And if he did, he would most likely dismiss the idea. He is a most pragmatic man, your father." She smiled. "One of his few faults, I'm afraid."

She put the opened box with its glittering contents in Nicholas' lap.

"You are free to use six of these. To convert into money if your need is sufficient. No, hear me out. I want you to understand this fully; I think you can accept what I'm going to tell you." She took a deep breath. "There must never be less than nine emeralds in here. Ever. No matter the reason, you must not use more than six.

"This is a mystical box, Nicholas. It has certain powers." She paused, as if waiting. "I see you're not smiling. Good. I believe it as did my father, So-Peng. He was a great and wise man in all matters, Nicholas. He was no fool. He knew well that there exist on the Asian continent many things which defy analysis; which, perhaps, have no place in the modern world. They relate to another set of Laws; they are timeless." She shrugged again. "So I believe." She took her hands away from the box, watched his face. "You are old enough now to form your own opinions about the world and its mysteries. If you believe, then the power will be there for you when someday you need it."

Night. Nicholas in the living room, cross-legged in front of the window.

High in the sky, clear now of clouds, the full moon sent reflected light scattering down across the treetops and, closer to him, the formal garden. Intense black shadows streaked the window as the tall pine near the front of the house was illuminated as if by some celestial spotlight. Now and again, as the wind disturbed the branches, the shadows moved up and down, up and down, the motion of a fairyland boat from tales his mother used to tell him as he was falling asleep years ago. That time seemed long gone and Nicholas wondered now whether this was something all people felt: that childhood belonged to another, simpler time when all decisions were minor and seemed of little consequence.

In times gone by, on sleepless nights, that lone pine had been his protector. He knew every configuration, every angle of its branches, every knot along its thick trunk. Now it seemed to him to have been transmogrified. He saw it as an old soldier, a guardian in the night, a friend and an ally. *To be a true champion...*

His world was changing so swiftly now.

Haragei allowed him to become aware of her presence as she stepped into the room. He did not move. He heard her coming toward him. Softly. Softly. Appalled, he found himself getting hard. He willed his erection down but his body would not listen.

She sat down gracefully, facing him, away from the moonlight. Her face black in the dense shadows, her long blue-black hair haloed faintly in platinum light. He thought he could see her entire body beat with the rhythm of her pulse.

He was so acutely aware of her, it was almost painful. The musk of her body mingled with a perfume he could not identify; a certain heat that transmitted itself physically. But there was more, an almost tangible force. He felt enveloped by her aura.

The house was so still that he could hear the white noise soughing in his inner ear like an internal storm.

He stood up so abruptly that he felt rather than saw her start. Reaching down for her hand, he pulled her up and, opening a *shōji*, took her outside.

Unmindful of the cold, he took her to the periphery of their property, along the verge of the cryptomeria wood, searching for the half-hidden path Itami had shown to him years ago.

At length he found it and plunged with her headlong into the forest. There was no light to speak of, just dim luminous patches like odd floating flora where the moonlight penetrated the green canopy high above their heads. Cicadas called shrilly and, to one side, came a soft scuffling of leaves, a pair of bright red eyes.

They flew along the jungle trail, Nicholas guiding them unerringly as if he were a bat with radar. They leaped over roots, ducked under black swinging branches and, at last, broke through into the moon-drenched clearing. Before them was the circular path and the closed double doors of the rearing shrine.

She dragged him back to the grass verge, pulling him down beside her. "Now," she whispered fiercely. "I can't wait anymore."

Her robe parted slightly. She was incredible. Her flesh glowed as if with an inner light. He could not keep his hands off her. He leaned forward, parting the robe farther. He stroked her thighs until she moaned and reached out with both arms, drew him over her. Her panting was hot in his ear as his mouth opened, enveloping one nipple, as much of the surrounding breast as he could take. He sucked hard, felt her indrawn breath, the hot scoring of her nails on a line down his ribs. Her thighs surrounded him, her flesh scorching, drawing him inward to her moist center. She sounded as if she were choking. He could smell her strongly on the night air. Moving snakelike down her writhing body, using his tongue and his lips until he reached her high mound. He raised up, then descended to the soft flesh of her inner thighs. He moved so slowly that, at length, he heard her cry out in longing, felt her fingers in his hair, pulling him up her.

Her buttocks were off the soft damp ground in an attempt to get him to suck her there, where she desired it the most. But he held on, circling, circling, so hard he thought he might never be soft again, until finally he moved, stabbing through the wet dark hair, spreading the flesh beneath. Her hands turned to fists and the cords of her neck tautened. She screamed again and again. There was no stopping the convulsing of her sweat-flecked body.

"I was born to be something," she said much later, "more than what I am now."

The cryptomeria rustled contentedly above their heads. The earth was soft beneath their spent bodies.

"I'm nothing now." Her voice was so soft it could have been the night wind. "Nothing but a reflection." He did not understand that. "All my life no one has said one word to me that's meant anything." She turned her head in the crook of his arm. "It's all been lies."

"Even your parents?"

"I have no parents." She turned over, her buttocks against his thighs.

"Are they dead or..."

"Did they leave me, do you mean? My father died in the war. He was Satsugai's brother. My uncle never approved of the marriage in the first place."

"What happened to your mother?"

"I don't know. No one ever said. Perhaps Satsugai gave her a sum of money to leave."

A whippoorwill trilled, seeming far away. The air was dense with mist though there seemed few clouds in the sky. The moon was low, bloated, tinctured orange.

"I'm surprised Satsugai didn't take you in," he said.

"You are?" She gave a tiny bitter laugh. "I'm not. Itami wanted me, I know that. But Satsugai arranged for a couple to take care of me in Kyoto." She was silent for a time, thinking. "I asked Aunt Itami once and she said that Satsugai thought they would have many children of their own and he didn't want anything to interfere with his family. It didn't turn out that way, obviously."

"Then you do have parents."

"There's something odd about that household." She was still talking about her uncle. "I can't put my finger on it. It involves Satsugai and Saigō. Itami's not part of it, though I'm sure she knows what's going on." There was a dry fluttering over their heads as a plover took off southward. "I think it has something to do with where Saigō goes."

"In Kyūshū."

"Yes."

"It's a *ryu*, I'll bet."

She turned over, her eyes luminous and huge in the dark. The heat of her body, its musk penetrated him. "But why travel so far? There are plenty of *ryu* in the Tokyo area."

There are many ryu *in Japan.* Kansatsu's words came to him as clearly as a tolling bell. Did he know? Good and evil. White and black. Yin and yang. *One must explore the darkness, too.*

"It must be a very special *ryu*."

"What?"

He'd said it so softly, thinking out loud, that even this close she had not heard him. He repeated what he had said.

"But what kind?" she wanted to know.

Nicholas shrugged. "I'd need to know the town he is going to."

"But I can find out!" she said excitedly, sitting up on one elbow. "He leaves tonight for Kyūshū. I'll only need to take a peek at his train ticket."

"Would you do it?"

She gave him a little conspiratorial smile. Lights danced in her eyes. "If you wanted me to."

He watched her for a moment, then lay back, hands underneath his head. "I want to know something." His throat felt tight. "I want to know if what you said...before is true. Did you sleep with Saigō?"

"Does it matter?"

"Yes, it matters."

She threw her arms around his neck. "Oh, Nicholas. Don't be so serious always."

"Did you?"

"It might have happened—once."

He sat up, staring at her. "Might?"

"All right. Yes. But—it just happened."

"The way it just happened with us," he said nastily.

"Oh no." Her eyes looked into his. "That's not the way it happened at all. He's nothing like you."

"You mean you planned the whole thing with me?" His voice was demanding.

Her eyes flickered down for a fraction of a second. "I—didn't know what to think when Aunt Itami told me she was taking me here. I remembered I wanted to fuck you that night on the dance floor but that was—"

"You told me you didn't remember that!" His tone of indignation concealed his inner delight.

Her eyes danced. "I lied about that." She smiled and stuck out her tongue, a very un-Japanese gesture. "I didn't want to spoil the surprise. I knew the moment I saw you again what I wanted to do."

"I had no hint when we went out in the garden."

She shrugged. "I'm two different people. You've seen both sides."

"What was it like for you, growing up?"

"Why do you ask?"

He burst out laughing. "Because I'm interested in you. Why? Do you think I'm after something?"

"Everyone's always after something."

"Not everyone," he said softly, pulling her close. "I'm not." He kissed her with closed lips. "I care about you, Yukio. A great deal."

She laughed. "Well, at least you didn't say you love me."

"I might," he said seriously. "I don't know yet."

She tossed her head. "Oh, come off it. You know you don't have to say those things with me. They're meaningless. You'll get what you want, don't you know that?"

"I don't understand you."

"I told you before," she said patiently. "I don't need to hear those things. I don't need that illusion. We give each other pleasure. That's enough for me."

"Is that how it was with Saigō, too?" he said harshly. "I meant what I said. I do care about you. About what happens to you. How you feel. If you're happy or if you're sad."

She stared at him for a long time as if she could find no words to utter. She was watching him carefully. At length she settled back onto the grass.

"When I was a little girl," she said in a small voice, "we'd go into the mountains for the summer, to a small town perched high up on the sloping wooded side. The houses, I remember, were all on stilts. It was the first time I'd seen anything like that. It looked like a town out of a storybook.

"My foster parents never had much time for me though Satsugai gave them enough money each month. They never wanted children. So I had a lot of time to myself. I remember that during the days I'd sit in the tall grass, hearing the cicadas in my ears—the shrill metallic sound of the locusts late in the summer..." She breathed deeply, staring up at the nodding foliage of the cryptomeria. "The afternoons seemed endless. I'd sit on the mountainside, overlooking the valley. There were two long furrows etched into the foliage, brown and sere, mysteriously bare, as if some giant had scored the land in anger. I used to spend hours wondering what had made those cruel marks."

"The war, perhaps," Nicholas said.

"Yes. I never thought of that." She turned her head away from him. "But I'd get beaten for staying away so long even though I knew they didn't want me around. There was never any compassion. Never even any understanding. I was like an alien to them, some freak, a miniature adult. It seemed as if they had never been children themselves, had no conception of what it was like to be a child."

"Yukio," he said softly, leaning down to kiss her tenderly.

When they broke apart, she said, "And then there was the bamboo grove. It was somewhat farther down the mountainside. I discovered it quite by accident, early on, when I was lost one afternoon. I used to creep out of the house at night; the darkness stifled me as I lay in bed, sleepless. It became solid, a crushing weight pressing against my eyelids until I had to get out of there.

"It was quite near a stream which bubbled constantly.

When there was a moon it looked like it was made of silver. The water was so frigid, it numbed your mouth.

"It was like being at a shrine, standing in that grove, the tall straight bamboo rising like columns over your head. Their tops sometimes speared the huge orange harvest moon late in the summer, when the locusts were at their most shrill." She moved against him as if making herself more comfortable. He felt her bare flesh against his. "It was the only place I could call my own. My secret place. I had sex there for the first time." He felt the musculature of her body beginning to tremble as if she were cold. "I brought a boy there. He lived on a nearby farm. It was his first time, too, I think. He'd only seen the cattle do it and he wasn't very good. He was so nervous, wanting to do it the way he'd seen the horses performing. He was so excited, he went all over my thigh."

"In the West," Nicholas said, "they say, 'I'm coming.' Here, we say, 'I'm going.' There's a complete reversal."

"With death, too," she whispered, "I've heard it said. Westerners don't understand *seppuku*, do they? They'll turn outward, instead of inward, jump off a building—"

"Or blow some poor bastard's head off before they turn the gun on themselves."

"Odd, isn't it?" She giggled. "Perhaps they're barbarians, after all." But she shivered nonetheless.

"Don't let's talk of death," he said, holding her.

"No," she whispered. "We won't." She reached between his thighs, caught gentle hold of him, stroking.

"Is that all you can think of?" he said thickly.

"It's all I have," she said in a moan.

Fourth Ring

THE FIRE BOOK

West Bay Bridge / New York City

SUMMER PRESENT

No, no, no, no!" she said, laughing. "Let's just forget all about it."

She ran at him instead of away from him as she had been doing. She leaped in a shallow dive, skidding across the top of a sand dune, wrapped her arms about his ankles, bringing him down.

Justine laughed again, half atop him. Nicholas spit sand out of his mouth, rolled over on his back.

"Very funny!"

She jumped on him, on all fours, and they spun about on the dark sand. A cool breeze came in off the sea, ruffling their hair. The porch lights from the house were diffused by the ground mist, haloed, comforting.

Her face was very close to his, her eyes wide. He could see the red motes as they caught the light. Her long hair was like a bridge between them. Her long delicate fingers were on his cheeks. They had the firmness, the lightness of touch of a sculptor's hands. "I don't want you to be sad, Nicholas," she said softly.

He kissed her lightly.

"I'm here."

"I know you are."

"It's a big thing for me to say. And mean." She was totally serious now, the playful mood had slipped away. "I had a lot of time to think about...things."

"You mean in bed."

She shook her head. "No. In the water. It wasn't my life

267

that flashed before me." She laughed but it was a rueful sound. "There was one time when I didn't think I was going to come back up. I had been fantasizing about you while I was swimming. You know, a harmless kind of thing." Her eyes were almost out of focus, she was so close to him. "That's not what I thought about when I was under. I thought about what it would be like never to see you again." Her voice was so soft now that, despite her nearness, he could barely make out what she was saying. She swallowed hard as if the words were sticking in her throat. "I'm frightened. Frightened of what I'm telling you. It's one thing to admit to the feeling, quite another to voice it, you know?" She gave him a long hard stare. "I love you," she said. "I can't think of anything else when I'm near you. I usually like to go to certain places, be with specific people, but I don't care about any of that when I'm with you. I know that sounds juvenile and romantic but—"

He laughed. "Romantic, yes. Juvenile, no. And anyway, what's so terrible about being a romantic? I am. Maybe there aren't many of us left, though."

Her eyes were clear and searching. "Do you love me, Nick? I want you to be honest. It's all right if you don't. I just need to know the truth."

He did not know what to say. His mind was alight with memories both pleasurable and painful and he knew then that Yukio was still not gone from him. He felt like a salmon struggling upstream, fiercely fighting the current. But he was no fish and he wondered why he was doing it. What was he fighting, anyway? And what made it so important?

He felt that he had the answers to those questions inside of him if only he could pin them down. He still stung from the jibe Croaker had given him in the restaurant and he was angry at himself that it had affected him so. What if Croaker had been right? How deeply had he been affected by Terry's and Ei's deaths? Surely he felt *something*. He must. He was no machine. But he could summon no tears. Perhaps there were other ways to grieve; he knew he was like his mother in that respect. He was far too controlled to allow certain emotions to surface. But with that he was denying a part of himself and that could prove to be disastrous. Without full understanding of himself, he could control no situation. He could be champion of nothing, not the light, nor the dark. That thought made him jump as if someone had pricked him.

An idea rippled like a banner at the edge of his consciousness....

"What are you thinking?"

His eyes focused to see her. There was concern on her face. "You shouldn't make sacrifices," he said. "Not for me, not for anybody. It can be dangerous."

"Damn it! I'm not making sacrifices. Not anymore. I'm through with all that. I won't give anything up for you. Not until I'm quite certain it's what *I* want." Her eyes glittered, fine pinpoints of energy in the darkness. "Is it so awful that you satisfy me? That I'm content with that? Does part of you rebel against that notion?"

She had cut him to the quick without realizing it. "Christ, what made you say that?" He sat up, feeling his heart hammering.

"Because it's true?" She tried to look in his eyes. "I don't know. But I do know how your body reacts to mine. That's communication on the most basic level, the way it was done a million years ago before there were books to talk about or films or plays, any entertainment. When people just had each other. I want to know why you reject that out of hand. Don't you trust your body to tell you what's right? It knows better than your mind what's good for you." She laughed. "I can't believe it. You of all people. You've been working with your body all your life and still you don't trust it."

"You don't know anything about it," he said shortly.

"Oh, I don't?" She sat up. "Then you tell me. Explain it to me simply so my poor female brain can understand."

"Don't be childish."

"It isn't me who's being childish, Nick. Just listen to yourself. You're terrified of revealing anything of yourself to someone."

"Didn't you ever think there's a good reason for that?"

"Oh yes. That's why I'm asking you what it is."

"Maybe it's none of your business."

"Right. All right," she flared. "I can see how far I'm going to get with you."

"Nowhere, Justine. You don't own me."

"This is what I get for being honest with you."

"You want honesty?" Knew he shouldn't do it and didn't care. "I met your father in the city today."

Her head came up. She looked incredulous. "You met my father? How?"

"He picked me up in his limo outside the station. I got the first class treatment."

She stood up. "I don't want to hear about this." Her voice was abruptly harsh. She remembered San Francisco all too clearly. Rage built up inside her. She felt impotent against him. Always had. Always.

"I think you should," he said cruelly. Some part of him egged him on, reveling in the pained expression on her face.

"No!" she cried, putting her palms against her ears. She wheeled away from him.

He got up and went after her, across the cool sand. "He wanted to know all about us. He knows all about you. What you've been doing. What you haven't."

"God damn him!" She slipped at the crest of a dune, pulled herself up, whirled on him. Her eyes were feral sparks, as large as beacons. She was white with rage.

"Christ but you're both bastards! Him for doing it and you for telling me. You're a real sonovabitch, you know that?"

All he could think of was pushing her away now. "He thought I might be another one like Chris—"

"Shut up! Shut up, you cocksucker!"

But he pursued her relentlessly. "He offered me a job, and you know, the joke of it is I took it. I'm working for him now."

"How could you do this to me?" she cried. She wasn't talking about the job. "My God! My God!" Weeping, she hurled herself from him and, stumbling up the sandy stairs to her house, she disappeared from his view.

Nicholas broke down and cried, falling to his knees in the unforgiving sand.

"He will soon be here," said Ah Ma. "Is everything in readiness?"

"Yes, Mother," Penny said from her spot at Ah Ma's feet. "Willow has just returned with the last of the...ah, items." Penny's perfect white face bent over a leather-bound ledger in which she was writing Chinese characters in vertical lines. She used a thin brush which she dipped periodically in an open bottle of Higgins ink. Her movements were deft and sure.

She considered her mistress's silence, then made a decision. "Do you think we should be letting this man in here?" She kept her eyes on her writing and, for just an instant, felt

270

her heart contract coldly in her chest at the thought of Ah Ma's possible outburst.

Ah Ma did nothing more, however, than sigh. Penny was quite correct, of course. In days gone by she would never have allowed this to happen. She shrugged mentally. Ah well, times had changed for them all and one must accommodate oneself as best one could. Her voice, when she spoke, conveyed none of this inner dialogue.

"Penny, my precious one, there is, as you well know, a great deal of money involved. I am not a prejudiced person; neither should you be." But she knew these words to be false although Penny never would. Ah Ma, now in her late sixties, was Fukienese, from that district of coastal China midway between the cities of Hong Kong and Shanghai. She was one of fifteen children but she had always felt quite apart from them. Perhaps her name had something to do with that. There was a legend of a poor Fukienese girl by that name who sought passage on a junk. In all the port only one would grant her request. Out of port they were beset by a furious typhoon and it had been Ah Ma who had brought the junk safely through. There was a temple to her, Ah Ma knew, at the base of Barra Hill on the island of Macao.

She shifted in her chair and it creaked. She felt the slide of silk against her arm. Through the open window she could clearly hear the clatter from Doyers Street. There was a fish market on the corner which stayed open late. They carried marvelous squid this time of year. She heard several voices raised in argument and she winced at the Cantonese. Up here in the large suite of apartments which took up the entire third floor of the building only Mandarin was spoken. That was the way it had been in Ah Ma's house when she was a child; that was how it was now.

Ah Ma got up, padded silently over to the window, peering down at the narrow crowded street. She could, she knew, have had her pick of virtually any location in Manhattan. Over the years there had been many attractive offers to move elsewhere. She had always refused. It seemed right to her that her business should be square in the heart of Chinatown. The area was dim and slightly seedy but it was atmospheric. In many ways it reminded Ah Ma of home. That was what she wanted. Now a millionairess, she was still no more comfortable among the steel and glass towers of uptown Manhattan than she had been with structures like the Chrysler Building when she had first arrived in New York.

Yes, Ah Ma thought now, looking down at the night-dark street, the bright bustling clutter of the throng, the intermittent odors of fresh fish in the early morning when the catch was brought in downstairs, the delicacy of the steamed dim sum from the dumpling house next door, I am very comfortable here. Very much so.

She sighed again. Of course, the Chinatown Planning Council might not be too pleased with her if they knew her real business. But the police were certainly happy with the thousand dollars they picked up each month. She was careful to perform this duty herself and to serve them tea each time they came; it increased her face.

Her home in Foochow was always with her but, oddly, more so as she grew older. Being in Chinatown gave her some small illusion of being home. Not that she would ever consider going back now. She had no great love for the communist Chinese and even now, when it might be feasible for her to return for a visit, she could not bring herself to contemplate the reality of it.

No, she had all that she wanted of Foochow right here.

Around the corner the red and blue neon lights of the restaurants turned the darkness watery with reflected light. It was the Japanese, of course, whom she had learned to hate long before the communists. They had come down the coast, those wealthy arrogant businessmen, from their deals in Shanghai, already jaded with that city's nightlife or just wanting to see a bit more of China. They are so different from the Chinese, Ah Ma thought wonderingly. But of course they do not have our centuries of history to learn from. The Japanese are a relatively new people. When we had already forged dynasties, were experimenting with gunpowder, their islands were inhabited only by the barbarous Ainu—unintelligent savages. If the modern Japanese are descended directly from those people, it's no wonder they're so warlike.

She turned away from her window on Doyers Street, said, "I want to see him, now, Penny. There must be no mistake."

Penny nodded, put aside her ledger and pen, stood up and crossed the room.

"Penny..."

She stopped short, her hand on the doorknob. "Yes, Mother?"

"He is not from here?"

"No, Mother. He's from uptown."

Ah Ma nodded. "Good. I do not want neighbors...involved."

In the short space of time Penny was gone, Ah Ma thought about her. She had made the right decision in elevating the girl. She was clever with her mind as well as with her hands. Ah Ma would never admit it openly but there were times when she relied on Penny's judgment, and it disturbed her that she seemed set against the Japanese.

Penny was the name Ah Ma had given to her when she had first applied for a job; Ah Ma gave names to all her girls and henceforth they were known by that name and that name alone. It was neat and tidy and as anonymous as Ah Ma believed her business should be. Besides, it gave her great pleasure to name her "children"; it pleased her, too, that they should address her by the honorific "Mother," a word not lightly used in her land.

There would come a time, Ah Ma thought, when she would have to relinquish her hold here. When that eventuality occurred she wanted to be certain that precisely the right hands took over.

Penny came back, ushering in a boy of about eleven. She stopped just inside the threshold, both hands on his shoulders. He stood perfectly still, his eyes incurious. Through the partially open doorway Ah Ma could hear the quiet bustle of the preparations. As planned, there were only one or two guests expected tonight; this, too, was built into the enormous fee she was charging the Japanese. She did not mind.

She looked the boy over. He had clear smooth skin, a slight Mongol cast to cheeks and eyes. His irises were like chips of coal. His mouth was wide, the lips slightly sensual.

"This is Philip Chen," Penny said.

"Close the door, precious," Ah Ma said softly. Her hands were clasped in front of her, the fingers interlaced. She looked at the boy. "You will have another name while you are here," she told him. "Sparrow. This will be how you are summoned, how you will be addressed. Is this understood?"

The boy nodded, then smiled slowly.

"Call me Mother."

"Yes, Mother."

"Have you been properly instructed? I don't want any surprises."

"Yes," he said happily. "Penny has explained everything. No problem."

"Really?" Ah Ma's eyebrows arched. "That remains to be seen. All right. Leave us now, Sparrow. Find Willow. She will take you to the proper room. You know what to do."

"Yes, Mother." He turned and left.

After Penny had shut the door behind him, Ah Ma said, "Parents?"

Penny shook her head. "He lives with an uncle who is too drunk to care if he's out all night."

"The situation is totally secure?"

Penny nodded her head. Her black hair tossed like an animal's mane, "Willow saw to it personally."

Ah Ma allowed herself a small smile. "You have done well, my child."

Penny bowed her head to cover the flush in her cheeks. It was rare indeed to be addressed in such a loving manner by Ah Ma. "Thank you, Mother," she murmured.

Ah Ma went silently to stand in front of Penny. She lifted a hand, tilted her chin up. "Now tell me what's bothering you," she said quietly.

Staring into those all-knowing eyes, it was difficult to find words. Penny felt as if her throat had constricted so much that not even air could pass through.

"Come, come, child. Is it the Japanese? What is it about him that offends you so?"

"I am ashamed that my feelings are so transparent," Penny said sadly. Her eyes dropped for a moment and she felt at any moment as if she might burst into tears.

"Nonsense!" Ah Ma said, irritated. "What is apparent to me is not to others. You have lost no face with me. Please tell me now what I wish to know."

"It is the drug which bothers me so," Penny said. "This is something I don't think we should become involved in."

For a moment Ah Ma said nothing. She recalled a trip she took as a small girl into Shanghai. She could still smell the overpowering cloying stench of the burning opium. Her nostrils quivered at the memory; she had never smoked but the odor remained with her like a brand.

It had been in the air the night the communists had come for her husband. There had been no sound, no warning. They had been in hiding but the communists had known precisely where to look. They had been traduced.

Ah Ma's husband had been a political activist. His fore-sight was long-range. He had seen the impending storm of the Communist Revolution, perhaps had even understood its inevitability. Yet he fought against it with unequaled ve-hemence. "For once," he had said in speeches, had written in pamphlets, "we are in a position to learn from the Japa-nese. What good did the closed regime of the shōguns do them? There came a time when it became apparent that the country was stagnating, strangling in its hard-bound tradi-tions of iron. The way of the future for the Japanese became Western capitalism. Now see where they are. Can we here in China ignore such a historical example? A communist take-over will seal us off from the West, from the very cap-italism which has made such thriving cities of Hong Kong and Shanghai. Thus will China fall behind the rest of the world, a true sleeping giant."

They burst in, throwing Ah Ma against a wall so that her head banged into the edge of a cupboard. They dragged him out of bed, stripped him, beat him with their heavy sticks, the butts of their rifles. The red star embroidered on their peaked caps, the epaulets of their stinking uniforms. They had dragged Ah Ma's husband, unconscious and bleeding, from the house. It was the last time she ever saw him. To this day she could not be certain whether he was alive or dead. But she hoped for his sake that he had died quickly. Perhaps he had found a bit of wire or a length of bedsheet. She did not want to think of what they might have done to his mind.

That was a long time ago but sometimes, on the dismal gray days, when rain lashed the windows and even the street below was obscured, Ah Ma thought that the wound had never quite healed.

She brought her thoughts back to the present, smiled into Penny's eyes. She was so beautiful. Perfect and beautiful. "It is good you feel that way, my precious," she said. "As a rule you know I don't allow drugs of any nature in here. This man is an exception." He fights the communists in China, in his own way, Ah Ma thought. He believes that his security is total but I know. Of course I know. I would not be who I am otherwise. I know all about everyone who comes here. Without exception. This one merely took more time, more *baht*. But there are always palms willing to be greased; there is a price on all such matters.

"May I know the reason?" Penny asked softly.

Ah Ma patted her shoulder. "It does not concern you." She smiled. "Now go help Willow. It's almost time."

Penny bobbed her head, her eyes on the floor in front of her. "Yes, Mother. Right away."

Ah Ma watched her silently pad out of the room, wondering what the world was coming to.

As for the Japanese, he was, at this time, exiting the movie theater via its side entrance. He immediately crossed Forty-ninth Street and ran the last several steps to catch a downtown bus. It was fairly crowded but thinned out not long after they passed Thirty-fourth Street.

He swung off one stop from the terminus, walked the rest of the way into the Village. On Eighth Street he turned east until he came to Cooper Square with its black metal cube sculpture balanced on one point. Along one face someone had spray-painted in white "Zombie loves Karen R." It seemed to fit.

He caught the City Hall bus on the corner of Eighth and Third Avenue, traced the Bowery as far as Canal Street. There he found the first phone booth. He stared up at the chunky old-fashioned clock above the jewelry store on the corner. Immense semis, spewing diesel fumes, rumbled westward and across the avenue the mock-Roman columns of the Manhattan Bridge rose.

He dialed a number, got the correct time. He hung up and waited precisely one minute and fifty seconds. Then he dialed a local New York number. He detested this procedure but it was a built-in factor and a logical one; he did not fight logic.

At the other end the receiver was picked up. The Japanese read off the seven digits of the number from which he was making the call, then immediately replaced the receiver. He held down the bar while lifting the receiver, placing it against his ear. A woman who had been looking at him turned around disgustedly, searching for another phone.

Four and a half minutes later the phone rang. The Japanese lifted his finger from the bar. The conversation was in Japanese.

"Yes." He could hear the hollow sound of the overseas line.

"Status."

"We're running."

"Tell me more. What results have you?"

"Results?" He seemed somewhat taken aback. "I'm in place. The buy is running." *Buy* was his own word for mission.

"I see." There was a pause during which it was just possible to hear the sibilants of another call far in the open background. "The line is secure?"

"From this end, absolutely."

The voice at the other end appeared to disregard the discourtesy. "We wish a rapid denouement."

"That was made clear to me in the beginning." Every fifteen seconds he checked his immediate area. Not that he expected to find anything; one should never forget security. It was all one ever had.

"Precisely."

"These things can't be rushed. You know that. I work a certain way. This was agreed upon or I never would have taken on the buy."

"Oh yes. We are well aware of that. But life is ever changing and recent events—events which have taken place while you were out of the country—necessitate a more precipitate closure."

"I never do things that way. I—"

"You will now." The voice was as soft as silk, the tone even. There was no haste to the words, no heavy-handed menace. "It is imperative you close the buy within the next seventy-two hours."

"I do not think that—"

"Your fee is doubled."

The line was dead in his hand.

"Good evening," Ah Ma said. She stitched a smile on her face, extended an arm. "You honor this house w—"

"Is it all ready?"

Ah Ma kept her annoyance at this serious breach of ritual courtesy out of her voice. She was an extremely orderly woman; she did not take well to disruptions. Or to rudeness. She thought briefly of throwing the Japanese out. Certainly she did not need his money. But he had killed communists in China. Three high officials that she knew of; that surely meant the true figure was higher. She hated the communists far more than the Japanese. Besides, the arrangements had already been made. It would have been a cruel waste of time for her people had she sent him away now.

Ah Ma gave the Japanese her warmest smile. "All is in readiness, as we discussed." Covertly, her wide-apart black eyes, as alert as a bird's, studied him. His mood was different, she thought. He seems less relaxed, almost on edge. Perhaps he goes from here to kill another communist. She shrugged inwardly. It was none of her concern.

"Would you care for some tea first?"

"No."

"Dumplings are just now being prepared."

He shook his head.

Ah Ma lifted her shoulders. "As you wish." Barbarian! she thought. The amenities mean nothing to him. Time rushes him as if he were a Westerner. Ah well! The Japanese are much like the Westerners now; they are great mimics. "Willow," she called softly.

A woman glided up. She was tall and slender, her face bony. This set off her long eyes and full wide lips. She was most striking. Yet she possessed a remarkable icy detachment. No one could mistake her for one of Ah Ma's girls; one knew immediately, almost instinctively, that she was far more. One had no idea what that might be.

Willow looked at Ah Ma and at no one else.

"Take the gentleman," Ah Ma said softly, "to the Gold Suite." All of the rooms used for professional purposes were designated by color.

Willow bowed and led the man down a dimly lighted hallway. The walls, save for the decorative molding at floor and ceiling, were papered in a blue-green Shantung silk. The carpet was a deep beige, as were the molding and the closed doors they passed.

They came to the last door on the left and Willow halted. Her hand reached out for the knob.

"Wait a minute." The man's fingers encircled her slender wrist. He pulled her around to face him. "Are you going to—" He was speaking in Cantonese, saw the blank look on her face, switched to Mandarin. It was too much to expect that they'd know Japanese. "Has the old woman fixed you up with me? I told her I didn't want anyone tall." Willow stared at him mutely. "Listen, I don't want you. Understand? There's been some mistake."

Willow dropped her gaze to his fingers holding her.

"Tell the old lady there's been a mistake. For the money I'm—" He stopped, puzzled. She had made no move to break

278

away from him. He had wanted her to struggle, even to whimper. He increased the pressure of his fingers but there was no response. He let go her wrist.

Willow turned and silently opened the door. She did not step over the sill.

The Japanese went inside and turned around to look at her but the door was already closing behind him.

The room was large. Green carpet covered the floor. The walls were gold; the ceiling, an eggshell white. The room contained a large double bed, a wide sofa and a trio of matching chairs, all done in gold cotton. An open door in the right wall led to a rather large and, upon closer inspection, ornate bath. A highly polished oak armoire stood along the left wall next to a large window.

He crossed to this, looked out on Pell Street. There was a conventional black iron fire escape running up the side of the building; there was no window in the bath. Normal security precautions. He turned around.

He saw a young boy and, behind him, a young woman.

"What is your name?" he said to the boy. He did not ask for the woman's name.

"Sparrow."

"Do you have it?"

The boy nodded, took a step toward the Japanese.

"Stop," he commanded. "Give it to the girl."

The boy turned and handed her something.

"Bring it to me."

The girl bowed. On her way to him, she stopped to pour a cup of hot sake. She handed it to him.

He stared at her, his eyes boring into hers. His hand flipped out in a blur, knocking the cup from her outstretched hand. She stifled a cry at the blow. Her fingers stung terribly.

"Do nothing," he said coldly, "unless I command it. Then be quite certain you do precisely as you are told. Is that clear?" The girl nodded dumbly. These remarks seemed directed solely at her. "Let me see what you have."

She opened her hand. In it he saw two brown tablets and, beside them, a chunk of a black substance. He picked this up first, sniffed it. He nodded. He placed it back in her hand, picked up the tablets. These he tasted with the tip of his tongue. Satisfied, he told her to grind them up.

This combination of opium and synthetic DMT was not new to him. He had acquired a taste for it from a fellow student years ago. The pressure at the *ryu* had been enormous. Sake, of course, was often used as a source of relaxation. But it was not for him; it was not enough.

He watched glassy-eyed as the girl, on her knees, ground the mixture in a stone mortar she had produced from within the armoire.

When she had finished and had filled a pipe for him, he told her to run the water for his bath.

"I can do that," Sparrow said.

"Stay where you are," the Japanese barked. His gaze shifted to the girl. "Do as you are told."

She bowed her head, half ran across the room. By the time he had the pipe lit, he heard the muted sound of running water.

The Japanese took three long drags at the pipe before he took it out of his mouth. "Come here, Sparrow. Now inhale. No, deeply. That's right." He returned the pipe to his mouth, finished smoking. He could hear nothing but the distant water, tumbling. It sounded like a falls.

Every time he breathed in now, the air felt chill; on the exhalations, it seemed to burn the lining of his nostrils. He felt his heart pumping, the blood squirting through his veins and arteries. He felt hot.

Gravity pulled upon him as if he were underwater. He felt its drag on his arms and legs, on his head and on his penis. His balls seemed to have grown within their sac.

"Come," he commanded the boy and together they went into the bath. The tub was three-quarters full. The girl was on her knees testing the temperature.

"Undress the boy," he told her. Every time he spoke, he could feel the rumbling vibrations in his chest. The words, gaining substance, seemed to roll around within the cavity, like ripples set in motion, eddying outward. Some words were as small as insects, as bright and shining. Others were as large and ungainly as giraffes.

The Japanese watched avidly as the girl went to where Sparrow stood on the doorsill. "Do it on your knees," he told her. He was gratified to see how well she took instructions. He must remember to compliment the old woman.

The boy stood naked, his thin body just beginning to form the musculature of adolescence. The Japanese stared, his pupils dilated. In and out. His breathing like the bellows in a busy forge. The girl sat with her legs folded beneath her.

Her head was bowed. Her long black hair hung, shining, down her back.

He bade her undress him next, his shirt first so that she could perform the rest on her knees in front of him. He did not watch her; he watched the boy.

He was hard by the time she had finished and the boy's penis was no longer soft. Without looking at her, he grabbed the girl by the back of her head, pushed her face against his scrotal sac. Her mouth opened. The boy was hard and quivering.

He pushed the girl away from him, stepped into the hot tub. "Now," he said to her, "wash me."

When this had been completed, he stepped out and instructed her to scrub the bathtub. Only when it was washed and rinsed did he step back in. She ran the water for him again.

Lying back, soaking contentedly, he stared up at the gleaming white ceiling just as if he were alone. He thought about the call and what it meant. He smiled. He had meant to kill Tomkin within three days anyway. He had not been about to reveal that to his employers. The less they knew the better. Once you gave anyone information of any kind, you risked giving them an advantage. That was something the Japanese had never done. He was successful because it was he who held the advantage always. This he had been taught well.

He had to laugh. His body moved, sending wavelets bouncing off the porcelain of the tub. By not revealing his plans, he had just had his fee doubled. It had been high enough to begin with and rightly so. Others had tried to kill Raphael Tomkin; none had succeeded. The Japanese had no doubts about his success; none at all. It was, rather, the method that occupied his mind so fully. Yes, his first assessment had been the correct one. Tomkin was most vulnerable in his new office. It was high up, it was isolated, it was surrounded by a warren of tunnels and half-completed passageways into which he could disappear in an instant.

There were, of course, the long-range methods: the rifle, the bomb, and so forth. These were not in the Japanese's repertoire of murder. They were the coward's way; totally Western forms of assassination. He did all his work firsthand, with his own weapons. There was no honor in killing otherwise. Thus he had been taught. The ninja, too, had their code of honor. It was far from the laws of weak-minded *bush-ido*, he thought contemptuously, but it governed him none-theless. A buy was simply not worth doing if one could not get to within an arm's length of the objective. And that was all he needed.

So it would happen on the top floor of the office building, in the plush office—that would be superbly fitting. Not to-night and perhaps not the next; there were too many matters to tie up, too many things yet to be settled. The night after next, then. No need to rush it. He went over every phase of the buy again, feeling a tingling in his groin beginning. The only matter that now concerned him—because it was out of his control at the moment—was whether he had been too obvious. Perhaps he had miscalculated in killing Ito. Then he thought: No, it's what I had planned to do from the start. It's what he needs.

The tip of his erect penis breached the water. He stared at it, fascinated.

"Time," he said and the girl opened the drain. He stood up. The hot water rolled down his flesh. His torso and limbs were hairless.

He stepped out of the tub, brushed aside the thick towel the girl had opened for him. "No," he said. "Lick the water off me." He watched the boy, who had not moved all this time, as the girl bent to her task.

Yes, he thought. There is plenty of time. Enough for me to return here tomorrow night. Release was instrumental to his functioning properly. Between his spread legs, the girl continued to lick at him.

In the bedroom, he smoked another pipeful, repeating his offer to Sparrow. The girl was the only one who was still dressed. She came and stood before him when he commanded, her eyes at her feet. With one blurred gesture he ripped the silk robe from her. She had small firm breasts, the nipples long and hard. Narrow waist and hips, thick pubic triangle. Her skin was raised in goosebumps. Still she would not look at him; he liked that.

He reached his left hand up. It was so big that his fingers were able to completely encircle her slender neck. Her skin was so soft there. With his other hand he touched her briefly where her flesh was raised, interested in the oddity.

Holding her thus, he drew his right hand away, slapped her breasts so that they shook. She grimaced but made no

282

sound. The Japanese turned his head slightly so that he could see the boy's reaction; he had not moved. The Japanese swung at the girl's breasts again, this time from the opposite side. She gasped and immediately bit her lower lip. Sweat started out along her hairline; her flesh was damp beneath his fingers.

When he hit her a third time, it was with considerably more force. She gave a short cry and her legs collapsed from under her.

The Japanese took her under the arms, threw her on the bed. There was a piece of silk tied to each of the bedposts. He took these and, one by one, tied them around her wrists and ankles until she was spreadeagled, unable to move. Her chest was heaving and it glistened with sweat. She moaned, half-unconscious.

The Japanese crossed the room, took the ceramic bottle of sake back to the bed and fed it to her. She coughed twice. Her eyes flew open and she swallowed convulsively. He kept the lip of the bottle to her lips until all the liquor was gone. Then he got onto the bed, straddling her. He faced her crotch and spread legs; her breasts were beneath him.

"Come here," he said to Sparrow. The boy moved to the side of the bed, climbed up into the position the Japanese indicated. He crouched between the girl's legs. His eyes went to her crotch. He fell over, dazed. The right side of his face was numb. Moments later, it began to sting. It was very red.

"Don't do that," the Japanese said. "Look only in the direction of *this*." He pointed to his rampant penis.

Now the Japanese settled over the girl's face. He felt the heat of her breath, the soft tickle as her lips opened. Her tongue began to probe his anus.

"Now," he commanded the boy. Sparrow leaned forward, opened his mouth.

Soon the Japanese closed his eyes. He began to talk in expletives. Neither Sparrow nor the girl understood his words; they were in Japanese. They could not, however, mistake his tone.

As his excitement mounted, so did the obscenities he uttered. He reached down without knowing it, grabbed painful handfuls of the girl's inner thighs, leaving marks and red welts, and, as he exploded into Sparrow's mouth, he hit her once between her thighs so hard that she fainted with the pain.

Seeing the look in the Japanese's eyes, Sparrow backed away off the bed. It was his turn now.

Doc Deerforth was thinking about the war. He sat in his old wooden chair behind the desk in his office, a cup of steaming coffee half on the pale blue blotter in front of him. His head was turned slightly so that he could gaze out through the screen window, past the ancient oak, out along Main Street. This time of the morning there was little evidence of activity. It was hot yet seven o'clock.

Without looking, Doc Deerforth reached for his cup of coffee, took a long sip. He scalded his tongue but he took no notice.

It was quite like malaria, he thought now. Once caught it could never be cured entirely but would return over and over in diminished attacks like an unpleasant reminder of the past. It might even be seasonal, he suspected, coming on most strongly during the hot days of July and August, the dog days when even out here in West Bay Bridge the sun was so withering, the atmosphere so sticky that the leaves on the trees seemed to wilt.

He never seemed to think of the war during the winter.

He picked up the phone, dialed Ray Florum's number at the police station. He let it ring six times before cradling the phone. He had dialed Florum's private line. No one would pick it up but Ray himself.

Where the hell was he? Doc Deerforth thought irritably. Then he glanced at his watch, saw how early it was. Ray didn't come in until around eight. Still, Doc Deerforth wanted to know if there had been any progress toward capturing the ninja. He felt an irrational anger which, he knew, stemmed from fear.

The front doorbell rang and he jumped. For a moment he considered ignoring it, but when it came again, he got up and went through the house.

"Nicholas," he said, blinking into the light. "Come in." He closed the door. "What brings you here so early? Are you ill?"

"I didn't wake you up, did I?"

Doc Deerforth laughed. "Hell, no, son. Just sitting here

dreaming." He peered closely at Nicholas. "You don't look at all well. I think you better come along with me."

"I haven't slept, that's all," Nicholas said, allowing himself to be led into the house. But instead of taking him into his office, Doc Deerforth led him to the kitchen.

"A good breakfast will do you a world of good," he said. He opened the refrigerator, took out a carton of orange juice, handed it over. "Here, help yourself." He looked up. "Bacon and eggs all right with you?"

"Hey, you don't have to—"

Doc Deerforth waved away his words. "Course I don't have to. I *want* to." He smiled, carrying eggs to the stove. "Besides, it's been a while since I had a guest for breakfast. Do me good. I've been sitting around too much lately." He began to prepare the food. He got more coffee going, then put up the bacon. The sizzling of the meat gave him a peculiarly warm feeling. He wondered over that until he recalled he used to cook breakfast for the girls. That seemed so long ago. "I s'pose you want to know what Florum's been up to," he said. Nicholas sat down at the table, poured himself some juice. He looked up expectantly. "Nothing," Doc Deerforth continued. "There's not a damn thing for him to go on."

"I'm not surprised," Nicholas said. He told the other about what had taken place in the city.

"Friends of yours, huh?" Doc Deerforth said when he had finished. "That's a bit of bad luck. I'm sorry." He turned the bacon. "You think he's really after Raphael Tomkin?"

Nicholas nodded.

"Then why these other killings? None of the victims seem to have any connection with Tomkin."

"They don't. At least, not as far as I can tell."

"Then what's he up to? He could have been in and out a half-dozen times by now."

"I've thought about that." Nicholas glanced down at his juice as if he might find answers there. "For one thing, it's not so easy to get to Tomkin. That kind of penetration takes time."

"All the more reason for him to keep a low profile. They don't like the limelight." He drained the bacon, started on the eggs.

"Normally that's true," Nicholas agreed. "But this man's different. He's shrewder than most. Look, he's going up against a man who's been a target three or four times before.

There are good reasons why Tomkin is still alive. The ninja figures a simple penetration won't do it. Something a bit more complex is called for. You know how they are. He'll have to go in himself. There'll be no remote-control gadgets; he won't use the long gun."

"I know." The kitchen was filled with the smell of the food. Doc Deerforth took out the bread, gave it to Nicholas to toast.

"All right. The idea is to confuse the enemy. It's an ancient form of strategy in kenjutsu and on the battlefield. Use different forms of attacks; attack from different sides. While your enemy is wondering what you're up to, you attack decisively and he's defeated."

Doc Deerforth eyed Nicholas as he brought the plates over to the table. "And you think this is what the ninja is doing?"

"It seems logical, yes."

Doc Deerforth began to eat, frowning in concentration. "You've thought of other possibilities, naturally," he said after a while.

Nicholas looked up. "What other possibilities?"

"I don't know. But they're devious bastards. I could never pretend to know what was in their minds."

Nicholas looked away for a moment. "I knew several in Japan."

Doc Deerforth's eyes blazed briefly. "Did you?"

"That was years ago."

"Time doesn't mean anything to them." Nicholas knew he was talking about his own experience. He put down his fork, said nothing. "They're not human," Doc Deerforth said after a time. It was so quiet between the words that Nicholas could hear the ticking of the clock on the wall. "At least, there's something quite inhuman about them—as if they were vampires or something. Something supernatural." His eyes had turned inward as he strung out the banner of his memory.

"Our war," he continued, "was quite different from any other, from what it was elsewhere. Where we were, it was never a matter of companies taking a ridge and holding it in the face of an enemy counter-offensive. There were no front lines, separate territories, retreats or attacks. There was only a kind of holding on. A desperate stubborness against this terrible fluidity which brought you to the front in the morning and behind the enemy at sunset without having moved at all during the day.

"We were never quite sure just where the enemy was.

286

Specific orders were sporadic at best and, when they came, it seemed clear to us that the generals had no idea of the actual situation. We lived in a kind of loosely controlled state of anarchy. It was our only protection from the panic which continually besieged us.

"The time I'm telling you about was late in the war. Almost all of us had been in the Pacific Theater from the beginning. Many of us were in no condition to fight. Malaria, amoebic dysentery, those and other diseases I had never encountered before were what we lived with. But, after a while, we began to fear even the cholera less than the nights.

"The nights brought the infiltrations, silent and lethal. We seemed incapable of stemming them. We doubled the perimeter guard, began patrols of the compound itself. Nothing helped. The commander, in desperation, mounted a series of night patrols. They shot at shadows or the calls of night birds. They hit nothing and were, in turn, silently killed.

"These incidents built themselves eerily. Then some idiot mentioned *Dracula*. He had a dog-eared copy of the Bram Stoker novel and it quickly made the rounds. The fear magnified itself. What else could you expect under such circumstances? Man is notorious for inventing creatures to explain away the otherwise unexplainable. It was something out of a Gothic horror novel. Even now, with so much time in between, it doesn't seem like a joke. We were used to fighting soldiers of flesh and blood, not shadows which melted away in the light. If we could have caught just one, even—caught a glimpse—we'd have had some idea of what we were up against.

"Fear has an uncanny way of escalating. We were none of us cowards. We had all done our share of killing. Even I— even I had been called upon several times.... We were in danger of being overrun. But now we were experiencing something else—something quite beyond our ken. It sounds foolish, I know, but believe me, Nicholas, when I tell you what happened...."

We were struggling across Leyte. The enormous naval battle of Leyte Gulf was behind us. On the sea the Japanese were destroyed, but on land it was another matter entirely. We did not yet own this small island and Luzon, the main island, was still in Japanese hands. They were undermanned and frightfully undersupplied. We thought we had them beaten at Leyte Gulf; that it was the end.

It wasn't.

A new Japanese commander had arrived from Tokyo just before the battle began. Vice-Admiral Ōnishi of the First Naval Air Fleet in Manila. Two days after he arrived, he traveled to Mabalacat, a small town fifty miles to the northwest. It was the site of the Two Hundred and First Air Group. There he chaired a meeting that was, although none of us knew it then, one of the war's most fateful conferences.

Not long after, we heard the first reports. Many of us, knowing the wildness of scuttlebutt, did not believe it. But then, no more than a week later, we saw it for ourselves. At first we thought the Zeros were after us but they screamed by overhead as if we had not existed. Then we saw our ships out to sea, an aircraft carrier and two destroyers. They did not strafe our ships, these Zeros, nor did they dive-bomb them. They merely careened into them. We were certain that the first one had been hit and crashed. But as they one after another followed the same suicidal course, we began to understand. Yet we understood not at all. How could rational men do this? It seemed inconceivable. We thought perhaps they had been brainwashed; the Japanese were notorious for their methods. Anyway, that was the prevailing opinion.

Yet something about this theory stuck in my mind. I could not believe it. Psychological reorientation takes time, I knew that. Certainly it could not have been accomplished overnight. It took time and that was the one thing the Japanese did not have. No, I was convinced it had to be something else. But what?

It was the season of rain; there seemed no dry ground on all of Leyte. We made progress but not without casualties, of course. One night the unit was forced to move on. There were a number of wounded who needed taking care of. I volunteered to stay behind for a short time so that I could properly bandage them. There was a relief column due in the morning. But the situation was far too volatile and my C.O. insisted I move out with the rest of the unit.

We made camp just before dawn. Many of us were too tired to fall asleep. We sat around and talked about Dracula. Three men had been killed the night before; the vampire theories were at their height.

At last I left them, pitched my tent and crawled inside. For a time I could hear their voices as they continued to talk, then the sounds stopped. I wasn't sure whether I had fallen asleep or they had just broken up for the night.

I was in that odd state between sleeping and wakefulness. I thought I dreamed someone was there, watching me. I tried to wake myself but I couldn't. My head felt like it was too heavy to lift up. I strained but nothing happened. It was as if my consciousness had somehow been severed from the nerve impulses which mechanized the muscles. I wanted to look behind me, you know, over my head, certain that was where the danger was coming from. I could make no move.

Above me a face hovered in the air, disembodied. I don't know when my eyes had actually opened or whether they had ever really been closed. My chest felt heavy and I seemed to have trouble breathing. I felt cold. Not as if the night was chill but from inside. I shivered.

It was a Japanese face, coal-black as if it had been coated with charcoal or lampblack. It was dull so that no light would reflect off it. His eyes seemed very large. They had an odd light to them as if, while they stared right at me, they were focused on another universe. It was eerie. I had seen something like it once in a hospital when I was in my last year of medical school. We went into the psycho wing and I saw several patients. One was a young man, not far past twenty. His hair was cropped close. He had high cheekbones and a long thin nose. He could have been a scholar. He was in a straitjacket. I watched his eyes for a long time, while beside me the resident droned his spiel like a carnival barker. I felt like a shill. This man, this...creature was far beyond the supposedly modern and humane treatments the resident was describing in such loving detail. This man had reverted. He was certainly no longer human but had returned to the animal state of his ancestors. There was no hint of what we might term "intelligence" in his eyes; at least not as modern man defines intelligence. But I saw cunning there, of a kind and in a strength which terrified me. For a moment I fantasized what it would be like having this man loose in the world. Richard Speck? Gary Gilmore? Jack the Ripper? It was beyond imagining. For this was a man who was clearly beyond morality.

Now you know some of what I saw in the eyes hovering above me that night on Leyte. But not all. To call this "madness" would be to seriously underestimate it, for it was far more. Ours is a world of order, ruled by laws. From science to morality there are parameters within which we all live. This man did not. He lived outside time as if residing within him, lending him all its ferocious energy, was the essence of chaos. I don't know how to better describe it, but seeing him thus in the flesh only underscored the fact rather than the fiction of his supernatural origins. Perhaps, after all, our vampire stories had not been so far off the mark. I know, I know, this all sounds rather fanciful—pulled out to give a good Gothic kick to this story. I assure you that nothing could be further from the truth.

While I thought of all this, I felt his movement. He produced a matte black length of cloth and, folding it upon itself, wrapped it painfully tight across my mouth. He was quite close to me now and I saw that he was dressed all in black.

He hauled me out of the tent and, stooping, slung me over his shoulder.

He ran.

He ran without sound. No shadow trailed behind us; we were never in the light. He took a route out of the encampment that was neither direct nor circuitous. It was merely undetectable, as if he were following a path no one else suspected of being there; a path made just for him.

I didn't struggle. I found myself wondering why I hadn't been killed as the other victims of these silent infiltrations had been. I was amazed. Even upside down I could see well enough to know that he was a magician. No one I knew could possibly have gotten in and out of our encampment totally undetected as this man had. He moved without seeming motion. That must sound like a contradiction but it's not. He ran with such fluidity that there was no up and down motion, merely the sensation of forward movement.

We were in the jungle now, traveling extremely quickly. In fact, even though the way was now more choked with foliage and underbrush, our speed actually increased. His strength and endurance were exceptional. We were totally alone in the world, or so it seemed to me. It was that time of the night when the nocturnal creatures have crawled back into their holes to sleep and the diurnal animals have not yet awakened. The jungle was quite still, just a sleepy bird calling here and there, the sounds quite isolated and seeming part of another world.

We traveled thus for perhaps thirty minutes. Then the man stopped abruptly and, spinning me off his shoulder, widened the cloth around my mouth so that I was now blind-folded also. He led me, stumbling, through the jungle. His fingers were at the back of my jacket so that, each time I fell, he suspended me as if I was hanging from a coat hook. It was a terribly dehumanizing thing to do and I tried to shut my mind to it.

After a time I began to hear voices. I did not speak Japanese but I understood enough to get by; it was something I did not want him to know. At length the blindfold was removed. We were in the midst of a Japanese camp. It wasn't anything like what I had pictured. In fact, I was aghast; I thought for an instant that he had taken me to a hospital; it hardly seemed like a military camp at all. For one thing, most of the soldiers were either lying down or sitting. I saw no troops as such; no guards.

We were near the water, though on which side of the island I could not tell. I saw the water clearly through a gap in the vegetation. I watched for a time, totally unmolested, while the man who had brought me spoke with several of his fellows who were identically dressed. These seemed to be the only operational men in the camp. At first I tried to pay attention to what they were talking about, but either they were speaking too fast or in some dialect I had never heard because I couldn't understand them.

Dawn had broken and there was a white line just above the horizon; I knew I must be looking east. I saw a smudge coming into view and then another. I heard, simultaneously, a heavy drone from the northwest, in the direction of Luzon. It was the Two Hundred and First. I looked up. The Zeros were black and bloated against the pale sky. The night's clouds had melted away.

The Zeros passed low over us, headed out to sea, toward the dark smudges staining the horizon, coming closer.

"You know they go to attack your ships."

I started. A thin Japanese stood beside me. He was on crutches. His left trouser leg was pinned back at the knee but he'd surely die of malnutrition before his stump would begin to bother him.

"You speak English very well," I said.

"Yes." He was still staring out at the moving targets as they closed with one another. "They will not come back. None of them. Ōnishi has seen to that." I understood that he meant the new Vice-Admiral. He shook his head sadly. "They say, you know, that he helped Yamamoto plan the Pearl Harbor attack." He clucked his tongue against the roof of his mouth. "It's hard to believe. It seems so long ago." His head turned. "Do you speak Japanese? No? Pity." He turned back. The Zeros were nearing our ships. You could see the batteries begin to fire. Black clouds with orange bits in their centers exploded, eerily silent until, moments later, the reports found us, shook the air. "No, they won't come back, those boys. They're on a one-way mission."

Abruptly, his words penetrated the fog which had surrounded me since I had come into the camp. "Do you mean to tell me," I exclaimed, "that they're on suicide missions? The plane and the pilot...?"

"One big maneuverable bomb, yes." The Japanese stood quite still. Tears seemed to be standing in the corners of his eyes but there was no change in his voice. "Vice-Admiral Ōnishi's idea. It's a desperation move. He had a time convincing the others but he managed it." He said something in Japanese which I took to be a curse. "Not enough of us have died for this 'noble cause.' The Emperor still sends his sons into a war which we have already lost." Far away, on the white and black horizon, the Zeros were leaving the sky.

There came a sharp call from behind me. I did not need to understand the language to know that my captor wanted me. I walked away from the crippled soldier, saying, "You ought to get something to eat."

He laughed shortly. "If I could, do you think I'd be here now?"

"What about a hospital?"

"Won't take you in unless you bring your own food," he said. His eyes were clear. I could see his ribs underneath his uniform blouse. I thought: What am I doing? He is the enemy. "We're all dying of malnutrition. We can't get into the hospital and our unit's booted us out because we can't fight anymore. It's not a soldier's end. There's no honor in any of this." He stared at me and, for a moment, there seemed to be no difference between us.

Then my captor had hold of me and, barking harshly, he pushed me toward another part of the camp. Here, too, soldiers littered the ground. It seemed pathetic.

He carried with him a small black satchel which I hadn't noticed before. It was over this that they seemed to be arguing. There were perhaps four of them. They might have been brothers. Now I regretted not asking my unexpected friend who these men were. It was clear that they weren't regular army. To one side, I saw what was obviously a cooking fire. There was a black iron pot. By its side was a small pile of what the Japanese called *kamote*, the diminutive Philippine potatoes that taste rather like a conventional sweet potato. There were also some withered tubers. These were obviously their rations: all the food they possessed.

The man who had brought me produced a series of cans he had obviously stolen from our camp. How he had spirited this food away I could not imagine, but there it was.

They began to argue all over again—I suppose about who would get how much. My captor hustled me away, shoved me down toward several of the supine men. It was clear that he wanted me to work on them. Now I understood why I had been spared. He knew very well what I was. I began to wonder what else he knew about me.

I turned to the soldiers. In truth there wasn't much I could do for them. I was without my instruments and my medicines. But they would not have been much help. My friend had been quite correct in his analysis of the situation. The Japanese were dying of malnutrition.

At length I got up, went over to the man who had brought me.

"I'm sorry," I said, "but there's nothing I can do."

He hit me without warning. I didn't even see where the blow came from. One moment I was standing and talking to him, the next I was on my ass in the mud.

"They need food," I said inanely.

He reached down and hauled me up. There seemed to be no expression in his eyes. He hit me again, this time harder, with the edge of his hand. It felt like I had been struck by a cement mixer. I went down and stayed down.

It was dark when I awoke. I had a splitting headache and my right shoulder didn't seem to work. It was odd. I could wiggle my fingers, even make a loose fist, but I couldn't raise my arm even an inch off the ground.

I was in a tent, lying on something hard. Now I could tell it wasn't the ground. I had my jacket and fatigue shirt on but no pants. I was naked from the waist down. I tried to move but couldn't. If I strained hard enough I could just about move the table or whatever it was I was on. But my head began to throb so powerfully that I soon had to stop. My entire body seemed to pulse with the pain. There were flashes behind my eyes and I wondered what he had done to my nerves.

Shortly after, he came in. I didn't hear him but felt some stirring of the humid air. His face loomed over me. He had removed the lampblack from his face but not the black clothing. This, apparently was his uniform.

"What is your troop strength?" he asked.

I understood. Having proved useless in my healing capacity, I was now a full-fledged prisoner of war. I knew what that meant.

I told him my name.

"How much firepower have you?"

I told him my name.

"With which units will you rendezvous?"

I told him my name.

"What is the American timetable for linkup?"

This time I varied it. I gave him my rank and serial number.

"When do the Americans plan to launch their invasion of Luzon?"

"Luzon has already been invaded," I said. "By the Japanese."

Then he began to work on me. He used nothing but the ends of four fingers: his two thumbs and forefingers. No blades, no heat, no drugs, no wire, no water. None of the traditional interrogator's tools. He had no need for anything so crude.

He worked on me for all of the night—more than ten hours. Oh, not constantly, of course; I never could have taken that. And at the end of that time there was not a mark on my body.

He was, truly, a magician. He worked on the nerves. Not just the major nerve centers as might be expected, but the nerve chains themselves. Just his fingers squeezing.

Everything else ceased to exist. He saw to that. It became, after a while, a kind of sensory deprivation situation: I felt nothing but pain. Even the two or three times I urinated, I couldn't feel it, only smelled it for a time. Then that, too, was obliterated.

He used pain the way a clever woman can use pleasure. You know the way a woman leads you up the pleasure curve, slowly, lovingly, gently, until you're throbbing for release.

She'll bring you to the brink, hold you there for exquisite moments, then stop until the excitement subsides and she starts all over again. Finally, when you come, the sensation is better than it's ever been before. This man used the same principle. You know terrible pain can become its own anesthetic—just like when you fuck too much, you go numb for a while. So, too, with pain. Even your nerves have a limit, and after a while they just shut down and you feel nothing. That can be your only advantage in intensive interrogation.

By his very technique, this man avoided that. Again and again, he would bring me slowly up the pain curve, keep me hovering on the brink for long moments—but he never let me topple over into the numbness of the other side. He knew precisely how long I could take it and brought me down each time.

All the while the questions were repeated over and over. Not shouted, the tone calm and even friendly, he spoke in an intimate voice as if we were close friends meeting in a bar, talking about old times.

It was odd, this combination. We became, after a while, as intimate as lovers. I wanted to trust him, to tell him all my secrets, to break down the last barriers between us. The pain, too, changed over time. It became—how shall I put it?—less painful? Yes, that's it. Less painful. I still can't understand how it was done. Of course, I knew even then that he was working on my mind as well as on my body. But somehow that didn't help any. I seemed powerless to stop what was happening. I felt things slipping away from me, as if I were losing my balance on slippery ice. Then even the ice was gone and I felt myself settling down into a kind of muddy slime, sinking lower and lower. There seemed to be no bottom.

All this time the pain was ebbing and, as it did, I felt myself wanting to trust him more. He was my friend and I became guilty at holding out my secrets. How selfish I was! How unworthy of his friendship.

It was not numbness which overtook me now—I told you he would not allow that. It was another sensation. Pleasure. It crept up on me while I was concentrating on not answering his repeated questions. This was taking more and more energy and once or twice I had to bite my tongue in order to stop myself from telling him everything he wanted to know.

I felt, at that moment, my self slipping away from me, revealing, underneath, another person I knew not at all. It seemed to me, then, that this man knew more about me than I did and this terrified me.

Now I found myself wanting to tell him more than ever. Once I did, I was convinced he would hold and comfort me. The pleasure grew. I began to rejoice in the pain, to want it, for it was my link with him and I began to feel that I would be lost without it, that once it ceased I would have nothing and, therefore, be reduced to nothing. Time ceased to have any meaning. There was no past, no future, just an endless now with its bright connection. My mouth was hot with my own blood as I fought to hold back telling him everything.

Abruptly, it was gone. The pleasure-pain. Everything. I was lost. Alone in the tent, I began to cry, great dry racking sobs—my body had been so depleted of moisture during the night that even tears would not come. I was terrified of being alone, like a child cruelly left by its mother. I had been reduced to a kind of psychological infancy in which I now depended on my inquisitor as a baby does its mother. I had been left alone so that it would be hammered home. I knew then that the moment he returned and started on me again, I would talk and talk and talk. Nothing would stop me.

I became abruptly aware of a sound in the tent. It came from behind my head. I thought he had returned and I wept for joy. There came some scraping sounds. I tried to twist my head but I could see nothing except the heavily fluttering tent top.

"Get up!" It was a harsh whisper in my ear.

"What?" It sounded moronic. A combination of the dehydration and my swollen tongue made me sound like a cross between a heavy drunk and a lobotomy case.

"Get up! Get up! Get up!" the voice hissed.

I felt hands under my back, forcing me to sit up. It seemed a novel experience. For a moment I stared stupidly down at my body, perhaps expecting to find the flesh shredded into ribbons or blackened bamboo shoots under my nails. There was no mark on me. I shuddered as I forced myself to remember the pain.

"This way!" the voice said, urgently. "Come on! Move yourself! There's no time to sit around!"

Gingerly, I swung off the wooden trestle table and turned. It was my friend, the crippled Japanese. His face was drawn with worry. His extended arm held open a flap of the tent on the far side. Through it I could see the bright green of the jungle. The daylight hurt my eyes and for a moment I felt a sense of intense vertigo.

I stumbled across the room and he had to reach out to stop me from falling over. "I'll never make it," I said.

"Yes," he whispered "you will. They won't follow you in the daytime." He gave me some water then looked away from me as I gulped it greedily down. "We've all had enough of this," he said softly. "It's no use, so pitiable." He moved on his crutches. "Come on. There's no time to lose. We can't let them find you like this, can we?"

I went to the open tent flap. My chest seemed to be pounding so hard that I thought I might drop dead of a heart attack before I had taken ten paces.

"I don't know how to thank you," I said as I passed him.

"Don't," he said. "We're from totally different worlds. We could never understand each other."

"Oh no?" I stuck out my hand. He touched it for a moment, then released it quickly as if he was embarrassed again. "One last thing," I said. "Who are they?" He knew who I meant.

"You don't want to know." He began to turn away. The tent flap was coming down like the curtain between our two worlds.

"Yes I do. Very much."

His back was already to me. "Ninja." I heard his voice float back to me as if from a great distance.

"I wished him luck," Doc Deerforth concluded, "but I don't think he heard. I turned and ran into the jungle, away from the camp, away from the ninja."

He sat staring down into the remains of his eggs as if they were a doorway into the past. The skin of his high forehead where the white hair had receded over the years was shiny with sweat. For the first time in what seemed like hours, Nicholas heard the stertorous ticking of the clock on the wall.

After a while, Doc Deerforth lifted his head. His eyes seemed weary as they looked into Nicholas'. "I've never told anyone what happened," he said softly. "Not the men in my unit; not my C.O.; not even my wife. I told you, Nicholas, because I was certain you'd understand." His gaze was steady now, the eyes seeming to bore holes right through Nicholas' skull, X-raying his brain.

"You know, then."

Doc Deerforth didn't need to nod; his eyes told Nicholas what he wanted to know.

"What are you going to do?"

"Do?" Doc Deerforth seemed genuinely surprised. "Why, nothing. What *should* I do?"

"I know how you feel," Nicholas said, "about them."

"About that one," Doc Deerforth corrected him.

"They're like that, most of them."

"Are they."

"It's the way they're trained. Their training is even more rigorous than a samurai's because its tradition is bound in such secrecy."

"Tradition. Odd, isn't it, that such stringent traditionalists should be the perpetrators of such violent anarchy."

"I never thought of it that way but, yes, you're quite right."

"I want you to get this one, Nicholas." Doc Deerforth pushed his cold plate away from him. "I know you're the only one who can. The police don't know—"

"No, they don't."

"—anything at all about this. It's very fortunate that you've become involved. Have you thought about that?"

The day was bright, not a cloud in the sky. The dazzle off the car's chrome was so intense that he put on his sunglasses.

Nicholas left the town behind as he drove back out to Dune Road. He slid into the driveway at the side of his house, picked up the *Times* lying outside his door. He glanced uninterestedly at the headlines, went down the steps onto the beach.

He came up on Justine's house from the right, so he could not tell if her car was there. Both the screen door and the outer door were closed but the *Times* had been taken in. He went up the sandy stairs.

"She's not in."

Nicholas turned. Croaker was just coming around from the left side of the house. He was dressed in a rumpled brown suit. His tie was pulled half off. He looked as if he hadn't slept in two or three nights.

"Car's gone."

"What are you doing here, Croaker?"

"Let's take a walk."

He led Nicholas down to the beach.

"You're not exactly dressed for it," Nicholas observed.

"That's all right. I like sand in my shoes. Reminds me of

298

when I was a kid. We used to stay in the city during the summer. Never had any money to go anywhere. We used the hydrants. Turned them on and cooled off." The water crashed and creamed past them on the right. Far down the beach, blankets were being set up. A portable radio blatted out disco, all booming bass and tattoo percussion. "There were seven of us. I don't know how my old man made ends meet. But you know, once a month during the summer, as regular as clockwork, he'd call me over just before he went to work. 'Lewis,' he'd say, 'c'mere. I have something for you.' He'd give me enough money for carfare out to Coney Island and an ice cream. He knew I loved the beach. 'Promise me one thing,' he'd say every time. 'Take a towel. I don't want your mother to worry. Okay?'"

Someone went running out into the surf, laughing. One could see heads bobbing in the water past the surf line. A woman in a Danskin one-piece walked toward them, a bright beach towel slung nonchalantly over one shoulder. Nicholas thought of Justine, wondered where she'd gone.

"Yeah, we're old friends, the sand and I."

The woman was close enough for them to see how beautiful she was. Her long hair had been streaked by the sun. She ran past them to meet her lover.

Croaker squinted up at the sun for a moment. "I threw Alison out of the house last night."

Nicholas looked at him silently.

Croaker gave him a quick smile that didn't quite reach his eyes. "Well, it wasn't really like that. I think she wanted to go, too. Getting restless. Yeah. We both were." He stuffed his big hands in his trousers pockets. "It was bloodless. Relatively. She'll get over it. These things"—his shoulders lifted and fell—"you know, they pass and—"

They both stopped at once as if on cue. The sea rolled up near them. Over the slight hump of sand lay a dark straggle of sea grape.

Croaker looked down at his shoes, half sunk in the sand. When he looked up, he said, "Nick, Vincent's dead. They found him last night." He didn't say where. "His neck had been broken."

Nicholas took a deep breath and sat down in the sand. He wrapped his arms around his legs, stared out to sea.

"Nick..."

He felt numb, as if his brain had been anesthetized. He

299

recalled Doc Deerforth talking about pain. This seemed more than enough. This was the day of Terry's and Ei's funeral.

"Jesus," he said. "Jesus."

Croaker crouched down next to him. "Nick," he said gently, "there was no other way to tell you. There was the phone but I couldn't do that."

Nicholas nodded. Through the numbness, he understood. Croaker had recognized the debt he owed him. He appreciated the fact that the lieutenant had come all the way out here when he only had to have someone pick up a phone and dial. He remembered that the two had had dinner last night and wondered if this was, in part, Vincent's legacy. If so, it was a fitting one.

"Nick," Croaker said. He hesitated.

Nicholas' gaze swung around.

"What's going on? You have to tell me."

"I don't know. What do you mean? I—look, Tomkin's involved. Up to his armpits. He received a ninja warning about a week ago. It fits in. I've seen it. It's authentic. He has a lot of business deals with a number of high-powered Japanese firms. No one's very buddy-buddy in business, least of all them. He crossed them in some way. Anyhow, it's a mortal offense he's committed. There's no doubt they've sent one over to kill him."

"It's been tried before. Tomkin's a grown-up bastard now. He doesn't need your help."

Nicholas shook his head. "That's where you're wrong. Without me, he's a dead man."

"But it makes no sense, don't you see? The two deaths out here, the three in the city. None have any link with Tomkin."

"They must," Nicholas said, stubbornly. "Look, he's even made an attempt to frighten Justine." He told Croaker about the furred thing thrown through the kitchen window.

Croaker looked at him for a moment. Beyond, he could hear the surf hissing as it sucked at the beach front. The sounds of laughter were bright and brittle as if they had been made to be broken.

"What if," Croaker said slowly, "that message wasn't meant for Justine."

Nicholas stared at Croaker.

"What do you mean?"

"I think it's time we faced the facts. I think that warning was meant for you."

Nicholas gave a short sharp laugh. "For me? Oh, don't be idiotic. There's no reason—"

"There must be," Croaker said earnestly. "Look at the pattern. The two deaths out here. Terry and Eileen, now Vincent in the city. You're the central point to all the deaths."

"I didn't know the second man out here."

"No, but the murder happened close to you."

"Lew, they happened close to a lot of people."

"But only to one who's had three friends murdered subsequently."

It was logical of course, but, Nicholas knew, logic was often not the answer.

He shook his head. "I don't think I can buy it. As I said, there's no reason. It's a smoke screen."

"A hell of a smoke screen!" Croaker snorted.

"It wouldn't matter to him, don't you see? He must know that I'm involved through Justine. *I'm* the danger to him, not you or Tomkin's muscle. He knows that. No, he's after Tomkin, plain and simple. He's just trying to muddy the water."

Croaker held up a hand. "Okay, okay. It was just a theory. But I gotta tell you, I hope you're right because I cared a hell of a lot more about Vincent Ito than I do about Raphael Tomkin."

Nicholas looked at him. It was as close as they both could come to the outward recognition of their friendship. He smiled. "Thanks. That means a lot—to me. I know it would to Vincent, too."

They stood up. Croaker had kept his suit jacket on despite the heat of the day. Now he was sweating profusely and he shrugged out of it. His thin white shirt was stained with sweat.

"You ready to go back?"

Nicholas nodded. "One thing, Lew." He hesitated

"Shoot."

"You may not want to tell me."

"Then I won't. Okay?"

Nicholas smiled. "Okay." They began to walk up the beach toward Croaker's car. "What is it between you and Tomkin?"

Croaker opened the door, slung his jacket onto the backseat. He got in behind the wheel. He had parked in the shade but the interior was still hot. Nicholas got in on the passenger's side and Croaker started the engine.

"You're right," he said. "I might not want to tell you. And a few days ago, I wouldn't have." He made a broken U-turn, began to drive up Dune Road toward the bridge across the canal. "But everything's different now and I guess I figure if I can't trust you, there ain't nobody *to* trust, and I can't live my life like that."

They rumbled across the bridge, heading past the houses and the small bobbing boats with their stowed outboard motors, toward the highway.

"You know about the Didion thing."

Nicholas was surprised. "You mean the murder of that model? Sure, but only what was spread across the papers. I used to see her in practically any magazine I picked up."

"Yeah," Croaker said meditatively. "Beautiful lady. Just beautiful. Like they invented the word for her."

"It sounds like—"

"Nah. Not what you think." They swung onto the highway and Croaker picked up speed. The wind was still hot enough to keep them from cooling off. "But it struck me, you know, that this girl's a person just like everyone else. All anyone thinks of is the image, you know? Her face, her body like that; the façade. No one would stop to think that she might be just as fucked up as all the rest of us, huh? That she belched after a good meal; that she might fart once in a while. Human things."

He switched lanes, avoiding a blue and white bus, its diesel exhaust asphyxiating. He jammed his horn as they came abreast, then they were shooting away westward.

"Then she was dead and everybody was making a stink. She was a celebrity and responsible for a helluva lot of bread, not to mention the hold she had on a multiple million fantasies. But nobody, I guarantee you, said: There's another life stupidly wasted. Well, buddy, that's what I thought about when I stood there in the middle of her bedroom and looked at her cool body. I thought: She's a human being and I want to know who did this to her." He shrugged. "But, hell, I'd do the same for any two-bit whore who got knocked over. Done it mucho times. Doesn't go down well with my captain. But, shit, I never cared a rat's ass about that fucker. 'A waste of the taxpayer's money, Croaker,' he'd say to me. 'Find something more valuable to do with your time.' Jesus!" He hit the steering wheel with his fist. "Can you beat that? Christ, that bastard's always got one finger in his nose and the other up his ass!

"Anyway, this case turns out to be the ballbuster of all time. I mean, there isn't one goddamned break. All I get is mystery and for that I can go to the movies.

"From what I get from her bedroom, there was someone else there that night. A woman. A woman who had, it appeared, been intimate with Angela Didion and who might conceivably have seen the murder being committed. Only problem is, she's disappeared as if she'd never existed.

"So I'm left with nada and the papers are screaming for a solution, which puts the commissioner to screaming at Captain Finnigan, who—but why belabor the point, right? You get the picture."

They turned off before the multiple exits leading to Manhattan and, in a slow curving glide, moved onto Queens Boulevard. The westbound traffic was only moderate and they made good time.

"Two or three uniforms went through the building doing preliminary checks—seeing who saw what. But it being the Actium House, they were told to step softly and whisper at all times. The result they come back with is nobody knows nothing.

"Okay. Fair enough. But a week later, with everyone screaming for blood—my blood—I decide to take a peek myself. To give you the *Reader's Digest* version so you won't fall asleep from boredom on me, it turns out that the uniform assigned to canvass Angela Didion's floor missed one tenant. Turns out she was away when he came around and just came back. A little careful digging turns up the interesting fact that she left the morning after the murder—early—for Palm Springs. She stayed for seven days and then returned. She was an older woman. In her late fifties but looking a good ten years older. An alcoholic. I interviewed her at ten in the morning and her breath stank from gin. Her hands shook and she couldn't stop herself from going to the bottle while I was there."

He turned off Queens Boulevard at Yellowstone Boulevard, went south. They were in Forest Hills.

"But even more interesting was that she swore she saw a man visit Angela Didion—the same man—over the past six months. It might have been going on longer. Six months is when she became aware of him. Apparently there was a fight there one night and from then on she kept a sharp lookout through her door peephole. Nothing better to do with her time."

He pulled up in front of a medium-sized one-story building with a white brick façade. It had dark green, rather ginger-bready trim. A swinging sign on the lawn in front, black and white, read: PARKSIDE FUNERAL HOME. A large shade elm stood on the other side of the lawn. The wooden doors stood open. As they sat there, several people walked inside. Nicholas recognized one of the *dōjō's* instructors.

"She gave me a detailed description of the man, Nick. There's no doubt he's Raphael Tomkin."

"So Tomkin was having an affair with Angela Didion. It's not that surprising, two high-powered people living in the same apartment building. Could she place him there the night of the murder?"

Croaker looked toward the elm. It rustled slightly in a warm desultory breeze. "She's afraid of flying," he said finally. "She took a chloral hydrate with a large slug of gin and passed out at 6 P.M. She didn't get up until about five the next morning."

"When she left for Key West."

"Yeah, right." Croaker turned to him. "But I know what I know. I've checked and rechecked the movements of all her known intimates. It was Tomkin, all right."

"You've got no proof, Lew," Nicholas said. "You've got nothing."

"Less than nothing, buddy," Croaker said morosely. He got out of the car and Nicholas followed him up the flagstone path to the funeral home.

Another of the *dōjō's* instructors stopped Nicholas on the steps, said several words to him. Nicholas nodded.

"Listen," Croaker said, pulling Nicholas close to him and lowering his voice, "the Didion case is officially closed. Finis. Kaput. I got the word the other day from jellybelly Finnigan. This came right from the top; no one would be stupid enough to grease *his* mick palm."

"Are you saying the police were bought off?"

"What I'm telling you is that if I had any lingering doubts as to Tomkin's complicity in this, they went bye-bye with that order to shut down. Very few people can command that kind of strict hush. He's one of 'em." His voice was a harsh whisper now, sibilant, lethal. "But now I got a lead. One of

304

my contacts came through with a make on the other woman in Angela Didion's apartment the night of the murder. I'm waiting for her name and address. When they come through, I'm gonna nail that sonovabitch's hide to the goddamned wall."

The service was brief but expressive, half in English, half in Japanese. But it was, basically, an American ceremony, which they had both wanted. Nicholas had been asked to eulogize both Terry and Eileen and he did so. He spoke in Japanese. There was music. A couple, friends of Eileen's. They were professionals and it showed. They played traditional Japanese music on *koto* and *shakuhachi*. And there were the traditional flowers.

Croaker waited until they had walked away from the grave site. Behind them, the workmen were beginning to fill in the graves. There seemed to be no sound as the brown earth filled the spaces.

"Nick," he said, "what do the names Hideyoshi, Yodogimi and Mitsunari mean to you?"

Nicholas stopped and turned away from the sun. He did not want to put on his sunglasses. "They're famous names out of Japanese history. Why?"

Croaker seemed to ignore the question. "Could they be people who are alive today?"

Nicholas shrugged. "It's possible, I suppose. Sure. They're family names. But those three are linked together by history. The chances—"

"I see what you mean."

Past them, along the black macadam road, a car door slammed and a motor coughed into life, the sound seeming to float on the hot air. Plane and maple trees rustled their leaves by the side of the path they were on. The heat was mounting.

"You'd better tell me what this is all about."

Croaker reached inside his coat pocket. He handed over a thin folded slip of what looked like scratch paper. As Nicholas opened it, he said, "I found this when I was going through Terry's effects the M.E. gave me. It was in his pocket. It might have been made the night he was killed."

"So?"

"So there was a man—a *Japanese*—at the *dōjō* the afternoon Terry and Ei were murdered. Two of the instructors—karate and aikido *senseis*—"

"*Sensei.*"

"All right, whatever. They said this man was the best they had ever seen. Afterward, he had a kendo match with Terry. Vincent told me Terry had been troubled by it when they had dinner together. That was the night of the double murder."

Nicholas looked at him, ignoring the paper in his hand. It was thin and limp, seeming stained with sweat. "What's the punch line?"

"This Japanese gave his name as Hideyoshi."

Nicholas looked away for a moment, out over the cemetery. The white marble headstones were brilliant in the burning sun and even the dark gray or striated stones seemed as light as feathers, threatening at any moment to shake free of their moorings and float away into the sky as serenely as clouds. It was the middle of the week; there was little movement along the neat narrow paths, the close-cropped lawns. Bright blobs of color, flowers placed precisely at the doorways to heaven, gave the panorama a rather false festiveness as if they stood in the middle of a newly abandoned state fair. At the periphery of his vision, a yellow bulldozer moved fallow earth. Beyond, the highway arched in a steel and stressed-concrete rainbow, its traffic so muted its hiss seemed like the sigh of endless surf.

"In 1598," Nicholas said, "Hideyoshi, the Kwambaku, he who controlled all the warring *daimyo* of Japan, died. It is commonly believed that he, being a farsighted man, bequeathed his power to Ieyasu Tokugawa, the strongest member of the governing council. This is not so. Hideyoshi's mistress was Yodogimi and she had given him a son. He loved them both and wished, above all else, to have his heir one day rule Japan. Just before his death he asked to see a close friend, Mitsunari the policeman. He told him in strict secrecy to guard Yodogimi and his son. In effect, he set Mitsunari against Ieyasu. 'Mitsunari, my friend,' he said. 'Ieyasu exults in my death though you will see him act otherwise. Do not be deceived. Ieyasu is as clever as he is dangerous. He will, within a short time of my death, seek to become Shōgun. Mitsunari, my friend, you must oppose this with all your might for, to do this, Ieyasu must destroy Yodogimi and the true heir.'

"Then, just moments afterward, Hideyoshi received Ieyasu. 'You are the strongest of the council,' he told him. 'Thus you must take over the reins of power after I am gone.' 'Do not speak of such sad matters, Kwambaku,' Ieyasu said, but Hideyoshi waved him to silence. 'Listen to what I have to say. There is little time. When I am gone, there will be anarchy among the council members. Undoubtedly they will split into factions and the country will be plunged back into civil war. This must be avoided at all costs. You must seize power, Ieyasu. Those other three *daimyo* are as nothing to you. Sweep them aside; rule to forestall a civil war which would rip Japan asunder.' And Ieyasu Tokugawa bowed his head in acquiescence.

"Thus did Hideyoshi set in motion at the very moment of his death a complex plan for the eventual succession of his heir; thus he hoped to manipulate the destiny of Japan even from beyond the grave. He knew that the moment of his death was most inopportune. His son was still far too young to be able to defend himself or to hold for long the loyalty of all but a tiny fraction of those who were loyal to him. He knew of Ieyasu's ambition to become Shōgun and this he would not permit. That honor must go to his own heir."

Off to their left, a small funeral procession made its lentitudinous way from the black macadam road from which heat waves rose, along one of the narrow paths toward an open grave. The gleaming casket was already in place, surrounded by garlands of flowers. The mourners were forming up and a slight commotion began as one of the family members collapsed. Distance and the heaviness of the air dampened the sound so that it appeared as if they were viewing a mime show.

"Was Hideyoshi successful?" Croaker asked after a time.

"No," Nicholas said, "he wasn't." He was still watching the crowd of people. The person—a woman, it appeared—had recovered and the service commenced. "For one thing, Ieyasu Tokugawa was far too clever and powerful. For another, Mitsunari gathered a coalition of *daimyo* around him who were just not up to the task of defeating Ieyasu. In 1615 Ieyasu led his forces against those who sought to protect Yodogimi and the heir. They had retreated into the nearly invulnerable castle at Osaka. On June fourth of that year, Ieyasu's forces breached the castle's defenses but by that time both Yodogimi and the young heir were already dead; she had killed her son and then committed *seppuku*."

"Is there a villain in this story?"

There came a flash in the sky and a drone, heavy with vibration, as a 747 headed in to Kennedy.

"I suppose it depends on your point of view," Nicholas said. "But I can tell you that Ieyasu was one of the greatest leaders in the history of Japan. Whether Hideyoshi understood those qualities in Ieyasu is open to debate. In any case, they were two different kinds of men, and it is impossible, I think, to make an overwhelming case for one against the other. They were both crucial to the development of their country."

"Yet, in the end, Hideyoshi is the loser," Croaker pointed out. "His line died with him." Nicholas said nothing. There was a kind of stillness over the cemetery. People looked like statues, caught within a moment as if part of an old photograph. The hazy spires of Manhattan, sitting astride the horizon in the west, seemed out of place, dropped there by mistake by some drunken stagehand. Croaker's voice had lowered in volume when next he spoke. "Why would this man take Hideyoshi's name—we can be certain it's not his own—when that man failed?"

Nicholas smiled thinly, turned to look at Croaker's face. Odd, he thought. Depending on the intensity of the light and which way it struck, one could see his face as either rugged or battered. But perhaps they were the same, after all. "That's a totally Western way of viewing history," he said softly. "In Japan there is what we call the nobility of failure. Many of our greatest heroes failed in their ultimate objectives. But their *vision* was heroic, as were their subsequent actions. In the West, you revere only the victorious. That's a pity, don't you think?"

Croaker squinted against the glare of the sun. "You mean this Hideyoshi was a hero."

Nicholas nodded. "Yes."

"What about the other names on the list? How would they fit in here?"

"Frankly, I don't know, but Terry wasn't just doodling." He handed the paper back to Croaker.

"Well, I don't get it."

"Neither do I," Nicholas said.

There was a kind of stillness in the air that had nothing to do with sadness and death and defeat. Nicholas thought, wonderingly, that it had been some time indeed since he had felt as close to another man as he did now to Lew Croaker.

"You know," he said, "when I came to this country years ago, I deliberately put aside a certain part of my life. That is not an easy thing to do—for anyone—but especially for someone brought up in Japan. There was a debt I felt I owed to my father—to the West, really—where it resided inside myself." Croaker's eyes seemed silvery with the sunlight as he regarded Nicholas silently. He had come to understand the immense importance of this gesture.

"But, abruptly, I stopped. Just like that. It was as if I had suddenly awakened from a long dream-filled sleep. What had I been doing all these years here? What had I accomplished? I would not have myself, as my father had at his death, feel as if I had squandered the time allotted to me. It was enough that I had been encompassed by *his* sorrow, *his* bitterness. I could not countenance the same thing happening to me."

They were silent for a time, listening perhaps to the unsteady wind reaching the elms. The sun was very hot.

"And now?" Croaker said with a hint of hesitation; he was still in unfamiliar territory. "Has anything changed?"

Nicholas laughed, not unkindly but with a sword-sharp edge. "My whole world has turned upside down. It's as if the intervening years since I came here never occurred."

"I'm trying to imagine something like that happening to me."

Nicholas looked at him for a moment in pleasure.

As if by mutual consent, they began to walk slowly down the path toward Croaker's waiting car. Both seemed somehow reluctant to be on their way as if dreading the freneticism of the city. Just before they reached the car, Croaker said, "What's your opinion of Justine's old man?"

Nicholas looked at him. "That's an odd way to put it."

Croaker shrugged. "A figure of speech."

But Nicholas suspected his friend of having inserted a subtle warning. "I started out by hating his guts," he said slowly as if formulating his thoughts as he spoke. "But that's hardly surprising, given Justine's point of view and the way he and I first met. He's deliberate and heavy-handed and used to getting everything he wants. I don't like any of that."

"I hear a 'but' hanging around there someplace."

Nicholas stopped and faced Croaker. "Look, it would be very easy—and expedient for us all—to write him off as a rich villain out of some dime-store novel but it's not as simple as all that."

"He's a murderer, Nick."

"He's vulnerable—"

"Oh, Jesus—"

"He loves his girls, no matter what they think of him. He'd do anything to protect them. And he's not as sure of himself as he ought to be. There's something—"

"It's the grand act he's putting on for you. He needs your help and he knows you're no dummy."

"I really think you're wrong. He's not as two-dimensional as you make him out to be."

"All right. Your ninja goes out and kills people," Croaker said. "But there must be someone somewhere who he comes home to and loves. He is still what he is."

"You're ignoring the complexities—"

"He's a fucking shark, man. You'd better face up to it."

"You're looking at it from only one point of view."

Croaker shook his head. "No, Nick. I just know him longer, that's all."

On the way into the city, Croaker told Nicholas all he knew about the circumstances of Vincent's death. It wasn't much.

He dropped Nicholas at Tomkin's building on Park and continued downtown. At the office the M.E.'s report on Vincent was waiting for him. He slung his sopping jacket over the back of the gray and dull green chair, took a MintyPick out of his breast pocket, flipped it into his mouth and opened the folder.

What he saw brought the sweat out on his forehead and along the line of his upper lip. He ran a hand through his thick hair and swore under his breath. Then he reached for the phone. There was the minimum of delay.

"Nate?" he said when he got the M.E. on the line. "Croaker. Thanks for the report on Vincent Ito. Someone must have broken his back to get it here so soon."

"I did it myself." Graumann's voice sounded tired. "We're all still a bit stunned here and—"

"Hey, Nate, I'm working on it."

"What's up? And don't give me any *schmeer*."

"Not much," Croaker admitted. "Only that it seems related to the deaths of Terry Tanaka and Eileen Okura. They were friends of Vincent's."

"Yeah, I remember the files. Vincent did the autopsies himself. But how? There's certainly no similarity in M.O."

Croaker rubbed at his eyes. "Right now, all I can say is that M.O. doesn't seem very relevant."

"I see. I phoned Doc Deerforth out on the Island. I wanted it to come from me."

"How'd he take it?"

"Not well. Look, Lew, we'd—*I'd* appreciate anything you can do—you know...." His voice trailed off.

"I know you two were close. Believe me, the minute I have something, I'll be in touch." He looked up. Vegas was in the open doorway, grinning like a Cheshire cat. He put one finger in the air, put his hand over the speaker, said, "Hold on, I'll be off in a minute."

"...the funeral arrangements," Graumann was saying.

"Do that," Croaker said, "I want to be there." He looked down at the report. "About this chemical substance you found—are you certain—"

"Like I said, I did the autopsy myself. There's no doubt about the finding."

"Good. That narrows things down considerably."

"There's absolutely no way the substance could have been introduced accidentally. It happened shortly before his death."

"So I see," Croaker said, reading the typescript. "A modified nerve toxin; slowed down his muscular responses enough so that—"

"I'd say he was pretty near helpless by the time—by the time it happened."

"It wasn't injected."

"No. It would have no effect that way. This is an organic compound we're talking about, not a laboratory synthetic. It had to have been sprayed and from close range. He might have known his murderer."

"Or just not suspected. Anyone—even someone coming quickly out of a crowd—could have sprayed him. Listen, I'll get back to you."

"Yeah. I just hope it won't be long."

Croaker cradled the receiver thoughtfully. Still no word from his contact. What was taking so fucking long? "Come on in," he said to Vegas. He shifted the MintyPick from one side of his mouth to another. "Where you been all duded up?"

Vegas was wearing a plum-colored suit with wide lapels and modified flare trousers. Underneath, he wore a pink shirt with a high collar.

"Been out pickin' up the shit," Vegas said, the wide smile still stitched to his mouth. "Yeah, real bad shit this time, my man. Took us three months settin' it up."

Croaker grunted. "Business as usual." His mind was on the M.E.'s report.

"No way, man. No way a-tall." Vegas lounged his huge frame against the open doorway, disdaining the chair inside the office. "This time I got me a fox among all this shit I just hauled in."

Croaker clucked his tongue. "Don't tell me you're planning to mix business with pleasure."

Vegas shook his head and his grin seemed to expand. "Uh uh, not with *this* fox. This fox is special."

"Yeah? They're all the fucking same, man, those cunts you come across."

Vegas was waiting for this. He poked his forefinger toward Croaker and said, delightedly, "Not this one. This one's *your* fox, man. I just been her guardian angel till I got her here."

Croaker looked up, puzzled. "What the hell are you talking about?"

Vegas laughed good-naturedly. "What I gots downstairs in the wagon is one piece of high-priced property, man. C'mon, follow me." Croaker swung his jacket off the chair back, followed Vegas down the hall.

"This better be worth it," he said shortly. "I ain't got time for any of your jive."

"Oh, no jive, man. No jive." Vegas laughed again, stabbed the elevator button. "What I got on ice down in the alley is goin' make your day. Trust me." He gave a hearty laugh and slapped Croaker on the back as the elevator doors opened and they rode down. They shared the car with a uniform bringing a scruffy-looking Puerto Rican collar down for prints and pics and nothing more was said until they went out through the side entrance.

They came abreast of the police van in the cool dimness of the concrete alley. In this tightly enclosed space, Vegas' body size was magnified; he was as big as Paul Bunyan amid the White Mountains.

He put an enormous hand on Croaker's shoulder and Croaker was automatically reminded of one of the cases on

312

which they had been teamed. The Atherton thing. Christ, he thought, but that was a bitch! Thought sure we were gonna float away on a sea of blood and never see this goddamned world again. Jesus! He could see it as clearly as if it had just happened: he down with his shoulder shattered by a .45 slug and Vegas rising from the shadows of the burned-out car like an avenging angel. Croaker had fired on his assailant, spinning him around, his second and third shots a useless reflex aimed at the stars. But there was the mountain of a black man with the tire chain and the snub-nosed pistol the bastard had modified so that it could blast a hole in a brick wall at ten feet; and Vegas took him on with just his bare hands and I never saw anyone go down so hard or so fast from one blow as that motherfucking hood. There were three other corpses that night; Jesus, what a fucking mess! Croaker felt the pressure of the other's grip.

"Don't you worry none," the big man said softly. "We look out for each other, don't we? I don't give a rat's ass for anyone around here, you know that? They're all a bunch of god-damned hypocrites. I got my job to do, I do it. The rest of them, well, they all got an ax to grind, one way or another. There's always an angle to play out here, ain't that right. War's a perfect place for angles, you know that. The smart make out in wars. They ain't got no conscience, they ain't got no emotion. All they gots to worry about is keeping their tails on straight; after that, they got all the time in the world to look for the gravy rollin' in under the dirt and the scum and the—" Vegas stopped abruptly, aware that his grip had tightened painfully on his friend's flesh. He shook his head like a wounded animal. "Sorry, Soldier, it's been a heavy day." He smiled ruefully. "Real heavy duty."

"It's okay, Spook." They each had given the other nick-names long ago when they had first met; it gave them both a comforting feeling of privacy amid the openness of their days and nights on the force. At times, Croaker thought that this was the falsest feeling in the world, on those days when he felt completely invaded by his job. "We're two fucking heroes who think that shovelin' shit is heroic." He laughed. "But cheer up. What the hell, it could be worse. We could be the ones *makin'* the shit."

Vegas threw back his head and laughed, the rich sound rolling off the high walls. "Now, look, here's the dope," he said. "We been working, like I said, on this Scarsdale bust for three months, no less. We get a tip to move. We move. Lots of stuff there—enough pills to keep the goddamned Chinese Army awake for a year, a whole lotta horse, carload o' coke an' about a half a ton of reefer madness. Okay, not so bad. That's going on in the back of the place. In the front they got a party going on and everyone gets busted, you know? That's when I saw her. Thought I'd bring her in myself, just in case. I think she's clean but"—he shrugged—"you know how that is sometimes. Anyway, she's yours if you want her—I can straighten them out upstairs."

"How can I know if I want her," Croaker said, "if I don't know who she is?"

Vegas transferred his hand from Croaker's shoulder to the lever of the back door to the van. "Sittin' in the dark right in here, man, is Raphael's eldest daughter, Gelda Tomkin Odile."

Croaker felt a jolt race through him just as if he had been doused with ice water.

Vegas leaned on the lever, grinning; the reinforced-steel door swung outward and Croaker stepped in. The door slammed shut behind him.

He stood for a moment in the dimness unmoving, letting his eyes adjust to the low light seeping in through the windshield, washed to a pale gray by the mesh screen dividing the blessed from the damned.

She sat on one side of the plain metal benches riveted along either side of the van. Her head was tilted back, resting against the wall. This put her profile into prominence so that he could see the arch of her long forehead, the straight patrician nose, the flair of the highly sensual lips, the long cool sweep of her curving throat. He knew without having to see them now the dark sparks of her eyes, the rather heavy torso with its thrusting breasts and ample hips. Knew, too, the long sweep of the perfect legs from thigh to calf to slim exquisite ankle palely limned as they stretched out before her; those magnificent legs which, quite inexplicably, made of her heaviness an overwhelming asset.

"Well..." He felt a great weight about his body and an inarticulateness that obliged him to clear his throat and begin again. "Well, Gelda, what have you been up to now?"

The sharply delineated profile dissolved into sweeping shadow as she turned her head to look in his direction.

"Who the hell are you?" Even in anger there was a rich

luster, a silkiness to her voice that made it seem as if he had spoken to her yesterday instead of several months ago. Even alarm could not diminish its effectiveness.

"Croaker," he said, moving toward her. "Lieutenant. Remember me?"

"Should I?" The tone had turned aqueous, soft and languid. The air between them seemed to tremble.

"Maybe. I met you once before." He stood over her now, not seeing anything in the twilight except the pale sheen from the whites of her large eyes. But he felt her presence acutely and it gave him pleasure to stand thus. "I interviewed you at the beginning of the summer regarding the Angela Didion murder; we talked about your father."

"That shit!" Even though she spit it out, there remained an elegance to it. He heard her take a breath. "Yeah. I remember you. Big dude with a face like Robert Mitchum's."

His laugh was a brief bark. "How flattering! Thanks."

"Don't get cocky. His face looks like it's waged World War Three. So does yours."

He waited for a moment, then said, "Mind if I sit down?"

"You mean I've got a choice?" When he didn't answer, he felt her shrug. "Suit yourself. This isn't my house."

"That'd be on Sutton Place, right?" he said, sitting down next to her.

Abruptly her head came away from the wall. "What the hell's going on, anyway?" she snapped. "Am I going to be booked?"

"That depends."

"On what?"

But his hand, having dipped into his suit jacket pocket, was a blur and he was already moving. His left hand reached across the space between them. He grasped her wrists together, pulled. At the same time, he flicked on the pocket flash, searching the pale flesh on the inside of her elbows. He tried not to think of the softness of the skin here.

He let her go, sat back. "I could check the insides of your thighs, too," he said softly. "Or you could tell me." He had used a fair amount of pressure and her wrists must hurt but she made no move to rub them; he liked that. She had a great deal of pride.

"I shoot up through the eyeballs," she said acidly. "You've heard of that, I'm sure. Leaves no tracks." Her head turned then and her cheek lit up as a grillwork of gray and black fell obliquely across her face. She looked like a heroine out of a fifties' *film noir*. Some of the air seemed to go out of her all at once. "I don't do anything any of you guys don't do. Probably a good deal less. I don't blow coke, for instance."

He said nothing, sat beside her smelling her scent until she turned her head and she was in absolute darkness again. He felt like a blind man, wanting badly, irrationally to see her again. "Do you believe me?" Her voice had turned small and he wondered how much of an act she was promoting.

He decided to be honest with her; anything less would be useless and potentially dangerous. "Yes," he said slowly. "I believe you."

"Then I'm free to go?"

"In a minute." He didn't realize how gentle his voice had become. "Why the hell are you involved in all this?"

"What, you mean break my poor old father's heart?" She laughed sardonically. "Come on, what do you want me for?"

"I'm just talking to you," he said reasonably.

"Yeah, sure. In a police van, home from a bust."

"That was your choice, not mine."

She was silent for a moment and, though he couldn't see her, he knew that she was studying him. It could all break apart now, he knew, and held his breath.

She laughed again, a bell-like sound, slightly echoey within the confines of the metal van. "All right," she said softly. "I'll tell you why I do it. I like it, it's as simple as that. It's fun to get paid to fuck. I'm an actress, a model, selling things, just like Angela Didion was. It's all come-on, there's no involvement."

"Never?"

Her head tossed like a bridling horse and he saw a flash of light across her eyes. "Sometimes," she said truthfully, "with a woman." She was thinking of Dare. "Does that shock you?"

"Not really," he said. "Did you think it would?"

"I don't know what kind of man you are."

"I'm just your plain ordinary New York slob."

"Yeah, I can see that." She had hurt him and she knew it; she felt he had asked for it.

"What about the booze?" Croaker asked her.

"What about it?" He could hear her voice go hard as her defenses came up.

"Still hitting the bottle hard?"

Perversely, she felt herself wanting to tell him the truth, stopped herself in time. "Not so much anymore," she said. "I've got my work to keep me warm."

"No men?"

"What is this, twenty questions?"

"If you want to call it that."

"I don't want to call it anything," she said shortly. "I want to get out of here."

"I can't detain you any longer."

"You mean I'm free to go?"

"There are no charges."

"Now I'm supposed to thank you?"

He knew it was over with; that he might just as well have not begun this at all. He felt tired and depressed. "You're not guilty of anything. You're free to go." He deliberately used her phraseology.

Still she made no move to go.

He sat stiffly with his back against the wall, his buttocks jammed up against the joining of the bench to the wall. His wrists lay loosely on his thighs. He stared at his hands, could barely make out the pale sheen of his nails.

"What do you want from me?"

Her voice was so soft that for a moment he thought it might be a whisper from his own mind.

"Nothing," he said. His voice sounded dead. "I don't want anything from you."

"In a horse's ass."

"All right." His head swung around and he saw that she was staring at him. She blinked once and it seemed that she did so in slow motion. "I can help you, Gelda."

"What's that supposed to mean?"

He knew then that he meant what he said, that it was not just his desire to probe her for information about Raphael Tomkin; he knew that he had been dreaming about her for the past two weeks. A current of electricity went through him and he half turned toward her. Her eyes seemed to be searching for something in his face.

"Just what it says."

"I wouldn't trust you if I were drowning and you had the only line."

"But you *are* drowning," he said softly. And then, after a time, "It doesn't have to be like that. The booze and the pills and the—work." He paused. "You could go away somewhere."

317

"Go away!" she exploded. "Christ, there's no place far enough to get away from myself." She put her head back against the metal wall and he saw her soft throat again. "You want to know how I got my name? Gelda." She said that last word as if it had a bitter taste. "I got it because my mother hated." She laughed humorlessly, the first ugly sound he had heard her utter. "Oh, not me personally. She would never stoop to anything so personal. She was far too busy detesting the life which bound her like a jealous lover. Being so powerfully rich had been her one dream in life, her overriding goal. . . . Yes, I guess you could call it that: her goal. Anyway, she found it with my father. Found, too, that it was not what she'd expected it to be—not by a long shot. Oh, she had all the power she had dreamed of and all the money, but living with my father was pure hell and with every moment of their marriage he ground her down." She sighed. "I think, in the end, it became a game with him, to try and see how much he could take away from her. Not material things, of course. My God, she had more than enough of those. No, it was in the area that matters most to my father that he denied her: in the mind. I suspect that if she had fought back, she would have eventually emerged bloody but victorious, as they say.

"But she would not. She wanted to hold on to her dream so desperately that she forfeited any kind of courage. She was my father's slave, a slave, more accurately, to his wealth. She was a weak-willed bitch who must have loved the pain which my father inflicted on her. I mean she put up with it, didn't she? Even after—" She stopped suddenly, putting the palm of her hand over her mouth for a moment. "Christ, what am I saying? And to a cop of all people." She stifled a nervous laugh. "I must be out of my mind."

His heart beat faster as he heard himself say, "What does all this have to do with how you were named?"

"What?" she said almost absently.

"You were going to tell me about your name."

"Oh. Oh, yes." She folded her hands one over the other. She rubbed them against her long thighs, back and forth in a hypnotic rhythm. "I really believe that about the last thing my mother wanted was a child. But my father, as always, insisted on what he wanted. And what he wanted was children. Strangely enough—or not so strangely"—here she gave an odd little laugh—"he didn't care whether they were boys

318

or girls, just as long as he became a sire. He's old-fashioned that way; he feels it's a sign of manhood.

"But my mother misunderstood him. She supposed that he wanted sons to carry on the Tomkin line and that anything else would be considered a failure. I suppose it's a measure of how far she really was from him that she could have been so wrong about him.

"She was naturally ecstatic that she had given birth to a girl. So she named me Gelda. It was a way of getting back at my father without him knowing, you see. Gelda. Gelding. Get it? Sure you do." She turned away as if from the memory.

"You could change it," he said reasonably and for the first time she gave a completely natural laugh. It was quite beautiful, he thought. "I guess I'm just perverse," she said. "I carry it now as a reminder."

"Of what?"

"What's it your business?" she snapped. All the warmth that, so soon, had suffused her voice, was abruptly gone.

"Look," he said, "I'll tell you the truth." It was a desperate gamble; one which he had hoped not to make. He had no choice now. "I need your help with an investigation."

"With what?"

This was it. "I think your father murdered Angela Didion."

"So?"

It was not what he'd expected and he was momentarily nonplussed.

Gelda seemed pleased. "I see you're speechless," she said laughing. "Good for you. Did you think I'd say, 'I hate his guts, copper, but he's still my father'? Bullshit. It wouldn't surprise me if he did kill her."

"You mean, in your opinion, he's capable of murder?" His heart hammered in his chest; this seemed like a gift straight from heaven.

"In my opinion?" She laughed. "Yes. In my opinion my father's quite capable of murder. Laws, I remember, were not things for him to be concerned with."

She had moved fractionally so that she was facing him in three-quarter profile and he could see her eyes and the hurt within them, deeply buried.

"Did you know about Angela Didion?" he said quietly.

"You mean that he was balling her? Sure. I was there one day when she walked in. She did it so you knew right away it was like she owned the place, you know?"

319

"Did you talk with her?"

She smiled. "We didn't exactly get along. There was a kind of instant repulsion, as if we were magnets with the same polarity."

"I thought you and your old man don't get along."

"We don't." She seemed quite close to him now, though he had not been aware that any shift had taken place. "But sometimes my father is impossible to ignore. That happens maybe twice a year." She shrugged. "Who knows? Maybe he wants to see if I've changed any."

"Changed in what way?"

"It's none of—" The fire in her eyes died and she said, quite sweetly, "That I've given up girls. He can't stand that in me. I suppose that's one of the reasons I like them more than men." She shrugged. "A shrink said that to me once. I walked out. I didn't need to pay him fifty dollars an hour to tell me what I already knew."

"How'd Tomkin come to know at all?"

"About me and girls? Oh, he found me at it one day on the summer estate on Gin Lane out near Southampton. That was after we'd sold the Connecticut estate; after Mother ...died."

"What did he do?"

"My mother was a suicide. He—"

"No, I meant when he found you and the other girl."

"You know, even my sister Justine doesn't know this part of it; I'd never tell her and, God knows, my father never would. He treats her like my mother always did. He dotes on her as if she were a cripple. She was the baby, after all. But she was slim and athletic while I was heavy. No matter what kind of diet they put me on and, believe me, they put me on them all, I never could lose weight. My mother never let me forget that; she made me ashamed of it."

She paused. "I don't know how I got on to that." She wasn't really talking to him anymore. "Anyway, my father found me with this girl. It was about a week before my mother died. Deepest summer. I had met Lisa on the beach—her parents had the estate at the other end of the Lane—her father and stepmother whom she hated. Our hate brought us together, I suppose. But we also loved each other's bodies. Truly. There was a purity to our love that I've never been able to find again.

"It was so hot that day, even so near the water. Everything

320

was lying limp and bedraggled. We were lying at the edge of my estate in the lee of a line of high hedges. We were on the border, clad only in our bathing suits. It was like we were naked, only better. We couldn't keep our hands off each other. We took off our suits and made love. It was very beautiful.

"We were still holding each other wetly when I saw my father. I imagine he had been there for a time, perhaps from the very beginning although I have no true way of knowing.

"He saw me looking at him. His face was red and he seemed to be having trouble breathing. He scrambled toward us in a crouch, screaming. His hands flailed the air. Lisa was terrified. She grabbed her suit and ran off down the beach. My father hadn't even looked at her.

"I lay on the ground, paralyzed. With fear, I thought. Now I know better. That first moment when I had looked in his eyes, I knew what he had been doing while he was watching us—it was as unmistakable as the mark of Cain; he made it that way. I might have been horrified but I was not. The idea made me excited; he had watched me make love and I had turned him on.

"I watched him come toward me. There was something clouding his eyes which I couldn't place then. I had never seen him this way before; I was seventeen. He seemed a totally different person than the one I had known as my father; he had come out of himself.

"He took me there where I lay, staring up at him, thinking myself helpless under him. He plunged into me with such force that I cried out and, immediately, I felt his wrist between my lips. I bit down on it with my teeth; I sucked up the blood I had caused to come out of him. I felt as if I was being stuffed all the way up to my throat.

"It was over so quickly that for a moment I thought it had never happened. But there was the salty taste in my mouth and the wet soreness between my legs; I couldn't walk without some pain for two days after."

She stopped and her head turned. She became aware of him again. "There, I've said it; I've spewed it all out and now that's supposed to make me feel better. But you know, it doesn't. I still feel the same lousy rotten feeling inside. I loathe myself. Not because he did that to me. But because I didn't fight him; because deep down I didn't want him to stop. I reveled in feeling his come jetting deep inside me. Oh,

God! Oh, my God!" She was weeping now, her frame shuddering as if it might shake itself apart.

She fell forward and he caught her. His hands slid under her arms and he stood up with her. Her legs had no strength and he had to support her half propped against him. Her shudders transferred themselves to him as if they were seismic quakes, the vibrations entering him. He felt her long silky hair gently brushing back and forth against the side of his face; the strength of her perfume; the heat of her flesh beneath her elegant clothing.

She cried for a long time and even after her sobs had subsided she continued to cling to him, her hands locked behind his neck.

Then he heard her whispering, "I must be mad. I must be mad."

"C'mon." He said it softly but with a great deal of force. "Let's get you the hell out of here."

Nicholas thought about the three names as he went up in the elevator to the top of the tower and Raphael Tomkin's plush office. Hideoshi. Yodogimi. Mitsunari. What the hell had Terry meant? Nicholas knew him almost as well as Eileen had but he couldn't fathom this cryptogram. All right. Start at the beginning. Hideoshi is the ninja. Assume? No, it's a given. Then who are Yodogimi and Mitsunari? Were there three people involved? It seemed to go against all the laws of ninjutsu but, of course, it couldn't be ruled out. Deduction was so easy in literature. Elementary, my dear—he wished Holmes were here with him now.

Yet he felt a kind of familiarity with the names. Of course he knew all about the historical personages, their personal histories: the sweep of the past come alive. But this was the present, divorced from the past.

He looked up, watching the neon indicator moving relentlessly from left to right as if ticking off the seconds, the minutes, the years. Time, he thought.

My God! What am I thinking? I've been too long in the West; I've become one of them. He felt then a kind of secret shame, something that was difficult to admit to, even within himself.

Wasn't I taught that the present is never divorced from the past? Why have I pushed that away continuously? Why have I suddenly, at age thirty-three, dropped out of life? Given up my job, left the city, begun to hibernate—yes, that's the right word—out on the beach like it was Malibu, some far-off lotus land devoid of worries or responsibilities?

Abruptly he felt something rising within him; something dark and ugly and unstoppable. A *tsunami*—the tidal wave. It reared up at his back, rushing recklessly toward him. Had there been no warning?

There had been plenty of warning. He had just been too preoccupied or merely too dense to see it. Or far too close.

He felt as if he were suffocating and he put his hand out, palm against the textured wall. It was slippery with sweat. He imagined that he was Amelia Earhart blithely flying through the cotton-candy skies on her way to—where? He couldn't remember. No matter. Traveling, working the controls. When suddenly.

Nothing.

Not a thing. No sky, no clouds, no land below, no stars above.

Had the past overtaken her, too?

The elevator doors sighed open and he stepped out into the corridor, stiff-legged. He went to the outer edge, looked out at the streaming city through a pane of glass so newly installed that it still carried the wide white *X* through its center. He seemed so oblivious.

It seemed so obvious to him now. Yukio should have given him the clue. His memory of Yukio stood between him and Justine like a guardian ghost baring her teeth. It was this specter within him that had hurt Justine so. He clenched his fist unconsciously. Still a part of him after all this time. But he knew how hollow a statement that was. The psyche bore no notion of time, that was a rational response to a basically irrational question.

Abruptly, the force of his feelings for Justine broke the surface like a geyser rupturing the glass surface of a still pond. How stupid could he have been!

Having made up his mind, feeling calmer than he had for a while, he quickly went down the corridor and pulled open the metal doors to Raphael Tomkin's office.

Frank stood just inside. His eyes blazed when he saw Nicholas and his right hand twitched. Nicholas went by him without a second look.

"Hey, you can't—"

But Tomkin had looked up from behind his desk and had already waved him to silence. "It's all right, Frank," he said amiably. "Nicholas is now on the payroll, isn't that right?" He redirected his gaze toward Nicholas.

The office was immense, perhaps slightly smaller than a grand ballroom. This seemed, outwardly, impossibly excessive until one saw that the space was divided up not by walls but by furniture groupings, forming out of the whole a kind of mini-apartment.

Here to the left was what amounted to a living room with a one-step-down sunken parquet floor surrounded by a C-shaped sofa in crushed velvet from Roche Bobois. A low smoked-glass and chrome coffee table sat in the center, above which swooped a crescent-necked floor lamp.

To the right, nearer the long bank of windows, was what could be classified as a professional engineer's workroom, complete with drafting table, flexible light source and a black plastic tabouret. Nearby was a vertical metal file for storing architectural plans. There was, on its top, even a scale model of the tower as it would look when completed, including the ventral atrium garden, plaza and trees along its eastern and western peripheries.

Far to the left, in the dimness of the office's interior, Nicholas could make out a tiny kitchen with half-refrigerator, a stainless-steel sink and, above, an electric oven. Next to it a door stood open revealing a full bath. The rear corner on the left had been transformed into a library. Bookshelves climbed two walls. There were two strong, shaded reading lights hovering at the side of a pair of clubby high-backed leather chairs which, rather than new, looked well lived in. All that was missing was a massive glass ashtray holding a meerschaum.

Lastly, there was the office proper, directly ahead of him, where Tomkin sat now. The magnificent hardwood desk had quite obviously been custom-made. It was a beautifully blank piece of furniture from this side but, on walking around to its reverse side, one found it revealed itself as housing a complex data center. Nicholas thought it more resembled a console of a 747 than it did anything else. There was a bank of four phones, each color-coded; a telex; a NYSE ticker; the set of TV monitors for the now obligatory interior surveillance system and a number of other gadgets whose functions totally eluded him.

Tomkin was on the phone. He waved Nicholas to a plush chair in front of the desk. Nicholas looked down. The left armrest contained its own phone. He lifted the receiver, pressed an unlit button for a clear line, dialed Justine's number in West Bay Bridge. He let it ring six times before he hung up. She might just be out on the beach. On impulse, he tried her city number. No answer.

He got another line, asked Frank for Abe Russo's extension, dialed it. When he got the construction foreman on the line, he asked him for a list of all oriental men currently working on the tower project.

"That'll take some time," Russo said shortly. "I got a lotta work. I don't know—"

"Let me put it this way," Nicholas said slowly. "If we don't get these names, this project may be halted—permanently."

"Okay. I'll get it right up to you."

"I appreciate your assistance," Nicholas said. "And, Abe. I want you to do this all yourself. Don't involve anyone, is that clear? And, listen, when you've got the list, I'm going to want to see all the men on that list. Think about how you're going to do that without giving them any advance notice. No leaks, all right? Good." He hung up, suppressed a desire to try Justine once more.

Tomkin was on the phone for another ten minutes. During that time there was no movement in the office. In the brief silences, Nicholas could hear the gentle hiss of the central air conditioning. Frank was immobile near the closed doors.

Nicholas got up and, skirting the conversation pit, went back to the library. There was an old-fashioned rolltop desk to one side that he hadn't noticed before. On it he saw several pictures in silver frames that looked Mexican. There were a number of color shots of the same women at ages varying from perhaps sixteen to late twenties. One was Justine; the other, he surmised, must be Gelda. They were both quite beautiful in very different ways, yet they seemed linked by a hidden quality that defined both. He saw only one photo in which the sisters appeared together. It was a black and white shot, torn at one corner. The two girls stood on a lawn. In the background he could just make out the corner of a building, brick-faced, ivy-covered. It appeared to be part of an estate house. They were ten and seven years old. Justine held up a painted egg. At her feet was a tiny wicker basket. She was smiling at the camera. Gelda, a step behind her, taller and a good deal heavier, had been caught looking off to her left. There seemed, even at that young age, a peculiar gulf between the two, as if one had no cognizance of the presence of the other. They might have been pasted together from different pictures for all the relationship they bore to one another.

"Nicholas?"

Nicholas turned and walked back to the side of the desk. Tomkin stood up, came around. He wore a fox-colored silk suit, deep yellow-and-white-striped shirt with solid yellow collar and cuffs and a brown silk tie. He extended a hand. It was thick, the back dark with curling hair. He wore a ring of white gold or platinum on his right ring finger; his left hand bore no jewelry at all.

"Glad to see you," he said. His blue eyes seemed to have a touch of gray to them today. "I was wondering when you'd show up. What did you find out?"

"I beg your pardon?"

"Information, Nicholas." He formed the words slowly as if trying to capture the attention of a retarded child. "You went out to West Bay Bridge because you thought the ninja might be there. At least, that's what you told me over the phone."

"He wasn't there."

"Is Justine all right?"

"Perfectly."

"I don't like your tone of voice."

"You're not paying me to like my tone of voice, merely to protect you."

"I have been wondering how you were doing that from Long Island. Remote control, I suppose."

Nicholas laughed shortly. His eyes were steely. "Let's cut the crap, Tomkin. You don't have to like me, just be cooperative. Otherwise, I can't do my job."

"But I do like you, Nicholas. Whatever gave you the idea that I didn't?" Affable now, he guided Nicholas down into the living area. They sat on the couch. It was chocolate brown and luxuriously comfortable.

"Surely you're not surprised to find that I'm—curious, shall we say—about your methodology. After all, Frank here never leaves my side. He gives me a great deal of comfort."

"Frank is useless," Nicholas said, "when it comes to the ninja. He'll get through Frank as if he's not there."

Tomkin smiled thinly. "He may get through Frank but if he does, he'll do so with a couple of .45 bullets in him."

Nicholas shrugged. "If you choose to take this matter lightly—"

"I assure you, I am not taking this lightly. At all. Else I would not have hired you, understand? Now—" he slapped his thick thigh—"tell me what you're up to."

"I'm expecting Abe Russo any minute."

"What the hell we need him up here for? He's got his hands full keeping to our deadline."

"The ninja's hallmark is infiltration," Nicholas said quietly. "He won't try to kill you by...remote control, as you say." He grinned. "He's got to come right up to you—do it himself from arm's length. When Abe gets here, we'll find out if he's in the tower building."

"Here? But how?"

"The most likely probability is as a worker. He'd be anonymous, have the run of the place. It's only logical."

At that moment there was a knock on the door and Frank let Abe Russo in. He carried a sheaf of computer printout paper in one hand. His clothing was rumpled and he wiped a stray lock of sandy hair from his forehead.

"Here it is," he said, dropping the paper on the coffee table in front of them. "I've circled all the oriental males. There's thirty-one of 'em," he continued as they both began to look over the list.

"What are you looking for?" Tomkin said. "You know his name?"

Nicholas shook his head. "Even if I did, he'd never use it here." It was a long shot to expect to find the name Hideoshi on this list but it would have been foolish to have ignored the obvious. "This it?" he said to Russo.

The other nodded. "Yeah. Every one. Twenty-five are on the day shift, the rest are on at night."

"All twenty-five here today?" Nicholas asked. "None called in sick?"

"None sick. They're all here as far as I can tell."

"And no one knows about this?"

"Not a one," Russo said. "I worked on it alone."

"Okay," Nicholas said. "Let's go." He stood up.

"What's happening?" Tomkin said.

Nicholas rolled up the paper into a tube. "I'm going to see

all of these men face to face. Every one's a candidate for our ninja."

Russo took him through the labyrinth of the building and, one by one, the men on the list were interviewed and crossed off the list.

The thirteenth name was a Richard Yao. Russo didn't know precisely where he was working at this time of day, so they sought out his unit foreman. They found him supervising the welding going on in one section of the bottom of the atrium lobby. He was a heavyset man with almost no hair and close-set eyes.

"You just missed him, Abe." He took a thick cigar stub out of his mouth, used it to point over his shoulder. "He split."

"What for?" Russo asked.

"Said he was sick." He put the cold stub back into his mouth. "Didn't look too good neither."

"How long ago did this happen?" Nicholas said.

"Oh, I'd say fifteen—maybe twenty minutes ago. Like I said, you just missed him." He looked at Russo. "Anything wrong? He's a good worker."

Russo's eyes flickered briefly in Nicholas' direction before he shook his head negatively. "Thanks, Mike. You need another man down here?"

"I could use one."

"Okay. I'll see to it then."

On the way back up to the top of the tower, he said, "What do you think, Mr. Linnear?"

"I think," Nicholas said, "that we have our man."

"Well, hey, give me this for a sec—" He took the sheaf of paper from Nicholas' grasp, leafed through the accordion sheets. "Here!" His forefinger stabbed at the sheet. "Here's his address, 547—hey, wait a minute! That address is too far west. It's a phony!"

"I'm not surprised."

The doors opened and Nicholas sprinted down the corridor, leaving the other behind, staring at him. He pushed past Frank. Tomkin was on the phone, behind his desk. He put a palm over the mouthpiece. "Well," he said, "what gives? Did you find—"

But Nicholas was already at the verge of the desk, his fingertips moving quickly but surely around the rim of the top.

"What the hell—"

"Hang up," Nicholas said. He was circling the desk, probing. His fingertips never left the surface of the oiled wood.

Tomkin stared down at Nicholas' hands as if they were disembodied entities. He lifted the receiver to his ear, mumbled a few words and hung up.

"Good," Nicholas said, still moving. "I'd like to talk to you—"

"About what happened downstairs. Yeah. Yeah." His blue eyes were open wide as he watched. Across the room, Russo had come in. He stood quietly next to Frank, looking on.

"Right. About what happened downstairs." Nicholas knelt, began to search under the desk. He spoke as he worked. "I think we found our man." Wiring and computer modules. "The thirteenth. A man named Richard Yao. He was transferred here from a Rubin Bros. site in Brooklyn." Ridged templates: the computer grid. More wiring. "Not too long ago." As thick as a rat's nest, color-coded for easy repair. "Quite a good worker, so his foreman says."

"Yeah, so what?" Tomkin's deep-set eyes never left Nicholas' hands. "What's it to me?"

"He's our man. He split just after I made the call to Russo requesting the list of oriental male workers here at the tower." One ridge higher than the other and he backtracked with the tips of his fingers just to make certain. He gave a little pull. "Russo didn't speak to anyone about this little job and there was no time for anyone to get a peek." Fingers still in darkness with their minuscule prize. "Just Russo and me and"—he lifted it into the light at last, deposited on the gleaming desk top in front of Tomkin, a bright bit of plastic and metal, thin as a wafer, less than an inch in diameter— "of course, the telephone."

Tomkin's face had gone red and his head seemed to tremble somewhat. He reached out one forefinger, pushed hesitantly at the thing as if he thought it might bite him. "Goddamn it!" he cried. "Goddamn it! Under my own nose!" He pounded the table, looked up. "Frank, you sonovabitch! How'd you let that cocksucker in here? I'll kill you!"

Frank stood rooted to the spot, bewildered.

"It's not his fault," Nicholas said quietly. "He couldn't know what to look for."

But Tomkin was beyond calming words. He moved out from behind his desk, the forefinger that had touched the electronic bug waving in the air at his bodyguard. "Is this what I pay you for, you asshole? That—that *shit* was in here, prowling around! Where the fuck were you? Tell me that! Where the *fuck* were you?"

"I was here all the time, Mr. Tomkin," Frank said hastily. "Even when you were out to lunch, I was here. I never left, you gotta believe me. This guy must have busted in here at night, after you and me were gone. I don't—"

Tomkin soared forward, slammed Frank with the back of his hand. "Nobody broke in here, you schmuck—not without my knowing about it the next day." He watched the bright red stain on Frank's cheek; he could almost feel how hot the skin was. "No, he was here all right, under our noses. You were just too stupid to have seen him."

"But I didn't even know who to look for," Frank said.

"Shut up! Just shut up, will you?" Tomkin turned his back on him. "Christ, you sound like a baby crying."

Nicholas had been moving in a half-crouch outward from the epicenter of the desk in a tight spiral. It took him ten minutes of intensive search but he found a second bug under one section of the chocolate couch. No one said anything until he was finished.

"I think," Nicholas said, dusting off his hands, "that under the circumstances we'd better go downstairs."

"What for?" Tomkin looked puzzled. "The room's secure now, isn't it?"

Nicholas nodded. He was already moving toward the door to the corridor. "Tell you on the way down, okay?"

Tomkin's heavy voice broke the whirring silence of their descent. "I don't mind telling you that was a good piece of work you did up there, Nick. Damned fine. Thanks." He sighed. "You know I routinely have my office and homes electronically vacuumed every six months to weed out surveillance but, Christ, I haven't even moved in here officially." He ran his fingers through his iron-gray brush of hair. "Sweet Jesus, when I think of what he might have overheard over those lines! I'd like to rip his throat out!"

The doors slid open and they stepped out into the atrium.

"You don't think the bastard's here somewhere, do you?" His head moved from side to side.

"No chance," Nicholas said, guiding the other man along the lobby. "He knew security had been broken the minute he overheard my conversation with Russo. He's split. For the time being."

They went out into the hot sunshine on Park Avenue. Like stepping out onto the surface of a bloated, slowly turning planet, the burning atmosphere so thick it felt like gravity; locked in a pressure chamber.

As they approached the car, the thin bony chauffeur got out, stood waiting on the broken sidewalk, one hand grasping the door handle.

Nicholas stopped them midway along the plank walkway. The jarring sound of the jackhammers filled the air like a battery of dentists' drills. Tomkin had to lean close in order to hear what Nicholas was saying. He nodded and they climbed into the dim cool interior of the limo.

They started up immediately, nosing out into the traffic flow. Nicholas began to work. He went to the phone first, unscrewing both ends of the receiver, drew a blank. It had to be a place of easy access, he reasoned. The ninja might have been able to take his time in Tomkin's office but certainly not here. He looked into the well where the receiver was placed; very little room. He used one finger all around the sides. And came up with it. He depressed a button and an inch of window slid silently down. He threw the bug out. The window sighed up.

"Clear?" Tomkin asked.

He held up a hand, inspected all the obvious places; nothing.

"All right." He sat back up in the seat. "We're secure."

"Good." Tomkin's face relaxed visibly. "All of this has given me the creeps because it's come at the worst time imaginable." He leaned forward, depressed a hidden stud. A smoked-glass panel slid upward, cutting them off from the front of the car. Nicholas saw the cross-hatching of the wire mesh embedded within the glass. "I'm in the middle of one of the biggest deals I've ever made. It takes in corporations on three continents. The amount of money involved, well, it's incalculable. Christ, what I need now is not to be disturbed, so I get this—asshole—hanging around my neck." He chuckled, his mood shifting abruptly. "Well, I shouldn't complain, really. This idea originated with the Japanese. Only they were far too timid; they refused to go all the way with it even after I outlined the perfect methodology. Scared, is all. So we had a falling out—of sorts." He laughed. "I stole the idea. Shit, they were going to just sit on it for a while, 'study' the sampling they already had." He snorted. "No one'd get rich *that* way. Then they wanted back in after I had it running. Can you imagine? I told them to fuck off. They had lost a lot of face by then—too much, I guess. So they've sent the ninja."

Tomkin settled himself more comfortably against the plush velvet seat. "Might as well go somewhere now that we're out." He flicked a switch, gave the chauffeur an address on the West Side. "I'm hungry. How about you?"

"I could eat something."

"Okay. Good." He closed his eyes for a moment. "I don't want anything to happen to my girls, understand?"

Nicholas said nothing. He was thinking about what Croaker had told him about this man. He was wondering at the truth.

Tomkin turned his head sharply like a dog at the point. "I'm quite certain you think I don't give a shit about them. I can imagine the kind of fantasies Justine has told you about me."

"She really doesn't talk about you much. Does that surprise you?"

"Don't be impertinent with me," Tomkin said coldly. "It won't get you very far." His voice softened somewhat. "But, to be quite frank, I *am* surprised she hasn't told you all about me." He waved a hand as if in dismissal. "It doesn't matter, really. I still love them both. I know I'm not the world's best father but then they leave a lot to be desired as daughters. Let's just say we're all at fault."

"Perhaps if you didn't use your power with them the way—"

"Ah, then she did talk about me."

"A bit, yes. Once."

"My dear boy," Tomkin said, "I don't mean to be pompous but money *is* power or, more accurately, it's the other way around. It amounts to the same thing. That's my gift, you see. It's what I excel in. Making decisions, building power, watching the money pour in." He lifted a knowing forefinger to the side of his nose; absurdly, it made him look like an avuncular character out of a Dickens novel. "It's also what keeps me alive. I'd be dead tomorrow without that excitement; I can't give it up for anyone, not even my girls."

"Would you even want to?"

"To be honest, I don't know." He shrugged heavily. "But what possible difference could that make? It's a moot point. I don't love them any less for it; I'm merely denied certain things."

"So are they."

332

"Life is tough, huh? I'm glad you figured that out." He turned his head. "I guess I was right about you. I like the way you work."

They crossed Fifth Avenue on Fifty-seventh, heading west. Heavy traffic brought them to a standstill midway along the block. Behind them was the white modernistic sweep of Nine West. Fuel exhaust and the heat combined to streak the air as it rose in waves from the asphalt of the street.

"You know," Tomkin said while they were stalled, "money's a funny thing. Most people who don't have it want it very badly. But the ones who have it, if they have any sense at all, know what a fantastic burden it is. There are mornings I don't want to get up and go to the office, despite the excitement. I feel as if my body weighs tons, as if every breath I take is made painful by pressure." Up ahead, at Sixth Avenue, the light turned green. No one moved. After a moment, horns started blaring.

"But there are decisions to be made," he continued. "Decisions involving millions of dollars and the lives of thousands of my employees throughout the world. There's nobody but me to make them." His voice turned reflective. "That's excitement enough, don't you think? To know you're performing something in a way no one else can. You know about that as well as I do, eh? You do what you do better than anyone else."

"And what's that?"

Tomkin's eyes narrowed as if he were looking through cigarette smoke. "You're a very deadly man, Nick. Don't think I can't feel it. Even before I saw what you could do to Frank and Whistle. Oh, it was nice to see a graphic example of what had been in my mind's eye, of course. But I was as certain of you as I have been of anything. To tell you the truth, I'm glad Justine likes you—I think you'll be good for her. She should get to know what a real man's like."

The light had turned red again but the horns hadn't diminished.

"What's the problem, Tom?" he said into the grille.

"Bus broken down, Mr. Tomkin," came the electronically filtered reply. "Won't be long now."

"Buses," Tomkin said, readjusting his position. "Christ, I haven't been on a bus in over thirty years."

"Money'll do that to you," Nicholas said blandly.

"The only thing that money does," Tomkin said sharply, "is corrupt."

Nicholas turned his head. "Does that include you?"

"We're all susceptible; we all succumb. There're no exceptions, none at all. In that respect, money's the great leveler. It makes fools of us all." He barked a laugh. "All those assholes who tell you that money hasn't changed 'em are full of shit. Of course it has. They just like to stare at illusions they build for themselves. As for me, I'm a realist. I take the drawbacks and accept them. Everything has its price tag—you just gotta make sure you got enough to pay.

"Now take my late wife, for example. Jesus, there was a woman who knew sure as hell what she wanted only she didn't have the guts to come to grips with what went along with it. People like her, they piss me off no end, 'cause all they want is to stand and squat in a stream all day long while someone comes and wipes their asses for them three times a day. You think they ever heard of the word *responsibility*? Not a chance."

They began to move now and the limo slid to a stop at the far corner where Wolf's Delicatessen stood.

"Come on," Tomkin said. "I don't know about you but I can't wait to taste a Number One Combination."

Behind them, in the limo, the second bug, perfectly hidden under the carpet, remained undetected and undisturbed.

"You're not impressed?"

"It seems like a lot of space for one person."

"I'm claustrophobic."

Croaker laughed. "Yeah, well, I could see where you wouldn't be in this place." He came back from the windows overlooking the East River and Queens. His fingers stroked the butter-soft leather of the brown couch.

"Beautiful," he murmured.

"It gets a lot of attention." Her topaz eyes regarded him playfully. "Why, Lieutenant, I believe you're blushing. Don't tell me you've never met anyone of my profession before—that would be too much to swallow."

He groaned at the deliberate double entendre. "Do you always talk like that?"

"Only when I'm—only occasionally." He wondered what

334

she had been going to say. "Hey, I'm hungry." Immediately her face fell. "But, oh, there's nothing here—"

"That's okay, I've got to—"

"Oh, don't go. Please. Not yet, anyway." She crossed the room to the phone. "You deserve some time off—at least to eat. And they know where to reach you if something really hot comes up."

Yeah, he thought. Like the address of the lady who'll nail your old man to the bathroom wall. He felt immediately embarrassed and wondered why. He'd never felt that way before.

Gelda had her ear to the receiver, was saying, "I'll order us up some food. How about Italian? Do you like Italian food? I love it."

"Okay. Fine."

She nodded, dialed a number, waited a moment. "Philip," she said. "It's G. Yeah, fine. What about you? You sure? You sound a little funny. No? Hey, how'd you like to get me some food. Mario's, yeah. For two. You know what. Okay. 'Bye." She turned around.

"Who's Philip?" he asked. "Not a runner or something stupid like that? You wouldn't do something like that to me, would you?"

"Don't worry. No. He's just a kid who hangs around. Does stuff for some—of us." She saw the look on his face. "Cut it out. He's got no family but us. We all love him and he knows it. Is that monstrous?"

He smiled. "Sounds all right." He moved around to the front of the couch, sat down. "Feels nice."

She followed him, said when she was very close, standing over him, "You should feel it without clothes on."

He gave a slightly uncomfortable laugh.

Gelda walked toward the bedroom doorway. She began to take off her silk blouse. Before she had disappeared through the doorway, he had seen the flawless expanse of her naked back. Despite the fullness of her breasts, she wore no bra.

"What are you doing?" He got up from the couch, stood uneasily with his hands in his pockets.

"Just changing." He heard her voice drift back to him. "Don't worry, I won't attack you."

"I wasn't thinking of that," he said not quite honestly.

"Good."

He heard the sensuous rustle of silk against firm flesh.

"Do you want to come in," she said, "so I can see you while we talk?"

"I'm all right out here." He felt like a schoolboy on his first real date.

"Listen," she said, "you've seen my mind. I can't imagine what would embarrass you about seeing my body."

"Nothing," he said automatically.

"All right, then."

He stood where he was for a moment, feeling an outsider in this plush yet intimate landscape. In his mind, he tried to summon up clear images of what she did here but he could find nothing. He had an active imagination; at the moment it had shut down entirely.

He walked to the doorway, stood looking in on the threshold, a voyeur at his first peephole.

She stood with one leg up on the bedspread, putting on a stocking. A stocking, he thought, not panty hose. The perfect foot was dark, the flesh shining through the silk mesh so that the black was made pale, an altogether new color. The toes indented the spread as if she had stepped along the crest of a sand dune. Her legs seemed endless.

She wore bikini panties, a garter belt, both flesh-colored, soft and lacy. Otherwise, she was nude. The effect was startling.

She twisted her head over her shoulder to look at him. Her topaz eyes were very light. She smiled ingenuously. "There." The voice was but a wisp. "That wasn't so bad, was it?"

"I wish you'd put on some clothes."

She walked across the room. He tried not to stare at the movement of her breasts at each step but he had given himself an impossible task. When she reached the closet she raised her arms and his temperature at the same time. She drew out a forest-green silk satin robe, came toward him. "Is that better, Lew—I *can* call you Lew? After all, I threw up all over you in the van; I ought to be able to call you by your first name. At the very least." She brushed by him, went into the living room with the ghost of a smile.

He detached himself from the doorjamb, wondering what he was still doing here; always on the job, that's me, he thought. But what was really on his mind was his dark apartment crouching as deserted as Wall Street on a weekend, waiting for him to return. Going home to that seemed as out of the question as when it had been filled with Alison's scent.

"Should we go to bed now or after the food gets here?" He could not quite keep the anger out of his voice. There was a degree of control he felt had abandoned him sometime when his attention had been elsewhere.

Gelda turned in the middle of the room. Her belted robe opened as if on cue and he saw the gleaming length of one leg. "Is that what you think?" She was still smiling softly, like the gentle glow from a heavily shaded lamp.

"It's obvious, isn't it?"

"Is it?" One eyebrow arched. "You know my sexual preference."

Of course; he had forgotten. Deliberately? He felt an idiot. He put his hands in his pockets again, turned away, too embarrassed to apologize. Mental sets, he thought savagely. Isn't it odd how the eyes see one thing and the mind—that great complex monstrosity—makes leaps of illogic to form conclusions. He felt, abruptly, just as he had that scorching summer's day in Hell's Kitchen when not even the turned-on hydrants helped, when the steaming air hung like layers of blankets your well-meaning but misguided mother had wrapped you in when sick, impossible to take off. Tempers were short and incendiary as if everyone had an itch they couldn't scratch.

The cry came through the wide-open window and he was racing down the dark narrow stairs and into the baking sunshine. Just two doors away, he lay in the alley, his uniform dark with sweat and blood. Trash cans lay tumbled around him, having divulged their slimy secrets as if in one last paroxysm. The gray eyes were open and already glazing; eyes that had always reminded him of a storm-tossed sky. Gentle eyes.

So this was how it ended for Martin Croaker. After twenty-nine years on the New York City Police Force, lying sprawled in an alley piled high with garbage, surrounded by summer stink, fearful rats and incurious roaches, the wail of sirens forlorn in the distance, closing, shot four times forty feet from his own home.

He stared down at the corpse of his father and the world had spun around, canted dangerously on its axis. He felt that, at any moment, its momentum and crazy angle would combine to throw him off.

That's what he wanted, of course, to run far far away from this stinking hole; never to return. Never.

But that was the easy way out; the coward's way. Not Lew Croaker's way. His father had taught him too well.

So he stayed on. To join the police. Old and gray, his mother had come to his Academy graduation and had cried as he was sworn in.

He had never found the man responsible for his father's death but, after a time, that pain, too, had been put to rest.

He felt her touch his arm; he hadn't realized the wound was still sensitive. After all this time.

"I'm sorry," she said. "I shouldn't have teased you. I was just..."

"What? You were just what?"

Her eyes lowered. "Happy to be with you." She tried to make a half-joke out of it, failed. "You make me feel..."

"What?"

She looked up. "Just feel."

He felt torn. "I bet you could do that and not feel a thing."

She nodded. "I could. I'm an actress, of course. Do you distrust me? You couldn't. Not after what you said to me in the van. You took an enormous chance, telling me what you suspect about my father. It was an idiotic thing to do."

"That's me. Always the idiot."

"Yes." Her voice was as soft as silk.

"You know, you could sell me anything." He said it defensively, because she was so close. He wanted her to know he knew. He felt he needed that precaution now.

"No," she said, "I couldn't. Not now, anyway." She put her fingers along his arm; they seemed very warm. "The challenge, for myself, is to be honest with you. It's what will make me happy."

There came the sound of muted chimes.

She disengaged herself from him, disappeared into the old-fashioned foyer. Her voice floating, "Hi, darling. Come on in." Returning with her arm around a rather tall boy, dark-haired, almond-eyed. Philip. Croaker turned his back on the proceedings, stared out at the dazzle of the water. A long barge laden with garbage wallowed slowly upriver, a tug at its side. A man in a red and white track suit was jogging along the promenade. He passed the barge, going the other way, and disappeared from view. He and Gelda in bed—flash of flesh against flesh.

"What happened to you, darling? Your face looks awful."

Her voice was like the background chatter of a TV left on at low volume. He wanted that call to come in so bad he could taste it: the satisfaction of putting a bastard like Tomkin away for twenty years.

"What in God's name happened to you, darling? You look like you've been in a fight."

"No fight, G."

"Well, what then?"

"Nothing. I fell down...."

There was a sailboat out there—can you imagine? In the middle of the goddamned week. The sail white against the patchwork colors of the buildings on the far shore, scudding along as effortlessly as a cloud. No pressure out there on the river, just the wind and the salt spray and a long way until you reach port. Your own master. Her breasts heavy in his hands; her lips parting.

"...in an alley. The garbage cans—"

"Don't be an idiot, Philip. And don't lie to me. Darling, you must tell me what happened. Here, let me put some ice on it—do as I say." A soft clatter. "There."

There would be time, after Tomkin was put away, to take some time off. Go to the sea as Melville did when he was sick at heart and he felt like screaming at anyone who came too close. Yes, the sea. Not to fish; he hated fishing. But to sail, perhaps. He'd never done that and it might be time now to try her.

"At Ah Ma's—I worked there last night."

"Well, she'd never do that to you."

"No. A man—"

"A bastard, that's what. Here, keep the ice on for a little longer. I forbid you to go there again."

"But the man is coming there again tonight. She wants me to be there—"

"I don't care *what* Ah Ma wants, you're not going. She'll have to learn to do without you."

"It won't be any good without me."

"What do you mean?"

"The man wants me. That's how he—ejaculates. I said that right, didn't I?"

"My God—who is this man?"

"I don't know. A Japanese. A very strange man. Eyes like dead stones—you know, like he was from another world."

But Croaker was already turning, his face flushed with the adrenalin building in his body. "Talk to me, Philip," he said slowly and carefully, masking his excitement. "Tell me about the Japanese with eyes like dead stones."

Croaker was waiting for them at the tower's Park Avenue side. His big figure was leaning negligently against the side of his unmarked sedan. The detachable red light revolved atop the car, piercing the long twilight's sapphire haze like a lighthouse beacon's unerring warning.

Nicholas emerged from the limo as soon as it pulled over to the curb just to the uptown side of Croaker. As he went quickly toward the detective, he was acutely aware of Tomkin's presence blooming behind him as Tom, the thin chauffeur, held the heavy door open.

He was aware, too, of the city around him, everything shrouded in blue. The sun was just a memory but its heat refused to leave the asphalt under his shoe soles. The atmosphere was thick with exhaust fumes. The strings of dull yellow cabs along both sides of the avenue seemed like streaming caravans entering and leaving the bowels of the gilt-edged Helmsley Building.

"How's your boss?" Croaker's voice was flat and hard and unyielding; he stared past Nicholas' right shoulder.

Nicholas, feeling the live-wire buildup of tension, said, "Leave it alone, Lew. Forget about—"

"Too late for that, buddy."

He felt the presence directly behind him even before he heard Tomkin's voice say, "Still patrolling the streets, I see, Lieutenant. Keeping New York safe for us citizens?" The note of sarcasm was unmistakable.

"This city's still dangerous for some," Croaker said pointedly.

"What the hell's that supposed to mean?"

"Figure it out for yourself, Tomkin."

"I don't like veiled threats, Lieutenant. Not from anyone. Perhaps I should have another talk with the commissioner and—"

"I knew it was you, you dirty—"

"—we'll see how long you remain a lieutenant—"

"—reassigned now to this case Nicholas was hired for, so I guess we'll be seeing a lot of each other."

340

"What?"

There was a malicious grin on his face now, his skin yellow, alternately lighter and darker with the wash of passing headlights from the traffic flow.

Brake lights turned Tomkin's face reddish. "My God, I won't be saddled with you again!"

"Nothing you can do about it now, I'm afraid. The transfer came down directly from the commissioner himself. Even you won't get him to change that order. He'd look far too foolish, scurrying to rescind a reassignment."

"Christ, haven't I had enough of you, already? You've hounded me about—"

"I'm only here to protect you," Croaker pointed out, "and to nail the ninja before he gets you."

Tomkin's eyes narrowed. The peculiar monochromatic light had washed out all color from his eyes; they looked oddly pale. "Wouldn't you just love to sit back and let him do your dirty work? Sure, sure. You could say, 'Well, I'm sorry, Captain, but I did my best. I got beaten, is all. Can't blame me for that.'"

"Listen, you bastard"—Croaker lunged forward, trying to get around Nicholas' body—"I do my job better than anyone else in this creepy city and if that means making sure you don't buy it, I'll do it. When I nail you, buddy, it's gonna be for all the right reasons—"

"What reasons?" Tomkin snarled. "You got nothing—"

"No, but I will have," Croaker shouted. "And when I do, I'll be coming for you with a warrant that'll stand up to any of your high-priced attorneys!"

"You've got nothing," Tomkin sneered, "and you'll get nothing. I was nowhere near Angela Didion the night she was murdered. There's nothing linking me to—"

They were pushing and shoving now. Nicholas heard swift reports on the asphalt as sharp as rifle shots as Tom headed their way. He shouldered the two roughly apart, said, "Knock it off, both of you."

Then Tom had hold of his boss and was pulling at him. Tomkin allowed himself to be drawn away from the confrontation but lifted a finger, swung it in the air in Croaker's direction. "I'm warning you," he cried, "this is harassment. I don't want you near me!" And then, lowering his voice, said to Nicholas, "He's after me. I don't know why. It's a vendetta. I've done nothing, Nick. What's he doing to me?" He turned away abruptly, walked silently back to the limo with Tom at his side casting a worried glance or two over his shoulder. The revolving red light played on their backs intermittently.

"Well, that was pretty stupid," Nicholas said, turning around.

"Oh, who gives a fuck? What are you, my nanny? Jesus!" Croaker disappeared into the car.

Nicholas went slowly around to the passenger's side. He took his time climbing in. Croaker stared fixedly out through the windshield.

"Sorry," he said, after a time. And then, "That bastard really boils my blood."

"The antagonism isn't going to make anything easier."

Croaker turned his head; looked at Nicholas for the first time since he got in the car. "You know, I worry about you, Nick, I really do." Their reflections in the windshield like a neon sign, blinking on and off in the backwash of traffic headlights, a product advertisement. "You're a man who never loses control. Don't you ever get angry? Or sad?"

Nicholas thought about Justine. He wanted to see her now, to talk to her more than anything.

"Because I feel sorry for you if you don't."

"No cause to worry," he said softly. "I'm as human as the next person. All too human."

"Hey, you know I'd swear you're making that sound like a liability. We're all born into it, buddy."

"But me," he said. "I grew up thinking there was no room to make a mistake; that it was some kind of failure if I did."

"But you made them—"

"Oh, yeah." Nicholas laughed softly, without humor. "I made plenty of them, especially when it came to women. I trusted when I shouldn't have; now I guess I'm afraid to try it again."

"Justine?"

"Yeah. We had a heavy row. It's mostly my fault, I see now."

"You know what I think, buddy?" Croaker said, starting the engine.

"What?"

"I think the problem's not with you and Justine but in the past. What's so wrong in trusting someone? Like I said, we all do it. Sometimes it pays off and sometimes..." He shrugged. "But what the hell, right? It's worse never to trust anyone." He put the car in gear and they edged past Tomkin's limo, pulling over to the left to make the U-turn downtown.

The flood was coming, Nicholas knew. His face was awash in yellow and red, blue in the shadows between light sweeps. The *tsunami*, his personal tidal wave, was roaring blackly just behind him, looming over the world. The past will never die, he thought. Pain surged inside him, threatening to engulf him. All the bitter days, hanging like frost on the ledges of his soul, were returning again despite his careful compartmentalizing; the agony returning like a dull river of lead, climbing through him once more. He lacked the strength to push the memories away anymore.

Come! He thought savagely. Here I am; let it happen.

But before the *tsunami* hit, he heard Croaker saying triumphantly, "But cheer up. We got a break. We may not know who this ninja is but I know where he's gonna be at exactly 11 P.M. tonight.

"We're gonna be there, buddy, waiting. You and me and two blue-and-white backup units. We're gonna nail this bastard before he even gets a chance to get to Raphael Tomkin."

Osaka / Shimonoseki / Kumamoto / Tokyo Suburbs

WINTER 1963

At this time of the year the countryside was bleak and pale. The searingly spectacular deep reds and oranges of the autumnal foliage had already faded, dropped away to dull brown mulch under animals' hooves, and the first snow had obstinately yet to fall to leave the sere land hidden beneath its ghostly luminescence.

Rolling by rail under a low sky full of incipient rain reminding him of a child's face full of an emotion unacknowledged, it seemed sad to see the lines of bare trees like rough wire approximations of next year's model in among the eternal dark green of the sentinel pines. So forlorn, almost as if God had, after much effort, at last given up on this part of the world.

Nicholas allowed his eyes to focus on the far horizon. The speed-blur of the landscape passing closer about on a funhouse ride. Yukio, leaning half across him to get a better glimpse, pressed the side of one hard breast against him. Fingers spread on his thigh to brace herself against the rocking. Nails digging in, giving her purchase. Warmth spread upward into his groin and he wondered, half-afraid, half-expectant, if her hand would move up with it to cup him.

Opposite, on a seat facing them, a Japanese businessman in a dark-colored pinstripe and a scrubbed face; calfskin attaché case placed carefully on the seat beside him as mute company, surmounted by a charcoal-gray cashmere overcoat folded meticulously and, atop that, like the miniature couple on a white wedding cake, a black bowler hat—in all, an arcane archaeological pyramid offering no ancestral clues— glanced up from reading the paper. His eyes were given the unnatural size and annularity by his thick round glasses. He

345

blinked much as a fish might upon encountering an unexpected foreign object close to hand. Was he staring at the proximity of her fingertips to his crotch before he returned to his reading? The paper rustled slightly. It might have been a brick wall.

Nicholas could see the flash of reflected light from the curving edge of the thick gold ring. He imagined the man to be an important member of the *zaibatsu*. But which one, he wondered? Mitsubishi, perhaps? Or Sumitomo or Mitsui? Not one of the groups, surely, Fuyo, Sanwa, Dai-Ichi Kangyō. Of the seven lesser konzerns, he was obviously not from Nippon Steel, Toyota or Nissan. No, he had the look about him of the burgeoning electronics firms like Tōshiba-IHI, Matsushita, Hitachi—on second thought, scratch Hitachi—or Tōkyū. Did Tōkyū manufacture electronics, come to think of it? He wasn't all that certain.

Perhaps this man's family had started Mitsubishi—the families, he knew, were back running the *zaibatsu* as they had since the beginning. The American laws that had forced a hiatus had been stricken after only a brief term.

Nicholas stared at the paper barrier as if he had X-ray vision. He could see in his mind the round yellow face, slightly burnished with a light film of sweat, and, below it, the perfect collar white as snow, stiff and starched, the thin dark silk tie the color of the midnight sky. Here was a symbol of the new Japan: the painful climb out of the stone-age isolationism—oddly, still more pressing than the much more recent war—the human memory is so deliberately and depressingly selective. Adopting the Western mode of dress was just one manifestation of the Japanese cultural drive to catch up with the West. As monomaniacal as Tojo still. Or MacArthur. Our savior.

Parity was already a fact in Japan and the country was gearing itself up for overdrive, for the great push to surpass those countries from which it had learned. And there would come a day now, Nicholas was convinced, when the Japanese, having proved his economic strength, would shed his Western apurtenances, returning in rewon security to the traditional kimono, robes of state.

They were on the fast train—the express—from Tokyo to Osaka. Out the window on their right was all of the width of Honshu, the main island. On the other side they could see from time to time the glintings of the sea, throwing bright golden reflections in abstract patterns across the car's ceiling. The vibration from the rails was minimal, as was the noise on this sleek blue and silver liner, quiet, spacious and serene.

Yukio sat back in the seat, linked her arm through his. "Why don't we stay overnight in Osaka?" she suggested and then, as if in explanation, "I hate trains."

Nicholas thought about that. Perhaps it wasn't such a bad idea. The night life there was bright and glossy and he needed cheering up right now.

The little bit of clandestine cloak and dagger that Yukio and he had concocted regarding Saigō—he had quite conveniently forgotten whose suggestion it had been—had proved unnecessary. Astoundingly, before she had even had a chance to leave for the dinner at Satsugai's house, where she was to take a peek at Saigō's ticket destination, a note had been delivered to Nicholas. It was in Saigō's hand and it invited him to come to a town called Kumamoto in Kyūshū for a visit during the next few weeks. No reason was given for the invitation. Like everything in Saigō's life, this, too, was meant to be secretive.

Nicholas had read the note with a mounting sense of deflation. Irrationally, he felt as if Saigō had somehow read his mind and he could not throw off the anticipatory overtones the words set off in him, like a far-off bell tolling from some fog-shrouded hillside. "This will all be unexplored territory," Kansatsu had said to him, "if you decide it's what you want. It is totally your decision to make, Nicholas. I cannot guide you. Only say that here you can go no further. For that you must look to the darkness—and the light." Squelched, his plan had been cruelly revealed as just so much juvenile fantasy and, instead of thinking about why he had been asked south, he made himself busy feeling unhappy, defeated. And to make matters worse, Yukio went to dinner at Satsugai's anyway.

Mountains reared silently through the perspex window, blue-gray, ragged with streaks of snow running down from their summits like spilt cream. One of the three ranges of Alps—the most southerly, headed by Mount Shirane—passed like a cincture about Honshu's waist. Where was he headed now, he wondered. Into the light or the darkness? Did it matter?

"Especially this one," Yukio said as if there had been no space of silence between. "I hate this one. All the wide seats, the chrome trim, the bigger windows don't mean a thing to me. It's worse on this one. Because of the silence. The silence makes me restless." She made a face. "My foot's asleep." She shifted, stretching out legs on which she had been sitting. The businessman across the way rattled his paper, peals of warning.

"All right," Nicholas said. "Yes." There seemed no good reason to rush headlong into Kumamoto. Anyway, he'd only been to Osaka once when he was much younger and he was curious to see how much it had changed. Would he recognize it? He thought not.

He felt Yukio's presence close and warm beside him and he wondered if it had been intelligent to take her. In truth it had not been his idea. But after making his decision to accept Saigō's summons, it had proved quite impossible to deflect her. "It was you, after all," she had said in her most persuasively accusatory tone, "who got me involved in this in the first place." He could not recall whether or not that was so. "It's only fair you take me along now." She had flung her head back defiantly, sensually—but then, even in anger, she was superbly sensual. "Besides, if you don't, I'll only come with you on your own. Do you think you could hide from me?" He thought not. Decidedly un-Japanese, he had said to himself while acquiescing. Did the Colonel give in to Cheong in this way?

He often trembled when she was so close to him, his muscles jumping and twitching quite beyond his control. He sometimes clandestinely watched this phenomenon as if he were an outsider. This helped stymie the feelings of terror that rose, fluttering like leathery bats, from the pit of his stomach, rising toward his head. This he knew he must not allow to happen, otherwise he felt he might go mad. She passed a hand across his flesh and thus stirred that hidden pool at the core of his being which he had, for a time, thought closed even to himself. It remained inaccessible to him.

Mr. Mitsubishi, face glossy as a horse's hide after a canter, had put his paper down, folding it lengthwise. He proceeded to destroy the pyramid beside him, opening his attaché case, closing it again. On its spotless top he unfolded waxed paper in which was a chicken sandwich. Light lanced from his round glasses as he ate, turning him blind for moments at a time. Perhaps somewhere, Nicholas thought, he had a small bag of potato chips or a bar of chocolate.

348

Behind him, a group of Japanese businessmen, in all respects identical to Mr. Mitsubishi, rustled inside their dark three-piece suits like chrysaline insects, black bowlers on their laps, chattering animatedly about the two Jacks, Ruby and Kennedy.

One did not travel to Osaka for culture—one went to Kyoto, the country's original capital, for that. It was commonly said—mostly by the inhabitants of Tokyo—that Osakans were money-mad businessmen, greeting each other on crowded street corners with the all-too-familiar phrase "*Mō kari makka?*" Making any money?

Nicholas had little first-hand knowledge of such affairs yet it was true that secreted along the city's riotous streets, like tiny pockets of the past encysted within the neon age, were numerous shrines to Fudōmiyō-ō, the deity overseeing such matters that concerned the dedicated businessman. These shrines never seemed to lack for attention.

He took them to a smallish modern hotel not far from the Dōtombori where they checked into separate but adjoining rooms. It being still too early for dinner, they immediately set out to see the city.

Yukio insisted on seeing Osaka Castle, that last bastion of refuge of the Toyotomi family, besieged by Ieyasu Tokugawa after he had already assumed the mantle of Shōgun in 1603. It had been erected by Hideyoshi Toyotomi—as had much of Osaka—and was completed within three years, in 1586.

"There was a time," Yukio said as they strolled through the park bordered at their backs by the modern Osakan skyline, "when the Lady Yodogimi was my ideal." The castle loomed through the lowering afternoon, seeming larger than life, a squat pagoda, stolid and boxlike. It was not, Nicholas reflected, the kind of structure that Ieyasu would have had built.

The crowds grew in size as they approached the castle's outward fortifications. "What I thought was so...special ...was how she carried on the will of Hideyoshi, even after his death, just as if she were a samurai herself. She devoted herself totally to the safety of the heir."

"Oh yes," Nicholas said. "Yes." They had reached the first of the stonework, massive and hulking in the lengthening shadows. "To the detriment of the rest of the country. She and Mitsunari plotted—"

"They *plotted*—as you choose to put it—to protect the Shōgun's son. They did what honor dictated."

Nicholas shook his head from side to side. "Yukio, Yodogimi was the Shōgun's mistress, not his legal wife. Her aspirations were a bit grandiose." He waved a hand as if in dismissal. "In any event, Ieyasu proved a far too potent foe for them." He stopped.

"You talk as if Yodogimi was some kind of villain in some children's storybook."

"Well, she hardly had the best interests of Japan in mind, you must admit that."

"Perhaps the child would have grown up to be this country's finest leader."

Nicholas looked past her. To their left was a small shedlike structure. The arms house. It was here that Yodogimi had brought her son and their retainers when the end had become inevitable; it was here she took her son's life before committing *seppuku*. "That's all rather irrelevant, don't you think? In the years it would have taken him to come of age, without one *daimyo* strong enough to become Shōgun and lead Japan, the country would have been plunged again into the civil war from which Hideyoshi had saved it. Without Ieyasu's strength, Japan would have been doomed."

"Still, such a brave woman. Loyal and brave." Yukio's voice might have been the whisper of the wind. "So selfless." She watched the parade of tourists before the shed. "I admire her so much."

Hidden, the sun slid downward to the earth as if too heavy to sustain its own weight. The sky was like gray ribbons fluttering across an excited girl's breast, parting at the soft advance of her lover. There was a brief flash of gold, stonework in flickering torchlight, then it was gone.

"Come on," he said, taking her hand. "Onward and upward."

Of course, the original Osaka Castle had been razed in 1615, when it had been overrun by the forces of the Tokugawa; a structure, like Nicholas, previously regarded as impregnable. This one they strode had been constructed of ferroconcrete in 1931.

Nightside. Along the Dōtombori, jammed with restaurants, shops, newsstands, movie theaters, nightclubs, restless crowds and, above all, the vast spotlit signs glittering in the night, pushing the darkness away as if it held no dominion here. Colors spun, neon lights blinking on, off, on in time to the heartbeat of the shifting traffic.

Time seemed suspended here, as if in a dream these dazzling colored lights, celebrants of power, called here to summit, would brook no outside interference even from such a basic concept.

A great replica of a crab, crimson and white, its spiny carapace gleaming, so many centered spots focused upon it the light seemed to drip from it like honey, hung over them, a temptation to enter and eat the night away.

They dined in a place of glossy emerald-green lacquered wood and thick bars of mirror-bright chrome as incandescent as neon tubing, replicating portions of their faces as they moved. In a private tatami room, shoeless, stuffing themselves with sashimi and sake—did they both appear so much older?—she would not let him forget the castle's awesome history or its daunting inhabitants.

"I suppose I adore her because I am so little like her." She poured more rice wine with a steady hand.

"Meaning?"

She met his gaze for a moment before her eyes slid away. "I'm not loyal and I'm not in the least brave. I am only Japanese." She gave a tiny deprecatory shrug. "I am a Japanese coward. No one is interested in that. A Japanese without any family: therefore without loyalty."

"You forget your uncle."

"No." She shook her head; her black hair gleamed in the low light. "I don't forget him. Ever."

"He's family."

Her eyes flashed. "Must everything be spelled out for you? I hate Satsugai. How would you feel about an uncle who would not have you with him, who put you into the hands of—" She swallowed sake convulsively.

"One day," he said, eyes on his plate, "you will find someone. Fall in love."

"No loyalty, remember?" Her voice held a tinge of bitter-

351

ness. "I was born without it just as I was born without the capacity to love. They are alien concepts to me."

"Because you think that sex is the only thing you have."

"The only thing that makes me happy," she corrected.

He looked up. "Don't you see that's just because you think of yourself as worthless?" He reached out, covered her hand with his. "What you really can't conceive of is anyone caring about you—I mean you as a person, not wanting to be with you because of what you can do with your body."

"You're being an idiot." But she did not take her hand away and this time she did not look away either.

"If that's what you choose to call it."

"I do. I have no trust. Truly. Can't you just accept me for what I am? You can't make me over."

"It's not a question of that. I want what I feel is inside you to have a chance to come out—"

"Oh, Nicholas"—she put her fingers against his cheek—"why torture yourself by thinking about some future that will not come about. Who knows? I may be dead in a year—"

"Shut up," he said quickly. "I don't want to hear you talking like that, understand?"

"Yes," she said, surprisingly meekly. Her head dipped as if in penance and her thick hair slid across one side of her face like a midnight waterfall. She was the model Japanese wife bowing before the inevitable authority of her husband's words.

"And anyway, who says you're not brave?" He wasn't used to this. He wanted desperately to lean over the table and kiss her half-open shadowed lips but lacked the nerve. "Just think of what you've been through, growing up with that couple. That took a lot of strength."

"You think so?" A little girl now.

The waitress rustled in and knelt by the side of the low table, delivering more food and drink. Nicholas watched her leave as she slipped on her *geta* at the threshold.

"I just said so," he whispered fiercely. "What's the matter with you?"

"I don't know." Dark eyes on the tabletop. "I don't know."

He filled her porcelain sake cup, white and tiny.

* * *

They went out walking, she chattering on animatedly as if nothing untoward had happened, clutching his arm, aimlessly drifting from topic to topic.

Stealing the dark, hiding it in their side pockets as they filtered through the honky-tonk night life, through swirling colors and blaring noise. The air smelt of incense and petrol fumes, the walls of the evening brilliant with the unrelenting marquees here in the city of merchants, erected almost overnight, this new class universally despised by the noble samurai and the lowly peasant alike.

An enormous arcade of pinball wizards they passed up after staring for long moments like the most ignorant of country bumpkins and, farther along, the electronicized insistency of American rock 'n' roll, a quicksilver pulse projecting from a music store's loudspeaker. The wail of harmonized black voices drenched by a wave of strings and the backbeat, always the backbeat like a burnished path guiding you through the melodies. They dance before the lighted window on which is taped a black and white publicity photo, streaked by reflected light: John, Paul, George, Ringo. *Close your eyes and I'll kiss you / Tomorrow I'll miss you / Remember I'll always be true*... Around and around. *And then while I'm away / I'll write home every day*... Red and green and yellow neon bars, swinging her from one to the other; a rock 'n' roll fan overnight. *And I'll send all my loving to you....*

"Who are they?" says Yukio, slightly out of breath.

"The Beatles," says the shopkeeper. "A new band from England."

And he buys her the record, imported and exorbitant.

But down the next block they heard the stentorian tones and the intermittent music of the *samisen*. Culture shock. And turned in to investigate.

It was the Bunraku, the traditional puppet theater, indigenous to Osaka, as the Kabuki was to old Edo. Yukio was delighted and, clapping her hands together as if she were a child, implored him to take her inside. He dug into his pocket, bought them two tickets.

The theater was nearly full and they had some difficulty finding their seats. The play had just begun but he knew from the billboards outside that it was the famed *Chūshingura*, "The Loyal Forty-Seven *Ronin*."

The puppets were magnificent, the principal ones dazzlingly dressed, so complex that they required three men to manipulate them successfully. The master puppeteer for the head, body and right arm, a second for the left arm and the third for the legs or, in the case of the females, the kimono skirts.

They were seated near the back and, some time after they arrived, a couple of marines drifted in. Why they had come to the Bunraku on leave Nicholas could not imagine. One was white, the other black. They might have been waiting for their girls or, perhaps, a third buddy. The white man slid into a row but the black marine turned, stood waiting in the center aisle.

Nicholas saw Yukio's eyes drifting from the color of the stage. He saw where she was looking. Like a retriever on point, her gaze locked on the large bulge of his crotch. Colors swam in reflected light, reminding Nicholas of an aquarium his parents had taken him to in Tokyo. It all seemed so unreal. Her lips slightly open, he saw the sharp rise and fall of her breasts as she breathed, as she watched.

In the dimness, he felt her fingers between his thighs, caressing, the zipper of his fly being drawn down, the heat enveloping him. Hard. And still she stared, never turning her head, her eyes wide and glittery. His loins turned to water. He wanted to shout to her: *Stop!* But he could not. Had she blinked in all this time? He wanted to take her fingers away from him but he did not. Just sat there watching the Bunraku, the black marine's crotch in the periphery of his vision, ballooning ominously. How big was he? How big could a man be? Was that a criterion for sex appeal, the way Americans felt about big breasts? Did it drive women wild?

The *samisen* played on. The *ronin* fought with proper valor. Yeah, yeah. *Yeah!*

"You know what it is I hate about being Japanese?" she said. Street-light, blue-white through the blinds, threw angular bars of light-shadow-light across the top of the far wall and part of the ceiling.

He turned in the bed. "What?"

"Not having light eyes." She sighed and he knew her wide, sensual lips were drawn in a pout. "The French girls I see in Kyoto and the American ones, too, with their short hairdos and their blue eyes. Funny, I've always dreamed of having green eyes like emeralds."

354

"Why think about it?"

"It makes me realize, I think, just how much I dislike myself. Here"—she reached out, took his hand in hers, guided it to the heat between her legs—"this is the only thing that matters. Right here."

"No," he said, taking his fingers away, "that's not important at all."

She turned on her side; her voice was light now. "Not even a little bit?"

He laughed. "All right, yes. Just a little bit, then." He rose up, leaning over her slightly. Her skin was pale in the half-light, her thick hair a black forest. "Look, Yukio, I was interested in you before we danced that night."

"Before I—"

"Rubbed yourself all over me."

She put her hand out, lightly stroking his chest. A muscle fluttered and he felt the familiar tightening of his stomach. It felt as if a hand were pressing against his lungs, pushing powerfully down so that he had difficulty breathing. He might have been an asthmatic in fog.

"What is it?" she said just before he whirled away to sit on the edge of the bed. "What are you afraid of?" She sat up and he felt her looking at him. An odd way to put it. "Is it me, Nicholas? Are you afraid of me?"

"I don't know," he said miserably.

And that was the trouble.

They left Osaka on an old prewar train which, despite its perfect cleanliness, was in marked contrast with the superliner that had brought them to the city.

There were rattles, squeaks and a fair amount of jounces. The swaying, too, was more pronounced but, oddly, the added vibration produced in him a calming effect. His mind kept returning to the Bunraku performance; to, more accurately, Yukio's performance. Was she a nymphomaniac, he wondered? But how could he tell? He did not even know the clinical definition. Was someone who was sexually insatiable a nympho? Could it be that easy to define? He couldn't even say that Yukio was insatiable. Her sexual thirst *could* be slaked. It just took an enormous amount of energy. And, anyway, what if she was? Would that make any difference to him?

355

He turned away from her presence, staring out the window. Rattle, rattle. Someone came down the aisle, half-fell against her as the train lurched around a turning. The land fell away in a sharp gradient here, giving onto flat fields and rice paddies. He thought he saw cattle standing motionless in the distance. In less than an hour the tracks would turn southeast toward the sea.

The day was bright, the sun burning away the white ground fog by late morning.

Kobe, along with Yokohama, the busiest port in Japan, was already far behind them with its scores of freighters and its international settlement comprising fully a quarter of the city's population.

We're well away from there, Nicholas thought. Such strictly business-oriented places, like parts of downtown Tokyo, made him nervous. Like airports, they all had a frightening similarity that cut across language and even race. He never knew where he was in airports—he could be anywhere at all in the world and never know it. Train stations, however, were quite different. Oddly enough, there were no two alike that he had seen and this kind of old-world individualism was comforting to him. Of course, on trains, one could look out the window and see far more than just gray clouds like wisps of an old man's beard, parting like gossamer. What held the goddamned thing up, anyway?

He tore his eyes away from the ribboning land, glanced around the car. The passengers, too, on this train were different. The last businessman had debarked at Kobe and now, all around him, he watched the people of the land. A man in blue overalls and thick-soled, high-topped shoes sat with his thickly callused hands crossed over his lean belly, chin on his chest, legs stretched out, ankles crossed. He had very short hair which was white and a stiff-looking mustache which was black. A farm worker, perhaps, on his way home. Across the car, a fat woman in a bright white and crimson kimono slept peacefully with her mouth open and the breath hissing in and out. Beside her, a squat stack of brown-paper-wrapped parcels. Two kids in Western clothes knelt, arms and elbows along the seat top, making faces at anyone who passed.

"...in the back."

"What?"

"Nicholas, have you been listening to me?"

356

"No. I'm sorry. I was thinking about the Bunraku."

She laughed. "You mean the way I jerked you off."

"I don't," he said, "understand why you feel you have to talk like a sailor. Why, for example, must you say 'fuck' instead of 'make love'?"

"Because," she answered seriously, "'fuck' is exactly what I mean. Have you ever *made love*, Nicholas? Tell me what it's like."

"I make love to you."

"What are you talking about? We *fuck* like bunnies."

"I don't even think that is what you do."

"Oh no?" Her tone rose slightly. "Listen, Nicholas, I fuck you the way I fuck everyone else. You know what I do with you? Well, I do it with other men, too. With Saigō, for instance." Now why did she bring him up? "I come on the edge of his hand, against the instep of his foot, his tongue and his nose, his—"

"All right!" he cried. "Enough! What the hell do you think you're doing?"

She rubbed herself against him, began to purr like a giant cat. "Me? I'm just trying to get you excited, that's all. You weren't paying attention to me and I—"

"Jesus!" he said, getting up. "Is that the way?" He went roughly past her, out into the aisle to the end of the car, stood watching through two sets of glass at the jouncing car behind his. Christ, he thought, did she think telling him about her past conquests would turn him on? What a twisted idea. He felt cold and slightly nauseated. He braced himself against the swaying with a stiff arm against the door frame.

On his right a town flashed by, becoming smaller as they pulled away toward the southeast. He glanced at his watch, calculating distances and speed. That should be Kurashiki. Good. They were but moments away from sighting the northern end of Seto Naikai, the Inland Sea, which he had always found so peaceful and calm during the summers his parents had taken him there as a child.

They plummeted through thick stands of tall gaunt pines, the car darkening abruptly and eerily as if they were in the midst of an eclipse. Then, just as swiftly, the sun broke through again and the foliage fell sharply away on the right, revealing the high bluff along which they raced. Below them, Seto Naikai, glittery with sunlight, dancing like ten thousand golden scimitars, a jewel field.

He watched, transfixed at the sight. But still. Part of his mind was in a film. This was the point when Yukio should come silently up behind him, put her arms around him and tell him she was sorry. This was no film and it never seemed to happen to him that way. And why should he expect it? He did, nevertheless. The eternal romantic.

Islands, so far from home, humpbacked and flat-faced stretched one after another across the waters of the Inland Sea, all the way to the horizon. Was there really, as he had been told as a child, more land than water here? He could not say and he thought then that it did not matter. They looked like pieces of intricate knitting, these islands, terraced to make them productive; usable land was at a premium in Japan.

One day, he thought, I would like to spend my time just traveling from one island to another, talking to the people there, sitting down to eat with them after helping them in the terraced fields, spending a night here and there. I think that if I did that, I'd probably live out my life and die before I got to the last one. What an idea! Never to go back, only forward. Each day different from the one before and the one after. Never to get tired; never to get bored. As he was now. Awfully young to feel this way, he mused. But he knew that he was not bored or tired but merely feeling the symptoms of each, hiding what he really felt.

Fear.

In Hiroshima it was a completely different story. In the bay, above which they passed like a wisp of smoke, they saw Miyajima, marked by the great orange and black *torii*, the gate of the Itsukushima Shrine. It was one of the most spectacular sights in all the islands, one that he had seen many pictures of but, until now, had never seen in person.

It hung there as if in midair, rising out of the tidal water like a great three-dimensional cuneiform character written upon the world, mark of the old Japan, a warning never to forget the past.

The train seemed to stand, huffing, for a long time in the Hiroshima Station. All about them were the squat ugly in

358

dustrial structures dominated by a kind of incandescent silence hanging in the air, as thin and brittle as a robin's egg.

The seat facing them, long vacant through the afternoon, was taken by a gaunt, spare man in a gray and brown kimono. His head was hairless save for a few wisps of white beard hanging from the point of his narrow chin. His skin seemed as translucent as parchment, stretched across high cheekbones, but underneath his eyes and at the sides of his mouth one could see the masses of wrinkles like the vast accumulation of the years, an ancient tree whose age one could count by the number of rings in its flesh.

His eyes were bright chips as he nodded to them. His hands were lost within the folds of his formal robe.

Soon after, the train gave a little lurch and they began to move slowly out of the station. On the way out, the feeling of oppression only magnified as if all the air had been sucked away and what remained to breathe, if only they would open the window and stick their heads out, was the frosty vacuum of space. They might have been on another planet.

Nicholas felt a creeping in his flesh and he looked out the window, upward into the bright porcelain sky, certain he had heard the heavy drone of an airplane.

The train moved with unutterable slowness through the city. For a moment they could see, silhouetted against the near horizon, the shell of the old observatory, standing just as it had been left in 1945, its surmounting hemisphere a bird's-nest skeleton, a lonely, forbidding eyrie for the gulls that swooped low near it but would never touch its inimical skin. Perhaps even after all this time they could still feel the incendiary heat, the hissed outpouring of radiation, carrying it in their bones like a race memory, the survival instinct.

"You want to know the real me?" Yukio said into his ear as they both stared at the only monument to what had happened here such a short / long time ago. "There. You see it. That is what I am like inside. What you see on the outside is all that's left standing."

Now he thought she had become maudlin, turning full circle from her usual sardonic tough-as-nails stance. But, he thought, it was this dichotomy that most intrigued him about her. And he did not for a moment think she was as uncomplicated as she made out. He knew that to be a defense—her ultimate defense perhaps. Still, he could not stop himself

359

from wondering what manner of unfamiliar territory lay beyond the stone wall she had so effectively erected.

Streamers of cloud flew obliquely across the sky as they left Hiroshima behind, seemingly to begin from the ground, reaching up into the very heart of heaven.

"Pardon me," said the old man across from them. "Please excuse this intrusion but I could not help wondering."

He paused and Nicholas was obliged to ask him, "What were you wondering?"

"If you have ever been to Hiroshima."

"No," Nicholas said and Yukio shook her head.

"I didn't think so," the old man said. "In any case, you would be too young to remember the old city, to have seen it before the annihilation."

"Did you?" Yukio asked.

"Oh yes." He smiled, almost wistfully, and when he did the wrinkles seemed to fade from his face. "Yes, Hiroshima was my home. Once. That seems very far away now, I think. Almost as if it were part of another life." He smiled again. "And in an important way it was."

"Where were you," Nicholas said, "when it happened?"

"Oh, I was away in the hills." He nodded. "Yes, safely away from the fireball. Trees shook miles away and the earth convulsed as if in pain. There was never anything like it. A wound in the universe. It went beyond the death of man or animal or even civilization."

Nicholas wanted to ask the old man what it was that went beyond all those things but he could not bring himself to do it. He stared, dry-mouthed.

"It was lucky you weren't in the city when the bomb fell."

The old man regarded Yukio. "Luck?" he said as if tasting the flesh of some unfamiliar fowl. "I don't know. Perhaps luck might be a modern equivalent, though an inadequate one. If anything, it was karma. You see, I had been out of the country just prior to the war. I was a businessman in those days and went quite often to the continent. Mostly to Shanghai, where a majority of my selling was done." For the first time his hands came into view and Nicholas saw the unnatural length of his nails. They were perfectly manicured, buffed and gleaming with clear lacquer. The old man saw the look in Nicholas' eyes, said, "An affectation I picked up there from the Chinese mandarins with whom I did business and who befriended me. I do not even notice them now, I've grown so accustomed to them. But, of course, these are only of quite a moderate length." He settled back more comfortably in the seat, began to speak as if telling a bedtime story to his grandchildren. He had a remarkable speaking voice, commanding yet gentle, as well modulated as a seasoned lecturer's. "We took some time off over a long weekend and, all our business completed, we went into the countryside for a bit of relaxation. I had no idea what to expect, really. These were Chinese, after all. The mandarins have, ah, peculiar tastes in many things. But in business one must learn to be cosmopolitan in one's thinking—especially when it comes to the matter of your clients' personal tastes. Yes, I do not believe that it is good policy to be closeminded or, ah, traditional here. The world supports a myriad of cultures, is that not so? Who is to say which is the more valid." He shrugged his thin sharp shoulders. "Certainly not I."

Outside, the afternoon was waning, the oblique cloud banks streaked with gold and pink on their undersides, a charcoal gray above. The sun was already out of sight below the horizon and in the east the sky was clear, a vast cobalt porcelain bowl, seeming translucent. High up, several first-magnitude stars could already be seen flung aloft as if by a giant hand. The world seemed suffused with an absolute stillness as at the midpoint of a long summer's afternoon when time itself ceases to have any meaning. It was a magical time, made up of fantastic elements having all miraculously arrived at the same spot at one instant, the inaudible sigh the inner ear hears in that last moment in a theater before the curtain rises.

"They took me on a journey, my mandarin friends. To a town within a town, as I said, outside of Shanghai. It was—excuse me, my dear—a bordello. Not merely the building we went to, oh no. The entire town. Yes, that's right, a city of pleasure. You will forgive me, young lady, parts of this tale. A man on business for weeks at a time—one can ill afford to take one's wife along on such trips for many reasons. And these things become, well, almost an expected part of the trip.

"The mandarins regard sex very highly, oh my, yes, they certainly do. And I cannot say that I blame them." He gave a little chuckle, not at all smutty but rather avuncular. "It is, after all, both a necessary and an important part of life, so why not honor it.

"Uhm, in any event it was the most sumptuous, the largest such place I had ever been to. The clientele was strictly mandarin and further, I gathered, only certain families. Extremely exclusive, yes." His eyes were big and dreamy. "One could live the rest of one's life there quite easily, I daresay. But, of course, that is not possible. Such places are only for a small amount of time. That kind of rarefied atmosphere would, I imagine, pall after a time. Anyway, I wouldn't want to chance it. Life would most certainly be not worthwhile if all such spectacular dreams were shattered. Everyone needs times in their life when reality can be set aside, hm?"

The train rattled onward, across a trestle bridge, plunging into a bleak and scraggy forest of deciduous trees, as forlorn as the ragtag remnants of some defeated army. The light was dying, the clouds stark now in their blackness, only losing definition near the horizon where the haze rendered all color indistinguishable. Night had swept them up as swiftly as a remonstrating parent.

"So. Here we are in this place. But my purpose is not to tell you all the goings-on there." He smiled winningly. "You're young enough not to need any help from me on that score. No. Rather, I wish to tell you about a man I met there." He held up one long bony but perfectly straight finger. The long nail gleamed in the artificial light of the car, causing it to look like a street marker. "Curious. About this man, I mean. He was no client, of that I am certain. Yet neither did he appear to be an employee of the establishment. Certainly I never saw him at work.

"Late in the night, or early in the morning, to be completely accurate, he could be found in the great first floor parlor—the building had two stories; it may have been British-made, though certainly for quite a different purpose originally—sitting in one of the overstuffed wing chairs playing a game with red and black marked tiles I had never seen before—"

"Mah-jongg?" Nicholas asked.

"No, not mah-jongg. Another game entirely. One I could never fathom. He would sit there silent and motionless while the girls cleaned up and when they had finished and had left he would begin to play. *Click-click. Click-click.*"

The old man lifted out a cigarette and, with some difficulty, owing to the length of his nails, lit it with a thin gunmetal Ronson. He smiled as one eye squinted up with the smoke. He might once have been an oriental Humphrey Bogart, the expression came so naturally to his face. He twisted the lighter's wide face so that the light glanced off it in a flare. "A memento of those days, so far away. Belonged to a British diplomat whom I helped out of a spot of trouble there. He insisted I take it. I would have lost face had I not." He pocketed the Ronson, drew briefly on the cigarette, let it out so that his image was as hazed as the countryside rolling by outside.

"It was impossible for me to sleep in that place—even after I had been satiated. I hope I am being delicate enough, young lady."

'Perfectly," Yukio said. Nicholas wondered what the old man would think if he heard the way she threw words around.

"It was my habit to read late at night—I am an insatiable reader. Have been all my life. But one night I felt restless enough to put my book down—I was reading *Moby Dick*. In English, mind you—I don't trust translations; you lose too much—and take a stroll through the first floor.

"*Click-click. Click-click.* I heard the tiles as he moved them. I sat next to him and watched. In those days I was certainly a brash young man. Not rude, mind you. I was far too well brought up by my parents. But I had a spot of—what shall I say?—the impetuosity of youth, yes?

"Now this man was older than I am today, a good deal older, I would say, but then I am an abysmal judge of age so you must not go by me. Still, he was old. Anyone who saw him would certainly say that, yes.

"The odd thing about him was that his nails were so long that he was required to wear sheaths to protect them from breaking. These sheaths were something I had read about before. The mandarins were fond of wearing them, as an affectation, I had always supposed, during the turn of the century. However this was the late 1930s. Who in China still kept their nails thus? No one, I had thought. Now I knew differently.

"Usually these sheaths were of lacquer but these, if my eyes did not lie, were made of gold. Solid gold. But how could this be? I asked myself. How could the nails support such a weight? Still, I know gold and there was no doubt.

"'Why have you come here?' asked the man without looking up. *Click-click*, went the tiles. *Click-click*.

"I was so startled that for a moment I could not find my

voice and he was obliged to prompt me. 'Come, come,' he said. Just like the *click-click* of his tiles. The same cadence.

"'Can't sleep,' I said, still rather tongue-tied.

"'I never sleep,' he said. 'But that is because of my advanced age.' He looked up at me. 'When I was your age, I never missed a night. Perhaps that is why I don't miss it now.' He spoke in a rather peculiar dialect. It was Mandarin all right, but the inflections were odd, some nouns clipped at their ends, and so on. I could not place where he was from.

"'I don't often have this trouble,' I said, still the dazzling conversationalist. 'But you're not that old.'

"'Old enough to know that I am going to die soon.'

"'Oh, I doubt that.'

"He eyed me critically. 'Well, sentiment is never very accurate.' He began to stack up his tiles, nine to a pile. 'But there is no need for concern. I have no fear of death. In fact, I will happily leave here now. I do not want to see what is coming.'

"'Coming?' I said like a half-wit. 'What is coming?'

"'Something terrible,' he said. His hands on the small lacquered folding table looked like shining alien artifacts, newly unearthed. 'A new type of bomb with a power beyond anything you can imagine. With enough force to destroy an entire city.'

"I shall never forget that moment. I sat as still as a statue, barely breathing. I remember hearing the chirruping of a cicada so clear and near that I thought it must have gotten itself trapped inside the house. Oddly, I found myself wanting to get up and find it to free it into the vast darkness which surrounded us.

"I could not move. It was as if his words had pierced my heart, riveting me to the chair in which I sat.

"'I don't understand,' I said with a kind of opaque astonishment.

"'It is not likely that you would,' he said, finishing stacking his tiles. Then he put them away into an inside pocket of his robe.

"He rose and, for an instant, I thought I might have known him or at least seen him at another, previous time. But I think now it was just the light which made it seem so."

"What happened then?" Yukio asked.

"What happened?" The old man looked momentarily nonplussed. "Why, nothing. Nothing at all. 'Good evening to you, sir,' he said in his somewhat formal way. 'I wish you pleasant dreams.' Though how he could have meant it after what he had just told me I could not imagine.

"The place was very still after he left and, slumped back in my chair, I imagined I could hear the sound of the grass growing outside where the tree frogs slept. A cloud of mosquitoes whined against the netting.

"At some time I must have gone upstairs—though I have no real remembrance of doing so—to Ishmael and Ahab and the *Pequod*, though I could not well concentrate on even so great a world as Melville's that night.

"His words ran around my head as if he had somehow engraved them upon the grooves of my brain with a cunning scalpel."

"But how could he have known?" Nicholas asked. "At that time not even the Americans who eventually comprised the Manhattan Project knew."

The old man nodded. "Yes," he said slowly. "That is often what I ask myself. From that day in August when I stood on that secluded hillside and felt the earth shake and the sky burn with color and heard the heat wind coming, I have asked myself that same question. How could he know?"

"And what is the answer?"

The old man looked at them and smiled wanly. "There isn't one, my friend." The train was slowing as it came out of a downgrade. Cinders flew, whirled up and around by the wind eddies created by their passage. He stood up and bowed to them, long hands clasped against his flat stomach, nails like translucent chopsticks. "My station," he murmured. "Time to get off."

"Hey!" Nicholas said. "Wait a minute." Forgetting, in his anxiety to know more, his modes of speech, lapsing into the common formation; it lacked the necessary respect a younger person must show toward someone his elder. It did not matter, however, for the old man had gone, swinging lithely down off the car even before the train had come to its full panting stop. Clouds of steam obscured the windows.

Nicholas came back down the aisle, slumped down in the seat next to Yukio. "Too late," he said. "Too late."

Now the train picked up speed for the last part of the journey toward Shimonoseki. It was quiet in the car. Even Yukio was silent. She stared at her hands while he looked out the window.

The night was aflame. They were passing fairly close to one or another of the southern cities—he had no idea which one—which had been turned into a supportive structure for a vast oil refinery. Giant flames leaped and spewed into the darkness like the corona of the sun seen close up in a kind of silent hellish dance. It seemed an inhuman place to work or live, a desolate dreamscape from which there was no exit. It went on and on as they traveled, the lines of red and orange lights leading in inevitable precise rows toward the refinery's main building bulking blackly against the skyline, the bloated billowing flames.

"What did you think of the old man's story?" Yukio said.

He turned his head. "What?"

"The old man. Did you believe him?"

For some reason he thought of So-Peng. "Yes," he said. "I did."

"I didn't." She crossed her legs at the knees, very American. "Something like that couldn't have happened. Life's just not like that."

They spent the night in Shimonoseki, so near the water they could hear it though they could not see it for the thick ground fog. Horns hooted mournfully, deepened by the night air, made somehow mysterious.

She lay with her head on his bare chest, her night-dark hair spread in a fan across his pale flesh. He was a long time falling asleep. He felt her breathing gently, rhythmically through his fingertips, the weight of her on his sternum and rib cage. He wondered what it was about her that drew him so powerfully. And could not even decide why it seemed so important for him to know.

Yukio stirred and it seemed a part of him.

"What is it?" he asked her.

"Oh, nothing." Her voice was very soft. "I was just thinking of a story. It's the one my mother told me. The only one I remember. Want to hear it?"

"Yes."

"Well, once upon a time there was a lady. She lived in a castle in Roku-No-Miya. Where that is no one knows to this day—that's just how my mother used to say it. Anyway, after this girl's parents died, she was brought up by a governess—

366

she was an extremely well-protected girl—and, as the years passed, she grew up into a beautiful young woman.

"One evening she was introduced to a man and, every evening after that, he would come to the castle and she would entertain him until gradually the place took on a festive air.

"But during the long afternoons, while she was alone walking her gardens, the lady thought of the power of fate. She thought about being dependent upon this man for her happiness. Then she would shrug her shoulders and smile wanly into the sun.

"At night she would lie awake beside her lover, neither happy nor unhappy. What satisfaction she could possess was fleeting.

"But then, one day, even this was to end, for her lover informed her solemnly that he must go with his father to another district to assist him in his new political post. 'But,' he said, 'the assignment is but for five years. At the end of that time I shall return for you. Please do me the honor of waiting for me.'

"The lady openly wept, perhaps not from love itself but from the idea of separation.

"In six years, nothing was the same at the lady's castle in Roku-No-Miya. The man had not returned and all the servants had gone as both time and money withered away. The lady and her governess were forced into the old, long-abandoned samurai's quarters to live.

"Now there was only rice to eat and great gaps in the wooden frame of the place let in both wind and rain. At length the governess beseeched her lady, saying, 'Forgive me, lady, but your lover has abandoned you. There is a certain man who has been inquiring about you. Since we have so little money...'

"But the lady would not listen. 'I have no use for other adventures now,' she said. 'I only wish for the solace of death.'

"At that moment, in another district, the lady's lover lay with his new wife. Startled, he sat up in the dark, saying, 'Did you hear that?'

"'Go back to sleep, my lord,' his wife answered him. 'It is only a cherry blossom falling.'

"Not over a year later, this man returned to Roku-No-Miya with his wife and retinue. He had paused at a roadside inn to wait out inclement weather and there had sent a number of notes to his former mistress. Not one was returned and

367

thus, piqued, he left his wife at the house of her father and set off in search of the castle at Roku-No-Miya.

"When he arrived, he almost passed it up, so changed was it. The great wood and iron gates that had become so familiar to him were but stumps in the loamy earth and, down the road, the high blue lacquered *torii*, around which he and the lady used to stroll in the spring and summer, was gone.

"The castle itself he found uninhabitable. Some immense storm had completely demolished the east wing and the rest was in shambles.

"In the old samurai's quarters he found only an old, time-weary nun. She was, she said, the daughter of one of the lady's servants. When he inquired after the lady's whereabouts, she said, 'Alas, my lord, no one knows.'

"He went out searching for her but no one in the district claimed to have seen her.

"One dreary, rain-filled night, he stopped at a crossroads beside a monk and, hearing a voice he was certain was familiar, peered through the loose slats of a board house. Instantly he recognized the withered woman on the floor as his mistress. Rushing with the monk to her side he looked upon her face. She was surely dying and he asked the monk to recite a sutra over her. 'Invoke the name of the Amida Buddha,' the monk implored the lady. To which she replied, 'I see a blazing carriage.... No, it is a golden lotus.' 'Please, my lady,' the monk cried, 'you must call out to the Amida Buddha. We have no power over transmigration, otherwise. You must call to Him with all your heart.'

"'I see nothing,' the lady cried. 'Nothing but darkness.'

" 'My lady—'

"'Darkness and a cold wind blowing. A black wind, so cold.'

"The monk did his best to assist her while the man prayed to the Amida Buddha. Gradually the lady's cries grew fainter, at last mingling with the sound of the wind whistling through the trees.' "

Yukio was quiet for some time.

"Is that the end of the story?"

"Not quite. On the night of the full moon, some days later, the old monk sat by the same crossroads, pulling his ragged cloak about his bony knees in an effort to keep out the cold.

"A samurai came by singing a song and, seeing the monk, paused to hunker down next to him. 'Is this the place?' he

368

asked. 'It is said in the district of Roku-No-Miya the weeping of a woman can be heard sometimes at night. What do you know of this?'

"'Listen,' was all the monk would say. And the samurai listened. He heard nothing at all save the tiny night sounds. Then, of a sudden, he thought he heard a woman's cry of grief. 'What is that?' he said.

"'Pray,' said the monk. 'Pray for a spirit that knows neither heaven nor hell.' But the samurai, having no God, merely looked at the monk before he walked on."

They ate breakfast at the hotel and then went outside. It was cold and damp, the fog still swirling with curled tendrils underfoot. They saw the train on which they had arrived still standing at the station—way station was more like it. It was merely a central platform between two sets of tracks with enormous rough-hewn pillars of wood supporting a slanting, pagoda-like roof, lacquered on top against the debilitating effects of the weather and the salt air, but was quite naked underneath. The scent of cedar was still powerful.

As they watched, a skeleton crew swung onto the train and, several moments later, it crawled a small distance onto a section of track set into an enormous disk which, as the train stopped, turned one hundred and eighty degrees. The train now pulled slowly into the opposite side of the platform, ready for the return journey north to Osaka.

The show over, they walked slowly away. The sky was perfectly white, the sun diffuse and ragged within the mist.

They were quite near the harbor and Nicholas could already make out two or three high white sails of the fishing boats maneuvering carefully away from the quay. Past them, he knew, though hidden now, lurked the flatlands of the Asian shore.

As they came up on the headland, he thought he could make out the dark brown hills, due south, of Bunzen Province across the narrow straits on the island of Kyūshū.

"How peaceful here," Yukio said, stretching like a cat. "How different from Tokyo or Osaka or even Kyoto, as if the war never touched this place, nor industrialization. We might be in the seventeenth century."

"Full of samurai and the ladies of samurai, eh?"

She took a deep breath. "It's like being at the end of the

world—or the beginning." She turned to him, put her slender fingers around his wrist. He was startled at the nonsexual intimacy it conveyed. The sharp smell of drying fish hung heavily in the air, clinging to their nostrils like paint. Great gray and purple gulls wheeled, crying, in the low sky, half seen. "Why don't we stay here, Nicholas."

"Here?"

She nodded her head like a child. "Yes. Right here. Why not? It's idyllic. The rest of the world doesn't exist here. We can forget. Be free. Start all over. Like being born again without hurt or sin." He looked at her and her grip on him tightened convulsively. "Oh, please," she said, her voice as hushed and echoey as if she were talking in a cathedral. "Let's not go on. What for? What can there be waiting in Kumamoto to compare to this? You have me; there's the sea. We could go sailing. Out into the ocean. Even to the continent. It's not so very far away. How much time could it take? And then. And then…"

"You can't really mean that," he said. "You have to be realistic, Yukio."

"Realistic?" she cried. "What do you think I *am* being? There's nothing for me back there." She flung her arm out to the north, from where they had come. "There's no love, no life. And to the south, in Kumamoto? What's there? Saigō. Saigō and his damnable secrets. I don't want any part of all that. It terrifies me."

They had passed a street vendor, shrouded in fog, and Nicholas detached himself from her for a moment, went back, bought two small paper cups of tofu in a sticky sweet brown glaze. He gave her one. A wooden spoon was stuck in the center of the sweet.

She looked at it, then at him. "What's the matter with you?" she said. A strong gust of wind, humid with the fecundity of the sea, whipped around them and she had to peel her hair away from her face. A few strands clung to the wet corner of her lips. The rest of her hair, unbound, was like a scarf worn in midwinter, flying out behind her. "You treat me like a child. You buy me a sweet as if I've just awakened from a nightmare." She batted the paper cup from his outstretched hand. It hit the ground with a fat splat and stayed there, a misshapen lump of white and brown. "What I'm feeling is not going to go away, despite what you may think. I go to sleep at night and wake up the next morning hoping that it *is* all a dream. But it's not. Don't you see that?" He began to walk, she with him. "Nicholas, please." Her body was bent slightly, either against the wind or against her emotions; perhaps both. "I'm begging you. Let's stay here. I don't want to go across to Kyūshū."

"But why not? You knew where we were coming when you insisted I take you along. What did you imagine would happen?"

"I don't know," she said miserably. "I didn't think that far ahead. I'm not like you in that respect. I can't plan ahead. I never know what I am going to do, how I am going to feel until I do it. I didn't go with it all the way until the end. I just wanted to be with you—" Her hand flew to her mouth and her eyes opened wide. She whirled away from him, bent over.

"Yukio—"

"Leave me alone. I don't know what I'm saying anymore."

He threw away the cup, held her by her shoulders. "I don't understand," he said. "Please talk to me."

"You know I can't do that," she said, "very well." Her back was still to him.

"Yukio"—he held her tighter to him—"you must tell me."

"I can't do it. I can't."

He spun her around. "Yes you can. I know you can." He stared into her frightened eyes, enlarged now by incipient tears. "Will it help if I tell you?"

"Yes. No. I don't know." But at least she knew what he meant.

"I love you," he said. "I don't know how long I've known it and not said it. I—" Was this why he was terrified?

"No. No," she said. "Don't say it. Please. I can't bear it. I can't bear it."

"But why not?"

"Because," she said fiercely, her face wrenched in a snarl, "I believe you."

He almost laughed with relief. "And is that so bad?"

"Don't you understand yet?" Her face was so close to his, her eyes seemed crossed. "I feel like I'm going to die. I'm not equipped—"

"Yes you are!" He shook her so that her hair flew across her face and her lower lip trembled. "Everyone is. You just don't know it."

"I can't handle it." Her voice was almost a sob. A boat

hooted over their shoulders, the rhythmic rumble of its diesel reaching them as a vibration up their legs until it had passed, its green and gold stack lost in the mist. He could not even see as far back up the foreshore to where the vendor must still be, hawking his sweet tofu.

"I am committed now," he said, deliberately changing the subject. "I've said I'd come."

'You can always change your mind. No one's locked you into one decision." Her voice had taken on a pleading edge. But was it for him or for herself?

"My commitment is to myself," he said softly. "I must find out what Saigō is doing in Kumamoto."

"Why? Why is that so important? Who cares what he's doing? Who is it going to affect? Neither of us. Why can't you just let it go? It's such a small thing."

"It's not," he said despairingly. "It's not a small thing at all." But he wondered if there was any way he could explain it to her. How could he when he was not even sure he could explain it to himself?

"It's come down to that fight you two had in the *dōjō*," she said cannily. "It's like you have each other by the throat and neither of you will let go. You'll destroy each other that way, don't you see? One of you has to let go, otherwise . . . Why can't it be you?"

"There's a matter of honor." He only knew it now, a revelation like the sun as it first slips over the horizon, beginning to defeat the long night's chill.

"Oh, don't give me that one," she said shortly. "That kind of honor went out of style a long time ago."

How little she must understand of life, he thought. "For some of us, it's never gone out of style."

"For the samurai," she said tartly. "The elite of Japan. The warriors who hurl themselves unhesitatingly into battle. Who live to die in combat?" She laughed, a harsh, discomforting sound. "Now who needs a strong dose of reality? You're the same, the two of you. Two rabid dogs who'll worry a leg off before they'll give up and let go."

"Not the same," he said. "Not the same at all. Saigō hates everything I stand for. My mixed blood; my love of Japan combined with my *abominable* Caucasian features. It rankles him that someone who looks the way I do should be better than him at anything, especially something so important as bujutsu."

372

"Important? What's so goddamned important about bu-
tsu? What has any of that to do with living, with feeling—"
"You're a good one to talk about that." Knew it was the
wrong thing to say as soon as it was out of his mouth. He
saw the look on her face, said, reaching out for her, "I'm
sorry. You know I didn't mean—"
"Oh, you meant it, Nicholas. I'm quite certain of that. And
you've a right to say it, I guess. I've been frightened these
last few days and now you know how I get when I'm frightened. You've made me feel—something—I was sure was impossible for me. I still don't quite—well, part of the time I
want to run away from you and hide and never see another
human being for the rest of my life. Is it okay to trust you?
I keep asking myself. Isn't it just my cunt and my mouth he's
after? But then I think, he's already got those so why go into
this at all? It must be real even though every instinct that's
still functioning tells me it's not. The past dies very slowly.
I keep hearing echoes all around me. When you talk to me,
say things, I hear what you're saying but, in my mind, other
meanings, hidden and secretive like invisible hieroglyphics,
burn themselves into my brain and I hear two different things
and I begin a debate as to which of those signals is the real
one, the one you mean for me to hear." She looked at him.
"Does any of this make any sense to you?"
"I think so."
"I see it doesn't." Her eyes were so bright they seemed to
glitter despite the lack of any direct light. "I suppose I am
trying to tell you I love you."
Her arms were around his neck, though how they had
gotten there he had no idea. Hadn't they been at her sides
just a moment ago? Had there been any movement since
then? What was happening?
They kissed in a kind of timeless moment where even their
breath hung suspended, condensed clouds on a chill winter's
morning.
They took their bags down to the ferryboat ticket taker's,
a ramshackle wooden building no larger than an outhouse
with an arched window in its front, glassless and inade-
quately hooded against inclement weather. One could easily
freeze to death within such a place.
A young boy in his late teens took the two rail ticket
passes Nicholas handed him, stamped and punched them in
several places, handed them back.

"The next ferry sails in seven minutes," he told them Even here, in such an out-of-the-way town, there was th typical Japanese concern with punctuality.

Yukio was unnaturally quiet until they cast off. But onc away, her melancholy seemed to slip away. "Perhaps ther will be a new show in town," she said gaily. "Or a ridin stable. We could picnic and ride all afternoon." It was as the episode on the near shore had never occurred. Still, N cholas was disturbed in its wake.

Behind them, Shimonoseki drifted away like a dream beyond the churning white wake of the ferry. Gulls swun gracefully across their bow, wheeling obliquely like a fighte squadron, calling plaintively to each other.

They passed, quite close it seemed in the mist, a pair o fishing boats lying low in the swells, their black nets haule up the masts like a moron's idea of a sail. A young boy o one of the boats waved excitedly as the ferry passed him b but there were none aboard, it seemed, inclined to return th gesture.

His gaze shifted subtly to regard Yukio beside him. He head was thrown back as if to catch the wan sunlight on th wide planes of her cheekbones, her hair flying to one side a raven's spread wing. The long line of her neck was exposed shadowed softly because of the thrust of her chin in thi position. The hard jut of her breasts. Was it his imaginatio or could he see the slight protrusions of her nipples as the poked, erect, through the lace of her bra?

"Why is it, do you think, that Satsugai is afraid of th Colonel?"

The wind tore at her words flinging them over the ferry' side, out toward the bobbing fishing boats, mere black point now, misting to dull gray, and for a moment he was not sur he had heard her right.

"I was not aware that he is."

She turned toward him, studied his face. "Oh, yes. But o course. You mean you haven't noticed it? Well, I suppose shouldn't be so surprised, really. I've spent more time with him than you have."

"They argue a lot." He put his elbows along the railing leaned overboard. He felt her hand on his arm.

"Don't do that. Please." She laughed. "If you fell in I' have to go in after you and I hate the water."

"Water and trains."

374

"Water worse than anything. I don't mind being near it. like that, in fact. I'm just terrified by the tides and undertow nd that."

"About Satsugai," he said. "He and my father are from e opposite sides of the tracks, politically speaking. But aat's, well, just talk."

"Do you imagine that they would be together if it were ot for Itami and your mother?"

He looked at the water, dark and light. "No, I don't suppose ."

"Right. Well, I know Satsugai. That kind of hate only ems from fear and let me tell you he is not a man who is asily frightened. Whatever the Colonel has on him is potent deed."

"I think it's just that Satsugai, being in the *zaibatsu*, was nder suspicion as a war criminal for a time. You know, uring the purges when the Americans disbanded the tra- itional family structure of the *zaibatsu*. My father inter- ened in Satsugai's behalf. I don't know the details but that ind of debt would be a heavy burden for Satsugai to bear."

"Yes. He prides himself on owing no one and he's more owerful now than he was during the war." She shook her ead. "To think that's due in part to the Colonel."

"It's family. That's something my mother is adamant bout. Politics are relatively unimportant next to that. Next my father and me, Itami is her sole family. There is nothing ney wouldn't do for one another."

The fog closed in on them and the day turned chill. The rry's deep horn sounded at regular intervals, hoarse and ournful. The gulls had gone and now it was even impossible see the water. They might have been skimming through ne air. The whiteness seemed stifling. There was no breeze speak of. They heard voices, muffled and odd-sounding, om the ferry's far side as if coming to them from across a ast and unfathomable gulf.

All at once the land loomed before them out of the intense ist and, with only a slight bump, the ferry docked against ne jute-covered slip. Nicholas wondered how the captain had een his way across. They could hear the creak of the pilings. hen a dog began to bark hysterically.

*   *   *

To Nicholas the train ride to Kumamoto seemed inter
minable even though it was merely a fraction of the time
had taken for the bulk of the journey. Perhaps the fog ha
something to do with it, but he felt now a kind of desperat
longing to know what it was that had brought Saigō dow
here. Kansatsu had been concerned about it. He realized tha
now, so belatedly. The *sensei* would never have come out an
said such a thing, merely implied it. But what could it b
about Saigō's visits here that would be so disturbing? An
why should it concern Kansatsu at all? These question
gnawed at him as they rode across Kyūshū and he wishe
with all his might that he had the answers but, of course
that was a useless wish. In fact, any wish, Cheong had tol
him more than once, is useless. "If you want something badl
enough," she had said, "then you must do it. Those who si
and wish for things accomplish nothing."

Abruptly, he felt resentment welling up inside him fo
that part of him which was Western in nature. But even so
he knew that that was his turbulent side, filled with energ
and longing, impatience and changeability. It was, in short
what made him different.

Yukio, as usual, was filled with lust and, in the jouncin
empty car, she sat on his lap, lifting her skirt up and makin
the hot connection. Neither of them needed to move at all.

Kumamoto was a town that no doubt in feudal times ha
been dominated by the stone and mortar castle perched hig
on a dun-brown hill that in the spring would turn lushl
verdant. In these modern times, however, the castle, thoug
still quite imposing, seemed over-shadowed by the industria
plant flung across the valley to the northwest. Its fifteen o
so smokestacks seemed like inelegant fingers stretchin
themselves irreverently toward the heavens.

This afternoon, as Nicholas and Yukio stepped off th
smoking train, one could not see their tops and the mist mad
them seem as if they had been covered by gloves.

Oddly enough, Kumamoto itself was not as modern as thi
new appendage might lead one to believe. There was littl
evidence of Western erosion and they saw more traditiona
Japanese garb than they had anywhere else in their travels
Even through the mist, which now appeared to be at las
lifting, they could see how mountainous Kyūshū was. Dar

376

masses loomed on every side, filling the land with a kind of undulating light and shadow pattern of the kind one might see from an airplane riding high above patchy clouds.

They booked into a hotel along the Street of the Wrestlers. "Here," the bustling proprietor said, flinging open the doors to their rooms, "you will have a perfect view of Mount Aso." He put down their bags, crossed to the window of Nicholas' room. "Of course, you'll need a clear day but no doubt by tomorrow you will be able to view, well, perhaps not all five summits but most assuredly Nakadake." He turned around, rubbing his palms together. "It's actively volcanic, you know, and always smoking." He waved one pudgy hand toward the mist outside. "We get this kind of weather when the wind's the wrong way." He walked to the door and his finger touched the knob. "We've had ash and pumice, the sky so dark you'd think it was night, when it erupts." He shook his head. "Can you imagine? Coming all that way." He clucked his tongue against the roof of his mouth. "Still, one shouldn't complain. Mount Aso brings many people here every year and where would I be without tourism?" He shrugged deprecatingly. Nicholas tipped him and he gave them a rather stiff little bow. "Anything I can do to make your stay here more pleasant," he said, opening the connecting door between their rooms before leaving.

Nicholas phoned Saigō but he was not there. He left a message including the hotel's number.

They spent some time searching for a stable but there seemed to be no riding, at least within the town's limits. Yukio could not hide her disappointment.

They ate a light lunch at a tiny teahouse in a square surrounded by trees. Birds called as they flitted from branch to branch. The food was impeccable but Nicholas was not able to eat much. His stomach was tense and he needed to move around.

When they left, they proceeded to walk aimlessly around, through the wide main avenues, down small shop-lined streets, filled with mingled scents and clamoring customers.

They returned to the hotel in late afternoon with the light receding swiftly from the sky. The mist was gone and the hard shell of the cobalt sky seemed distant indeed.

A message from Saigō was waiting for him. Dinner. Saigō would come to the hotel.

"How long will we be here?" Yukio asked as they were dressing. The door between their rooms was open.

"I don't know. I hadn't thought about it. Why?"

"I want to leave. That's all."

"We've only just gotten here."

"I know, but it already feels like we've been here a year. This is an odd city."

He laughed, pulling on his trousers. "You just don't want to be here. Listen, we're not so close to the water here." He smiled. "No chance I'll fall overboard."

Her smile was a bit bleaker than his. "Yes. Yes. I know. But haven't you noticed? The air here smells different, almost as if it were burnt."

"It's only the refinery," he said. "Or maybe Mount Aso. I've never been near a volcano before. Isn't there one on Hokkaido?"

Saigō arrived promptly just after six. Nicholas opened the door to his room.

"Well, Nicholas, I didn't—" His dark eyes slid across Nicholas' face, over his shoulder. The color seemed to drain from him. "What's she doing here?" It was said in a hiss but, just as important, in a different speech mode; the polite form had been abruptly dropped.

Nicholas turned his head. "Yukio? She decided to come with me. Didn't you know she was here?" But of course how could he?

Saigō's angry eyes flicked back to regard Nicholas. The stare was hard and cold. "You set this up deliberately, didn't you?"

"What are you talking about?"

"You know, don't you? Don't lie to me, Nicholas. She told you everything."

Nicholas felt her presence close and warm behind him.

"I told him nothing." Yukio's tone was chill enough to freeze the blood. "But now that you've brought it up like an hysterical child, perhaps you ought to tell him yourself."

"Tell me what? Hey, wait a minute!" Saigō had begun a lunge around him toward Yukio. Nicholas stepped into his path, using his shoulder and left arm as a wedge against the doorframe. Yukio stepped lithely away.

"I think you had better tell me what this is all about."

Saigō heard the warning note in Nicholas' voice and he felt his blood boil. Leaned forward with the left side of his

378

body, half-concealing the horizontal movement of his right hand and wrist.

Nicholas brought his forearm down in a blur, striking the exposed bone in Saigō's wrist. Physical damage was minimal but nerve disruption was considerable. The hand went numb.

They were very close together and Saigō used his foot, aiming for the side of the knee. The doorjamb was his ally; caught in the force of the blow, Nicholas' knee would shatter like crystal. But he stepped back and the side of Saigō's foot slammed into the wood with a crack as loud and as sharp as a house collapsing.

Saigō recovered enough to whirl around and head off down the corridor before Nicholas had a chance to react. Without a word, Nicholas went after him.

Yukio ran to the door. "Nicholas!" she cried after him. Then she, too, followed in Saigō's wake.

The angelfish, all gray lace, hovered near the bottom. Its tiny mouth opened and closed. It might have been trying to eat the algae off the side of the tank.

A pair of gouramis passed close by it, disturbing its concentration, and it darted off behind a group of three or four water plants twisting gently in the clouds of rising bubbles from the aerator.

They stood across the street, in the deep shadow of a doorway. The street was quiet, every step of the few passersby discernible.

"What are you waiting for?"

"Quiet," Nicholas said, thinking, twelve, thirteen, fourteen.

A young couple turned a corner, came down the street. He gave the man a quick glance, went back to watching the front door of the fish store where Saigō had disappeared moments before. Twenty-one, twenty-two, twenty-three. When he had reached thirty and there was still no sign, he took her by the hand and went across the street.

A tiny bell rang in the back of the shop like a call to the penitent. It was a narrow, bare-floorboarded place, its walls stocked with glass tanks of varying sizes. Only one or two were dry, cloudy with dust.

A man, thin, worn down by the passage of time, his skin as gray as yesterday's mist, sat on a high wooden stool in front of a wall filled with filters, rolls of clear plastic tubing and stacked boxes of dried fish food.

No one was in the shop.

"Is there a back way out of here?" Nicholas asked him.

"Hm?" He looked up belatedly. "Oh, yes but—"

Nicholas, with Yukio a step behind him, was already loping past him, through the short, dark passageway and out the unbolted back door.

They found themselves in a dim brick alleyway that was more a cul-de-sac. Only one way for Saigō to have gone and they followed.

They spotted him, already a block away, heading west. Twice he doubled back and once, when he thought he had lost him altogether, Nicholas began to sweat because he didn't think now that he would get a second chance; Yukio had seen to that. But they got lucky. He had been hidden within a small jostling crowd around a news kiosk, in plain sight, really. It might have been accidental or an extremely sophisticated maneuver. There was no way of telling. But the question remained. Why was Saigō taking any precautions at all? Why was he concerned about being followed?

Above their heads a full moon rode, blue-white, as large as a hanging paper lantern, harbinger of winter's first snow. Clouds appearing as flat and substantial as curtains turned the illumination inconstant and, with it, perspective kept changing so that he was obliged to stop them now and again to check their proximity to the dark hurrying figure in front.

Once Saigō turned around, his face a pale blur struck by the moonlight, and Nicholas forced Yukio into a doorway, hearing only the soft rasp of her violent breathing and the hammering of his own heart.

Saigō's silhouette was fast diminishing down the dark street and he grabbed her hand, pulling her along until, at length, he saw his quarry pause before a narrow doorway in a rather run-down wood-frame building, windowless and hulking. Disappeared like a nocturnal animal.

Nicholas stood perfectly still in deep shadow with Yukio by his side for several moments. "Now," he said in a low tone and took her, running, across the wide street.

There was no sign on the building's face to indicate what it might contain; no bells to ring. Nothing. The door was metal, painted in deep red enamel. He grasped the brass handle half-expecting it to be locked. Pulled it open.

Inside, they found themselves in a plain hallway without a true ceiling. A wide industrial-type stairway led upward; it too was metal. There were no doorways on the ground level. Nor were there any on the first floor, they discovered. There seemed to be a lot of empty space, however.

The building seemed silent but for a peculiar kind of intermittent vibration coming through the rough wooden planks of the vast landings.

They found the one door—closed and padlocked—on the third floor. Yukio coughed twice before putting her palm against her mouth; there seemed to be a great deal of sawdust hanging in the unquiet air.

One had an odd feeling here. Not merely the prickly sensation of trespassing but the uncomfortable hollowness in the pit of the stomach that might come from standing in the foyer of a haunted house at midnight.

"I want to get out of here," Yukio whispered in his ear. She tugged at his arm.

"Shhh."

He went slowly, cautiously across the landing toward the closed door. He had thought—yes. The light was so dim that he had not been certain. But now as he approached, he saw clearly the sign that had been hand-painted in black ink squarely on the center of the door: a circle within which were nine black diamonds. They in turn surrounded an ideogram, *komuso*.

Nicholas stared at the sign. Where had he seen that before? Surely he had—a *ryu*. It was a *ryu*. But which one? He had seen this sign quite recently. Just before he had left Tokyo, in fact. A regional offshoot, perhaps. Or—

Abruptly, he reached for Yukio's hand, backing away.

"What is it?" she whispered. "Where are we?"

"Come on," he said. And then, jerking her along with him. "Come *on!*"

Outside in the street he found that he still could not breathe. He began to run down the street with her in tow. The night seemed terribly still, Kumamoto deserted, and he had the impression they were the only people abroad that night, that they fled through a dreamscape from which they might never emerge.

His head pounded as if it might burst and a kind of fever careened through him. His mind whirled uncontrollably and he only vaguely heard Yukio's panting questions.

He had recognized the sign on the door and, with it, both the reason he had come here after Saigō and the nature of his immediate future.

Back at the hotel, he left Yukio to go to her room alone. "Won't you tell me anything?"

"In a while," he said, still half distracted. "Take a bath or something. I'll be in in a little while."

"You're not going out again," she said worriedly. "I don't want to be here alone."

"Don't worry. I'll just be next door."

Once inside, he crossed to the window. The darkness seemed absolute. But still, perhaps only because the proprietor had mentioned it, he thought he could see the white plume of pumice belching from Nakadake, Mount Aso's fifth column.

There was no doubt in his mind now why Saigō had traveled such a distance to become a part of this particular *ryu*, for there were none such as this in the Tokyo area. Kansatsu's words haunted him now with an intensity impossible to ignore: *There are many* ryu *in Japan, Nicholas. Among these, the variety of disciplines taught is virtually limitless. Good and evil are sometimes propounded indiscriminately.*

No wonder Saigō has been so furtive in his movements: so careful to backtrack.

It would be a natural precaution for a ninja.

For that is precisely what he had become. This Kumamoto *ryu* was no regional offshoot but a center. *The* center, to be more accurate.

The ninja are not bound by the Way, Kansatsu had said, and that was correct. Yet ninjutsu was more complex than that and, as in bujutsu itself, there were many types propounded and taught. Good and evil. The black and the red. Kansatsu himself had shown it to Nicholas before he had left Tokyo. Of the red, he had said, far and away the most dangerous, the most virulent *ryu* is the Kuji-kiri. "It is the Chinese word for the 'nine-hands cutting,' the basis for much of the ninja's real or imagined power. It is said by many that these hand signs are the last remaining vestiges of magic in this world. As for me, I cannot say, but as you yourself have come to understand, there are times when the dividing line between imagination and existence can disappear." That was

382

when Kansatsu had shown him the symbol of the Kuji-kiri ryu. It was the one he had seen on the warehouse door just moments ago.

He heard the water running in the bath next door; Yukio disrobing.

A suspicion was forming in his mind now and the more he thought about it the more certain he became. Had Kansatsu known what it was he would find here? How? Perhaps he had only suspected. But why was Kansatsu involved at all?

Abruptly, Nicholas had the cold sensation of being manipulated by forces he had not even suspected of existing. It was certain that Kansatsu knew quite a bit more about this situation than he had told Nicholas. Why hold back?

Outside, the moon had slipped its cloud mooring and now rode, unbridled, in the sky. The world was tinged with a blue light, cold and harsh and monochromatic. Far on the horizon—he was certain now—he could make out the rising oblique volcanic cone, its pale umbrella billowing like the aftermath of an explosion seen in slow motion. The still air held the pumice dust in languid suspension like a decadent sprawled across his silk-covered settee.

It seemed to him now that the lines of his life had already been drawn by some other hand at a time when he had been looking elsewhere. As he had said to Yukio this afternoon, he was committed. They had been set against one another, he and Saigō, from the moment they had first met. For what reason he could not yet say, yet it was a reality with which he must now deal.

What to do now?

He knew. He knew. And it terrified him.

The bathwater had drained some time ago. He got up from where he had been sitting in the windowbox and opened the connecting door into Yukio's room.

He paused on the threshold. The lights were extinguished and all seemed still.

He called her name softly.

Blue moonlight was a wash along part of the floor interlaced with the oblique bars of shadow from the casement.

"Yukio?"

He went silently into the room.

And immediately stopped. *Haragei*. Someone else was in the room. He turned his head without moving his body. Saw

Yukio lying on the bed, a last bit of light limning the bridge of her nose. She was atop the covers. The other side of the double bed had blanket and sheets drawn down. An impression had been made there, as if by another body. She was naked. Her breasts and belly rose and fell in even breathing.

"Welcome, Nicholas." He turned his head. The chair in the far corner, facing into the room. Moonlight fell partway along its back; its face was in shadow. "So nice of you to join us."

"Saigō. How did you get in here?"

"How do you think, Nicholas? How do you think?"

"I imagine there are many ways—for a ninja."

He seemed unperturbed. "Quite so, oh yes. But, you see, I didn't need any of them." He waited a beat. "Yukio let me in herself."

"Yukio..." He took two steps toward her.

"It won't do any good, Nicholas. She can't hear you."

"She—"

"Oh no no no, nothing like that. She's merely sleeping. That's a waste of time. You won't be able to wake her. But don't fret, she's perfectly safe."

"Wake her up," Nicholas said. He was sitting on the bed. Her flesh felt cold, raised in goosebumps, but she seemed to be breathing normally.

"I don't think so. At least not yet, anyway." At last Saigō stood up. He was dressed in a black raw silk suit, rather old-fashioned, somewhat like the ones Chinese mandarins used to wear on formal occasions. His hair had been cut so short that he looked almost bald; the black stubble seemed somehow far more ominous. "The obvious thing to say now is that I'm sorry to be proved right. About you, I mean. But that would be a lie. I'm not in the least sorry. In fact, I'm delighted. I was right about you all the time. So was my father." He went into the center of the room and Nicholas followed him with his eyes.

Saigō shook his head. "How you ever found out I cannot imagine. I have to give you credit for that."

"What," said Nicholas, "are you talking about?"

Saigō's eyes flashed and his lips curled in a snarl just as if Nicholas had struck him. He flew across the room, grabbed Nicholas by his shirtfront. "All right," he whispered savagely, "I'm through being courteous to you. I see there's no point. Did you really think I didn't know that you were following me? Do you think you could have if I hadn't wanted you to? You really *are* a fool!"

Nicholas reached up, slammed Saigō's fists from him. They stood, a little apart, eyeing each other, controlling their breathing, like two titans about to do battle over dominion of the world.

"What do you think you're doing to yourself?"

"I'm saving myself," Saigō said. "I would have thought it was obvious. I have been accepted into the elite. Beyond *bushi*, Nicholas. Way beyond." He took a step forward. "And you can join me."

"What?"

"Why did you think I asked you down here? This is no vacation spot. And then you show up with *her*. Idiot!"

"I love her."

"Forget about her. She's nothing. Less than nothing. A whore. Fucking—"

"Shut your *bloody*—!"

"Yes, I forget about your English heritage. So chivalrous!" He took another step forward so their chests almost touched. "So. Whatever she is or isn't. She no longer exists for you or for me. I am offering you the world, Nicholas. You have no idea. None at all. Ninjutsu is—"

"But why the Kuji-kiri? Why black?"

"Oh, I see. I see how it is now. That scum Kansatsu has been talking to you. Yes, it's black ninjutsu, but that is as it should be. We are the strongest, the most potent. With Kuji-kiri you become invincible. In all the world, there will be no one to stop you. Think of it, man, unlimited power!"

"There is nothing in that that appeals to me," and he was spinning down obliquely across the bed, away from Yukio, using the wrist blocks against the darting eye-strikes Saigō drove at him with monstrous swiftness. He retaliated with sword-strikes, three in rapid succession. Thwarted, but that was all right because they had served their purpose and the adrenalin was surging through him like a tidal wave.

He rolled over, Saigō atop him and his immediate concern became the elbow-strike feint followed by a sword-strike aimed at his larynx. He worked his way out of that, found his left arm pinioned beneath the full weight of Saigō's right shoulder. He was in trouble, he knew. Inside, Saigō, with the ninjutsu training, had an enormous advantage. His only hope was to break away, get some reasonable distance between them.

He began a knee-strike, twisting away at the same time, but Saigō was not fooled and a blow caught the ridge of his collarbone; his frame flexed involuntarily. Still, he was fortunate that the strike was a near-miss.

They were locked now on the floor, part of the counterpane drawn under their straining bodies. There was very little real movement for long minutes as they struggled, fingers grasping wrists, elbows against sternums, a kind of perverse engine, stifling on its own energy output.

It became time to try something else and he slashed upward with his kneecap, heard Saigō's grunt and, almost simultaneously, a soft metallic click in front of his face. Saw a small blade, glinting in the moonlight, standing out like a deadly toothpick from between Saigō's first and second finger knuckles. A conjurer's trick. But it was no illusion. He turned his head away as the blade moved infinitesimally toward his eye. There was a peculiar odor and his nostrils flared briefly. Then it was gone and he was concentrating on stepping up the pressure of his forearm against the hand with the blade. He pushed upward, using all the available leverage. Sweat had broken out along the line of his hair and now it drooled with cruel slowness down his forehead, threatening to blur his vision.

But the deadlock was breaking as, bit by bit, he brought the hand backward, away from him. Then he was free and on his feet. His chest heaved with the intense exertion of the past few moments. He staggered a little, waiting for Saigō to stand. When he did, Nicholas attacked, but perhaps the blow to his collarbone had affected him more than he had thought because he was just a little off balance and, as Saigō countered his thrust, he seemed to take an inordinately long time to react.

Now Saigō was at him, seeming faster than ever before. Barely he was able to deflect a fork-strike, but he failed to counter a sword-strike to his neck.

He went down then in a heap. Coughing and gasping, he could not seem to fill his lungs with air. On his back, he saw Saigō standing over him, grinning, as if he knew there would be no more resistance.

Tried to stand up but he had no legs. He used his hands, raised them. Or thought he did; no feeling there, either. He blinked several times, unbelieving. Trapped within a useless body. He glanced down. His hands lay like pale flowers, part of another world. He felt the pounding of his heart unnaturally loud in his inner ear. But that was all.

Saigō bent over him, a sardonic smile on his face. "Did you think I came unprepared this time?" he said, almost amiable, as one friend to another. "No, it has all been planned from the very beginning. Yes, Nicholas, even down to Yukio's involvement. She knew about it all. In fact, some of this was her idea. Surprised?"

Nicholas could only open and close his mouth soundlessly like a fish dying of the air. His tongue worked like an idiot's. No, he thought wildly. No no no. It's a lie. It *must* be.

"Well, you shouldn't be. Didn't I tell you she was a whore? Surely she told you we were lovers. Yes, I thought so."

He turned away and in the half-light Nicholas saw him reach over toward the bed. He grasped Yukio's sleeping form, dragged her across the counterpane. A lamp in front of Nicholas went on and he blinked slowly while his eyes adjusted to the glare. Like having the sun in his eyes.

Yukio! he cried out silently. Yukio!

Saigō had her sitting up now. He had a small capsule in his hand. He broke it in half, waved it under her nose. Her head went back and he followed with the capsule. She shook her head from side to side as if wanting to get away from the expelled contents.

Her eyes came open and her features arranged themselves in a slow sensual slavish smile. Her arms came up around Saigō's shoulders. He kissed her roughly and her lips opened like a flower.

Yukio!

Careful to continually stay within Nicholas' line of sight, Saigō caressed her. He rubbed her breasts so that her nipples stood out hard and quivering. He spread her legs, rubbed her there. Yukio began to pant. His fingers came away wet.

He turned her over, bending her across the bed. Her buttocks were pale globes in the harsh light. He dropped his black silk pants. They puddled around his ankles. Spreading her thighs, he rummaged again, anointing his phallus. Then he rammed himself into her anus.

Yukio cried out as he moved on her flesh. From his vantage point Nicholas could see the reddened member sliding in and out. He tried to close his eyes but the gruntings and pantings

387

overwhelmed him, pummeling his brain until his eyes flew open in self-preservation.

Yukio's arms were flung out over her head, her fingers clutching convulsively at the counterpane, drawing it up into bunched sweaty hillocks. Her eyes were squeezed shut. Her thighs writhed against the bed, pressing her mound down in time to Saigō's thrusts.

All at once, she gave a cry. The counterpane shredded between her frenzied fingers and her thighs drew up convulsively and she shuddered powerfully.

At that moment, Saigō withdrew and a tiny moan of disappointment escaped her lips. His reddened member flicked upward at every pulse.

Saigō bent over Nicholas, flipped him over. It was only then that Nicholas understood the true nature of what was happening.

He felt the first burning penetration, heard Saigō's heavy grunt, felt the great weight of him upon his shoulders and buttocks, coming into him again and again like the tide.

The Colonel returned home quite late.

He sat for a long time behind the wheel of his car smoking his pipe, thinking of nothing. It seemed like days since he had smoked it last and he savored the mellow bite of the dark tobacco on the back of his tongue and against the roof of his mouth. He thought he might want a drink in a little while.

The moon was a dim smudge low on the horizon, ready to rest for the night. Whatever remained of it. The Colonel slowly rolled up his side window, preparatory to getting out, but he was abruptly suffused with a curious kind of lethargy that left him incapable for the moment of taking any action no matter how minuscule.

I suppose that is to be expected, he thought.

He looked toward the darkened house and he thought of Cheong asleep on their *futon*. How he cherished her. How he had failed her. And himself. And especially Nicholas. He had done the only possible thing but he knew that it was far from enough. He had bollixed it long ago. Tonight just took some of the sting out of it for him.

What he thought of now was lying to Cheong. He had never done that before and he had no strong desire to do it now. Still, there was no help for it; he understood all too well the consequences of the alternative.

At last he climbed out of the car, shut the door behind him with a soft thunk. The night seemed terribly still.

He went silently around to the side of the house, found the small pile of leaves Ataki had left for the morning's burning. Kneeling down, he set it to flame, listening meditatively to the crisp crackle, inhaling the pungent odor.

He stared into the fire. Odd what one remembers, he thought, in times like these. Like a submarine suddenly surfacing, the memory came to him of the bright summer afternoon when he had been locked in the crucial meeting with Prime Minister Yoshida, debating the specific consequences of the Korean War with John Foster Dulles, General Bradley and Defense Secretary Johnson. Dulles was in Tokyo because among the first American troops being sent into Korea were those who had been occupying Japan since 1945. But that left the bases and approximately a quarter of a million U.S. dependants left unprotected in Japan. The Americans were, of course, against this and they proposed the commencement of a Japanese military.

It was a bombshell proposal because such a force would be in direct violation of Article 9 of the Japanese Constitution written in 1947: "Land, sea, and air forces, as well as other war potential, will never be maintained."

In the best of American traditions, Johnson assailed Dulles' stance and the P.M. reacted negatively to Dulles' pleas for Japanese remilitarization. However, it was clear that something had to be done. The Colonel proposed that the existing Japanese police force be expanded to approximately 75,000 men, calling it a National Police Reserve. "We will have an effective army without having to call it that," the Colonel had said.

For Dulles, of course, this was not enough, but Yoshida, seeing that the Colonel had given him a way out without any loss of face, readily agreed. The plan would have to be, by definition, Top Secret. Even the recruits, Yoshida insisted, must not know the true purpose for which they were being trained.

The P.M. then set up the Annex of Civil Affairs Section within the existing bureaucracy to be responsible for recruitment and training, and an American officer was put in charge.

Afterward, Yoshida had asked the Colonel to remain. Tension still laced the room like rancid fruit and the P.M. suggested they take a walk in his gardens.

"I owe you a great debt of thanks," he had said after the usual amount of conversational courtesies which, even in such a signal situation, could not be ignored.

"The problem is, sir, that the Americans still do not understand us." He saw Yoshida glance sideways at him. "Perhaps they never will. They have been here a long time."

The Prime Minister smiled. "Remember, Colonel, that there was a time when we did not understand the Americans."

"But there is, I think, in Japan, a greater ability for cultural absorption."

Yoshida sighed. "Yes. Perhaps that is so. But, in any event, I am most grateful to you. Mr. Dulles was most anxious to back me into a corner. What he was no doubt leading up to was a Japanese involvement in the Korean War. Why else ask for a sudden enormous military buildup here?" He shook his head, his small hands clasped behind his back. "It is unthinkable, Colonel, for us to send troops into Korea."

Unthinkable, the Colonel thought now, kneeling in the brittle night. That time we avoided the unthinkable, by the grace of God. Now it had happened.

The fire was going strong. He reached the cord out of the pocket of his dark nylon jacket, dropped it into the center of the tiny conflagration.

He was not surprised to see that the knot in its center was the last to blacken and fall into ashes.

Said goodbye to Mount Aso, hello to Mount Fuji.

It rained most of the way back, drops beading the windowpane, streaking in fat rivulets as they combined. The low sky was black, filled with evil fulminating clouds. A stiff wind out of the north quarter plummeted the temperature; winter was here at last.

Nicholas shifted uncomfortably from one buttock to another, finding it painful to sit normally. Someone, farther along the car, kept fiddling with the tuning dial of a transister radio: brief bursts of rock music interspersed with a dry cultured voice announcing the news. Saburō, the leader of the Japanese Socialist Party, was under fire again for his "structural reform" policies which the Party had adopted a little over two years ago. Speculation was that he would be out soon.

Just north of Osaka, the rain turned to hail, pattering against the windows as it tap-danced along the hull of the train.

Nicholas, scrunched down in the seat, shivered slightly despite the adequate heating. Vaguely, as if the feeling belonged to another person and he had, perhaps, gotten his lines crossed, he felt hungry. But he had not left his seat since he had boarded this train at Osaka, had collapsed into it. Any movement at all seemed a chore to him now. Perhaps, before they pulled into the station at Tokyo, he would be obliged to relieve himself. He preferred not to think about that now. But then any kind of thought was difficult at the moment. His mind was a wind tunnel, leaves suctioned by the same currents, creating precisely the same patterns no matter how many times it was replayed.

Hear the groaning, feel the heat on his face: the light—shade off the lamp? Shadows moving, rising, falling, larger than life. Saigō, oddly, making the bed. Yukio, dressed in skirt and blouse, packing rather mechanically. He tried to say something but it was as if his mouth had been packed with dry sand. Was his larynx paralyzed as well?

Saigō took her by the arm, bag in her other hand. They both had to step over him to reach the door. Lay there like a quadriplegic, eyes blinking salt sweat and tears. He strained to see her face but it was in partial shadow, her long hair swinging across her cheek.

Saigō stopped her with a word in her ear, leaned backward and down, his face, shiny with sweat, hovering just over Nicholas'.

"You see how it is now, don't you? There's a good boy," he sneered. "And don't bother coming after, hm? There's really no point. Because this is good-bye. No *sayonara* this time. Get it?" He reached out, patted Nicholas' cheek almost tenderly. "If we ever meet this way again, I'll kill you."

Shadows looming—were they really people?—and then gone, just the after-image, dark on his retinas. He closed his eyes at last and concentrated on breathing.

The paralysis began to fade sometime after dawn, he estimated. He could not be certain of the time because he must

391

have fallen asleep at some point. Only knew that when he awoke just before eight, he could move his fingers and toes.

Within the hour he could stand and even walk steadily. He went into his own bathroom and stayed there for a long time.

His first stop was the warehouse. The character of the street was totally different in the daytime. This was near the center of the business district and during the day the area was jammed with traffic and pedestrians.

He tried the front door but it was locked. After two complete circuits of the place, he was convinced that there was no other way in. Picking the lock was out of the question.

He went into a nearby teahouse for breakfast, sitting at a table that gave him an oblique but clear view of the building's front. He drew a blank and after an hour gave up.

While paying the bill, he asked directions to the local police station. It proved to be a short walk away. He was sent up to the second floor of the wood and brick building. The place smelled of cement and turpentine.

The sergeant on duty sat behind a desk that was as battered and scarred as a war veteran. He was a small man, rather young, with a very yellow complexion and a wide mustache meant to disguise his splay teeth. His uniform was so neat that Nicholas could see the creases in his blouse.

He seemed sympathetic, even helpful. He took down all the particulars, including the address of the warehouse. But his eyebrows shot up when Nicholas told him what was behind the red lacquered door on the third floor.

"A ninjutsu *ryu*? Young man, are you certain this isn't some sort of prank?—a college hazing, that sort of thing. Because if it is, I under—"

"No," Nicholas said. "It's nothing like that."

"But surely," the young sergeant said, stroking his mustache lovingly with one forefinger, "you know that the ninja no longer exist. They died out, oh, almost a century ago."

"Do you have any proof of that?"

"Now see here—"

"Please, Sergeant. All I am asking is that you send some men around to the warehouse to check."

The sergeant took his hand reluctantly from his upper lip, held it out palm first. "All right, Mr. Linnear. All right. Just leave it to me. You go back to your hotel and wait for my call."

392

It wasn't until after three.

"Yes?"

"Mr. Linnear." The sergeant's voice sounded weary.

"Did you go to the warehouse?"

"Yes. I went myself. With two patrolmen. It is owned by Pacific Imports."

"Did you see the sign on the door?"

"There was no sign. Just a plain door."

"But there must be—"

"The warehouse was closed today but we were able to scare up the watchman. He was good enough to take us through. It's a warehouse. Nothing more sinister."

"I don't understand."

"Mr. Linnear, perhaps I should send a man over to take a look at your girl friend's luggage. Perhaps we might find some clue to her present whereabouts."

"Luggage?" Nicholas said, somewhat bewildered. "Her luggage is gone, Sergeant. I told you."

The voice at the other end of the line seemed to contract, become somewhat colder. "No," the sergeant said, "you didn't. Mr. Linnear, did you and your girl friend perhaps have a row last night? Did she walk out on you?"

"Now listen—"

"Young man, perhaps I should call your parents. Where did you say you were from?"

He waited until long after dark before setting out. It was colder, with a dankness that hung in the air like a steel curtain. What people remained on the streets at this late hour hurried past him, eager to reach the warmth of their destinations.

He went around the block once just to make certain. He saw no one more than once. He stood in a doorway, staring at the front door, shivering slightly as the wind picked up. A bit of newspaper fluttered across the gutter, lifted, then fell like a mammoth moth searching for a flame.

It took him four minutes to get inside. He was extremely careful. For what seemed a long time he stood with his back against the door, listening for sounds. He needed to pick up and memorize the aural pattern of the place so that, when he began to work, his mind would be attuned to any deviation from the pattern. That kind of thing could mean the difference between making it back out and being trapped in here, the subject of a manhunt. He gave himself ten minutes to be certain; the pattern contained outside traffic sounds and these took the most time to assimilate principally because they were intermittent. Then he went silently up the stairs.

The place appeared deserted but he discounted that, assumed that he was on enemy territory. The sergeant, at the very least, would not be pleased if he was caught trespassing and he had no desire to involve his father's name in these precincts; the less the Colonel knew of his activities in Kumamoto, the better.

Windowless, the warehouse was just as lightless during the day as it was at night. Time had no meaning here. On the third-floor landing, he reached out a pocket torch, played it on the door.

He stood perfectly still for some moments. Wood creaked somewhere downstairs, a settling rather than from a footstep. Outside, in an alley perhaps, judging by the hollowness of the sound, a dog barked twice and was still. The brief rumble of a truck.

The sergeant had not lied. The door was completely free of any sign.

He went across the landing for a closer look. Rubbed his fingertips over the surface in the light of the torch. Nothing. Had it ever been there? He sprung the padlock.

Fifteen minutes later he was away, walking stiff-legged from the pain down the street. A warehouse. Only a warehouse. And not a sign that it had even been a *ryu*. *Don't bother coming after*. Because we won't be there?

In the railroad car, the radio played a pop song he did not know. Its tempo was fast, its tone optimistic. The passing landscape was blurry with mist and, out of it, the hail, rattling and jumping like Ping-Pong balls.

Nicholas leaned his head against the perspex, glad of the chill it afforded. He tried to make sense of it all. What a superb actress Yukio had been. And what a naïve little boy he had proved to be. It was almost amusing. He working so hard to gain her trust when it was she for whom trust was a meaningless word. No, it was far too dispiriting to be in the least amusing.

But ironic, yes. So ironic.

There was a kind of numbness inside him as if Saigō's cruel intrusion had somehow anesthetized him, shorting out some spark of current. He thought of Yukio's remark at seeing the bombed-out observatory in Hiroshima. *That is what I am like inside.* Another part of her lie, but it was all too true now for him.

It began to snow, the sky turning white. The silence seemed appalling and absolute after the long siege of the hail. The radio had been switched off at last.

It was the reverse of the story she had told him, he thought, his head pounding. Except he was the lady waiting in vain for the broken promises of her lover to come true. Would Yukio, returning to find him gone, become a nun? For the first time, he began to think of America as more than just a country on the other side of the world. Forsake his beloved Japan? Yes, he thought. Yes. But first...

With a raucous burst, the radio broke into renewed life.... *I'll pretend that I'm kissing the lips I am missing / And hope that my dreams will come true / And then while I'm away / I'll write home every day / And I'll send all my loving to you....*

It hardly seemed surprising that Nicholas did not go straight home from the station.

He threw his bags in the back of a taxi and, climbing in after them, gave the address of Kansatsu's *ryu*.

Apparently the snow had been falling in Tokyo for some time. There was already more than an inch on the ground and traffic was snarled. This first snow had come so late in the year that everyone had given up on it and so had been taken by surprise.

The heavily laden windshield wipers gave off a hypnotic *hiss-thunk, hiss-thunk* as they crept through the city in maddening herky-jerky fashion. But once on the highway at the outskirts they made better time; the sanding crews had done their job.

He sat slumped in one corner of the backseat and did not open his eyes until they came to a stop outside the *ryu*. The driver called to him and he asked the man to wait until he was certain someone was still there.

The taxi seemed to sit there in the snow, panting, its exhaust expelled in tiny white bursts. He returned in a moment, paid the driver and hauled out his bags.

Kansatsu served him green tea in one of the *ryu*'s back rooms. The *dōjō*, itself, was deserted. There was no one here save the *sensei* and himself.

"You have had a most difficult trip," Kansatsu said.

Through an open *shōji*, Nicholas could see the snow silently falling, muffling all sound. In the twilight it seemed more blue than white. Fuji was invisible now, in the weather.

"I can see it on your face."

So Nicholas told him.

There was a great silence after he had finished, or so it seemed to Nicholas.

"Kansatsu—"

But the *sensei* stopped him. "Drink your tea, Nicholas."

Nicholas threw the gray porcelain cup away from him; tea spilled across the tatamis. "I am tired of being treated like a child! I know what I want to do now—what I *must* do."

"I think," said Kansatsu, unperturbed by the outburst, "that you should go home now."

Nicholas stood up, his face red with rage. "Don't you understand what has happened? Have you been listening to what I've been telling you?"

"I have heard every word." Kansatsu's tone was calm, soothing. "I sympathize with you. You have confirmed what I have suspected for some time. But no decision can be made in haste. You may think that you know what it is you want to do now but I doubt that you do. Please take my advice and return home. Take some time to think—"

"There are some answers I want from you," Nicholas said harshly. "You set me up for this. You knew—"

"I knew nothing. As I said. *Now* I know, as do you. That is better, you will admit, than being unsure. No decisions can be accurately made, no course of action taken, in such circumstances. That is basic. You understand that." There was a slight interrogative at the end.

"Yes."

"All right." Kansatsu sighed and stood up. They faced each other across the low lacquered table. "Let me tell you that which I withheld from you was for your own benefit—"

"My own bene—!"

Kansatsu held up one hand. "Please allow me to finish my thought. I had, at the time, only conjecture to go on as regards Saigō." His tone of voice changed, softening somewhat. "As for yourself, I told you what was in my mind. Working here will no longer well serve either of us. That you have survived your journey to Kumamoto is proof enough of that—if you might be inclined to mistrust my word."

"I would never—"

"No. I know. You would not." Kansatsu came around the table, touched Nicholas on his biceps. It was the first such gesture he had ever made toward Nicholas. "You have been my finest pupil. But the time has come for us to part ways. You must grow along your own path, Nicholas. Too long in this *ryu*, any *ryu*, can be detrimental to that growth. But"—he raised a long forefinger—"before you decide on where to go, your mind must be clear. And you will admit that you cannot claim such clarity now, hm?"

Nicholas was silent, thinking.

"Take several days, as long as you need, in fact. Then, when you feel you are ready, come to me. I will be here. I shall answer all your questions as best I can. And, together, we will decide on your future."

"There is something," Nicholas said at last, "that cannot be ignored."

"And what is that?"

"I have an enemy now." *Don't bother coming after.* "I invaded their territory; ignored their warning. When they come, I must be prepared."

Beside him, Kansatsu never seemed so old and frail as he stared out at the falling snow.

"I am afraid there's been some bad news."

He stood with his bags in the doorway of his house. Immediately he thought of Cheong. "Where's Mother?"

"At your aunt's. Come inside, Nicholas." The Colonel seemed pale and drawn.

The house seemed subtly different. Emptier.

"What's happened?"

"It's Satsugai," the Colonel said evenly. He had his pipe in one hand, unlit. "We tried to reach you in Kumamoto. I finally got hold of Saigō this afternoon. Itami was surprised to learn Yukio decided to stay with him."

Nicholas felt a knife twisting inside him. *All my loving darling, I will send to you.* There was a silence. He could hear the clock on the mantel in the Colonel's study. All the way in here. Nothing moved outside. It was as if the world had frozen over in a new ice age.

The Colonel cleared his throat. "Satsugai's been killed.

I'm sorry, it's a hell of a homecoming. I can see you didn't have the best of trips."

Was it so indelibly etched across his face; skywriting that he refused to face?

"How did it happen?"

The Colonel put the pipe stem to his lips, blew sharply outward to unclog it. He looked at the bowl. "Robbery, the police think. Satsugai must have surprised the thief."

"No one else heard him?"

The Colonel shrugged. "No one else was in the house at the time. Itami was at her sister's."

"Which one? Ikura?"

"No. Teoke."

Nicholas disliked Teoke.

"Well." He went to take his bags into his room. The Colonel stooped to help him and together they went through the house.

"It's so quiet," Nicholas said. "Nothing seems right."

"No," the Colonel agreed, something far off in his eyes. "It's never the same." He sat on the *futon*, pressed his thumb and forefinger against his eyelids. "The servants have gone with your mother and Ataki won't come today."

Nicholas began to unpack, separating the soiled clothes from the unworn ones. "Dad," he said after a time, "what do you know of the ninja?"

"Oh, not very much. Why?"

He shrugged, looking down at the shirt he was holding. "Kansatsu's been talking about them. Did you know that when firearms were first introduced here in 1543 by the Portuguese they were immediately incorporated into ninjutsu techniques? No? And because of that, firearms were shunned by the majority of the other classes—most especially the samurai—until the Meiji Restoration."

The Colonel got up, went across the room to stand beside his son. "Nicholas," he said gently, "what happened between you and Yukio?" When Nicholas said nothing, he put his hand on his son's shoulder, said, "Are you afraid to tell me?"

Nicholas turned around to face him. "Afraid? No. I—It's just that I know how you felt about her. You disliked her from the beginning."

"So now you won't tell me—"

"I love her," Nicholas said in anguish. "And she told me she loved me. And then. And then, it all fell apart just as if it had never existed." The Colonel's heart ached at the look he saw on Nicholas' face. "How could she go off with Saigō? How could she do it?" Tears stood in the corners of his eyes. "I don't understand any of it."

When he had seen Nicholas standing there in the doorway, the Colonel had felt an enormous urge to tell him everything; to confess. Now he knew that he would never do that; it would be far too selfish. It was a burden designed for him alone. How unfair to make Nicholas carry it for the rest of his life. But he wanted desperately to say something comforting to his son. He was dumbfounded now by his inarticulateness. Is this how I have been with him all his life? he wondered. I don't know what to say; what would calm him. He wished that Cheong were here now and was instantly ashamed of the thought. My God, he thought, am I that estranged from my own son? Is this what my work has done to me? It seemed to the Colonel to be the final irony. And now he realized how he had envied Satsugai's close relationship with Saigō. It was something he could never have with Nicholas. The fault, he saw, lay within himself.

He heard the door chimes ringing. "Come on," he said, and they both went to answer it.

A detective sergeant of the Tokyo Metropolitan Police stood on the steps. He was a heavyset youngish man, seeming ill at ease; he knew all too well where he was. He saluted smartly as the Colonel opened the door.

"Colonel Linnear," he said. He had restless brown eyes. "Lieutenant Tomomi asked me to inform you of the investigation's progress." He did not have to say which investigation. "Our latest findings indicate that your brother-in-law—"

"He's not my brother-in-law."

"Sir?"

"Never mind," the Colonel said. "Carry on."

"Yes, sir. We have ruled out burglary. At least, it's no longer at the top of our list."

"Oh?"

"The coroner's report indicates a double fracture of the cricoid cartilage. In the larynx. He was garrotted. And by a professional. Lieutenant Tomomi believes there is now reason to consider a radical leftwing connection."

"You mean assassination?"

"Yes, sir. We are bringing suspects in now. You know, the usual activists from the JSP, the Communists, so forth."

"Thank you for informing me, Sergeant."

"No trouble at all, sir. Good day." He turned away. Gravel crunched under his high black boots.

In the weeks that followed, the family life slowly restored itself to a semblance of order. But, as the Colonel had remarked, it was not the same.

There was Satsugai's funeral, of course, a strict formal ceremony, delayed for a time until Saigō returned home.

Nicholas found no sadness inside himself at Satsugai's death. This, of course, was not surprising. But he also found himself oddly anticipating the funeral and did not realize what it was he was anticipating until he saw Saigō and Itami arrive. Then his heart sank. Yukio was nowhere to be seen. For his part, Saigō neither looked nor talked to anyone save his mother.

With Saigō's return, Nicholas had expected Cheong to return home. Such was not the case. She continued to stay with Itami for more than a week. She might have, perhaps, stayed indefinitely had not Itami insisted she leave.

The tragedy had aged his mother, Nicholas saw, as much or even more than it had his aunt. She rarely smiled and she seemed distant as if holding herself together by a supreme act of will.

Further, and, to Nicholas, quite inexplicably, something had changed in her relationship with the Colonel. For as long as Nicholas could remember this had been an unwavering bulwark in his life, the backbone he could always count on. True, the shift was subtle and, perhaps, an outsider might not have picked it up, but it was there nonetheless and it frightened him. It was almost as if she blamed the Colonel for the tragedy. He had saved Satsugai's life once, wasn't that enough? Nicholas asked himself. He felt she was being unreasonable and, for the first time in his life, he felt himself being pulled by the increasing polarization of his parents.

Itami came almost every day for lunch. On several occasions she brought Saigō along when he was in town. Nicholas missed these meetings, being either at the *ryu*, talking with Kansatsu, or at classes at Tōdai, Tokyo University, but

Cheong spoke to him about them when he returned home in the evenings.

The Colonel had taken a week off from work, though he had not taken a vacation in almost a year and a half. He said he was ill and, for the first time since Cheong knew him, he went to a physician. He seemed pale and drawn but she was relieved to find that there was nothing physically amiss.

For his part, Nicholas became engulfed in college life. It was a strange business, Tōdai, but he soon got the hang of it. Once he had passed the enormously difficult extrance exams, he found that he had become a member of the famed *Gakubatsu*, the university clique. He found that Tōdai was one of the world's most exclusive clubs, grooming its graduates for top-line executive positions in government. Had not five of the postwar prime ministers come from Tōdai?

This period of intense self-involvement took Nicholas away from his family and it wasn't until weeks later that he recognized something was amiss. The Colonel had extended his leave of absence. He would rise early in the morning, as was his habit, and wander around the house touching objects as if for the last time. Often he got underfoot and the servants, quite good-naturedly, would steer him into another room or, increasingly— as he had a tendency to wander aimlessly back—outdoors. Then he would spend long hours sitting by the side of the Zen garden as if studying the swirling lines of the gravel. For a man who had been both strong and extremely active all his life, this behavior was most out of character.

Itami, when she visited, seemed totally attached to Cheong. Increasingly now, she spent the weekends, often taking long walks with Cheong through the cryptomeria and pine wood to the Shinto temple where she had taken Nicholas that afternoon so long ago. Perhaps they even passed through the spot where he and Yukio had rolled over one another as they had made love. Of what things Cheong and Itami spoke at those times Nicholas had no idea.

One day he came home from his studies earlier than usual and found the Colonel still outside. He was huddled inside his old English greatcoat. It seemed far too big for him now.

Nicholas skirted the house, went to sit beside him. He was appalled to see the sharp bones standing out along the ridges of the Colonel's cheeks.

"How are you?" he said. His breath frosted in a miniature cloud in front of him.

"Fine," the Colonel said. "I am just—tired." He smiled wistfully. "Just tired, that's all." His thin hands fluttered like birds. The backs were dark with liver spots. They settled restlessly on his thighs. "Don't worry about me. You know, I am thinking of taking your mother away somewhere for a rest. She's still not gotten over this thing. She needs to get away from here for a while. Forget all about grief. Your aunt hangs on to her now as if she were her only lifeline. It isn't fair."

"It'll be all right, Dad."

The Colonel sighed. "I don't know about that. The world is changing. It's become too complex. I'll never understand it. Perhaps you will. I hope so." He rubbed his palms up and down his thighs as if they ached. "Nothing's the way it once was." He looked away, into the sky. The last of the geese were moving south in giant vees; two fingers lifted triumphantly: the victory sign. "I had such dreams when I came here. There was so much I could have done."

"And you have. You've accomplished so much."

"Like ashes," the Colonel said. "I feel as if I've done nothing, merely slid with the tide, taken by forces I knew nothing of." He shook his head. "I cannot escape the feeling that perhaps I didn't try hard enough."

"How can you say that? You gave them everything. Everything."

"I thought it was the right thing to do. Did I do wrong? I can't say now. I'm pulled in two directions. I wish I had given them more, gone to Washington, pleaded our case there. I wish I had given them less, spent more time with you and your mother."

Nicholas put his arm around the Colonel's shoulders. How thin they had become. Where had all the hard muscle gone? Not even to fat. It had just disappeared.

"It's all right, Dad." Such an inane phrase, connoting nothing. He seemed tongue-tied. "It's all right."

What was it he really wanted to say?

But something irrevocable had taken place in the Colonel's life and it wasn't all right.

Despite repeated trips to the physician, despite a prescrip-

ion of potent pills, eating and, finally, injections, he continued to lose weight until there was nothing more anyone could
do to sustain him. Ten days after his talk with Nicholas in
the Zen garden, he died in his sleep.

The funeral was immense. Most of the arrangements were
taken care of by the American military in Tokyo. Mourners
came from all over the Pacific and President Johnson sent
a personal envoy from Washington. Nicholas thought this
man's presence highly ironic, given what he knew of his
father's failed ambitions. The Americans had been unwilling
to listen to him in life but were anxious to extol him in death.
He could not help but resent the man, despite his charm and
extreme courtesy, seeing in him not a little of Mark Antony.

The Japanese government, as was its wont, was somewhat
more honest. The Prime Minister himself attended, as did
many members of the Diet. The Japanese would not forget
the Colonel's awesome contributions to their country and
they paid their debt—some time later, after a decent interval,
Nicholas was approached for training for a high-level governmental post. He politely declined, pleased nonetheless.

As requested in the Colonel's will, the American Army
rabbi conducted the ceremony, which no doubt nonplussed
many of the attendees, especially those who had believed
they knew the Colonel well. The rabbi had known the Colonel
for a long time and when he spoke the eulogy it was with
enormous conviction. It was, in retrospect, quite a beautiful
ceremony.

"The Tenshin Shoden Katori *ryu* is the only answer now."
"I believe that is so. Yes."
"I want to leave and I do not want to leave."
"I understand this fully, Nicholas."
Kansatsu's cat's eyes were bright and alive.
He and Nicholas knelt facing each other. Around them
was the gleaming empty expanse of the *dōjō*, a deserted beach
in the sunlight.
"What will happen to me—there?"
"I am afraid that I cannot tell you. I do not know."
"Will I be safe?"
"Only you can answer that. But the strength to be so is
within you."
"I am glad you came to the funeral."

"Your father was a fine man, Nicholas. I knew him well."

"I did not know."

"No."

"Well…"

"I have prepared your letters of introduction. These include your graduation certificates—with highest honors—from this *ryu*." His eyes, focused on Nicholas' face, were unwavering; bits of flashing jet. He withdrew from his wide sleeve three tightly rolled sheets of mulberry paper tied with a thin black cord. He extended them and, when Nicholas touched them, it was the only physical link between them. "Remember," he said, "there is a chain. Thin. Link by link it goes. Take care you discover the identity of the next link on lest the chain break in your hands and you are left defenseless." Then he handed over the sheets. His hand lowered with a kind of grave finality.

"*Sayonara*, Nicholas."

"*Sayonara, sensei*." Tears filled his eyes so fully that he could see only a blur rise and leave the room. *I love you*, he thought. It was what he had wanted to say to the Colonel that day in the Zen garden and hadn't.

He hard no door click shut but abruptly he knew that he was alone in the house of cedar.

Oddly, the first thing he noticed was that the woodbine had died. Ataki no longer came, and during the last weeks the Colonel had been too ill to think of hiring a replacement. The hedges, always so carefully pruned even in winter, were spiky with branches left unchecked. The ground was hard with ice and frozen snow.

He felt a rising desire to run inside and tell Cheong that he was leaving but he was so uncertain of her response that he lingered awhile outside.

Above him the sky was a rich cobalt blue with just a few tracings of high cirrus clouds and, farther down, orange along the horizon where the sun slid through the thick haze. Far away, he thought he could hear the rumbling drone of a 707 coming down at Haneda.

Now he might have regretted canceling his dinner date with a couple of school chums in the city; he had told Cheong he'd be home late this morning. But, the decision being made to leave for Kyoto where the new *ryu* was located, he had felt the need for completion. And that would not come until he had told her.

Inside, the house was quite still as it had been since the moment he had returned home from Kumamoto, as if that had become some inexplicable nexus point in all their lives. Loss had followed gain and he wondered now if it had been worth it. He thought once more of the lady of Roku-No-Miya and her certitude of the implacability of fate. Thought, too, of the Colonel's conviction that he had been taken by forces he knew nothing of. Life could not be so cruelly unfathomable.

He went through the darkened hall, wondering that none of the lights had been lit.

The kitchen was deserted. No one answered his call. He shrugged off his coat, threw it over the back of a chair, went toward the back of the house. Stillness nodded deferentially to him, ancient as time.

He came, at length to his parents' room. The thin paper *shōji* was closed but, beyond, a light was on and he caught the edge of a shadow, moving.

He hesitated, reluctant to disturb Cheong if she was about to rest. Tomorrow, he promised himself, he would take her to the grave and together they would kneel before the marker of new cedar, lighting the incense and saying the prayers in English and in Japanese.

The shadow moved again and he called out her name softly into the falling night. No answer came and cautiously he opened the *shōji*.

He stood perfectly still, one foot in, one out, staring. All the breath had gone out of him. His head pounded and he felt a shock at the base of his neck as if from contact with a live wire.

All the tatami save one had been taken outside. The *futon* was folded in a neat pile in the far corner. One round white paper-shaded lamp was on against the right wall. Beyond, outside the glass panels of the far wall, lay the blue-whiteness of the snow, virgin, without one footprint to mar its granular surface. It seemed unnaturally pale against the black backdrop of the cryptomeria and pine forest. There were no lights in the sky.

The one remaining tatami had been placed in the center of the room; the surrounding wood floor seemed naked, like raw flesh with the skin stripped away. On it Cheong knelt

405

with her back to him. She wore a formal light gray kimono with obi. The one with the pink roses embroidered across it. Her back was bowed, her head down as if in prayer. The light gleamed on her blue-black hair, immaculately coiffed.

At her right side tiny Itami knelt, sitting at right angles so that he could see her profile. She, too, was dressed formally in a midnight-blue kimono, sleeves edged in crimson, milk-white obi.

The absolute stillness of the room was a tangible force, a rigid barrier holding him from further movement, even from speech.

Then one sound came, as sharp and near and startling as the first break of thunder from an unexpected storm.

It was the slither of steel against a sheath.

Cheong's right arm moved with unnatural speed and for the briefest instant Nicholas' mind was unaccountably filled with the sight of bursting cherry blossoms, impossibly pink against green foliage. Now that it had commenced, the transition from absolute motionlessness to rapid movement was irrevocable.

Saw the blade flashing platinum as its length caught the lamplight, as blinding as the sun, slashing inward in the blur of conviction that was necessary. Into the left side of the abdomen.

A thin cry like a startled bird but no fear and the body remained still. A slight tremoring, the perfect folds of the silk disturbed, an eyelash's flutter just before the violent jerk with both hands on the hilt, left to right, horizontally across the abdominal cavity. Only now the shoulders shook somewhat and he could hear a gasping as of a bellows desperately working. Droplets of sweat rolling down her forehead, dropping, darkening the tatami.

This must be a dream.

Saw the tension come into her elbows as she brought the blade upward toward her sternum. Such strength and force of will many men did not possess.

With infinite slowness, as if settling by degrees, fists still locked around the hilt, Cheong's body began to crumple forward, still in total control, a living monument. Her forehead touched the floor before the edge of the tatami.

As if that were a signal, Itami now moved. Her right hand fled to her side. With a harsh rasp, the *katana*, previously hidden within the folds of her kimono, was nakedly revealed

406

and, standing now, she raised it high over her head. The blade commenced its downward motion with a hot hissing sound as if those fearful shades of steel were anxious to feel the warm flesh part.

In an instant, Cheong's head was cleanly severed from her neck. Only then did the body lose its control and collapse completely. Blood seeped darkly, neatly, just a little of it as if sprinkled there by a decorator.

"No!"

At last released, Nicholas sprang across the room. Itami, staring down at the beautiful head, black and white and crimson, did not even look up.

"What! What!" He could not think. His tongue seemed an impossible weight in his mouth and he resisted the desire to rip it out. He could look at nothing but the body of his mother. And her head.

"It is done now, Nicholas." Itami's voice seemed distant and gentle at the same time. The bloody *katana* was at her side. "She is a child of honor."

Fifth Ring

THE NINJA

New York City / West Bay Bridge

SUMMER PRESENT

Someone began screaming, even before the lock shattered and the heavy door slammed inward in a crack of thunder.

The room was a shambles.

A bulky shape ran past him, across the room to the open window.

He began to struggle with it immediately because it had been his stupidity that had brought this on and if he did not work it out right now he would be no damn good in the next few hours and that would without a doubt prove fatal. He did not want to die.

Noted in passing the woman spreadeagled on the bed. Her flesh appeared to have been oiled, the light lying in long sweeps whitening the skin. Chinese.

He had known just as they had banged open the front door to Ah Ma's, in the wake of the *tsunami*. Took you bloody well long enough, he berated himself. Hideyoshi was not the ninja.

The woman stared not at him but at the muscled legs crisscrossing hers, wide shoulders at the edge of the stained coverlet, head off the bed at an odd angle. It was she who was screaming. The silken bond held her from moving. Her eyes were wide enough for him to see the whites all around. She might have been a madwoman and he saw why.

Upside down, Philip looked at him reproachfully, tongue half bitten through between his teeth.

The screaming seemed to go on and on in cadence, as effective as a siren.

"There's another way," Nicholas had said. "A better way." He dipped half a dumpling into its dark brown spicy sauce, popped it into his mouth. "I don't want any of your men getting hurt."

Croaker looked at him quizzically. "You're a strange bird, you know that? It's what we get paid for, us cops—taking risks."

They were in a dumpling house on Elizabeth Street between Canal and Bayard. The place was crowded, the noise level high.

"Reasonable risks," Nicholas pointed out. "The ninja's a sorcerer of death. They're not going to be prepared for him."

"Aren't you being just a little bit melodramatic?"

"No."

Croaker put down his chopsticks, pushed his plate away from him. A waiter immediately came to clear it away. "All right. What's your idea?"

"Let me go in alone."

"You're nuts." He leveled a finger. "Let me tell you something, Nick. This is a police operation. You know what that means? I could be suspended just for taking you along. And you want me to let you go after him on your own? The commissioner would publicly string up any part of me left intact after Finnigan, my captain, had gotten through. Uh uh. You'll just have to be content with the way it is now."

"You and me then."

"No dice. That would mean I'd have to leave you to cover the rear. Can't do it."

"There's going to be trouble, then."

"Not if we contain him in Ah Ma's. That's what we've got to do."

What worried him most in those last few moments as they had climbed the steps to Ah Ma's was the tactical disadvantage they were under. True, the element of surprise was in their favor, but only the man up in that suite knew the layout of the place, including the number of exits. Nicholas did not like any part of it.

On the first landing, he stopped Croaker, said, "You know, if we don't get him within the first few seconds, we've had it."

"Just concentrate on getting the bastard," Croaker had said and started up to Ah Ma's door.

Crouching in the dim hallway, Croaker had his .38 in one

412

hand, the warrant in the other. That piece of paper had not been easy to obtain; Ah Ma had many influential friends.

Somewhere, behind them, the intermittent buzz of a defective lighting fixture. A car passed in the street outside, honking its horn. The clatter of running feet. A sharp abrasive laugh.

Then the door was opening, Croaker was pushing aside a tall, elegant Chinese woman. The warrant flew through the air like a broken bird.

And Nicholas saw it all before him as if in a film. The killings, one by one, like links in a chain. One chain. Terry's historical clues. Three signposts: *Hideyoshi, Yodogimi, Mitsunari,* as obvious now as if they were glowing neon. Satsugai, Yukio, Saigō. The policeman sent to guard the dead Shōgun's mistress, a close enough approximation.

Idiot! he thought savagely as he stumbled into Ah Ma's after Croaker. Why did I withhold it from myself?

An American man, eyes wide in terror, stood up awkwardly, dumping a tiny Chinese woman onto the floor. He ran from them, through one of the living rooms, into a side suite.

Croaker was already midway down the long corridor leading to the back suites. Willow, who had opened the door to them, had been calling for Ah Ma. She was calm even in this seeming crisis.

Ah Ma appeared just as Nicholas began following Croaker back through the place.

"What is the meaning of this?" She grabbed at Nicholas. "How dare you break into my apartment? I have many friends who will—"

"The Japanese," Nicholas said in perfect Mandarin. Ah Ma started. She was borne along as he rushed through the long corridor. "Where is he?" Nicholas said. "He is all we want." He turned his head slightly. Doors passed them up, half-open, empty rooms lurking, mockingly. "Are you Ah Ma?" Noise up ahead. Croaker kicking at a locked door.

"He will destroy the place!" Ah Ma cried. She thought of the communists coming in the dead of night, destroying the house before dragging out her husband. But this was America.

Nicholas perceived her agitation. "The Japanese is a very dangerous man, Ah Ma. He could hurt your girls."

413

This she understood immediately and she fell silent, looking at him.

"Where is he?"

"There. There. Take him then."

He broke away from her, calling, "The left one. The left!"

Croaker swiveled, put a shot through the lock on the left-hand door. He went in with his shoulder and that was when the screaming began.

A blur of movement and Nicholas instinctively threw his arm across his eyes.

Flash of light, blue-white. The stink of cordite.

Croaker reeled and, running, Nicholas saw the last of a leg and shoe disappear through the open window.

"Christ Jesus!"

He turned. Croaker had one hand over his eyes.

"What happened?" His voice seemed hoarse.

"Flash bomb," Nicholas said. "A miniature."

Noise from the corridor, quickening.

"He's gone, Croaker. Out of the rear window."

Patrolman Tony DeLong received his final instructions from Lieutenant Croaker via the two-way radio and drove the blue-and-white slowly along the length of Pell Street.

"There it is," said Sandy Binghamton, his partner. "Pull over."

DeLong doused the lights, parked the car on a diagonal, blocking the street. It served a dual purpose. It would help keep the suspect within their perimeter if he came out the back of the building and it would discourage civilians from poking their noses into a potential red sector.

Binghamton was out first, swinging his big black bulk around the right side of the slewed patrol car. He paused, one hand on the chrome, and turned his head back toward the beginning of Pell Street. DeLong, still in the blue-and-white, was at this moment in radio contact with the second car but Binghamton wanted a visual fix. Civilian infiltration could be disastrous at this point and curiosity was a powerful motivator. He took his cap off, wiped his forehead on the sleeve of his uniform.

He turned back, studying the configuration of the end of the street, the specifics of the target building.

DeLong shut down the radio and came out into the street

and together they melted into the deep shadows thrown by the architecture on either side. The lieutenant had been quite insistent on this score. No sound and no sight. He watched the line of windows three stories up and thought about this. It was an unusual procedure where more than one blue-and-white was being used. But DeLong had no worries. He had faith in the lieutenant. He had worked with him for just under a year and a half and was now virtually assured, the next time the exam was given, of making sergeant. He wanted that very badly. He had had enough of the uniformed division and now he longed for a permanent assignment to a detective squad. There, too, the lieutenant could help him. And the extra money would come in handy now that Denise was due.

He felt Binghamton's bulk reassuringly near him. They were a vet team and this was his long regret in moving up. He did not want to break up a partnership that had been so successful. But Sandy had no desire to become a detective. He was content to be on the street with the people. "It's where I belong, man," he had told DeLong often enough. "I don't want to be no desk jockey." It was just that they conceived of the same job in different ways. Lieutenant Croaker's life wasn't filled with paper work but he could not convince Sandy of that. Once the big man had made up his mind about something, it took the devil's own—

Binghamton nudged him but he had already seen it. A hot flash of intense light, followed by a surprisingly soft *phutt*.

"Trouble, maybe," DeLong said. They both drew their weapons, crouched in darkness, waiting tensely.

Movement at the windows, shadows flickering like a children's shadow play.

"Get ready." Binghamton's voice was a basso rumble. "I gotta believe he's on his way out."

DeLong nodded and, together, they began to edge closer to the rear of the building. They moved as quietly as they could, keeping to the shadows. For the first time, DeLong noticed that several of the streetlights were out. Odd, since the new Chinatown Association lost no time in bringing such problems to the city's attention. But that was New York for you.

They both saw the blur of movement at the same time. DeLong gave his partner a pat and ran across the street into the concealing shadows on the far side. The black man kept his eyes riveted to the building at the end of the street. He knew from long years of experience where DeLong was headed.

They began to close in, keeping the old-fashioned iron fire escape between them. Looking up, they saw the moving shadow racing over the slats and then—nothing. No vertical movement downward.

The two men glanced at each other, then, cautiously, they moved forward until they were almost directly beneath the vertical ladder of the fire escape. From this perspective, it seemed an angular jungle of stripes and deep shadows. Randomly spaced lit-up windows made detection that much more difficult—insufficient light in many areas, spurious illumination in others creating three or more shadows of the same object.

"What the hell happened to him?" DeLong asked.

"I dunno." Binghamton holstered his .38, swung the iron ladder down with a grate. "But I'm going up to find out. He may have gone over the roof." He scrambled up onto the first-floor fire escape landing and drew his gun. Moving quickly and quietly, he climbed upward. He had difficulty maintaining a clear view through the forest of metal striations.

He paused for a moment on the second floor at the sound of a police siren, rising and falling, as a blue-and-white sped along the Bowery. Apparently it was heading uptown because the sound dopplered abruptly away, sounding odd and echoey in the summer night. Nothing to do with him.

"Anything?"

DeLong's voice drifted up to him along with the background wash of Chinatown, the traffic, slowly along the narrow streets, the distant chattering of a foreign language, sing-song, rapid-fire. Gave a negative wave of his free hand and heard the buzzing in the same instant. Some kind of insect. But the impacts—one two three—pinpricks puncturing the flesh of his chest and spinning him around were from nothing so innocuous.

He stumbled, reached out with his left hand, saw a movement, fired, grasped the railing. He thought only of getting enough air into his lungs. The .38 clattered against the iron grillwork at his feet.

Turned drunkenly and saw the dark figure before him as if it had appeared out of nowhere. Looked spectral in the wreaths of light and dark stripes, broken into oblique shards

416

like a fun-house mirror as he lurched from side to side. He wanted to vomit.

Impression of a pale face dominated by black almond eyes. In a moment the eyes moved and a thin line of white lights appeared along their curving edges. Pupils dilated, he saw. Drugs, he thought, irrelevantly. His mouth opened and he grunted like a stuck pig. "DeLong." Had it been loud enough? His ears rang as if he had just come from a rock concert.

The figure came at him, ballooning dangerously. He reached out, barring the figure's way with a stiff left arm while he brought his right up to the horizontal so that the gun was brought to bear—where was his gun? His thoughts as slow and stupid as a Neanderthal's.

Felt as if he were at the bottom of the sea, gravity dragging as cruelly at him as if he weighed five hundred pounds. Almost all of his strength was now being used to maintain his standing position. His chest was on fire—a cool numbing flame that seemed to set him floating inside himself, his consciousness detached itself from the useless husk of his body. Freed at last, it shot upward through the top of his head and into the humid squalor of the night.

Now the entire blaze of the city was spread out below him, a pinky-blue shell of light pulsing above the buildings like a shroud. Beyond it, infinite space.

Peering down through the haze, he could just make out in dwindling perspective his swaying body as the shadow ran past it, arm outstretched. He could even make out the pale blob of DeLong's anxious upturned face, moving nervously in the shadows of Doyers Street.

When he looked again his body was toppling ever so slowly, losing its balance. It seemed as if he had to strain to see clearly now, so high was he. Everything cloaked in an aurora and he wondered, fleetingly, whether he had exceeded his limitations and had gone too high.

Like Icarus, he thought. And descended into darkness.

DeLong felt it before he even saw it. Like an elevator unexpectedly coming down, the sheer bulk was oppressive.

He sidestepped, though he had no idea what had been thrown down. Then it landed, quite near him, with a heavy sound that had no analogue in life.

"Jesus Christ!" he said under his breath. He began to

417

sweat. He knelt beside the crumpled body of his partner. "Jesus, Jesus. Sandy, what happened?"

Shock. He knew he must look for whoever it was that had done this, but for the moment he was incapable of looking away. The shock. And blood seeping silently in a rivulet along the asphalt. The left side of the head had impacted first, then the shoulder and so on.

DeLong got up and backed away two paces.

Heard a sound, soft as only a cat might make, and he tore his eyes away. Pell Street had become a trap now for him and he scuttled back into the shadows of a doorway, looking up. For the first time he found himself wondering what the lieutenant had gotten them into. Where the hell was he, anyway?

He caught the movement now, this time soundless, along the horizontal plane of the fire escape one flight up. In other circumstances he would have passed it up as an animal prowling the night. Not now. He raised his .38, and, leading the target, squeezed off a shot. The report was very loud in the confined space, echoing off the walls, zigzagging from left to right. The *spang* of the ricochet told him he had hit metal.

"Shit!" He aimed, fired again. This time, no ricochet. Had it been a hit?

There was a vertical and the last horizontal row before the suspect could get to street level and he would be most vulnerable, DeLong reasoned, in descent. With difficulty, he held himself in check. Binghamton's broken body was like a heavy weight close by him and he fought the rising desire to empty his pistol at the moving shape. Wait, he cautioned himself. Wait and get this bastard when he's closer and there's no doubt.

Now the shadow was at the end of the first-floor fire escape landing and DeLong sighted carefully, using both hands, one cupped over the other to steady his aim. He fixed on the point of the access to the hanging ladder. His forefinger tightened on the trigger. Wait. Tidal breathing. Wait. Now. Here he comes. Shots, three in rapid fire.

Nothing happened.

DeLong raised his gun, puzzled. Where was the bastard?

Then he picked up movement on the street in the periphery of his vision. Impossible, he thought. How the hell had he made the drop without using the ladder? And without a sound?

418

He swiveled, legs spread, aiming the .38 in the classic pose he had been taught so well at the Academy. Silence. No movement. He tried to recall the path of the motion and extrapolate....

Felt the presence so close that he was startled. He dropped to one knee, fired fast and accurately on reflex. But in the space of that last instant he saw the figure leap at him. The left hand was extended and DeLong could make out a short black-wood stick, blunt-ended, as big around as his own nightstick. He braced for an overhand blow and thus was totally unprepared for the horizontal thrust. He was dumbfounded by the useless gesture.

The rounded end just touched the cloth of his uniform over his heart. It was only then that he jerked to the searing pain lancing through him as the seven-inch stilletto blade, powered by a high-thrust steel spring, shot out from the end of the wooden stick, puncturing him from front to back. It speared his heart, went through one lung and DeLong was dead before he hit the ground.

The flying form was by him, veiled by the first gout of blood, heard DeLong's last gasp which, to the policeman's dying brain, sounded like the loudest shout in the world.

Nicholas led Croaker back through the apartment. Women, half-clothed, stood in the doorways, staring curiously at them.

Ah Ma, having received the warrant papers from Willow, stood stone-faced with Penny at her side. Willow was in the back suite the Japanese had used seeing to the boy and trying to soothe the girl's shattered nerves. Willow is wonderful in a crisis, Ah Ma thought, resignedly. The way I used to be. She sighed silently. I do not want to go in there, she thought. Once it would have been the first place I'd run. To help. But no more. Times have changed and so have I. She put one arm around Penny's shoulders, as much to keep the girl beside her as to reassure her.

"You should have caught him," Ah Ma said in Mandarin to Nicholas. "Now he may come back here. He won't be happy. His security was broken."

"He won't be back," Nicholas reassured her. "He has already killed the leak."

They had to go out by the front, the long way around,

surely, because in the dark and without radio linkage they could not chance egress via the back window. Gunfire still came to them, sporadic and muffled by the intervening walls of the building.

In the hallway a dog was barking and someone one flight down had turned up a TV set, perhaps to drown out the noise from outside.

"Christ!" Croaker said, rubbing at his eyes as they pounded down the stairs. "What a goddamned mess."

More shots as they emerged into the hot sticky night and they ran down Doyers, heading for Pell Street.

They saw the blue-and-white first, slewed at an angle. They raced past it.

Nicholas saw the two bodies immediately. One was outlined in the foreground, the other cloaked in a spider web of shadows at the end of the street. He paused, his eyes searching from left to right and back again.

Croaker brushed past him, his gun at the ready, but checked when he saw the first body. Slowly, warily he went toward it in a semi-crouch and, on one knee, turned it carefully over. He recognized DeLong at once, was appalled at the amount of blood. He searched in vain for any sign of life. His hand came away soaked.

He got up and, crabwise, scuttled quickly down the street, checked Binghamton's cooling body. He stood up and holstered his gun. He came back, passed Nicholas without a word and slid in behind the wheel of the patrol car.

He called dispatch, asking for the meat wagon and the associate M.E. on call. Then he sent out an A.P.B. He was still on the phone when Nicholas came up, leaning on the frame of the open door.

"He's long gone, I'm afraid."

Croaker cradled the receiver, put his head onto the back of the seat, closing his eyes. "They were my best team." His eyes snapped open and his big fist pounded the steering wheel so hard it jumped. "The best goddamned team!" He sighed. "I'm sorry now I didn't listen to you. I don't know who that guy out there is but—"

"Lew," Nicholas said, "slide over. I want to talk to you before the crowd comes."

Croaker turned to look at him as he slid over to the passenger's side. Far off, they could hear the wailing rise and fall of a siren. It could have been an ambulance.

"I know who the ninja is."

Croaker sat perfectly still for a moment.

"How long have you known?"

Nicholas blew out a breath as if that would relieve the heaviness he suddenly felt. The deaths in the present had combined with the deaths in his past, rushing forward to once again engulf him. He felt very tired and very sad.

"Not long, really. In the hallway outside Ah Ma's."

"I see."

And then he told Croaker everything, spewing it all out as if that might cleanse his soul, relieve him of a burden which, he felt now, he had been carrying far too long.

"Do you mean to tell me," Croaker said, when he had finished, "that Saigō isn't after Tomkin at all? That he's after you?"

"Yes and no," Nicholas said wearily. "He is going to kill Tomkin all right, unless we stop him, but I believe he took on the job to get to me also. It's the only way all of the killings make sense."

"I see that, of course, but this is like a blood vendetta."

"It's a matter of honor."

"But you must have known it was coming." The siren's wail was louder now, a cry in the night, and the sound of excited voices pitched back at them off the brick walls. "Weren't you afraid of—?"

Nicholas gave him a wan smile as he shook his head. Time to go, he thought. "I am prepared for it. I've been prepared for a long time now." He climbed out of the car. Every muscle seemed to ache and his head throbbed as if it were in a vise. He leaned in so Croaker could hear him as the blue-and-white drew up, followed by the ambulance. The street lit up red and white, red and white like the entrance to an amusement park.

"You see, Low," he said with infinite slowness, "I am a ninja, too."

"Nick, wait!"

But he was already walking past the oncoming people, crowding into the street, into the glare of the dense night.

"Sam."

Daddy. Daddy. Daddy. He had never said that word in his life yet he thought it now.

421

"Yes?"

"Sam."

"Who is this?"

"Are you still my rabbi?"

"Oy, Nick. Nick! Is it really you?" Goldman's voice was light.

"It's me."

"My God, how are you?"

"All right. How's Edna?"

"Edna? Edna's fine. Dying to see you. Where are you?" Silence. "Nick, are you all right?"

"To be honest, no."

"Just a minute. What...?" The sound of muffled voices came to him, a conversation from another world. A world where there were homes and families, children. Mortgage payments and, perhaps, a two-week trip to Europe in the spring. What was he doing here, anyway?

"Listen. Are you in the city? Edna says to come right up. It's Friday night. She's made chicken soup. With *lokshen*. Your favorite, remember?"

"I remember." He remembered everything now.

"So come over. We'll eat. We'll talk." Pause. "You'll make Edna very happy. She's been worried about you."

He rested his head against the acoustic panel of the booth. Traffic raced by him, just beyond his reach.

"Yes," he said after a time. "Okay. I'll be over."

He hung up and hailed a cab. The Goldmans lived in the Dakota on Seventy-second and Central Park West. They took the Bowery, which turned into Third Avenue, all the way up to Forty-second Street where the taxi turned left, heading crosstown to Eighth Avenue.

Just after Broadway, Nicholas leaned forward, tapped the intervening plastic partition. "I've changed my mind. I'll get off here." He paid and got out.

He had been idly staring out the left-side window as they passed the long line of movie marquees along that tawdry street when he had seen the film titles.

He watched the two-way traffic, crossed to the south side of the street. He walked west, past a couple of the new-era glass and chrome porno shops, proudly announcing "Couples Welcome." The doors were thrown open in one and a tall black man in wide hat and tight green pants lounged in the loorway. "Hits," he murmured, "loose joints, coke, speed. Quality stuff."

Now the movie marquees came one after another in a seemingly unending line on both sides of the street. Most were porno houses but one, the one Nicholas had seen from the cab window, was not. Here there was a kung fu triple bill. Two of the films starred Bruce Lee.

Nicholas dug out a buck-fifty and went inside. The place smelled old and musty. It was lighter than was normal in most theaters. There was a crowd of black and Puerto Rican kids clamoring around the soda machine in back.

He took a seat. The place was almost filled. On the screen Bruce Lee was talking earnestly with a couple of evil-looking Japanese in dubbed English. The audience was noisy, restless for the action sequences. Dialogue they did not appreciate.

Nicholas sat back, watching Lee for a time. The years had not diminished his aura. His spirit seemed to leap off the screen, making the most slipshod productions worth watching.

Nicholas recalled the first time they had met. It had been in Hong Kong, ironically, after the period Lee had spent in Hollywood, working as a bit player in films and TV and teaching stars enough of the martial arts to get by in front of a camera.

He was beginning to be somewhat of a star in his own right then. They had taken to each other immediately but time and logistics had worked against them and they had never seen each other again.

Lee's death had come as a shock to Nicholas. Not that someone would try to kill him—he knew enough about Lee by that time to understand that the man's uncompromising nature had become a thorn in some decidedly unsavory sides—but that an attempt had succeeded. He had always wondered how it had been done; now he thought he knew.

Outside, it was still stifling and, in this place of hot lights, fast food, dirty dope and even dirtier deals, more so than elsewhere.

It took him fifteen minutes to find an empty cab and half that time to reach the Dakota; there was little traffic.

He had stayed at the decaying theater just long enough to catch one of Lee's gorgeously choreographed action sequences, motivated, as usual, by revenge. Tonight there seemed nothing artificial about that.

423

Goldman, dapper as ever in a pale blue pinstripe shirt and midnight-blue linen slacks, met him at the door. He smiled warmly when he saw Nicholas, extending a firm hand. "Nick. We were getting worried about you." He turned, still in the doorway. "Edna, it's him." He pulled Nicholas inside, pushed a rum on the rocks into his hand. "Here. It looks like you need this."

Edna, a dark-haired chubby woman, bustled into the living room from the swinging door to the large kitchen. She beamed, raised her hands. *"Tateleh!"* She kissed him on both cheeks. She had the kind of incandescent inner warmth that made mere physical beauty irrelevant. "Where have you been so long, you haven't come to see us?" Her voice held just the right balance between love and reproach.

He smiled thinly. "It's good to see you both."

"That's it," she said as if she had discovered a rare artifact. "You've lost weight. Come." She took him by the hand. "We eat first. Whatever it is you want to talk to Sam about can wait for a full stomach."

They ate in the kitchen with the yellow and beige wallpaper and the old West Side fixtures, the oval table of fine-grained mahogany richly waxed, covered with a beautiful embroidered white-on-white tablecloth. A brass menorah stood on a wall shelf above the table, at its center.

Afterward, as Edna cleared the dishes, Sam nodded silently to Nicholas and they excused themselves. Edna kissed them both before they left. "Whatever is wrong," she told him with absolute faith, "you can fix it. Right, Sam? Am I right?"

"You're always right." He ushered Nicholas into the living room.

Beige and pale green predominated. Edna despised brilliant primaries, perhaps because she saw her childhood on 189th Street in those colors. The effect was a soothing one, like being in a cool forest during the heat of the day.

They sat on the beige velvet couch and Sam put his feet up on a matching ottoman. An antique clock ticked lightly from its owl-like perch atop the white marble fireplace. A great bunch of dried eucalyptus in a pale pink ceramic vase stood within, wafting its pungent scent into the room. There was a Utrillo on the opposite wall and, on another, a small Dali. In their bedroom, on pale blue walls, were a Picasso and a Calder which, of course, Edna detested. They were all originals but they were displayed with a pleasing lack of ostentation.

"It has come back," Nicholas said softly. "All my past, like a great tidal wave."

Goldman reached for a hardwood box, took out a cigar, lit it slowly.

"I've lost the present somewhere along the line. I no longer know where I am."

He deliberately blew the blue smoke away from Nicholas. "Nicholas, as Shakespeare so cleverly put into Ophelia's mouth, 'We know what we are, but we know not what we may be.'"

"Sam, I didn't come here for homilies!" he exploded.

"Nor did I mean to give you any." He took the cigar out of his mouth, laid it in a crystal ashtray. "Look, it is totally unreasonable to expect to know or understand everything about yourself. The human being is such a complex animal that we have to be content to muddle through things as best we can. Some days, it just doesn't seem nearly enough. At other times..." He shrugged with some equanimity.

"I understand all that. But you're the expert on history. I am only partly a Jew. I haven't had the training. I don't—"

"It has nothing," Goldman said seriously, "at all to do with training. One learns the meaning of being a Jew just as one learns the meaning of being a human being—by living life, not by learning the Torah.

"It comes from what you feel inside and the important thing is that you do not deny what is inside you. Doubt and fears; uncertainty of the present and the future all stem from that. Your self must be free to go in whichever direction it must go.

"The spirit flies, Nicholas—it is the only thing we possess which can. It is a sin to tie it down, to deny your spirit its breath. Life is nothing without it. We merely survive, from day to day, in a kind of unthinking limbo.

"Does this answer your question?"

In the nightsilence of the tower on Park Avenue, he sat with Raphael Tomkin. At the moment, Tomkin was on the telephone. Somewhere in the world, it was always some time between nine and five and that meant business was rolling.

Decisions, vital to one subsidiary or another, and thus vital to the corporation as a whole, required the mind of the mover and the shaker. Three continents awaited the outcome of such transatlantic or transpacific conversations.

While Tomkin talked on in mega-figures, a kind of semisecret corporate shorthand, Nicholas looked at the tiny bit of metal and plastic he held between his fingers. He turned it like a miniature world, though in truth it was a disk only and thus flat, so that it caught the lamplight, its face turning to a slow dazzle.

Just possibly, he thought, this little piece of the electronicized present could be the key to it all. The past, the present and the future. It could end right here, if he chose. If he chose.

And he wanted desperately for it to be his decision.

He felt, quite rightly, that Saigō had taken all initiative from him and he felt stripped bare, naked and defenseless because he had not seen what was happening.

Saigō had been leading him around by the nose until he was dizzy, laughing all the way. It was a technique from the *Go Rin No Sho*. What was its name? To Hold Down a Pillow. Restrict the enemy's useful actions while encouraging his useless ones. Lead him around as if he had a ring through his nose and, when he is in total confusion, strike.

"Where've you been?" Tomkin said, cradling the phone. He looked slightly rumpled at this time of the night, his cream-colored linen suit wrinkled at the insides of the elbows, his gray silk knit tie slightly askew. The flesh of his face had lost the pink glow it maintained for most of the day, seeming pummeled into a kind of uneasy truce—submission was a flat-out impossibility—by the long hours. Lines at the corners of his eyes had become noticeable but they merely made him seem that much more human. Nicholas still felt himself wondering which was the façade.

"In Chinatown."

Tomkin grunted, swiveling around in his high-backed leather chair. His hands played idly across his desk's electronic console as a Greek peasant might fondle his worry beads. "Chinatown, huh? With that bastard Croaker, I'll bet." He stared into Nicholas' face and his eyes, like chips of blue quartz, were merciless. They were sailor's eyes, Nicholas thought. The eyes of a man well seasoned to the sardonic tricks of the sea and the open sky. They were the eyes of a survivor; shipwrecked, his crew drowned, this man would

426

make it onto some beachy shore and, like Crusoe, vanquish time though perhaps not solitude. "You better not get too friendly with that cop. Just a friendly warning, 'cause I'm waiting for that motherfucker to step one inch out of line. Then I'm gonna break him in two."

Nicholas thought about what Croaker had told him of Gelda and he had to smile to himself. What would Tomkin do when he found out that Croaker and his daughter were seeing each other? Apoplexy might be an accurate term.

"That bastard's got a hard-on for me and I've got no idea why. He's got this crazy notion that just because I was balling Angela Didion, I killed her."

Nicholas watched him, rubbing the electronic bug back and forth between the calloused pads of his fingers.

Tomkin snorted derisively through his nostrils, giving Nicholas the image of a horse rearing. "Hell, that broad got around, you know? Doing people she didn't even know. Got a kick out of that, giving rim jobs to guys she pulled off the street. Just like that—Boom! Only it wasn't always guys, see. The broad was nuts. Definitely nuts. If I'd've known about that—you know, a closet lezzie—I wouldn't have—hell, she disguised it well enough." He waved a hand and gold glinted. "Anyway, it's all ancient history now—that's how I see it. But that cop won't let it alone, you know? He's like a fucking dog with an old bone nobody wants but him."

"He's doing his job."

"He *ain't* doing his job!" Tomkin cried. "That's the whole goddamned issue." He pounded the table. "The Angela Didion thing is a dead issue for everyone on the entire fucking New York Police Force except Croaker. What's he think he's got? A calling from God? Well, I'm telling you, he's got nothing. I got his number; loves to see his name in the papers." He swiveled back and forth in his chair, very fast, as if he had a surplus of nervous energy. "Goddamned glory hound. He's not gonna ride *me* to any headlines. He needs to be taught a lesson, that's all." He glanced up, no longer half-talking to himself. "What about this guy—the ninja?"

"Well, that's what I came to talk to you about. So far, he's been setting the pace. What I think we have to do now is reverse the situation. We have a chance if we can control the environment. We have to, in other words, be on the battleground before him."

"So? Set it up. That's what I'm paying you for, isn't it?"

"It's not that simple, unfortunately."

"Well, do what you have to do. I don't care what it is. I want him out of the way. Permanently."

"It involves you directly."

"Of course it does. He's been sent here to kill me."

"He's here to kill me, too."

"What?"

"I know this man. There is an old score to be settled. It's nothing to do with you."

"I see."

"Except that it may lead us to his entrapment."

"How?"

"Through one of his bugs." Nicholas lifted the tiny disk so Tomkin could see it clearly. "You see, this is currently inactive. It's one of the new contact type, which simply means that once it is reapplied to a surface, it becomes active again."

A gleam came into Tomkin's icy eyes; deceit was a currency he understood. "You mean—"

"We reactivate it. And use it. Chances are he'll believe there's been a minor dysfunction and—"

"What if he's smarter than that? This guy's an expert. I've heard stories about ninja—"

"I don't," said Nicholas, "think it will matter at all. He wants us both and, if he thinks he can get us together, he'll take the chance, even if there's the suspicion of a trap. It's one I've set up, you see. It's a challenge and he cannot back down without losing an awful lot of face. That he will not do."

"It amounts to inviting him over," Tomkin said slowly.

"Yes."

The blue eyes regarded him cannily. Nicholas could almost hear the sound of his mind ticking over, weighing probabilities just as if he were making a computer-assisted business decision. But then, in a curious kind of way, it *was* a business decision.

"Let's do it." His voice rang unhesitatingly.

Afterward, as Nicholas detached the bug and dropped it into the thick cotton bed he had fashioned for it in one of the desk drawers, Tomkin said, "Can everything be arranged by the night after next?"

"There won't be any problem."

"Good." He picked up the phone as Nicholas turned to

428

leave. "Hey," he said, "you didn't tell me you were having problems with Justine."

Nicholas froze, silently cursing Tomkin. Had he been spying on his daughter again? How else would he know?

"Hit a nerve, didn't I?" He laughed. "You got a damn good poker face, but I don't need to see your expression to know."

"Just what *do* you know?"

Tomkin shrugged. "Just that she's in the city; out with another guy. Don't know who he is but I will soon enough." He dropped his eyes, began to dial. "It's too bad, really. I would've liked you two to stay together. You're good for her. Now I'm afraid she's gone back to her old ways."

"Where is she?"

"Hello? Yes—"

"Tomkin—" Nicholas' tone cut through the space between them.

"Hold the line a moment—" Tomkin put his palm over the receiver. "What did you say?" His voice had turned a touch treacly.

"Where is she?"

"At a discothèque. On West Forty-sixth Street." He rummaged with one hand on his desk top. "I know I have the name of it somewhere. At least, I *had* it earlier.... Ah, here it is." He read off a slip of paper, giving Nicholas the name. His eyes lifted. "Know it?"

"I don't go to discos, normally," Nicholas said. His voice was as tight as a coiled spring. Across from him, Tomkin looked as if he had devoured a particularly tasty sweet.

"No, I suppose not. Otherwise you might have run into her before this. It's an old hangout of hers. Perhaps you ought to try it sometime." He turned away into the phone in dismissal.

For a time he spoke as part of a conversation that had no meaning, listening with his free ear to the sound of the elevator's doors sighing shut, the quiet hum of the machine as it took Nicholas down to the lobby far below.

When that sound had ceased, he reached out one hand and opened a desk drawer. Without turning his head, he replaced the receiver of the phone.

He stared down at the bit of plastic and metal with a kind of rapt fascination. A light line of sweat broke out on his forehead, the way it did every time he made a major business decision. His heart thudded and his pulse rate increased.

429

He licked his lips and, carefully, deliberately, he brought the bug out of its bed and attached it to the side of the desk.

He swung around, away from it so that he looked out on the winking late-night face of the city. West. The entire country was before him though, of course, he could not see it. At length he began to speak.

"I suppose," he said, almost meditatively, "it depends on how much you want him. But what if—what if I could *guarantee* Nicholas Linnear. I could hand him to you on a platter. As easy as pie, yes?" He swung around and now he addressed directly the bug hanging like a bloated spider. "I'll bet that's worth a lot to you. As much as a life. What do you say?"

He reached out and detached the bug, returning it to its drawer, precisely as Nicholas had placed it. Tomkin was a meticulous man.

Then he sat back with his hands behind his head, waiting for the phone call he was certain would come. The fully loaded pistol clinging in its holster to his damp shirt beneath his suit jacket felt heavy and warm and infinitely comforting.

In matters like this, he thought, one never knew.

"Someone wants to see you."

The phone had rung just after Croaker had walked in but, despite that and despite the fact that she had already put the machine on, Gelda had picked it up herself.

She had come into the living room to answer the door and both of them were still there in the semi-darkness. She watched him now as she listened to the voice in her ear, as he stood in the oblique bars of light and dark so that they climbed his legs to just above his knees. His face was illumined by the fat wedge of lemon light from the bedroom.

"G, are you there?"

"Yes, Pear."

"I thought you had drifted away for a moment. Have you popped anything?"

"Not tonight, no."

He seemed afflicted with a weariness that went far beyond a lack of sleep. It was as if all the endless hours in the office and on the streets and in the courtrooms had built up a sly accretion impossible to discard which now lay heavily upon him like a gray and ageless second skin.

"Just a professional question," Pear said, mistaking

Gelda's silence as an expression of annoyance, "that's all. Seeing as how there's—"

"Not tonight."

"I know I haven't given you any notice. That's because it's the senator."

Gelda knew what that meant. "Get him someone else."

"G," Pear said slowly and patiently, "he wants you. There *is* no one else. You know how he is."

He stood there in the half-light like some mythic animal come to life; a creature someone had mistakenly dressed in human clothes. He seemed only partially aware of her.

"The answer's still no." She could not be more aware of him.

"And what of Dare when she comes to town again?" Pear had obviously caught something in Gelda's tone of voice.

And, abruptly, Gelda knew that she had answered the phone *because* he was here. "No. Even for Dare. Those days are gone. I am out."

"I see." There was no hurt in Pear's voice, no hint of re-crimination.

Gelda felt light-headed, as giddy as if she had just consumed an entire bottle of Dom Pérignon. She also felt happier than she ever had before.

"We'll miss you, G. *I'll* miss you." It was like Pear, at a moment like this, not to mention the clients.

"I'll never forget you," Gelda whispered.

A soft laugh. "I should hope not. Good-bye, G."

Gelda put down the receiver, went over to Croaker. "What happened?" She put her arm around him, walking him into the bedroom.

In the warm lamplight, she saw the dried blood on his hands. "Won't you tell me?" she said in a voice calmer than she felt. "You look so sad."

"I've just come from seeing two families. A pregnant wife and a mother of three small kids." He looked at her despairingly. "Have you ever had to tell someone that the person she cares most about is dead?" He took a deep breath. "Well, I have. But never before when I knew those deaths were my fault." He stared at his brown hands, stained as if they had been dipped in dye, crusty as if covered in sea salt.

"Why don't we start at the beginning," she said softly, taking his hands in hers, drawing him forward. "The blood has to come off first."

431

I knew what I was doing / I knew right from the start / I knew where I was going / There's radar in my heart....

The place was all mirrored chrome and black smoked glass, multi-leveled like the hanging gardens with floors of translucent glass under which colored lights flashed in time to the music.

The air vibrated with percussion and electric voices, strung like a Christmas tree with garlands of perfume and perspiration and burning pot.

I felt your contact coming / Your star was on my chart / I heard your motors humming / Got radar in my heart....

Somewhere was the bar, obscured behind a forest of raised arms, swirling hair, shiny mindlessly concentrating faces. Dance dance dance: the imperative was clear, treading an atavistic path, the primitive's tribal revivals, an ecstatic communal orgy, trivalized to the point where all possible consequence was nullified.

The posters on your walls mark every fashion's rise and fall / Why try to keep the past alive / And though I know the time is almost 1984 / It feels like 1965....

Like moving through a dream. All senses assailed relentlessly until distortion grew like weeds in the abandoned front yard of reality. Every step forward carried with it the burden of two in retrograde. He thought of Alice down the rabbit's hole and wondered if Carroll could have had this in mind. Only Coleridge might have dreamsmoked this up; it seemed the habitat of a damaged archangel.

The music in my room is always slightly out of tune / My harmony is up on trial / And though I know the rhythm you'd prefer me dancing to / I'll turn my revolt into style....

At the bar there were leather-padded seats on which no one sat, a line of jackdaws ironically eyeing a busy cornfield in summer.

Nicholas sat and ordered a drink out of form. He was not thirsty. He watched the lamé glitter in the spiraling lights, the neon shoes with heels impossibly high. Multicolored eye makeup seemed to cover half the faces of women who turned toward him again and again in the course of the dance. Flesh was entirely incidental, it seemed; arms and breasts and

432

thighs were painted like lizard skin. Their expressions recalled to him vivid scenes from *Metropolis*.

He was searching for Justine but in this madhouse it seemed useless: like running after Yukio in Kumamoto. Doors closing in his face as fast as they were opened.

Then what Sam had said to him earlier in the evening began to seep through into his consciousness. What difference did it make what he was now as long as he knew what he wanted to be; what he wanted. It was no longer 1963, part of another lifetime. But he knew that he would never truly be free until he understood it all. Without understanding, he knew, assimilation was impossible. The *kijin*—the goblins of his past—would be appeased by nothing less.

"What are you doing? C'mon, c'mon, c'mon and dance."

She was a sloe-eyed blonde in a lavender crepe de chine dress which showed off her ample breasts to maximum effect.

I feel like a wog / People give me the eyes / But I was born just like you you you....

"Don't you wanna"—her bird's head swayed seductively—"get in the swing? C'mon, c'mon."

"No, I don't think—"

—like a wog / I don't mean you no harm / I just want to shine your shoes....

"—apricorn, right? You must be. Dour." She pronounced it *dower*. "All Capricorns are dour. But—"

"I'm not here to dance," he said, feeling foolish. "I'm here to find someone."

Golly gee / Golly gosh / Don't call me your golliwog....

"—do it together."

Don't call me, don't call me, don't call me / I'll call you if I want you....

"You don't understand. There is a woman here. A woman."

"So?" She took his hand, crimson nails gleaming, changing colors, lines of light flicking. "Let's dance, dance, dance until we find her."

He broke away from her grip.

"Don't you want to have fun?" she cried after him.

—made me feel like, feel like, feel like a wog....

Went up to the second level, blues and greens like a grotto of waving kelp. Synchonization had begun to set in and he felt his pulse throbbing to the beat of the music flailing the air with the abandon of a reaper at his wheat field.

And, at last, he saw her on the highest level, partly obscured by the scaffolding of the circular staircase. He had to wait several minutes, the narrow path clotted and blocked: dancing up, dancing down.

Disappearing in a wave of arms and heads bobbing and he went up the iron stairs two at a time. Black leather walls like a padded cell, smoked glass far too fragile for the height: what if someone should stumble in thrall and fall? What then?

Light in reds and yellows, turning white and gray against the black leather, disconcerting, like seeing a color TV show on an ancient set; everything somehow just slightly out of phase.

There she was. With a tall broad-shouldered man with lank black hair and the sallow skin of a Puerto Rican. He wore a sleeveless undershirt with a red, blue and gold Point Beer button, high-waisted deep red trousers.

Didn't I hear you cry this morning / Didn't I feel you weep / Teardrops flowing down on me / Like rivers in my sleep....

"Justine."

Her head whipped around and light caught at the crimson flecks in her near eye. Watched him silently until her partner whirled her around in a blur.

"Justine."

"What'a'you want, man? Don't hassle my chick, hey. Keep cool, okay?"

Didn't I hear your voice this morning / Didn't you call my name / I heard you whisper softly / But the words were never plain....

"Justine. Look at me." He reached out.

"Hey, man. Hey, hey. No way to act. You ain't listenin'. Drift away now. She don't want no part o' you."

Noted in passing, the dilated pupils, the reddened nostrils.

"Why don't you go to the men's room and do some blow?"

That's a strange way to tell me you love me / When your sorrow is all I can see / If you just want to cry to somebody / Don't cry to me....

"Now, hey man. I'm through talkin' to you." The *click* unheard in the throbbing of the leather room but the gleam of the switchblade was unmistakable.

"Justine."

"Don't talk to her, man." One shoulder lowered. "Now this's for you."

He was very fast and he knew how to use it, trained in the street where there are no rules except the need to survive. This kind could be far more dangerous than the professional because of the unpredictability. The eight-inch blade could rip open his abdomen in a fraction of a second.

Blocked the initial thrust with his left forearm and, pivoting, slammed the edge of his right hand into the Puerto Rican's hipbone. There was no sound save for the music; their violent motions, dancers' movements assimilated into the fierce kineticism of the leather room.

The Puerto Rican's mouth opened wide, his head thrown back in precisely the pose of the man in Munch's *The Scream*. He moved to right himself and Nicholas jammed his shoe against the outer edge of the other's right instep. All balance fled him and he pitched sideways, between two startled couples. His outflung arm smashed someone in the face as she whirled by.

It all might have been a scene from a comic opera but Nicholas did not feel like laughing.

Here are we / One magical moment / Subject the stuff from where dreams are woven....

Justine looked from him to the fallen man, clutching his hip. The switchblade lay on the mottled floor like a centerpiece at a bizarre wedding which no one seemed to want to pick up and take home.

"Justine—"

"How did you find me? What do you want from me?"

"Justine."

"I can't take any more. Please, please, please. Can't you see I've been crying—"

There are you / Drive like a demon / From station to station....

"—over you. Over you."

"Justine. I came here—"

"And I don't care anymore if you know it."

"—to tell you I love you."

Tears rolled silently from her eyes. The air was as thick as honey with music: aching voices, insinuating rhythms, erotic percussion. "Please." Had she heard him?

"I love you." They touched in a kind of radiation of energy and misspent emotion. "Justine, I—"

It's not the side effects of the cocaine / I'm thinking that it

435

must be love / It's too late to be grateful / It's too late to be late again / It's too late to be hateful / It's too late... / It's too late....

"...cried in the sand in front of your house with the night and the sea and that's never happened to me before." And he thought, lying on the long pale sea-foam sofa with Justine's long warm body next to his: You're wrong, Croaker. I can feel. I *do* feel.

"Don't be ashamed of it."

"I'm not." The first faint crumbling of his past, sliding downward to be buried at last beneath the churning waves of the sea. "I wouldn't have told you otherwise."

"It makes me happy." She put her fingers on his hip as if searching for a lock to open. "To know that you can be grateful to me for something." Stockinged, her legs whispered one against the other like cicadas' wings. "The way I am grateful to you."

"It's a new feeling." She watched his eyes turning inward, listening to his words. "What I did to you was so cruel. But I did it—I did it out of self-defense; a kind of survival instinct. I suddenly felt how close you had come to the core of me and it reminded me—"

Her long hair brushed his shoulder. "Of what?"

"The sea, a long time ago; the mist and a ferry ride through a cyclorama of Japan." His lips stayed half open even when he was silent, tidal breathing as one does when dreaming. "It reminded me of a girl I once loved. The trouble was then, I thought I was still in love with her."

"Where is she now?"

"I don't know. She could be anywhere—anywhere." She could feel the rise and fall of his chest and abdomen, as regular as the tide. "She told me she loved me—she convinced me—I didn't know anyone could be that good at deceit...."

She smiled, half hidden in the dark. "If you'd been a woman, you'd know all right."

"Sometimes I think sex is for the animals."

It was quiet for some time, just the intermittent hiss of late-night traffic passing outside, remote and inconsequential. Justine was surprised more by his tone; she had never before heard such bitterness and she found herself wondering

436

st what had transpired between him and that girl so long
ɜo.

"I'm jealous," she said. She thought she might be taking
n awful chance. "I'm jealous of how much of yourself you
ave to her." He was quiet, beside her. "Never again, Ni-
ᴊolas?" Only her side and hair touched him. "Who is being
unished?"

When he spoke, his voice was tight. With what was he
.ruggling? "She made me...feel..."

"What?"

"Feel, just feel."

"Is that so terrible?"

"And then she left me. She went off with..." And he told
er what he had never told anyone, flooded with shame.

Justine put her warm lips against his ear, whispered,
Unzip me, Nicholas."

He reached out. It came as the rasp of a log cracking,
urnt through, subsiding into the hot ashes of the grate.

The tops of her breasts shone palely in the werelight like
ɪe swelling crests of the sea at dawn. Here, too, there were
epths to be plumbed. But the tugging he felt now went
eyond his loins; a kind of tidal wash, covering his whole
ody, sweeping into his head. "I missed you so much." And
ot, anymore, Yukio.

She could feel how that had been torn out of him. "Yes,"
he whispered. "I can see that now. I felt old and tired without
ou there." She shrugged out of her shoulder straps.

"Let's not make love right away."

Her eyes were glittery so close to him, the little fire in the
ar one like a beckoning beacon homeward bound.

"Say it again."

"Justine, words sometimes have no meaning at all."

"Then what does?"

His arms encircled her. "I'll hold you," he whispered. "And
ou hold me."

Her fingers brushed his skin, moving.

Fukashigi, the kenjutsu master, awoke at first light with
he tendrils of something still in his mind.

The world, this early, was fog-shrouded, familiar land-
ᴊarks rendered as in a pointillist painting.

437

Not a dream. Fukashigi did not carry such things into the waking world.

Something had dragged him away from sleep. The tendrils swirled.

And immediately he thought of Nicholas.

It must be time then. And despite all his wisdom, Fukashigi felt the slight thrill of fear shiver him.

He had thought about this time often during long nights when sleep eluded him and now he knew that he had been deluding himself, thinking that this day might never dawn.

Here it was, after all this time.

Time, he knew full well, meant absolutely nothing.

Even with the distances involved, he felt the psychic tuggings like a storm pulling at the moorings of a ship.

The long years in China and Japan seemed like a mist-shrouded dream to him, like the world he saw outside his window. The mind, he knew, could do much, play many tricks, and he wondered this morning which world was truly more the dream. In a way, America could never be as real as those days and nights on the Asian shore with their spices and their mysteries.

There had been time then, unlimited time, it had seemed once, to plunge into each more involving puzzle. And the joy he felt at their eventual unraveling was still unequaled in his life.

There had been, of course, several times when he had cause to regret the life he had carved out for himself. It was, after all, a most perilous path, fraught with real and imagined dangers every step of the way.

Jealousy racked them all like a perennial ague that could never be fully assuaged. There was resentment of anyone new. And especially of one who sought to plumb the depths that had frustrated them all.

And conquered.

Fukashigi sat up on his *futon*, hearing his bones creak. Magic, he thought. What a misunderstood word. Typically Western. He had to laugh.

Then he thought about Nicholas. He did not envy him but then there was no envy in Fukashigi's heart. Had there been... Fukashigi shrugged his thin shoulders.

Who knows? He thought. But there was excitement inside him again.

Now he thought that he could see clear down to the bo
'he floor was full of silty hills and fish without color w
he pattern of their changeless lives through the mud an
ocks and sand.

This section of the Straits of Shimonoseki had been
aunted for seven hundred years or thereabouts. Ever since
he infant emperor Antoku Tennō perished here in a
pectacular sea battle along with every other man, woman
nd child of his Taira clan at the hands of the Mina-
ıoto.

There were frequent reports of sightings of the strange
leiké—another name for the Taira—crabs which have hu-
ıan faces on their carapaces and are said to house the *kami*
f the long-dead defeated warriors.

They cannot, it is said in legends, find peace and thus, on
ıg-blanketed nights, fishermen swear they can see odd spec-
ral fires upon the unquiet waters and they refuse to launch
heir boats, even when the fish are running, for during these
errible nights, the Heiké would rise from the deeps, inter-
ring with passing ships, pulling unwary swimmers down-
vard to their deaths.

And it was to help assuage these lost and unhappy *kami*
hat the Buddhists built the temple of Amidaji there.

But now, Saigō thought, it is more than ever a haunted
lace, this Dan-no-ura, for an outpouring of my own soul lies
ead and defeated in those waters, come to join the joyless
Ieiké in their endless journey: there would be no burning
re, no golden lotus hearth for either.

He could see the perfect face lying on the bottom undis-
urbed as if there were no intervening waves; perfect only now
s the features composed themselves in death. A traditional
eroine: the pious daughter, the loyal wife, heart filled with
acrifice; all her grievous sins expunged.

It was good, he told himself. It was right; it was just. A
eath decreed by history.

What else could he have done?

He felt the shortness of breath and the burning tears
hreatening to destroy his dead eyes with their pitiful flow
nd he automatically began to chant the *Hannya-Shin-Kyō:
'orm is emptiness; and emptiness is form.... What is empti-
.ess—that is form....Perception, name, concept and knowl-*

..age, are also emptiness.... There is no eye, ear, nose, tongue, body, and mind....

In darkness there is sin; in darkness there is death. Sin negates spirit; and the killing of beings without spirit can only be looked on as an act of charity.

But, but, but—how could there be love where sin exists? This was a question that had tortured him for years, more than any other one thing, shaping his life. And as he asked himself the impossible question again, he pounded his closed fists against his forehead and cheekbones, seeking to destroy that within himself which remained perversely recalcitrant. He could no more drive the memory of her from him than he could relinquish his name and it was just this terrifying obstinacy within himself which had driven him to the drugs. Besides, he believed now that they enhanced his powers.

But surely it had been Nicholas Linnear who had brought him to this sorry state. If it had not been for him, he would not...they would not...there would not...

Lights blazed against his closed eyelids as he beat himself but even they would not drown out the visions of the gentle pale fish at play in the straits. And, O Amida! How the wind howled on that night, snow swirling down like lace curtains, disappearing upon the changeless waves with the black sky so low that neither Kyūshū nor Honshu was visible. Alone in the rocking boat. Did the howling increase at the heavy splash? Did the Heiké know they were about to receive another unrepentant sinner? Unrepentant they must be or why else lie upon the darkest nights as unappeased *kami*?

Ghost lights upon the straits, just as the tales told, and he recited many prayers, as many as he knew, repeating them without surcease until the prow of the boat touched the wooden quay at Shimonoseki and he stood on solid land, shaking and wet with seawater and sweat despite the snow and the chill north wind.

Still today he could hear that eerie howling like demons calling him back, to complete terrors that had somehow been left undone, circling within his head like black kites descending upon a bloody carcass.

At last, his breath heavy with the aftertaste of psychedelics, drenched in so much sweat that he might have just come from the bath, he fell into a sodden sleep filled with dreams and, worse, the trumpeting echoes of dreams.

Nicholas dreamed: of land's end. And out from the near shore, the very end of it at least, arched a bridge of wood and stone very much like the one at Nihonbashi. And as he started across this bridge, he saw that to either side there was nothing but a hanging mist. He turned around, looking back the way he had come, and was astonished and not a little afraid to see that the strange mist had obscured the land from which he had come so effectively that he forgot which land that was as well as not knowing toward which land he was bound, as if the mist stirred about inside his head as well as without.

When he was approximately halfway across, he thought he could discern a sound, dim and muffled by the mist, but as he drew closer he became more and more convinced that it was the sobbing of a woman.

In time, he was able to make out a darker shape within the mist which, as he approached, coalesced into the form of a young woman. She was tall and willowy and she wore a clinging dress of white silk. It was, he saw now, dripping with water, as if she had just climbed out from the sea, which he supposed this bridge spanned.

She stood with her slim back against the bedewed balustrade, weeping into her hands, and such was the power of her lamentations that Nicholas felt compelled to move closer.

When he was only a few steps from her, he heard her speak: "Oh, you've come. At last! At last! I had given up all hope!"

"Pardon me." His voice reverberated within his chest as if it were a cathedral-like cavity. "My lady, I do not think that I know you, yet you seem to have recognized me. Have you, perhaps, made some error?"

As he said this, he moved his head back and forth in an attempt to get a clear view of her face for, as it was now, he could not truly say whether she was known to him or no. But this seemed quite beyond his present capacity. Between her long dark hair, spread like a sea fan and strewn with small shells and mollusks, and the long-fingered hands she continued to press to her face, she remained hidden from his gaze.

"No, there is no error. You are he whom I have sought for all these years."

441

"Why do you weep so bitterly, my lady? What ill has befallen you?"

"A most dishonorable death, sir, and until it is avenged my spirit must wander—wander here."

"I do not see how I can be of help to you, my lady. But if you will allow me to see your face..."

"It will do you no good to look upon me," she said so sadly that he felt his heart must break.

"Then I was correct. I do not know you."

She said nothing and thus he did not know what her answer should be.

"Take your hands away from your face," he said to her. "Please, my lady. I cannot assist you otherwise."

Slowly, as if more reluctant, her long fingers drifted down through the mist and he gasped.

Where the features of her face should have been—eyes, nose, lips and the rest—her skin was as flat and smooth as an egg....

"—God, Nicholas, what is it?"

His chest heaved as if he had just struggled to finish a marathon and sweat glistened across his face like rime.

Justine's face, lined with worry, hovered above him, her long hair draped on either side, an electric curtain, a tenuous link.

"What happened?"

"I don't know. You cried out in your sleep—"

"What did I say?"

"I don't know, darling. Nothing recognizable, at least not in English. Something like, oh"—her brow wrinkled in thought—"minamara no tat-something."

"Migawari ni tatsu?"

"Yes, that's it."

"Are you certain? Really certain?"

"Yes. Absolutely. You said it more than once. What does it mean?"

"Well, literally, it means, 'to act as a substitute.'"

"I don't understand."

"In Japanese folklore there is the belief that a person may give his or her life in order to save another's. It needn't even be a person. It could be a tree, just about anything."

"What were you dreaming about?"

"I am not certain."

"Nicholas," she said with her typical objective intuition, "did someone give their life for you?—In the dream, I mean?"

He looked at her, put his hand up to her cheek, but it was not her soft flesh he seemed to stroke, certainly not her voice he heard in his head then.

In that heated room of perfect death with his toes touching the hem of his mother's exquisite, perfectly folded kimono and, just a little way beyond, the rivulets of blood dropped like rubies along the floor, Itami said, "We both must leave now, Nicholas. There is nothing left here for outsiders such as ourselves."

"Where will you go?" His voice was as dull as lead.

"To China."

His eyes tracked upward to her white face. "To the communists?"

She shook her head slightly. "No. There are others there— who were there long before the communists. Your grandfather, So-Peng, was one such."

"You would leave Saigō?"

Her eyes were as bright as a bird's. "Nicholas, did you ever wonder why I had but one child? But no, why should you?" Her lips were turned in a grim smile that chilled him. "I can only say that with me—with *me*—it was totally a matter of choice, though Satsugai believed otherwise. Oh yes, I lied to him. Willingly. Are you surprised? Well." She stirred slightly like a sapling in a sudden gust of wind, giving way, giving way minutely. "I would not have another like him." Her dark eyes were slits now. "Do you understand me? I trust you do."

She looked down briefly at her *katana*, standing on its bloody point. "Do you hate me? I would not be surprised...But no, I see that you do not. That gladdens my heart, I cannot tell you how much.

"I love you, Nicholas. Were you my own I could not love you more but I think you already knew that deep inside yourself." Her head jerked as if she had been abruptly reminded of something. "These days of *kwaidan* pass through my fingers like so much sand. Time is short and I have much to do."

He stood in front of her, pale and drawn. He shivered once though no breeze stirred in the room.

"Will you tell me," he said, "what honor there is in this?"

"What honor there remains in all the world," Itami said

443

sadly, "resides in this room. There is little enough, I fear. Little enough."

"You must tell me. You must." His voice was almost a cry and he was certain then he saw tears standing out like soft pearls at the inner corners of her eyes.

"Ah, Nicholas. These tales are not so easily told. You ask me to expose the soul of Japan. I could sooner rip a blade into my own belly." Her eyes squeezed shut as if she were attempting to brush away a vision from her mind. Her voice was a whisper. "Ask me anything else. Anything."

"What will become of you—Aunt?"

Her eyes flew open and she smiled kindly. "In China I shall travel until I reach the place Cheong bade me go in her last breath. I will not be there long." Her hand tightened on the hilt of her *katana*; another drop of blood rolled from the blade's smooth steel surface onto the bare wooden floor.

I must see Fukashigi, Nicholas thought now, staring at Justine in the semi-darkness; time to renew the old vows. And she must leave here; she must be out of harm's way. *Aka i ninjutsu* was the only way now the forces of *Kan-aku na ninjutsu* were stirring, readying themselves to come against him: ancient, implacable enemies arrayed on a modern battlefield. He would need, he knew, all the fearful shades of steel to be victorious this one last time.

When Saigō awoke he was, for just an instant, convinced that it was into death's dark realm. Death held no horror for him but this might only be because life held so little for him. It was the meanest of gifts and, therefore, it meant nothing for him to part with it.

Then he remembered that he had not yet killed Nicholas and he knew that this was life only into which sleep had yet again deposited him.

There was much to be said for revenge, yes. It was all that kept his heart pumping now. He thought of all the money in his swollen bank accounts; the vast acres of land; the four small but rapidly growing electronics konzerns. What did it all amount to? Not even a part of the smallest steel filing from a master swordsmith's forge—ah, no!

Money was merely the sere gateway to power, and power, well, all that was good for was maneuverability. Once you

444

could maneuver in this atom age, you could accomplish ⌐
thing.

Yet there was but one thing that Saigō now wished to
accomplish and that was to seek out and expunge a life.

Tonight, he thought savagely, lying naked on the *futon*.
Pale gray light filtered through the blinds, traipsing across
the ceiling like an itinerant priest, his *koromo* torn and tattered, its ragged ends taken by the wind.

He marveled at the weakness of Americans. Such cowards,
they surely could not have powerful spirits. How they had
won the war he still could not imagine. It would give him
great pleasure to see the look on Raphael Tomkin's face as
he died beneath the blade of steel. To think that he believed
a deal could be so easily arranged. No deal was possible; not
after the commencement of a buy.

No, death would come to him tonight, just as it would
come to Nicholas.

Perhaps, even, there would be a stalemate between them
and death would come to both. This did not concern him. On
the contrary, he might have even looked forward to it, knowing that the importance of death lay not in the dying itself
but in the *manner* of one's death. How one died was recorded
by history and one was remembered as much for the manner
of one's death as for one's life.

For Saigō, as for all Japanese warriors from time imme-
morial, there were only two honorable ways to die: in battle
or by one's own hand with calmness and ritual. To die otherwise would mean terrible, insupportable shame throughout
eternity, an awful karma brought into the next life or, far
worse, carried into the infinity of limbo.

This intimate thanatopsis had made him hard and he almost regretted having killed the Chinese boy. He had been
so good. But there had been no choice just as, long ago, there
had been no choice—

Somewhere in the night he had been full of hate; a per-
nicious boiling that had all but swamped his long exquisite
training. It is a true measure of how emotions can warp the
soul, he told himself now, sitting up on his single black *futon*,
and he cursed the day that Yukio had come into his life. O
Amida! he cried silently.

But this early hour was like crystal for him. He had
thought, in the dark, to blunder into them tonight. To move
fast, fast, fast; to catch them both quickly, Nicholas and

Tomkin. But while he had slept in the land of death, his mind had been at work and now he knew that there might be more for him than just the death of those two. He thought of the straits and shuddered. Voices seemed to fill his mind, screaming louder as he inhaled, moaning like the autumn wind as he exhaled. He held his breath, squeezed his eyes shut for long moments until the voices faded.

Yes, he thought, rising and beginning to bathe, his training had taught him that there were things far worse for an enemy than merely slitting his belly.

The world, he knew, was one great wheel, an ellipse one was bound to by karma. Wheels within wheels; plans within plans. By day's end, his mind would be tranquil. Then, if death should come, he would fling wide his arms and welcome it.

It was a splendid day, clear and still cool with just a few touches of gauzy cirrus clouds high up in the west. Far too splendid to spend it hanging around the house, Justine thought, as she threw her bags on the bed.

The beach on Dune Road looked inviting as she went around the side of the house and took the car out on the road.

She went east on the highway, having no specific destination in mind, but seeing the exit for Watermill reminded her of a beach in that area she had heard talked about again and again, Flying Point.

It was no surprise to her that she got lost, but this far out on the South Shore it was difficult to get too lost and at length she found herself at Flying Point beach. She got out and, locking up, went out on the sand.

She was still far too full of energy to lie down so she walked. The beach was wide, surprisingly free of debris, with sand of a very pale color.

The surf was up, curling high in a translucent green arc crowned by white spume before tumbling forward onto the sand in a dazzle of silver spray.

It was far from crowded this early in the morning, though the beaches this far out were never jammed the way places like Jones Beach always seemed to be.

It was quiet, peaceful with the repetitive sounds of the sea and the gulls calling as they wheeled into the sun.

The character of the beach changed so subtly that for a

446

ong time she was not even aware of any difference, but presently it seemed to her as if it had become somewhat more amiliar. For instance, she knew that she was coming up on narrow spit of land before she turned the curve of the beach nd saw it lying before her. As this began to happen more requently she began to wonder where in fact she was.

Then, as she happened to look up from the beach to the nouses she was passing on her right, she saw the familiar pires. She felt a brief twist in her stomach as if she were lunging downward in a high-speed elevator, wondering how he could have been so stupid. Flying Point was just east of Southampton and Gin Lane.

There it stood in all its looming splendor. The family nouse.

As she stared, she saw the wooden gate swing open and figure come down the slatted redwood stairs onto the dunes.

My God, she thought. It's Gelda!

Her first instinct was to turn around and simply walk way but she was rooted to the spot, thinking: What the hell s she doing at the house?

On the sand, Gelda had poised and now she took off her unglasses.

She's seen me, Justine thought, panic-stricken. I can't valk away now.

Gelda came toward Justine. They stood facing each other n the near-deserted beach at a distance where a pair of luellists might stand preparatory to firing at each other.

"Justine!"

"Well."

"What a surprise." Her eyes had gone dull, as if an iron :ate had come crashing down behind them. They talked as tiffly as if they were two strangers awkwardly thrown to- :ether at a party neither of them had wanted to attend.

"Are you here with...anyone?"

The wind whipped about them, making streamers of their 1air as if they were pennants on a field of battle.

"No, I'm waiting for someone."

"I am too."

"Well."

"Yes." She did not want to admit to herself how much Gelda had changed. How beautiful she was now. How grace- ully she moved. And behind that, a kind of confidence that— vell, she had always had enough confidence for them both.

447

It was Gelda who always had the boyfriends, who was alway asked to parties and to football games. It was Gelda wh could ice-skate so exquisitely—her movements on the ice to tally belying her weight—her dates soon clung to the sid railings, watching her with unabashed awe.

Justine was always too young for this or for that; to skinny for the boys to notice her; too clumsy for sports. Sh drew instead and became more isolated, her envy feedin upon itself like a ravenous cannibal.

"Is Father here?"

Gelda shook her head. "No, he's in the city." She hesitate a moment, debating with herself. "He's in some kind of trou ble."

"That's nothing new."

"No, but I thought you would be concerned—at the ver least. You always were with Mother."

And there it was, staring at them both in the face like a ugly red sore.

"I can't help the way Mother felt," Justine said defer sively. Anger began to fill her up, and if she had ever er tertained the thought of telling her sister about Nicholas fled now.

"And I can't help being the way I am."

"That was always your excuse for doing just what yo wanted."

They stared at each other silently. Justine was appalle yet unable to initiate any action. My God, she thought de spairingly, we're kids again. We can't think like adults whe we're around each other, just intent on hurting each othe all over again.

Gelda squinted into the sun. "D'you want to come insid for a while?"

"No, I—"

"Oh, come on, Justine. You can unbend *that* much, I imag ine."

"You have felt it, also."

"Yes. During the night. This morning. I don't know when.

"It is important that you are here."

"There was nowhere else to go," Nicholas said.

Fukashigi smiled thinly.

There were no classes today and the *dōjō* seemed enormou

n its emptiness. Sadly, it reminded Nicholas of the last time he had seen Kansatsu in the *ryu* outside Tokyo. And it occurred to him that much of his life since then had been spent simply floating, the days and nights gently rocking him as they blended together, lulling him to sleep on the tide of their passage.

What had he really accomplished in America? What could he have done with that time had he stayed in Japan? So much time. And if he had never begun his studies in bujutsu? What then? What would he be now? Some high government functionary, no doubt, with a high salary and a perfect garden. Two weeks each year in Kyoto or somewhere on the seashore, even Hong Kong, perhaps, in a season when it was not overrun by Western tourists. A loyal wife and a family. Children to drool on him and laugh with.

The void, he realized, is only noticeable when it is no longer there. Justine. Justine. Justine. His reward for at last swatting down the past. He very much wished to see again the graves of his parents, to kneel before their *sotoba*, to light the incense sticks, to say the litany of prayer over them.

"You have brought it?" Fukashigi said.

"Yes, I knew I must one day, though I don't know why."

"Come."

Fukashigi led him through the abandoned *dōjō*, striped with shadow and pale sunlight bleeding through the ragged rents in the flying lengths of oblique cloud that marbled the summer sky.

At the threshold to the back rooms, Nicholas shed his shoes, Fukashigi his *geta*, and the old man took him to the very rear of the building, to a room with a raised floor of tatamis. He pushed aside the *shōji* and they entered.

Sitting cross-legged, Fukashigi waved his hand gracefully. "Please place it between us."

Nicholas put the parcel he had been carrying down onto the tatami and unwrapped it. There was the dragon and tiger box that So-Peng had given to his parents.

"Open it." Fukashigi's voice held a certain reverence.

Nicholas obeyed, lifting the heavy lid to display the nine cut emeralds.

All of Fukashigi's breath seemed to go out of him as he gazed at those nine bits of mineral which seemed to glow and spark in the low light.

"I never thought," the old man said softly, "that I would

449

see such a sight." He sighed. "And they are all here. All nin
of them."

He looked up. The square room was immaculate, spacious
harmonious, calming.

"Time changes many things. When you came to me s
many years ago in Kyoto it was, I think, only the letter fron
my friend Kansatsu that stopped me from dismissing you ou
of hand. Oh, so you did not know that. Well, it is true. And
to be completely truthful, even after I had read the letter,
thought that I might be making a grievous mistake. Afte
all, *Aka i ninjutsu*, history informs us, is no acquired trai
but a serious calling—quite as serious, quite as mysteriou
as the calling to serve Amida Buddha—to which one is bor
and bred.

"I can tell you that I had grave doubts concerning you
entrance into *Aka i ninjutsu*, despite what Kansatsu wrote
He is no ninja, I thought, therefore he cannot know. But
breach of our security had already been created and, o
course, you came to me appearing a Westerner. I knew onl
that Kansatsu had not lost his mind.

"Of course, to have sent you away would have been, I know
now, a mistake." His fingertips caressed the box before him
He smiled. "You see, I am not, as I understand was so ofte
said of me in those days, omniscient."

"It is still said."

The old man inclined his head slightly. "So? It is, as yo
can see, an untruth. It was through Kansatsu's intuitivenes
that you became the first student of mixed blood at the Ten
shin Shoden Katori *ryu*. The only one such. A signal honor
an unorthodox decision on my part. Still, I do not regret it
The *ryu* has had no finer student in all the years that it wa
mine."

Now it was Nicholas' turn to incline his head.

"But you came to us for a reason, did you not? And nov
the time has come. It has begun."

"I regret to say, *sensei*, that it began some time ago." An
he told the old man about the murders.

Fukashigi sat quite still and there was silence for a tim
after Nicholas had finished. His head swiveled and his coc
gaze swept over Nicholas' face. "When you joined us you too
certain vows, just as you did at every step of your training
You must have known what was commencing the momen
you discovered the *shaken* fragment. Yet you took no actior

450

Now, perhaps because of that, many people three of them your friends—are dead." His cold eyes seemed as luminous as beacons on a foggy day. "Are you dead, too, Nicholas?"

Nicholas watched the backs of his hands, stung by the old man's words. "Perhaps I never should have come to the West. I think I was merely trying to outrun my karma."

"You know better than that. Wherever you go, it will be the same for you."

"It sounds like a curse."

"If one chooses to see one's life in those terms, then it is. But I am surprised that you should think in such a curiously Western mode."

"Perhaps America has changed me as it did Vincent."

"Of course only you can know the truth of that—"

"I don't know anymore."

"I suspect that is only because you do not fully comprehend it yet."

"I am bound up inexplicably with Saigō—and with Yukio—yet—"

"Acceptance of karma should not be confused with fatalism. We are all, to a great extent, masters of our own fate. But also we must learn to bow before the inevitable: this is the true meaning of acceptance and it is only this which brings the harmony without which life is not really worth living."

"I understand all that," Nicholas said. "It is the specifics that still elude me."

Fukashigi nodded his head and, reaching inside his robe, he withdrew a series of rice paper sheets which had been folded very carefully. They had about them the look of age. Fukashigi handed them across to Nicholas.

"This letter is from Kansatsu. I am following his express instructions in giving this to you now."

It was a plain black Ford sedan.

Doc Deerforth tried to make out who was in it but the late morning sunlight spun like a nova across the windshield, completely opaquing it.

He watched the sedan long enough to make certain that it was following Justine's brick-red roadster and, still mindful of and not a little curious about Nicholas' warning, he spun the wheel of his car and set off after them both.

451

He had had a call out along the west end of Dune Road earlier that morning and had come east to look in on Justine. He had still been some distance away when he had seen her take the roadster east. That was when he had picked up the black Ford.

He stayed well back and turned in after seeing the brick-red roadster stop at Flying Point. But, curiously, no one emerged from the black Ford. He waited impatiently for what seemed a long time. He got out of his car, on the point of following her down the beach, when the black Ford started up. Slowly it began to pace her along the beach road.

Doc Deerforth went hurriedly back to his car and got in.

He was sweating profusely by the time he came around the last turn and saw the sedan parked some way from the beginning of Gin Lane.

He was grateful he had not lost it. The traffic was light and he had had to hang back farther than he would have wanted. More than once the Ford had disappeared for long moments around a serpentine turning.

Now he knew where they were both headed. He recognized Raphael Tomkin's house immediately.

The soles of his shoes crunched on gravel as he got out of the car. He snapped down the sunglass attachment to his glasses against the fierce glare.

Now he could see into the black Ford. It was empty.

It was quite still here. There was a lone cardinal in a tall pine but it would not sing. He could no longer hear the boom and hiss of the surf and the lack of that sound was like white noise clattering like thrown stones through his brain.

He began to walk toward the Ford. All sound seemed heightened in the hush. Not even a breeze stirred the high treetops. It was very hot.

The black Ford was nearer now, hulking like some sinister castle in the desert. Who would follow Justine? And why *Look after her*, Nicholas had said. Startled, Doc Deerforth realized he thought of the two of them as if they were his own kids. Just an old man's foolishness, he admonished himself. I miss my two girls, is all.

His shirt was soaked, sticking to his skin like loose folds of ancient flesh. Just as it did, he reflected, in the jungle so long ago. And abruptly, he staggered, experiencing a fierce stab of vertigo. It's the malaria, he thought, steadying himself against a resinous tree trunk. My own form of malaria. Because it's the summer. In the fall, it will pass.

He ran one hand along the burning flank of the Ford and, bending a bit, peering into the interior. There was nothing to see.

He was still stooped over like that, an old, balding man, sweating in the heat of the afternoon, when the shadow stretched itself across the side of the black sedan.

For a long moment, Doc Deerforth stared at it. It recalled to him a moment in a ballet he had seen a long time ago in the city: the entrance of the Dark Angel. On either side of him, his daughters—they were still young then—had cried at the vision. Black wings clouded the sun and he was abruptly cold.

He began to turn, heard the weird whirring sound at that same instant. A blur on the periphery of his vision and instinctively he raised his arm in front of his face.

Then something had wrapped itself about his ankles and he was dragged off his feet. Metal links scraped and dug painfully into his flesh. He gasped and twisted, feeling like a fish on a line.

He looked down. A long chain with a weight on its end was strung taut, pulling him into a stand of dense poplars beyond which stretched long fields of corn.

He rolled, puffing; tried to sit up. There was a blade at his throat.

He looked up. Before the sky, as rich a cerulian as he had ever seen it, he saw a face—at least part of one—that made him shudder. All the breath went out of him.

He stared into eyes as dead as stones. Madman's eyes. So different from those others long ago; yet the same. The ninja, Doc Deerforth thought. His mind seemed to freeze with the thought, as if there could be no room in the world now for anything else. His life seemed to shrivel down to the size of a pea and, disappearing altogether, become totally insignificant.

Cicadas chimed; flies buzzed. He was back in the Philippines, back in the tent, tied to the table.

And the soft, knowing voice said to him, "Why have you followed me?"

"Why have you followed the girl?"

There was absolutely no change of expression in those staring eyes, of that he was quite certain. But, without warning the ninja jerked on the chain and the saw-toothed steel links bit through skin, digging into tissue, ground against bone.

Doc Deerforth's head flew back and breath whistled through his half-open lips. Blood drained from his face.

"Why have you followed me?"

The words came again and again like a litany, a friar's prayer at day's end—what did they call that? Vespers?

"Why have you followed me?"

Time ceased to exist as the pain rose and fell like the tide—now faster, now slower, so that he had no clear idea of when it would make his jaws clamp together in a rictus, make the sweat fly off him as he jerked this way and that, make his thighs tremble and the muscles in his legs turn to water.

At some point, it was impossible for him to say when, Doc Deerforth knew that there was something different about this one. He was at once more cruel and less removed. And there was an elemental power to him that frightened him to the very core. It was as if the devil himself had come to strip him of life.

That it was his time to die, Doc Deerforth had no doubt. There would be no last-minute rescue this time and he was far too weak and old for muscular heroics. But a human being, until the very moment of death, has certain powers that can only be relinquished voluntarily. Neither time nor terror had dominion over these few last possessions.

The ninja now had one knee across Doc Deerforth's heaving chest. Gently, almost reverently, he took up Doc Deerforth's right hand and, using only the tips of his fingers, broke the thumb. He waited just the right amount of time—the shock had worn off and the pain was a sharp throbbing. He broke the index finger. And so it went, one by one, slowly and inexorably.

Doc Deerforth shuddered, heaved and sighed. He whispered the names of his daughters, of his long-dead wife. He felt, rather than saw, the ninja crouching low to hear his faintly expelled words. A curse and then a sharp crack. Pain flared as his right wrist shattered.

Someone, someone, he thought, hazily, will have to call the kids. Then the pain blanketed him and his nerves, vibrating, screaming with agony, pitched him at last into unconsciousness.

A child's high cry perhaps decided Doc Deerforth's fate.

It was close at hand and Saigō, abruptly deciding that nothing could be gained from prolonging this game, took up the other end of the saw-toothed *kyotetsu-shoge* and slit Doc Deerforth's throat with the double-edged blade.

"From the beginning," Nicholas read, "your father was suspicious of Satsugai. From the first time they met, the Colonel understood that behind the man's vast power in the *zaibatsu* stretched a hidden network of immense size and strength. He suspected, quite rightly, as further investigation bore out, that Satsugai was deeply involved with the Genyōsha. They were, perhaps, most responsible for sowing the seeds that led to the fateful decision to institute the preemptive strike at Pearl Harbor.

"Your father wished to crush the forces of the Genyōsha and it was to this end that he intervened in Satsugai's behalf when the SCAP tribunal was ready to try him for war crimes. He thought that leaving Satsugai free to pursue his plans would eventually lead to the arrest of the Genyōsha main body itself.

"It was a good plan except that Satsugai discovered it. Now he was eternally in the Colonel's debt—a man who was out to destroy him. This he could not abide. Satsugai was of the old school and most honorable. He knew that he could not touch or interfere with the Colonel in any way.

"Therefore, he set his son, Saigō, as his emissary of death, sending him into Kumamoto to the most feared of all the *Kan-aku na ninjutsu ryu*, the Kuji-kiri.

"Over the years, the Colonel came to understand the nature of his folly. He had gambled heavily and lost. Now Satsugai was forever beyond the law and this had been the Colonel's doing.

"Your father was an Englishman by birth yet he could not have been more Japanese had he been born here and he came to a decision that was uniquely Japanese. He killed Satsugai himself."

Stunned, Nicholas raised his eyes. And because of that shame to the family, Cheong had committed *seppuku*.

"Continue reading," Fukashigi said gently. "There is more."

"Your father was a fine warrior, Nicholas, and thus none suspected him. Until, that is, Saigō returned home. With the basic elements of *Kan-aku na ninjutsu* already at his disposal, it did not take him long to divine the truth. This knowledge he kept to himself and, while stoking the fires of his hatred in the secret depths of him, he meanwhile presented only the image of a grief-stricken son to the outside world. For already a plan of vengeance had formed in his mind.

"Thus he contrived to be home several times when he knew Itami was coming to your house for the afternoon, when you would not be home. I cannot say whether it happened the first or the second time but it scarcely matters.

"You must know by now what amazing *yogen*"—chemists—"the Kuji-kiri are; how many different and subtle ways they are taught to kill a human being without ever touching him.

"This, I fear, is what happened to your father. Saigō murdered him with slow poison."

Nicholas felt tears come to his eyes so that he had difficulty focusing on the last several sentences. His fingers gripped the thin rice-paper leaves, shaking.

"Here I must extend to you my most profound apologies. Even though I am not ninja, I feel responsible, at least in part, for your father's death. He was a great friend to me and I feel—even now after the initial sorrow has left me—that I should have known.

"You have become the symbol of my atonement. That you are reading this now with, I trust, my esteemed friend Fukashigi beside you, is proof of that. I am long past knowing.

"I imagine that you were quite surprised on arriving at the Tenshin Shoden Katori *ryu* to find that payment for your long study had already been paid in full.

"I trust you understand why I had to do that before I died and pray Amida Buddha that you will forgive an old man's lapse."

He saw the brush-stroke characters of Kensatsu's name through the well of tears as he cried for the Colonel, who had tried, in his own way, to tell him, and for Cheong. He felt now as if the years had been stripped from him like the red and gold leaves of autumn. And now he wept, too, for his friends, who had loved him and whom he had loved in return. Time enough for them all now.

Beside him, silent as sunlight, Fukashigi sat deep in contemplation, thinking about the cruelties time inflicted upon the young.

"Did you come here to dry out?"

"That's a bit direct, isn't it?"

"Sorry."

"That's all right. I suppose I deserved it. But, no, I've already done my drying out."

They sat within the immense oval of the starry living room. Fully half the walls were glass, open to the sunlight the beach and the sea. Above them, the skylight was like faceted diamond, the largest in the universe, so Justine had always believed when she was younger. Now, in the morning, the tardy sun had not yet slipped across its faces and thus they were bathed—as at evening—in a most flattering indirect light.

The couch upon which they both sat was completely circular with two breaks, as angular and distinct as the fitted edges of a Chinese sphere puzzle which someone had once given to Justine and which she could never quite conquer. They sat on opposite sides of the morning, their backs as rigid, their eyes as wary as a pair of cats' on unfamiliar territory.

Tall frosty drinks sat on the tables in front of them, untouched, as if for either of them to take the first sip would be to admit defeat.

"How long will you stay?" That was not what Justine had meant to say. She had wanted to say, "I'm glad" because she found that she was. No one wanted a lush for a sister. It was as if her tongue clove to the roof of her mouth when she wanted to say something nice to Gelda. I really can't give her anything at all, she thought in wonder. Not even the tiniest thing. She felt a wave of shame wash over her like her mother's long hands, slippery with soap, bathing her.

When she was older, she would wait until everyone had left the house. She would take a bath and emerge, moist and warm, one great snowy towel around her thin body and another smaller one wound about her long hair like a turban. And, as if she were in some far-off Byzantine city—that must have been from her constant reading—she would flop down on this very couch, her back against the foamy cushions, her legs up and dangling over the back. Thus positioned, she would turn her head, watch the slow wheel of the day as it

457

streamed in through the skylight and by its shape and it
position in the room could divine the precise time of da
without ever looking upward or out the window or at th
great clock on the mantelpiece behind her. But nevertheles
its heavy sonorous ticking caused her to dream of the sunligh
as drops of honey, seeping in through the panes of the sk
light, onto her out-thrust tongue.

In just this way she amused herself while Gelda was o
with her friends.

With a start, she realized that she had missed Gelda
answer. That was all right; she hadn't meant to ask the que
tion anyway and now had no interest in the response.

"You can stay here as long as you want," Gelda said.

"Oh, that's all right. I have to be going, anyway." But sh
made no move to get up and Gelda chose not to pursue th
matter further.

"You'll excuse me, then." Gelda rose and went throug
one of the narrow gaps between the couches. "I'll be around
She put her hands on the back of the couch. "You alway
loved this room best, didn't you?"

"Yes," Justine said, somewhat surprised.

"I always imagined you would have slept out here
Mother would have allowed it."

"Yes. That would have been nice."

"Well." Gelda's fingers plucked at the fabric. She looke
down at her hands, then toward where Justine lay ha
sprawled on the cushions. "You'll say good-bye before yo
leave, won't you?"

"Sure."

Then she was alone in the house—the servants were gor
for the weekend—as she had been when she was a child, an
her gaze quite naturally fell to the portion of the mornin
which the skylight let in, reflecting on what it might be lik
to be a great lady in some time past when there were no ca
or phones or even electricity—she always adored candleligh
and oil lamps to her meant taking to the sea for years at
time, hunting down the whales, imperiled and exhilarate
at the same time. It was something she, as a woman, wou
never know. Down to the sea in ships and back again wit
enough oil for all the lamps in Nantucket. I should have, sh
thought, been born a Starbuck.

And that was how Saigō found her, alone and dazzled, lo
within her imagination. She never knew that she had passe

458

nto unconsciousness or that anything was done to her while
he was out. She might have been sleeping. But she was not.

He worked over her for fifteen minutes, one ear alert for
he most minute sound that might herald an interruption.
Ie could not afford that now. He hoped that it would not
ccur because it would necessitate dragging her away from
ere and this he did not want to do. She was relaxed here;
t was a place she trusted. That made what he had to do that
nuch easier.

During this time, Justine's eyes were open and it could
ven be said that she saw, in a manner of speaking. But what
he saw was only his face; transfigured, like a geological
ault line after an earthquake. There was only a little fa-
niliarity among the change. It had become a face that was
nore than human.

It became the ground she walked upon, the food she ate,
he water she gulped thirstily down, the air she breathed. It
ecame her world and, finally, her entire universe.

Thus she listened as it spoke to her, this thing—being—
vhich engulfed her, far larger than the diamond that shone
bove her head. What he did to her was to hypnosis what the
tom bomb was to a bow and arrow. Here the will of the
ndividual did not loom like an unbreachable wall, stopping
hem from doing that which they could not do had they been
onscious. Now all was possible, for this was different. He
vas ninja. This was the Kuji-kiri and, beyond that, the
Kōbudera, that which even his *Kan-aku na ninjutsu sensei*
eared.

It was magic.

He waited patiently until Nicholas set aside the sheets of
ice paper, stained now with tears. It was the end of the long
teamy afternoon; the city was slowly cooling as the bloated
un slipped behind the backs of the high steel and glass build-
1gs. But that was outside. In here the West could not intrude.
Iere the eternalness of the East defied time, shrouding them
oth. Somewhere, a runic chanting like the call of the cicadas
rhen day is done.

"Kansatsu felt it most prudent to wait this time to tell
ou, Nicholas. Had you been told sooner, you would have, no
oubt, sought Saigō out and you were not ready then. He

would have destroyed you as easily as he could have done that night in Kumamoto."

"And now?" His voice was clotted with emotion.

"He may destroy you yet. I am afraid, Nicholas, that he has gone beyond even the Kuji-kiri teachings. He sought out *sensei* who, because of the nature of their teachings, would never be allowed into a *ryu*, not even the *Kan-aku na ninjutsu*. These were mystics steeped in the ancient lore of that portion of China—the central steppes of Mongolia—of which there is little known even today. There is magic in him now Nicholas, and it has taken him over completely."

"Well, there is a kind of magic inherent in many of our own ninjutsu teachings."

"There are imagined magic—that is, illusion—and real magic. The two should not be confused."

Nicholas knew better than to argue this kind of thing with Fukashigi and he was silent all through the simple meal the *sensei* had prepared. Afterward, in the darkness of the night Fukashigi began the ritual that would last until morning.

"Here"—his fingertips touching the opened box lid—"is the *Kokoro*." This was a word that, like almost all Japanese words, had many meanings: heart, spirit, courage, resolve affection, inner meaning, and more. It could, in sum, be said to be the heart of the matter. "It, too, is real magic. Your mother knew this and, although she suspected your father did not, she knew that you would. It was meant for you." His young eyes were watchful, full of life and—something more "Nine is the key number, Nicholas. There are nine emeralds here. One to break each arm of the Kuji-kiri—nine-hands cutting."

Saigō awoke in the hour before dawn and left his *futon* There was much to do this last day and the hours seemed to run ahead of him despite his precise organization. He had slept soundly and dreamlessly for the first time in more than a week.

He was on the streets early. He went deep into the East Village, to an enormous army-navy-camping store where he purchased a dark-colored heavyweight duffel bag with a triple-weight polythene lining. He tested the duffel bag's sling straps for strength.

Walking crosstown to the IND subway—he was most care

ful at this stage to take only public transportation hc emerged at Forty-seventh Street and walked the block over to Broadway. There he entered a theatrical supply house.

His third stop was at Brooks Brothers, where he purchased a light-weight tan business suit off the rack. The jacket was perfect but he dropped the pants off at a tailor to finish the length. On his way out, he bought a muted plaid porkpie hat which looked absurd on him in the light of day but which, he knew, would be perfect at night.

His last stop was in Chinatown, where he picked up a bamboo cane. Then, dropping off his parcels—which included the suit pants—he went out again, prowling in search of someone who looked just like him. This was something he had scouted on first arriving in New York. Height, weight, the physical semblance of his physique were all he was concerned with. The face itself would not matter. Not after he got through with it.

Croaker called in twice at half-hour intervals and it was a good thing he did. Either they had misplaced the message the first time or it had not yet come in.

He got it on the second call in.

"Matty called. Didn't leave his—"

"That's okay. I got it."

In the traffic he began to look for one and when he found it, pulled over to the curb. He dug a dime out of his pocket and dialed. No police lines on *this* call.

"Not-a here," Matty the Mouth said in a very bad Italian accent.

"It's Croaker."

"Oh. Hi."

"Cut the small talk. You got it?"

"Yeah but it's worth a lotta—"

"Matty, we've already settled on a price."

"Yeah, well, you see, Lieutenant, what we have here is a fluctuating market."

"What are you trying to pull?"

"The price is out of date."

"Look—"

"The situation's changed since we last spoke, is all. Nothing to get your bowels in an uproar about. I still got the goods."

"I got a notion to haul your ass downtown. How'd you feel about that?"

Matty clucked his tongue against the roof of his mouth. "Me, Lieutenant? Well, I'd be lying if I said I wouldn't mind, 'cause I would. But I really gotta say that you'd mind even more 'cause then you'd get zip outa me and you know there ain't anywhere else to go on this one."

Croaker felt a tightening in his stomach. His heart was racing. "What's happened?" he said carefully.

"This must be real important to you."

"Spill."

"The issue," he said, "was cold when we first talked about it."

"And now—"

"Now it's as hot as Lucifer's hind tit. Lotsa nosing around on the street. Someone else's looking for this dame, too. As a hot item, she's on the top of everyone's list. All of a sudden, like, y'know?"

"But you've got it all. Name, number and address?"

"Lieutenant, when I tell you I got something, it's not on its way in from the Coast. The information's in house."

"So give it."

"After," Matty said, "we've agreed on the new price."

"Okay, shoot."

"Triple."

"Triple! Are you out of your—"

"Lieutenant," Matty said reasonably, "we're talking about my life here. If anyone got wind—"

"Anyone like who? Who's been asking around about this broad?"

"Don't know directly."

Croaker sighed. "Maybe you could find out, Matty, there's a good boy."

"Maybe I could at that. What about the price? Agreed?"

"Agreed."

"Okay, here's the diamond load." The name Croaker got was Alix Logan. He also got a phone number and an address in Key West, Florida.

"About the other thing," Croaker said. "You better get it to me real soon 'cause I'm likely to head south at any time, get me?"

"That urgent, huh?"

"I can't remember the last time I had a vacation."

462

"Will do. You know, Lieutenant, you're really okay. No hard feelings, huh? Business is business, you know?"

"Yeah. Thanks for the vote of confidence. I have a feeling I'm gonna need it."

"Tell me something." There was an edge to his voice now as if he had just woken up. "How big is this thing?"

"What's it to you?"

"Huh! I'm involved, ain't I? Sure. Right up to my armpits. I just wanta know whether I'm standing in a pile of dogshit or—"

"I really can't say yet. The jury's still out. But it just could be."

"Maybe I oughtta fade, then."

"Strictly up to you. Might not be such a bad idea."

"'Preciate it, Lieutenant."

"I don't want my wells drying up. Like a Texan that way."

Matty the Mouth laughed, a dry rasp like a metal file going over an unstripped log. "Uh yeah! What I am today I owe to you."

"Just keep it up, Matty. Just keep it up."

Back in the car, he headed toward the office. Finnigan, the fat mick, would not be at all happy to see him this morning.

Well, to hell with him. Croaker braked savagely, jammed the heel of his hand against the horn rim, stood on the gas. When he returned from Key West with Alix Logan in tow, he only hoped the bastard would have a stroke.

If he could get her to talk. Fear was a most effective weapon wielded by a knowing hand. Unless he was severely mistaken, his little outburst in Tomkin's face had had its desired effect. A dead issue had become abruptly hot. Now there would be a direct link between Alix Logan and Raphael Tomkin. For a moment he debated bringing Vegas in on this. It would, after all, be helpful to have someone here to round up whoever it was who was nosing around while he was down in Key West. But he dismissed it almost at once. It wasn't fair to drop such a heavy bag of shit in Vegas' lap. No, he'd just have to look after both ends himself. Timing. He'd need timing.

And a good deal of luck.

* * *

"I saw Justine off yesterday," Nicholas said. "I asked her to go back out to West Bay Bridge until this is all over."

Croaker slammed the door to his car, came around to the front where Nicholas was standing. "Good idea. I asked Gelda to stay with a friend of hers or something. I just wanted her out of the apartment for a while."

Above them the tower on Park Avenue rose, half-skeletal, half-fleshed, so that it looked like an artist's cross section.

"He up there?" Croaker asked, indicating the building.

"He should be. I cleared all of this with him first." They began to walk across the wooden planks over the unfinished sidewalk. "He's got guts, you've got to give him that."

"Huh. I don't have to give him nothing. If he's agreed to it, five'll getcha ten he's got some angle figured."

"Sure. Like getting Saigō off his back. Do you think he wants to be hounded?"

Croaker gave him a sideways grin at that. "Naw. I don't think anyone wants that. Not even him." They got into the elevator.

"Where are the men?"

"Coming in"—he consulted his watch—"just about fifty minutes from now. All TPF—Tactical Patrol Force to you civilians. We've got the works this time: tear gas, submachine guns, even a pair of super-snipers with infrared 'scopes. Hit a dime at a thousand yards in the dark. And, of course, all the men will be wearing bullet-proof vests—they've all been cleared for hand-to-hand, by the way." The doors opened on the top floor and they stepped out. "Tomkin had just better behave himself."

"Listen, you leave Tomkin to me, okay? Just stay away. He only baits you because he's scared of you."

"Yeah?" Croaker grinned again. "Now that's the kind of thing I like to hear."

Just before they got to the doors of Tomkin's office Nicholas stopped him. "Remember," he said, "I don't want any of your men on this floor. Not for any reason, is that clear? If Saigō gets by them, they are to stay put. I don't want any of them getting in my way. This floor has got to be clear."

"No sweat. Not that I like it too much but this is his building and you're calling the shots. Seeing as how I didn't

464

o too well two nights ago. I think I can swallow this. Only"—e lifted a forefinger in warning—"don't expect me to stay own there with them. If he gets away, I'll be up here with ou."

Nicholas nodded. "As long as you come up via the route e mapped out together. Don't take any unexpected detours."

"I wish I knew what you had cooked up for this guy."

"Believe me, it's much better than no one else knows. It's oing to come down to him and me, anyway."

"But all you have is *that.*"

Nicholas hefted his scabbarded *katana.* "That," he said, is all I am going to need." He pushed open the door and they ent into the great corner office.

Tomkin, seated as usual behind his enormous desk, looked p, frowning. "Can you believe it?" he growled. "A god-amned garbage strike. And in the middle of the summer. hrist, those union bastards know how to get blood out of a tone. This place is gonna stink to high heaven before it's ven finished."

The old man stood on the west side of Park Avenue. Al-hough there was little traffic this late at night, he nonethe-ss waited for the traffic light on the corner to change in his avor. When at length it did, he started slowly across the ride avenue. He seemed a frail figure from a distance, tooped under the weight of the duffel bag he carried slung ver his rounded back. He had splay feet and his bamboo ane aided his slow passage. Because Park Avenue is divided y a rather wide concrete median, he could not make it across n one light.

Standing still on the strip, he looked quizzically about him s a grandfather might, caught dozing in his favorite chair uring the day. His head was slow moving and it was some me before his gaze took in the half-finished building on the ast side of the avenue. By that time, anyone who might be atching him, even casually, would not have thought it range that he contemplated the structure for the remaining me until the light returned to green and he made his limp-g way across the street.

Instead of turning right, he went straight on, due east, ward Lexington Avenue. Once there, he turned south to

the end of the block. He had now made a half-circuit alon
the perimeter of the tower.

There was an old-style phone booth on the corner. One o
those with green metal and glass walls all the way down t
the pavement. Beside it were black and tan polythene bag
of garbage awaiting pickup. He put this makeshift scree
between him and the tower as if he were about to head furthe
east.

Now he was in dense shadow and he stood perfectly stil
having first altered his image: the duffel bag was at his fee
and he stood straight, his shoulders squared. The bambo
cane lay in the gutter, out of sight of even the sparse traffi
along Lexington. He was invisible to anyone within the build
ing's periphery.

He waited twenty minutes.

Without bending, he unzipped the duffel bag and worke
with deft, economical movements. When he emerged from
his cover, he appeared to be a spare, dapper businessman i
a conservative suit and a porkpie hat. As American as appl
pie. He remembered to make his strides long and purposefu
knowing that even the most formidable of disguises could b
betrayed by the peculiar manner in which an individua
walked, the gait as singular as fingerprints.

There had been no movement along the east face but h
had seen two blue-and-whites parked along the verge of th
north face. They were dark, obviously meant to look empty
He did not think that they were.

Now as he completed his circuit of the tower, his est
mation of the New York Police Force rose a couple of notche
In all, he counted half a dozen men either within or aroun
the building. And once he had caught a tiny flash from some
where above that could only come from the barrel of a rifl

Not that he particularly cared one way or another ho
many men they had assigned to protect Tomkin. But one ha
of course, to be prepared. However, he detested estimates: o
anything. Estimates, he had been taught—and it was mos
assuredly so—were dangerous. How many men had gone t
their deaths by taking an estimated count for real?

He went south on Park, taking it slow and circuitou
arriving back at the phone booth on Lexington a half hou
later. Now was not the time to get careless.

The duffel bag was where he had stowed it, between pile
of plastic-wrapped garbage. He checked his watch. Thirt

econds. He unzipped the duffel bag for the last time. He took
•ff his light-colored suit, flipped the hat into the gutter. Then
¡e stooped and threw the contents of the bag over his shoulder
n a version of a fireman's lift.

The small but powerful incendiary device he had dropped
ınder a car at the end of the north face of the building in his
¡uise as the old man erupted with a white and green flash
nto the night. Even a full block away, he could feel the slight
oncussion as the force of the explosion shot the hot air away
·rom the epicenter. There was a pattering of metal and pow-
lered glass as bright as diamonds in the streetlights. Flame
icked skyward.

Crouching, he ran directly toward the building's façade
.nd, within its dense shadows, he went along its south face,
hrough the first-class cover of the dormant machinery—the
louble shifts had ceased two days ago, after they had dis-
overed he had infiltrated the place as a construction worker.
Within four seconds he had disappeared entirely.

Now he went from thick stanchion to thick stanchion, feel-
ng under his fingers the rough texture of the rust-retardant
ındercoat. Concrete dust still hung in the air and, as he
ropped down from the height, free of his heavy burden, he
aw the sharp shadows cast by the huge machines gave the
·lace the rather disconsolate air of a deserted carnival. There
.ad been a carnival once, at Shimonoseki. The thought of it,
.nd the sea slowly closing over, caused him to reach into a
ide pocket. He put a rough-textured square into his mouth
.nd swallowed.

He squatted, perched like a bird of prey, waiting for the
rug to hit. He had been forced to leave the Kuji-kiri when
.e had become careless enough to drop the stuff during prac-
ice. Not stupid, he reminded himself. He could not help it;
.e had been driven to it. By the rocking boat and the howling
vind and the heavy splash as the sea closed over—

Hit! In bright light. Form and line became stark, almost
wo-dimensional, like the backdrop on a theater stage. It
eemed to him that he could see in all directions at once. He
ecame at once more intensely aware of the driving dust in
he air. This, too, this little thing could be turned into an
dvantage. Because of the pollutant, his adversaries' eyes
vould be forced to blink more rapidly to avoid irritation.

That minuscule amount of time would be the difference be
tween life and death for some of them.

He raised his gaze. He hoped that he would not have t
use the thing on the ledge, but if he did...

He saw the first one. He was dressed differently than th
ones in Pell Street. Too, he carried himself more confidentl₁

Saigō spent several minutes studying the policeman. H
wanted to know several things before he made a move. Di
he have a specific territory assigned to him? And, if so, di
it intersect with someone else's?

When he was satisfied, he lifted the double curve from th
side and screwed the two pieces together. It became a bo₁
of high-tension plastic with a light aluminum center an
sight.

Interesting, he thought. The explosion had not caused a
much havoc as he had thought it might. It had, howeve₁
given him enough time to infiltrate the tower's perimete₁
But not much more. Now he could hear the piercing wail ₁
the fire engine as it approached. The policemen here, havin
at once determined that no person was inside the car or ha
been hurt while passing by, had left the mop-up to the fir
department.

From this vantage point he could see the slight clandestin
movement of the sniper. He waited until the policeman o
his level was at the extreme edge of his patrol. Fitting
steel-tipped arrow to the bow, he drew back and aimed. Thes
were not normal hunting arrows. Their points were made b
the careful layering of steel in precisely the same manne
katana were forged. In ancient times, they were known a
armor-piercing arrows. They could get through anythin
short of a two-inch steel block.

He let the arrow fly. There was a quiet humming as of a
inquisitive bee and a soft *thunk*. The glint of the rifle's barre
was no longer visible, but the unruffled feathers protrude
darkly from the sniper's neck.

The policeman on his level had turned around and wa
coming back. He stopped directly in front of Saigō and lifte
his head. Something dark and wet dripped down onto hi
shoulder. He shifted his submachine gun to his left arr
preparatory to phoning in via walkie-talkie.

Saigō leaped at him, an animated shadow. His left arr
was lifted high in an arc; it made a hissing sound as it de
scended. His hand was encased in a thin steel network, rur

ning from wrist out past the fingertips in what amounted to a set of claws, curved and razor-sharp. Articulated steel tendons across the back of the hand, along each finger.

The policeman had time but to open his mouth before the claws ripped viciously through his throat, embedding themselves in his chest, piercing cloth, bullet-proof vest, skin, flesh and internal organs.

There was a great gout of black blood and the body convulsed as if charged with electricity. Strips of flesh as if flayed flew through the air and the stench of death was abruptly as strong as jasmine in some far-off and peaceful clime.

He left the corpse, laughing silently at the ineffectual addition of the vest, and retrieved his bow from the dense shadows.

First the vast atrium, he thought. He was in no hurry. Upstairs, they could well wait for him. He visualized Tomkin's broad face slick with sweat in the tense period of not knowing what was happening below.

He moved with no more sound than the passing of the warm night wind through the pillars of the tower. In the next sector he came upon another of the plainclothesmen. He moved up behind him and, slipping the black nylon cord with its center knot around his neck, he pulled tight, whipping his wrists powerfully so that the knot bit cruelly into the man's Adam's apple. The back arched as the man fought for breath.

Saigō was momentarily taken by surprise. The man whirled and went for him instead of the encircling cord. He was monstrously strong and Saigō felt his balance going in these close quarters. He felt the arms, as thick as beams, around his waist squeezing as he squeezed. He stamped with his shoe onto the man's instep and he let go. Saigō hurtled to one side, the momentum too strong to compensate for.

The policeman was on him at once, gasping, his bulk nevertheless stultifying. He used kite and sword strikes which were only partially successful but his enormous weight made proper leverage impossible for Saigō.

He fought for the reverse, giving up all but token defense, taking massive punishment, struggling, sweat running down the sides of his neck, staining his black suit.

He cursed himself for the sin of overconfidence and, struggling to free his right hand, he let go a spring blade. It pierced the other's shoulder just center of the collarbone. The man grunted and, disconcertingly, applied even more force. Saigō heard a sharp *crack* in his right ear, knew his bow was now useless.

The policeman put all of his weight into his knees, which were on Saigō's chest, in an attempt to force all air out. This was a mistake. But how could he know that Saigō could last for at least seven minutes without any air at all?

Saigō now concentrated on the man's upper torso. He lacked the space to effectively use the claws. He stiffened the fingers on his right hand, using them as one would the point of a knife. He rammed them into the man's side just under the rib cage. This time, the protective vest did its work and the killing blow, though painful, was deflected.

In desperation, Saigō used the *tettsui* against the sternum. It cracked and all breath went out of the massive body above him.

Saigō got the reverse at last and now, sitting astride the policeman, rewrapped the cord about his throat, heaving with his arms and shoulders.

He heard it, escalating up the register until the decibels were so high they passed beyond human hearing. He moved at the same time. Felt the white-hot blast along his right temple and, half stunned, began to roll along the atrium floor. Scrambled for the shadows as the deadly sound followed him, whining away in ricochet.

Another sniper! He crouched in the shadow of a thick pillar, hearing the night erupt into sound and motion all around him. Blood seeped from the wound and he automatically put a hand up. Just a crease. Still, he had become careless. *We cannot advocate the use of drugs—any drugs whatsoever*—he heard his *sensei* say. *Drugs tend to narrow consciousness, intensifying the narrow-beam awareness while, at the same time, giving the impression of just the opposite. A false reality set is therefore presented. Narrow-beam consciousness becomes a tendency in any form of combat, especially during the latter stages. Even veterans must guard against it. You must effect the* Rat's Head, Ox's Neck *when this occurs. If preoccupied by minute points, step back and review the combat from a distant stance.*

This was precisely the trap he had set for himself and one into which he had neatly fallen. Otherwise he never would have been grazed by that bullet.

Hearing was still a problem and he scrambled away from

470

the epicenter of the commotion. He needed some time to recover.

Movement to the left and in front of him as he lay at an oblique angle within the building's interior. Above him, the partially completed atrium swept away in a narrowing pattern of dim light and deep shadow, the dark air hovering above him like a column of water, heavy and oppressive.

For the first time he considered the depressing possibility that he had seriously underestimated his foes. He felt helpless and terribly alone as he had that night of the howling winds upon the straits, carving out a part of him into the deep with dry eyes and trembling hands; as he had the moment he looked down on the face of his dead father. With the only person in the world who understood him now gone, there was room left only for Satsugai's last wishes. Nothing else had seemed to matter. It was as if he had relinquished all control of his life into the grasping hands of some powerful *kami:* a *jikininki*—the man-eating demon. Perhaps that was all his father had ever been. He had recognized this unassailable monomania even while feeling more respect for him than anyone else in the world—except perhaps for his namesake. It had occurred to him on first reading that earlier Saigō's history that the *kami* of that great patriot must surely reside within Satsugai. In Buddhist lore this was far from impossible.

Satsugai had taken him over completely from a very early stage. His life had been an extension of his father's and there had been, it seemed, no time at all to discover what it was about life that Saigō himself could come to enjoy. Now he knew that there was nothing about life he enjoyed: merely the knowledge of unfinished business which drove him onward toward its inevitable conclusion.

He no longer felt alone and afraid. The drug coursed through his system, heightening his senses. His muscles tingled with suppressed energy. It was time to move.

Out from the shadows, he encountered another policeman with a submachine gun at the ready. They saw each other at the same time. The muzzle of the submachine gun swung up, centering on Saigō's chest. His finger began to squeeze on the trigger; he stared into Saigō's eyes; his finger froze in place.

Still as a statue, he made no reaction as Saigō raised a blunt black stick from waist level. The man's eyes seemed

471

blank. Saigō depressed a hidden stud and with a whisper of sound a steel spike four inches long shot into the plainclothesman's gaping mouth, through the roof, puncturing the brain. He spun around, his finger convulsed on the trigger of his weapon so that it erupted in a short burst, a brief deadly arc.

Saigō was already moving away from the area as the man fell heavily to the patterned tiles of the atrium floor. He could hear the pounding of running feet, the hoarse shouts of the remaining policeman, the static of a walkie-talkie.

He skirted the area overseen by the second long gun, though this was one element which still made him somewhat uneasy. The sniper was potentially as mobile as he was. *Haragei* would protect him from direct assault and, in near-silence, it could negate much of the long gun's threat. But in this commotion he felt cut off from many of his unnatural senses and *haragei* was useless for the kind of distances involved.

He wanted to get upstairs now, but he knew he could not until he had nullified that last threat.

In a leap, he gained the catwalk halfway up to the mezzanine. Two shots in rapid succession spun off the metal close by his left side and had he not been moving he would certainly have been hit at least once.

He ran along the catwalk, his forebrain concentrating on what was directly before him as he let his subconscious work out the location of the sniper from the double flashes that had registered on the periphery of his vision.

He ceded conscious control of his body to this part of him, quartering in on the location. All the while, he watched for any movement.

Up ahead were two patches of light with a length of deep shadow in between. To circumvent them would mean to return to ground level. This he did not wish to do, for to do so he would relinquish his growing advantage over the sniper.

He paused six feet from the first patch of light and, standing perfectly still, surveyed the topography directly in front of him.

He took three deep breaths and sprang forward. One step, two and he was in the air, his legs jackknifed into a diver's tuck so that he passed through the first patch of light as a rotating ball.

He was already arcing downward when he heard the report of the long gun. In the midst of tumbling, he could not

472

ell how close the sniper had come to him but he took no
chances. Barely had his feet touched the metal catwalk than
e had relaunched himself through the air. But now the atmo-
phere around him seemed thick and humid, as turbulent as
loud turned to smoke.

Automatically he ceased to inhale. Briefly, as he turned
ver in midair, he saw the dull flash of the metal canister
olling along the catwalk in the pool of light. He counted the
bang and whine of four bullets, a quick heat sear along one
alf, and then he was in darkness again, on his feet, hurtling
own the catwalk toward the sniper. He ignored the pain in
is right leg, compartmentalizing and thus trivializing the
erve shock, the disruption to his thirstily questing senses.

The sniper, seeing at last the full outline of the onrushing
gure, did not drop to one knee and aim but turned his rifle
rosswise across his body, using it as one might an ancient
ongstaff. He jammed the heavy stock forward in an attempt
o wreck the figure's momentum, felt a jarring crash as it hit
protrusion, the figure's elbow perhaps.

He took one step back and to the side, bringing the muzzle
nd forward and down in an oblique slash. Saigō struck it
way and down with his forearm while extending his leading
eg. This brought him within intimate range and he used a
ite, the edge on his hand as hard as a block of concrete. The
ntire right side of the sniper's rib cage collapsed like an
ggshell.

The man had time only to grunt once, as if in surprise. As
is head and torso came forward, Saigō kicked high, catching
im on the bridge of the nose. Skin ripped away and cartilage
ore itself from its tendon foundations. Blood gouted and,
pinning, the sniper followed his useless weapon, cartwheel-
ng over the side of the catwalk.

Leaping, Saigō was away, racing toward the stairs. At his
ide, he gripped his scabbarded *katana*.

"They got him. Listen to all that noise."

He meant the firing.

Tomkin stood behind his desk, torso canted forward at the
ips, the way an athlete might hold himself. The columns of
is thick arms were rigid, his fists against the desk top.

The sounds of the machine guns had come like an echoing

roll of thunder, amplified and hurled upward by the vast core of air in the atrium.

Nicholas, at his post near the double metal doors, had not moved at all.

"What do you think, Nick?"

He wondered at Tomkin's sudden nerves. He had been as cool and relaxed as a man about to leave on a long vacation the last time he had seen him. Now he seemed on edge.

Across the room, faced with the reality of the situation, Tomkin was sweating. He was having serious second thoughts about his deal with the ninja. There seemed to be an inordinate amount of activity down there. He knew just how many men Croaker had deployed and with what armaments. Had they got him? It sounded like a world war down there. What if he made it up here? What if I can't trust him? My God, Linnear is my last line of defense and I've sacrificed him.

Tomkin opened his mouth to speak, bit back the words at the last minute. He could not tell Nicholas what he had done, no matter what. He put his shaking hand inside his suit jacket and felt his fingers slip in sweat against the warm edge of his gun. He felt wildly out of place, a piranha stripped of its teeth, watching the shark as it swam ever closer. The feeling did not sit well with him. He enjoyed being in control—at his desk, in the boardroom in the midst of proxy fights, overseas taming recalcitrant buyers—while others hung precariously on to the twists and turns of a destiny he was creating. Now, for this moment, others controlled his life and he felt a brief stab of a fear he had not known since one sun-drenched day sixteen years ago; the house on Gin Lane, the summer's heat, the sound the wind made as it raced through the high beach grass, the dryness of the sand like beads of glass, sounds on the sigh of the wind, a rising and falling tide, moaning, and movement and—Gelda. My God, Gelda. Gelda!

His heart pounded in his chest as upon an anvil and something sat astride his intestines, racing up from his genitals, squeezing, squeezing.

"... better sit down and do as I told you."

"What? What?"

"Sit down, Tomkin. He'll be coming soon now."

"Coming? Who?"

"Saigō. The ninja."

Tomkin's face was shiny in the half-light coming in through the wall of windows to his left. All the lights were off on the floor.

"They didn't get him?"

"I think not."

"What about all those men—down there?" He was thinking of them as lines of his defense. They could not all be crumbling so quickly, so easily.

Nicholas misunderstood him. "I'm surprised you care. This wasn't my idea. It should just have been me and you—and him. They're all innocents down there."

"Meaning," Tomkin said, moving a little toward the windows, wondering if Nicholas would follow him as the ninja had suggested he might, "that we—you and me and the cop—are not."

Nicholas might have been a statue. "No. Up here on Olympus morality has little meaning. When you get used to watching people from such a lofty distance their features blur, becoming at last so indistinct that they are as interchangeable as ants—and as insignificant. What does one less ant mean to the course of history? It's too insignificant even to think about."

"You're crazy," Tomkin said. "I don't know what the hell you're talking about." The trouble was, he thought, I *do* know what he's talking about. He pressed his hands against his temples, squeezing his eyes shut against the sun-dazzle tumble of images limned against his eyelids. Gelda and another girl. How his pulse raced! Now the hatred sluiced like venom through his veins. His head pulsed as if being blown up like a balloon. How could she have . . . He'd meted out retribution all right. Deservedly so. His thoughts began to race dangerously.

Where had the days of innocence got to? he asked himself. The Easter egg hunts in Connecticut, the school dances, the easy, laughing summers when the girls would come in from the surf like two brown-skinned mermaids.

Caught in faded photographs, irretrievably mired between Kodak paper and photographic chemicals, as real as Colerdge's dream of Xanadu; gone up in smoke like an addict's hopes.

"You said he's coming." Tomkin's voice was clotted with emotion and he had to clear his throat before he could continue. "What are you going to do?"

"Sit down," Nicholas said. "I want you away from the windows."

"I want to know!" Tomkin shouted. "It's my life!"

"Sit down, Tomkin." Nicholas' voice was even lower than it had been a moment before. "Keep yelling and you will guide him right to you."

Tomkin glared at him for a long moment. His chest heaved beneath his suit jacket. Then, abruptly, he collapsed into his chair.

Nicholas turned his head toward the rear of the office. Next to the open door of the bathroom was a narrow hallway leading first to the electrical and air conditioning circuits for the floor and then to the offices on the far side of the floor.

He did not believe that Saigō would come through the front doors. For one thing, they were bulky and slow-moving. Too much time and effort was involved in opening them. He could not, of course, discount the ledge outside the windows but, as in the manner of most newer, centrally temperature-controlled buildings, these windows could not be opened. Certainly they were easily breached but that also would take time and, worse, an inordinate amount of sound.

It was logical, then, to expect the attack from the rear of the office. He thought briefly about positioning himself more advantageously, in the air-conditioning alcove, perhaps. But if Saigō chose another way in, he might take too long recovering and he could not chance that.

That Saigō was at this moment on his way up he had no doubt.

It was quiet now, just the gentle white-noise hissing in the inner ear, as of the aftermath of a violent tornado. With the front doors secured, no sound seeped in from the street; all the glass was in place here.

He could hear the sound of Tomkin's heavy breathing, as if he were an asthmatic with his mouth partly open. Where he sat, behind his desk, he was in total shadow.

"Move a bit to your right," Nicholas said softly. "No, with the chair. That's right." He turned his head. "Now keep still." A bar of light shone over a portion of the steel-gray hair quartering the head.

The place was alive with them.
But, of course, that was to be expected.

Two at the entrance to the stairwell, three more guarding the cage elevator. He had not even considered using the main elevator bank.

The easiest thing would have been to use hypnosis. The plan was practical as well as amusing. The idea of having one of those plainclothesmen shepherding him skyward in the elevator appealed to him. But that would depend on a very specific set of circumstances. Given time, he had no doubt that he could execute them. He did not, at this point, think that he had the time. They would have begun to sort things out down there. They'd turn on the lights, roll up the casualty figures and send for reinforcements. He did not want to risk a get-out through a cordon of a score of men all on the hair-trigger lookout for one thing and one thing alone.

Not that he could not do it but it was foolish to take such risks when there was absolutely no need to.

In the shadows, he reached out four pads from his belt. These he carefully tied, one on each soft-soled shoe and over the palms of his hands. He slung his *katana* obliquely across his back. He could take no step now without attracting attention, for sprouting from the outer side of the pads were two-inch steel spikes set in a complex pattern.

Saigō unwrapped from his waist a long nylon cord, weighted on one end by a small sharp triangular hook. He looked up, studying the sides of the atrium though he already knew them quite well. He found what he was looking for and began to twirl the weighted cord about his head.

He let it go and it shot high into the atrium, arcing around a transverse iron beam. It was close enough to the wall so that, as he flung himself upward, he was swung inward by his momentum. He drew his legs up so that the soles of his shoes faced outward. He felt the impact as the spiked foot pads dug into the pitted face of the pseudo-marble facing.

This was one of the most ancient of ninjutsu techniques, used for centuries in infiltrating an enemy's castle stronghold. Mere walls, no matter how sheer, could not confound a ninja.

Upward he went with appalling rapidity. A fly on the wall, he was quite invisible to those below, even had they chanced to look this far up. He had, once again, total security.

To the shocked and bewildered men on the atrium's floor it was as if he had vanished into thin air and this was what they reported to Croaker via walkie-talkie.

The hallucinogen was raging full force within him. His involvement with his immediate environment was total. He could see-smell-taste-hear-feel simultaneously as he crawled up the wall.

Small sounds, brittle and three-dimensional, drifted to him from below, funneled by the peculiar acoustics. It was curious because he could hear specific sounds with more clarity from this vantage point than he might have if he were still down below: voices talking, shoes pounding against the cool flooring as they called for the ambulances. Do you no good, he thought. Talking, unanswered. The walkie-talkie, he thought. No matter.

The fine dust of his passage took to the slowly swirling air, a minute ineffectual cyclone passing through the light.

There was silence on the top floor; this was Nicholas' doing; this was why he had insisted that none of Croaker's men be on the floor. Sound was his greatest potential enemy now.

"I want you," he had said to Tomkin some time before, "to face away from him when he comes. Do you think you can do that?" Because it was a most difficult thing to turn your back on someone who meant to kill you. But this was essential. Nicholas was afraid of what the Kuji-kiri might do to Tomkin. Kick out the glass and take one last step down, that was only one possibility.

"Yes, I can do it."

He heard the fear shivering Tomkin's voice and wondered again at it.

"Is that where you're going to stand when he comes?"

"Don't worry about that. Just remember what I've told you. If you do anything else, chances are you'll be dead before you know it. This is no time to think about being in control."

"What can you know about that?" Part of his fear, Tomkin realized belatedly, was that somehow he had recognized a kind of a kindred spirit in Linnear. He had neither the knowledge nor the insight to understand in what way this was so, only knew that it was. This was a deadly man, a sort of a raw animal spirit held in check by a thin veneer of civilization. Tomkin shuddered to think of what might happen if that veneer should crack apart. Perhaps that was why he wanted to trust Linnear with his secrets yet could never bring himself to so unburden himself. Kindred they were and he judged Nicholas in the same light he judged himself. He would do anything to preserve himself thus—

"I know all about that. I've been too much in control all my life. That's hard to take. Calluses don't only grow on hands."

"What do you mean?" But already he suspected that he knew.

"I feel like my head's been full of novocaine for years." He paused for a moment, his head cocked at an angle as if listening to a far-off sound, and Tomkin felt his guts turn to water. Was he coming already? Dear God but he wanted to make a break for the bathroom!

"Your daughter's a very special person."

"Who, Justine?" Tomkin snorted, feeling better now that he was on safe ground again. "Sure, if you call loony special. I don't."

"You really are a fool, aren't you?" There was a small silence as they glared across the darkened room at each other. Nicholas wondered if Croaker had overheard all of this and was chuckling to himself.

"It's all a matter of opinion, isn't it?" Tomkin said, backing off somewhat. It would not do to have Linnear angry with him now. "I mean, I've been through a lot with her. You only know her a short time. But, listen"—he tapped a forefinger on the desk top—"I told you where she was, didn't I? I helped you find her. I want you two to make it, I've told you that and I mean it. You're good for her. Your strength can keep her from going back—"

"You don't know her at all," Nicholas said. "She's got more strength than a lot of men I know." He let that hang in the air. Had it been a glove thrown down at Tomkin's feet? If so, Tomkin chose to ignore it as such.

"Perhaps there has been some change. I haven't seen her for some time, I'll grant you that. I suppose I still think of her as the baby of the family. Gelda, my oldest, always seemed so much more capable of taking care of herself, even when they were both much younger. She was always so much more social than Justine." Oh yes, social. He had to laugh at that. Women fucking women. My God, where had she picked that up? "I am afraid we aren't exactly a closely knit family." How in hell could we be? "There is little sense of family loyalty between my daughters. I regret that most bitterly but it's to be expected, I suppose. When there is not

479

enough time"—Nicholas could sense the shrug in the dark of the office—"the children inevitably turn away from their parents, find others who can satisfy their needs." The finger stopped tapping, hung suspended for a time in the air. "I imagine you could say that both my daughters are arrested adolescents in a sense. Ah well."

No one had uttered a word in some time. The silence seemed absolute, totally antithetical to what one comes to expect in any big city. The outside did not exist for any of them. Here they were sealed into a violent world of their own manufacture where the laws of the world did not apply. Now dark and bloody gods stalked these angustate corridors as they did the warren chambers of the Great Pyramid of Cheops. Years falling away like crimson leaves whirled in an autumn storm.

Coming, thought Nicholas. At last he's coming.

He was born into the element earth. *Dai-en-kyō-chi*, as the *Aki i ninjutsu* had taught him: "Great-round-mirror-wisdom." This was his strength and he began the *Shū-ji*, the seed-word mantra that would bring him to the final state of preparedness, the death-and-night-and-blood that was ninjutsu combat.

And in the instant following the tiny sound of Saigō's leap onto the top floor, he heard that most unique sound in all the world as he drew his *katana* from its sheath.

Croaker, you bastard, Nicholas thought, you had better stay out of this. You have been warned. This is between Saigō and me and God help anyone who gets in the way.

Movement on the floor. No one heard but Nicholas. *Haragei*. He could feel the adept's approach. Like an itchy finger in the night, his senses felt the approach. He wore only a lightweight black silk shirt and cotton pants. He gripped the *katana* with both hands, standing in the attitude of *Happo Biraki*, "Open on all eight sides," a technique developed by Miyamoto Mushashi more than three centuries before. There was no possible kenjutsu opening for attack. This had been proved long before he had been born.

Energy flowed through him like current from a generator

The night beat on like a separate heart, with a will of its own, following a destiny no one could yet know.

He saw everything now as segments of a whole, parts fitting into the topography of the floor. The furniture: height, length, depth; fixtures, hangings; the world shrunken into a series of severely confined spaces within which would now take place the dance of death begun so many years ago.

A shadow shifted and Nicholas knew that Saigō was in the narrow hall. He leaped across the room, his *katana* held high above his head, a scream beginning in the recesses of his chest.

His nostrils flared and in midair he tumbled head over heels away from the hallway opening. He had caught the smell of it even before he had heard the soft click as it rolled along the floor.

The bathroom door was open and he used that. There was very little light but the percussion, abetted by the confined space, was awesome. He sensed Tomkin leaping to his feet, turning around.

Saigō was already in the room, moving at full velocity, using the noise of the blast for cover. He headed straight for Tomkin.

"Get away from me!" Tomkin cried, raising his hands defensively. He could be dead ten different ways, he realized, before he could draw and fire his gun. "He's over there!" He pointed frantically to where Nicholas was standing.

Saigō said nothing but his eyes blazed with a kind of cold fury that sent a tremor of terror through Tomkin's thighs. For the first time in his life he contemplated the coming of death as a real and substantial force. I am already dead, he thought, seeing an element in Saigō's face which, perhaps, had no place on this world. It might have been, had he believed in such a thing, Lucifer himself come to snatch him. He saw the terrible glint of light off the steel claws, extending from the left hand which was raised, beginning its thrust forward toward his chest where a fire burned already.

Then, in less time than, it seemed to him, the blink of an eye, the ninja was knocked sideways, across the floor toward the windows.

Nicholas, his right shoulder lowered, ran lightly after the spinning body, his *katana* held before him in a two-handed grip.

Saigō tumbled head over heels, came up on his feet facing

481

Nicholas. He withdrew his own *katana* with his left hand
made a flicking movement with his right.

Nicholas ducked and leaped at the same time. Something
no more than the size of a pea arced high into the air. It
bounced once on the floor directly in front of the desk. But
Saigō had been slightly off balance when he had tossed it
and, on the rebound, the thing hit the overhang of the desk
top and, instead of landing behind it, bounced back in front
of it.

As it was, the mini-blast blew Nicholas' *katana* from his
grasp as it tore away most of the front of the desk, ripping
up the carpeting.

Immediately Saigō hurled himself toward Nicholas, who
was still scrambling away from the concussion of the explo
sion.

In the periphery of his vision, Nicholas saw Saigō coming
He was vulnerable and he knew it. No textbook defense was
possible from his position, not against someone as skilled as
Saigō. His decision was made in a split second. He propelled
his body obliquely upward, using his palms, arms and shoul
ders for power, and, twisting, his soles caught Saigō's finger
as they curled around the hilt of his *katana*. The angle added
to the natural force of the blow and the weapon spun out o
his grip and away.

Saigō landed with the claw first and Nicholas countered
with sword-strikes to the liver and spleen, missing but de
flecting the attack at the same time.

It was the heart-kite Saigō immediately strove for. Beside
the fact that it was lethal, it had the added advantage o
forcing a break in a stalemate, a situation that would benefi
Nicholas more because of the time factor. Every added secon
that Saigō took here made the get-out that much more dif
ficult.

Saigō ignored the serpent-strike to his clavicle, biting bac
on the pain and concentrating on what he had to do. He wa
on top, part of him stunned by the mode of Nicholas' hand
to-hand defense. It was, in part, ninjutsu but a kind he ha
never before encountered. Could it be *Aka i ninjutsu?* h
thought wildly. That would be in character. By the Amida
It was ninja against ninja.

He worked out of the four-hands-lock Nicholas had presse
on him and was ready now. For the heart-kite. In less tim

482

than it took to think about it, Nicholas would be dead, training or no training.

He jerked away and down as the whine of a bullet passed through the air where his head had been moments ago. Amida! There was another one up here. He cursed himself mightily for becoming so involved with his new knowledge of Nicholas. It was this that had kept him from discerning the third man. Now where was he?

But Nicholas had thrown him the *tettsui-tō* and had already tied him up sufficiently for him to divert his full attention here.

With a frantic effort, he fought Nicholas off and bounded to where he had left his *katana*. Nicholas was after him in a flash, extending his body fully, wrapping his fingers around Saigō's powerful ankles. They crashed together into the drawing board. Saigō picked up his *katana*. Another bullet ricocheted off the corner of the board, spewing splinters into his face, and he rolled away, cursing.

Nicholas went for the sword arm, careful for all the many *shaken* he knew might pop into his face at any time. He went immediately into the air-sea change to throw Saigō off balance, for he had heard, as he knew his opponent had, the soft hum of the elevator working and when it arrived, he knew, Croaker's men might take no chances this time but flood the floor with tear gas the moment the doors opened.

Saigō knew that he was at the extreme end of his time limit. A new factor had been added that he had not counted on. Nicholas needed nothing more than a stalemate while he, on the other hand—

He attacked high with a rapid series of strikes aimed for Nicholas' esophagus but he was balked and he began to sweat hard. His mind raced but kept coming back to the same point. If both were out of the question, he would have to be content with one and plan for the other later. There was no question of choice.

He let a pair of blows in and doubled over, feigning more pain than he felt. His right hand, in cover, darted within his belt, palming another tiny sphere. This time he must make no error in judgment in his throw.

He turned his head fractionally to get a fix on Tomkin's position and that was when Nicholas knew. He threw himself from his opponent at the same time Saigō launched the sphere, diving across the desk top, slamming into the immobile Tomkin just as he heard the tiny popping sound behind him. As he pushed Tomkin out of the way, he kicked the massive high-backed chair backward. At about the same instant, he caught the sound of a shot and what sounded like a high crack of thunder. He hit the floor just as the explosion came.

It was a hot burst of green-white-yellow behind which came the concussion, the almost physical wave of sound and, just afterward, the soft pattering of the wrecked furniture like sleet on a frost-filled day.

Nicholas turned over on his back, sat up.

"What—?"

He put his hand on Tomkin's head, keeping it down. "Shut up," he growled thickly.

He saw Croaker's head peering out from behind the top of the long sofa.

"Jesus Christ!" He stood up. "Is Tomkin okay?"

"Unharmed," Nicholas said, thinking about how close it had been. Bitterly, he regretted letting Saigō get away. After so many years he wanted only death for death. But the decision had been inconclusive. In one sense, he knew he had been lucky. He had seen the shock in Saigō's eyes as he had learned that Nicholas was ninja. Well, that was some compensation but it only made the next confrontation that much more dangerous. Tonight he had been unprepared....

"Christ!" Croaker said again and Nicholas followed his incredulous gaze. "I wasn't sure that I had seen it just before the blast but now—"

Where the third window panel had been there were now merely shards of glass. Glass littered the carpet as the night wind had brought some of it back inside.

"Nuts," Croaker said, slipping his .38 back into its holster. "The guy must've been nuts—or suicidal." He turned as the metal door burst open and he waved the men off. "Downstairs," he said to a tousel-haired sergeant. "See what's left of the bastard for the M.E. to scrape off the sidewalk."

Nicholas had gone to the broken window and was peering out. Croaker came up beside him.

"Can't see anything from this vantage point," he said, "but the god-damned red-and-whites from the cars." He meant the revolving lights.

Tomkin was up behind them, brushing off his suit. It was ruined, whitened from the blasts, as if it had been abruptly aged.

Croaker left the room without looking at him.

"Nick." For the first time in his life he seemed to have trouble talking, and his legs felt rubbery. "Is he gone?"

Nicholas continued to stare out and down. He could see movement now and lights coming on. They had found the body.

"You saved my life." Tomkin cleared his throat. "I want to thank you." Maybe Nicholas had not heard the exchange he had had with that madman. He had been mad himself to trust him. He knew with a grinding certainty that tore at his guts that, without Nicholas' intervention, he would be dead now. He was in Nicholas' debt and this worried him. He felt anger forcing its way upward and, for the briefest of instants, he detested himself in precisely the same way he had detested himself as he had arisen, sticky and panting, from the supine body of his daughter so many years ago, in a summer filled with heat and the pounding of the surf. On Gin Lane.

On the street, Nicholas saw that they had already put the corpse into a body bag. He stopped them before they could load it into the ambulance. It was only one of a long line. The associate M.E., a light-haired woman with a pink complexion, glanced at Croaker, who nodded.

"Not much left after a fall like that," Croaker said with a curious lack of emotion.

He was right. There was not much left of Saigō's head, his face pulped. One shoulder seemed crushed and the neck at an odd angle.

"Legs're like jelly," Croaker said as if he relished the thought. "Not a bone in them now over an inch in length. That right, Doc?"

The associate M.E. nodded wearily. "Take it away," she said. "It's been tagged. I've got more work here." She turned away and Nicholas could see the parade of stretchers being brought out from the bowels of the building.

Croaker's face was white and drawn as his eyes ticked over the casualties.

"Four dead, Nick." His voice was a rasp. "That we know about for sure. There are two others missing and a couple

485

more are down recovering from gas inhalation. Jesus, your friend Saigō kills like other people eat." He rubbed his fingers over his face. "I'm glad it's all over. Glad as hell."

"I'm sorry it had to be this way," Nicholas said.

"Don't say 'I told you so.'"

"I wasn't thinking of that at all. I was thinking he's gone now. I can get on with my life. I just want to see Justine."

"What would make him jump?"

"He was a warrior. To die in battle was what he lived for."

"I don't understand that kind of philosophy."

Nicholas shrugged pragmatically. "It doesn't matter." He looked around. "Did you find his *katana*? I'd like to have it."

"His what?"

"The sword."

"Oh, that. No. But I don't think they've found all of *him* yet either. It's here, somewhere. We'll find it."

"I guess it's not very important, either."

Croaker's gaze swept over Nicholas' shoulder. "Your boss is looking for you, I think."

Nicholas swiveled and grinned back at his friend. "Ex-boss, you mean."

Tomkin, his suit streaked with gray and black, stood at the open door to his limo. Tom stood at his side, obediently holding the door. The motor seemed to be running. Sirens wailed in ululation for the dead and the night, where they stood at least, seemed very bright.

"Listen," Croaker said, taking his arm and leading him a few paces away along the avenue. "Before you go. I want to tell you I got that call I've been waiting for. The other woman in Angela Didion's apartment the night she was murdered. I know where she is."

Nicholas looked at him, then at Tomkin waiting silently beside the limo. "You're not going to let that go, are you?"

"I can't. I've gotta nail him on this. You should be able to understand. It's a matter of honor. If I don't do it, nobody's gonna be able to."

"But are you sure of what you've got?"

Croaker stuck a toothpick in the corner of his mouth. His eyes were dark pools. His face seemed more lined tonight than it had two days ago, but perhaps it was only the harsh light. He told Nicholas about his conversation with Matty the Mouth. "You thought I was just shooting off my big mouth with Tomkin, didn't you? Matty didn't know who else was

486

nosing around about this broad but I'll bet it's Frank who's doing it. You seen him lately? No? Why don't you ask your ex-boss, then, where Frank is, okay?"

"You won't know anything until you talk to the woman, right?"

"Right. That's why I'm taking off for Key West right away. But as far as the department is concerned, it's just a long-overdue vacation."

"I hope you know what you're letting yourself in for."

The last ambulance started up, its siren screaming. For an instant they were bathed in the intense crimson glow from its revolving light. Then it had turned a corner and was gone. The night darkened as if from a swiftly advancing storm.

"That's an odd thing to say," Croaker said, "coming from you."

"Nick! Are you coming?" Tomkin's voice floated across to them as unreal as a dream.

"In a minute," Nicholas called without looking over. To Croaker he said, "You going to see Gelda before you leave?"

"Can't take the time. I'll call her. Anyway, the number she gave me has a 516 area code. She'd never make it in." He looked down at his feet for a moment. "I just want to tell her that everything's okay now. And hey," he said as Nicholas turned to leave, "you ought to do the same. Justine's probably worried sick."

When Tomkin saw Nicholas coming, he ducked his head, slid into the limo. Tom held the door until Nicholas got in, then he shut it softly and went around the front.

All the night sounds were gone in the thick quiet interior. The motor purred richly. The air conditioning was on.

There was still a lot of police activity going on outside. Nicholas could see Croaker talking to a rather young-looking patrolman. He shook his head once in response to a question and pointed into the bowels of the tower.

"I'm grateful, Nick," Tomkin put his arm along the top of the back seat, his thick fingers partially curled. "I mean it. Tomorrow you'll come up to the office for your check. Plus a bonus. You deserve it."

Nicholas sat silently with his scabbarded *katana* across his knees. He put his head back and closed his eyes.

"And we can talk," Tomkin continued, "about you staying on in the firm."

487

"I'm not interested," Nicholas said. "Thanks just the same."

"Oh now, I wouldn't make a decision like that so hastily." His voice had lightened somewhat. But it was still as deep, ringing with sincerity. "I could use you. Somewhere high up. You've got remarkable talents." Tomkin was silent for a time. Even with his eyes closed, Nicholas could tell that he was studying him. "How'd you like to go back to Japan?"

Nicholas opened his eyes, stared directly ahead at the plastic partition. "I don't need you for that," he said slowly.

"No," Tomkin admitted. "Decidedly not. You could jump on a plane tonight and be there in ten hours. But if you went with me, it would mean a minimum of, oh, say, a quarter of a million dollars."

Nicholas turned to look at Tomkin.

"Oh, I am perfectly serious. Just because this ninja has been killed doesn't mean my problems over there are solved. Far from it. I need an expert who—"

Nicholas raised a hand. "Sorry, Tomkin."

The other man shrugged. "Well, you think about it, anyway. There's plenty of time now."

Behind them, Nicholas could see Croaker climbing into his car.

Tomkin spoke to Tom. "Let's go over to Third. I want to get a bite to eat before we drop Mr. Linnear off."

The limo started up, heading left on Park, around the median so that they could take the eastbound street fronting the south side of the tower. Nicholas saw Croaker right behind them as he prepared to head back downtown to file his report before driving out to LaGuardia.

"How is Justine?" Tomkin asked.

He really is beneath contempt, Nicholas thought. He wanted to get home so that he could call her. "Did you have me followed to the disco?"

Tomkin tried to laugh. "No, no. I knew I could never get away with that. No. Just a father's intuition."

If it had not been so sad, it might have been funny. Nicholas reflected. He just does not understand. "She's fine."

"Good. I'm glad."

The light changed and they went across the avenue. Tomkin cleared his throat. He almost said something, then seemed to change his mind. They came abreast of the tower.

488

The last few policemen were grouped on the broken sidewalk, talking amongst themselves.

"Nick, I know you don't like me much but—still—I'd like to ask you for a favor."

Nicholas said nothing. He watched as through the window the tower began to slide by.

"I want—that is, I *don't* want Justine to be estranged from me. I've done—well, I don't know what to do anymore and I thought maybe you could help—bring us together—"

This side of the building was filled with trucks and, midway along the block, a metal and wooden overhang three stories high that jutted out past the curb, used to maneuver the enormous panes of tinted glass into place.

"I think," Nicholas said, "that that has to be between the two of you."

"But you're already involved," Tomkin said in his million-dollar-deal voice.

The limo passed beneath the overhang and the night seemed to darken.

Nicholas turned away from the window to look at Tomkin. By the way," he said, "I haven't seen Frank around for a couple of days. Where is he?"

There came, at that moment, a tremendous crash as the left side of the windshield shattered inward. Tom seemed to leap from behind the wheel as if he were a speared marlin. He slammed backward with such force that the plastic partition cracked. His arms fluttered like wings and Nicholas heard a soft moaning sound like a child sick with fever.

Abruptly, Tom's suit jacket ripped and fully three inches of steel rammed itself past his spine. Blood spurted like a geyser and a terrible stench invaded the limo's interior.

"Oh, my God! What—?" Tomkin's face was pale.

The limo continued to head east along the street, passing the corner and crossing Lexington Avenue.

A great thrashing was coming from the front seat but Tom no longer screamed. Something or someone was squirming its way inside through the great rent in the windshield.

Driverless, the limo wandered to the left, running up on the curb until its front end smashed into a light stanchion that was part of the new building on the corner.

Blackness in the front of the limo as if the night itself had stolen in.

Nicholas had already taken the *katana* off his lap and was

holding it in his left hand. No use drawing it in such a confined space. Beside him, Tomkin was scrabbling at the door handle but it would not open. The automatic door locks were controlled from up front. It had been a security precaution. Now Tomkin cursed it.

Tom's corpse was flung to one side. The smell was so overpowering, it seemed as if there was nothing else in the world.

Something dark pounded at the cracked partition, trembling it. Nicholas waited until the third blow, timing it in his mind. Then as the fourth blow came he met it with a powerful kick with both feet flat against the plastic. The partition came apart at the force of the blow and Nicholas leaped into the front of the limo.

Saigō had come off the face of the tower, sliding carefully along the narrow ledge from which he had thrown the already dead body.

He had stayed in place long enough to ascertain that the decoy had worked, then slowly made his way within the shadows down the face of the building. Even those few cops still looking up at the shattered window in Tomkin's top-floor office had not seen him. Only Nicholas, had he been down on the street, would have had a chance.

Crouching in the blackness, he had cursed silently for now he felt the sodden touch of fear. Nicholas a ninja! His mind reeled and, reflexively, he popped another rough brown cube into his mouth, chewing on it to make it work all the faster.

Soon the psychedelic was flowing through his system speeded by the outlay of adrenalin pumping through his veins. Now the sky seemed to explode in a crimson and black mushroom cloud, his muscles bulged; his neck swelled with the power and his vision dazzled as it reached his brain. He was frying in energy.

Then the voices began in his left ear and he lifted one hand, touching a forefinger to the side of his head to settle more comfortably the electronic receiver in his ear canal. He heard Tomkin and Nicholas talking, heard "Third Avenue" and moved immediately toward the south side of the building where he knew the overhang jutted out into the street. When the limo passed by he swung down so silently and with such remarkable balance that no one inside knew.

He crouched on top and, unsheathing his *katana*, the night

490

wind in his hair, thrust it down and inward through the windshield, screaming in ecstasy as the car beneath him shuddered like big game being brought down.

Croaker had been about to head south on Park when he thought he saw some movement near Tomkin's limo as it went east. A sound came to him then. He could not identify it but he nevertheless braked hard, swinging the wheel abruptly to the left.

Tires screeched and his back end skidded outward. For a long moment he concentrated on holding the turn and not crashing into the median. Horns honked and he cursed softly, fighting the centrifugal force.

Then he was screeching uptown on Park back toward the tower.

In the first moments of shock he was at a distinct disadvantage. Saigō knew this and used it. He ducked under the initial force of Nicholas' lunge and, twisting around, began the *kansetsu-waza*—the dislocation—with the point of his left elbow.

Nicholas, above Saigō, felt rather than saw the lack of resistance and immediately went into the *osae-waza*—the immobilization—defense and got it, deflecting Saigō's elbow while, simultaneously, going on the offensive.

For an instant, Saigō had a short blade free. Then his hand clamped down and they were locked together, joined by the honed steel that was an extension of themselves—the most holy of holies, without which their lives themselves might have no meaning.

Muscles rippled along their hunched backs; sweat streamed from them. Saigō gritted his teeth. Nicholas pressed downward. It was as if the sun and the moon, offshoots of a single entity, had entered into conflict. Was this the awesome force which bound Cain and Abel, decreeing that their hands be raised against each other?

Now was the time of their desperation. For ninja they were; of *ryu* that were sworn enemies when the silent stars in the sky had different positions, when the summers were perhaps hotter, the winters far colder, the continents even showing the pimply faces of adolescence; such was the nature

491

of endless time into which they had both willingly entered in their youth.

Nicholas went immediately for the air-sea change, to break the deadlock, but this Saigō had apparently been waiting for, for he countered with *shime-waza*—the three-finger strangulation—and caught Nicholas off guard. But the liver-kite, severely foreshortened because of the tight space, broke that. And all the time, Tom flopped intimately against them, his slowly coagulating blood smearing their faces and wrists.

Muscles bulged like puffing engines, veins and rolling sweat ribboning their glossy skin. Their panting breath mingled, magnified in this tiny, overheated space, and their eyes crossed to look at each other. Mere words were, for the moment, beyond them and they hissed their hate at each other in a kind of elemental language that had not been heard since the dawn of man.

The blade of the *tanto* was turned away from him and Nicholas used the angle to force Saigō's wrist backward. But he was not *Kanaku na ninja*, not an adept in *koppo*. Saigō, however, was and he knew how to stop this maneuver. He drew his right knee up and, simultaneously, began a movement with his right hand. Which was the feint? Or were they both?

In the split second of deciding, Nicholas' grip on Saigō's left wrist loosened and then was dislodged. The point of the *tanto* blurred immediately upward toward Nicholas' face. He caught the end of the hilt on the outer bone of his wrist, deflecting its flight.

There was only destruction in their hearts; their minds, cleansing themselves of the years of enmity, poured their power into the emotionalism of the moment, stoked by pumping adrenalin and the *hsing-i*, the so-called imaginary mental fist: that is, the enormous force of will their disciplines had imbued them with.

Now Nicholas used the heart-kite to break the deadlock and Saigō, stung and surprised, swung outward, landing a blow on the side of Nicholas' head.

Immediately he rolled upward and out through the rent windshield. Nicholas followed, leaping from the hood of the stalled limo onto the sidewalk.

He saw Saigō, all in black, standing beyond the bent light post. He had thrown aside his *katana*'s scabbard and he held it now in the first position. He did not have to call to Nicholas

In the periphery of his vision, Nicholas saw a car brake to a halt. Croaker got out. Without turning his head, Nicholas called out, "Leave us alone! See to Tomkin. He's in the back of the limo."

Then he advanced on Saigō.

When one is ninja, one sees not only with one's eyes. *Haragei* allows one to see with the entire body. Thus it was that as Nicholas moved toward Saigō, it was his eyes which saw the other's one-handed grip but his body was already reacting.

Using the *iai* draw, he lifted the blade of his *katana* in time to deflect the pair of *shaken* Saigō had flicked at him almost nonchalantly. They buzzed away like angry bees clattering down the brick steps behind Saigō to the lower plaza of the building. Beside him a modern sculptured waterfall crashed and splattered downward to rectangular "rocks" in a pool on the plaza.

Their *katana* clashed together in the Fire and Stones Cut, shuddering them. Only the superbly forged Japanese weapons could survive such power intact.

Saigō seemed frantic. His pupils were so large his eyes seemed all black, so alien that Croaker was transfixed by the *hsing-i*, which he perceived as an almost physical blow.

Saigō attacked strongly and swiftly. His strength seemed appalling, even to Nicholas. He felt engulfed in a kind of magnetic storm which, swirling him around, threatened to disorient him completely. And he fell back under the onslaught.

He saw Saigō's lips moving slowly and softly and found himself wondering how high he was; how much of the drug was now coursing through him; and how he could use this to his own advantage.

He shook his head as a strike almost slipped through. Abruptly, his arms felt enormously heavy. His eyelids flickered. And there was a wolfish grin on Saigō's face.

Nicholas staggered back, felt running water against the backs of his legs. He was in the waterfall, a steep drop at his back. How had he become turned around?

He felt a sharp pain in his arm, saw Saigō's *katana* streaked with a line of blood like saliva from a mad dog and he knew what was happening to him.

It was the *Kōbudera*. The magic not even the most fanatic of the *Kan-aku na ninja* would touch. Except for Saigō.

Back went Nicholas under the ferocious attack until they were both in the water. Magic was all around him, turning the night crimson. He seemed not to be able to feel his legs; he staggered. His fingers were numb, the grip on his *katana* faltering. His breath came in pants.

And all the while, Saigō came mercilessly on, striking and grinning, his lips invoking the *Kōbudera*.

Nicholas' foot slipped on a slick piece of sculpture which he could not feel and he almost went down. He was immediately slashed again. Blood sparked the night air. His blood. Agony filled him and it seemed as if he could not breathe. Whatever Fukashigi did during the night, he thought, it is not enough.

The rushing water drenched him and he shuddered. And in that great breath, which reached from his throat all the way down to his toes, came a thin stream of crystal clarity piercing the fog that had shrouded him.

He thought of Musashi, the Sword Saint, standing in his garden more than three hundred years ago. "What is the 'Body of a rock'?" he was asked. In answer, Musashi summoned a pupil of his and bid him kill himself by slashing his abdomen with a knife. Just as the pupil was about to comply, the Master stayed his hand, saying, "That is the 'Body of a rock.'"

This, then, Nicholas did, reaching down inside himself where something he did not even know existed lay in wait. He dragged it up with all his strength and, as Musashi wrote, ten thousand things could not touch him, not Saigō's *katana*, not even the *Kōbudera*.

In a blur, Nicholas cut from left to right with his *katana*. In shock, Saigō lifted up his own blade, his eyes wide and staring.

Blood spurted, brilliantly red as a cardinal's plumage and Saigō's torso arched back, his lips pulled back from his teeth in a rictus.

Water sloshed and sucked as they both struggled to maintain their balance. For Saigō, who had been cut through skin and flesh and even sternum, it was a herculean task. His *katana* hung from his nerveless left hand, the fingers twitching relentlessly as they sought to do what their torn nerves no longer would allow them to. He weaved from side to side like a lush on one last monumental drunk. He grasped the top of his chest, near his shoulder blade, but Nicholas, using

494

the point of his *katana*, flicked away the deadly *shuriken* needles he had clutched.

Groaning, Saigō held on to the hilt of his *katana* now, using it like a walking stick to prop himself up. Without its aid, he would have collapsed like an old man.

"Kill me now." His voice was an harsh gurgle over the restless bubbling of the water rushing over the fall. "But not until I tell you, cousin, what I have waited long years to tell you." His shoulder twitched. "Come closer." His voice cracked, dropped abruptly in volume. "Come closer. We cannot have you savor your triumph, ah no!"

Nicholas took a step toward him. His chest and belly were streaked with blood and the iridescent seeping of his organs. For Nicholas, the pain was a dull throbbing all down his arm where Saigō had slashed him.

"You should have cut me when you could," he said. "Your spirit was not resolved; the *Kōbudera* consumed you and you slashed me instead. You see what one cut can do."

Saigō staggered. "What is that you say, cousin? Come closer still. I cannot hear you." He grimaced in pain, a fleet passing cloud, and then it was gone, hidden behind all the layers that they had both acquired. This was, perhaps more than any other thing, what set Japan apart from the rest of the world, this bit of hard unflinching stone beneath all the wrappers—the many many layers—of distilled duty and filial love. This was why they must go forward always and never take a step back. But, O Amida, their memories were long indeed, stretching beyond, it was said in many tales, the grave itself.

Nicholas wanted to sleep now. His body had dealt with the shock and now, as it damped down on the pain, he was calming. A kind of lassitude was running...

"You think that you have won but you haven't," Saigō gasped out. A thin trickle of blood was seeping from one corner of his mouth. His busy tongue flicked at it, as an adder's might, tasting it. "I see that I had better get on with it....But won't you come one step closer, cousin, so that I don't have to shout? Good." His eyes burned coldly. "You believe that Yukio is alive, somewhere, living the life of a married lady perhaps, and thinking every so often of the old days with you. But, oh no, this is not so!" He began a laugh which ended in a ragged cough. He hawked and spat pinkly between them. He looked into Nicholas' eyes as he said, "She lies at the bottom of the Straits of Shimonoseki, cousin, precisely where I dumped her.

"She loved you, you know. With every breath she breathed, with every word she spoke. Oh, I could drug her as I did that night with you and, for a time, she would forget you. But each time she would awake and it would be as before.

"At last it drove me out of my mind. She was the only woman, the only one...for me and without her there were only men and more men and still more...." His eyes blazed like coals, red-rimmed and mad. The trickle of blood had thickened, running like heavy drops from a careless painter's brush, darkening the water.

"You made me kill her, Nicholas," he said in sudden accusation. "If she had not loved you—"

"If life was not the way it was—" Nicholas said harshly. His arms were already in motion and the *katana* was a crescent of living light, as if he were the Lord's true messenger, whirring like a living entity through the hot wet air.

In a bright arc, Saigō's head sailed upward, tumbling over and over on its final journey like a miniature planet, a crimson streamer like a kite's or a comet's tail laced behind it. Over the edge it went, bouncing downward across the white steps, a child's lost ball, coming to rest at last at the bottom of the waterfall: on the ninth step from the top.

"—but it is," Nicholas said, finishing the sentence. At his feet, the water spun, rocking gently as if on a faraway tide, shivering. Caressing Nicholas' spread legs.

Of course, after it was all over, Croaker wanted to know just how he had done it, so he made Nicholas come down to the morgue with him to look at the body.

"Can't tell a goddamned thing from this," he said. "Christ on a crutch, we'd never have known."

Nicholas looked down at the battered and broken body. It was Japanese, the same height and weight as Saigō. An exhaustive autopsy would turn up the difference in the musculature, of course; this man could not have been trained as Saigō had been. But that would have happened only if you were *looking* for a difference.

He reached out, turned the head to one side, peered at the neck, touched the side with his fingertips. "There," he said.

"What?" Croaker looked at the spot. "His neck's broken.
o what? Happens all the time in a fall."

"No, Lew. It's the *way* the neck was broken. I've seen that
one before, years ago. Bones sheared through as if someone
ad used a surgical scalpel. No fall can do that. It's *koppo*,
ew. A ninja technique."

"Christ," Croaker said. "He killed a man just to snooker
s."

Nicholas nodded. "Plans within plans."

He listened, with nothing but the screen door between him
nd the coolness of the evening, to the quiet. To the breakers
ghing as they rose, curled, and fell again and again like
is own tidal breathing.

He was thinking of Japan. Of the Colonel, of Cheong, of
aigō, and especially of Yukio.

All in their rightful places now, the revenge done, all the
npossibly tangled cords laid out in their skeins, just as they
ad once started out; dying as they had been born.

The rage which had filled him up when Saigō had told
im seemed like yesterday's ember now. He recalled his
ream and the faceless woman was no longer faceless. Only
ow was he coming truly to understand the enormity of Yu-
io's sacrifice. She could have, at almost any time, run away
om Saigō. And where do you think she would go? Where
le wanted to be; at his side. And Fukashigi had said: *You
ere not ready then. He would have destroyed you....* Nicholas
new the full measure of the truth of those words. By staying
ith Saigō, Yukio knew she held in check a measure of his
eep anger; at least he had her and Nicholas did not. She
ave her life for me. *Migawari ni tatsu.*

*Why do you weep so bitterly, my lady? What ill has befallen
ou? A most dishonorable death, sir, and until it is avenged,
y spirit must wander—wander here.*

But no more.

He felt Justine coming quietly up behind him and he felt
vast peacefulness, like coming upon one's own stone cottage
: the edge of the sea, guarded by the tall pines one knew
well from infancy. A warm wind blew through his soul
d he closed his eyes as he felt her arms steal about him,
er lips trace the contours of his cheek.

"Are you all right?"

"Yes. Yes." They stirred together like two leaves on branch. "The sea is so blue now. Bluer than the sky."

"Because the sky is mirrored in it. See how they're bo there?"

"It's the artist in you. You see in colors."

"But you see it too, don't you?"

"Now you've pointed it out, yes."

She put her cheek against his shoulder. "I miss Doc Dee forth."

"So do I." He looked out to sea. "His daughters will here soon."

"Saigō must have been at Gin Lane looking for Fathe but why Doc?"

"I don't know," Nicholas said softly. "Perhaps he saw hi and became suspicious." But his thoughts were far far awa

After a long time, they made dinner and ate it outside his porch and the wind, taking her hair and pulling it to o side as a gentle mother might, whirled their paper napki out across the dunes to disappear in the surf, platinum a mauve.

A couple walked hand in hand, their bare feet scuffing t sand, leaving a trail of their passage like a pair of crabs. sleek Irish setter, its glossy coat burnished crimson by t setting sun, ran ahead, barking happily at them, its lo tongue lolling as it danced at the edge of the sea.

"Do you want to go back, now?" she asked, her hand his. "To Japan."

He looked at her and smiled. He thought about her fathe offer. "I don't think so." He sat back in his chair and it creak a little, a comforting sound like the rattle of lines in the wi aboard ship. "Oh, one day, perhaps—We'll both go to ha a look, as tourists might."

"You could never be a tourist there."

"I could try."

On the near horizon, boats were running back for sho their sails high and billowing. It might have been a regat except for the time of day. Music came from somewhere do the beach and was abruptly cut off, as if a door had slamme

Justine began to giggle.

"What is it?" He was smiling already as one does som times, in anticipation of a funny story.

"I was just remembering how you came and took me o

498

f the disco that night." Her face abruptly sobered. "I wish
ou'd told me," she whispered, "all about it."

"I saw no point in frightening you."

"I only," she said, "would have been frightened for you."

He stood up, his hands in his pockets, a very Western
tance.

"It's all over now, isn't it?" She was looking up at him, her
ace tilted so that the last of the light, reflected off the water,
oned her skin, cooling it, making it glow.

"Yes," he said, rubbing his bandaged arm. "It's all over
tow."

He was on his side, half dreaming, when Justine came out
f the bathroom. She turned off the light and, to him, it
eemed as if the moon had sunk beneath the rim of the ho-
izon.

He felt her silently get into bed, moving her pillow to a
nore comfortable position, then the warmth of her body close
against him: the line of her spine, the soft curve of her but-
ocks, her knees against his thighs. Electricity seemed to flow
rom one to the other.

He thought of Yukio, as the exhaustion rose like fluid,
uffusing his limbs and beginning on his torso. He knew now
hat his fear was the same as his love for her. Her purely
lemental sexuality was what drew him to her, what continually aroused him when he was with her. But he had been
inwilling, and thus afraid, to acknowledge the balancing
talf of the equation, that there was, to him also, an elemental
exuality. That Yukio had been able to draw this out of him
ie had both loved and feared at the same time.

It saddened him greatly that he should have been living
a lie for all these years, believing that she had deceived him.
But to know now that she had loved him as he had loved her
vas enough. She was gone from him, had been for a long
ime, except in his dreams. That memory was his and he
vould do for her what he did for his parents, light incense
and say the prayers for them on the days of their birth.

Justine stirred beside him and he turned over on his back.
ter right arm was beneath her head, the hand buried to the
vrist beneath the crumpled pillow. He heard her soft even
reathing....

In the high house filled with bars of bright golden sunlight
nd deep shade falling obliquely across the bare wooden
loors Nicholas encountered So-Peng. He seemed not to have

aged at all since the time the Colonel and Cheong had come
to visit him. Tall and thin with bright black eyes and long
hands, longer fingernails which clashed softly like the man-
dibles of some mythic creature, he stood in the center of the
vaulted room, studying Nicholas.

"You have brought me a fine present. I am most grateful.

Nicholas looked around, saw nothing. Only he and So-
Peng. He did not understand.

"Where am I?"

"Somewhere," said the old man, "east of the moon, east
of the sun."

"I don't remember how I got here." Nicholas felt panic
overtake him. "I'll never find it again."

So-Peng smiled and his nails clashed together, the brittle
sound of cicadas at noon. "You came here once. You will find
your way again."

And then Nicholas was alone in the high house, staring
at himself in a long panel mirror.

Dawnlight, gentle and pale, woke him as it came in
through the bedroom window. Justine was still asleep. He
lifted the covers lightly, got out of bed.

He washed and dressed silently, went down the hallway
into the kitchen to make himself a cup of green tea. He
whirled the crushed leaves around and around the cup until
they had dissolved. There was a fine froth on top, as pale
green as the mist in the mountains of Japan in autumn.

He sipped once, very slowly, savoring the bitter taste that
was like no other in the world. Then he went into the living
room. He turned on the light in the fish tank, fed the inhabitants.

It was a remarkably clear day. Clouds, very high up, stood
sharply delineated, their striations as well defined as those
in marble. They swayed in the high wind aloft. He opened
the door, leaving only the screen door closed against the
beach insects. The breeze swept in off the sea, rich and moist.

Justine was dreaming of a man whose face seemed to be
all mouth. It was a lipless scar, like the horizon on the brink
of a savage storm, black and ominous, opening and closing
as lurid lightning forked and flickered far out.

It was screaming at her, over and over, the voice just

500

hisper; each whisper a lash that stung her heart, raising
welt, leaving a scar in its insidious wake.

She tried to get her mind in gear, to think coherently, but
the screaming mouth confused her and she lay idling like a
car in neutral.

The words the mouth was screaming at her poured down
on her like hard rain, making her mind hurt until the only
thing she wanted to do was to put her hands over her ears
to blot out the terrible noise. But it went on and on and on.

The only way to make the mouth stop was to do what it
said.

Now she wanted to wake up. Or she did not. She could not
tell which. She began to whimper and cry. In her dream? Or
for real? Which did she want to do? Wake up? Or continue
to sleep? She was terrified and every moment she remained
asleep the fear intensified.

She began to struggle. She felt steel crossing the palms
of her hands.

Then her eyes snapped open.

Nicholas was on his knees, sitting straight-backed, facing
the windows: the water and the dawn, when Justine came
into the room. His eyes were closed, the handleless cup of
green tea steaming in front of him. His spirit expanded, gyr-
ing high into the clear sky, reaching toward the high clouds.

Justine, eyes opened wide and burning quiet cold fire,
stole silently past the bubbling fish tank. Her pale yellow
nightgown swirled about her as if she were immersed in mist,
rising up from the floor she walked, enwrapping her torso.

She turned and, reaching upward with her two hands,
unsheathed the *katana* which hung on the wall just below
Nicholas' *dai-katana*. She would have taken that but it was
just out of her reach.

Now she turns, transfigured. Her eyes are not her own.
The color is all wrong and the crimson motes have been obscured by the new blackness of the irises. Her face, she feels
with a mixture of terror and exhilaration, is no longer feminine, though her figure is not altered. Like dark lightning
flickering: adder, ant, man-thing. She shakes her head as her
vision blurs. Colors seem strange; shapes bulk at her in different proportions. All of it has lost the extra dimensions

with which she once saw the world. It is a cold and hateful place; joyless and as sere as the great Gobi.

Air bellows in and out of her lungs as if through some baleful force outside her ken and she curls up inside herself crying and shivering.

Still her hands are calm and controlled as she places them one over the other around the wound leather handle of the *katana*, feeling its weight and its balance, knowing—and not knowing how she knows—the perfection of it.

Now her bare feet are placed slowly one before the other at precise angles, as she draws ever closer to the muscular back at the front of the room.

Cool light floods her as she comes out from the shadow and she pauses a moment to allow her eyes to adjust to the glare.

Now she is so close that it seems her harsh breath must brush his skin. Her arms are raised high over her head in preparation for the one lethal blow. One instant and it is all over: the striking of a match in the dark, the flick of one fingernail against another. The difference between life and death.

The tip of the *katana* begins to quiver as the killing energy is built up. One cannot use the *kiai* in this situation—the great scream that releases so much energy. How does she know this? she wonders. One must draw the power upward from the lower abdomen—more, more, the muscles are so weak.

And it is at this moment, as the *katana* commences its dark downward rush, that her core, at last seeing, begins to uncurl.

No! she screamed to herself. *No no no!*

But the blade was already a blur, cleaving the air as it went down and down and down and, despairing, she knew that it was far too late.

In flight, his spirit seemed to take on the characteristics of an old man. Not any old man but a particular one.

Nicholas, unbound, was old yet seemed not to feel the years. Rather, they hung over one bare, insubstantial arm like a series of silk scarves, each one a different color, corresponding to its memories.

In the sky of the new day he danced the dance of life, a

elighted child who has nevertheless seen many things, experienced many days and nights. He fashioned stalks of heat from the stuff of the clouds and, grasping one in each st, swirled them around and around his head like crepe aper streamers.

Below him the continent of Asia stretched itself like an normous tiger, yawning in the early morning, just beginning to stir. Yet it was the Asia of another time, before the dvent of heavy industrialization, the revolution in China, ne devastation of Vietnam and Cambodia. The air was like ncense.

Nicholas became aware of Justine and the *katana* at the ame instant. Had he not been so far away, the *haragei* would ave picked up the intent far sooner. But he was relaxed and, r that moment, went unaware.

But in this last instant he had heard the bolt of black nunder and was already turning as the *katana* rushed down pon him.

There was, of course, no time for cerebration. Had he aused to think, even for the barest of instants, he would ave died. As it was, it was closer than he liked to think bout.

There are various methods of winning a battle without a word. The one he knew best was Letting Go the Hilt and he sed it now, instinctively reaching up with his arms crossed ast past the wrists so that he came in *within* the arc of the lade, slamming Justine's forearms away and up.

He was on his feet and she came at him with a horizontal ut from left to right and he knew then what had happened.

With a shattering cry, he extended his left leg, bending t the knee, and crossed his right arm over his left, applying blow to her fists with the flat of his hand.

He stamped, startling her, and broke toward the *katana*. lalfway there, he realized that the blow he was about to eliver would shatter the bones in her wrists and instead rasped them, wrenching backward, right over left, until she ried out and the blade clattered to the floor.

Her knee came up and struck him in the pit of his stomach. eflexively, he bent over and she pounded his back with both er fists.

The breath whooshed out of him but, in falling, he manged to use his forearms to sweep her off her feet. She fell eavily half atop him and immediately began to strike out.

Nicholas reached up through the rain of blows, touched the side of her neck. Something screamed. It came from her wide-open mouth, it used her vocal chords, but she never could have made that sound on her own. Her strange black eyes flew upward in their sockets until only the white showed and then the lids came down and she slumped, unconscious, across him, her long hair half-covering the shining steel blade of the abandoned *katana*.

It had been that second cut. Left to right. Justine was right-handed and would have cut from right to left. It was not Justine who wielded the blade. In any event, she would not have been able to handle the *katana* so well.

Saiminjutsu—the art of ninja hypnotism—was just one of the sub-specialities he had learned years ago. He worked over her for more than four hours—to undo was far more difficult than to do—using everything he had been taught, to exorcise the demon that had been planted in her.

Sweat dripped off them both like rain, mingling on the wooden floor, as he worked on and on until, at last, her body shuddered in his arms and she gave a fierce startled cry.

Within moments, she was in a sound sleep. But he would not give her up, even then, and held her, cradled protectively in his arms and lap, leaving her only once during the long heating day to relieve himself and to wet a towel with cool water so that he could place it over her forehead.

For almost all of the time, he stared down into her face, his features somehow different than they had been earlier. Once, the sound of the quiet bubbling of the fish tank intruded upon his thoughts and he looked briefly over at the denizens of the deep at play among the tall green columns of vegetation and the spiny backs of colored rocks. They regarded him impassively from beyond the glass, from another world entirely.

By the third day she had recovered fully. Before that, she slept on and off most of the time as one does when fighting off an evil disease.

During that time, Nicholas fed her and washed her, not minding at all. He would sit on the porch for long hours at a time, staring out at the sea, past the bathers and the sun

504

orshipers as if they did not exist, but he did not go onto the beach nor near the water. He would not go that far away from her.

And when that day dawned when she opened her eyes and they were perfectly clear, the tiny scarlet motes in the left one as brilliant as fires on a plain, he put his arms around her and kissed her.

It was not until he had made them breakfast and she had taken in the paper that he told her what had happened. He told her everything because this was something she must know, to understand that she had had the strength and the courage to pull through. Because he never could have accomplished it on his own. She had fought the *Kōbudera* from the beginning.

"I am strong now." She laughed. "As strong as you."

"In a way," he said, more seriously than she, "yes."

She shuddered. "Such power needs getting used to."

She read the paper while he cleaned up and the soft clatter the dishes in the sink as he washed them made her feel cozy and warm.

"Afterward," she said, "let's go out on the beach."

"We should. Summer's almost gone. We should make the most of these last days out here. Anyway"—he wiped his hands—"there are a couple of people in the city I want you to get to know—"

"Nick—" She looked up from the paper.

He came over to where she was sitting. "Why the look?" He kissed her.

"Look at this." She pushed the folded paper toward him. He took it, dropped his gaze from her worried face.

"I ought to call Gelda," she said as if from a distance.

Local Policeman Dead in Crash (he read). The dateline as Key West, Florida. "Detective Lieutenant Lewis J. Croaker was found dead late yesterday in a rented car, a spokesman for the Monroe County Police Department reported. The car had apparently left the highway at high speed six miles east of Key West, rolled down an embankment and caught fire. Heavy rains and high winds, which have plagued this area for a day and a half, may have contributed to the accident, the spokesman said.

"Detective Lieutenant Croaker, 43, was apparently in Key West on vacation. Contacted at his office at One Police Plaza,

Captain Michael C. Finnigan, Detective Lieutenant Croaker immediate superior, commented..."

But Nicholas had already stopped reading. There was pounding in his chest, a hollow kind of thudding, echoin away as if he stood inside an empty shrine. His vision blurre and he seemed unaware that the paper was shreddin through his clenched fingers.

"Nicholas..." Justine stood beside him, arms crosse hands clasping her elbows impotently, the physical for th moment put precariously at bay by the emotional. "I can believe it."

But he could, with that typically Asian perspective of th acceptance of events as they evolve. Karma, he thought sav agely. But Croaker's death was like a knife thrust into hi bowels, a kind of seething pain that would not dissipate.

Then he recalled why Croaker had gone to Key West. H read the article again, this time from first sentence to las On vacation, indeed. As if Croaker's *kami* hovered in clos asylum at his right hand, he heard again, *He's a murdere Nick. If I had any lingering doubts as to Tomkin's complicit in the Angela Didion case, they went bye-bye with that orde to officially shut down. He's a shark, man. You'd better fac up to it.* A hot wind from the cemetery, out from the shad elms, assailed him as he began to see past events in a chi new light. The confrontations between Tomkin and Croake had been deliberate. Croaker had wanted to needle Tomkir perhaps provoking him into making some precipitous mov like an attempt to silence Croaker. Now it had come, th whisper of the gibbet. And Frank, Tomkin's chief bodyguar had been gone several days, who knew where?

I've gotta nail him on this. It's a matter of honor. Ever remembered word a knife twist. *If I don't do it, nobody gonna be able to.*

He got up and went to the phone, his mind abruptly quit clear, and dialed a number. His whole body seemed to ach as if he had been recently beaten. He did not think it fa: that this should have happened to them; friendship as speci as this was meant to be savored, not snatched away by a thi in the night. He felt strongly as if they had both been cheate This, he knew, was Western thinking and he set it asid compartmentalizing it, as he had been taught, just as som one places a treasured item on a high shelf, out of harm way. Still, for the briefest moment, he could picture the fou them on a long sleek sloop, wet from the salt spray, laugh-g and carefree, the sun in their eyes. Then he banished the sion, letting it part from him as if it were the last ray of e sun slipping below the dark horizon. But did that change ything? Not at all, as he had already seen. Love and friend-ip were inextricably entwined in Japan and he was, after l the time in the West, the clothes, the new veneers, an asterner, now and forever. He knew this with an abrupt d wrenching conviction that both thrilled and calmed him. e had a sense of place now, as well as a sense of time.

And sacrifice, revenge, the cornerstones of Japanese his-ry, were both a part of him, too. This had been Itami's last essage to him, though, at the time, he had not fully under-ood.

Croaker's death made it all too plain.

Now a quote attributed to Ieyasu Tokugawa flew through s head like a bird of prey, circling in the sky of his mind. e knew what to do.

"What is it?" Justine asked him. Her voice was thick as she were still in shock.

He put his finger to his lips, said into the phone, "Is he .? It's Nicholas Linnear." He waited a moment. Justine came behind him, entwining her arms around him.

Frank answered. So he had returned. Bastard. But his ice was controlled as he said, "Had a good vacation? Yeah o bad you missed all the excitement." He felt the press of r breasts against his back. He put one arm around behind m, holding her. "Sure. Next time I see you, I'll tell you all out it." And thought: It might be a lot sooner than you ink. Frank said to hold on a minute.

He closed his eyes briefly, saw the sea at that time of day hen the sun, having left the sky, turns it into the brightest ece of topography; in twilight, the water shines like a carpet light

"Hello," he said. "I've thought about your offer. Yes. Yes, now what I said then." His eyes snapped open and Justine, close against him, felt the tension flooding through him d wondered at the disparity between his words and his elings. "But things have—changed a bit. I've reconsidered. es. I thought you might be." Oh, Ieyasu! How right I shall ove you! "Any time you say." His knuckles went white as ey gripped the receiver. "Yes. I just read about it in the per. Sure. A friend. I got to know him a bit." Justine,

sensing his mounting anger, pressed herself more tightly t
him as if her presence might mollify him in some way. N
cholas, feeling her warmth seep into him, knew that quit
soon—certainly before they went down to the beach—h
would want to make love to her, need to even as he grieve
for his friend. Perhaps because of it. He was returning to lif
now and so was she.

"In a week?" he said. "No, I don't think there will be
problem. You'll just need to fill me in on all the details. Bu
even that... Well, we can go over it on the plane, can't we
Yes. Yes." He listened for a moment more, his mind far awa
"I'll see you, then. Soon. Very soon."

He was one now with Ieyasu, with his words: *To come t
know your enemy, first you must become his friend.* He dre
all the warmth he could from Justine, now. Because he ha
gone cold with the realization that Tomkin had sent Fran
out to find the woman in Key West. And then Croaker ha
been killed in Key West. *Murder.* The word rang like a heav
bell in his mind. If not for you—he thought into the phon
as he cradled it.

*And once you become his friend, all his defenses com
down. Then can you choose the most fitting method for hi
demise.*

Afterword

There are, in Japanese martial philosophy—which incorporates many elements of both the Buddhist and Shinto religions—five cardinal signs: Ground, Water, Wind, Fire and the Void.

Miyamoto Musashi's *Go Rin No Sho* exists to this day.* It is, literally, *A Book of Five Rings*.

The Ninja, too, is a book of five rings.

* *A Book of Five Rings* by Miyamoto Musashi, translated by Victor Harris, is published by The Overlook Press, Woodstock, New York.

NEW FROM FAWCETT CREST

CURRENT CREST BESTSELLERS

THE NINJA
  by Eric Van Lustbader   24367 $3.50
SHOCKTRAUMA
  by Jon Franklin & Alan Doelp   24387 $2.95
KANE & ABEL
  Jeffrey Archer   24376 $3.75
PRIVATE SECTOR
  Jeff Millar   24368 $2.95
DONAHUE *Phil Donahue & Co.*   24358 $2.95
DOMINO *Phyllis A. Whitney*   24350 $2.75
TO CATCH A KING
  Harry Patterson   24323 $2.95
AUNT ERMA'S COPE BOOK
  Erma Bombeck   24334 $2.75
THE GLOW *Brooks Stanwood*   24333 $2.75
RESTORING THE AMERICAN DREAM
  Robert J. Ringer   24314 $2.95
THE LAST ENCHANTMENT
  Mary Stewart   24207 $2.95
CENTENNIAL *James A. Michener*   23494 $2.95
THE COUP *John Updike*   24259 $2.95
THURSDAY THE RABBI WALKED OUT
  Harry Kemelman   24070 $2.25
IN MY FATHER'S COURT
  Isaac Bashevis Singer   24074 $2.50
A WALK ACROSS AMERICA
  Peter Jenkins   24277 $2.75
WANDERINGS *Chaim Potok*   24270 $3.95

uy them at your local bookstore or use this handy coupon for ordering.

OLUMBIA BOOK SERVICE
275 Mally Road, P.O. Box FB, Madison Heights, MI 48071

ease send me the books I have checked above. Orders for less than 5 books
ust include 75¢ for the first book and 25¢ for each additional book to cover
stage and handling. Orders for 5 books or more postage is FREE. Send check
money order only.

Cost $	Name
Sales tax*	Address
Postage	City
Total $	State	Zip

*The government requires us to collect sales tax in all states except AK, DE,
T, NH and OR.*

his offer expires 1 March 82   8177